Yo, Dad! It's Reed. Can you come to the station and pick me up?

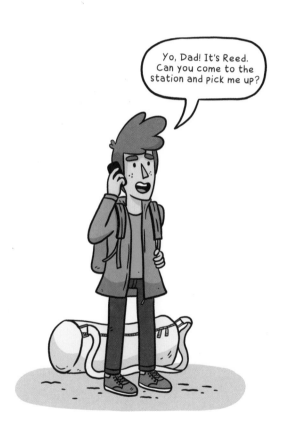

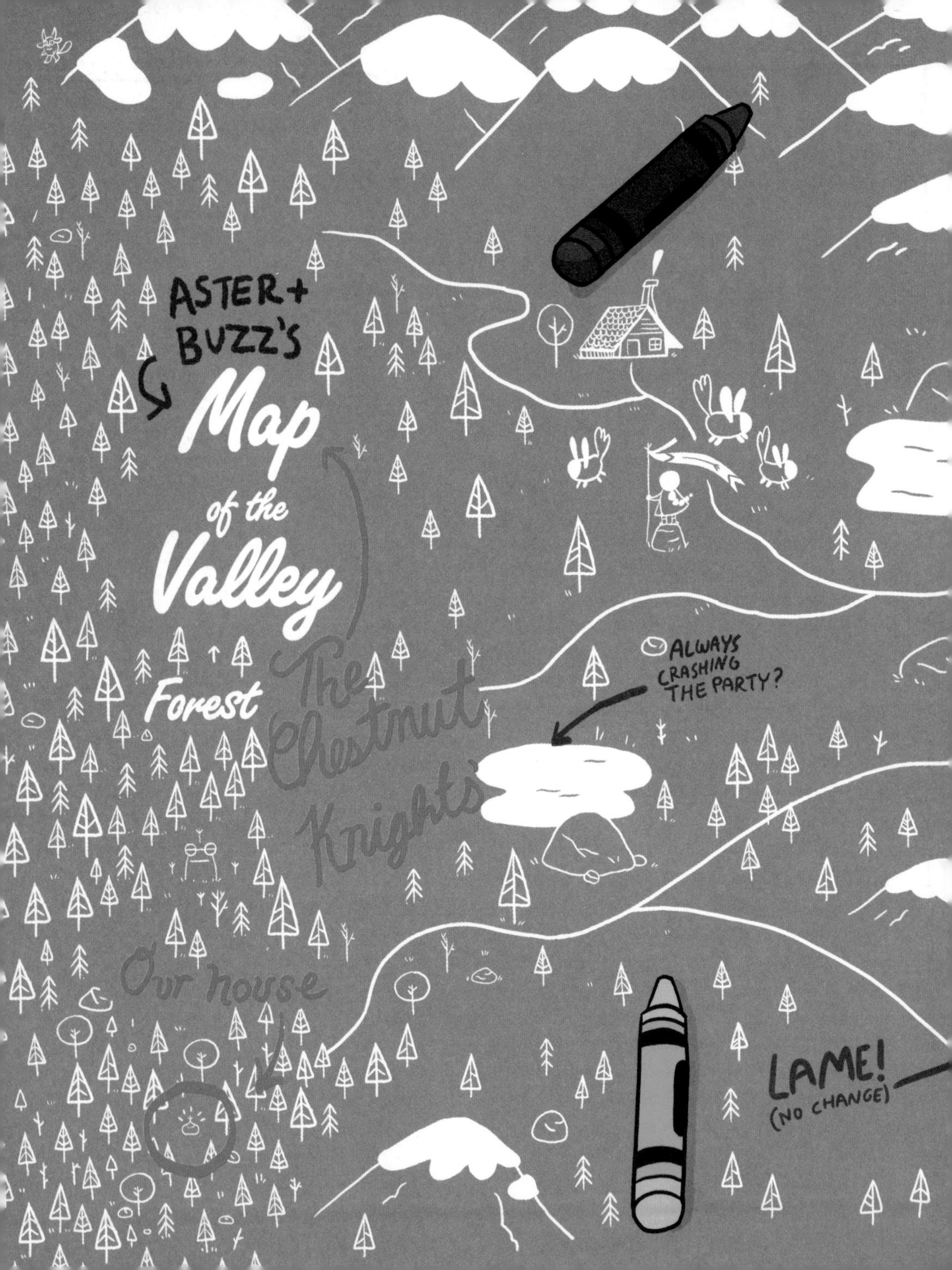
ASTER + BUZZ'S
Map
of the
Valley
Forest
The Chestnut Knights
ALWAYS CRASHING THE PARTY?
Our house
LAME! (NO CHANGE)

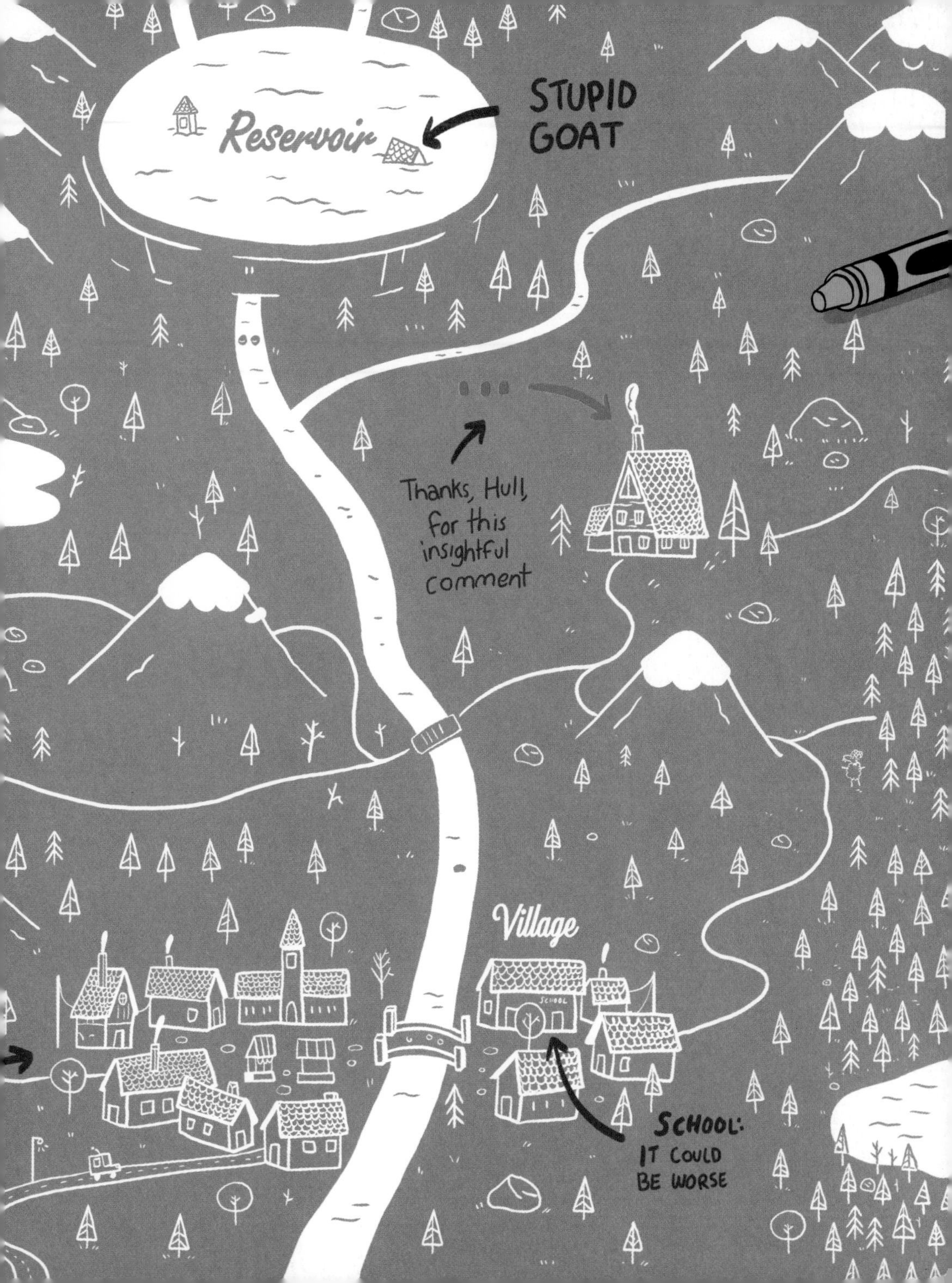
Reservoir
STUPID GOAT
Thanks, Hull, for this insightful comment
Village
SCHOOL
SCHOOL:
IT COULD BE WORSE

Thanks to Julien and Bolä for their help with the coloring.
Thanks to Élisa, Laurence, Stéphane, and Jonathan.
Thanks to Éveline.

Thanks to Anton, Gina, Patrick, Whitney,
and the rest of the American team.

Translation copyright © 2021 by Dupuis
Cover art and interior illustrations copyright © 2019, 2020, 2021 by Dupuis

Published in the United States by RH Graphic, an imprint of Random House Children's Books, a division of Penguin Random House LLC, New York. The titles in this work were originally published in two separate volumes in the French language in Belgium as *Aubépine 3: Pourquoi tant de laine?*, copyright © 2019 Dupuis by Thom Pico & Karensac, and *Aubépine 4: La fin de tout (et du reste)*, copyright © 2020 Dupuis by Thom Pico & Karensac, by Éditions Dupuis S.A., Marcinelle, in 2019. All rights reserved.

RH Graphic with the book design is a trademark of Penguin Random House LLC.

Visit us on the web and sign up for our newsletter! RHKidsGraphic.com • @RHKidsGraphic

Educators and librarians, for a variety of teaching tools, visit us at RHTeachersLibrarians.com

Library of Congress Cataloging-in-Publication Data is available upon request.
ISBN 978-0-593-11887-0 (pbk) — ISBN 978-0-593-12534-2 (trade) —
ISBN 978-0-593-11888-7 (library binding) — ISBN 978-0-593-11889-4 (ebook)

Designed by Patrick Crotty
Translated by Anne and Owen Smith

MANUFACTURED IN CHINA
10 9 8 7 6 5 4 3 2 1
First American Edition

A comic on every bookshelf.

Aster
AND THE
MIXED×UP MAGIC

Story and Script
THOM PICO

Story and Art
KARENSAC

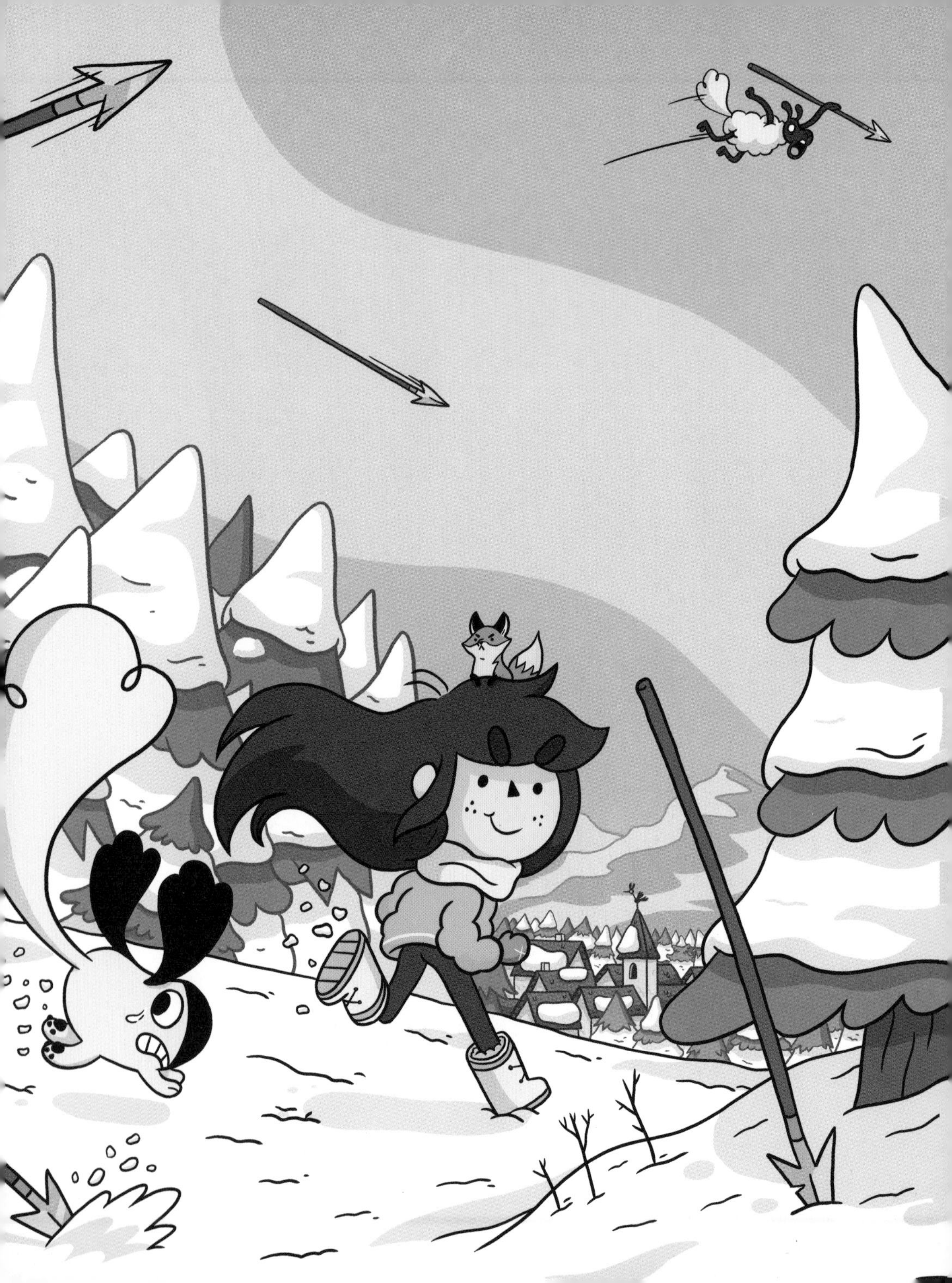

ALL'S WELL THAT ENDS WOOL

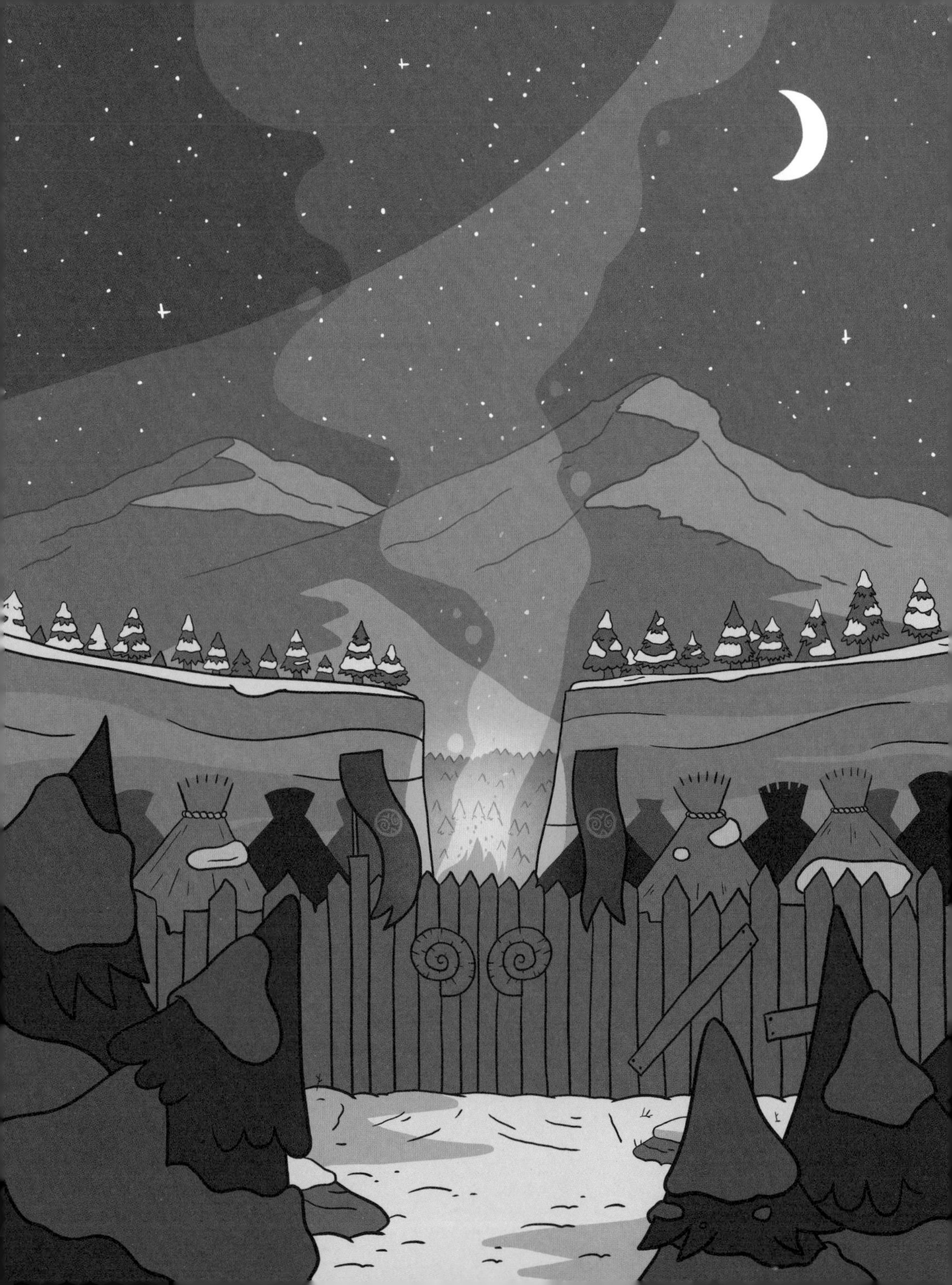

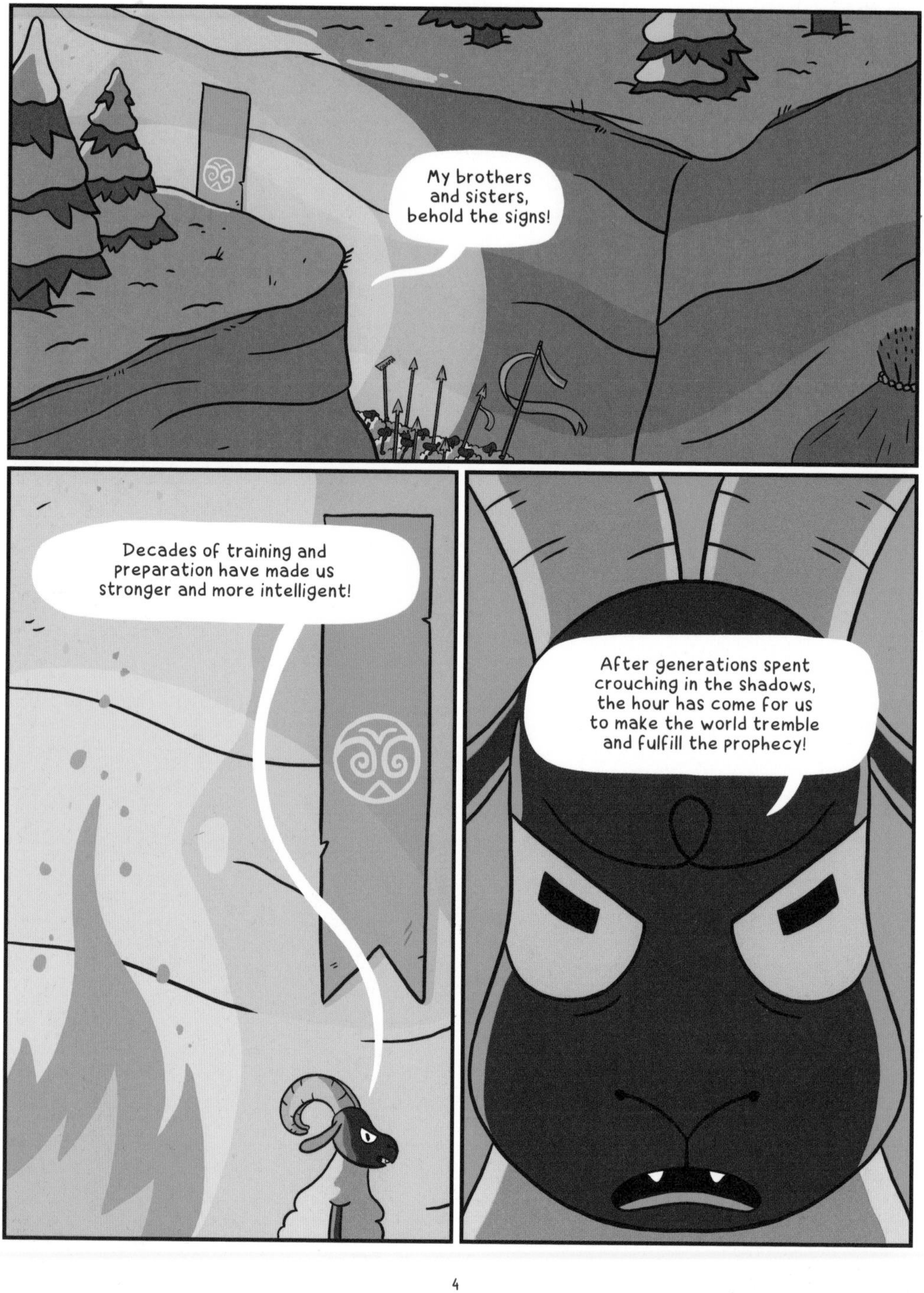
My brothers and sisters, behold the signs!
Decades of training and preparation have made us stronger and more intelligent!
After generations spent crouching in the shadows, the hour has come for us to make the world tremble and fulfill the prophecy!

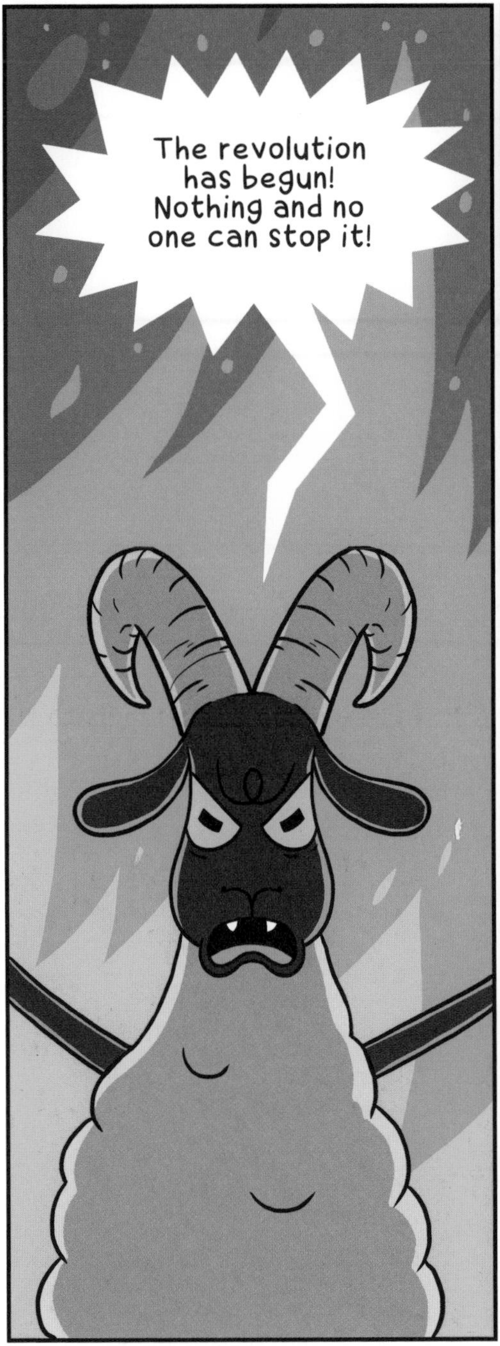
The revolution has begun! Nothing and no one can stop it!
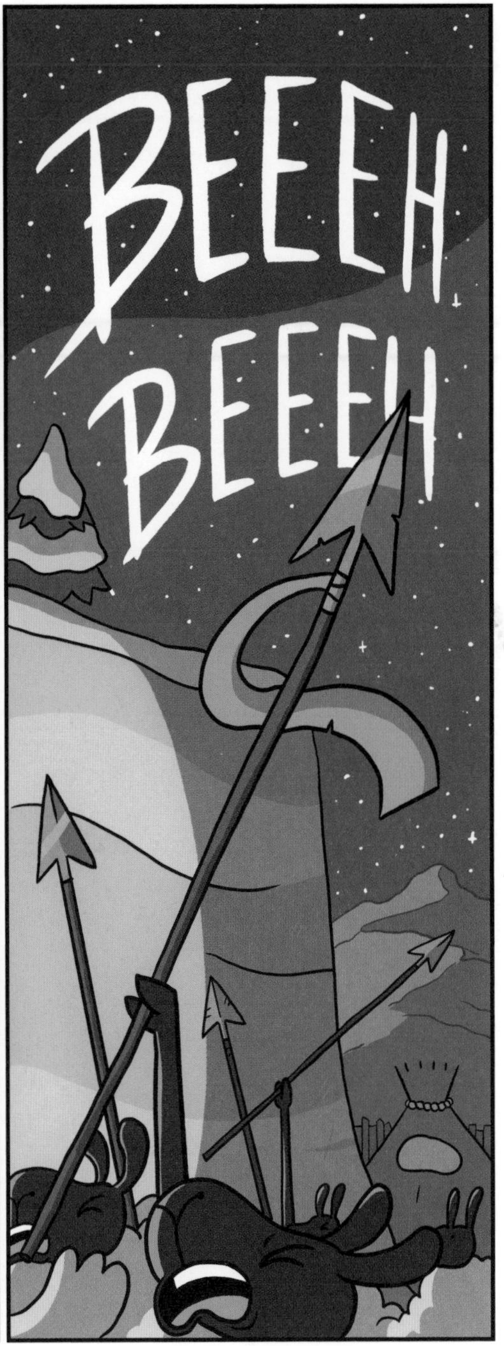
BEEEH
BEEEH

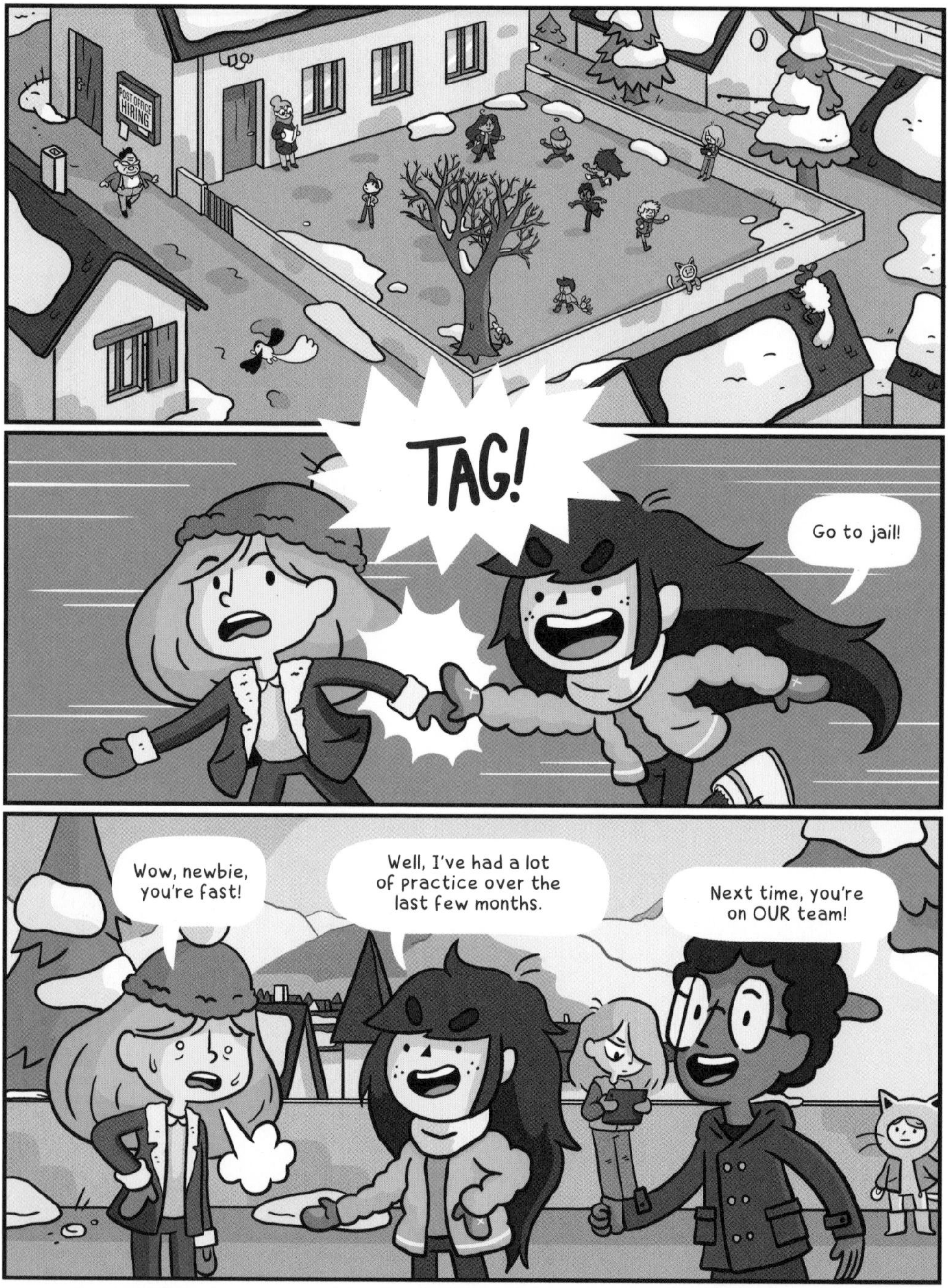
POST OFFICE HIRING
TAG!
Go to jail!
Wow, newbie, you're fast!
Well, I've had a lot of practice over the last few months.
Next time, you're on OUR team!

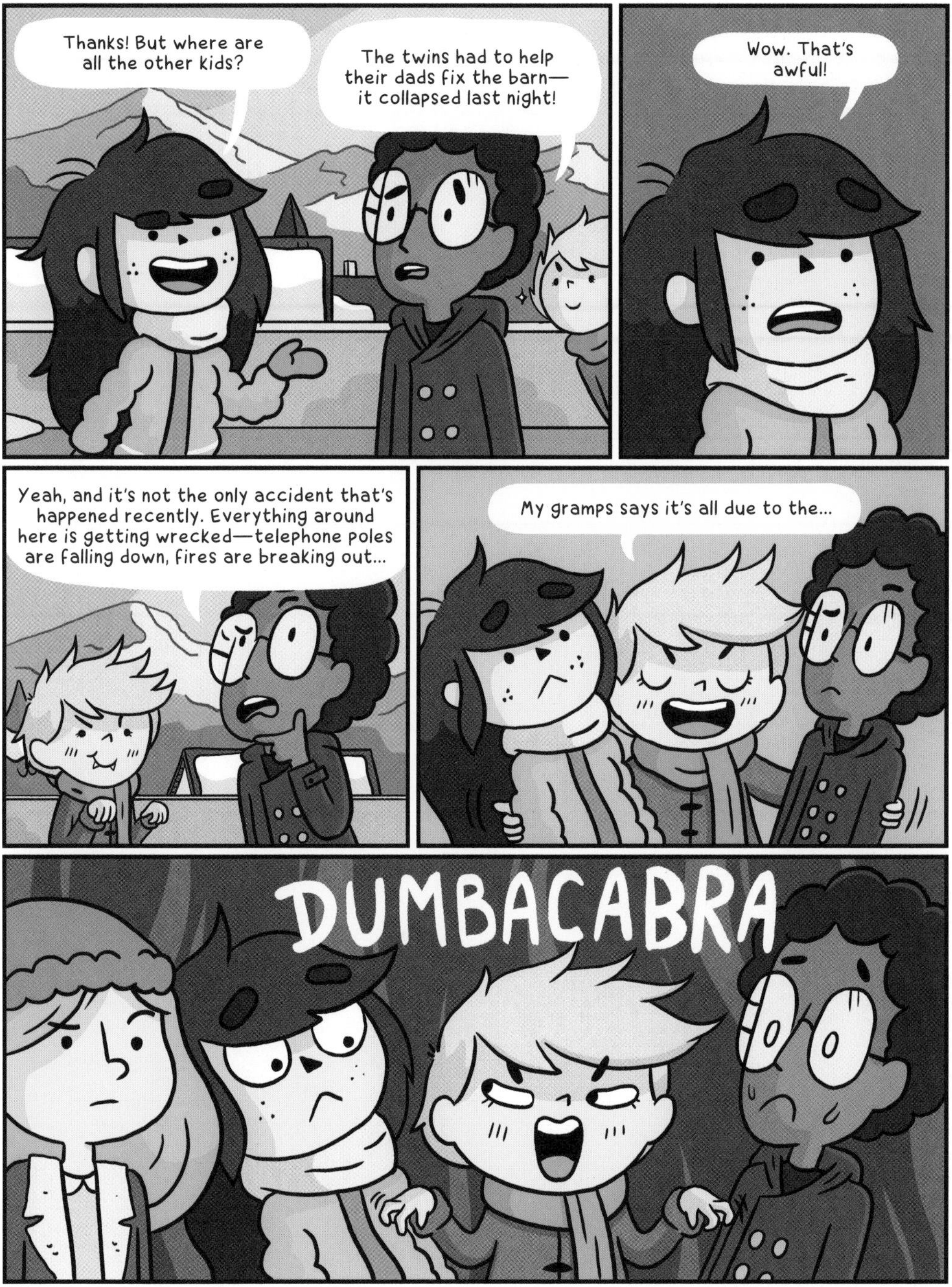
Thanks! But where are all the other kids?
The twins had to help their dads fix the barn—it collapsed last night!
Wow. That's awful!
Yeah, and it's not the only accident that's happened recently. Everything around here is getting wrecked—telephone poles are falling down, fires are breaking out...
My gramps says it's all due to the...
DUMBACABRA

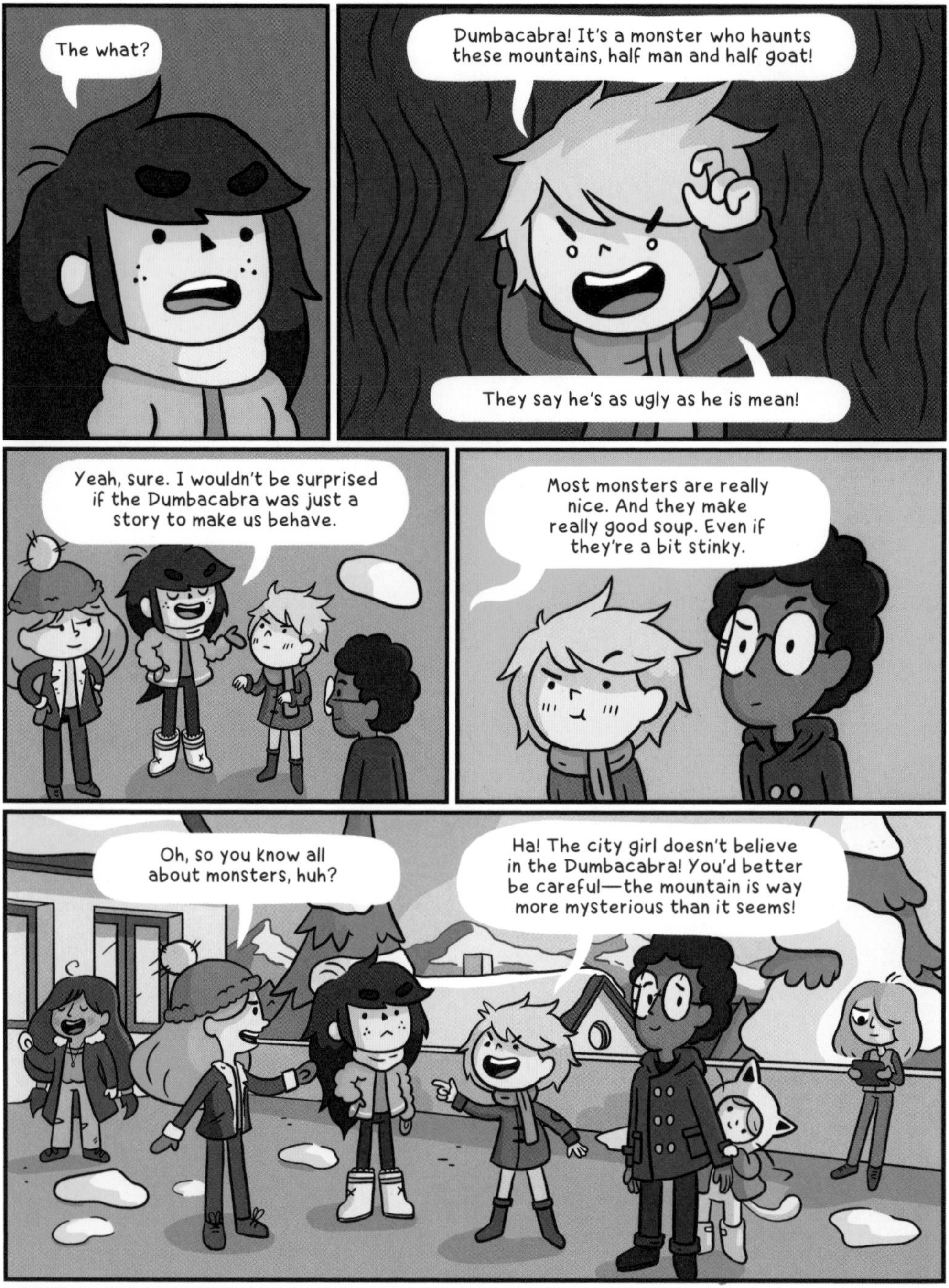
The what?
Dumbacabra! It's a monster who haunts these mountains, half man and half goat!
They say he's as ugly as he is mean!
Yeah, sure. I wouldn't be surprised if the Dumbacabra was just a story to make us behave.
Most monsters are really nice. And they make really good soup. Even if they're a bit stinky.
Oh, so you know all about monsters, huh?
Ha! The city girl doesn't believe in the Dumbacabra! You'd better be careful—the mountain is way more mysterious than it seems!

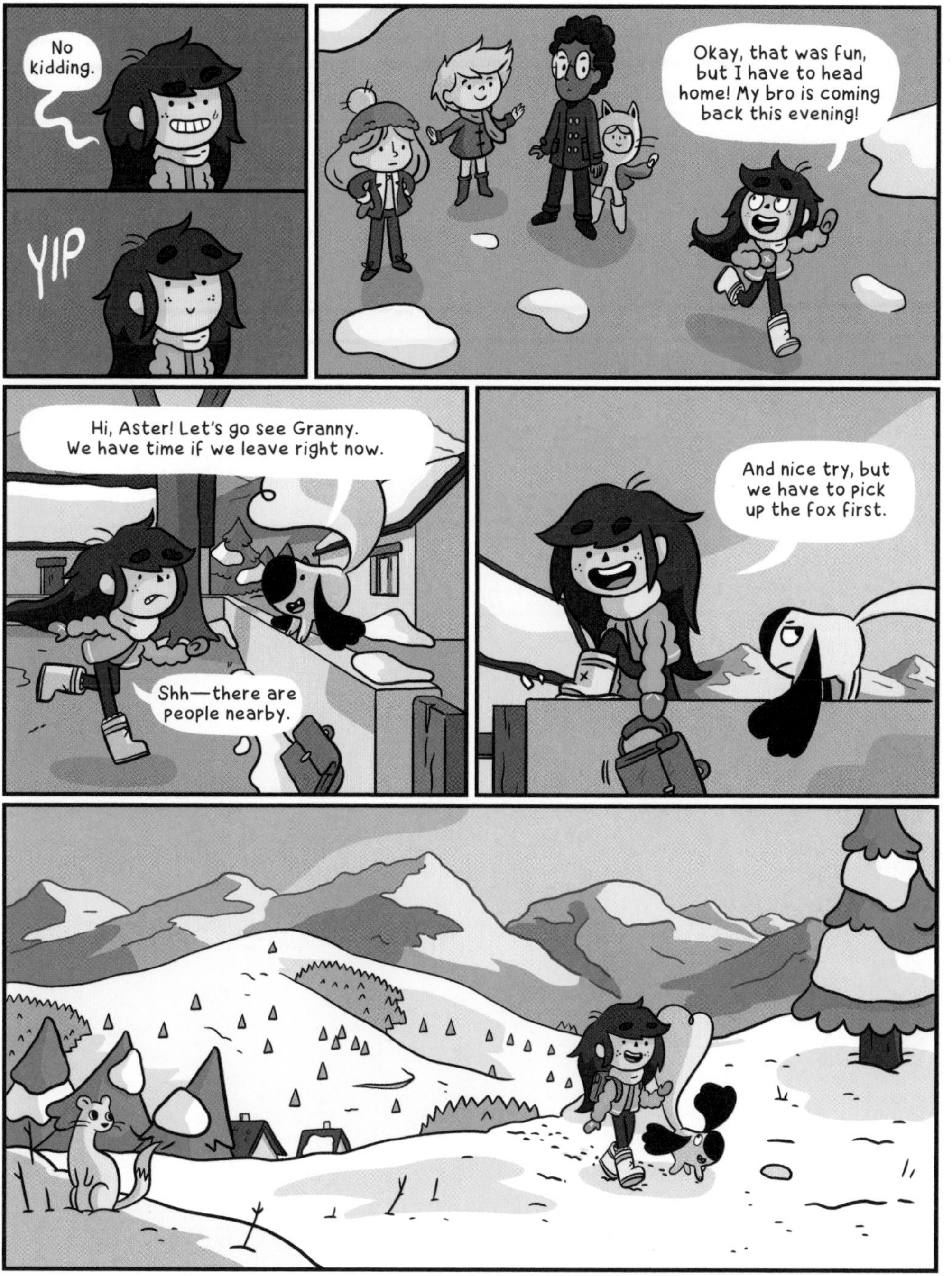
No kidding.
YIP
Okay, that was fun, but I have to head home! My bro is coming back this evening!
Hi, Aster! Let's go see Granny. We have time if we leave right now.
Shh—there are people nearby.
And nice try, but we have to pick up the fox first.

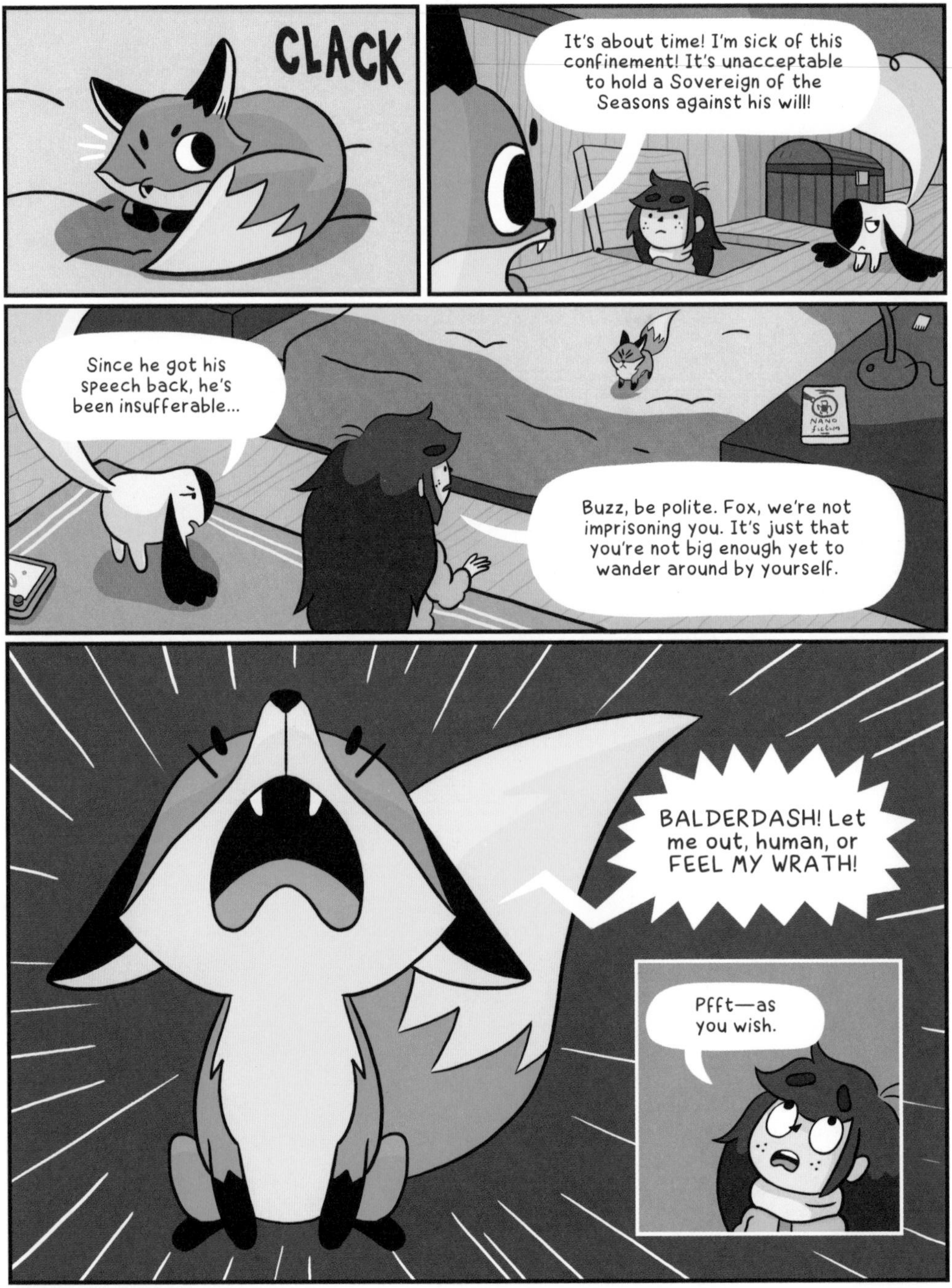
CLACK
It's about time! I'm sick of this confinement! It's unacceptable to hold a Sovereign of the Seasons against his will!
Since he got his speech back, he's been insufferable...
NANO
Buzz, be polite. Fox, we're not imprisoning you. It's just that you're not big enough yet to wander around by yourself.
BALDERDASH! Let me out, human, or FEEL MY WRATH!
Pfft—as you wish.

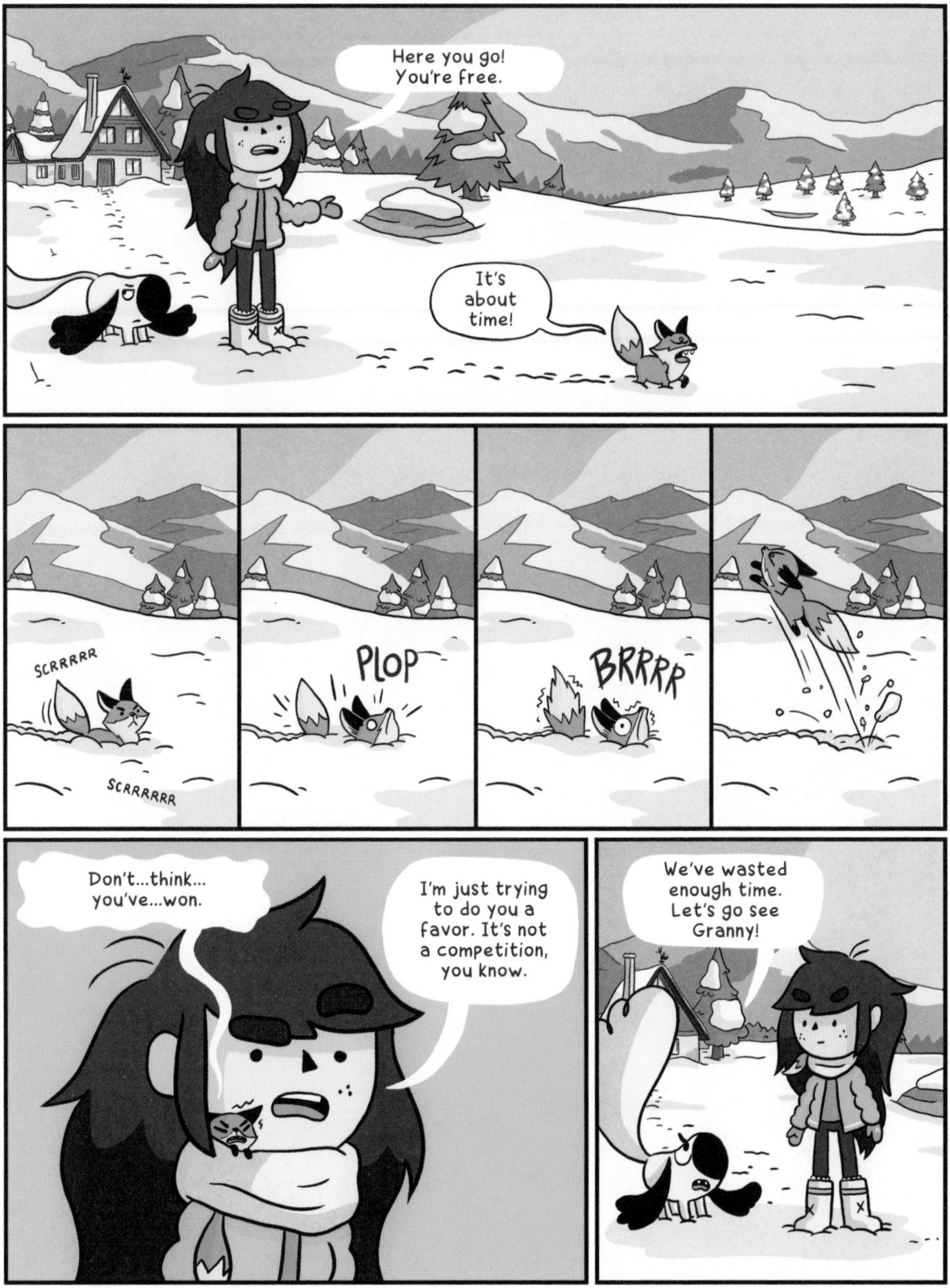
Here you go! You're free.
It's about time!
SCRRRRR
SCRRRRRR
PLOP
BRRRR
Don't...think... you've...won.
I'm just trying to do you a favor. It's not a competition, you know.
We've wasted enough time. Let's go see Granny!

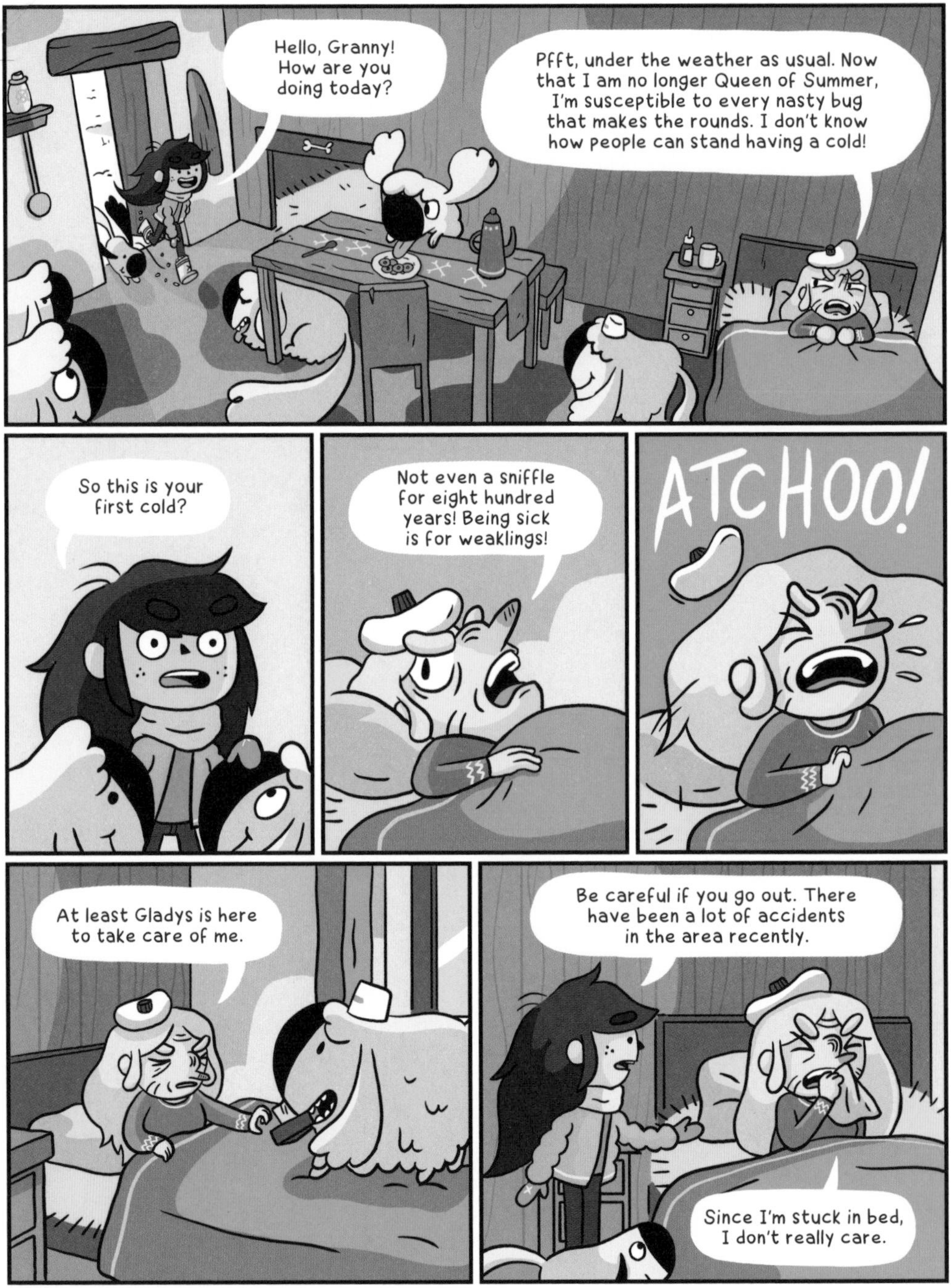
Hello, Granny! How are you doing today?
Pfft, under the weather as usual. Now that I am no longer Queen of Summer, I'm susceptible to every nasty bug that makes the rounds. I don't know how people can stand having a cold!
So this is your first cold?
Not even a sniffle for eight hundred years! Being sick is for weaklings!
ATCHOO!
At least Gladys is here to take care of me.
Be careful if you go out. There have been a lot of accidents in the area recently.
Since I'm stuck in bed, I don't really care.

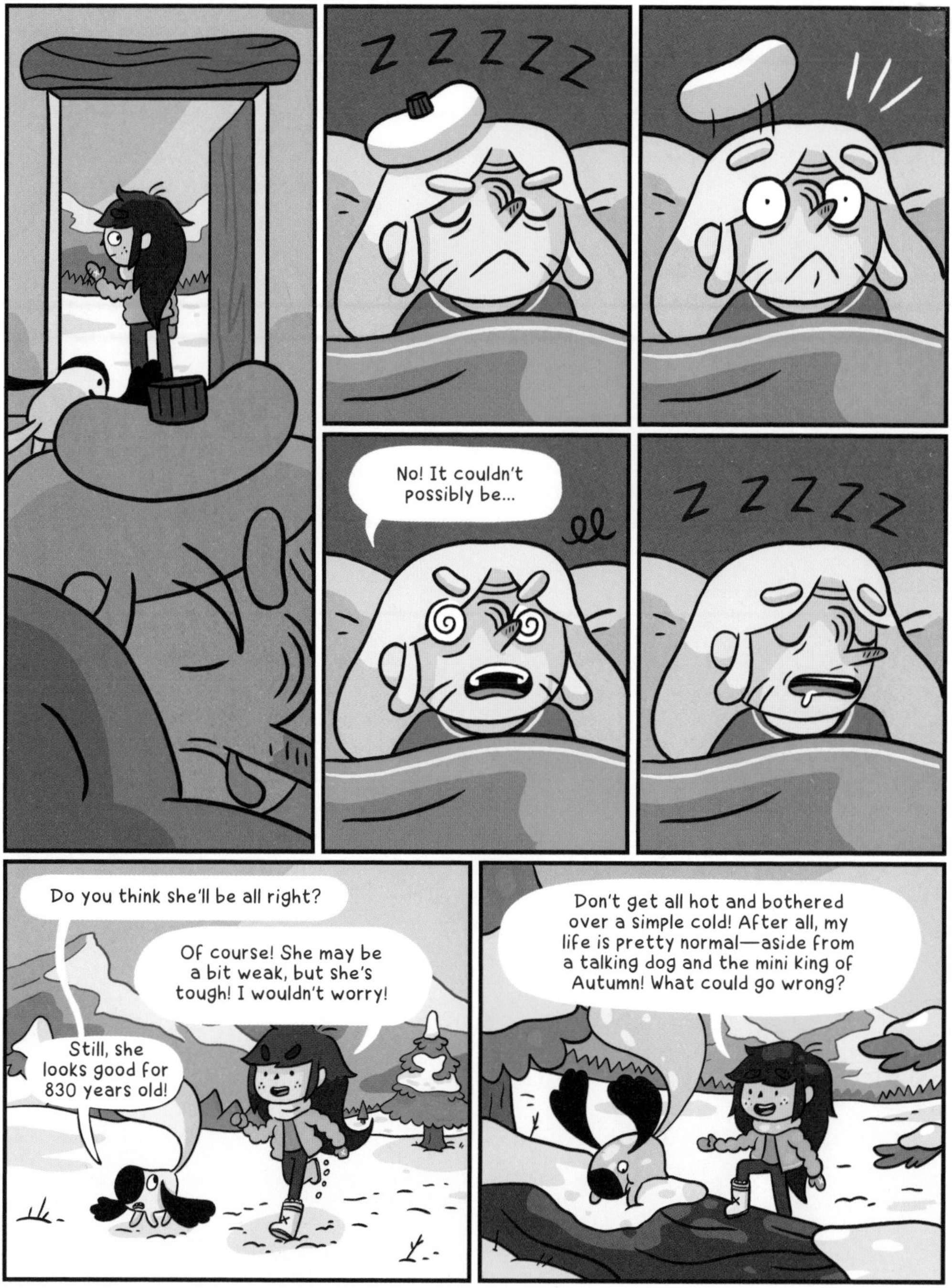

Z Z Z Z Z
No! It couldn't possibly be...
Z Z Z Z Z
Do you think she'll be all right?
Of course! She may be a bit weak, but she's tough! I wouldn't worry!
Still, she looks good for 830 years old!
Don't get all hot and bothered over a simple cold! After all, my life is pretty normal—aside from a talking dog and the mini King of Autumn! What could go wrong?

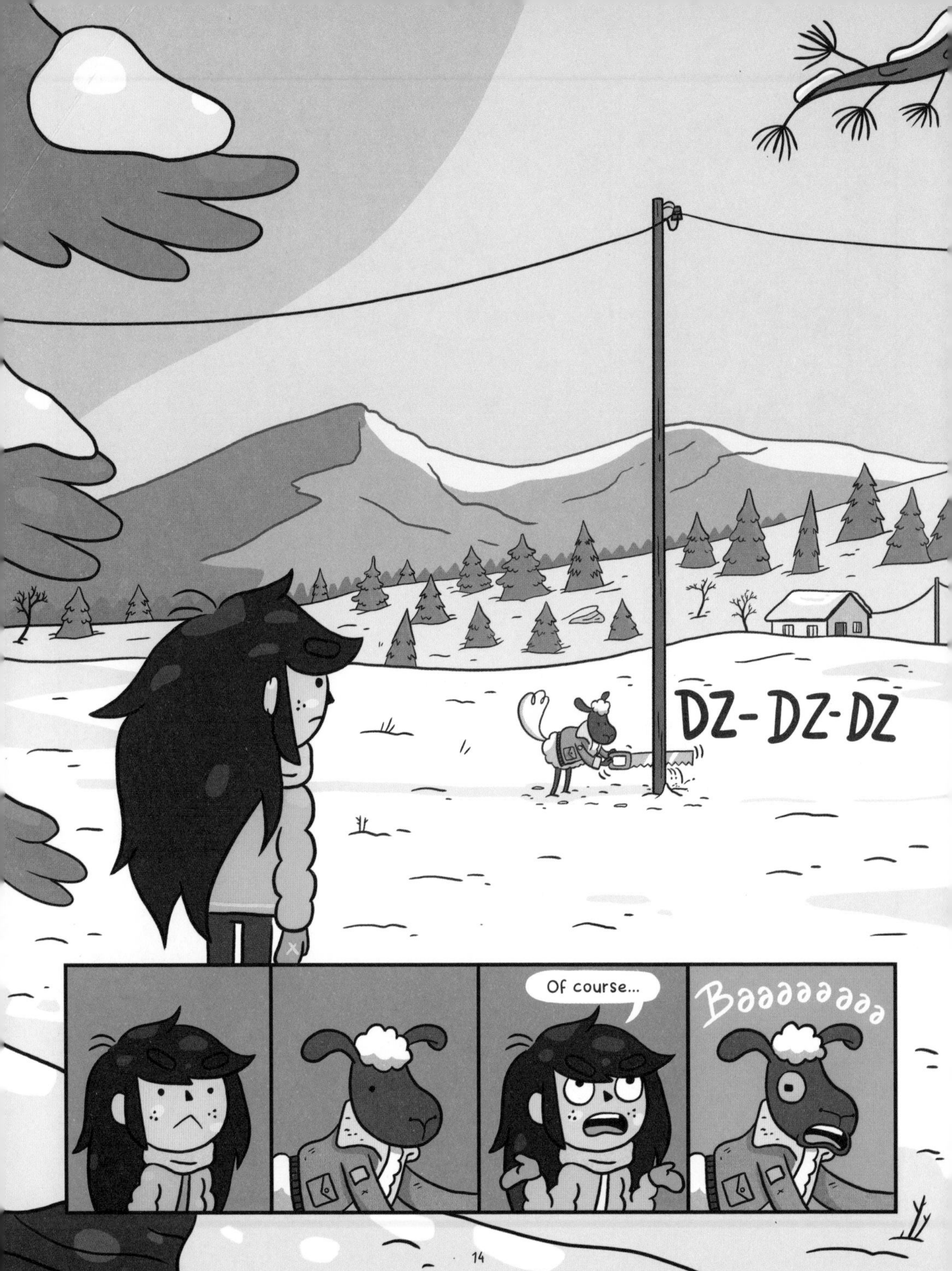
DZ-DZ-DZ
Of course...
Baaaaaaaaa

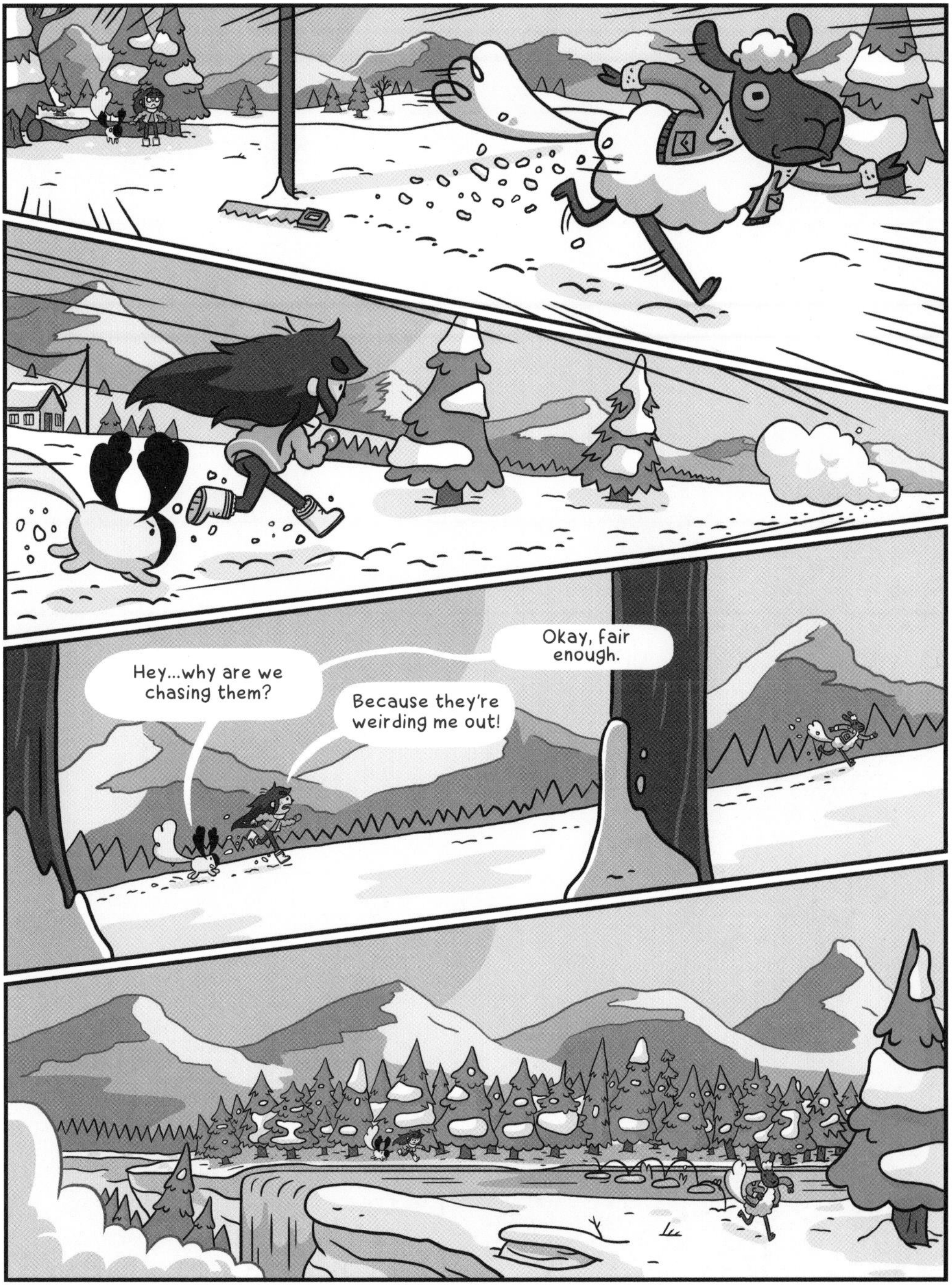
Hey...why are we chasing them?
Because they're weirding me out!
Okay, fair enough.

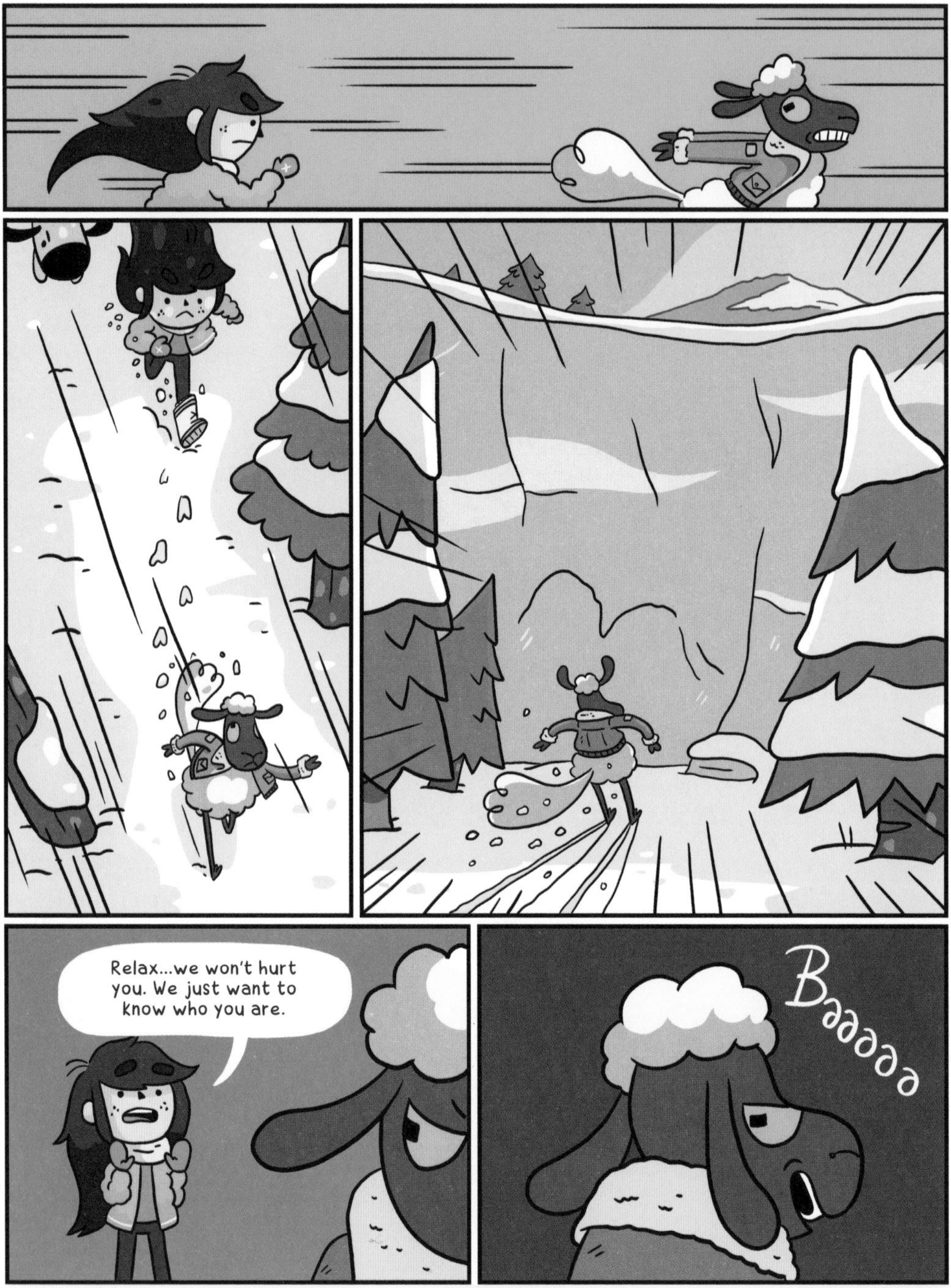

Relax...we won't hurt you. We just want to know who you are.
Baaaaaa

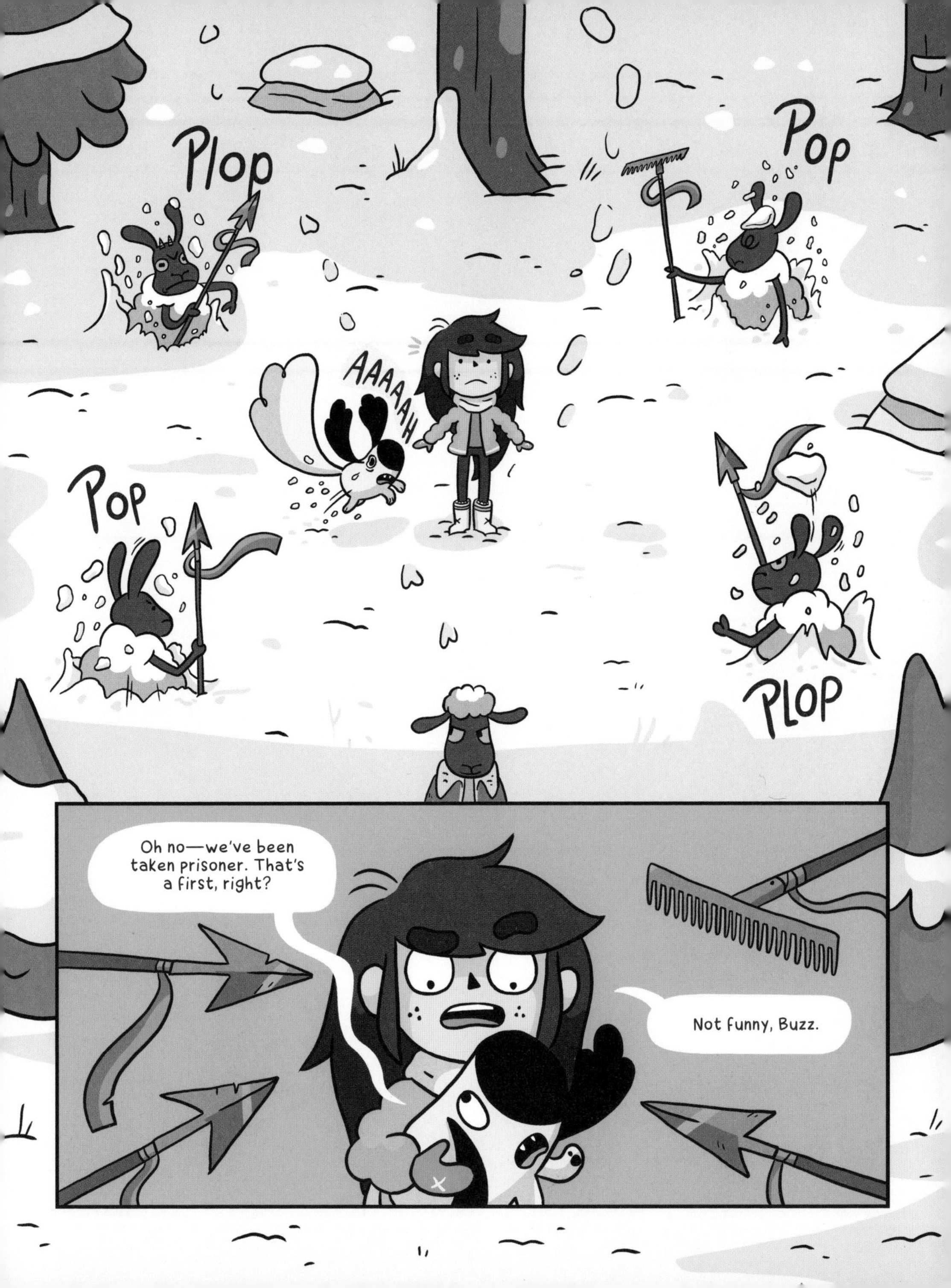
Plop
Pop
AAAAAH
Pop
PLOP
Oh no—we've been taken prisoner. That's a first, right?
Not funny, Buzz.

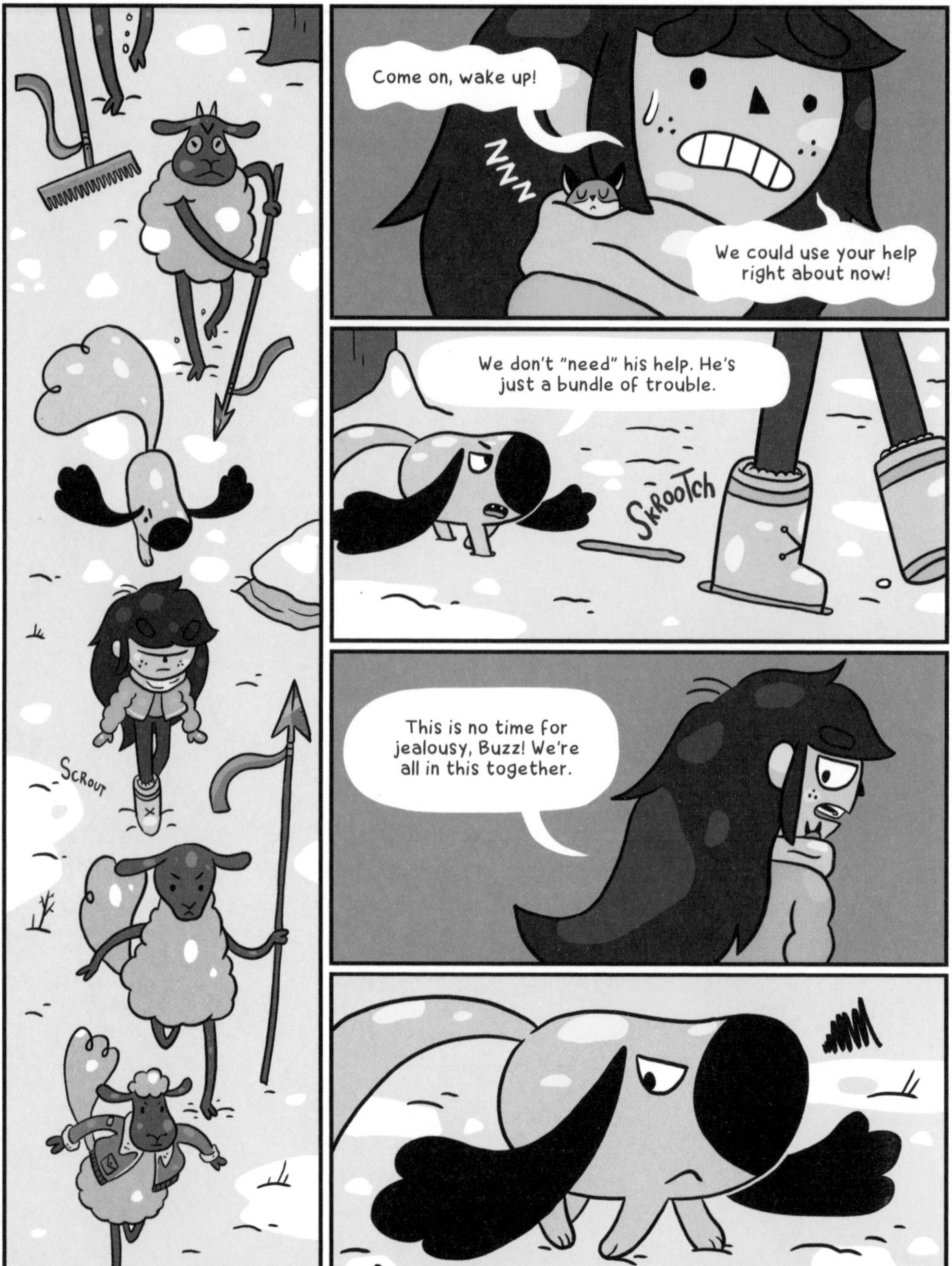
SCROUT
Come on, wake up!
NNN
We could use your help right about now!
We don't "need" his help. He's just a bundle of trouble.
SKROOTCH
This is no time for jealousy, Buzz! We're all in this together.

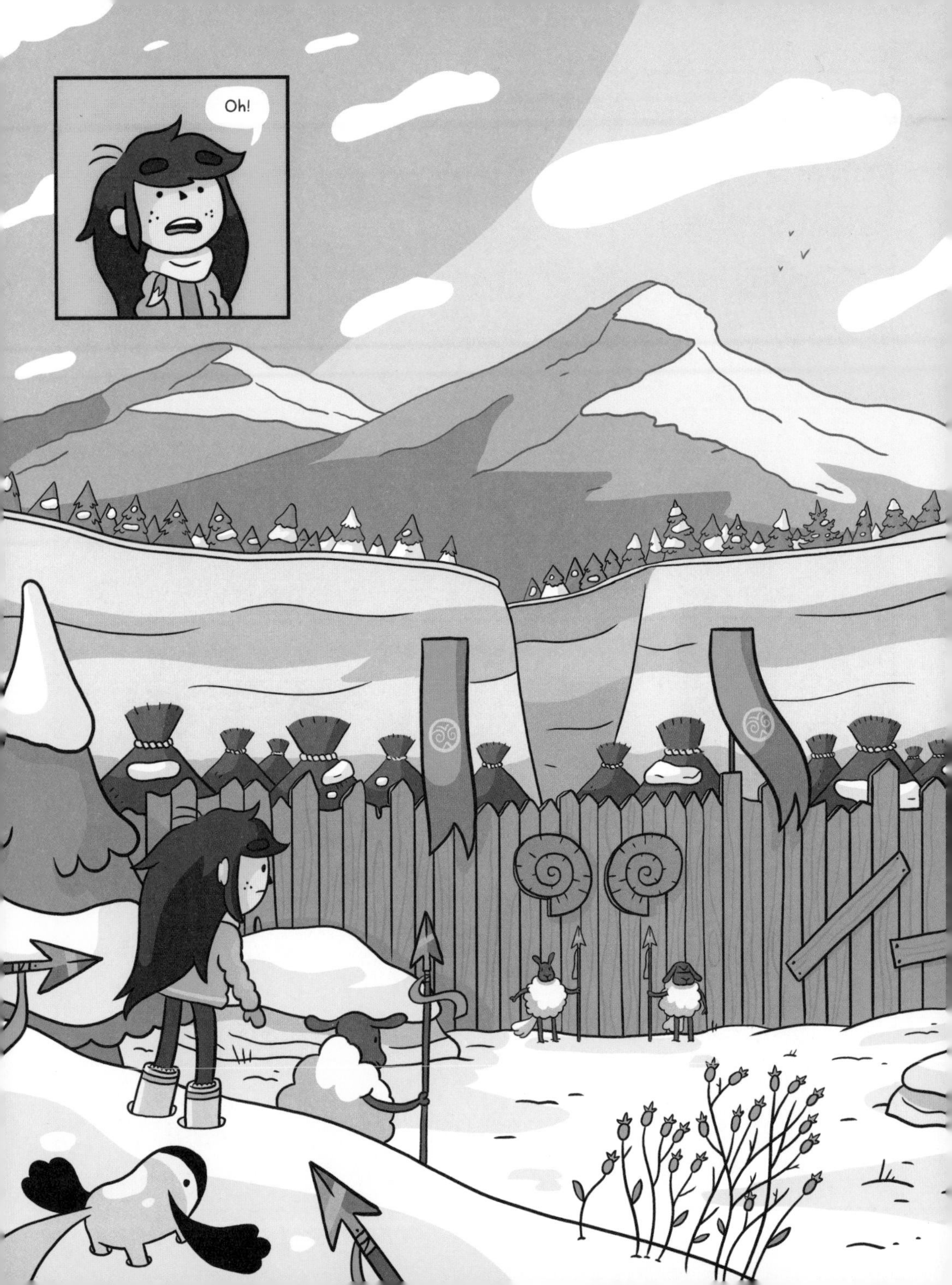
Oh!

BAAAAA
POW

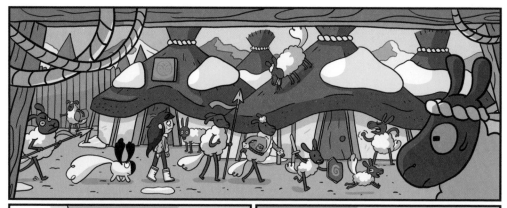

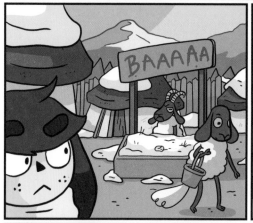

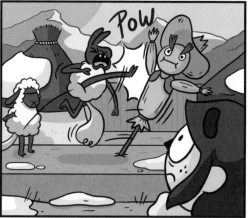

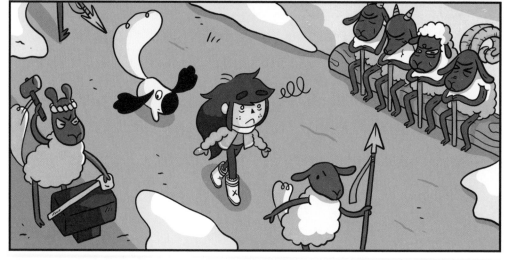

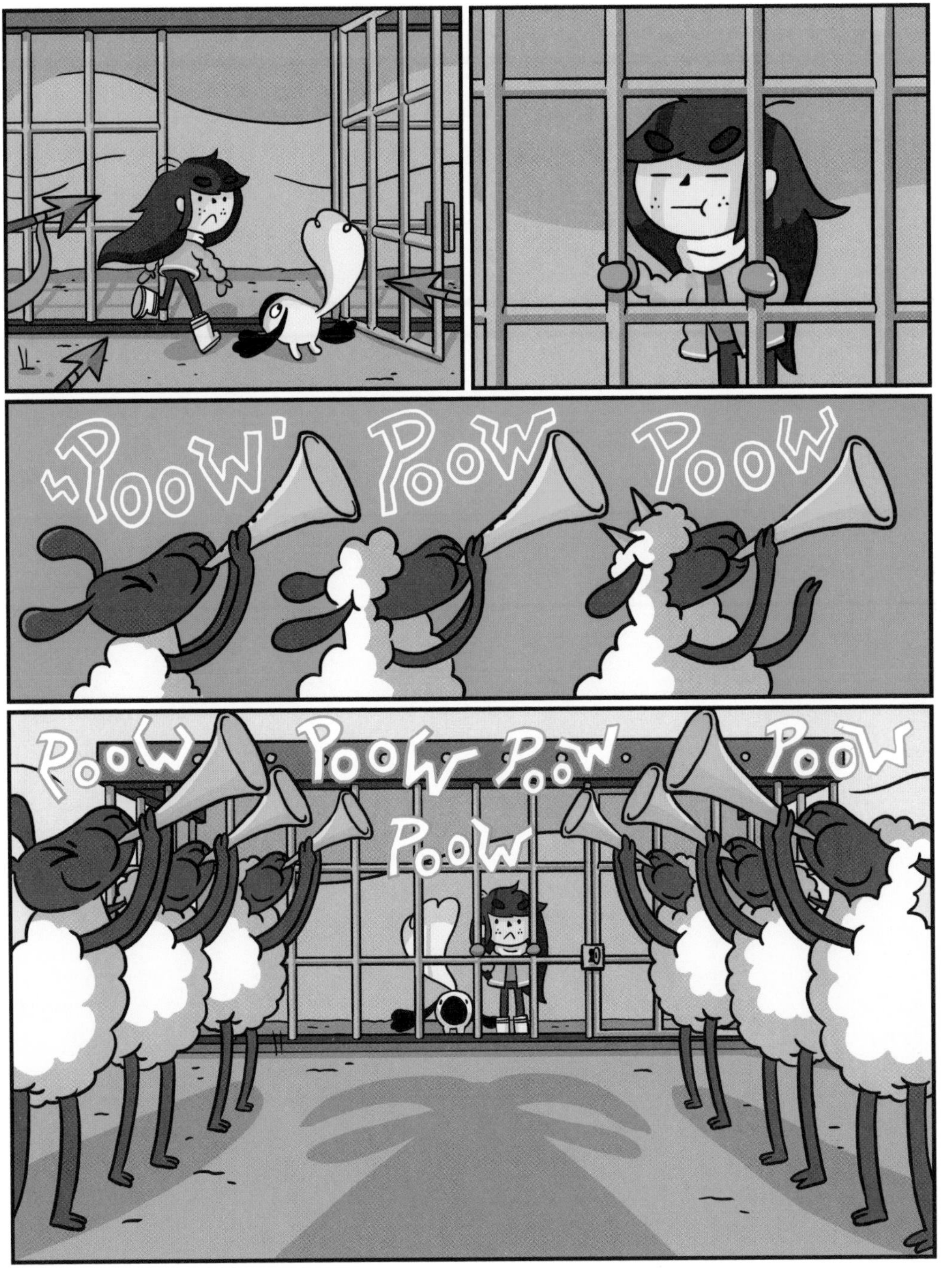
POOW POOW POOW
POOW POOW POOW POOW POOW

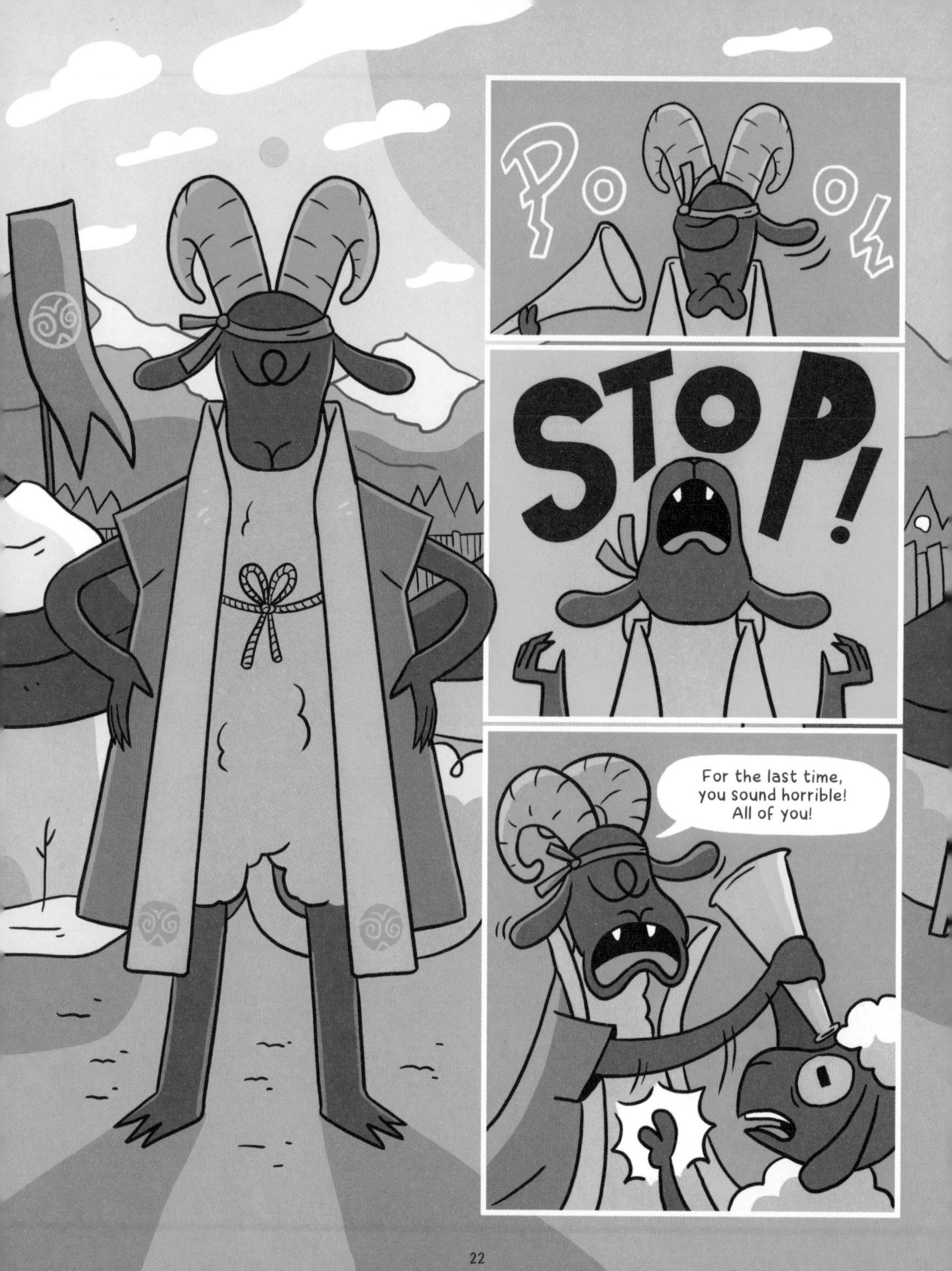
POOL
STOP!
For the last time, you sound horrible! All of you!

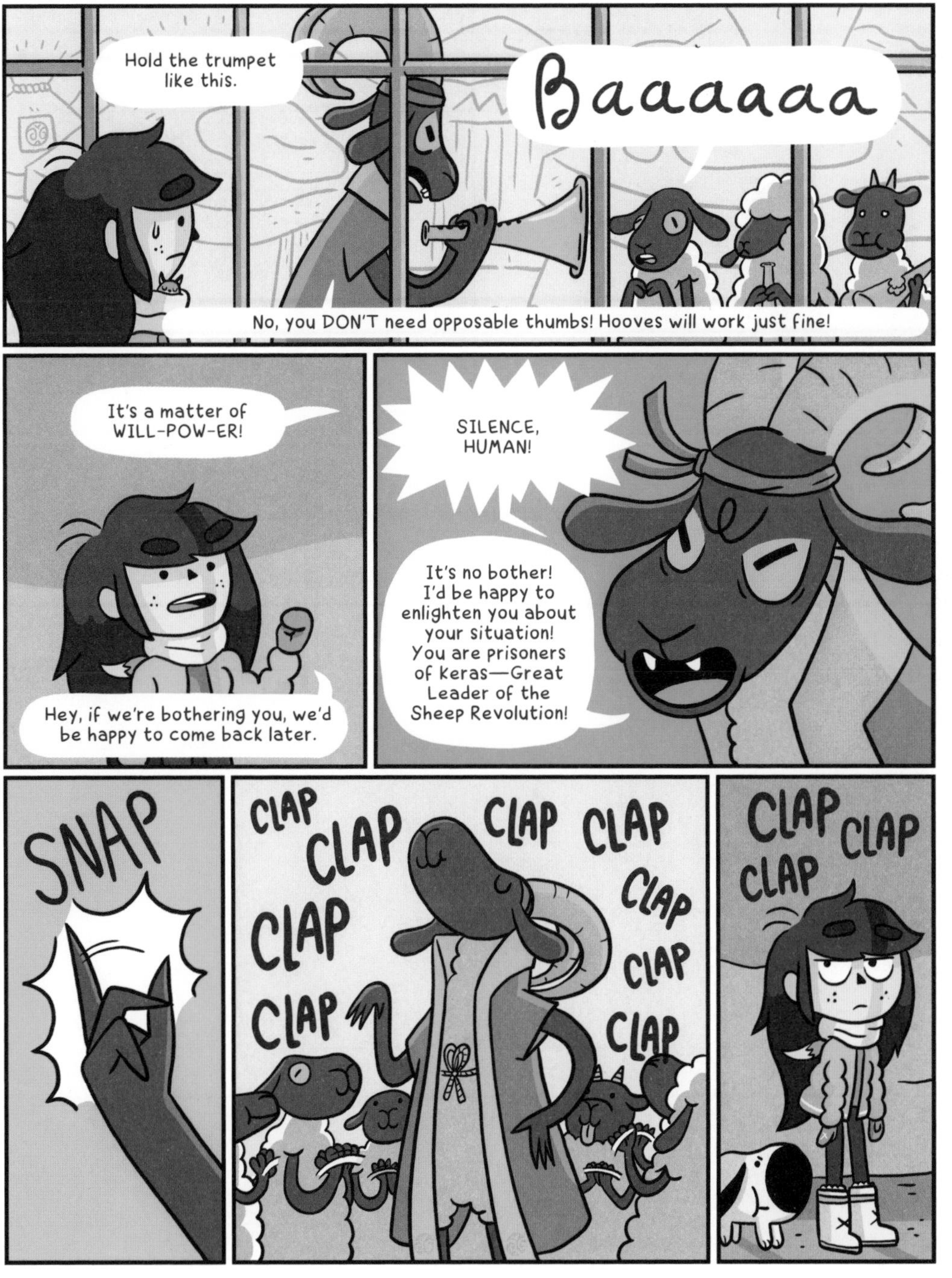

Hold the trumpet like this.
Baaaaaa
No, you DON'T need opposable thumbs! Hooves will work just fine!
It's a matter of WILL-POW-ER!
Hey, if we're bothering you, we'd be happy to come back later.
SILENCE, HUMAN!
It's no bother! I'd be happy to enlighten you about your situation! You are prisoners of Keras—Great Leader of the Sheep Revolution!
SNAP
CLAP CLAP CLAP CLAP CLAP CLAP CLAP CLAP CLAP
CLAP CLAP CLAP

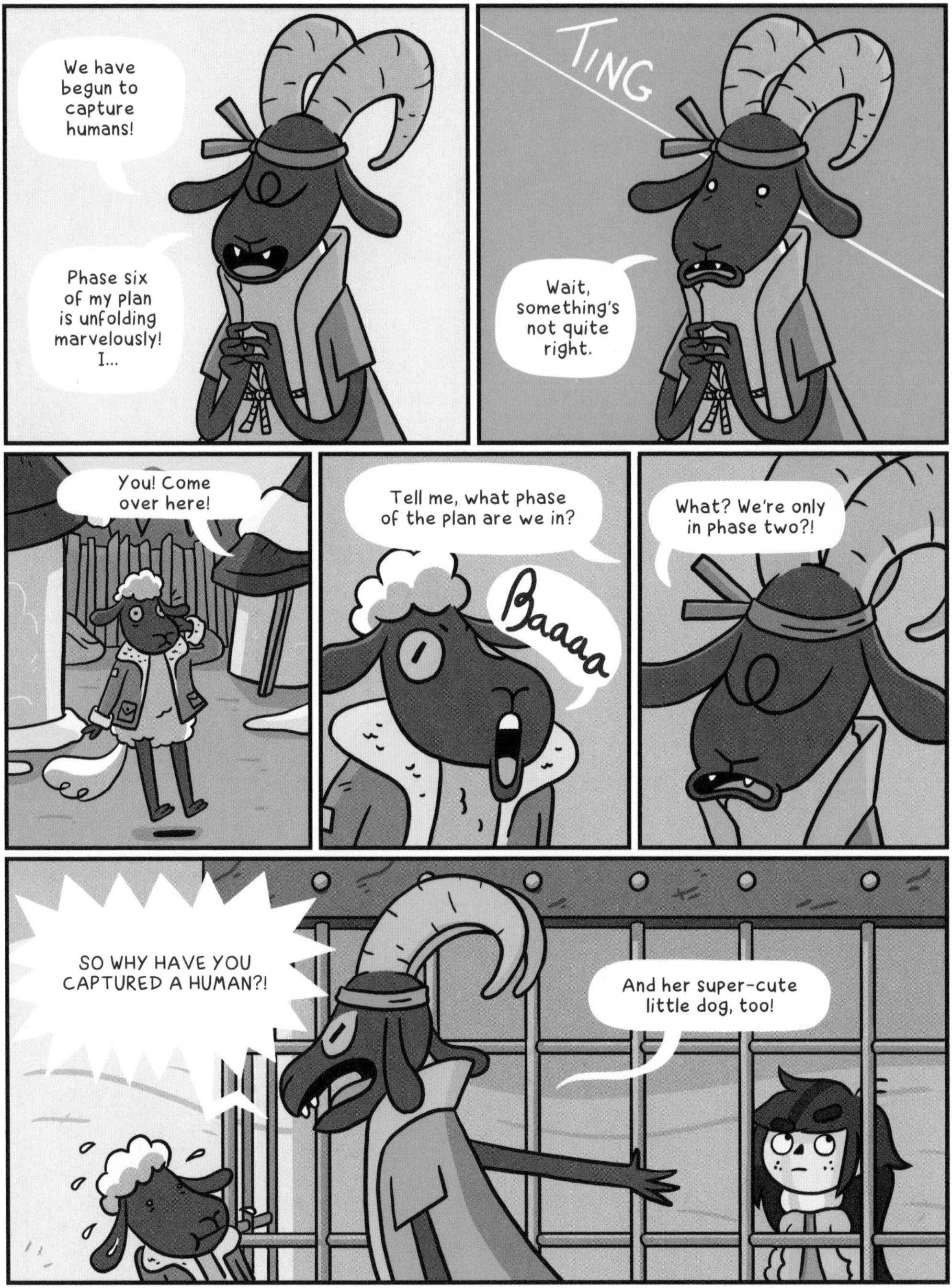
We have begun to capture humans!
Phase six of my plan is unfolding marvelously! I...
TING
Wait, something's not quite right.
You! Come over here!
Tell me, what phase of the plan are we in?
Baaaa
What? We're only in phase two?!
SO WHY HAVE YOU CAPTURED A HUMAN?!
And her super-cute little dog, too!

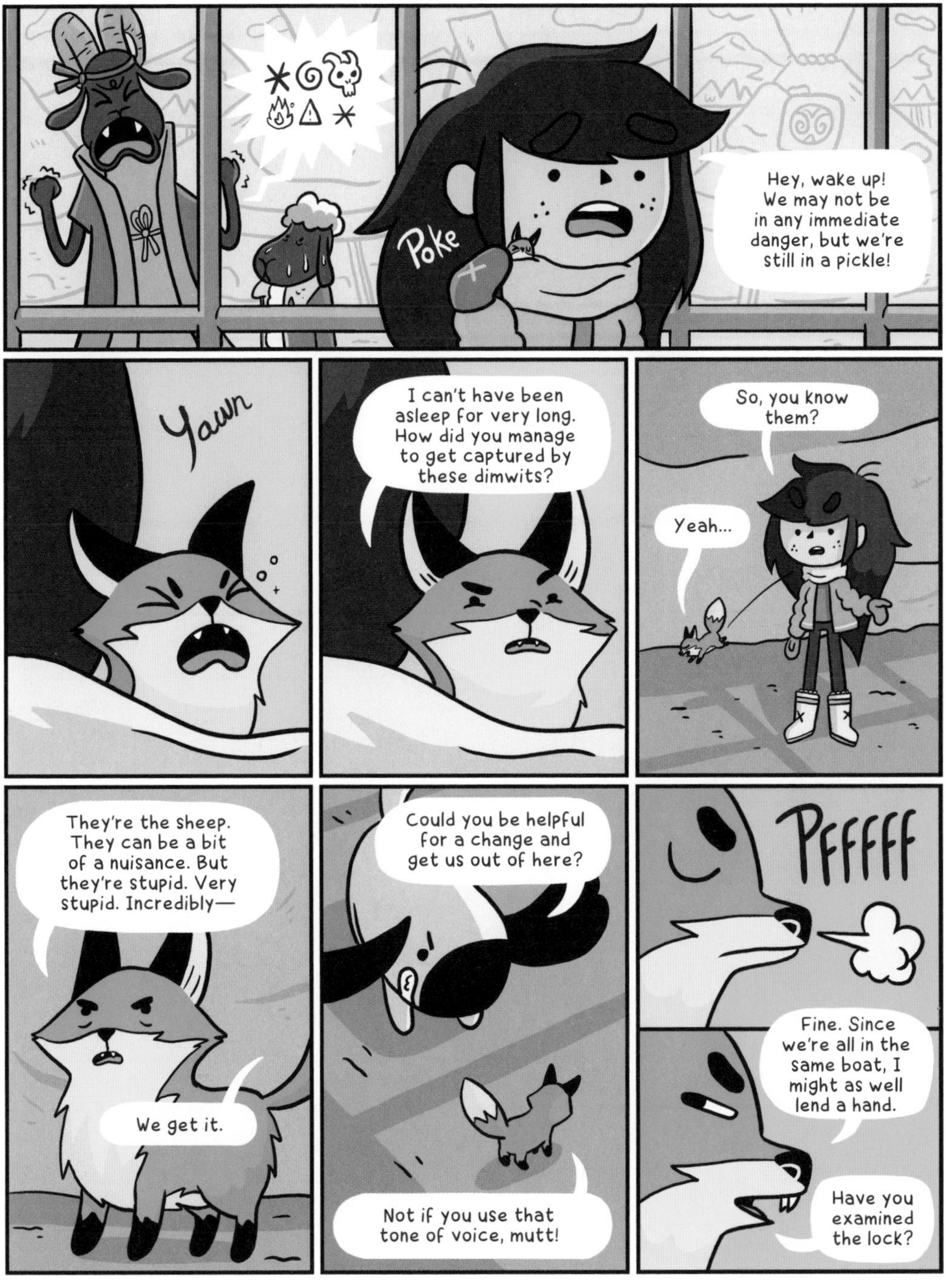
@☠ ♨⚠
Poke
Hey, wake up! We may not be in any immediate danger, but we're still in a pickle!
Yawn
I can't have been asleep for very long. How did you manage to get captured by these dimwits?
So, you know them?
Yeah...
They're the sheep. They can be a bit of a nuisance. But they're stupid. Very stupid. Incredibly—
We get it.
Could you be helpful for a change and get us out of here?
Not if you use that tone of voice, mutt!
Pfffff
Fine. Since we're all in the same boat, I might as well lend a hand.
Have you examined the lock?

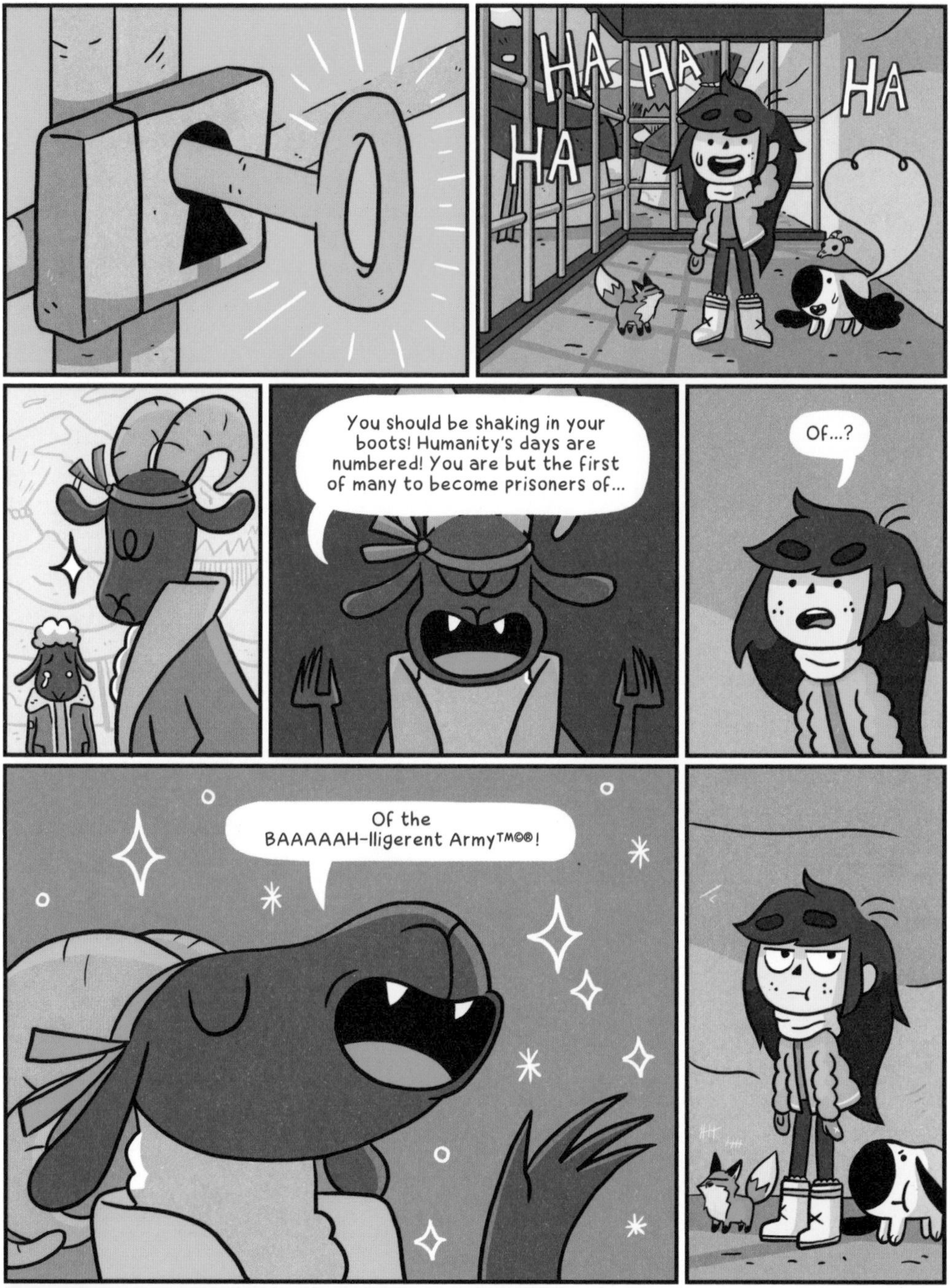
HA
HA
HA
HA
You should be shaking in your boots! Humanity's days are numbered! You are but the first of many to become prisoners of...
Of...?
Of the BAAAAAH-lligerent Army™©®!

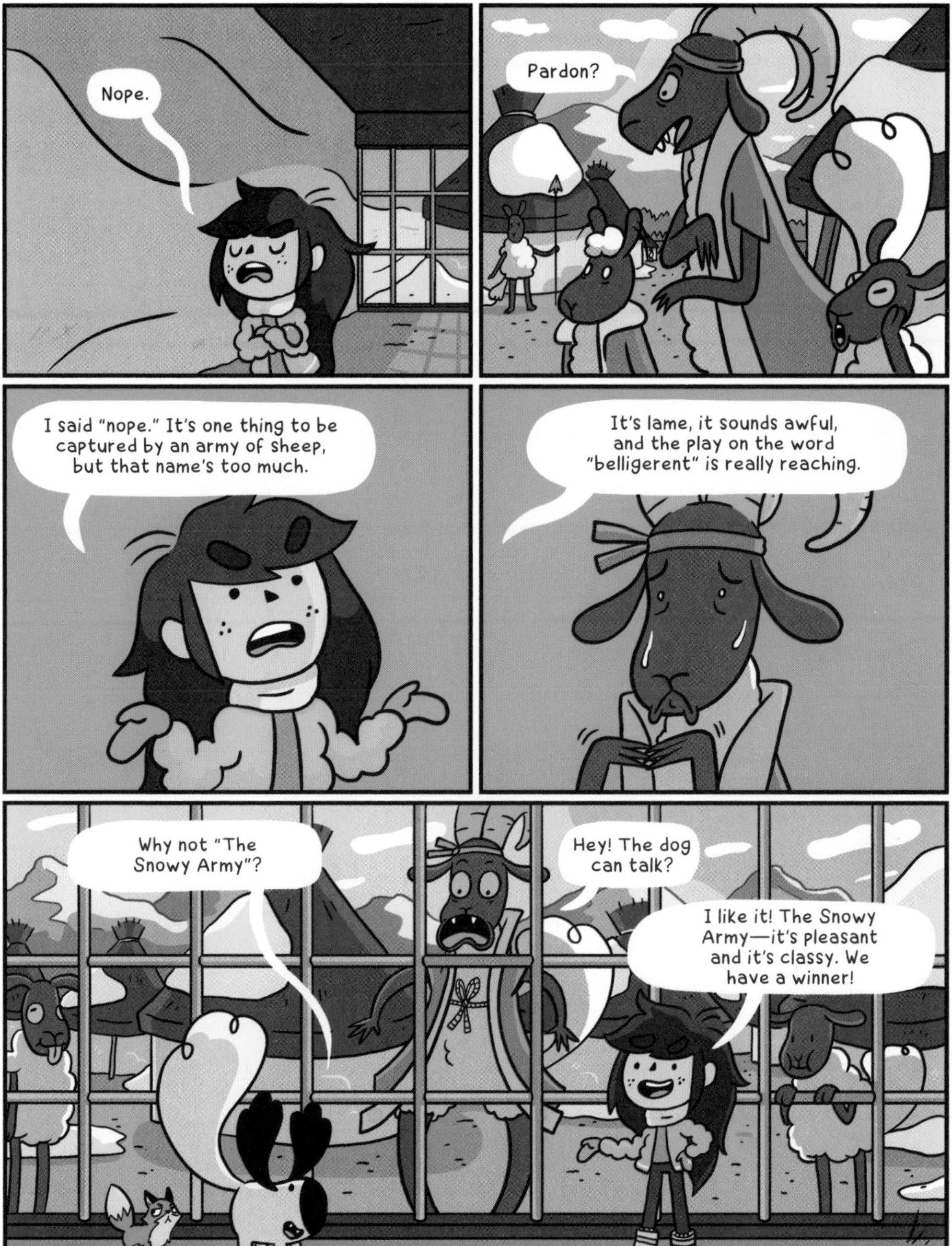
Nope.
Pardon?
I said "nope." It's one thing to be captured by an army of sheep, but that name's too much.
It's lame, it sounds awful, and the play on the word "belligerent" is really reaching.
Why not "The Snowy Army"?
Hey! The dog can talk?
I like it! The Snowy Army—it's pleasant and it's classy. We have a winner!

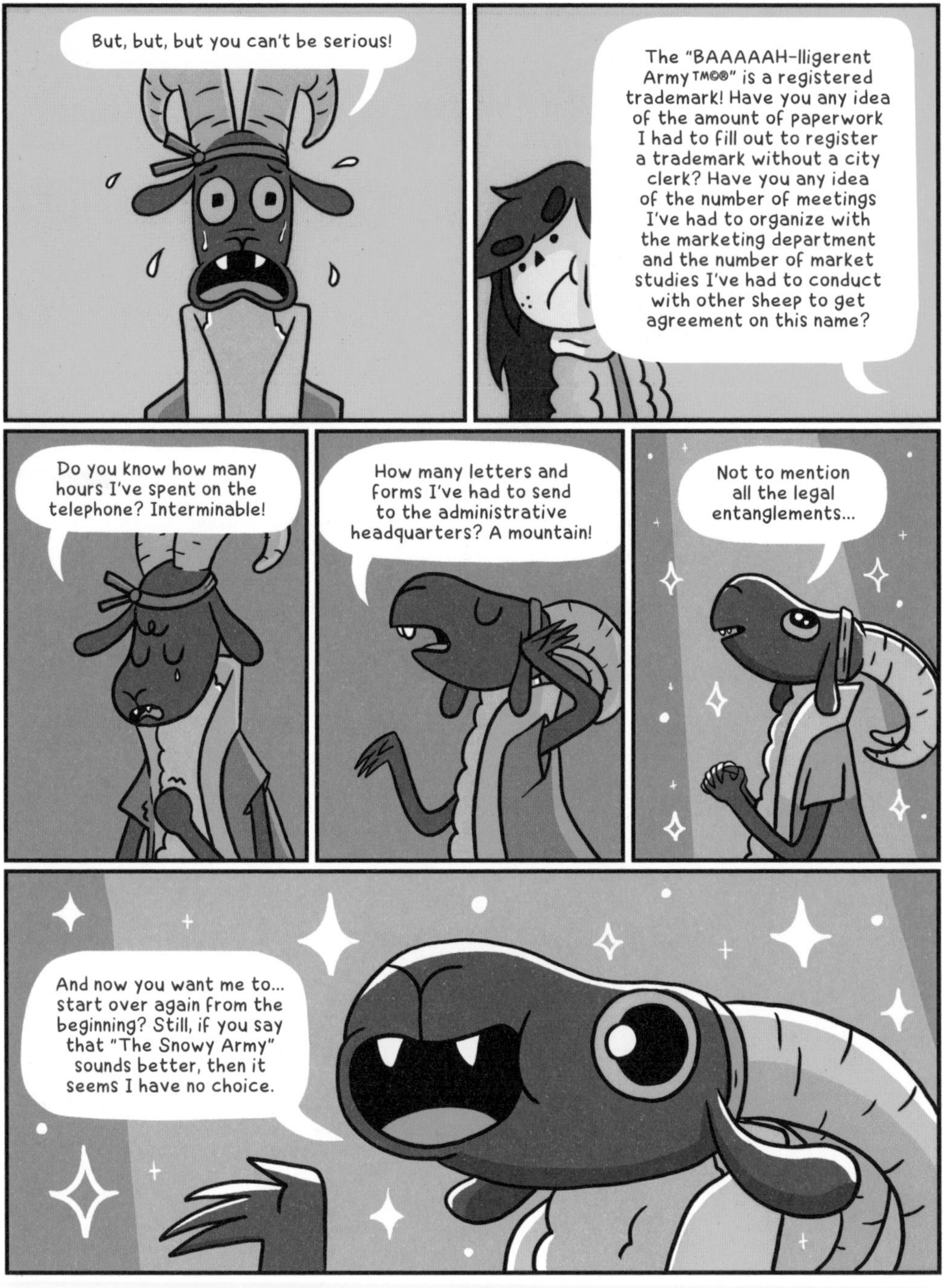
But, but, but you can't be serious!
The "BAAAAAH-lligerent Army™©®" is a registered trademark! Have you any idea of the amount of paperwork I had to fill out to register a trademark without a city clerk? Have you any idea of the number of meetings I've had to organize with the marketing department and the number of market studies I've had to conduct with other sheep to get agreement on this name?
Do you know how many hours I've spent on the telephone? Interminable!
How many letters and forms I've had to send to the administrative headquarters? A mountain!
Not to mention all the legal entanglements...
And now you want me to... start over again from the beginning? Still, if you say that "The Snowy Army" sounds better, then it seems I have no choice.

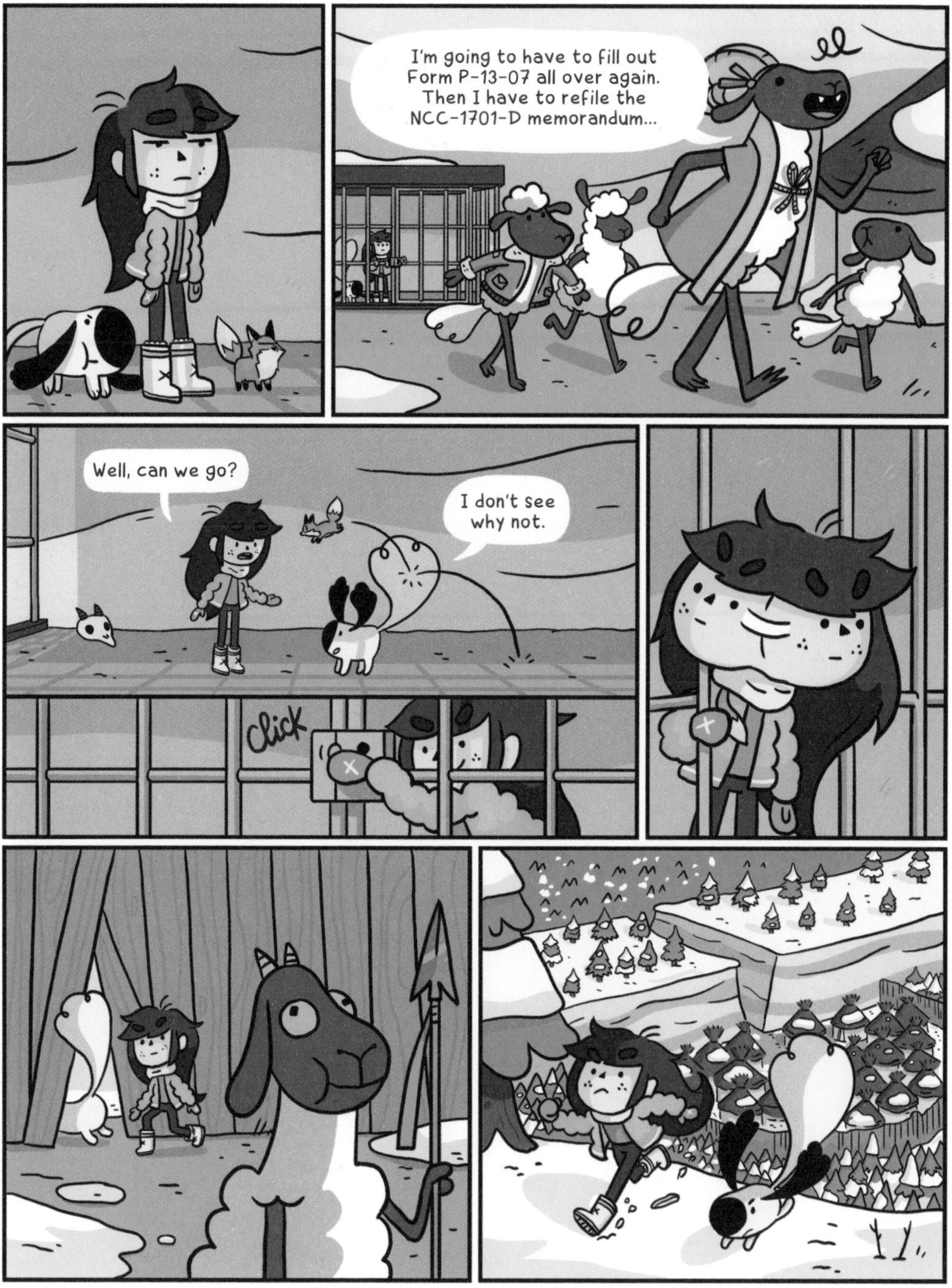

I'm going to have to fill out Form P-13-07 all over again. Then I have to refile the NCC-1701-D memorandum...
Well, can we go?
I don't see why not.
Click

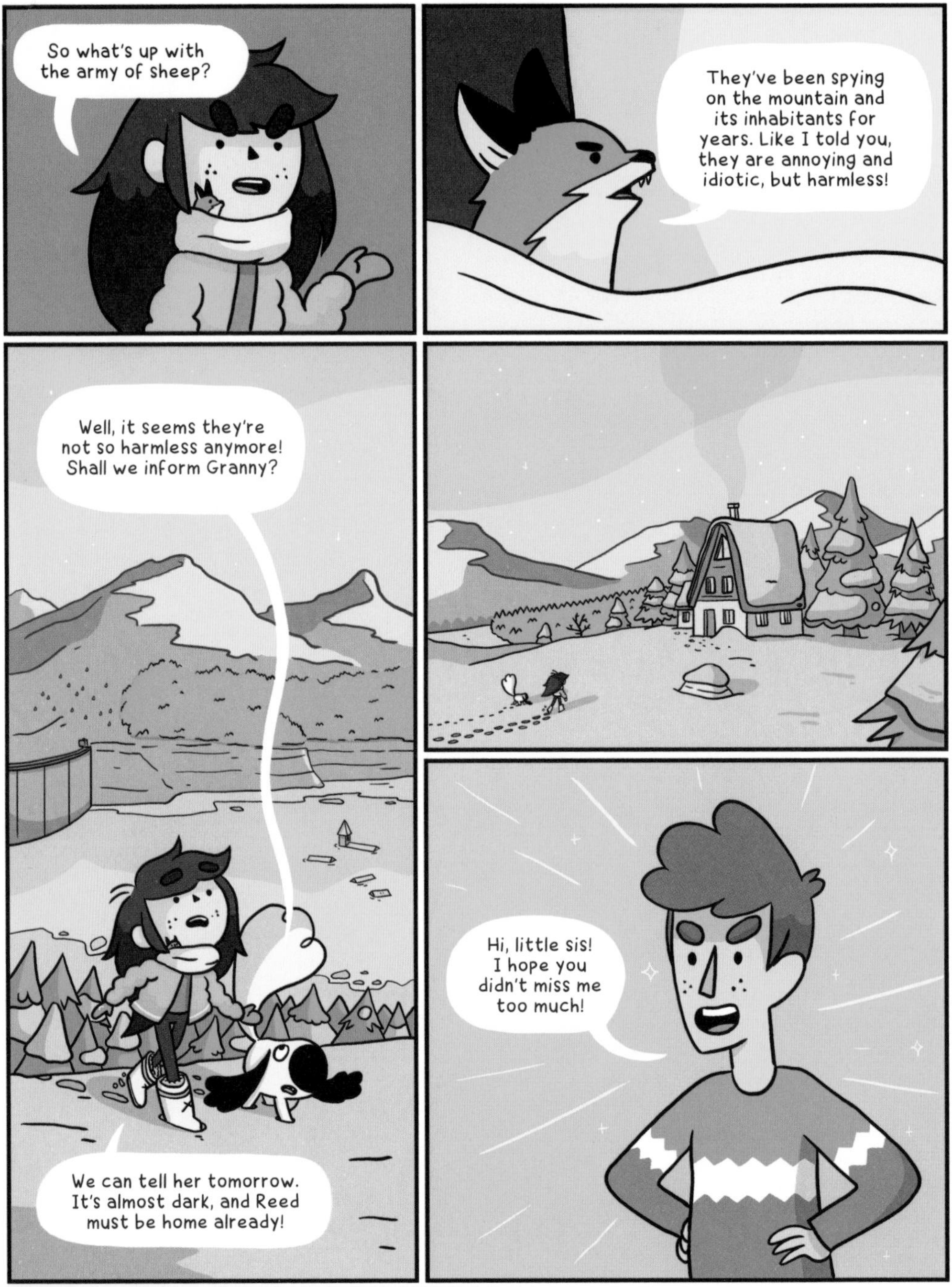
So what's up with the army of sheep?
They've been spying on the mountain and its inhabitants for years. Like I told you, they are annoying and idiotic, but harmless!
Well, it seems they're not so harmless anymore! Shall we inform Granny?
We can tell her tomorrow. It's almost dark, and Reed must be home already!
Hi, little sis! I hope you didn't miss me too much!

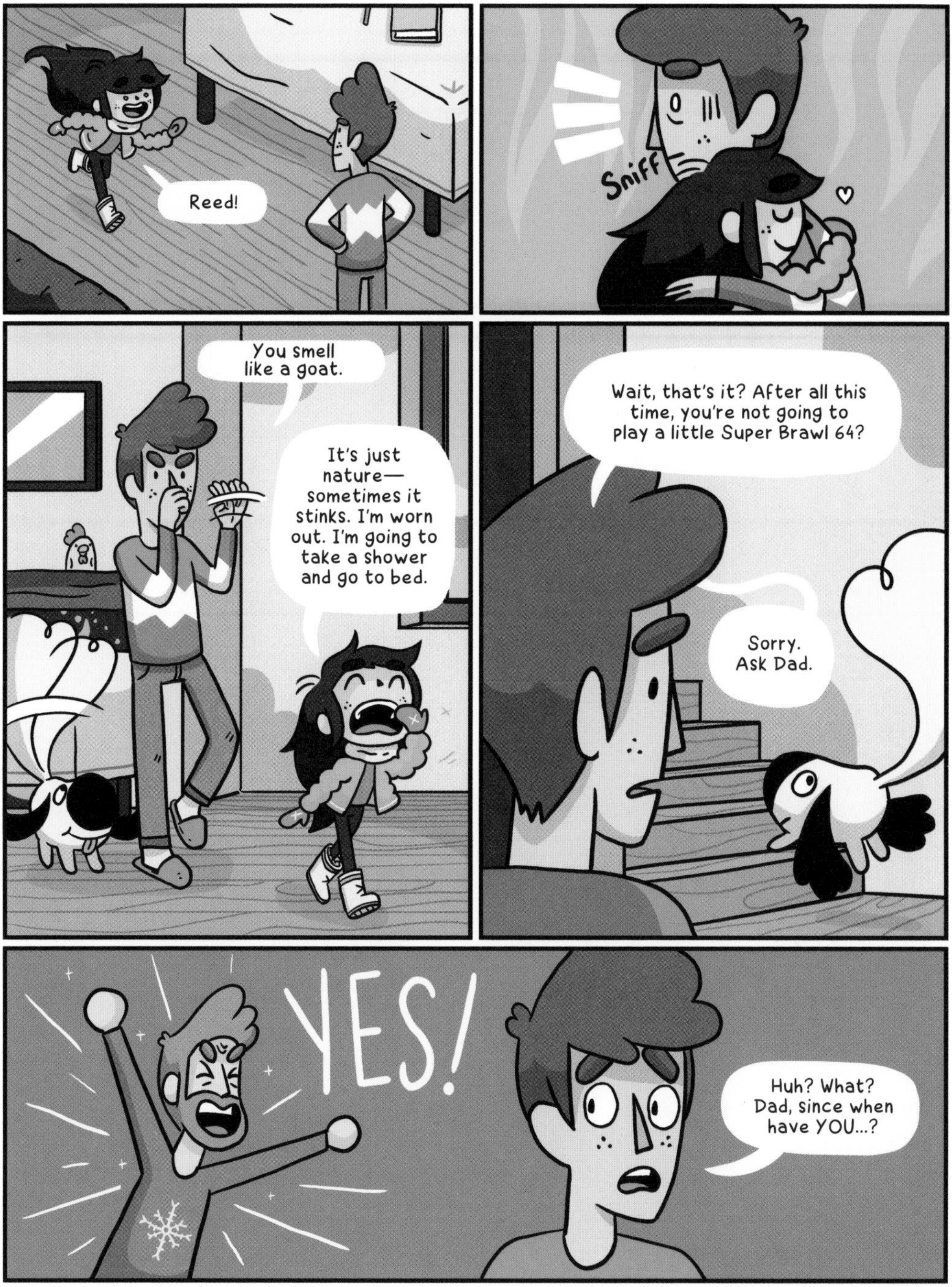
Reed!
Sniff
You smell like a goat.
It's just nature— sometimes it stinks. I'm worn out. I'm going to take a shower and go to bed.
Wait, that's it? After all this time, you're not going to play a little Super Brawl 64?
Sorry. Ask Dad.
YES!
Huh? What? Dad, since when have YOU...?

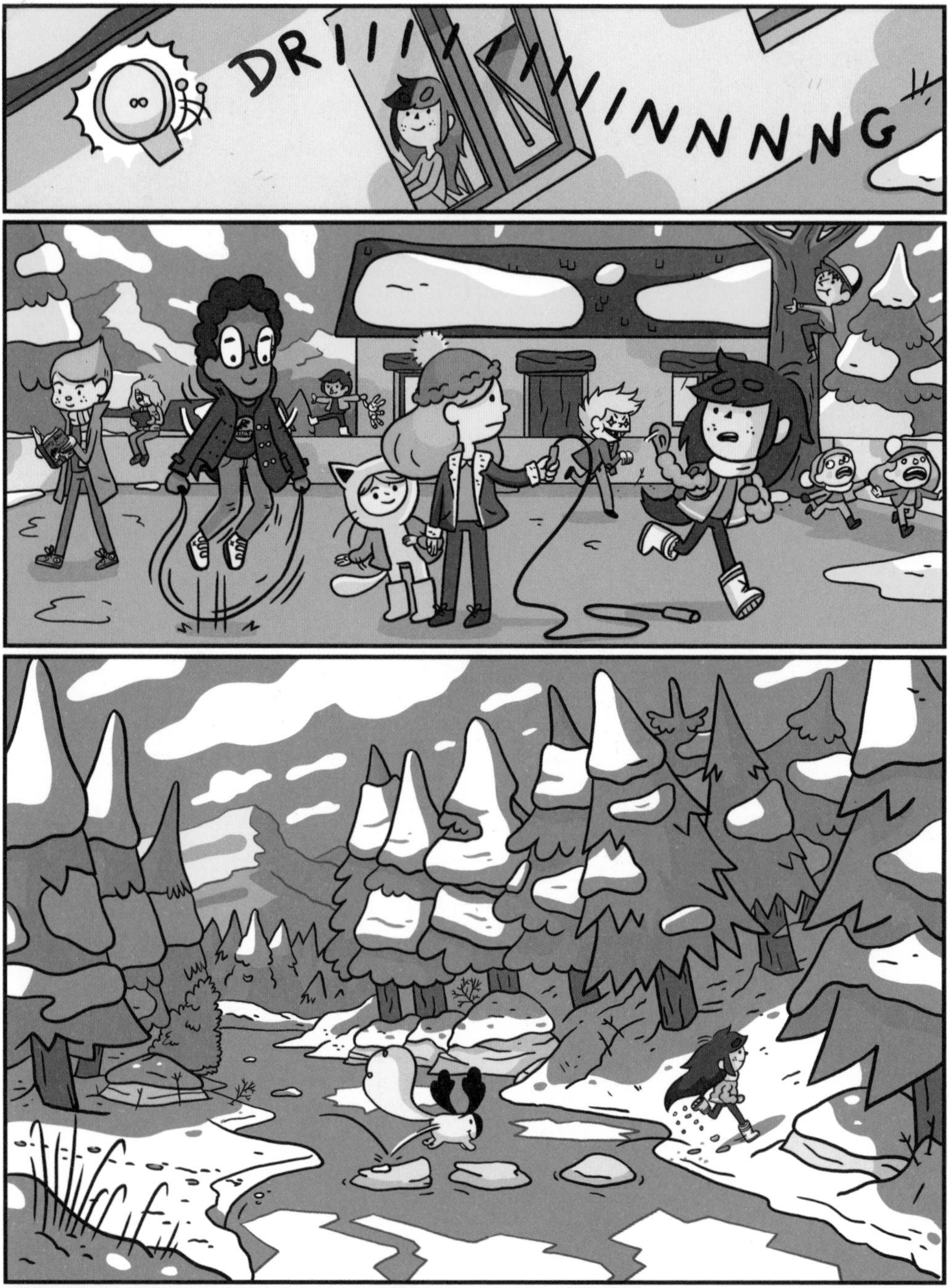
DRIIIIIIIIINNNNG

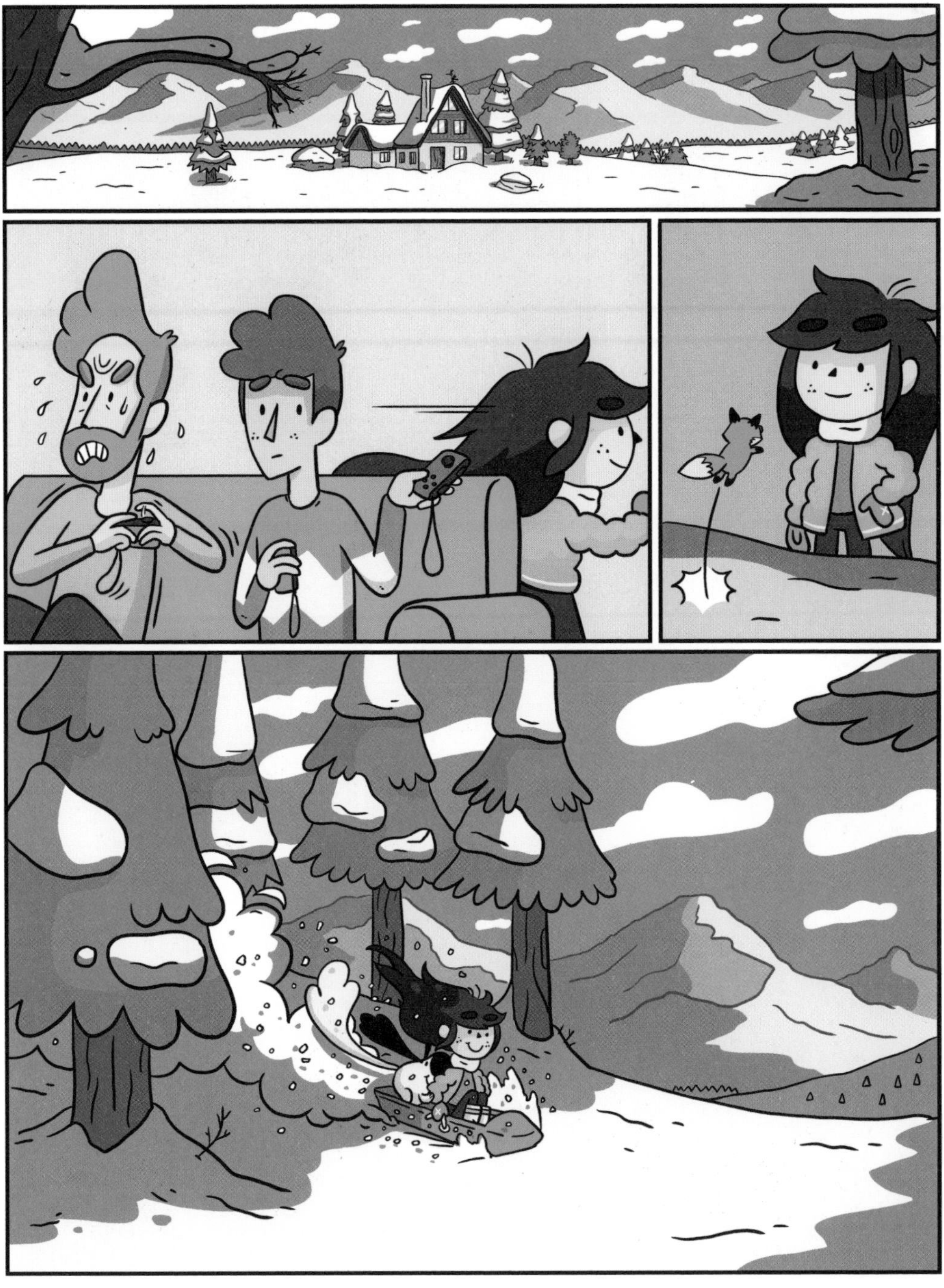

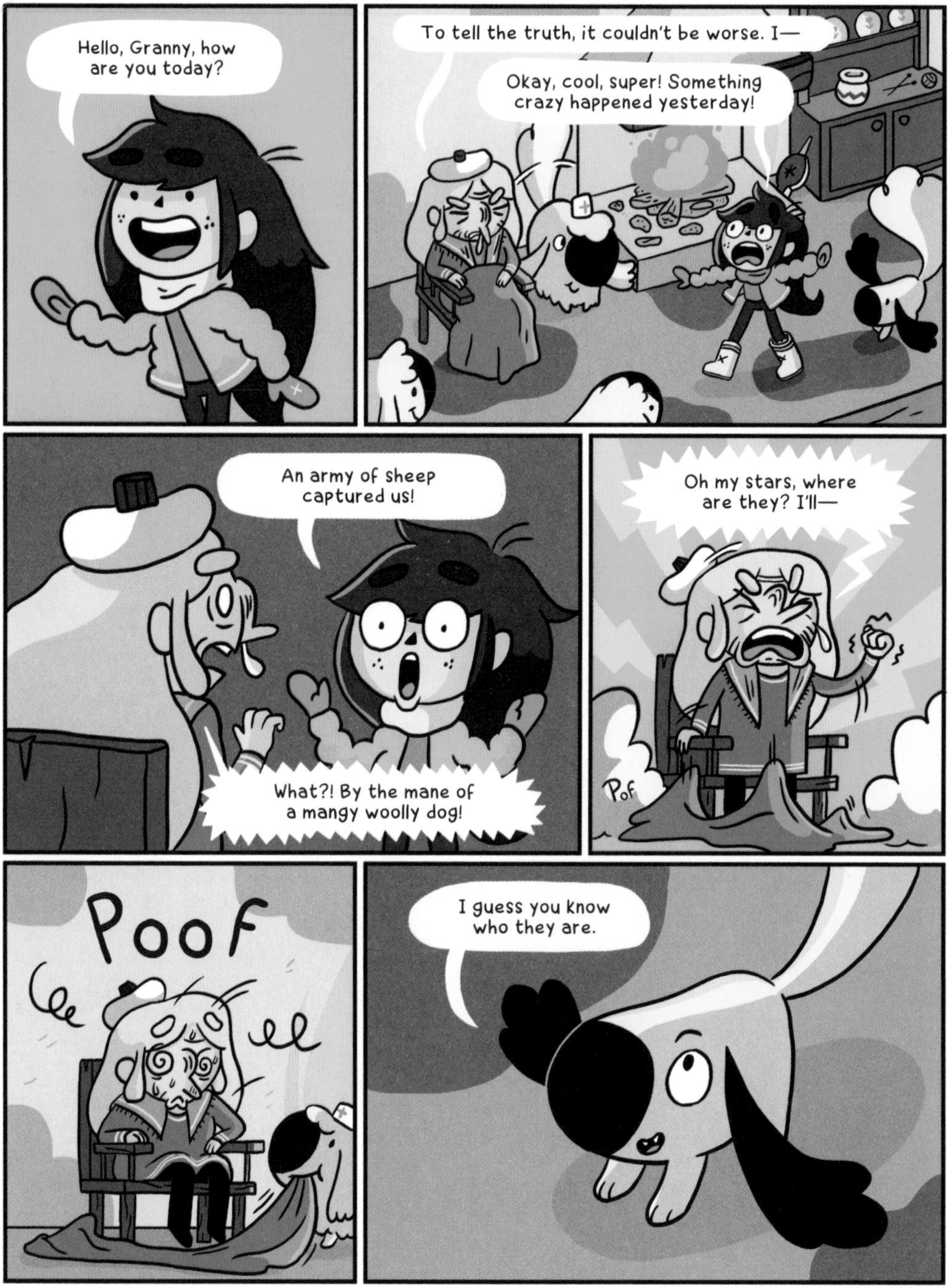
Hello, Granny, how are you today?
To tell the truth, it couldn't be worse. I—
Okay, cool, super! Something crazy happened yesterday!
An army of sheep captured us!
What?! By the mane of a mangy woolly dog!
Oh my stars, where are they? I'll—
Pof
Poof
I guess you know who they are.

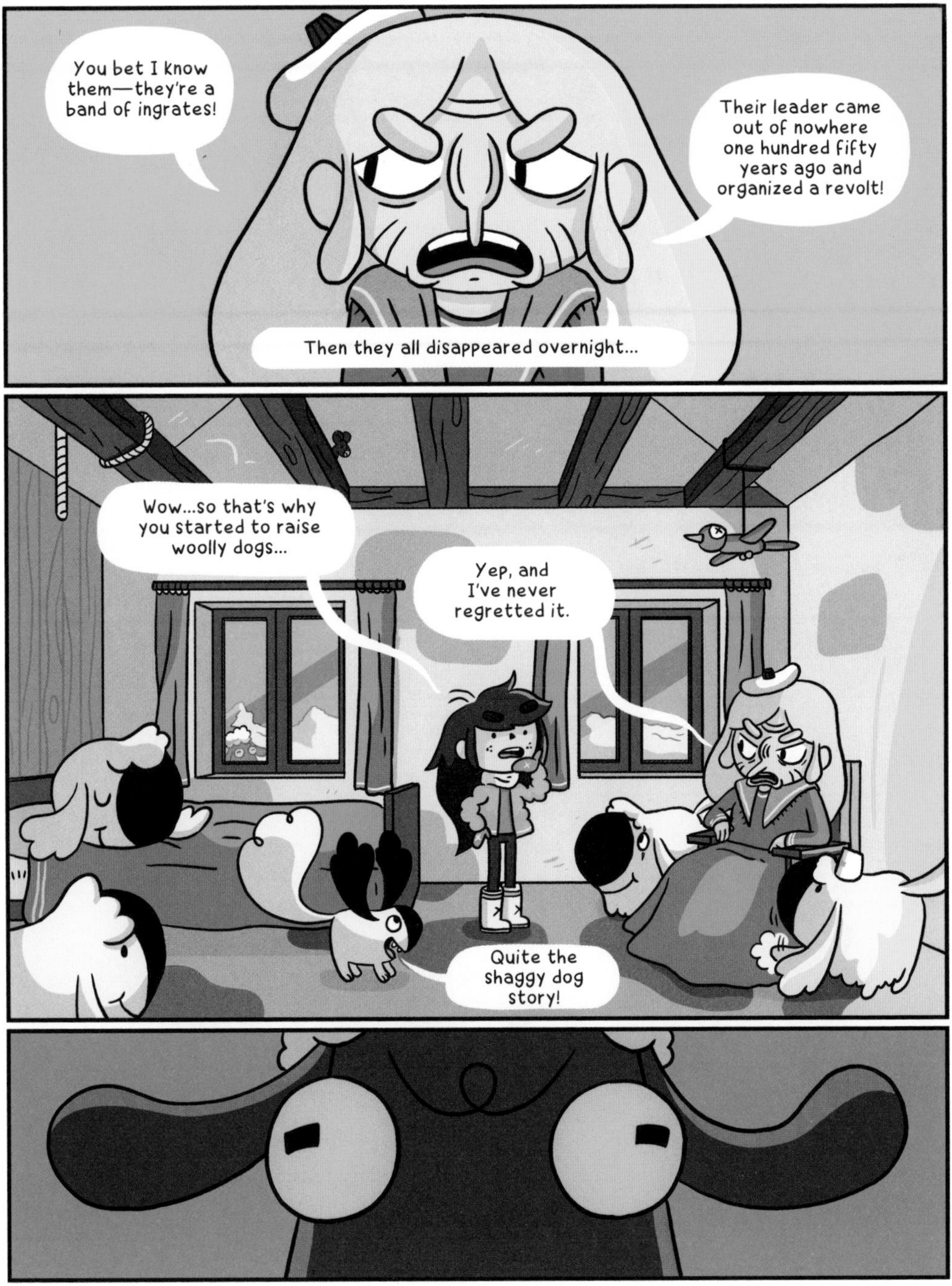
You bet I know them—they're a band of ingrates!
Their leader came out of nowhere one hundred fifty years ago and organized a revolt!
Then they all disappeared overnight...
Wow...so that's why you started to raise woolly dogs...
Yep, and I've never regretted it.
Quite the shaggy dog story!

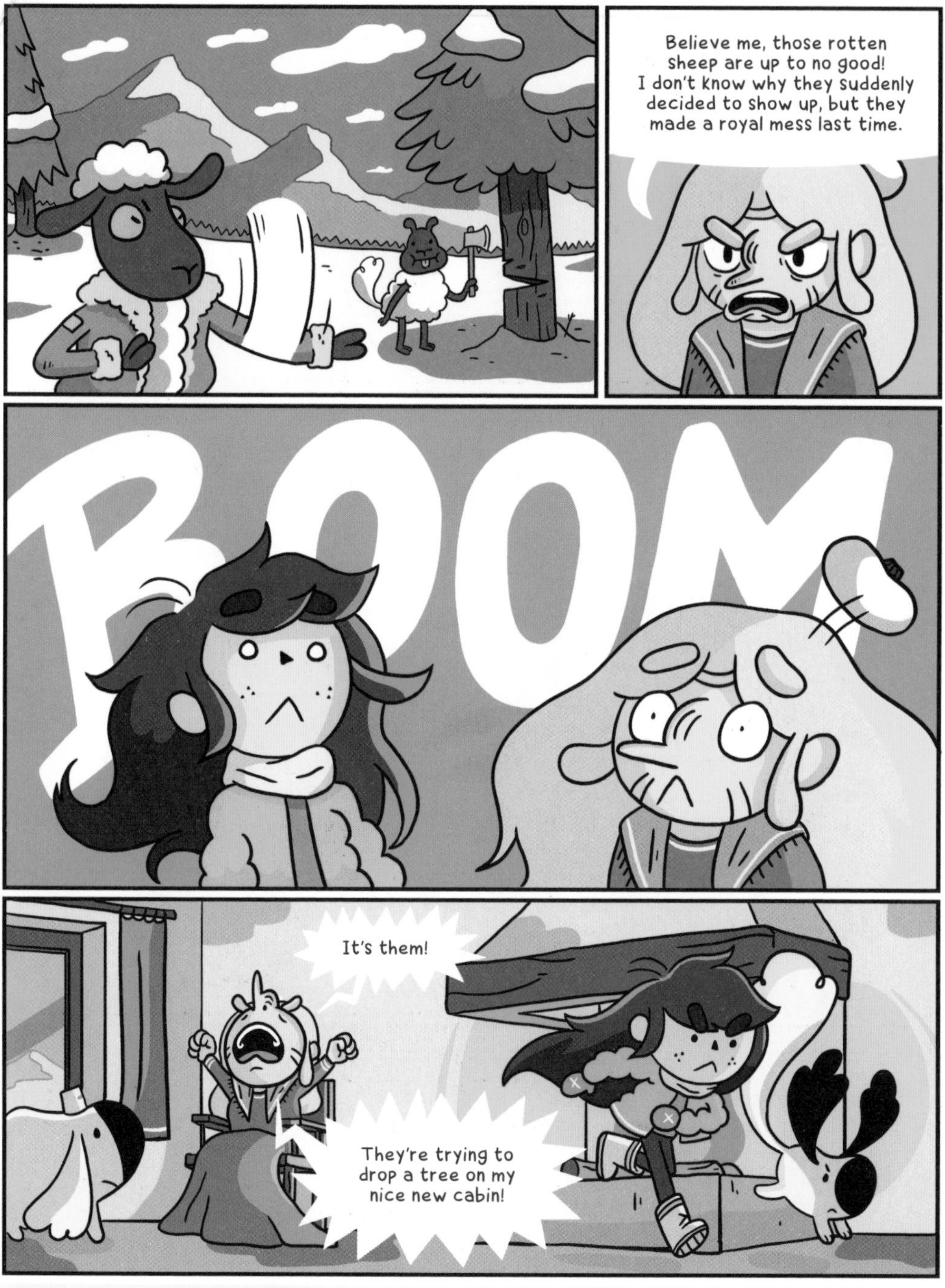

Believe me, those rotten sheep are up to no good! I don't know why they suddenly decided to show up, but they made a royal mess last time.
BOOM
It's them!
They're trying to drop a tree on my nice new cabin!

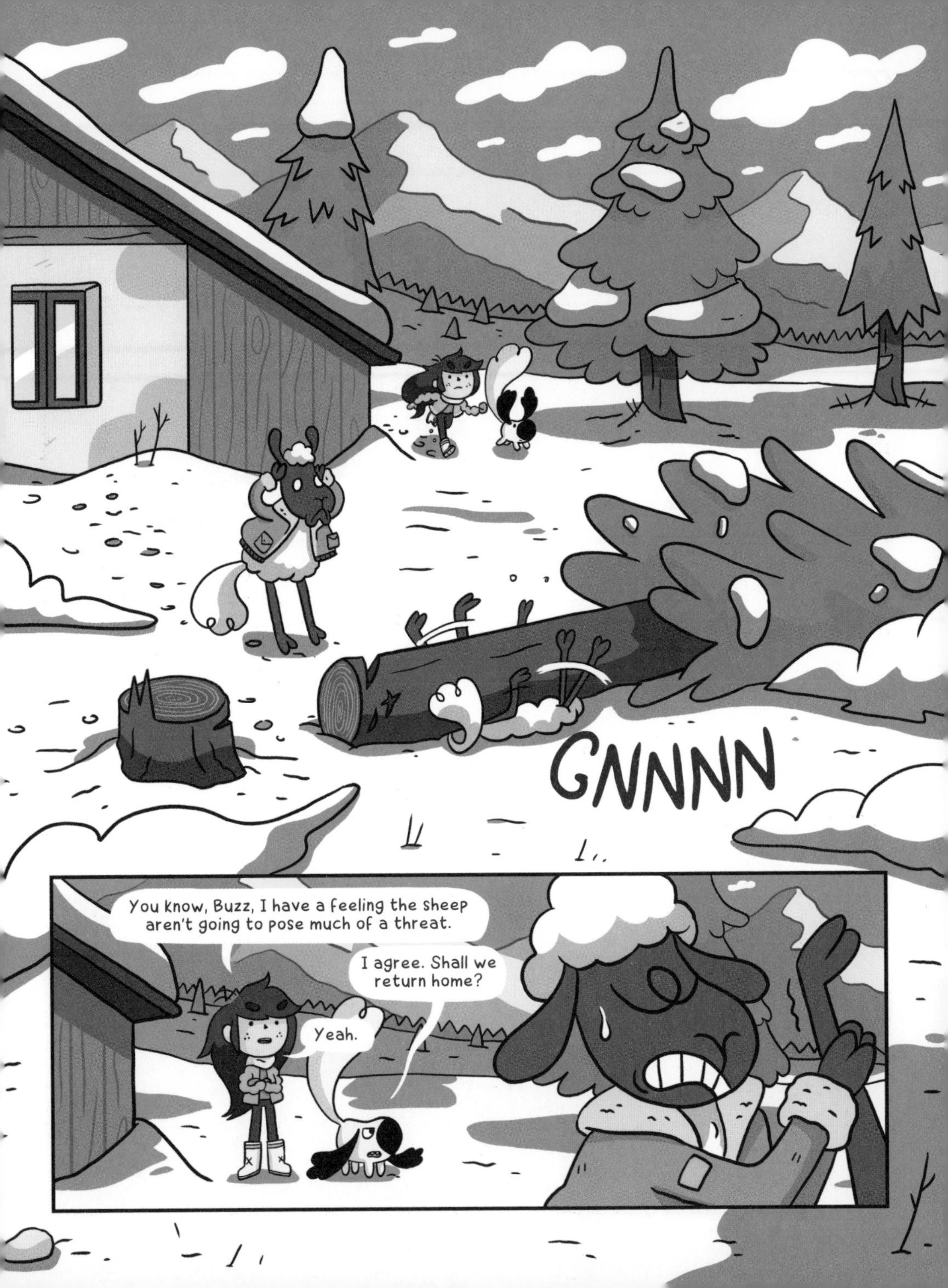
GNNNN
You know, Buzz, I have a feeling the sheep aren't going to pose much of a threat.
I agree. Shall we return home?
Yeah.

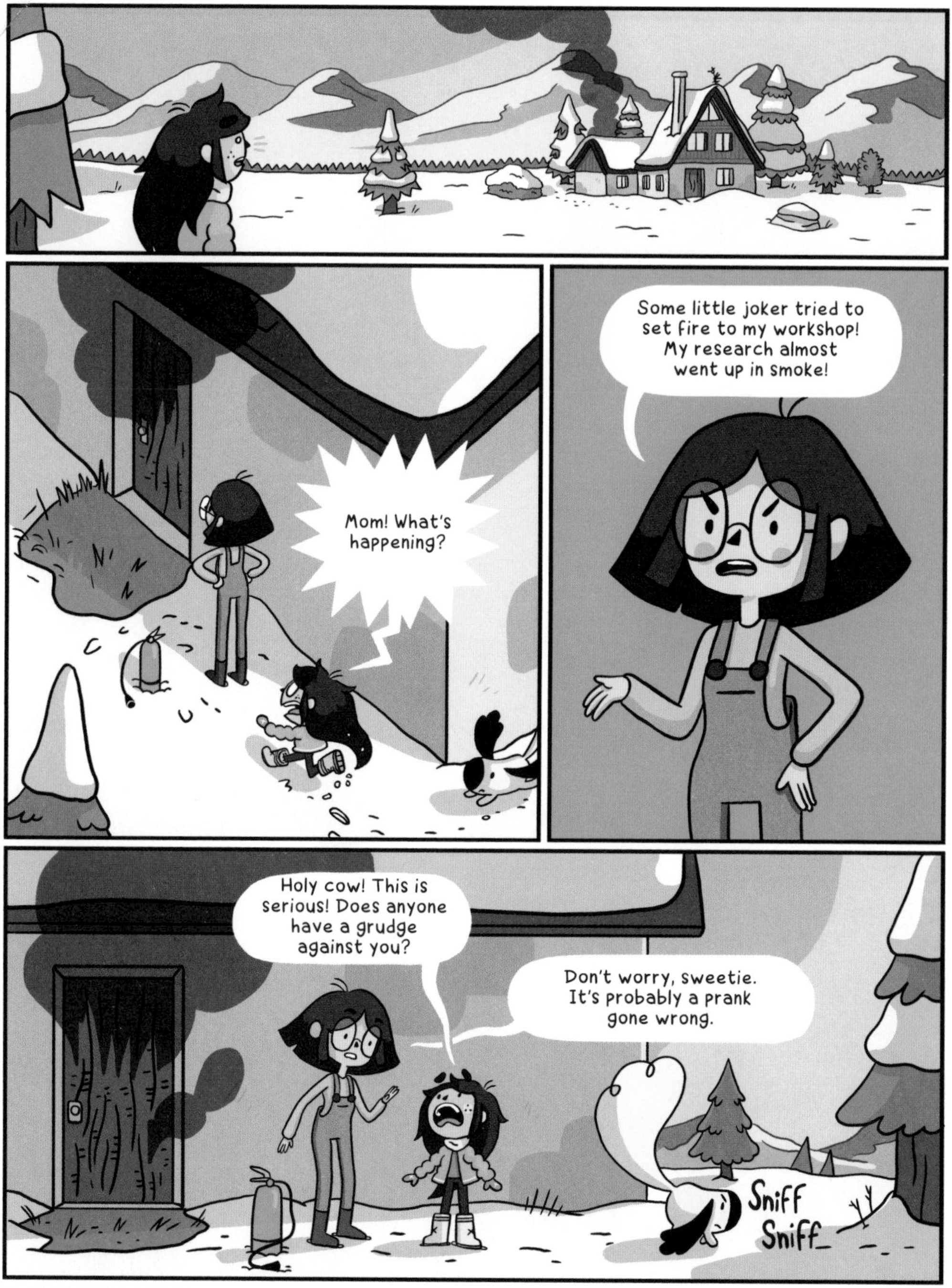
Mom! What's happening?
Some little joker tried to set fire to my workshop! My research almost went up in smoke!
Holy cow! This is serious! Does anyone have a grudge against you?
Don't worry, sweetie. It's probably a prank gone wrong.
Sniff Sniff

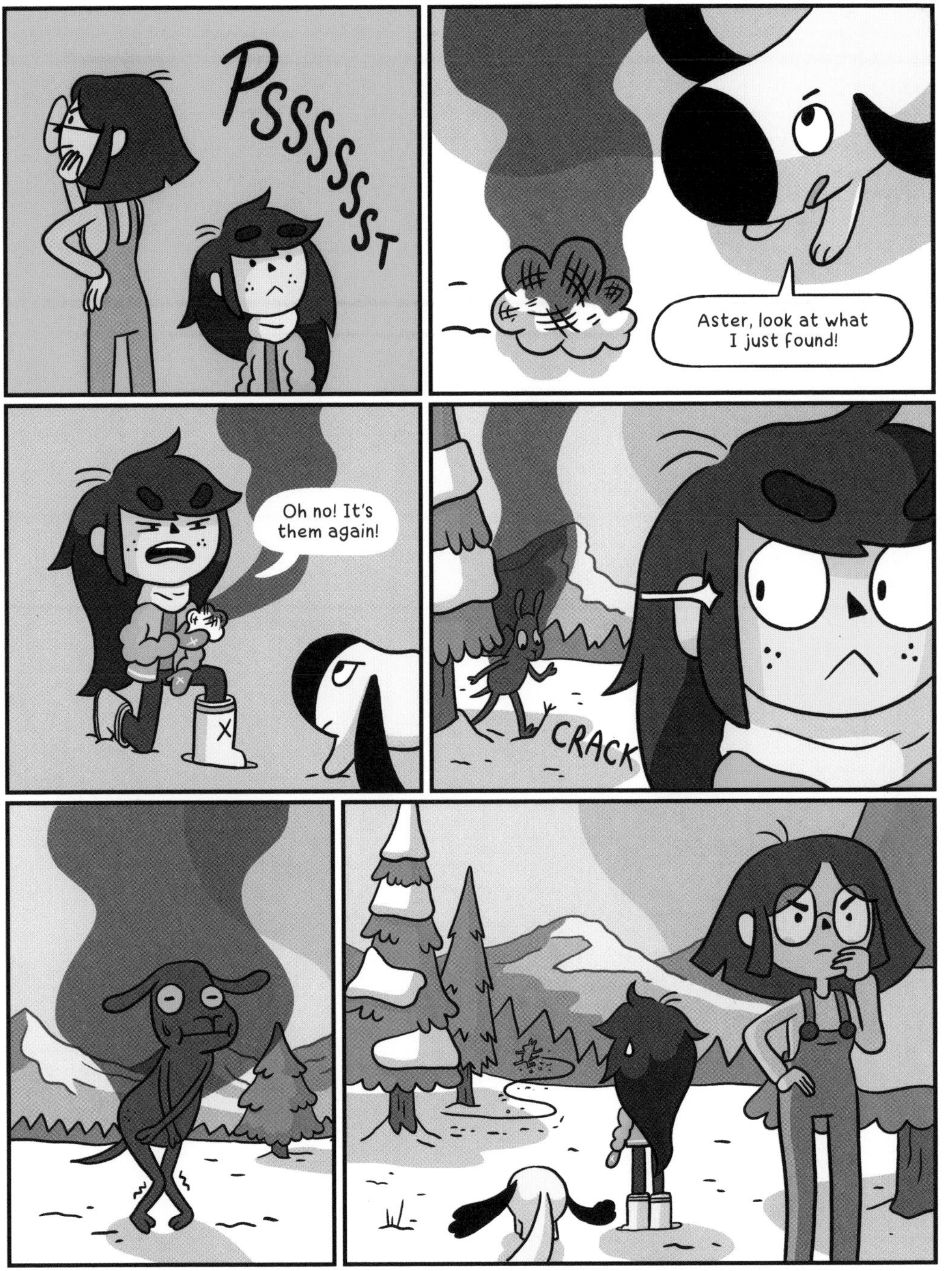
PSSSSSST
Aster, look at what I just found!
Oh no! It's them again!
CRACK

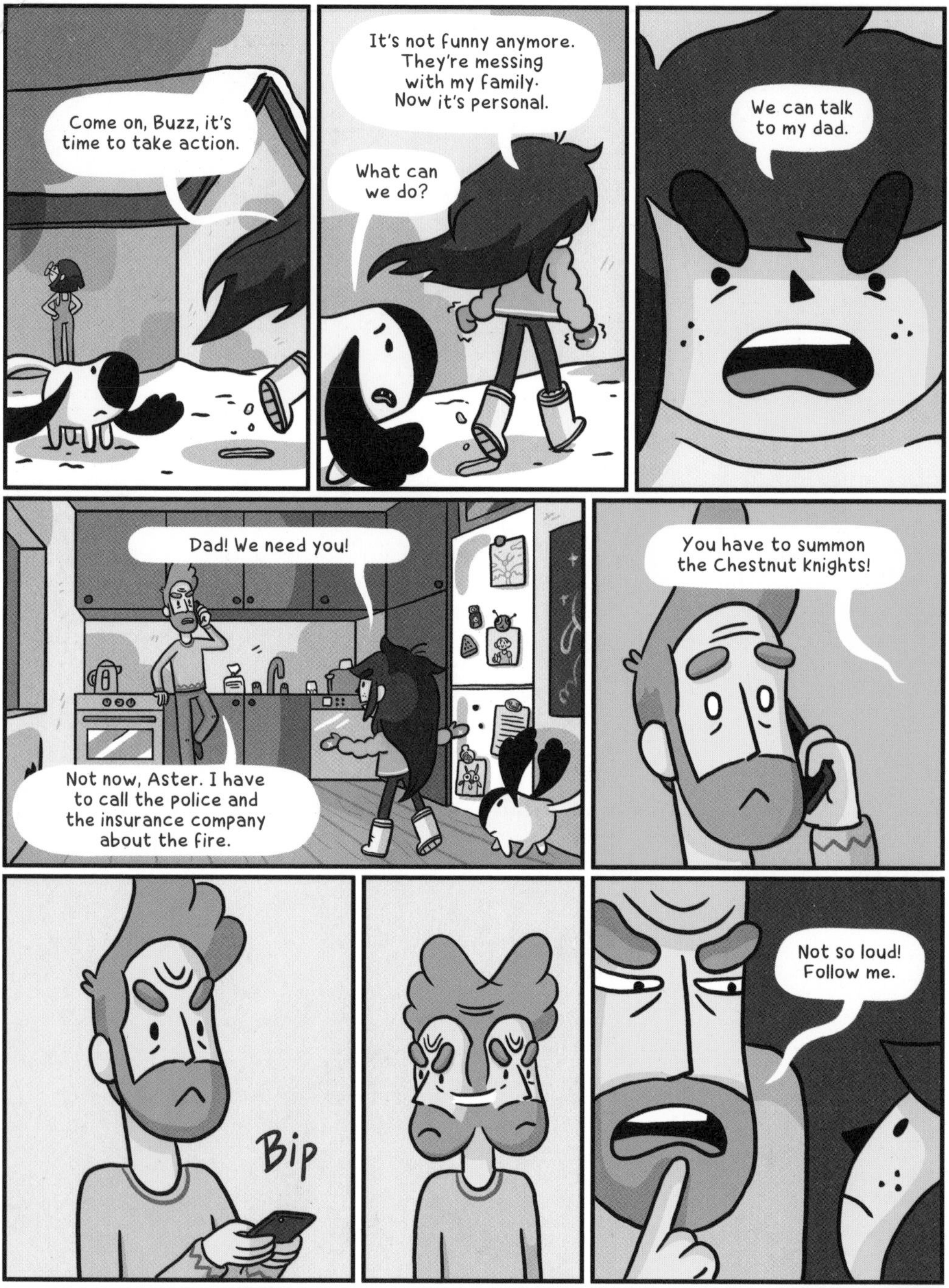

Come on, Buzz, it's time to take action.
What can we do?
It's not funny anymore. They're messing with my family. Now it's personal.
We can talk to my dad.
Dad! We need you!
Not now, Aster. I have to call the police and the insurance company about the fire.
You have to summon the Chestnut Knights!
Bip
Not so loud! Follow me.

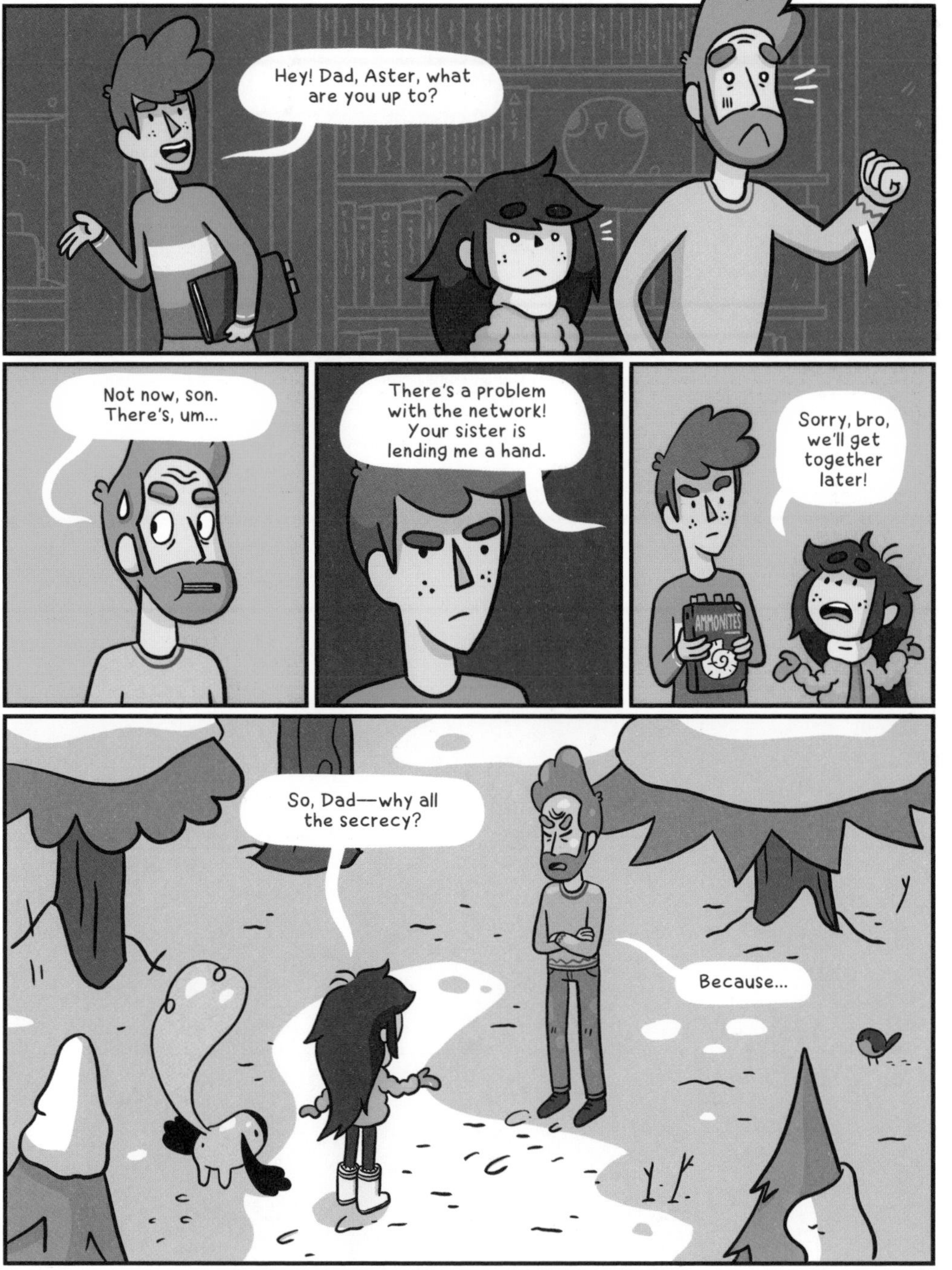
Hey! Dad, Aster, what are you up to?
Not now, son. There's, um...
There's a problem with the network! Your sister is lending me a hand.
Sorry, bro, we'll get together later!
AMMONITES
So, Dad—why all the secrecy?
Because...

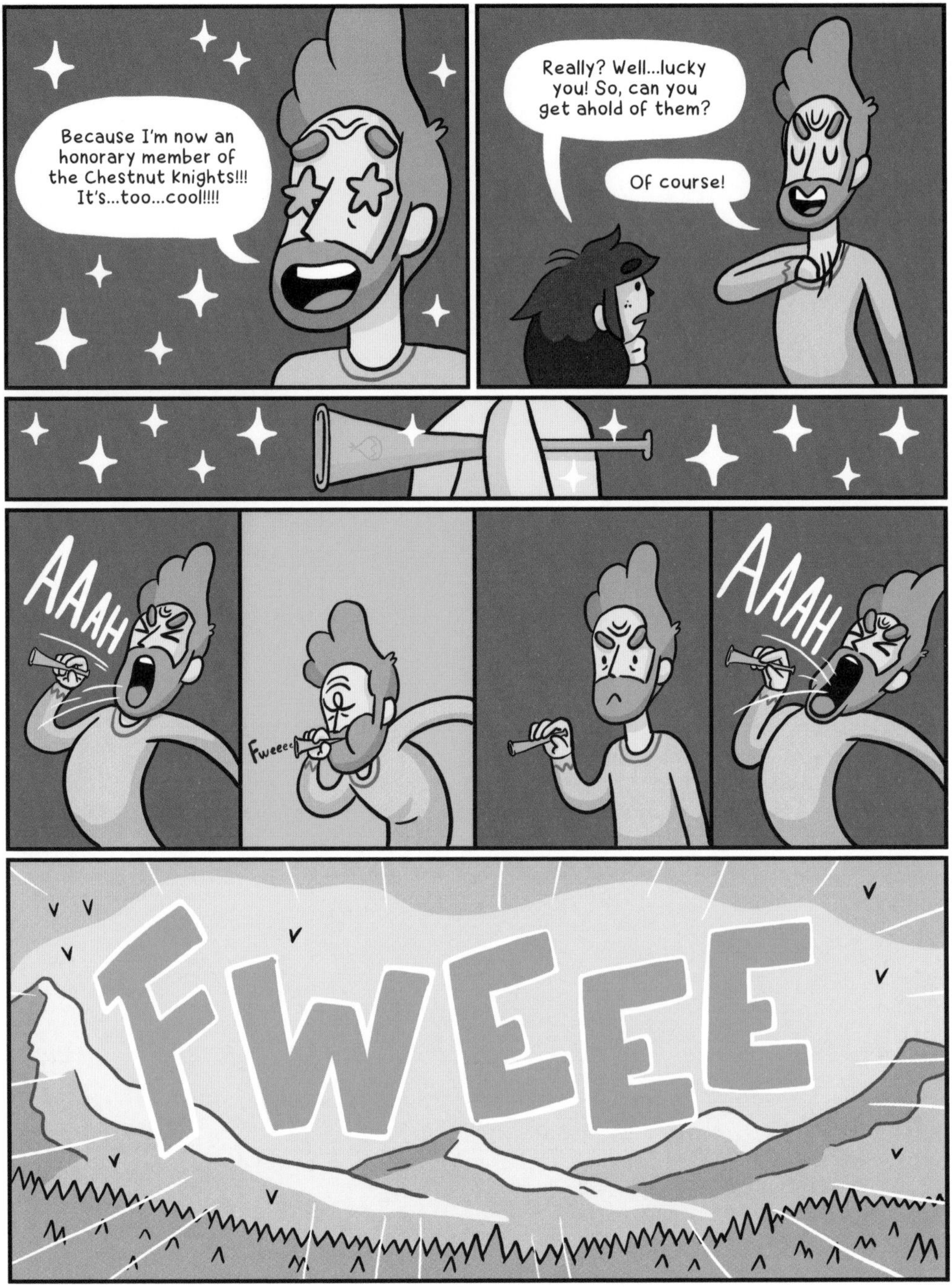
Because I'm now an honorary member of the Chestnut Knights!!! It's...too...cool!!!!
Really? Well...lucky you! So, can you get ahold of them?
Of course!
AAAH
Fweee
AAAH
FWEEE

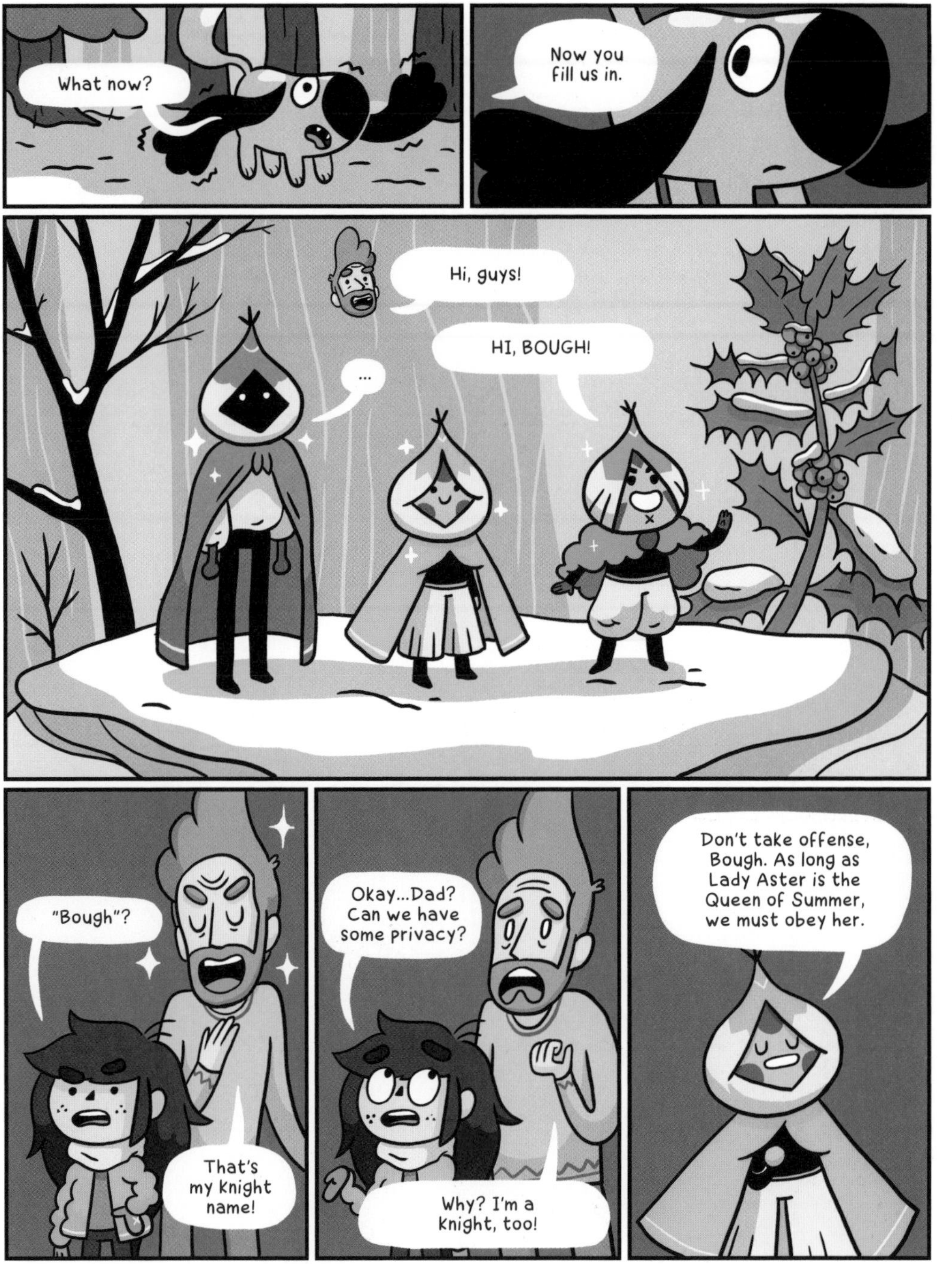
What now?
Now you fill us in.
Hi, guys!
HI, BOUGH!
...
"Bough"?
That's my knight name!
Okay...Dad? Can we have some privacy?
Why? I'm a knight, too!
Don't take offense, Bough. As long as Lady Aster is the Queen of Summer, we must obey her.

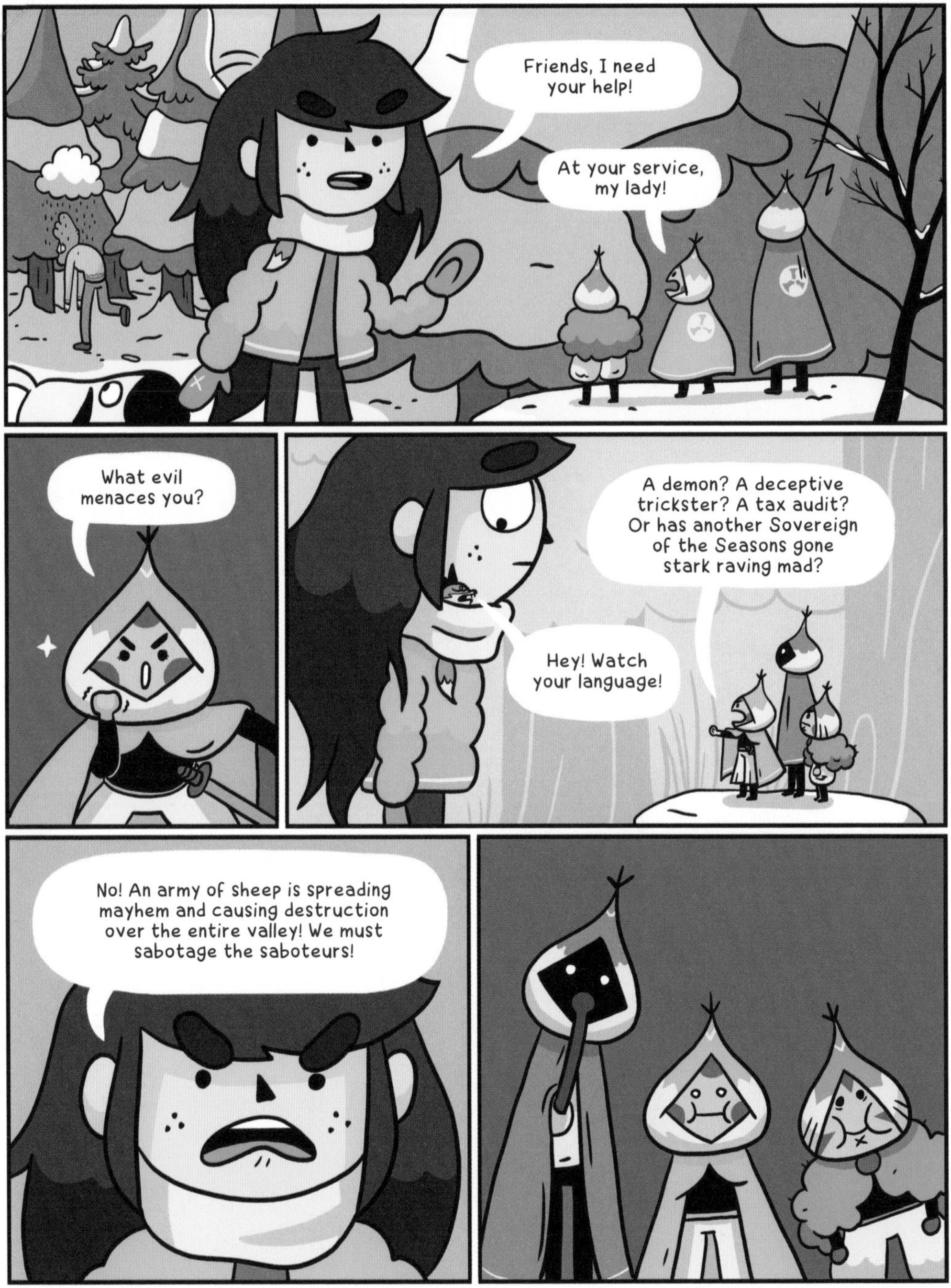
Friends, I need your help!
At your service, my lady!
What evil menaces you?
A demon? A deceptive trickster? A tax audit? Or has another Sovereign of the Seasons gone stark raving mad?
Hey! Watch your language!
No! An army of sheep is spreading mayhem and causing destruction over the entire valley! We must sabotage the saboteurs!

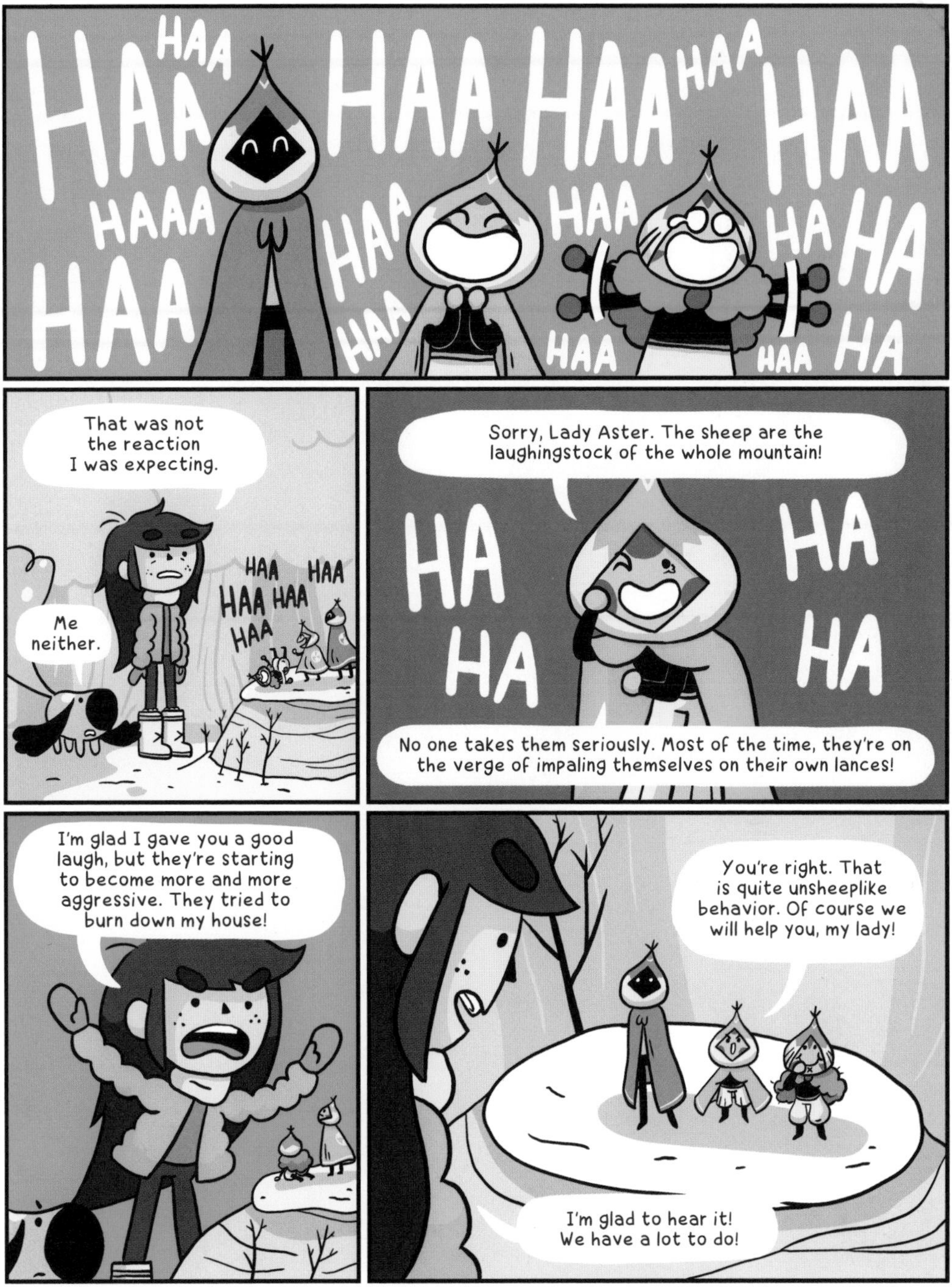
HAA HAA HAA HAA HAA HAA HAAA HAA HAA HAA HAA HA HA HAA HAA HA
That was not the reaction I was expecting.
HAA HAA HAA HAA HAA
Me neither.
Sorry, Lady Aster. The sheep are the laughingstock of the whole mountain!
HA HA HA HA
No one takes them seriously. Most of the time, they're on the verge of impaling themselves on their own lances!
I'm glad I gave you a good laugh, but they're starting to become more and more aggressive. They tried to burn down my house!
You're right. That is quite unsheeplike behavior. Of course we will help you, my lady!
I'm glad to hear it! We have a lot to do!

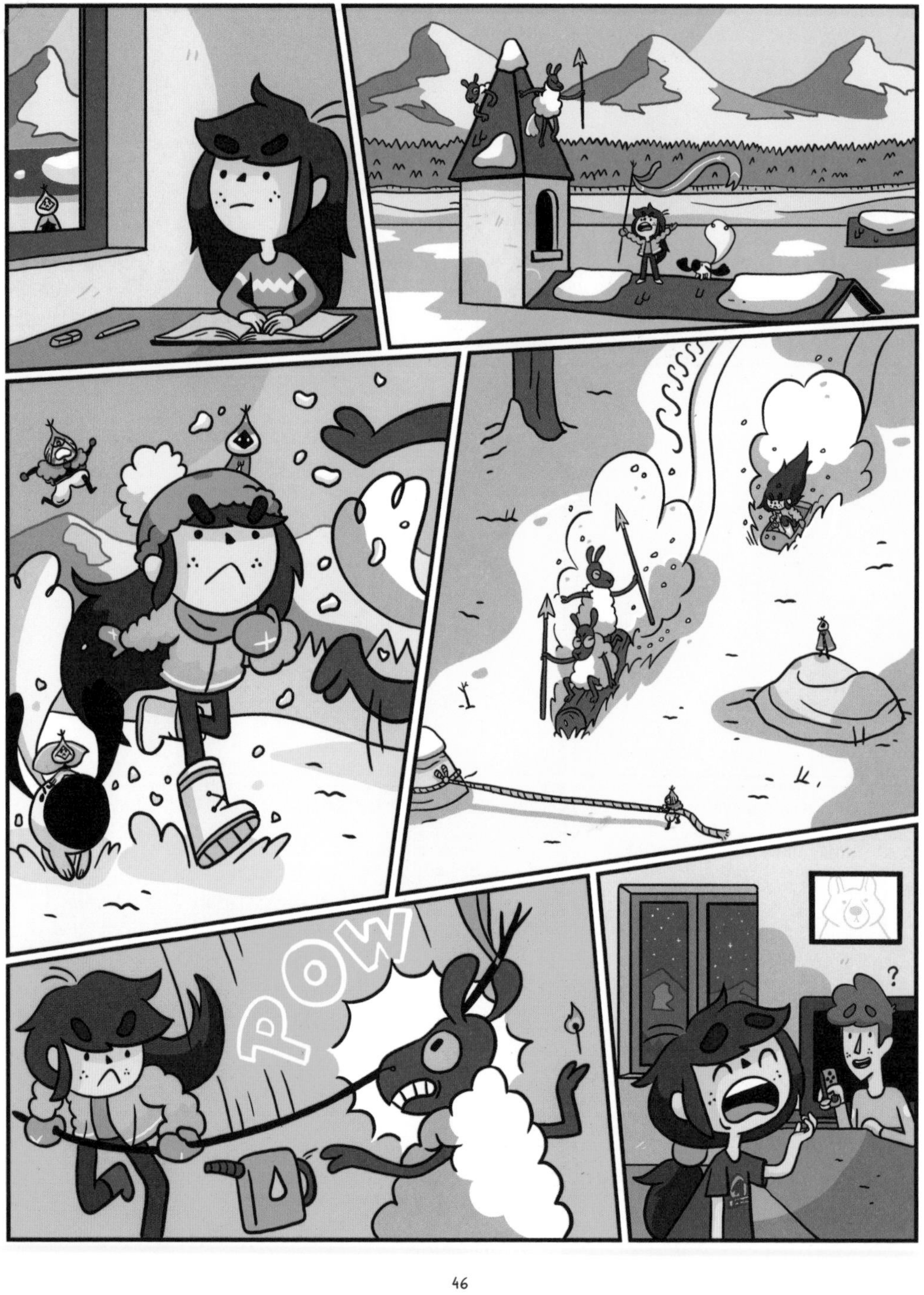
SSSSSS
POW
?

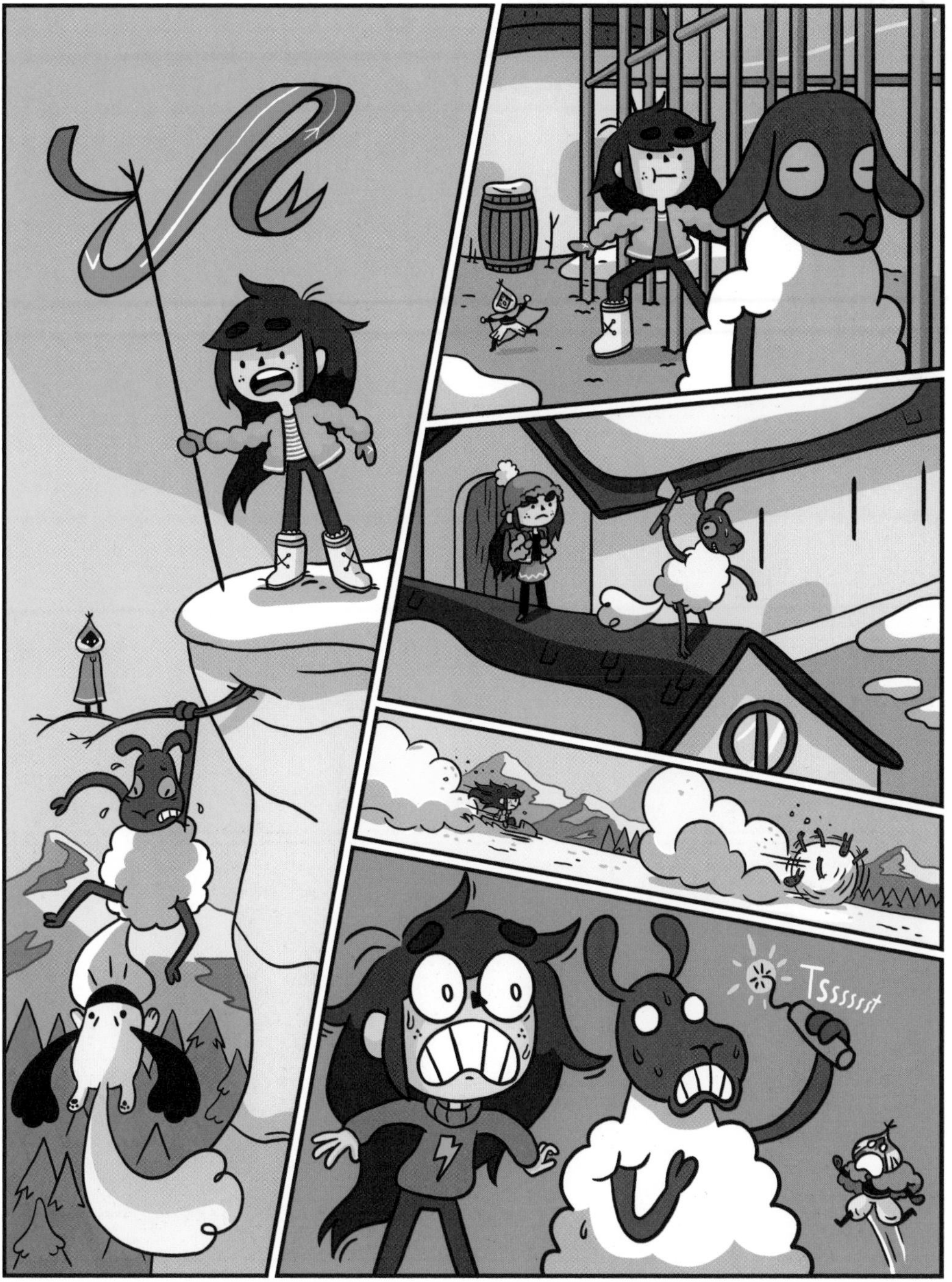
Tsssssst

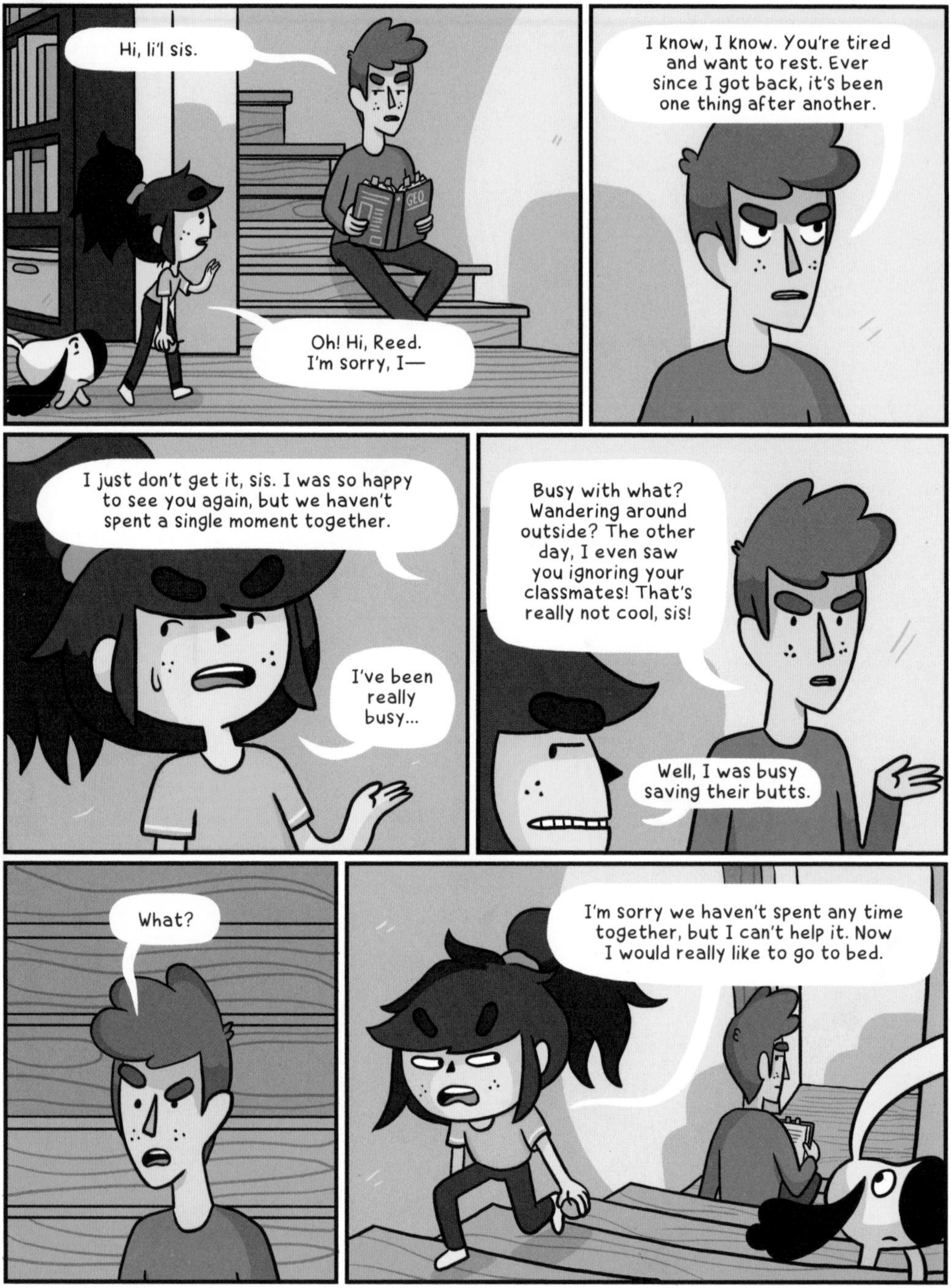

Hi, li'l sis.
Oh! Hi, Reed. I'm sorry, I—
I know, I know. You're tired and want to rest. Ever since I got back, it's been one thing after another.
I just don't get it, sis. I was so happy to see you again, but we haven't spent a single moment together.
I've been really busy...
Busy with what? Wandering around outside? The other day, I even saw you ignoring your classmates! That's really not cool, sis!
Well, I was busy saving their butts.
What?
I'm sorry we haven't spent any time together, but I can't help it. Now I would really like to go to bed.

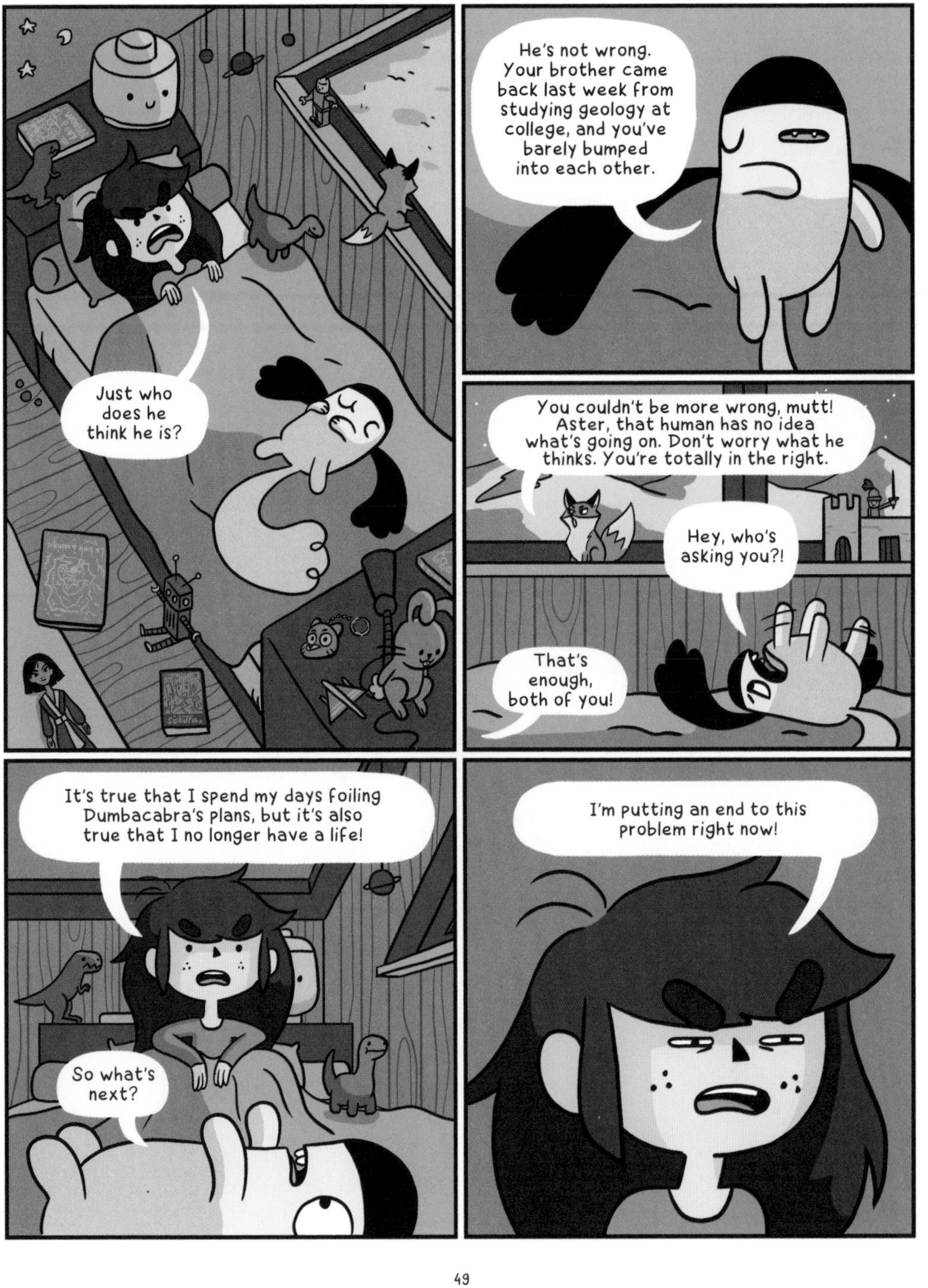
Just who does he think he is?
He's not wrong. Your brother came back last week from studying geology at college, and you've barely bumped into each other.
You couldn't be more wrong, mutt! Aster, that human has no idea what's going on. Don't worry what he thinks. You're totally in the right.
Hey, who's asking you?!
That's enough, both of you!
It's true that I spend my days foiling Dumbacabra's plans, but it's also true that I no longer have a life!
So what's next?
I'm putting an end to this problem right now!

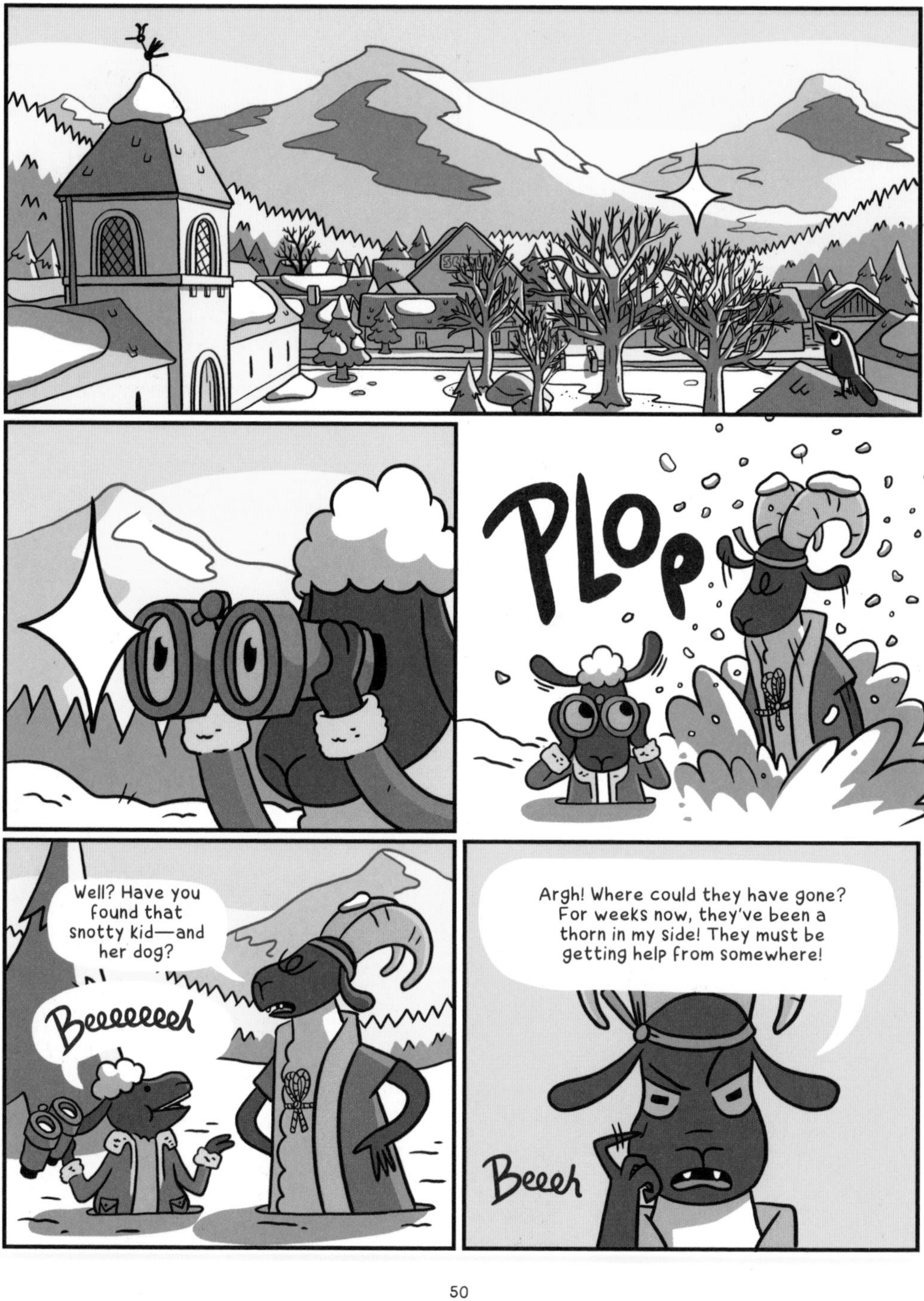

PLOP
Well? Have you found that snotty kid—and her dog?
Beeeeeeeh
Argh! Where could they have gone? For weeks now, they've been a thorn in my side! They must be getting help from somewhere!
Beeeh

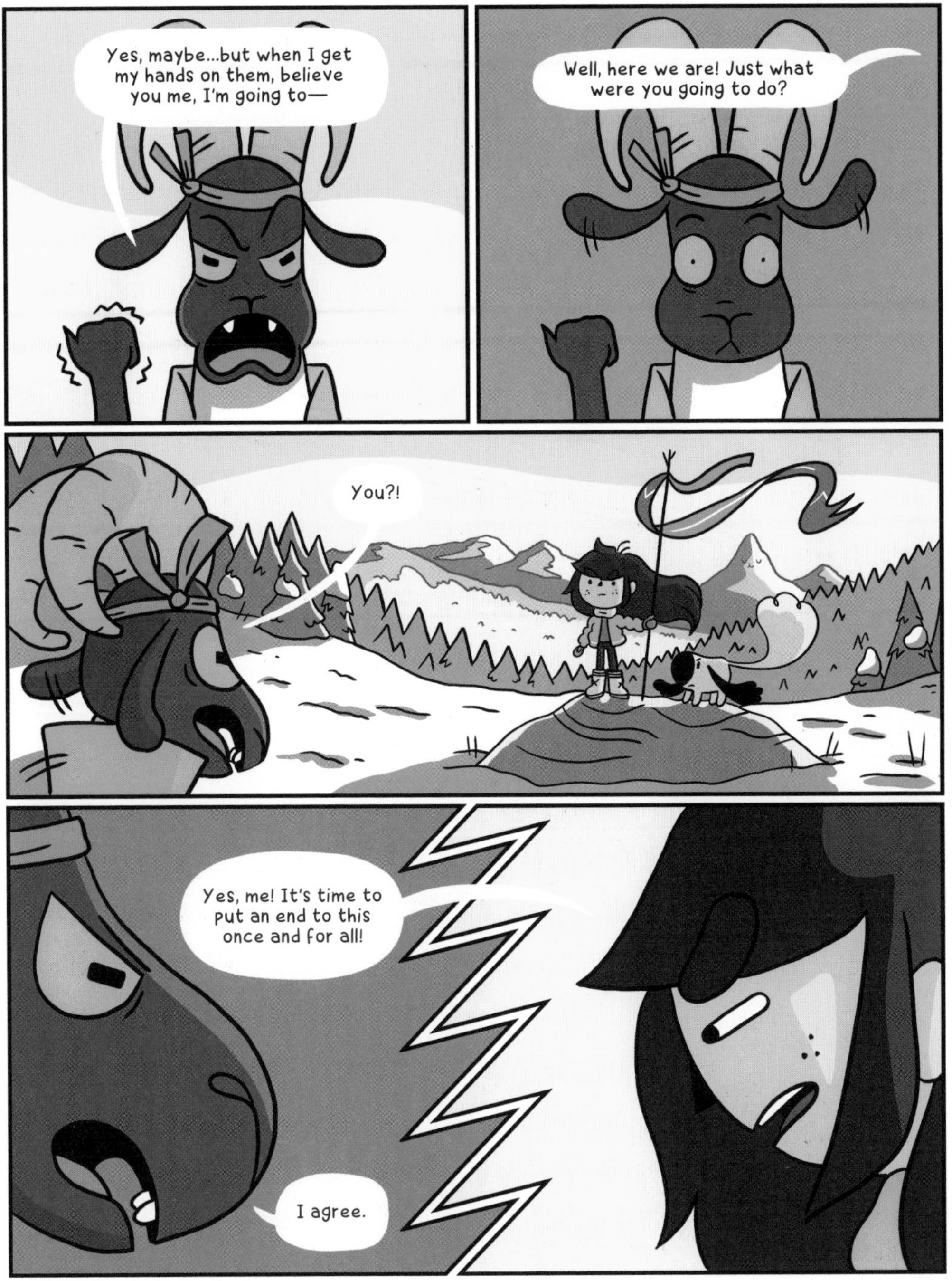
Yes, maybe...but when I get my hands on them, believe you me, I'm going to—
Well, here we are! Just what were you going to do?
You?!
Yes, me! It's time to put an end to this once and for all!
I agree.

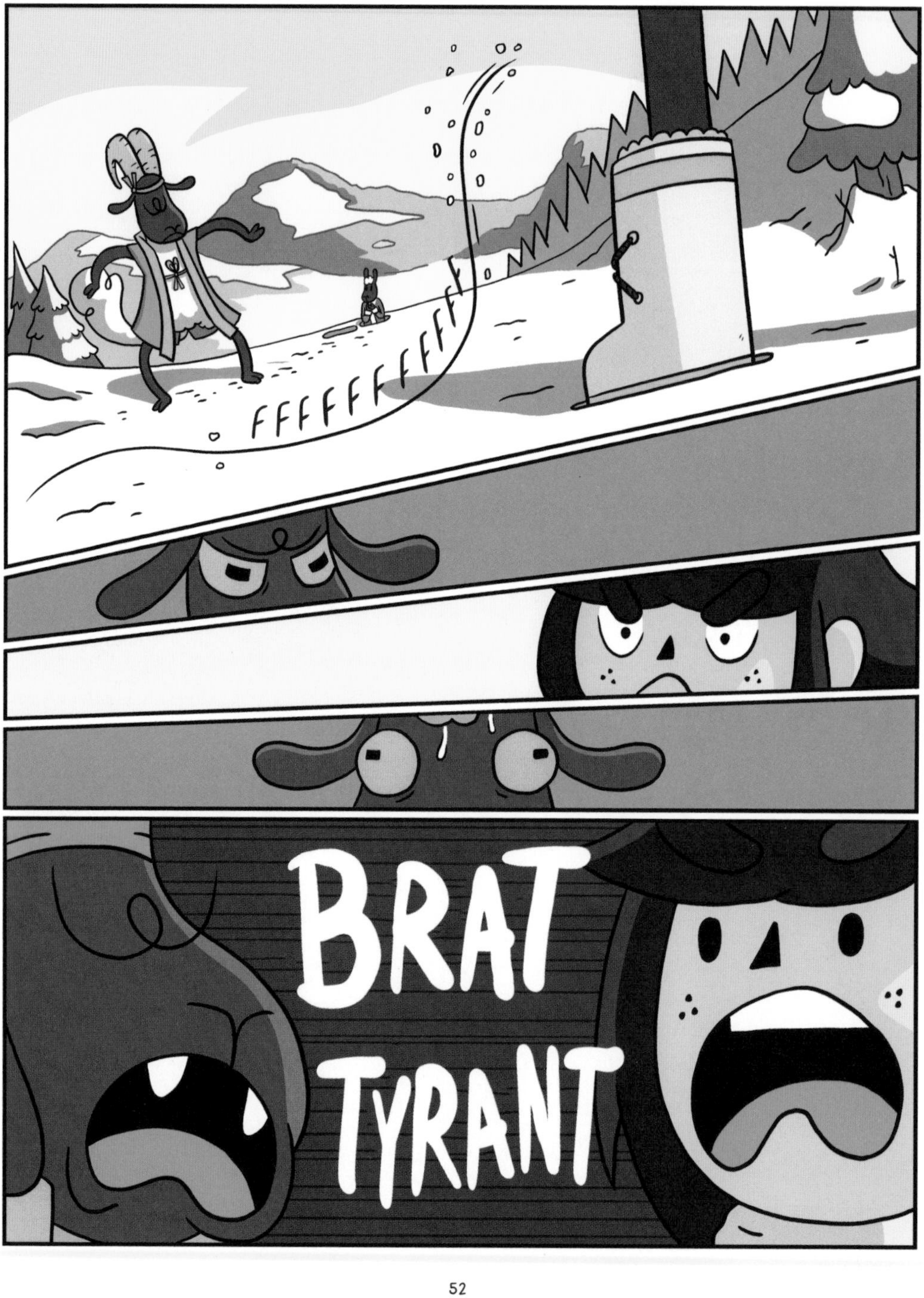
FFFFFFFFFFFFFF
BRAT
TYRANT

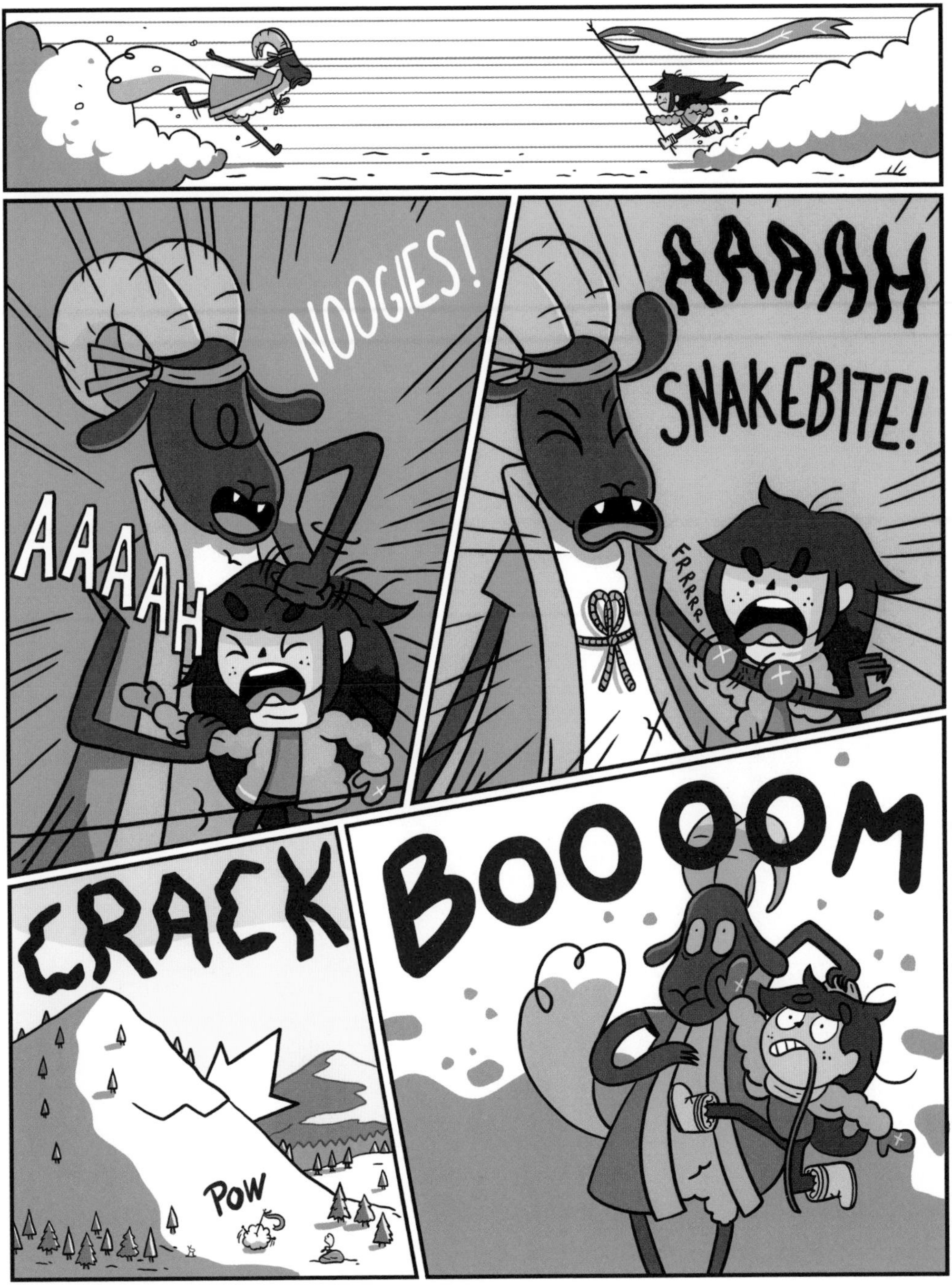
NOOGIES!
AAAAAH
AAAAH
SNAKEBITE!
FRRRRR
CRACK
BOOOOM
POW

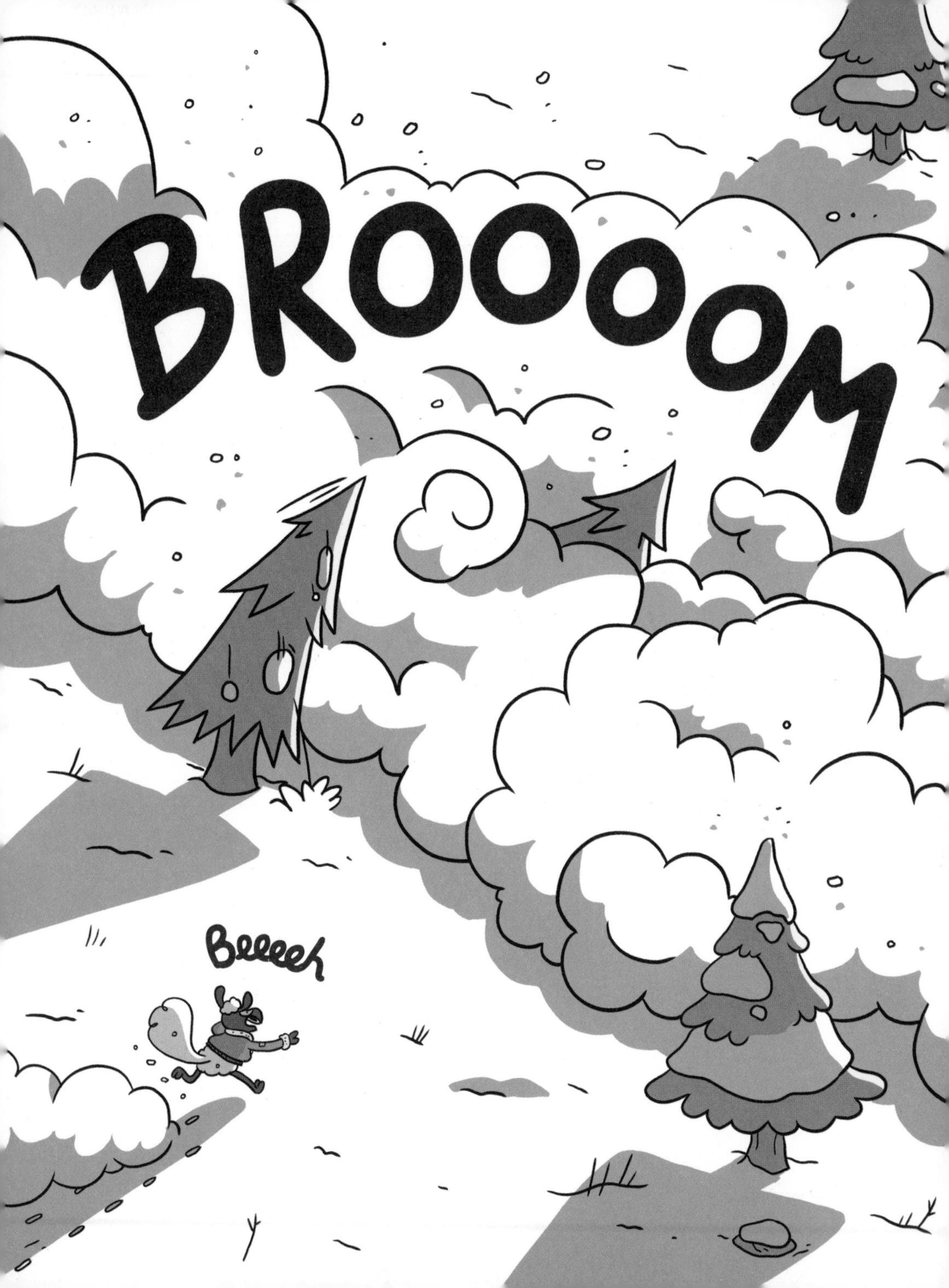
BROOOOM
Beeeeh

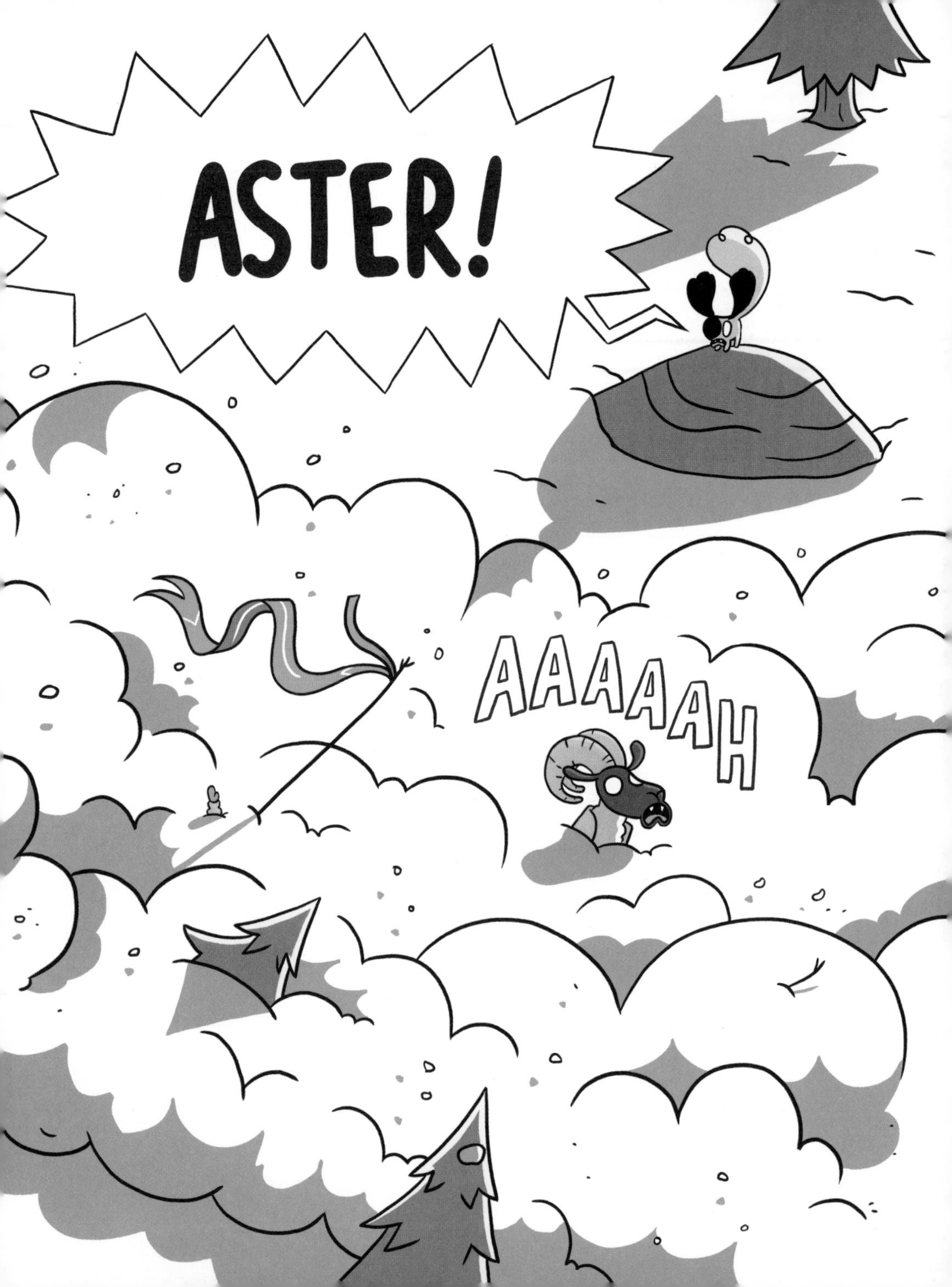
ASTER!
AAAAAH

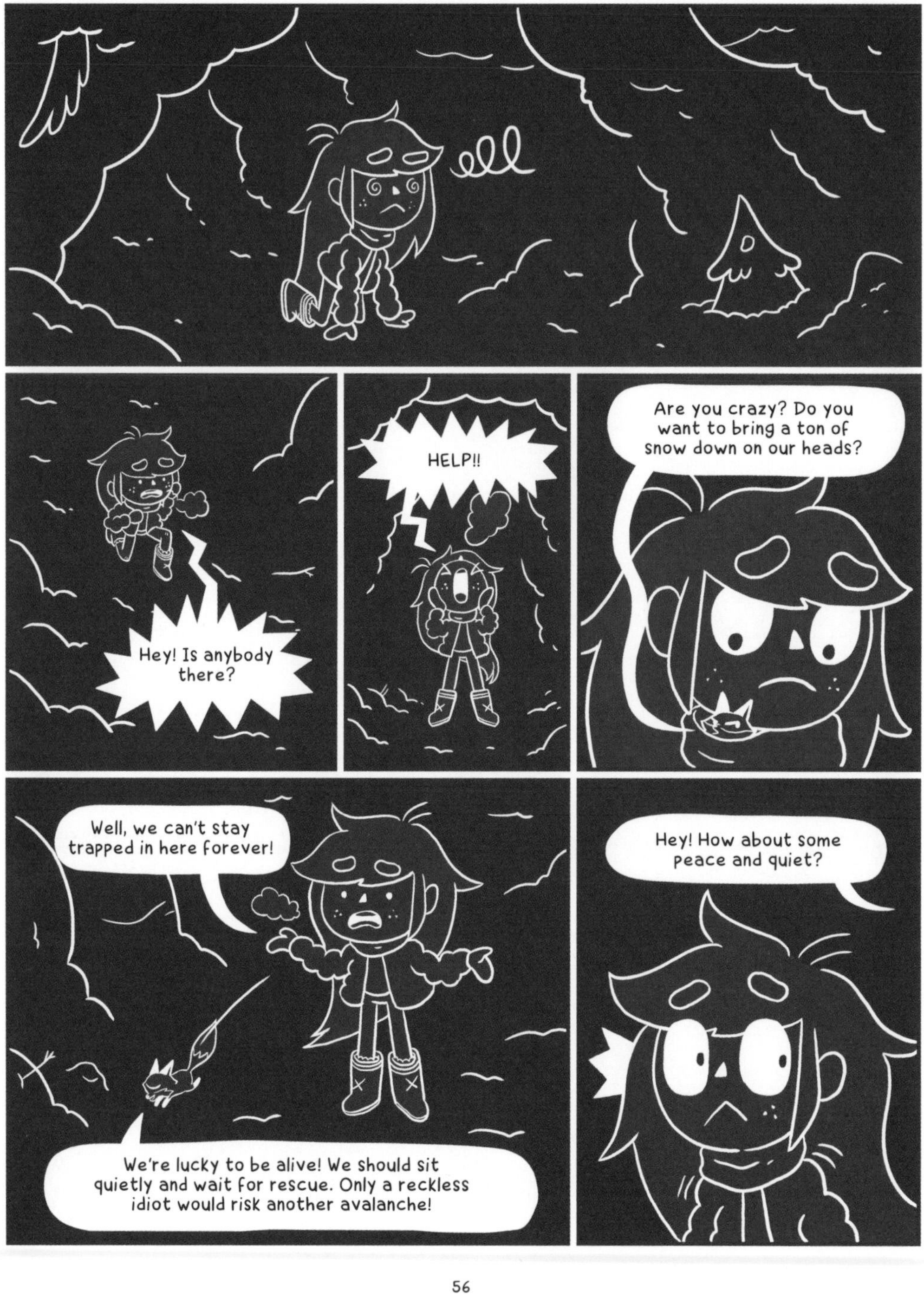

Hey! Is anybody there?
HELP!!
Are you crazy? Do you want to bring a ton of snow down on our heads?
Well, we can't stay trapped in here forever!
We're lucky to be alive! We should sit quietly and wait for rescue. Only a reckless idiot would risk another avalanche!
Hey! How about some peace and quiet?

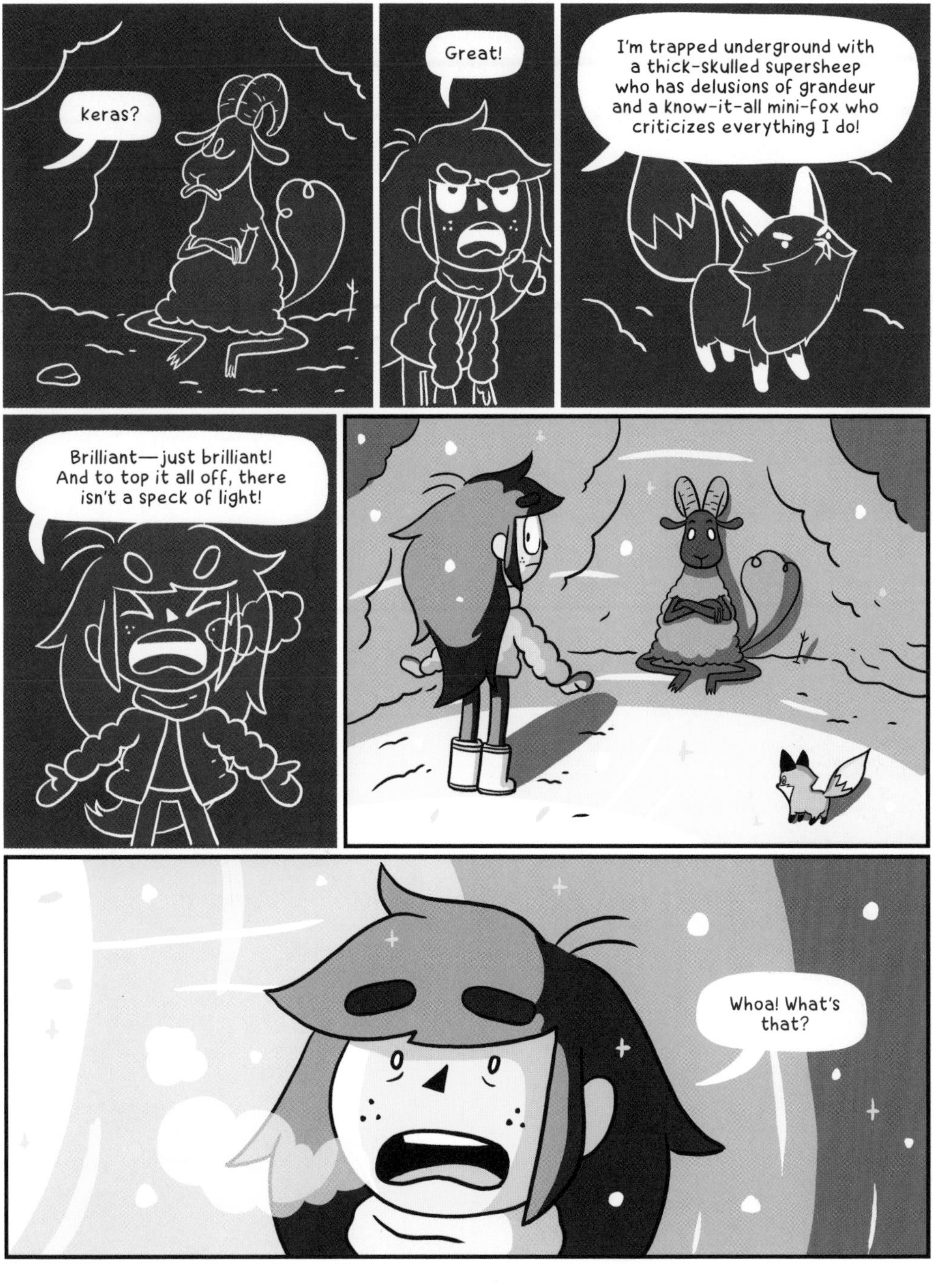
Keras?
Great!
I'm trapped underground with a thick-skulled supersheep who has delusions of grandeur and a know-it-all mini-fox who criticizes everything I do!
Brilliant—just brilliant! And to top it all off, there isn't a speck of light!
Whoa! What's that?

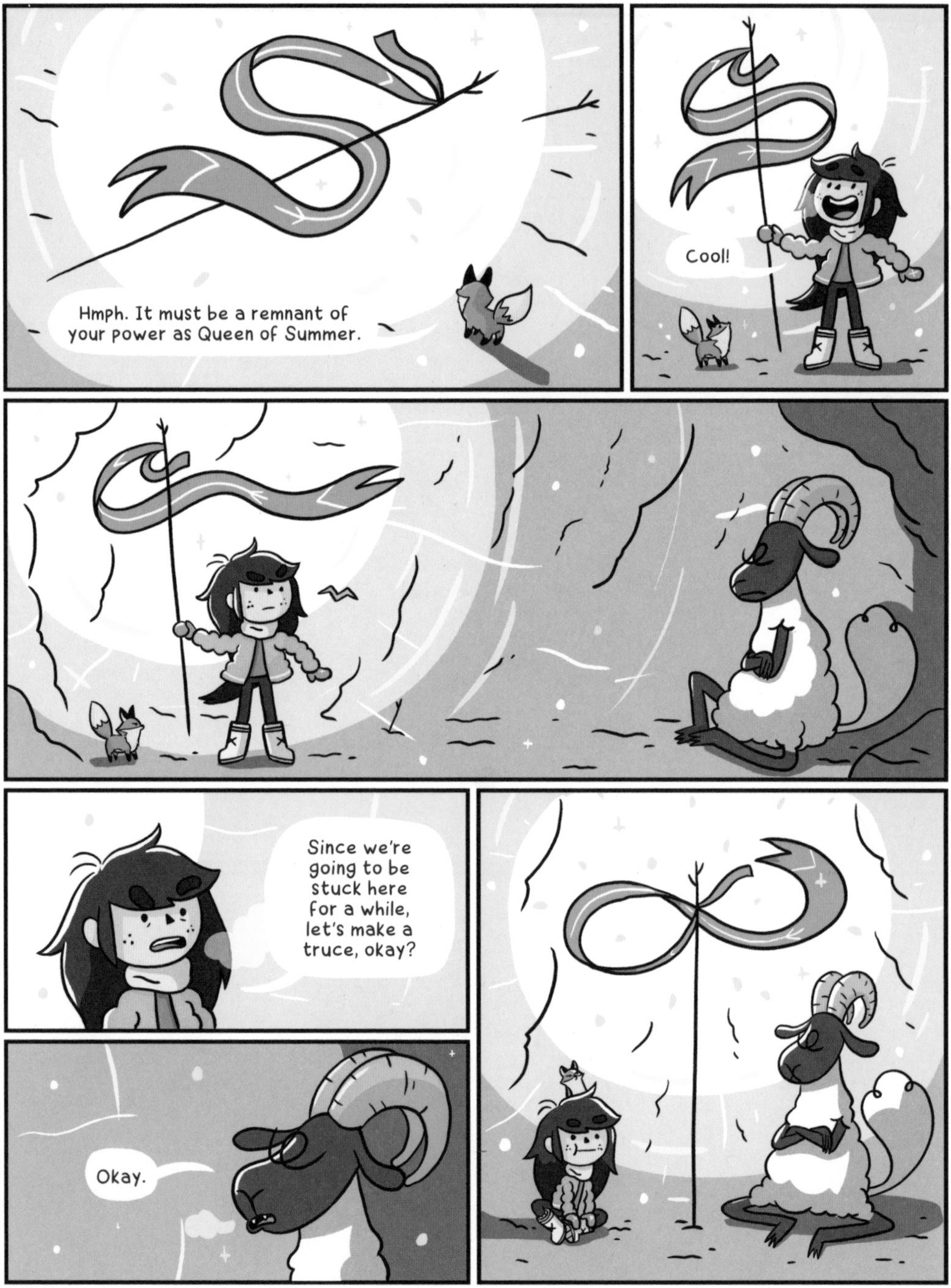
Hmph. It must be a remnant of your power as Queen of Summer.
Cool!
Since we're going to be stuck here for a while, let's make a truce, okay?
Okay.

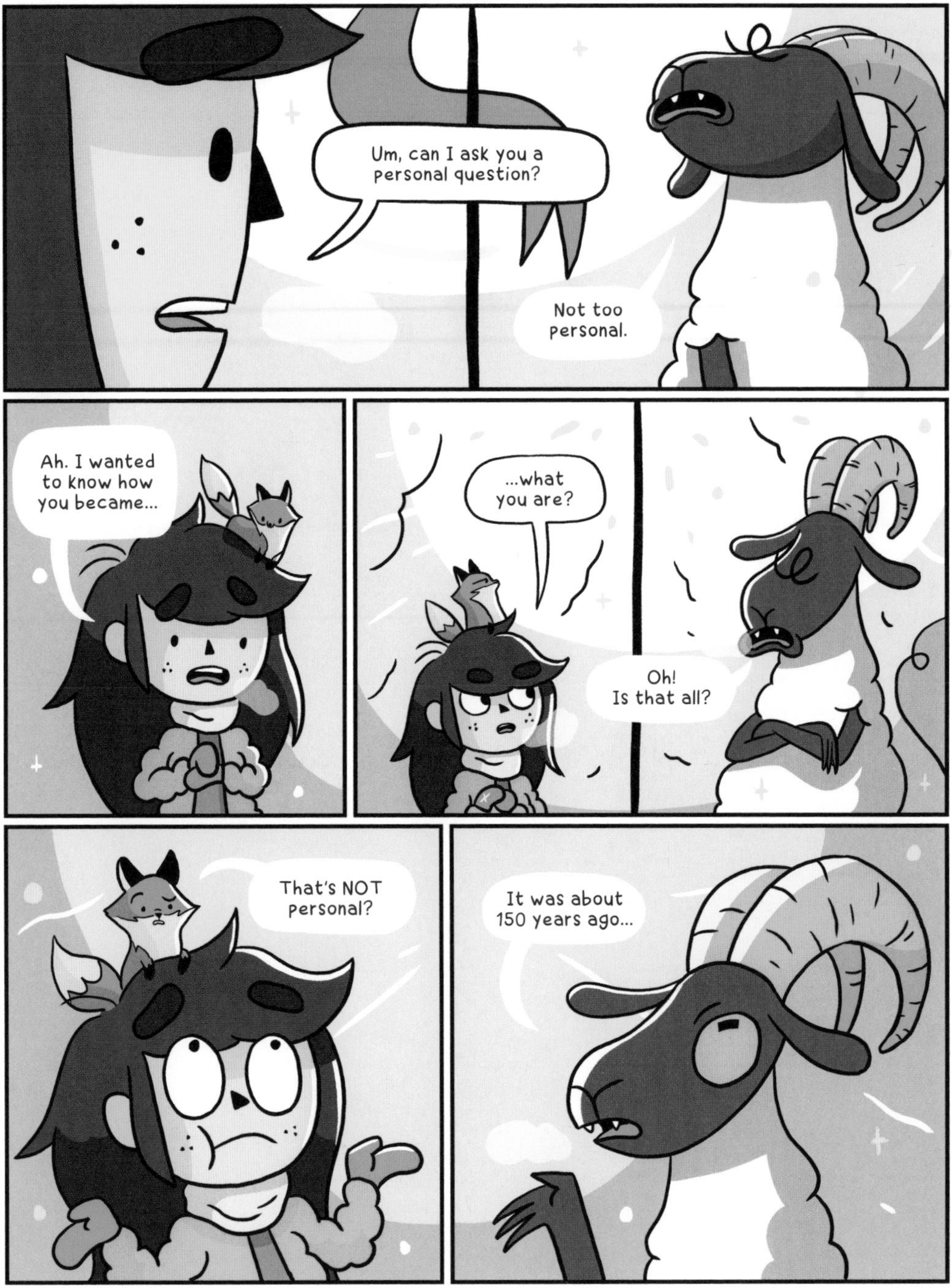
Um, can I ask you a personal question?
Not too personal.
Ah. I wanted to know how you became...
...what you are?
Oh! Is that all?
That's NOT personal?
It was about 150 years ago...

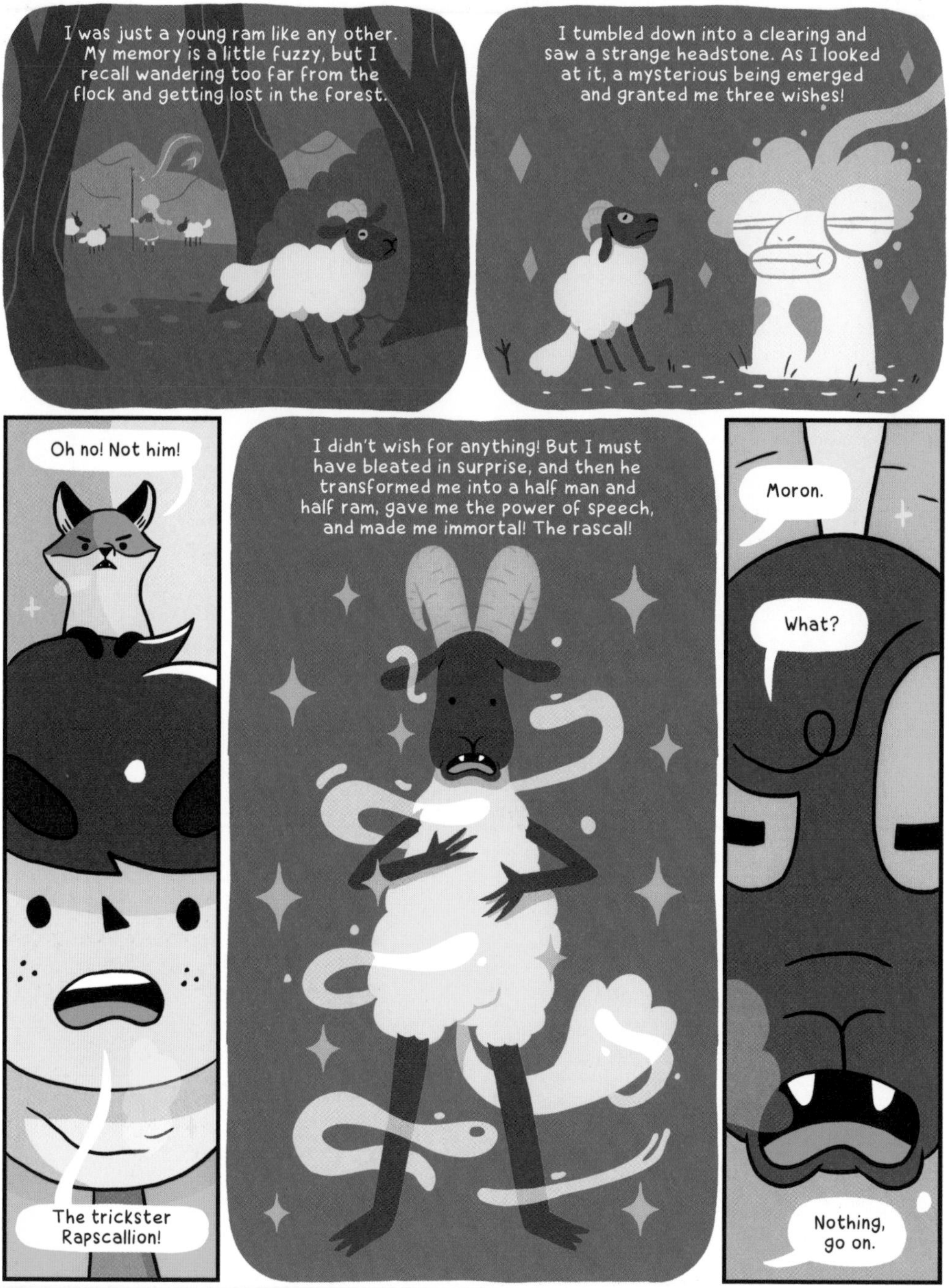

I was just a young ram like any other. My memory is a little fuzzy, but I recall wandering too far from the flock and getting lost in the forest.
I tumbled down into a clearing and saw a strange headstone. As I looked at it, a mysterious being emerged and granted me three wishes!
Oh no! Not him!
The trickster Rapscallion!
I didn't wish for anything! But I must have bleated in surprise, and then he transformed me into a half man and half ram, gave me the power of speech, and made me immortal! The rascal!
Moron.
What?
Nothing, go on.

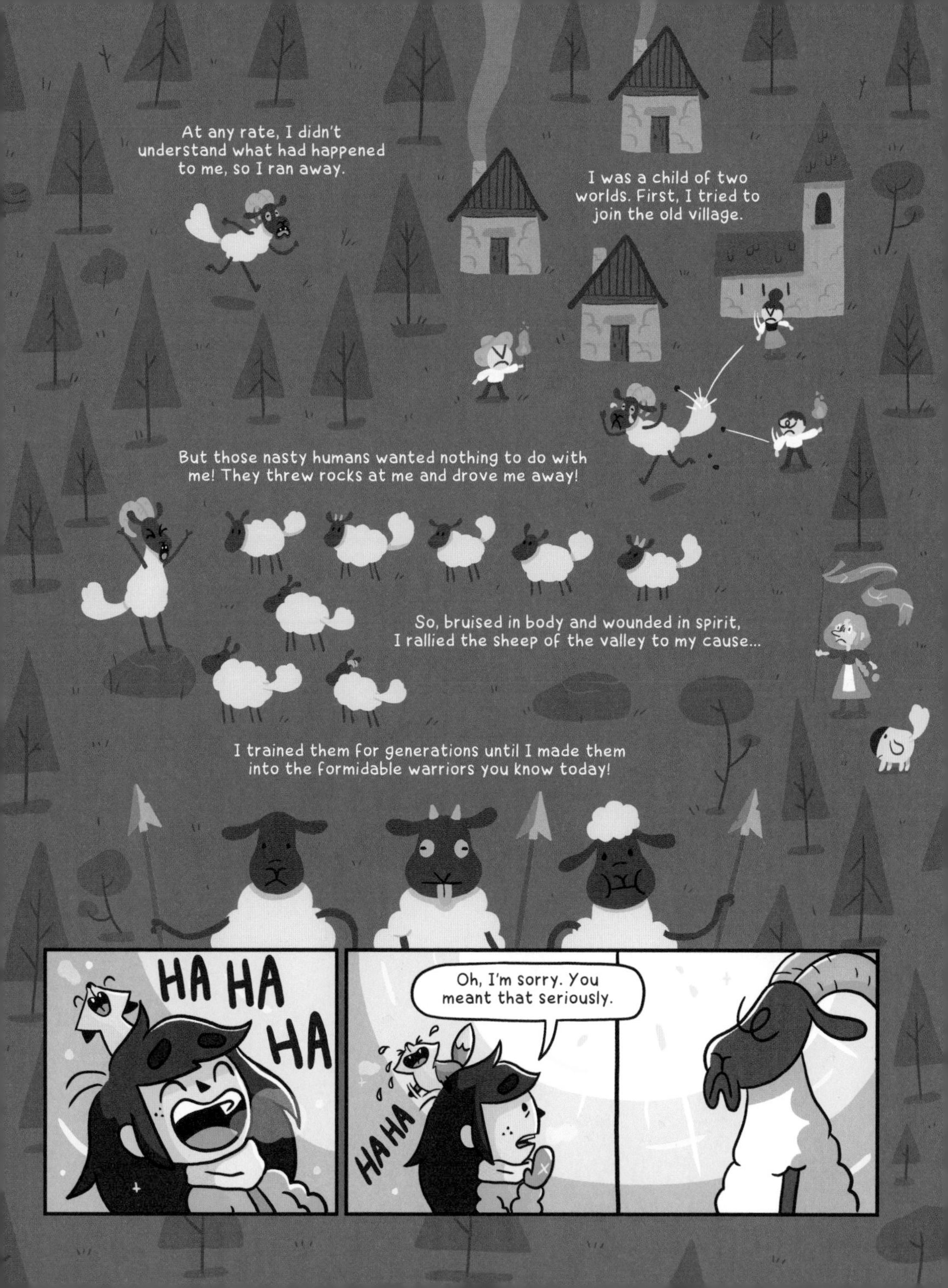
At any rate, I didn't understand what had happened to me, so I ran away.
I was a child of two worlds. First, I tried to join the old village.
But those nasty humans wanted nothing to do with me! They threw rocks at me and drove me away!
So, bruised in body and wounded in spirit, I rallied the sheep of the valley to my cause...
I trained them for generations until I made them into the formidable warriors you know today!
HA HA HA
HA HA
Oh, I'm sorry. You meant that seriously.

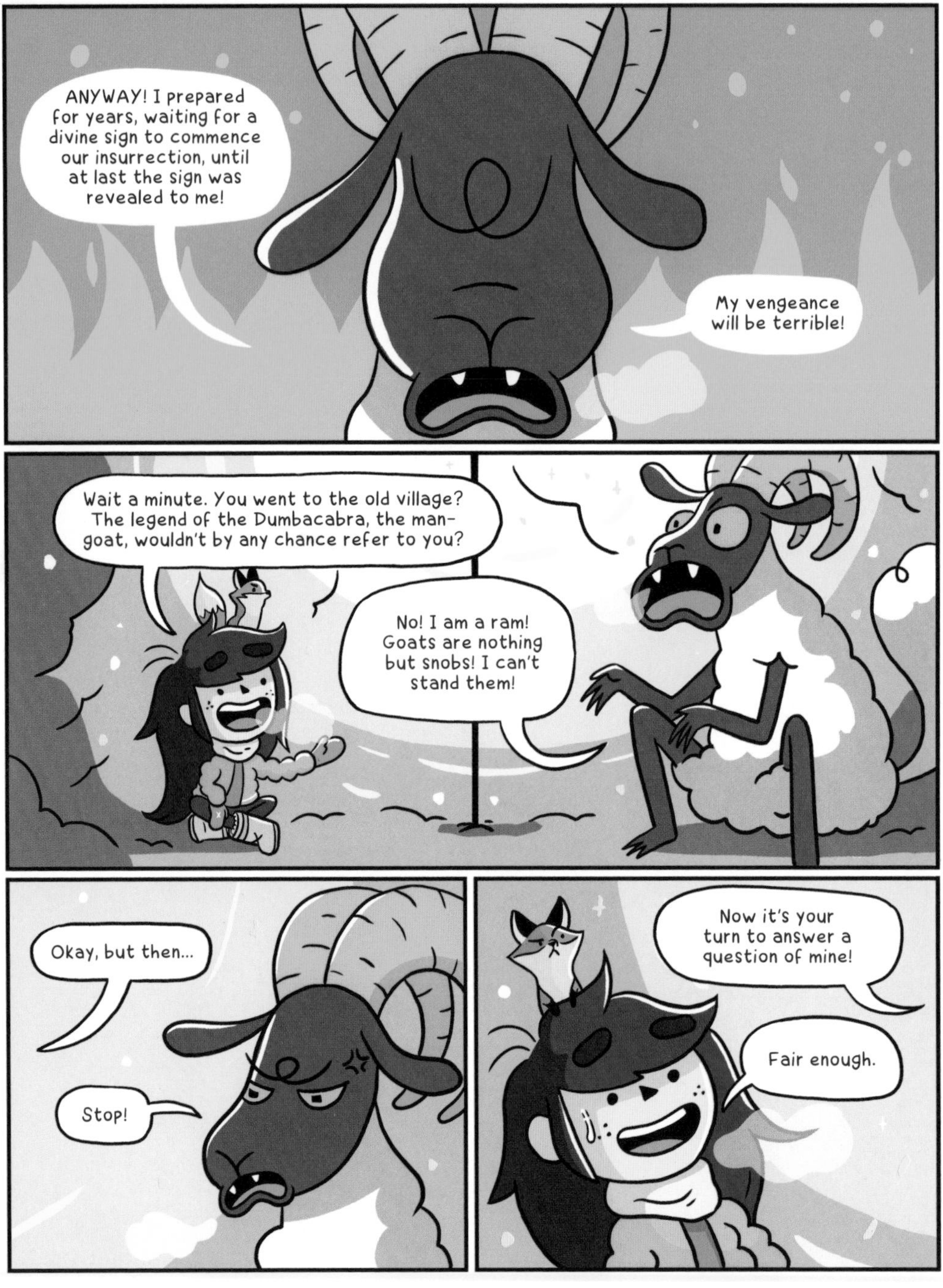
ANYWAY! I prepared for years, waiting for a divine sign to commence our insurrection, until at last the sign was revealed to me!
My vengeance will be terrible!
Wait a minute. You went to the old village? The legend of the Dumbacabra, the man-goat, wouldn't by any chance refer to you?
No! I am a ram! Goats are nothing but snobs! I can't stand them!
Okay, but then...
Stop!
Now it's your turn to answer a question of mine!
Fair enough.

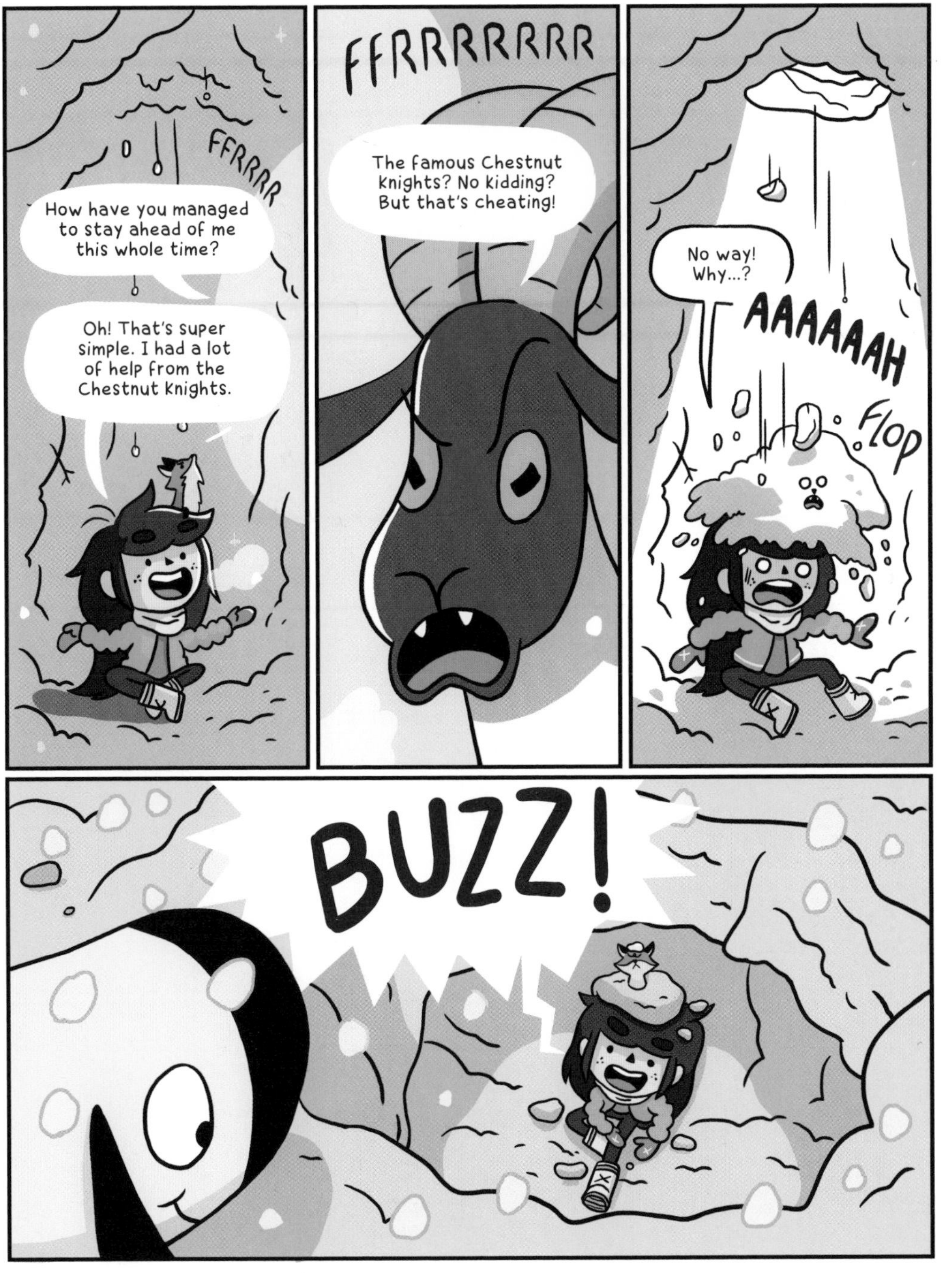
FFRRRRR
How have you managed to stay ahead of me this whole time?
Oh! That's super simple. I had a lot of help from the Chestnut knights.
FFRRRRRRRR
The famous Chestnut knights? No kidding? But that's cheating!
No way! Why...?
AAAAAAH
FLOP
BUZZ!

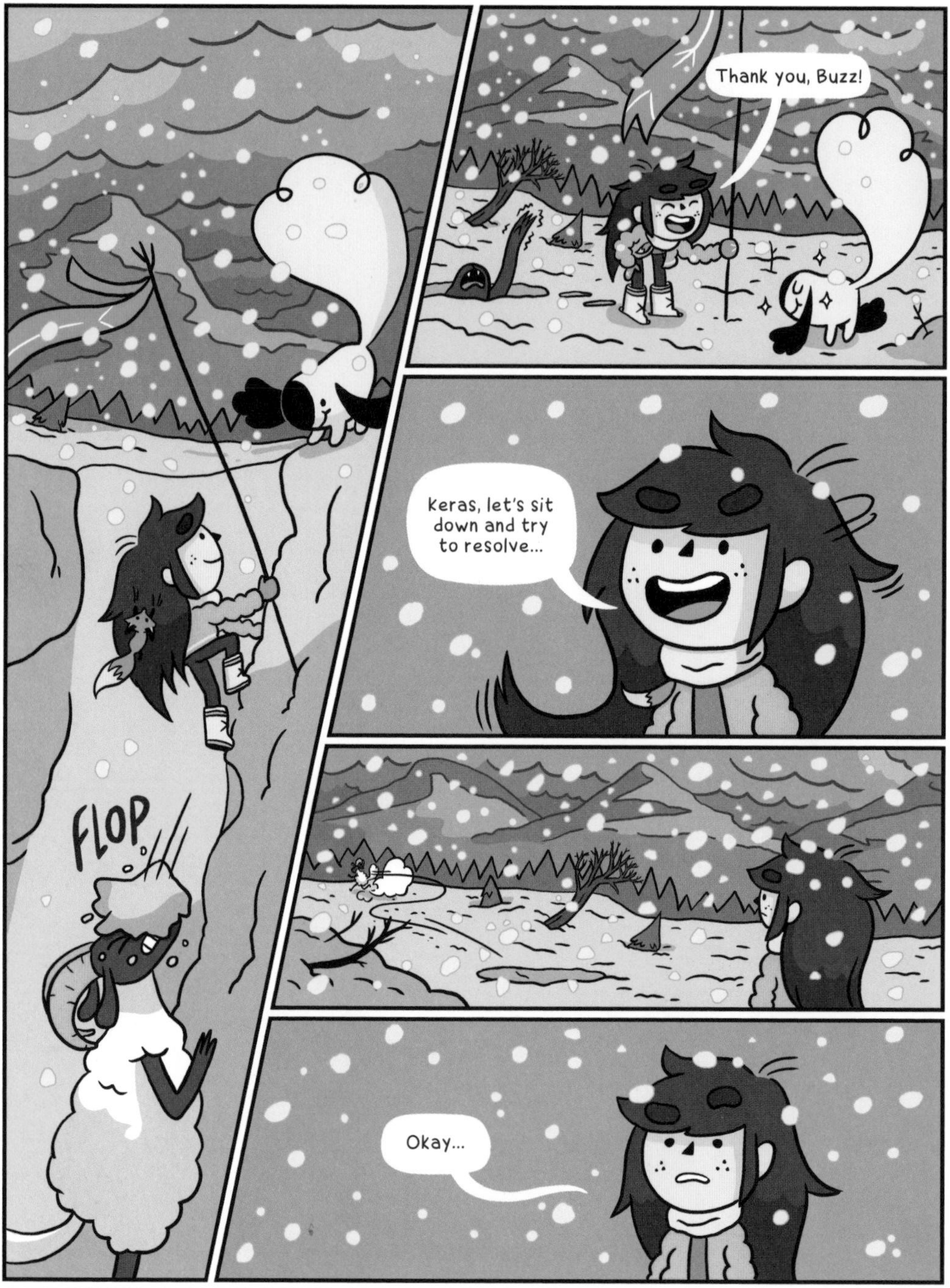
FLOP
Thank you, Buzz!
Keras, let's sit down and try to resolve...
Okay...

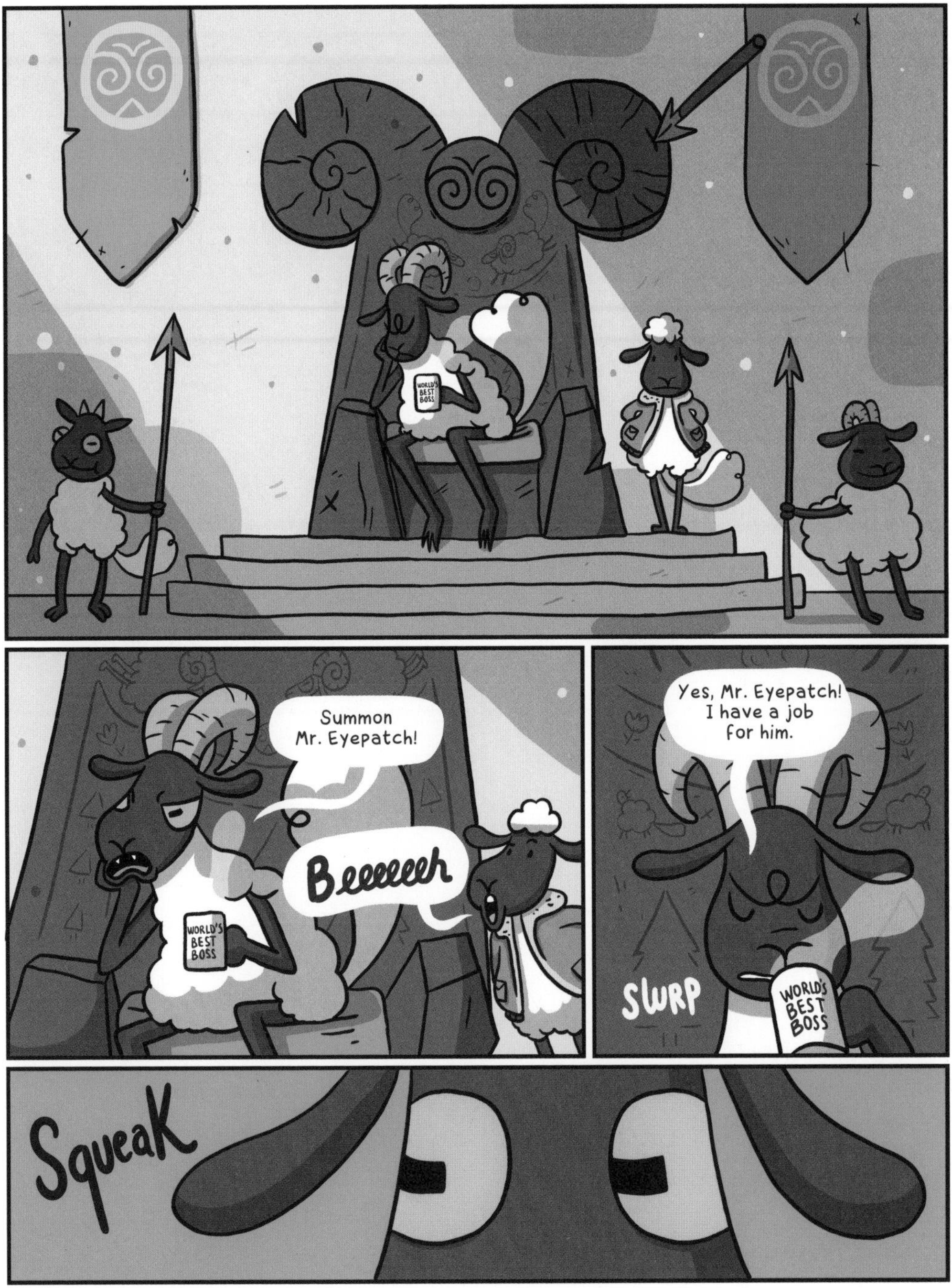

WORLD'S BEST BOSS
Summon Mr. Eyepatch!
Beeeeeh
WORLD'S BEST BOSS
Yes, Mr. Eyepatch! I have a job for him.
SLURP
WORLD'S BEST BOSS
Squeak

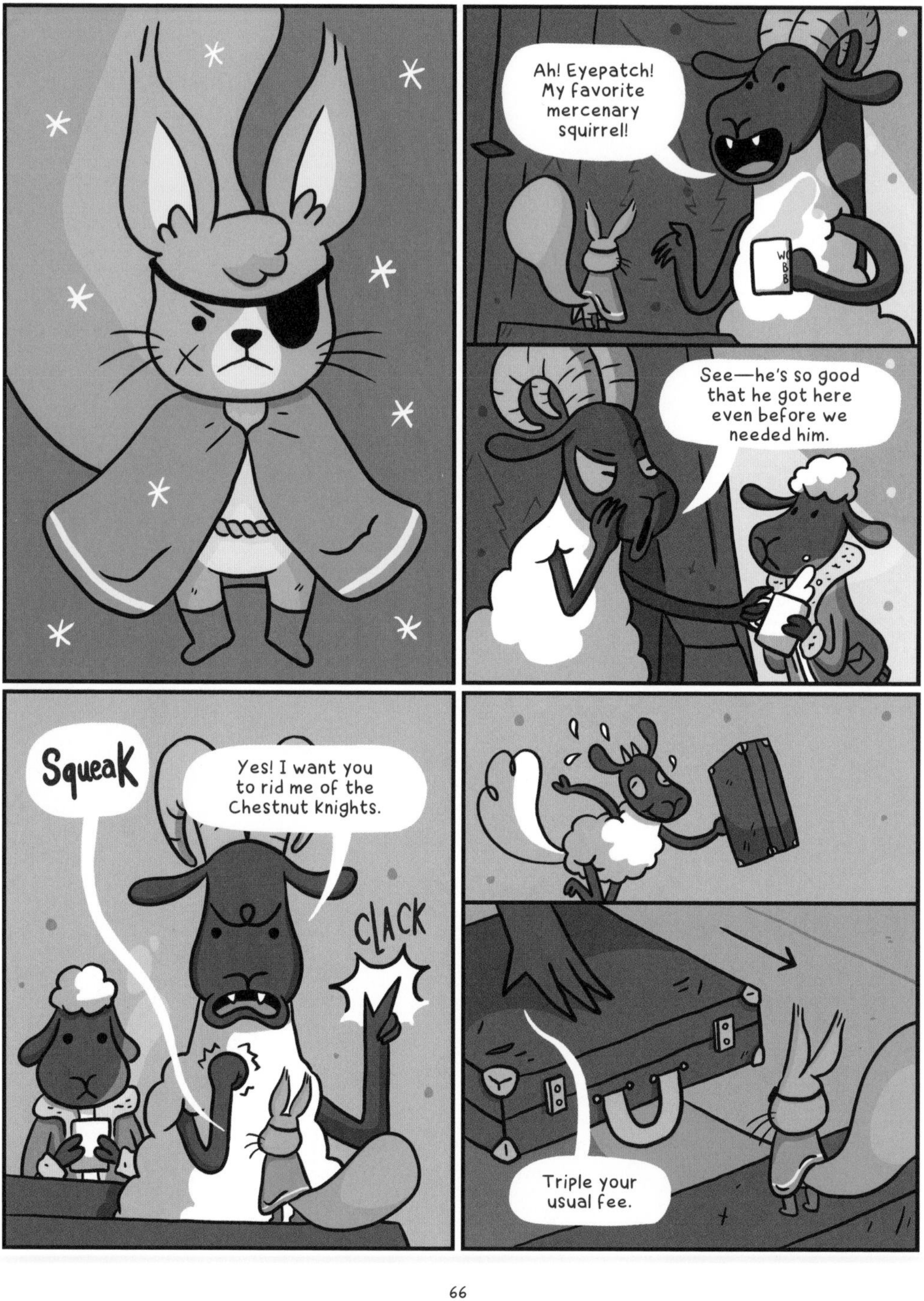

Ah! Eyepatch! My favorite mercenary squirrel!
See—he's so good that he got here even before we needed him.
Squeak
Yes! I want you to rid me of the Chestnut knights.
CLACK
Triple your usual fee.

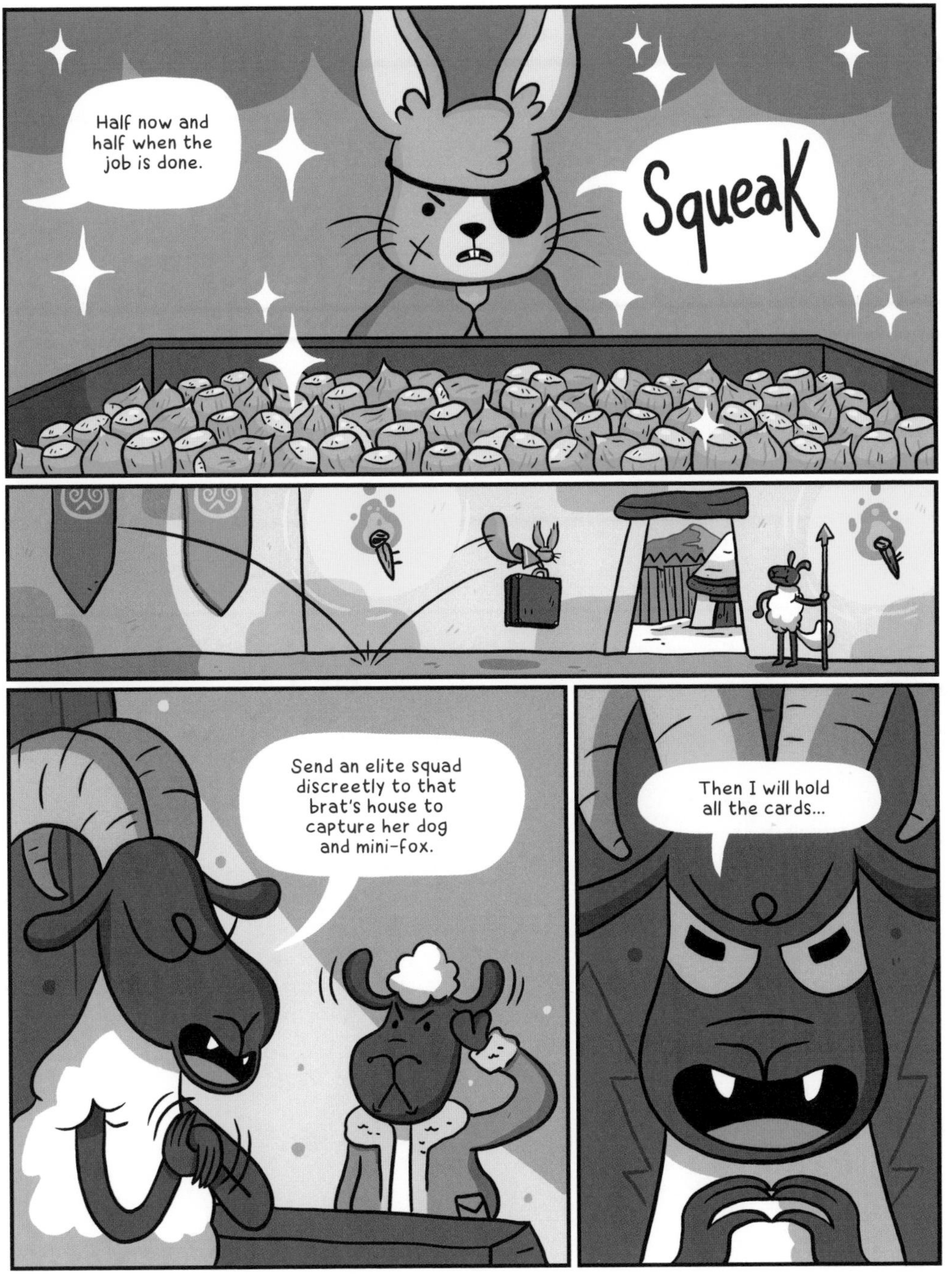
Half now and half when the job is done.
Squeak
Send an elite squad discreetly to that brat's house to capture her dog and mini-fox.
Then I will hold all the cards...

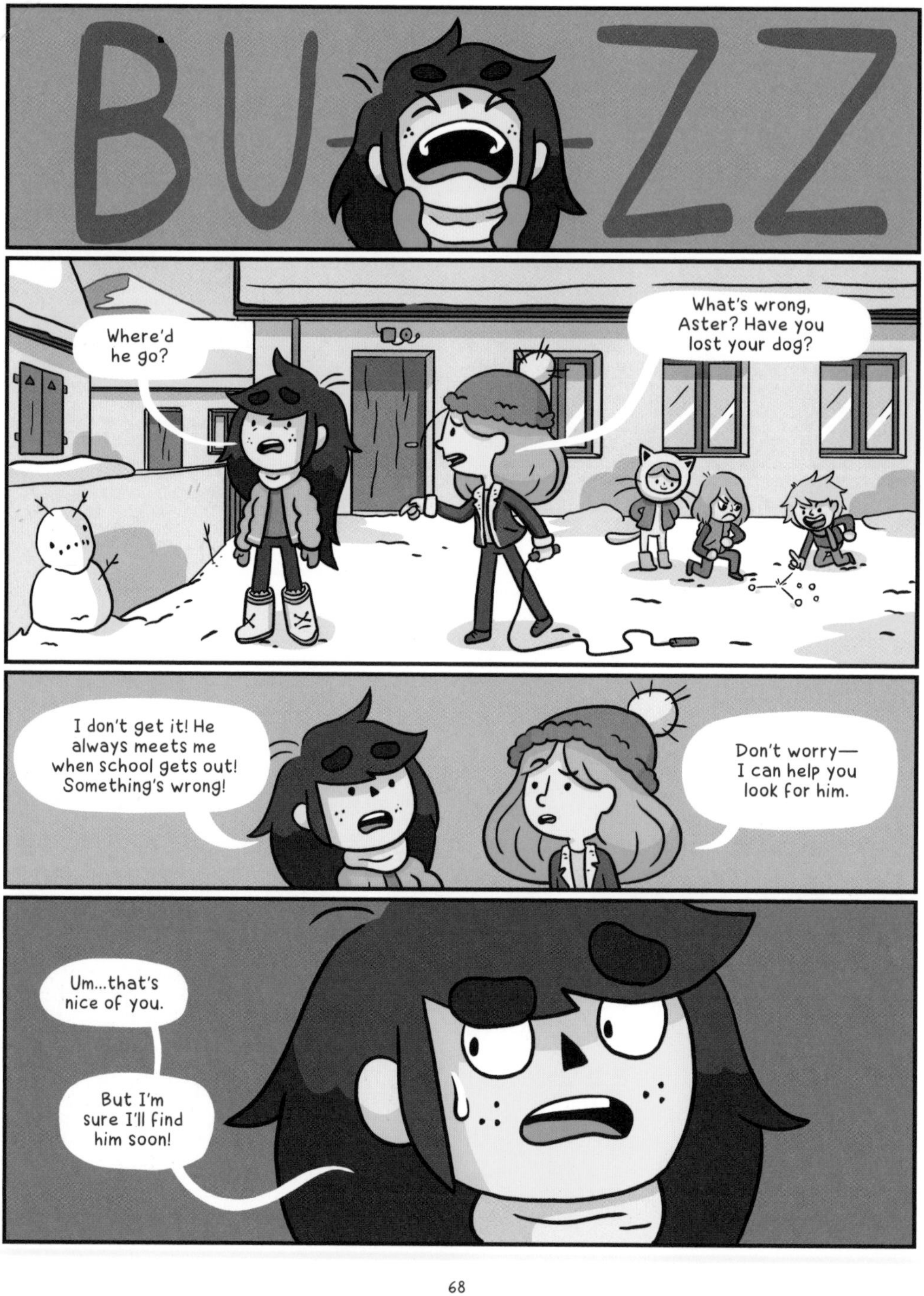
BUZZ
Where'd he go?
What's wrong, Aster? Have you lost your dog?
I don't get it! He always meets me when school gets out! Something's wrong!
Don't worry— I can help you look for him.
Um...that's nice of you.
But I'm sure I'll find him soon!

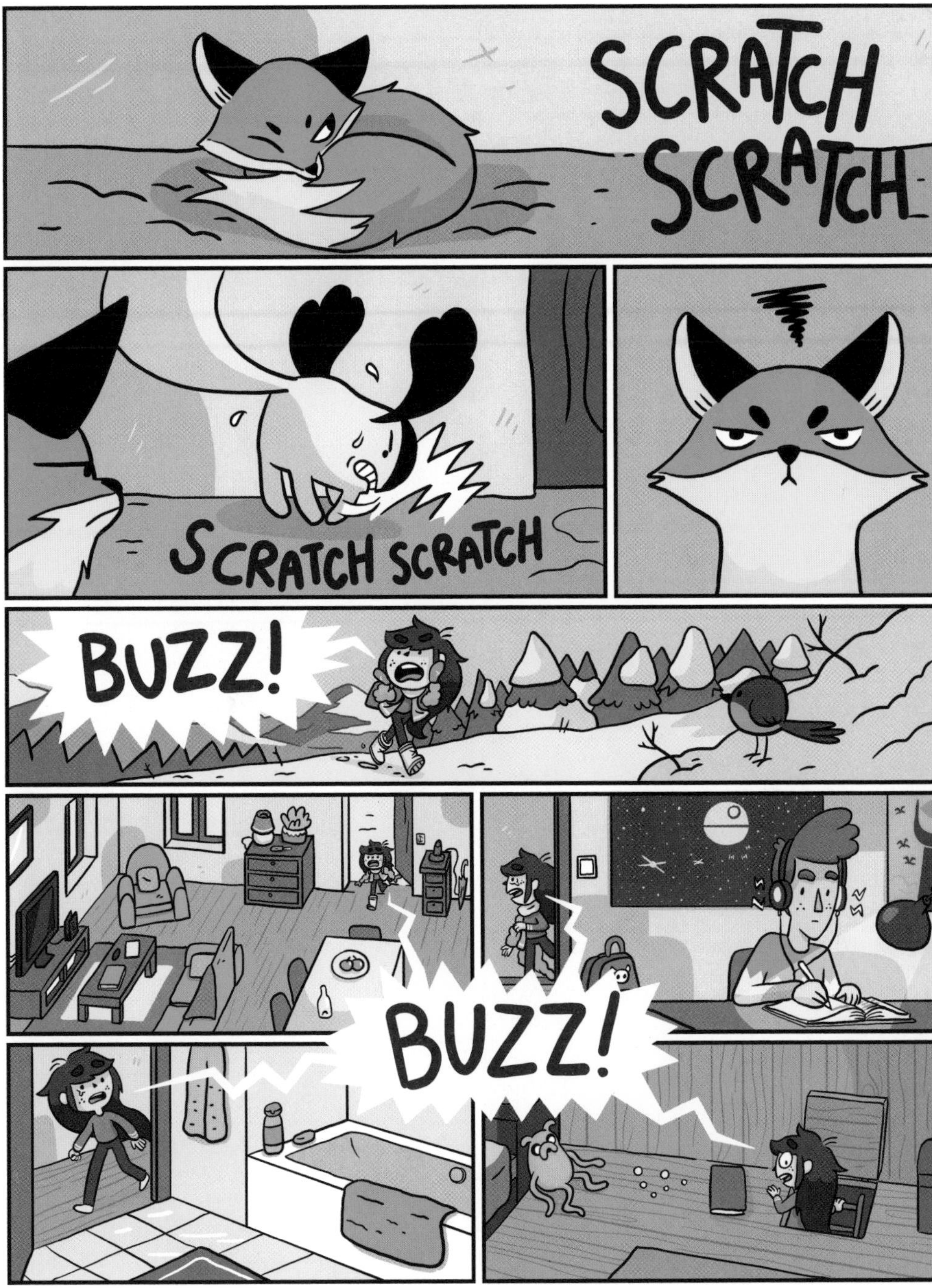
SCRATCH
SCRATCH
SCRATCH SCRATCH
BUZZ!
BUZZ!

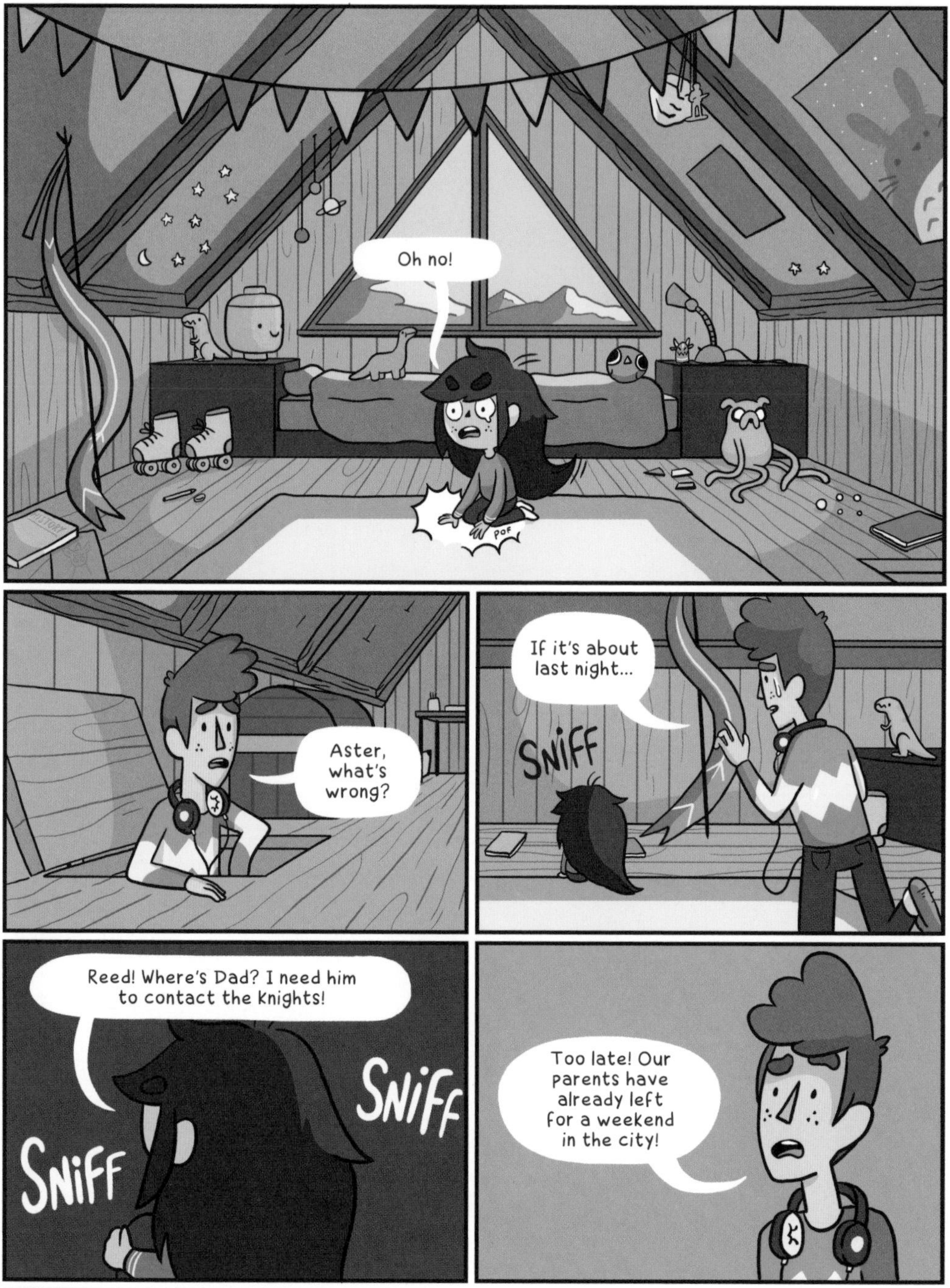
Oh no!
POF
Aster, what's wrong?
If it's about last night...
SNIFF
Reed! Where's Dad? I need him to contact the knights!
SNIFF
SNIFF
Too late! Our parents have already left for a weekend in the city!

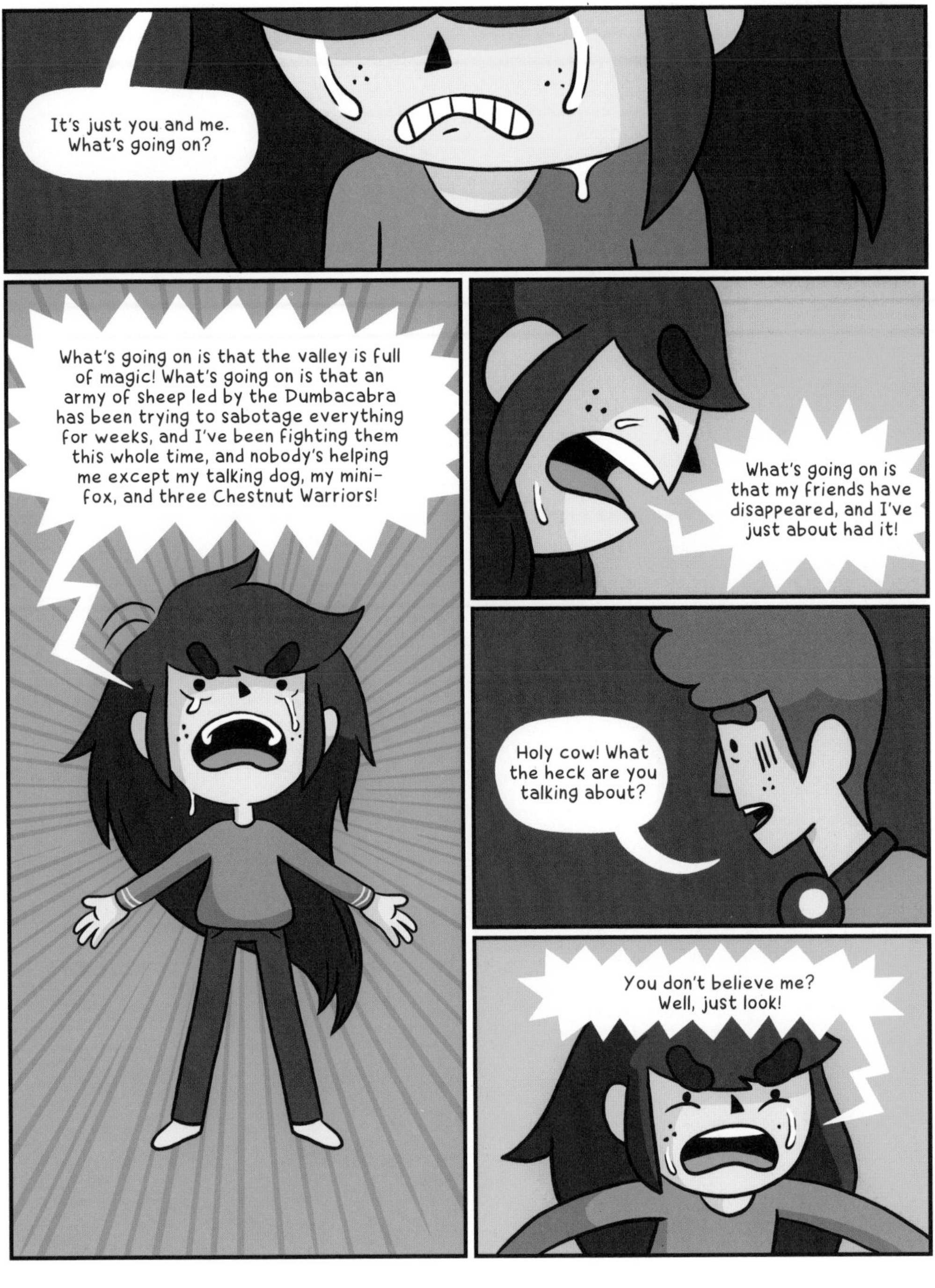
It's just you and me.
What's going on?
What's going on is that the valley is full of magic! What's going on is that an army of sheep led by the Dumbacabra has been trying to sabotage everything for weeks, and I've been fighting them this whole time, and nobody's helping me except my talking dog, my mini-fox, and three Chestnut Warriors!
What's going on is that my friends have disappeared, and I've just about had it!
Holy cow! What the heck are you talking about?
You don't believe me? Well, just look!

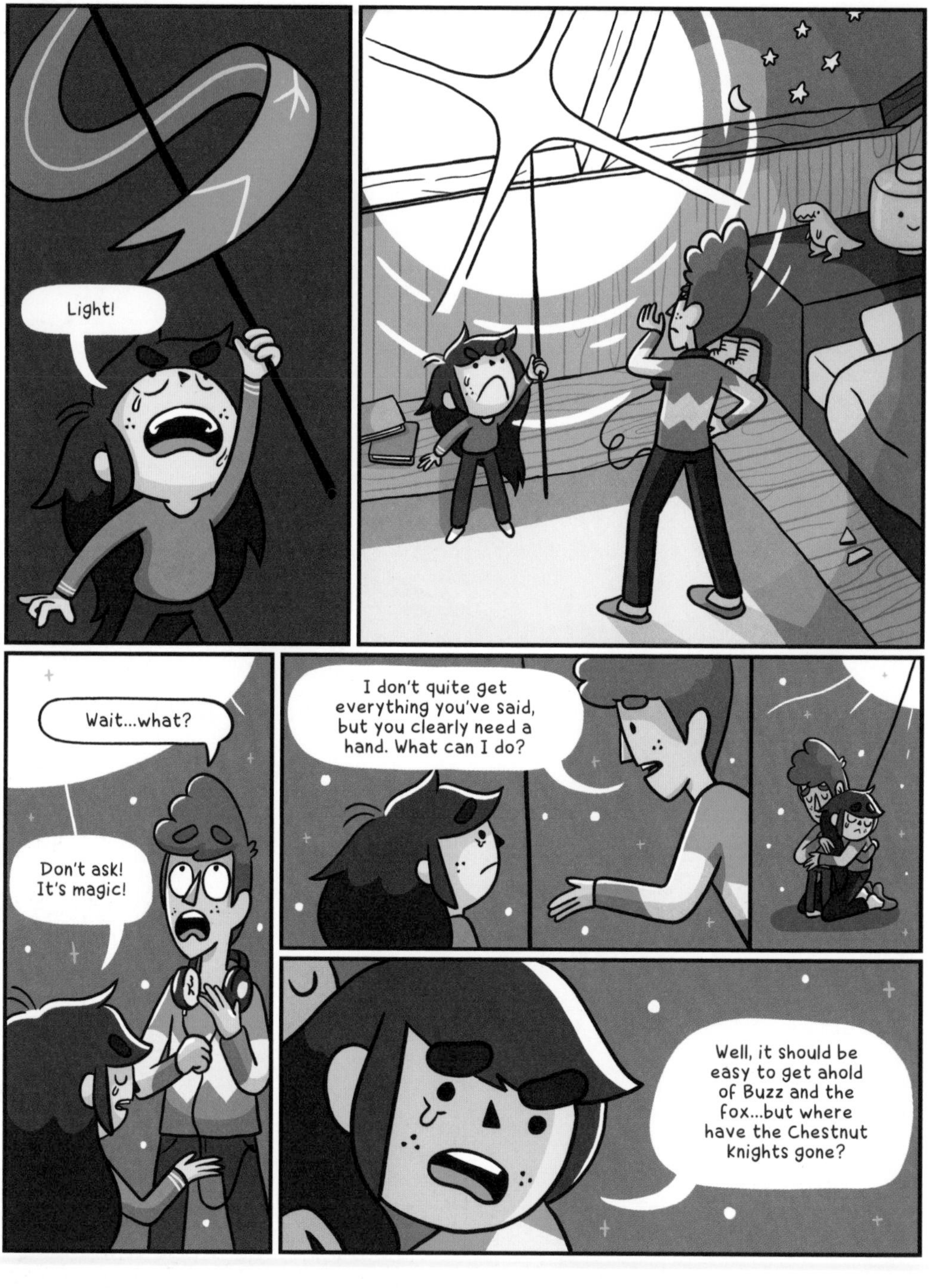
Light!
Wait...what?
Don't ask!
It's magic!
I don't quite get everything you've said, but you clearly need a hand. What can I do?
Well, it should be easy to get ahold of Buzz and the fox...but where have the Chestnut Knights gone?

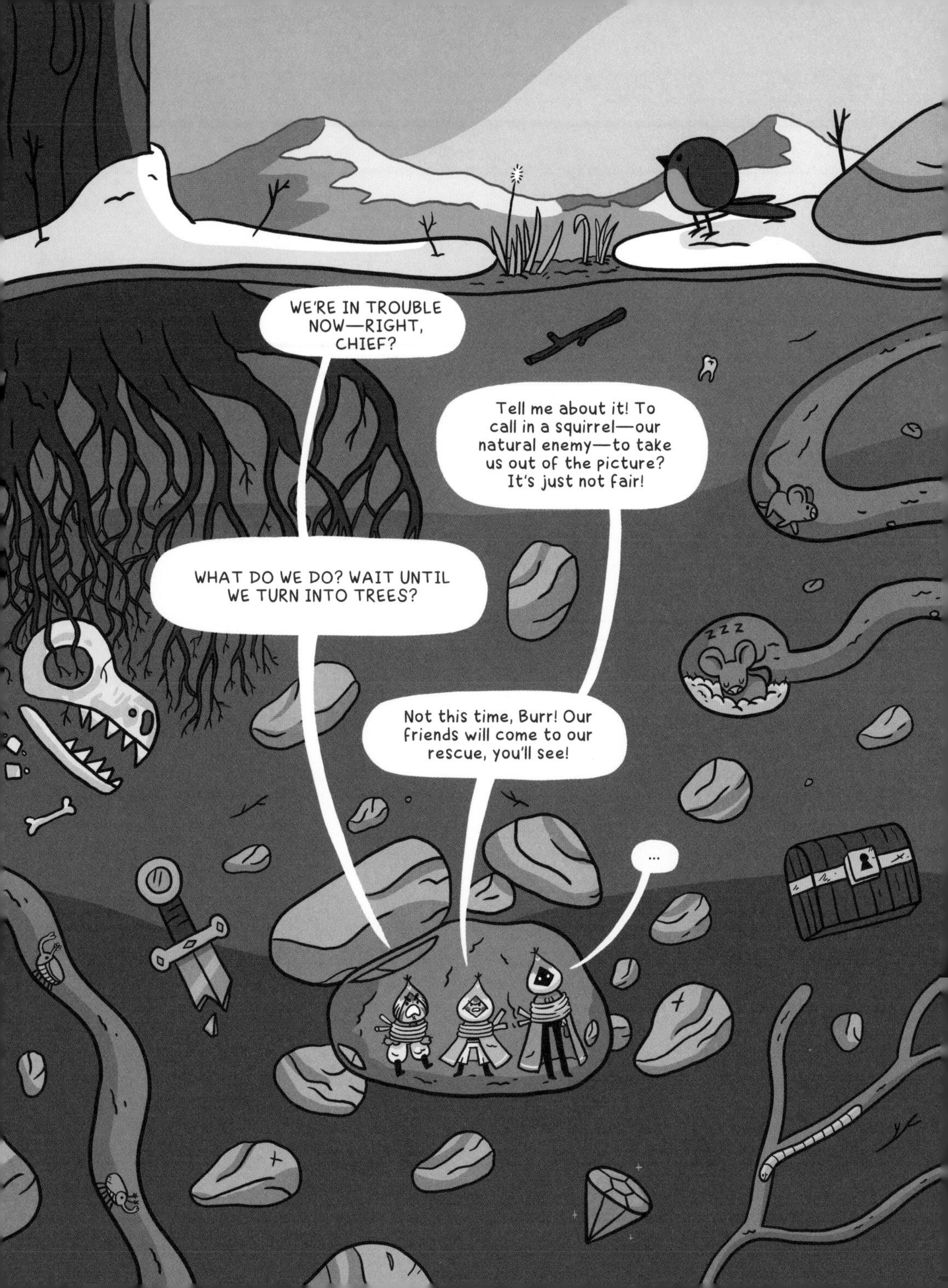

WE'RE IN TROUBLE NOW—RIGHT, CHIEF?
Tell me about it! To call in a squirrel—our natural enemy—to take us out of the picture? It's just not fair!
WHAT DO WE DO? WAIT UNTIL WE TURN INTO TREES?
Not this time, Burr! Our friends will come to our rescue, you'll see!
...

I'm just saying that we're not going to get out of here by digging through solid rock!

SCRATCH

SCRATCH

Maybe not! But at least I'm trying to do something! You're just standing there doing nothing!

PFFFT

Okay, listen. I know we're not exactly buddies, but we're going to have to bury the hatchet. All things considered, I'd just as soon be tucked up warmly in Aster's scarf.

So—you've changed your mind about us?

Let's say...it could be worse. So, do you want to get out or not?

Fine. Let's call a truce.

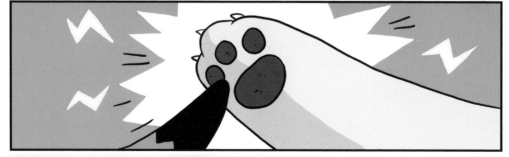

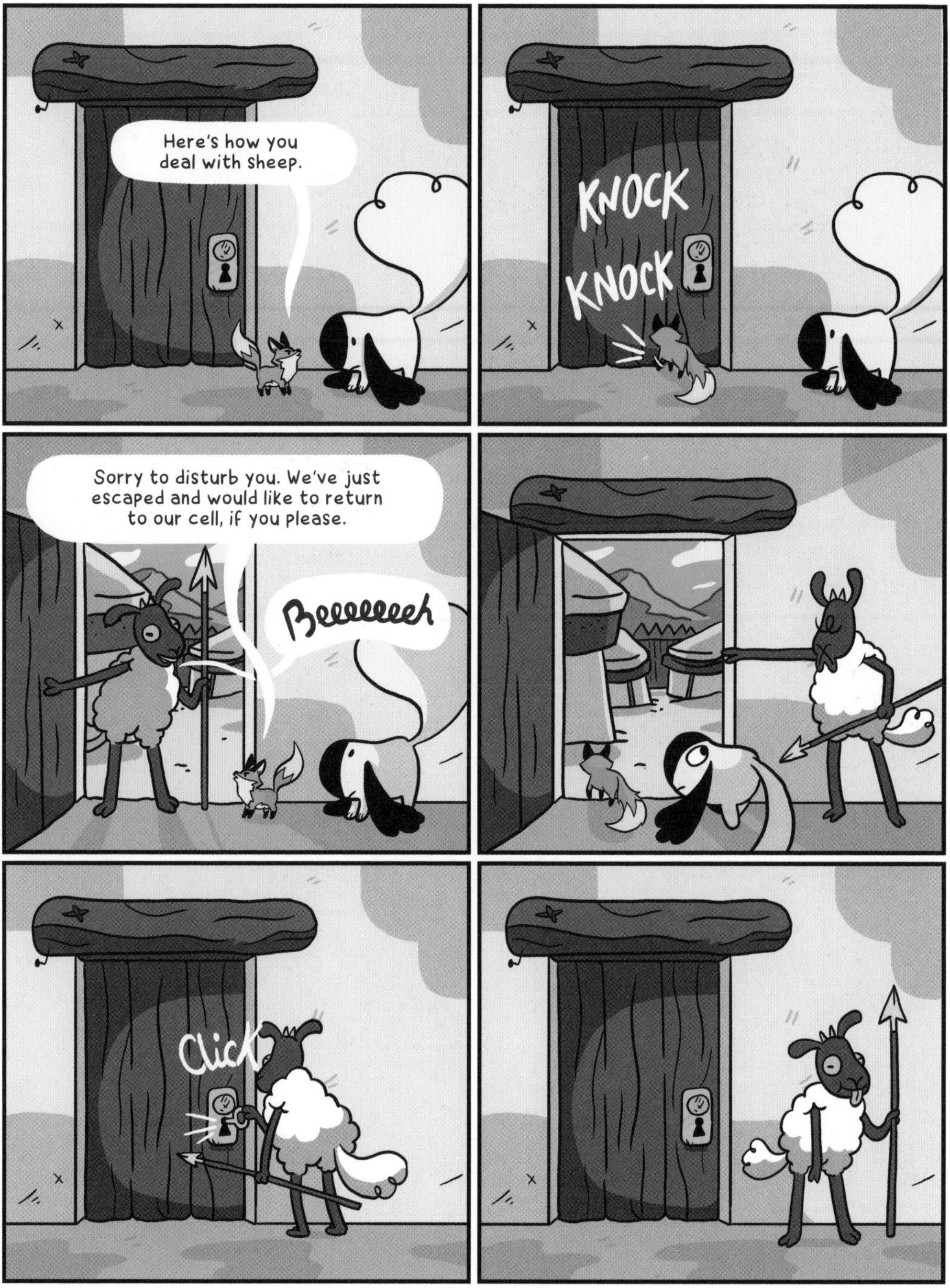
Here's how you deal with sheep.
KNOCK
KNOCK
Sorry to disturb you. We've just escaped and would like to return to our cell, if you please.
Beeeeeeh
Click

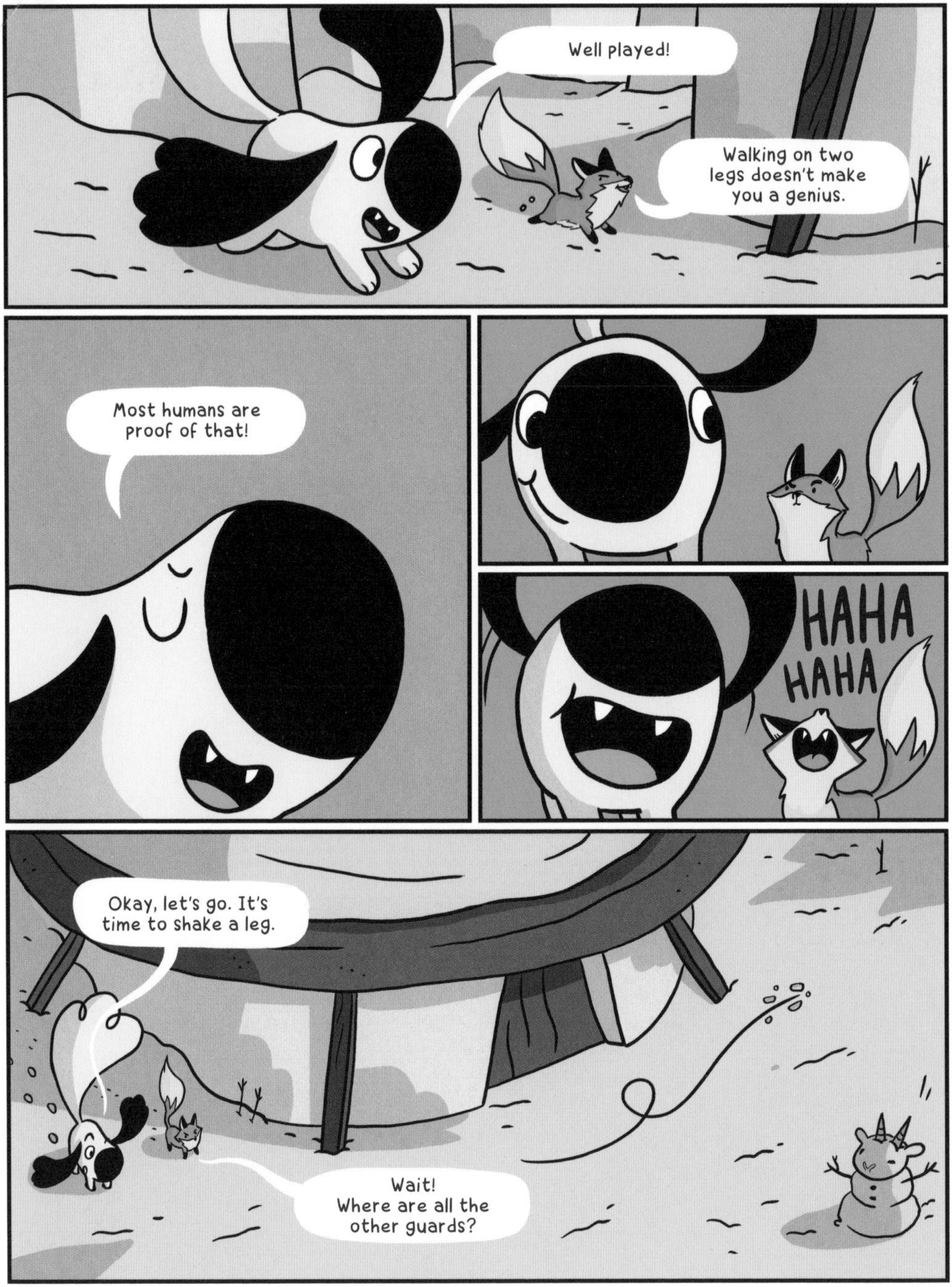
Well played!
Walking on two legs doesn't make you a genius.
Most humans are proof of that!
HAHA HAHA
Okay, let's go. It's time to shake a leg.
Wait! Where are all the other guards?

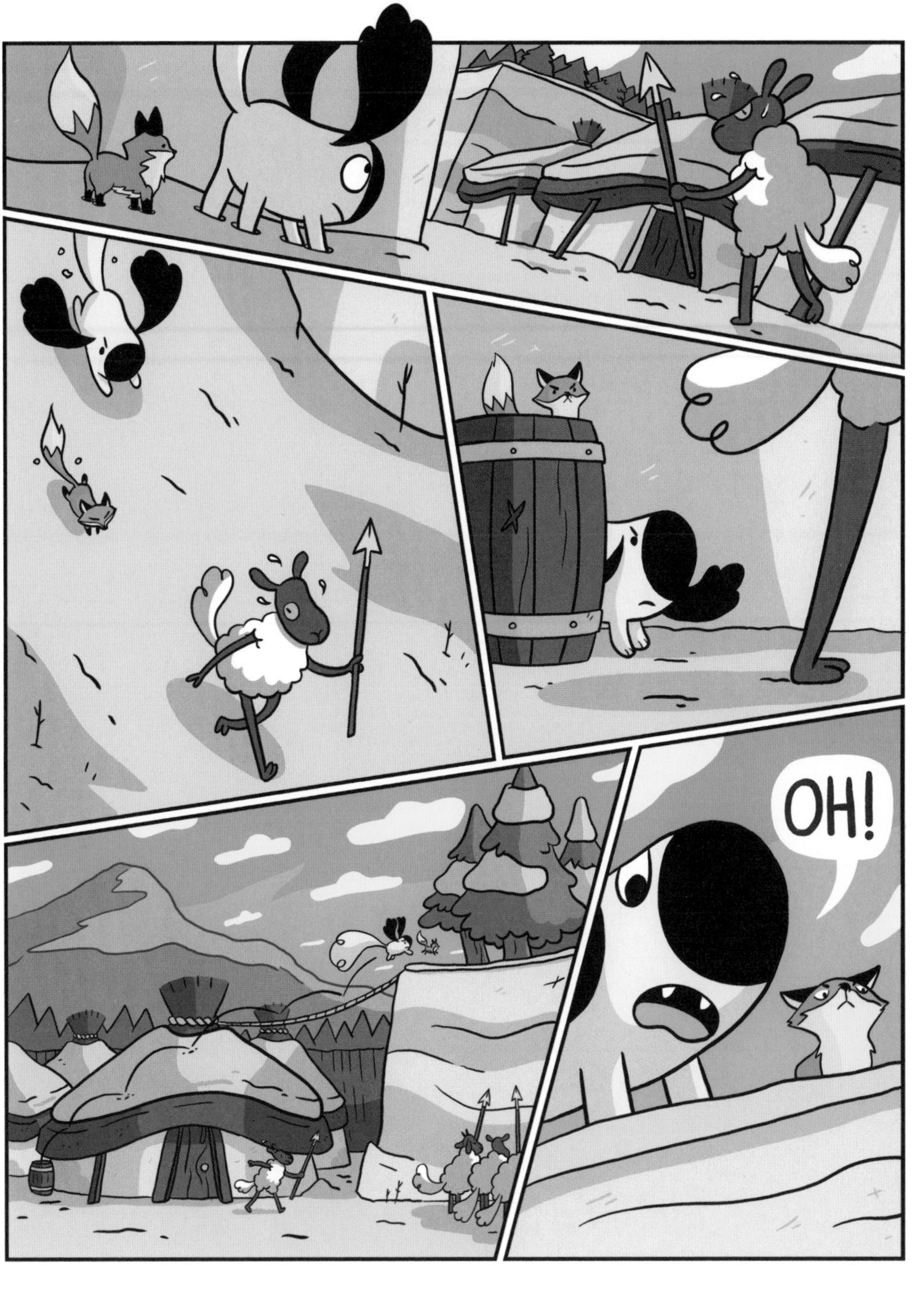
OH!

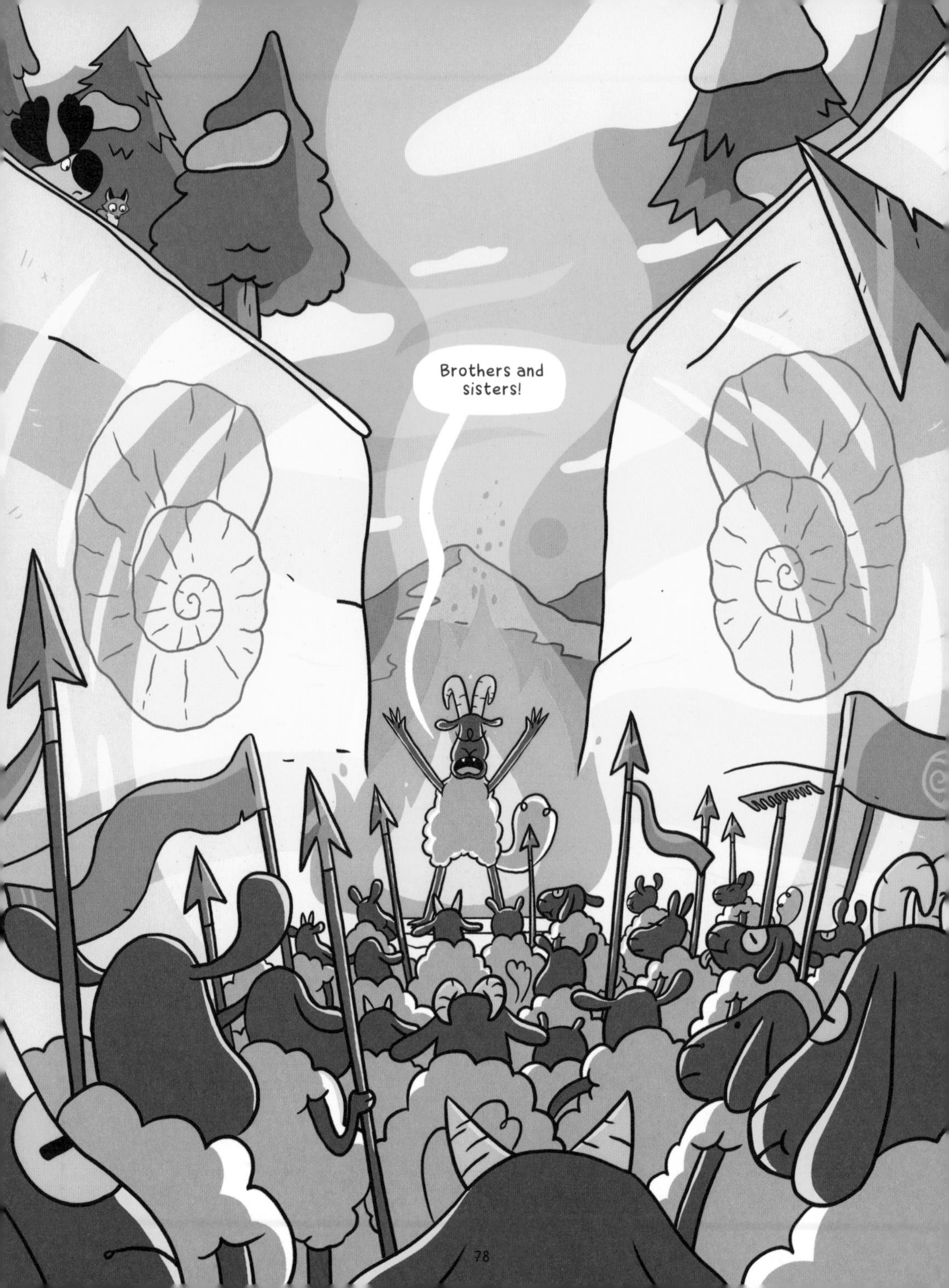
Brothers and sisters!

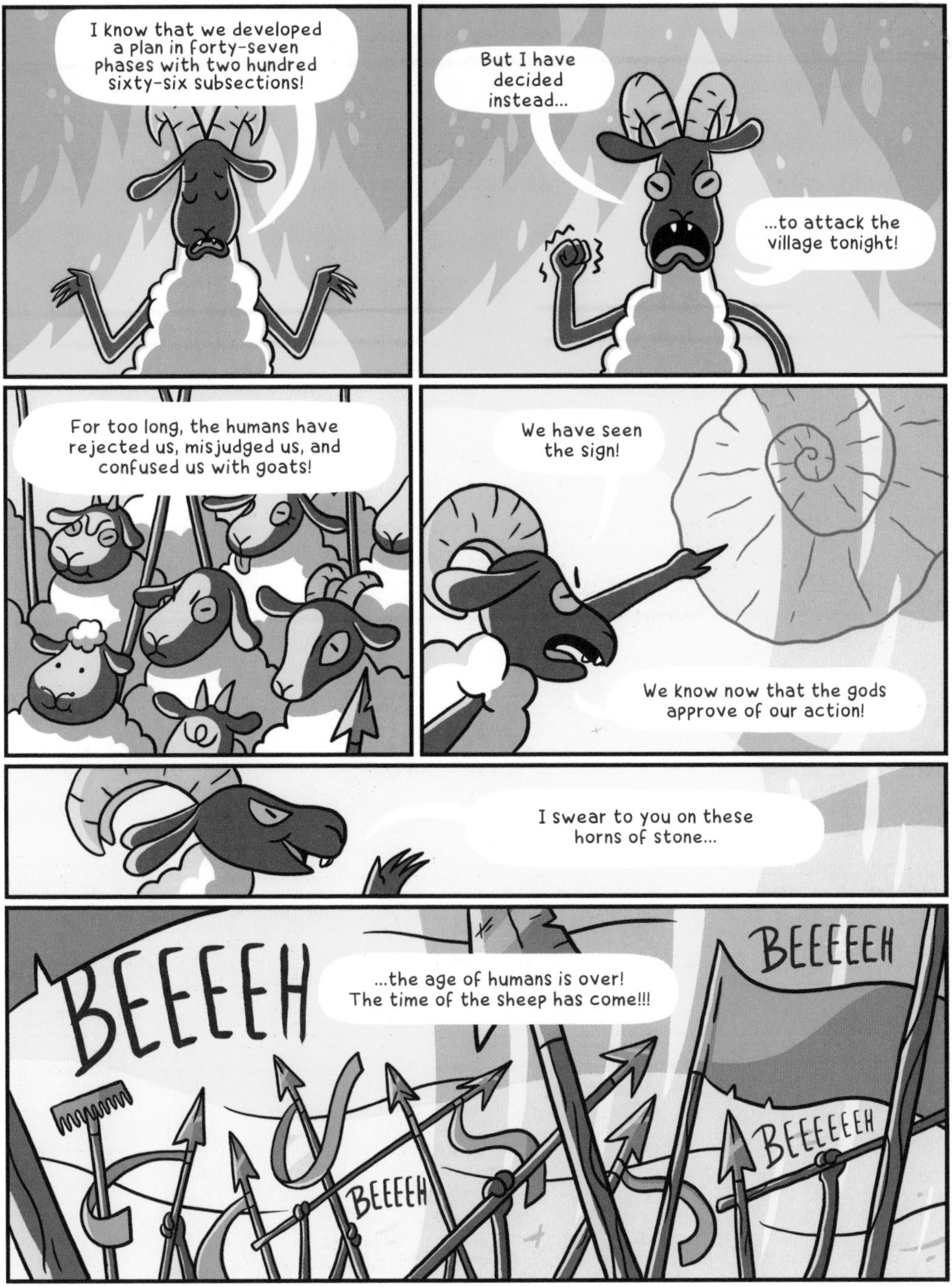
I know that we developed a plan in forty-seven phases with two hundred sixty-six subsections!
But I have decided instead...
...to attack the village tonight!
For too long, the humans have rejected us, misjudged us, and confused us with goats!
We have seen the sign!
We know now that the gods approve of our action!
I swear to you on these horns of stone...
BEEEEH
...the age of humans is over! The time of the sheep has come!!!
BEEEEEH
BEEEEEEH
BEEEEH

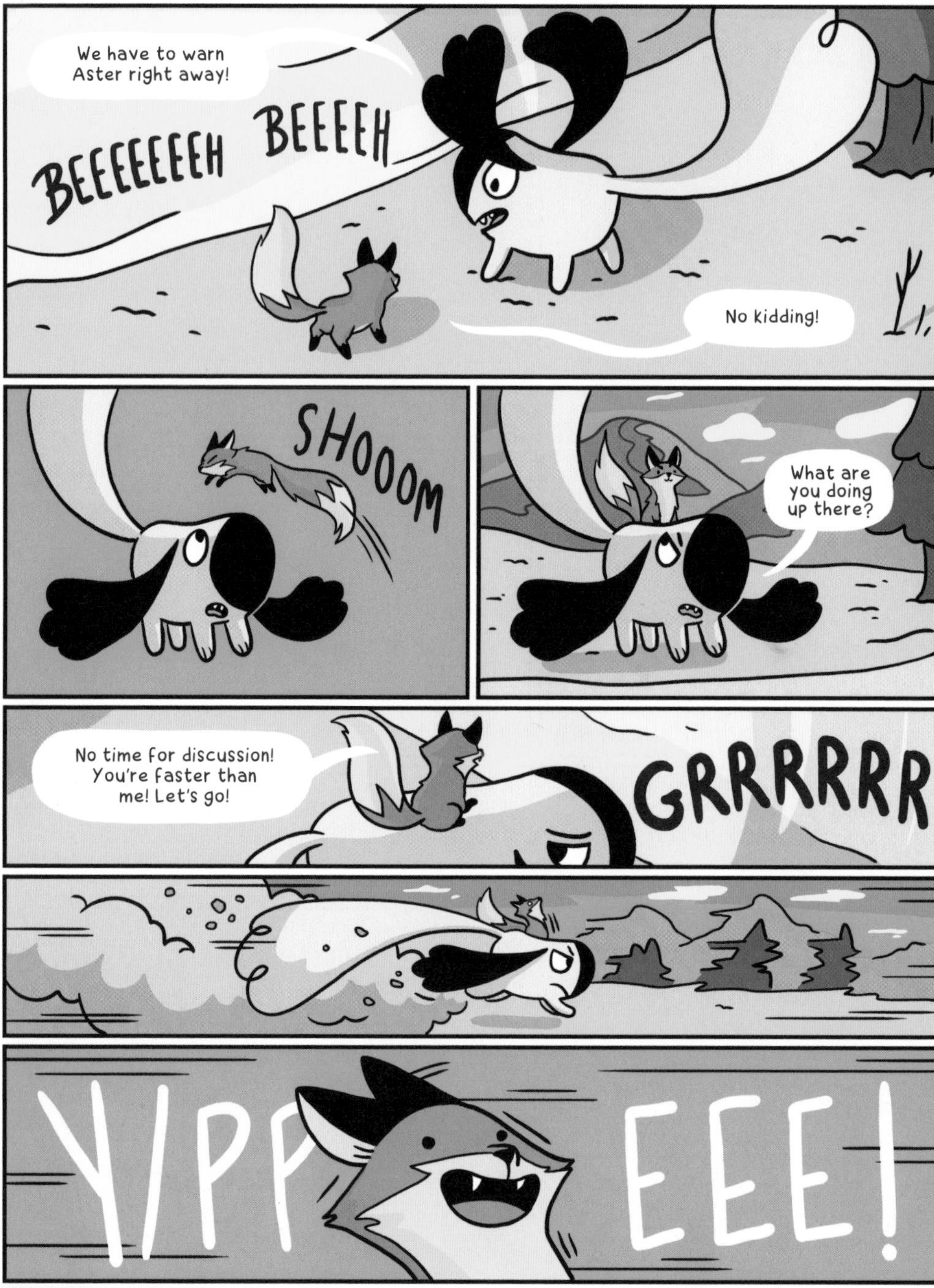
We have to warn Aster right away!
BEEEEEEEH BEEEEH
No kidding!
SHOOOM
What are you doing up there?
No time for discussion! You're faster than me! Let's go!
GRRRRRRR
YIPP EEE!

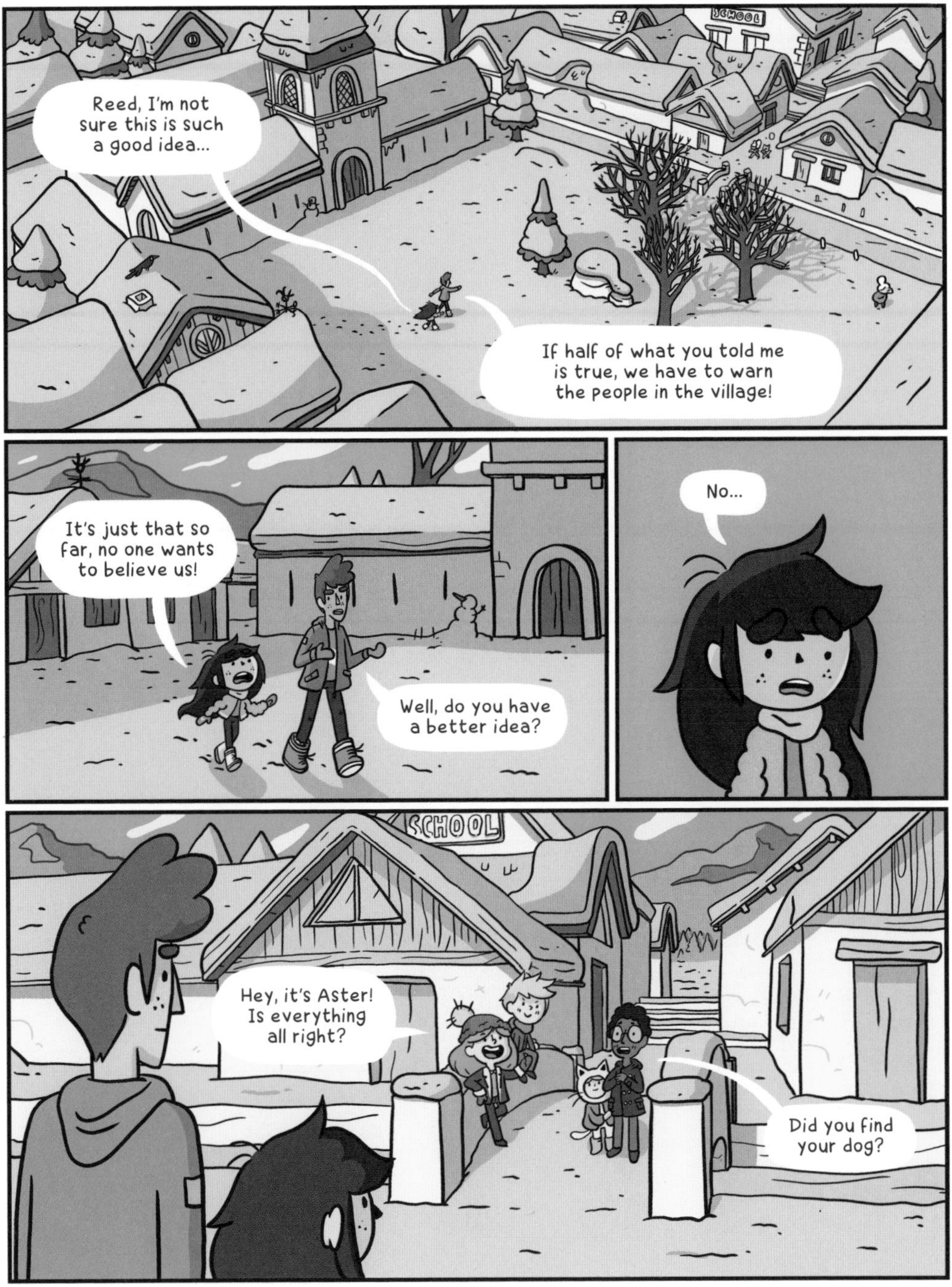
SCHOOL
Reed, I'm not sure this is such a good idea...
If half of what you told me is true, we have to warn the people in the village!
It's just that so far, no one wants to believe us!
Well, do you have a better idea?
No...
SCHOOL
Hey, it's Aster! Is everything all right?
Did you find your dog?

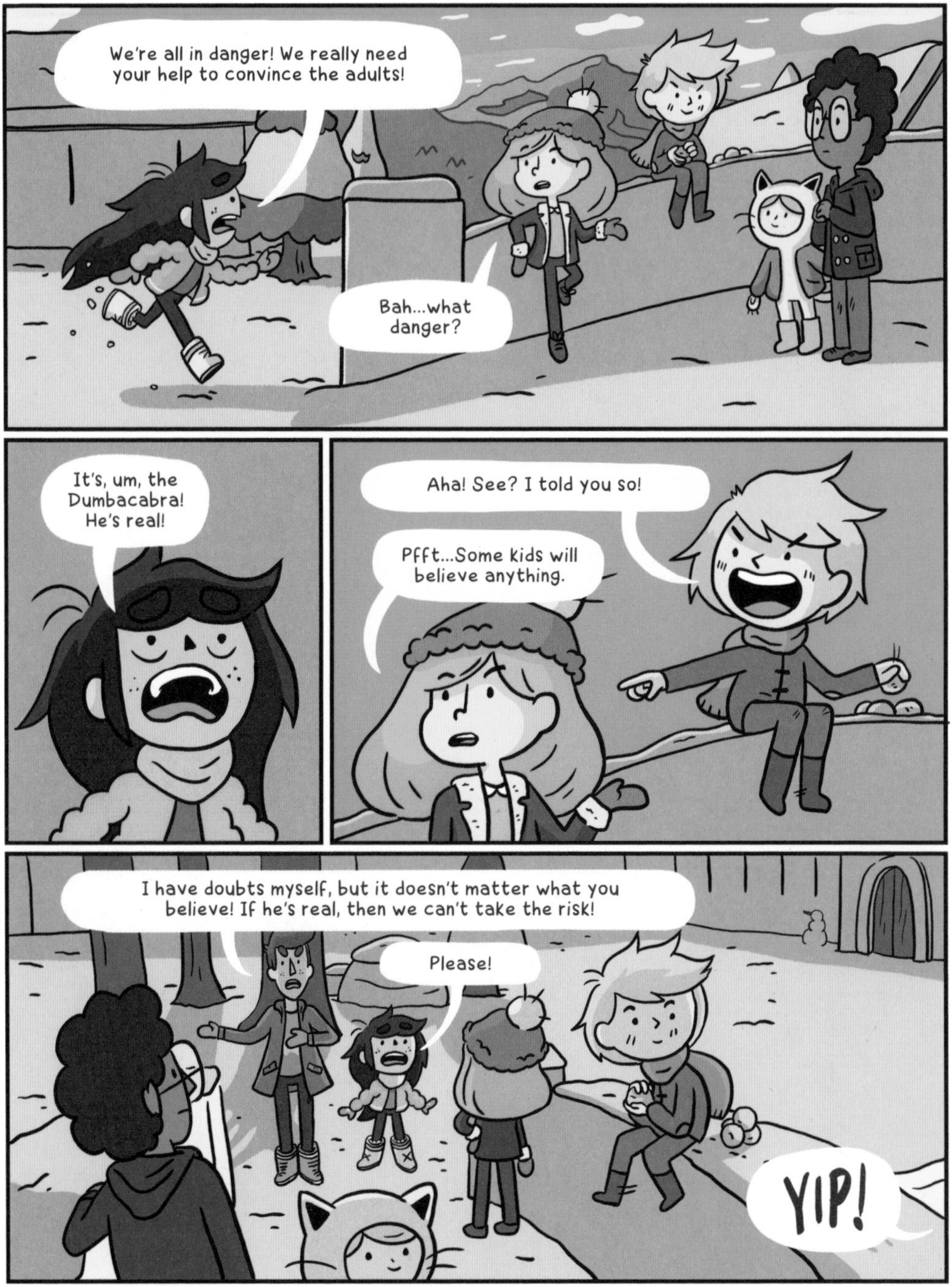
We're all in danger! We really need your help to convince the adults!
Bah...what danger?
It's, um, the Dumbacabra! He's real!
Aha! See? I told you so!
Pfft...Some kids will believe anything.
I have doubts myself, but it doesn't matter what you believe! If he's real, then we can't take the risk!
Please!
YIP!

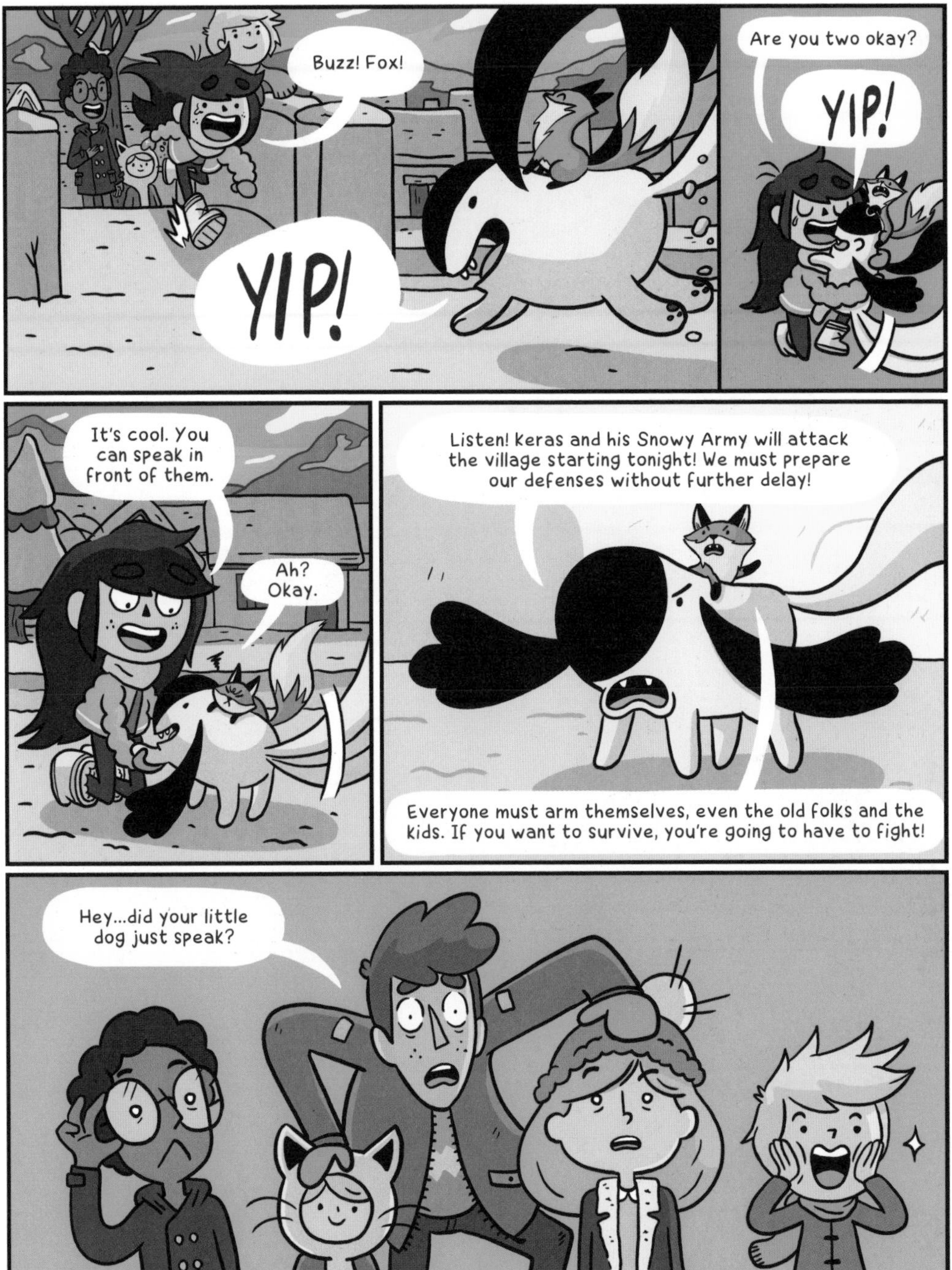
Buzz! Fox!
YIP!
Are you two okay?
YIP!
It's cool. You can speak in front of them.
Ah? Okay.
Listen! Keras and his Snowy Army will attack the village starting tonight! We must prepare our defenses without further delay!
Everyone must arm themselves, even the old folks and the kids. If you want to survive, you're going to have to fight!
Hey...did your little dog just speak?

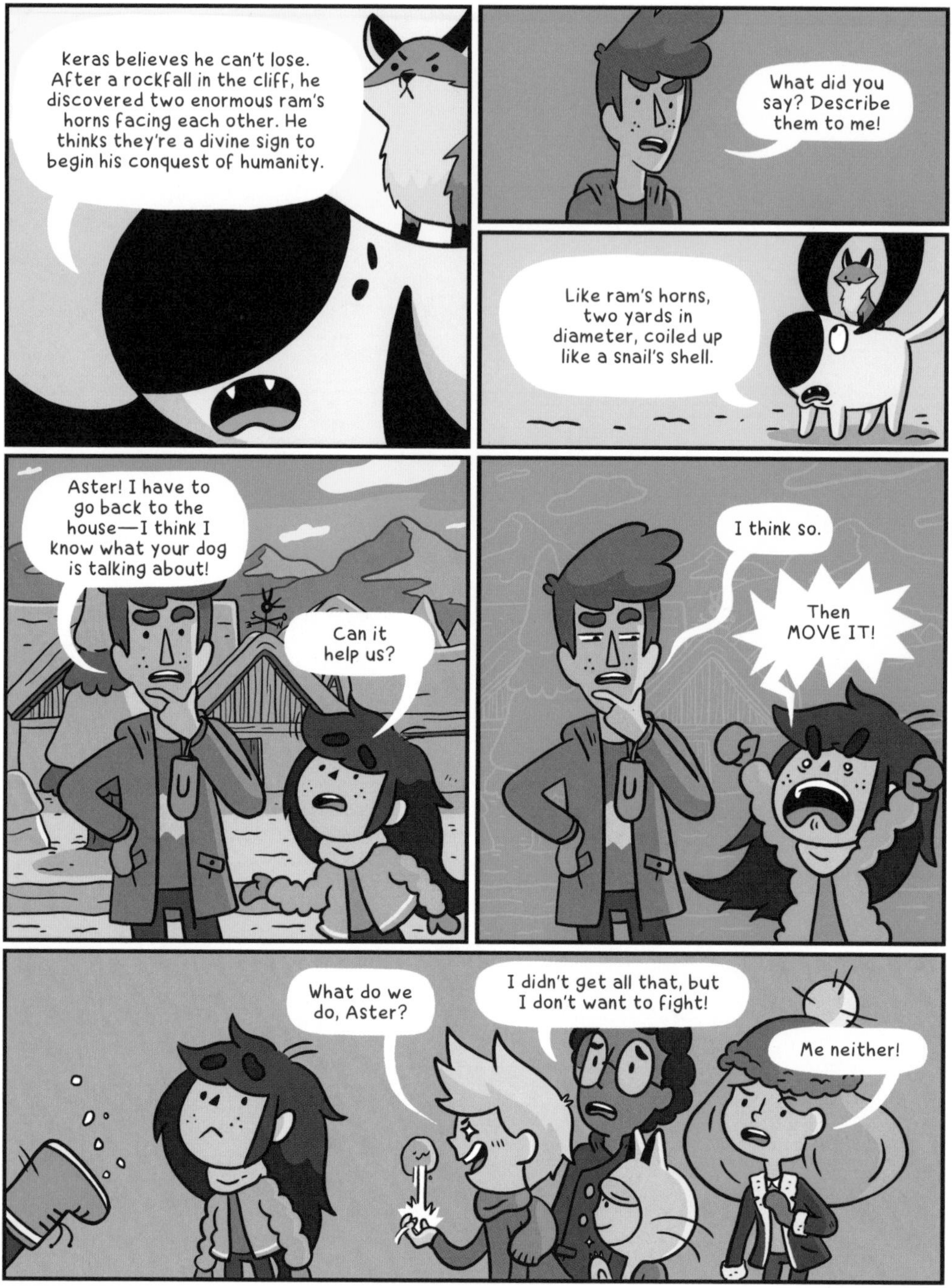
Keras believes he can't lose. After a rockfall in the cliff, he discovered two enormous ram's horns facing each other. He thinks they're a divine sign to begin his conquest of humanity.
What did you say? Describe them to me!
Like ram's horns, two yards in diameter, coiled up like a snail's shell.
Aster! I have to go back to the house—I think I know what your dog is talking about!
Can it help us?
I think so.
Then MOVE IT!
What do we do, Aster?
I didn't get all that, but I don't want to fight!
Me neither!

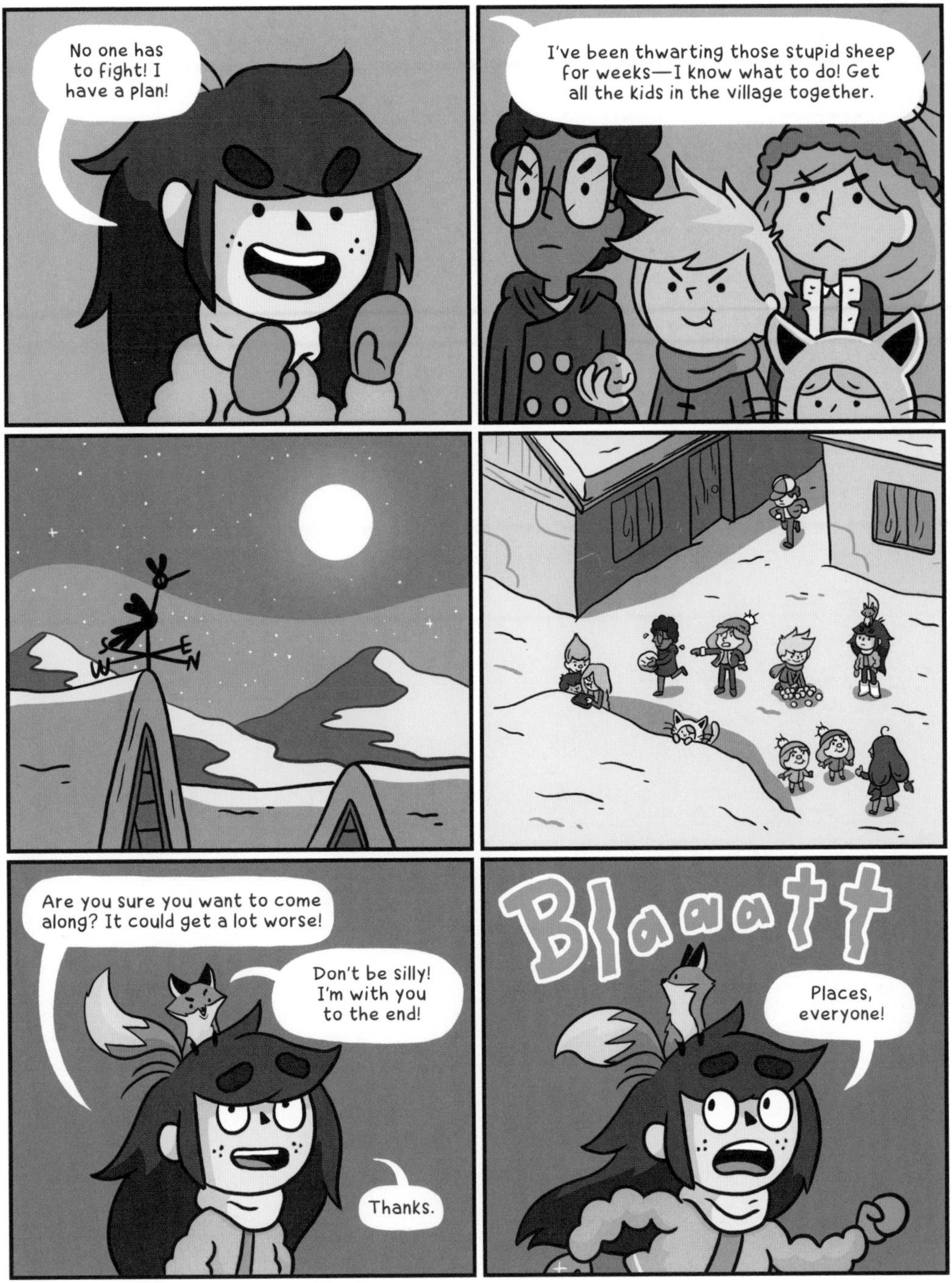
No one has to fight! I have a plan!
I've been thwarting those stupid sheep for weeks—I know what to do! Get all the kids in the village together.
W
S
E
N
Are you sure you want to come along? It could get a lot worse!
Don't be silly! I'm with you to the end!
Thanks.
Blaaatt
Places, everyone!

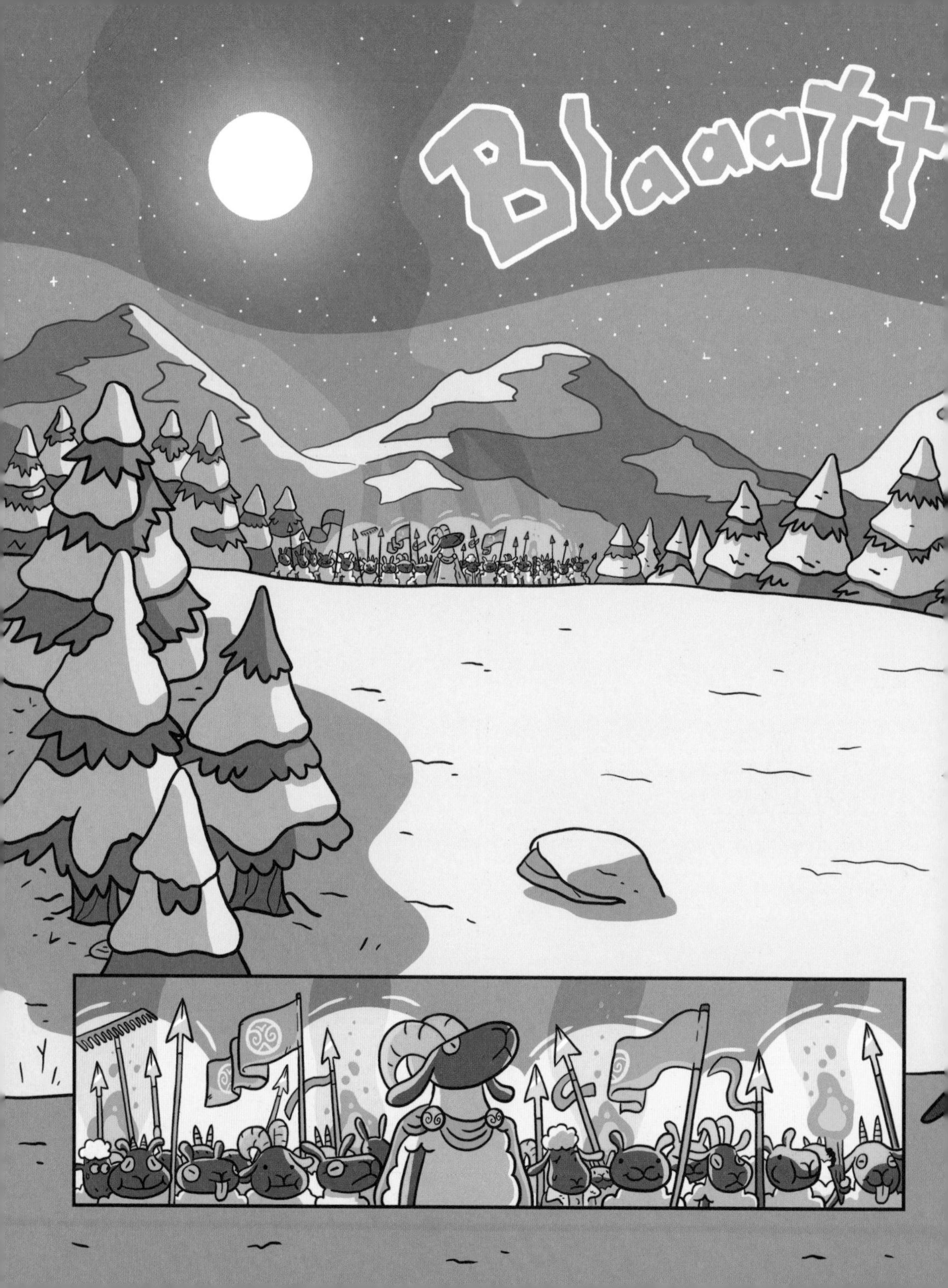
Blaatt

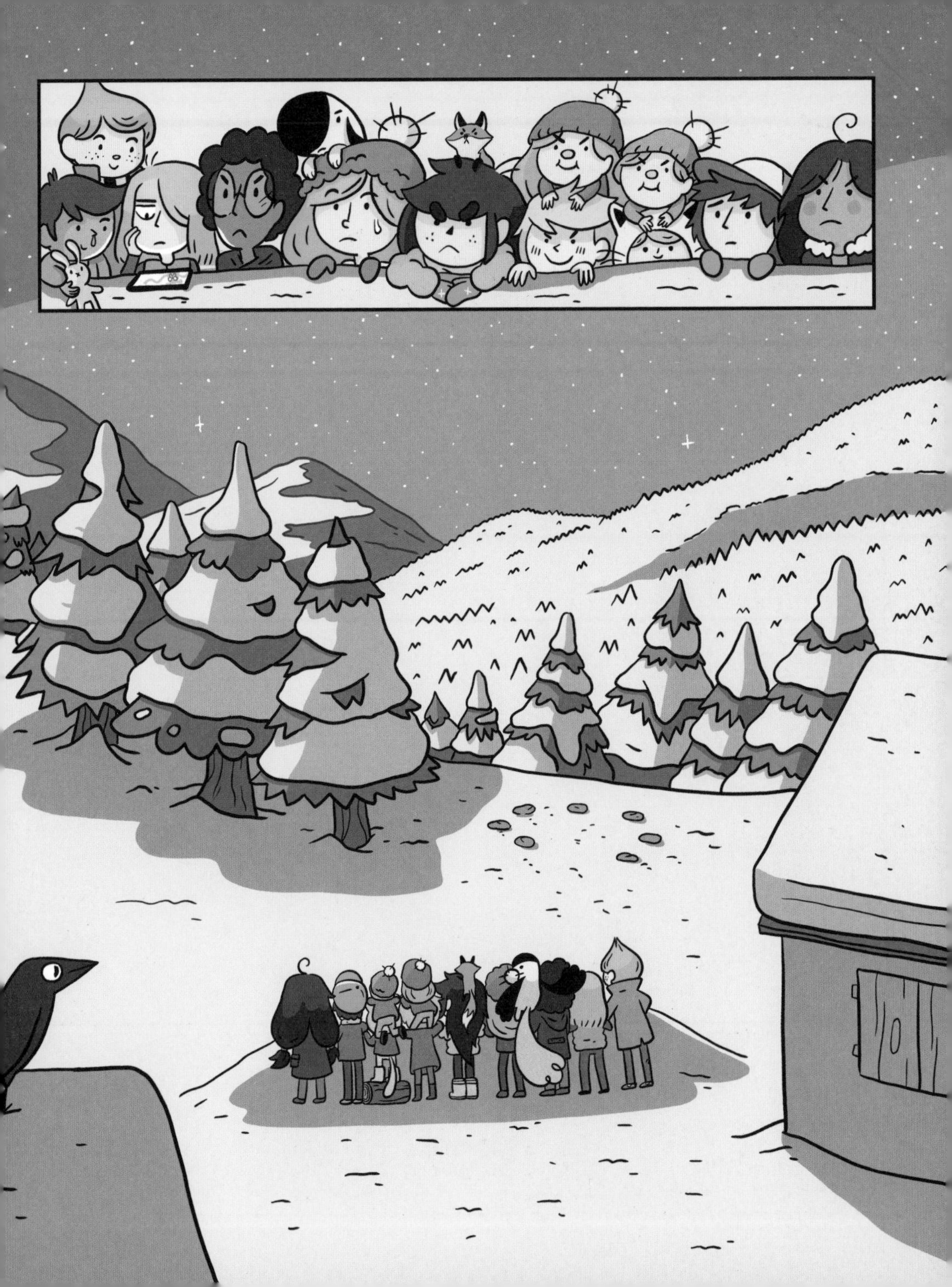

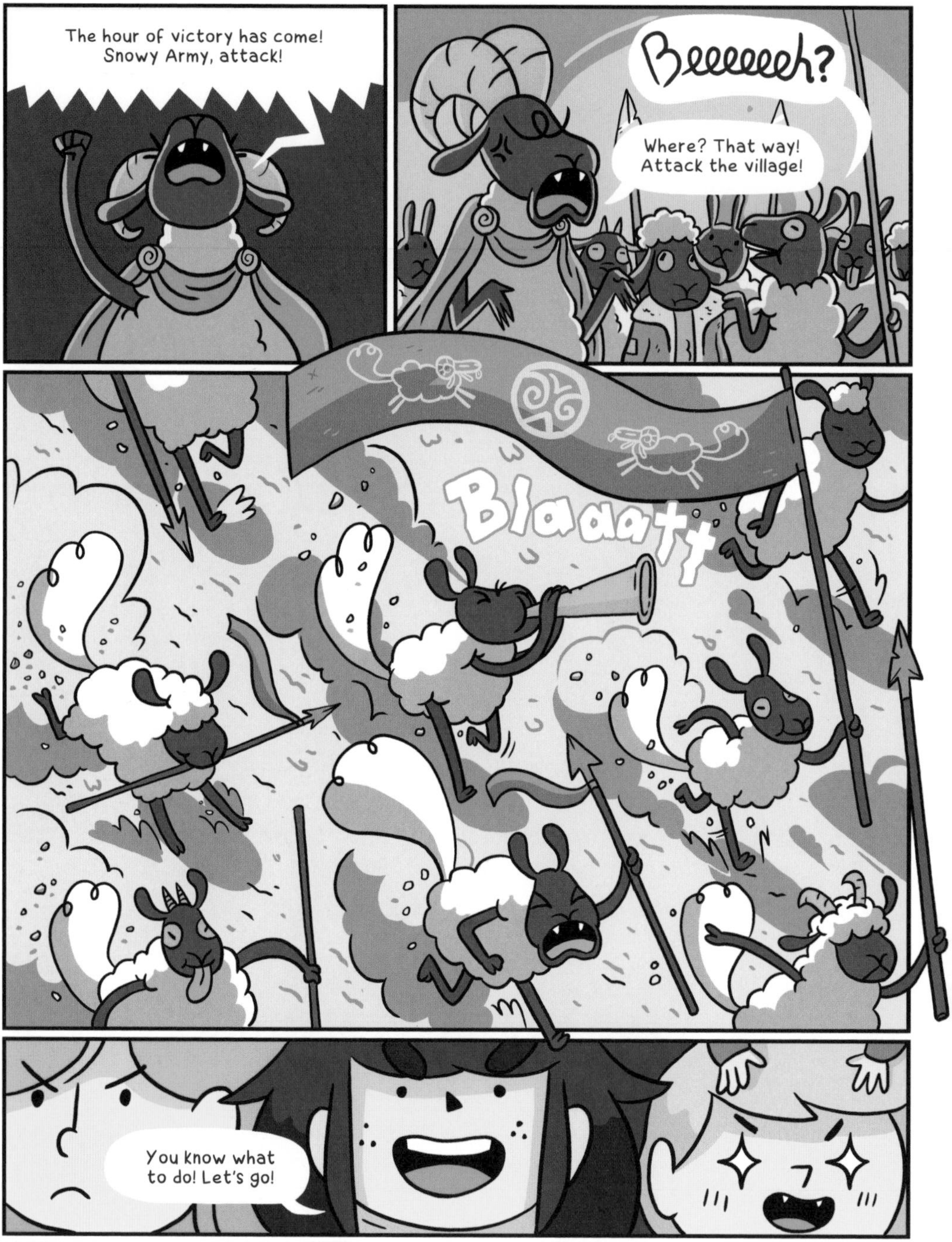
The hour of victory has come! Snowy Army, attack!
Beeeeeh?
Where? That way! Attack the village!
Blaaatt
You know what to do! Let's go!

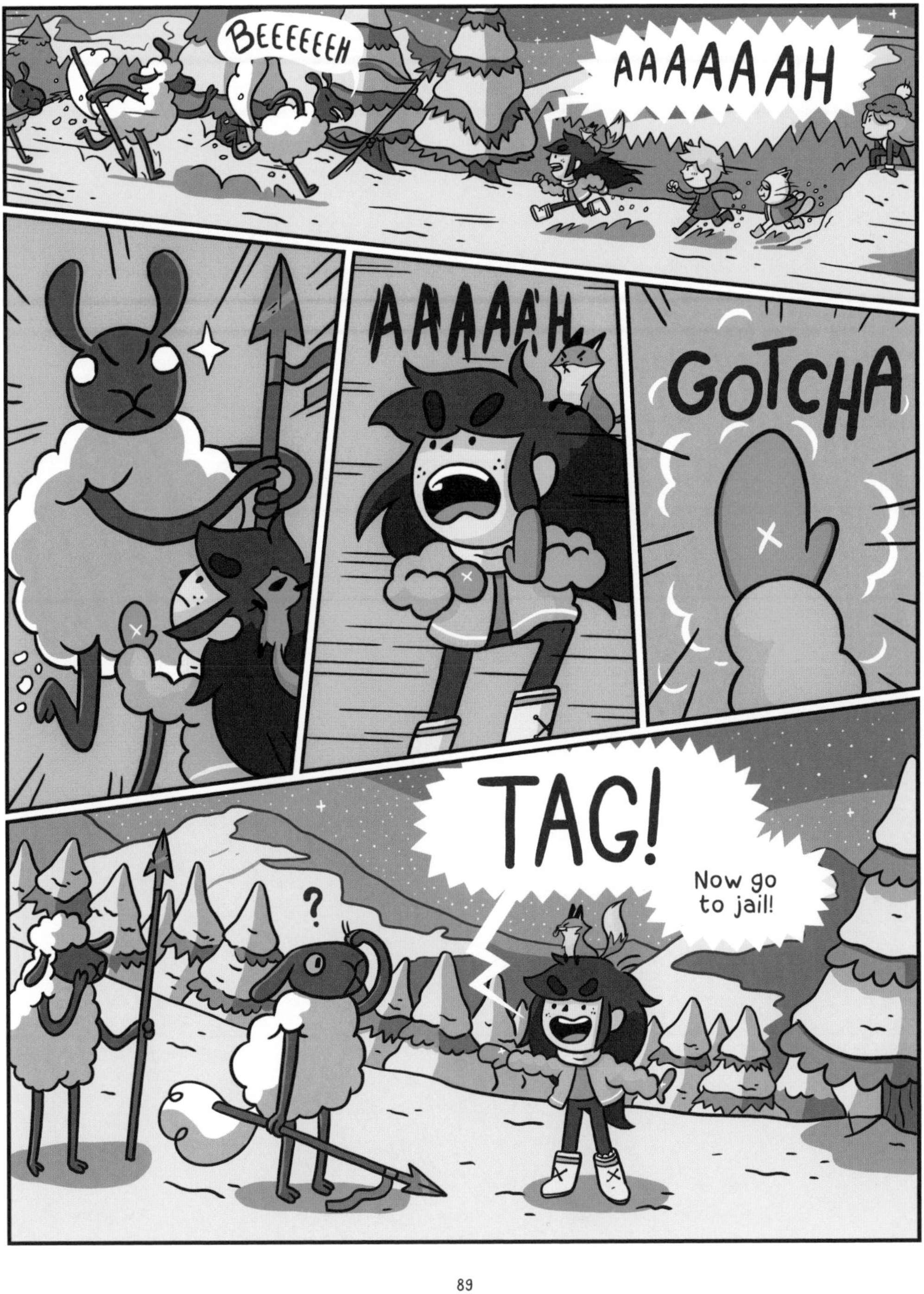
BEEEEEEH
AAAAAAH
AAAAAH
GOTCHA
?
TAG!
Now go to jail!

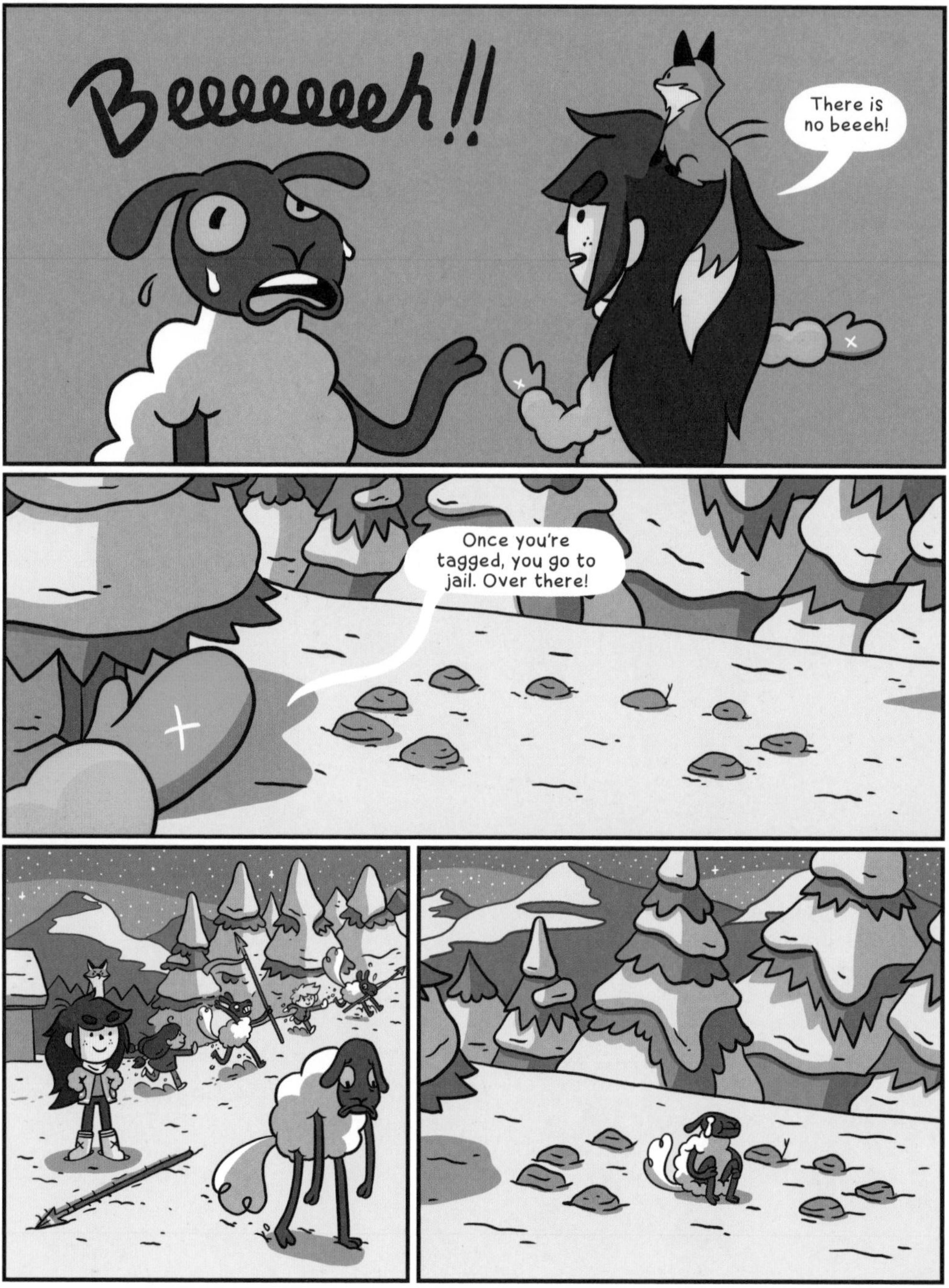
Beeeeeeh!!
There is no beeeh!
Once you're tagged, you go to jail. Over there!

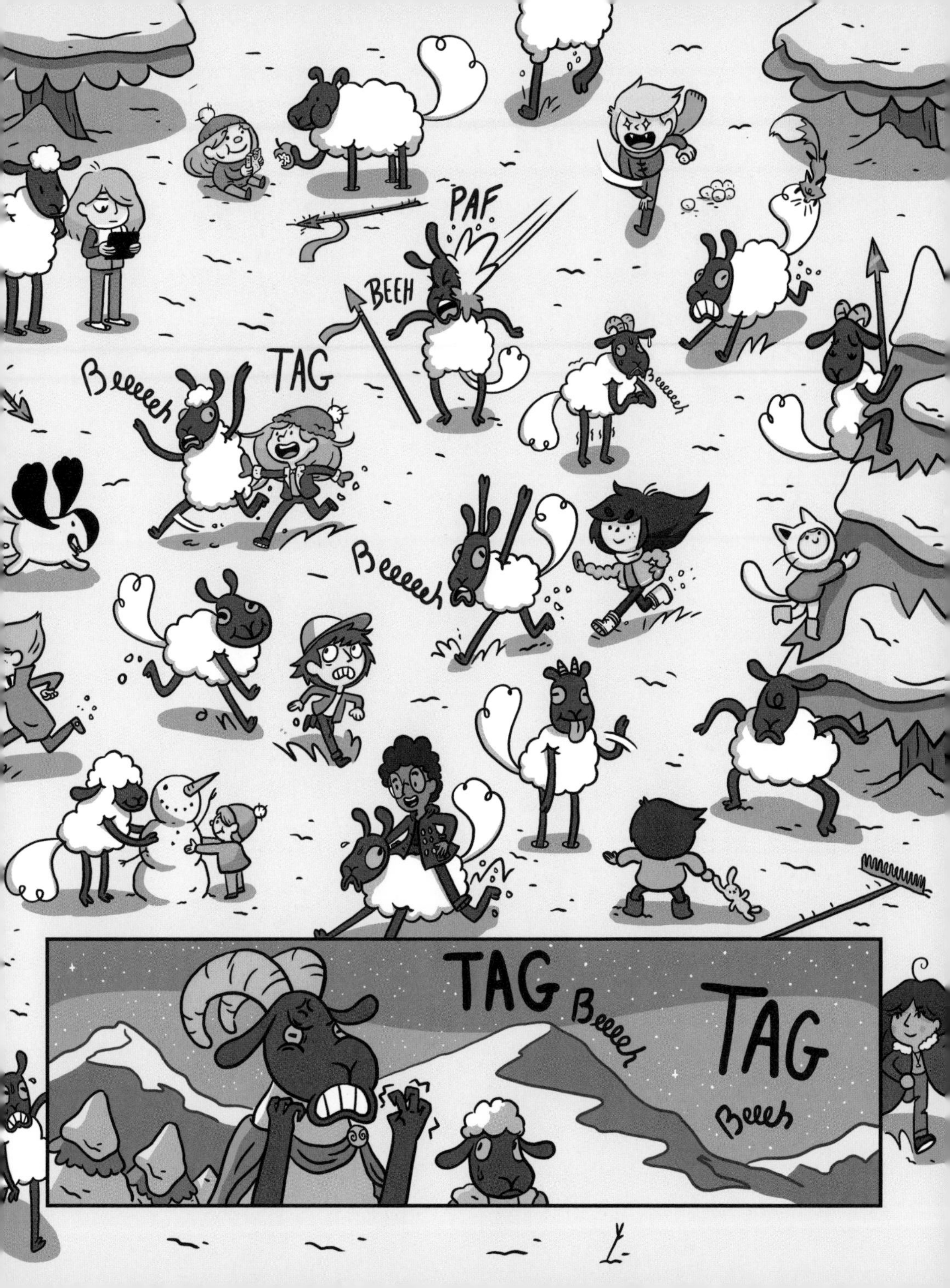
PAF
BEEH
TAG
Beeeeeh
Beeeeeh
Beeeeeh
TAG
Beeeeh
TAG
Beeeh

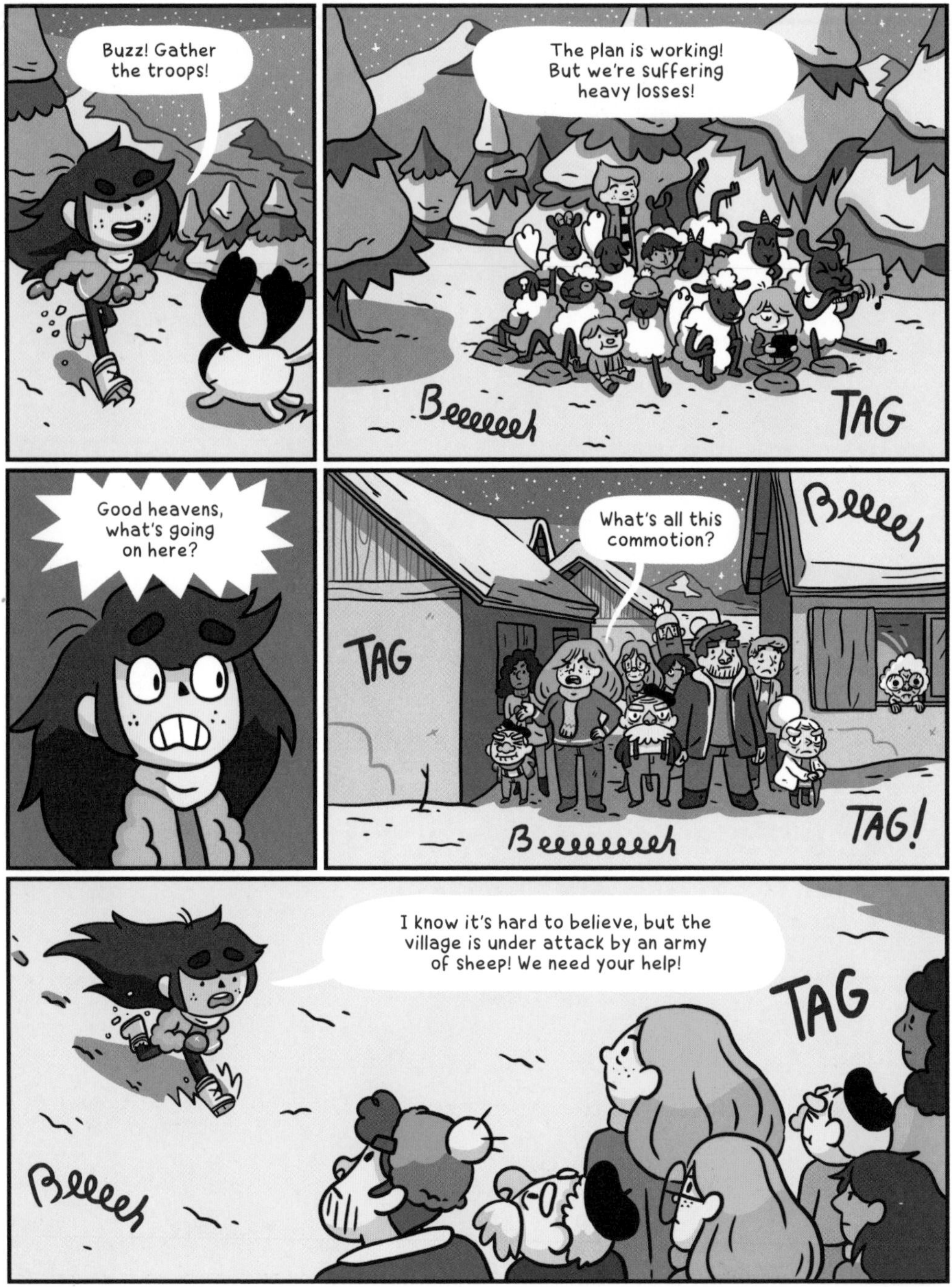
Buzz! Gather the troops!
The plan is working! But we're suffering heavy losses!
Beeeeeeh
TAG
Good heavens, what's going on here?
What's all this commotion?
Beeeeh
TAG
TAG!
Beeeeeeeeh
I know it's hard to believe, but the village is under attack by an army of sheep! We need your help!
TAG
Beeeeh

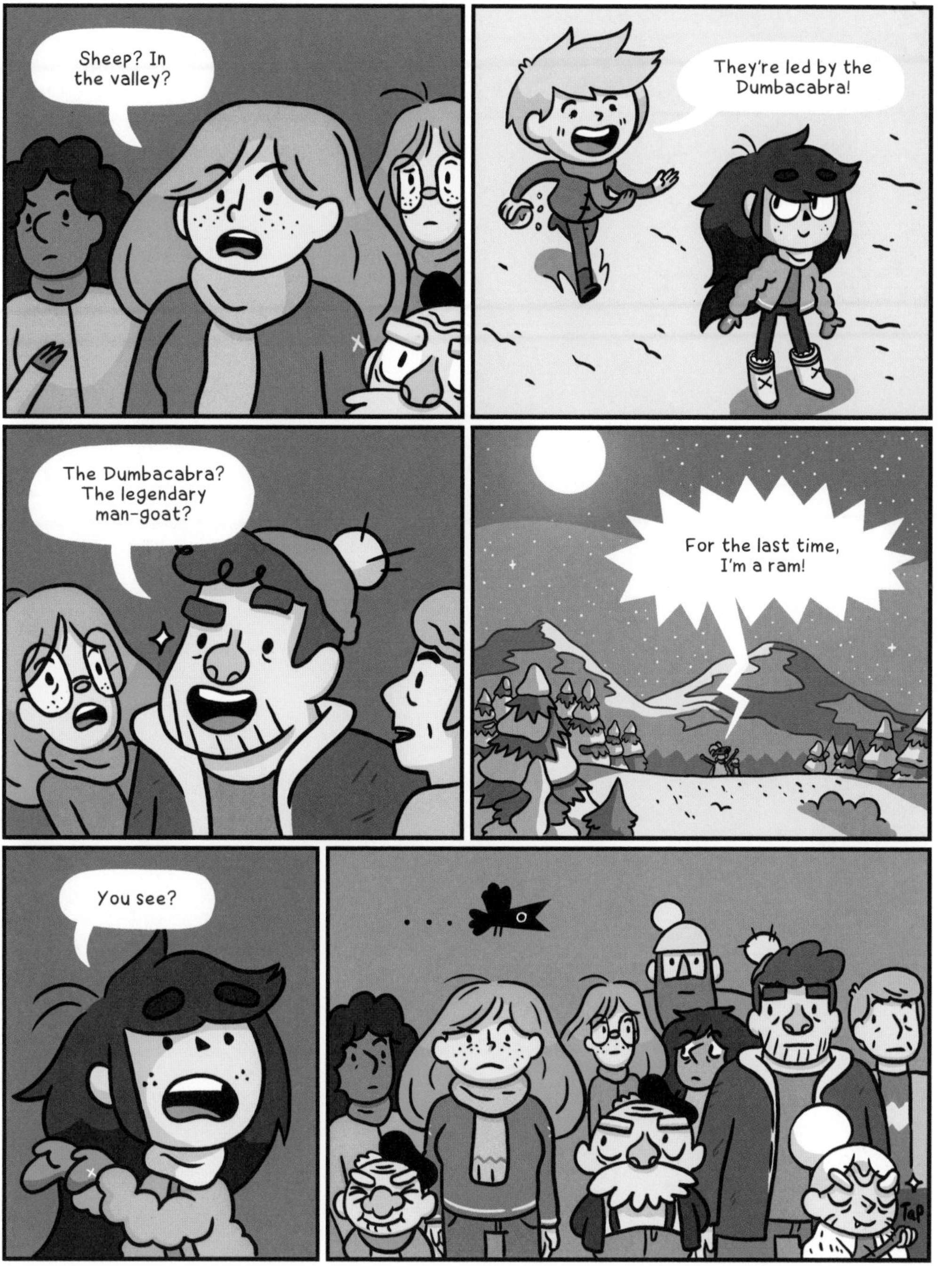
Sheep? In the valley?
They're led by the Dumbacabra!
The Dumbacabra? The legendary man-goat?
For the last time, I'm a ram!
You see?
. . .
TAP

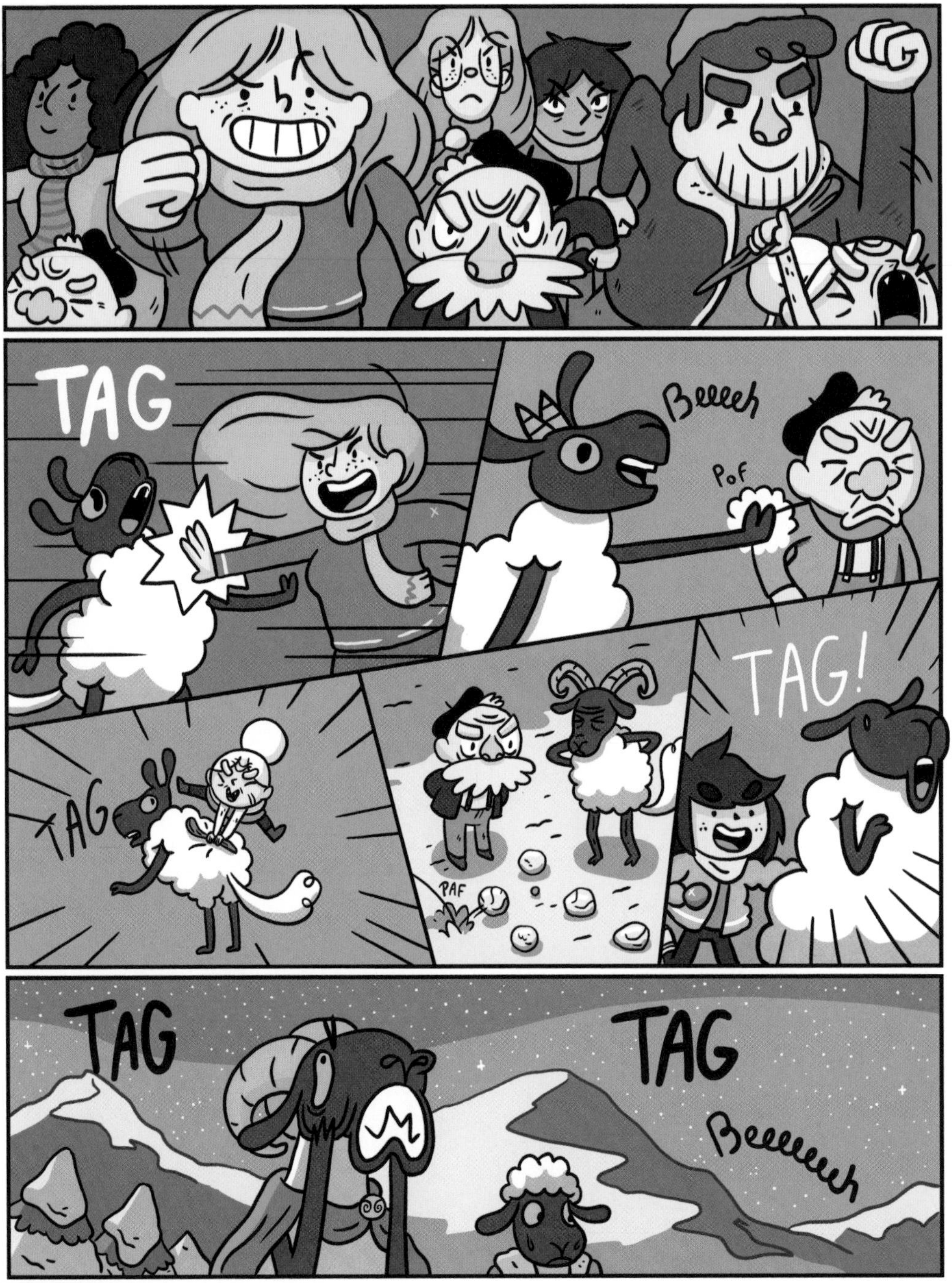
TAG
Beeeeh
Pof
TAG
PAF
TAG!
TAG
TAG
Beeeeeeeh

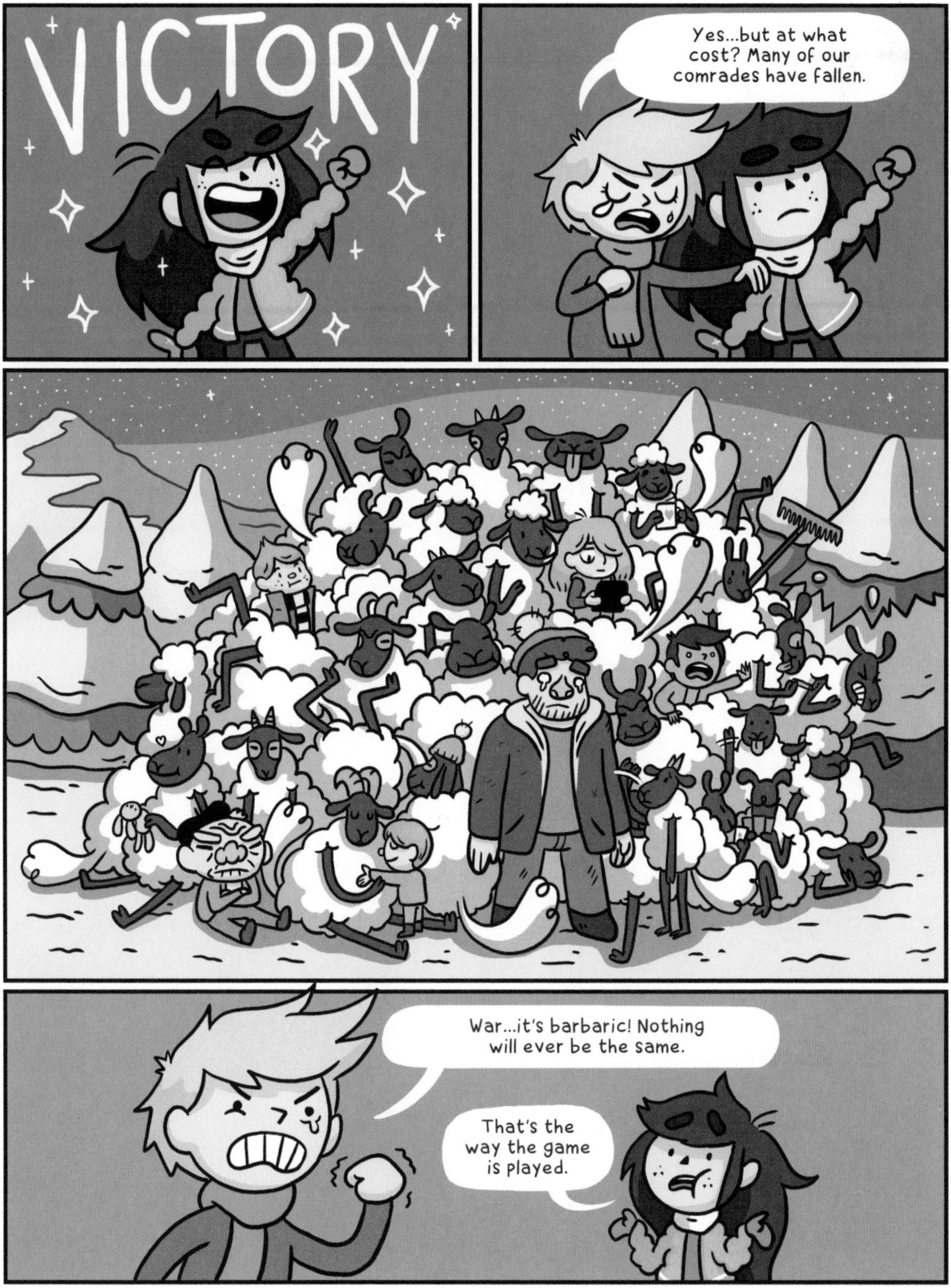
VICTORY
Yes...but at what cost? Many of our comrades have fallen.
War...it's barbaric! Nothing will ever be the same.
That's the way the game is played.

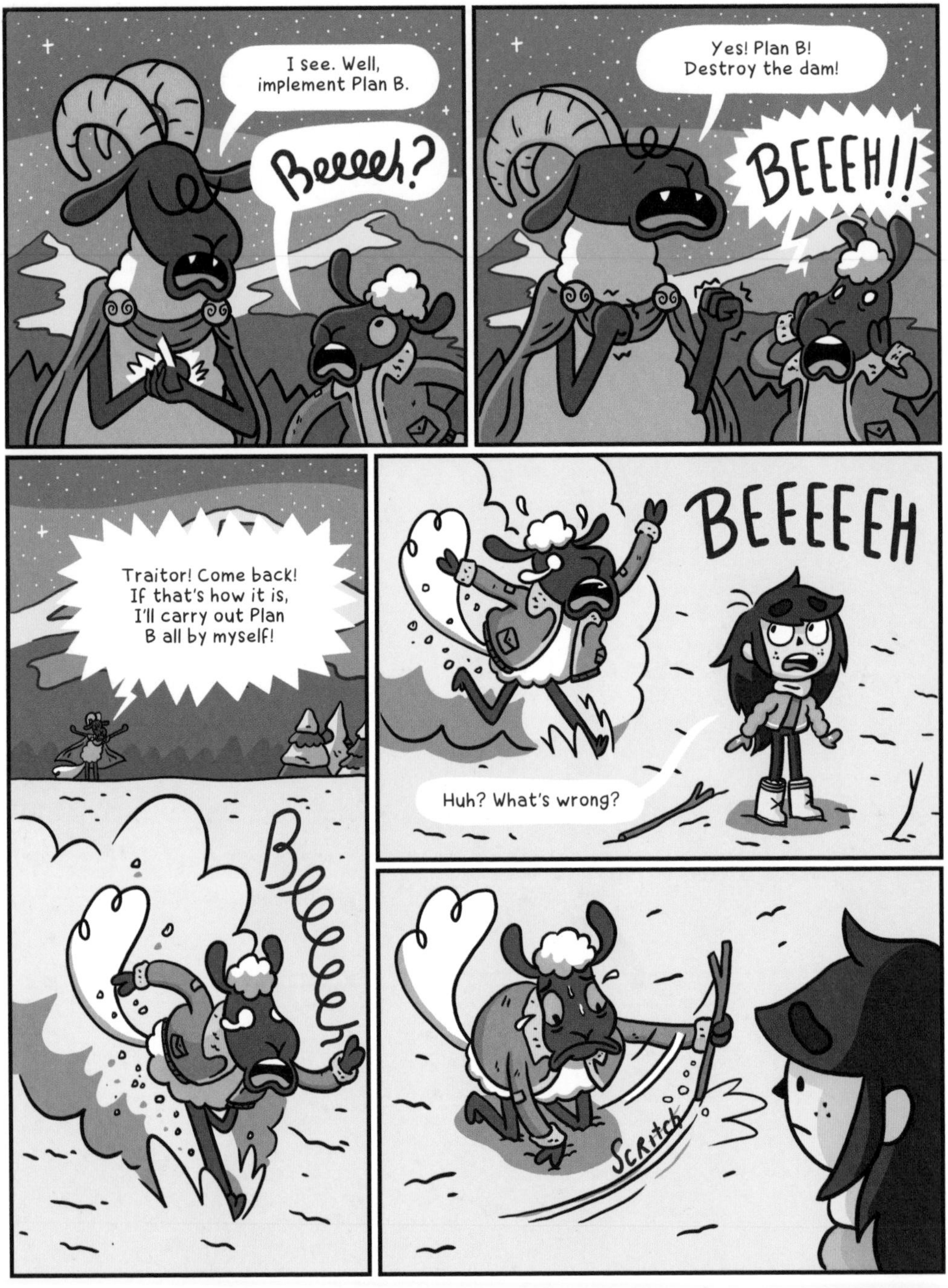
I see. Well, implement Plan B.
Beeeeh?
Yes! Plan B! Destroy the dam!
BEEEH!!
Traitor! Come back! If that's how it is, I'll carry out Plan B all by myself!
BEEEEEH
Huh? What's wrong?
Beeeeh
SCRITCH

What's she drawing?
Clearly, little one, it's a plan for blowing up the dam. See? There's the sluice gates, the spillway, and the control room.
How do you know?
Me...?
Young lady, I was a hydroelectric engineer back in the day.
The Dumbacabra is crazy! He's going to smash the dam and drown the valley! There's not a moment to lose.
Aster! I know you're busy, but you've got to see this!

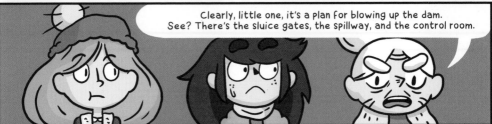

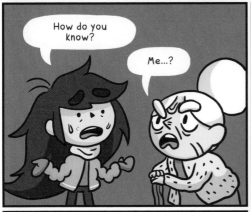

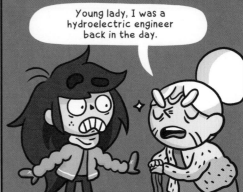

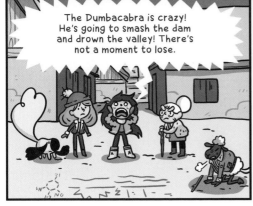

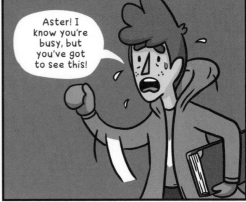

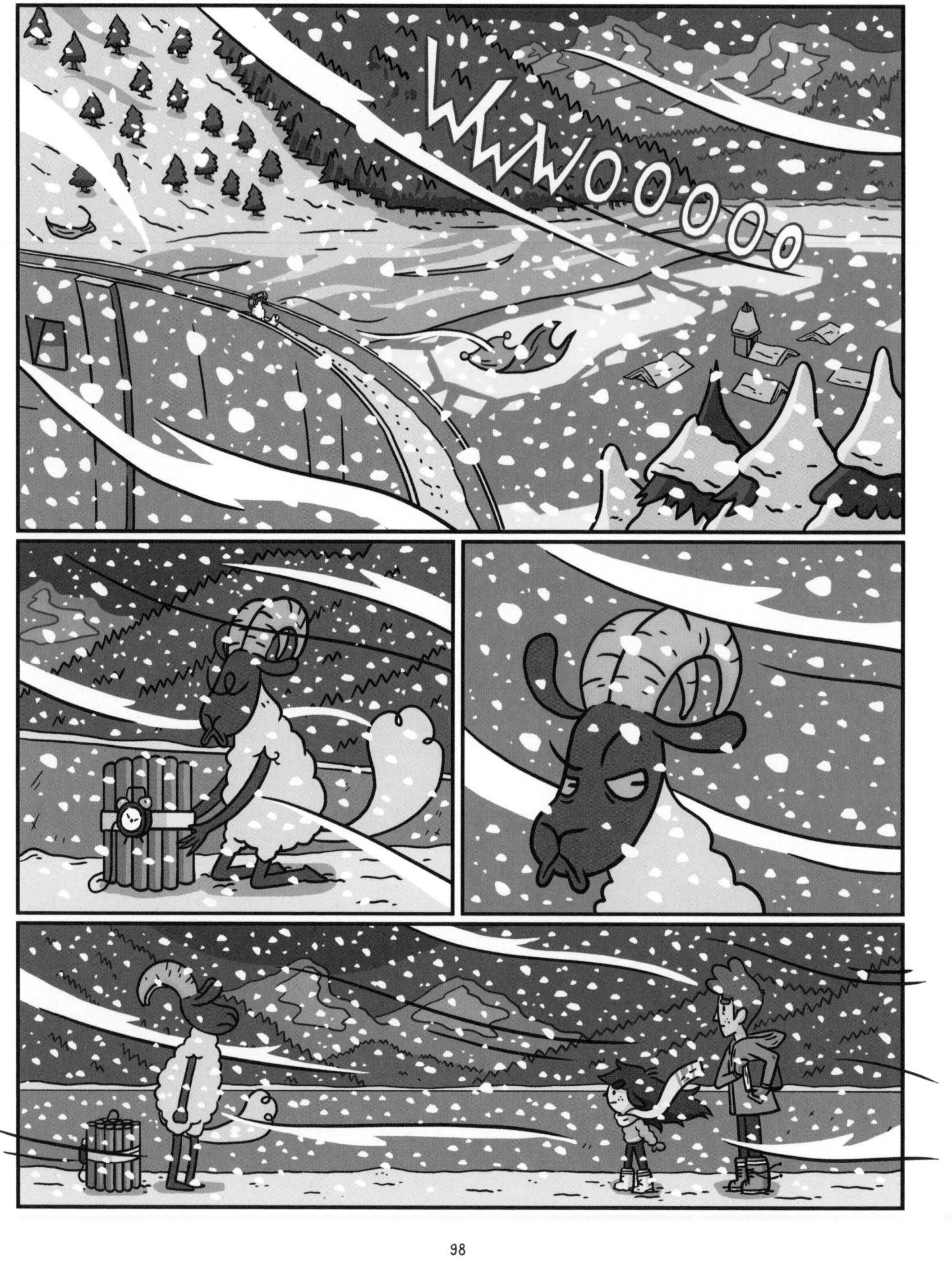
WWWOOOOOO

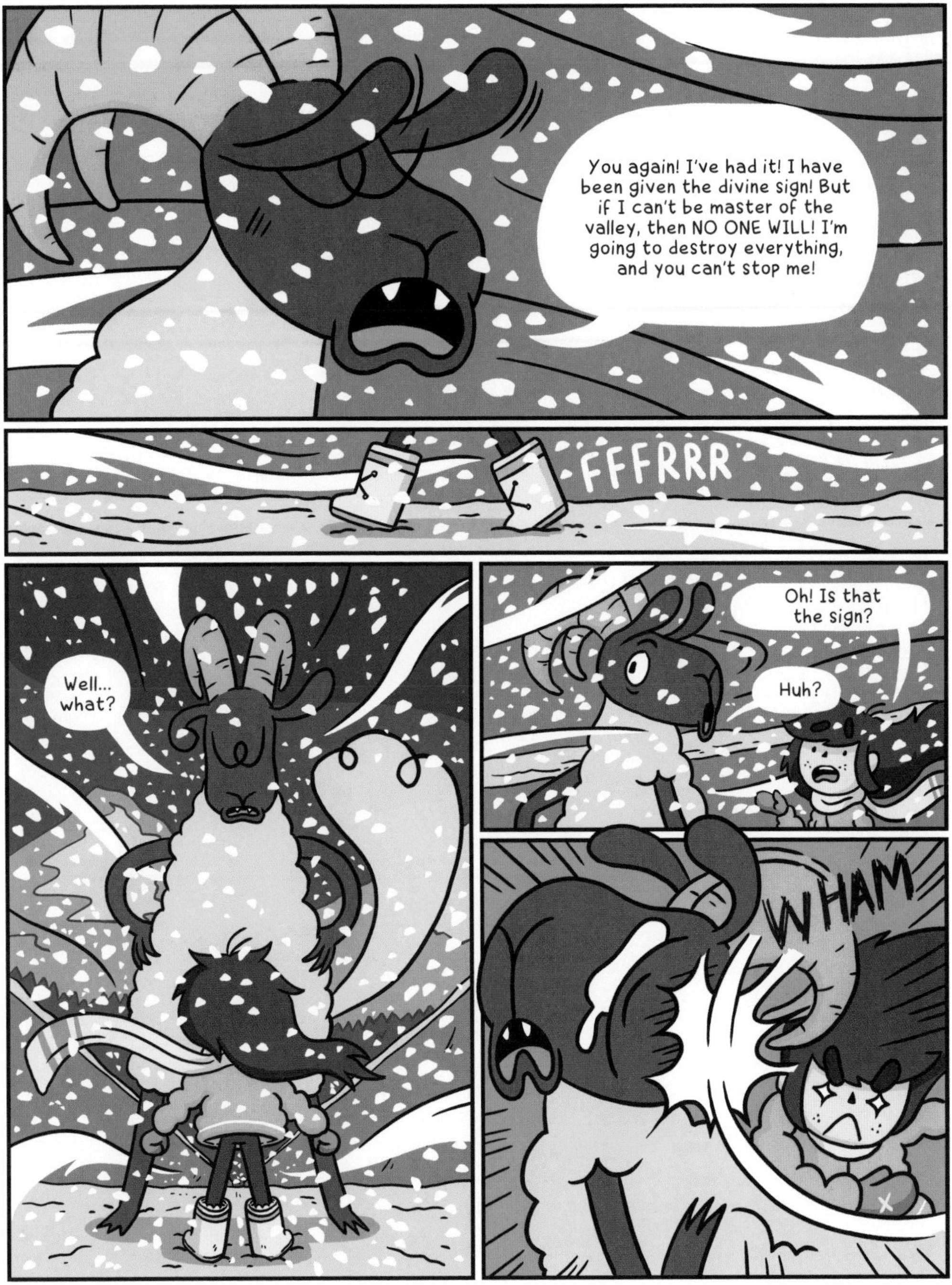
You again! I've had it! I have been given the divine sign! But if I can't be master of the valley, then NO ONE WILL! I'm going to destroy everything, and you can't stop me!
FFFRRR
Well... what?
Oh! Is that the sign?
Huh?
WHAM

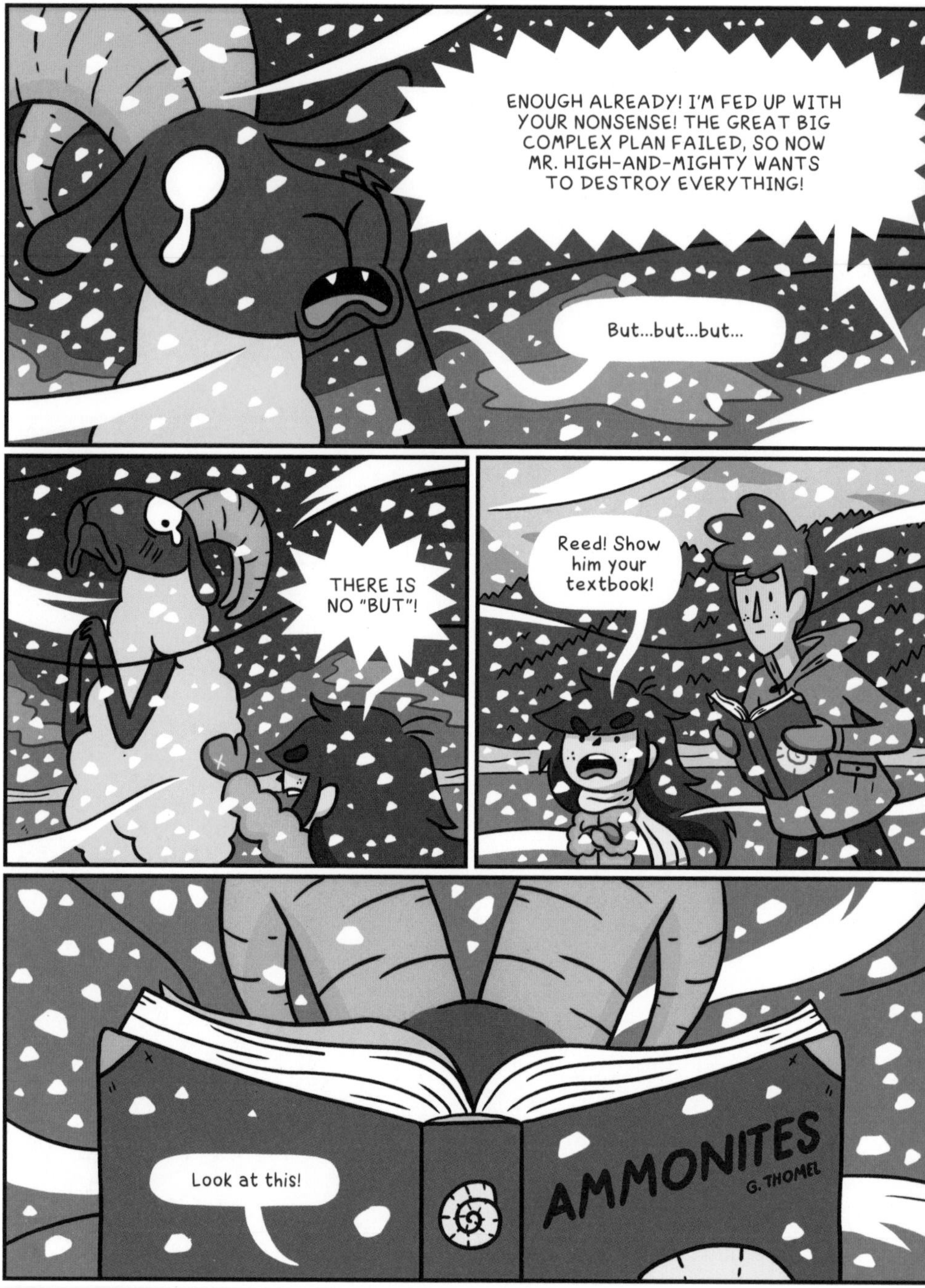
ENOUGH ALREADY! I'M FED UP WITH YOUR NONSENSE! THE GREAT BIG COMPLEX PLAN FAILED, SO NOW MR. HIGH-AND-MIGHTY WANTS TO DESTROY EVERYTHING!
But...but...but...
THERE IS NO "BUT"!
Reed! Show him your textbook!
Look at this!
AMMONITES
G. THOMEL

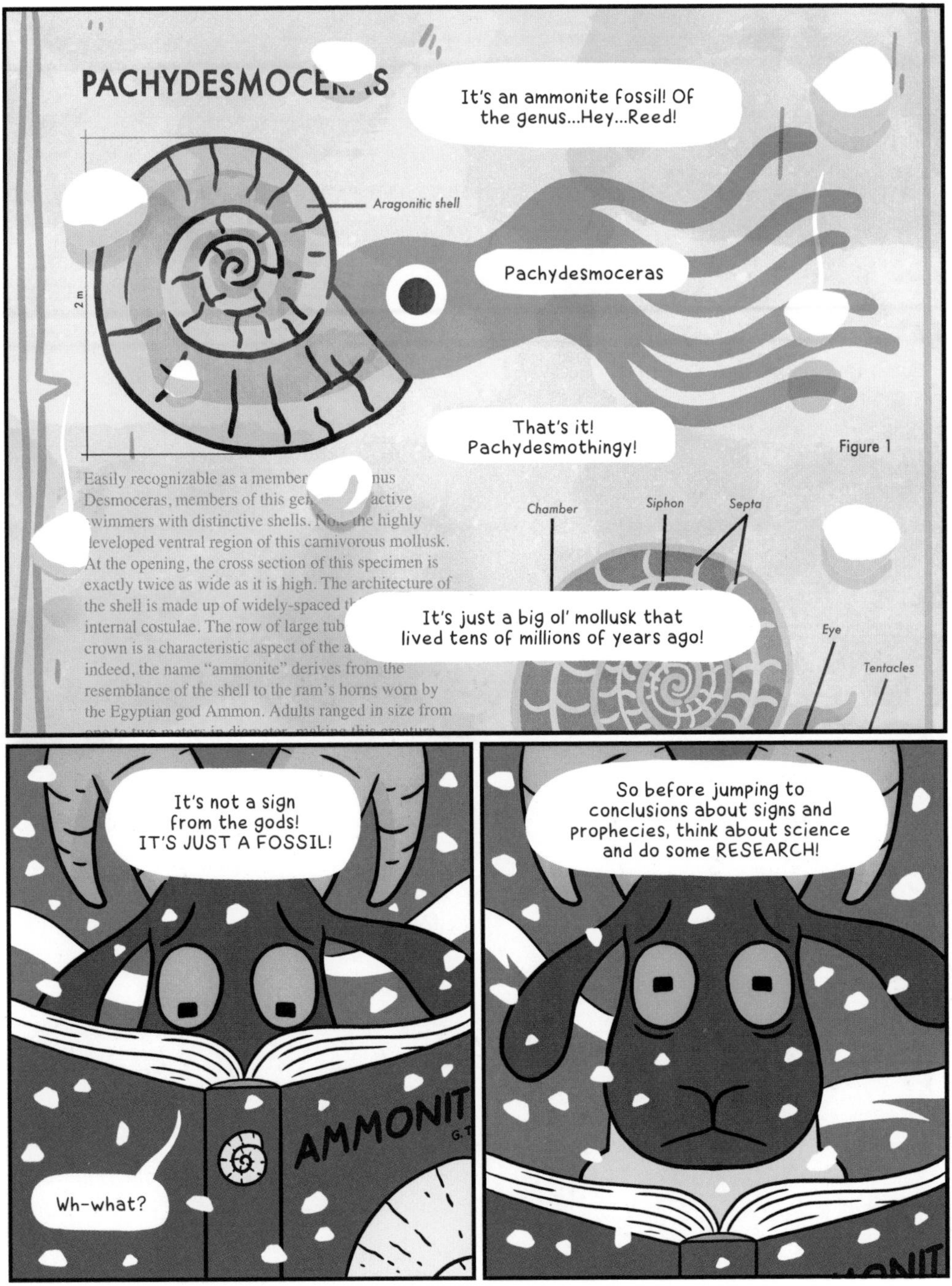
PACHYDESMOCER.AS
It's an ammonite fossil! Of the genus...Hey...Reed!
Aragonitic shell
2 m
Pachydesmoceras
That's it! Pachydesmothingy!
Figure 1
Easily recognizable as a member nus
Desmoceras, members of this ge active
swimmers with distinctive shells. No the highly
developed ventral region of this carnivorous mollusk.
At the opening, the cross section of this specimen is
exactly twice as wide as it is high. The architecture of
the shell is made up of widely-spaced th
internal costulae. The row of large tub
crown is a characteristic aspect of the a
indeed, the name "ammonite" derives from the
resemblance of the shell to the ram's horns worn by
the Egyptian god Ammon. Adults ranged in size from
Chamber
Siphon
Septa
It's just a big ol' mollusk that lived tens of millions of years ago!
Eye
Tentacles
It's not a sign from the gods! IT'S JUST A FOSSIL!
AMMONIT
G. T
Wh-what?
So before jumping to conclusions about signs and prophecies, think about science and do some RESEARCH!
ONIT

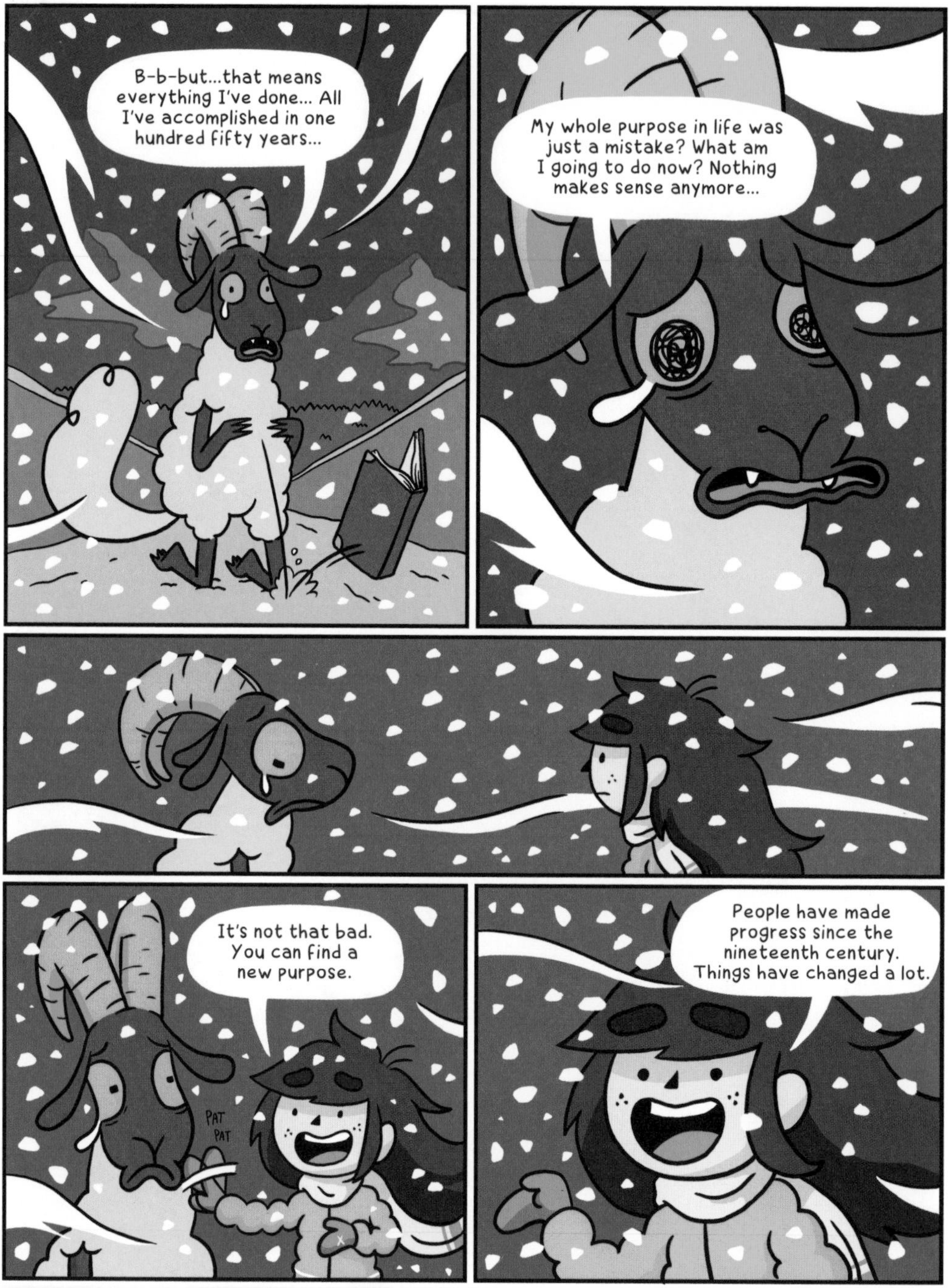
B-b-but...that means everything I've done... All I've accomplished in one hundred fifty years...
My whole purpose in life was just a mistake? What am I going to do now? Nothing makes sense anymore...
It's not that bad. You can find a new purpose.
PAT PAT
People have made progress since the nineteenth century. Things have changed a lot.

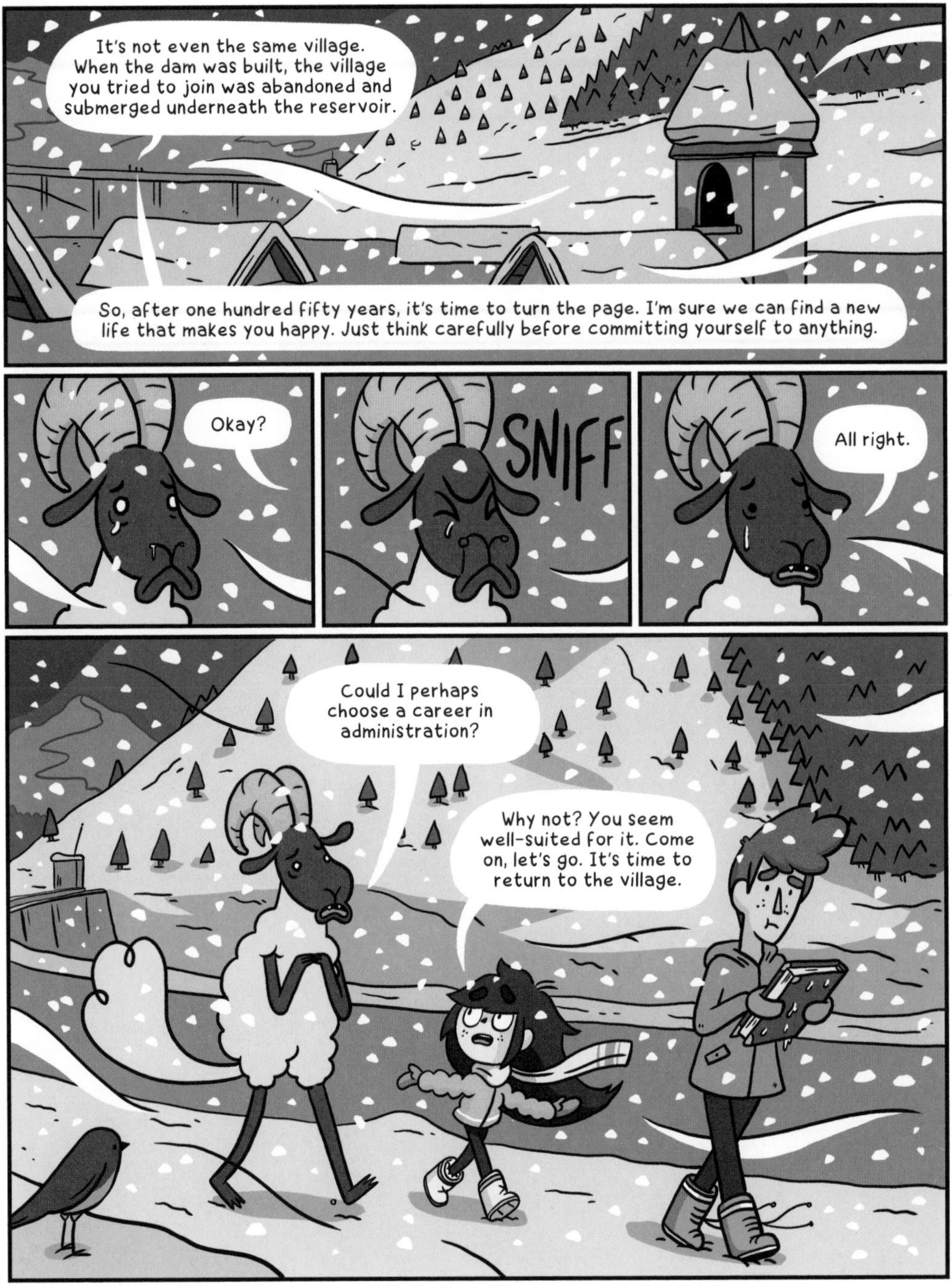
It's not even the same village. When the dam was built, the village you tried to join was abandoned and submerged underneath the reservoir.
So, after one hundred fifty years, it's time to turn the page. I'm sure we can find a new life that makes you happy. Just think carefully before committing yourself to anything.
Okay?
SNIFF
All right.
Could I perhaps choose a career in administration?
Why not? You seem well-suited for it. Come on, let's go. It's time to return to the village.

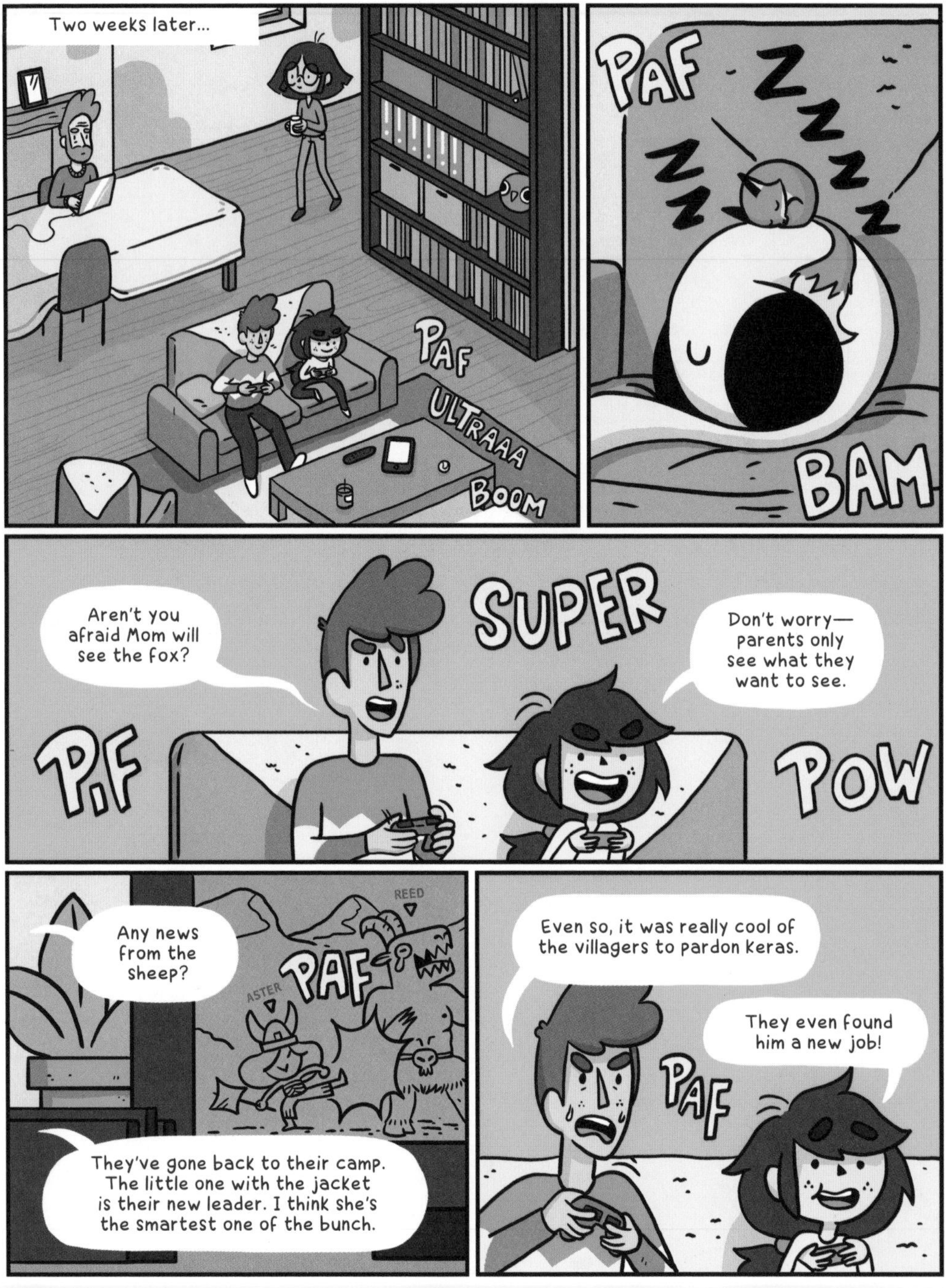
Two weeks later...
PAF
ULTRAAA
BOOM
PAF
ZZZZZZZ
BAM
Aren't you afraid Mom will see the fox?
SUPER
Don't worry—parents only see what they want to see.
PIF
POW
Any news from the sheep?
REED
ASTER
PAF
They've gone back to their camp. The little one with the jacket is their new leader. I think she's the smartest one of the bunch.
Even so, it was really cool of the villagers to pardon Keras.
They even found him a new job!
PAF

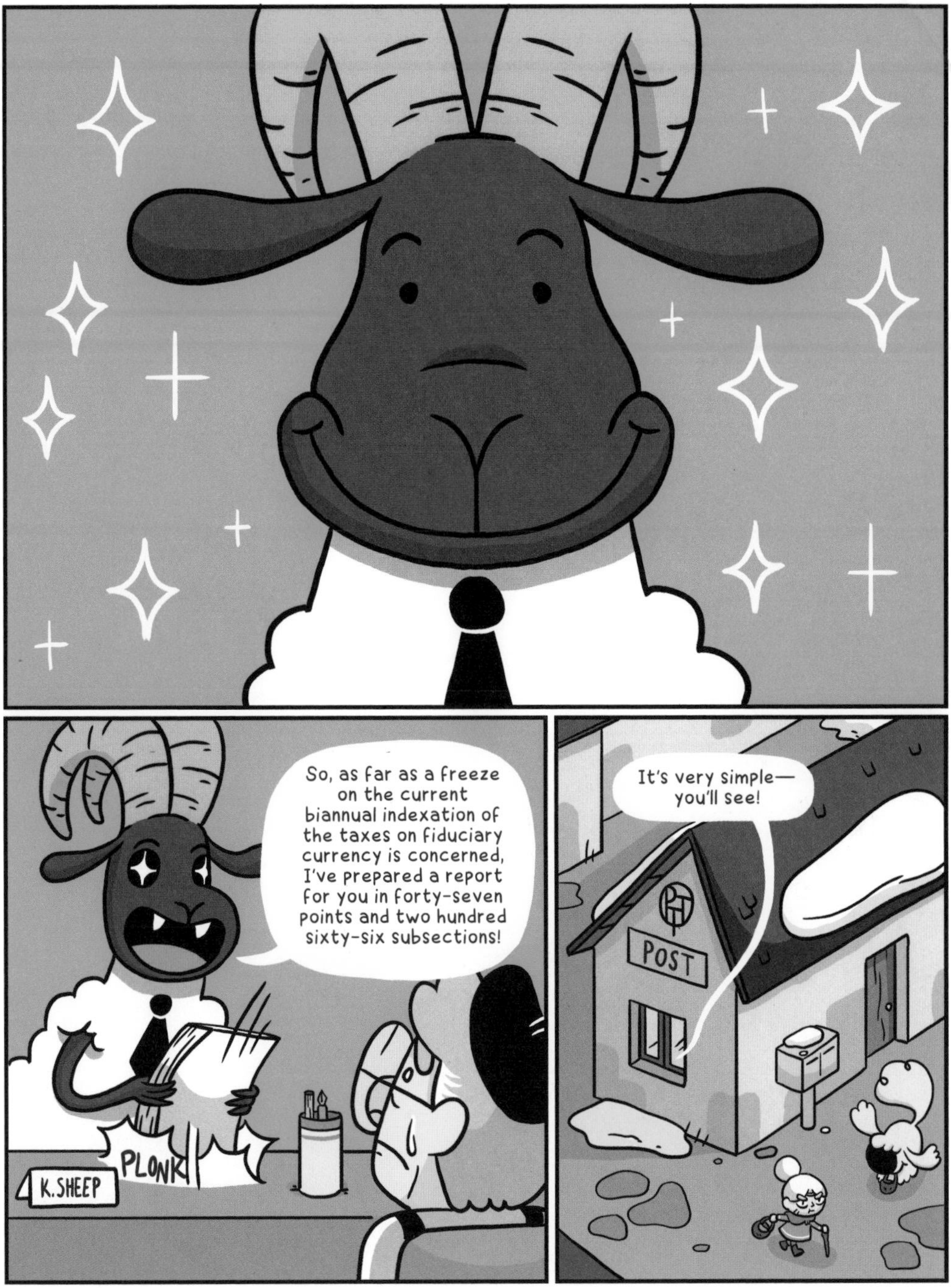
So, as far as a freeze on the current biannual indexation of the taxes on fiduciary currency is concerned, I've prepared a report for you in forty-seven points and two hundred sixty-six subsections!
PLONK
K.SHEEP
It's very simple— you'll see!
POST

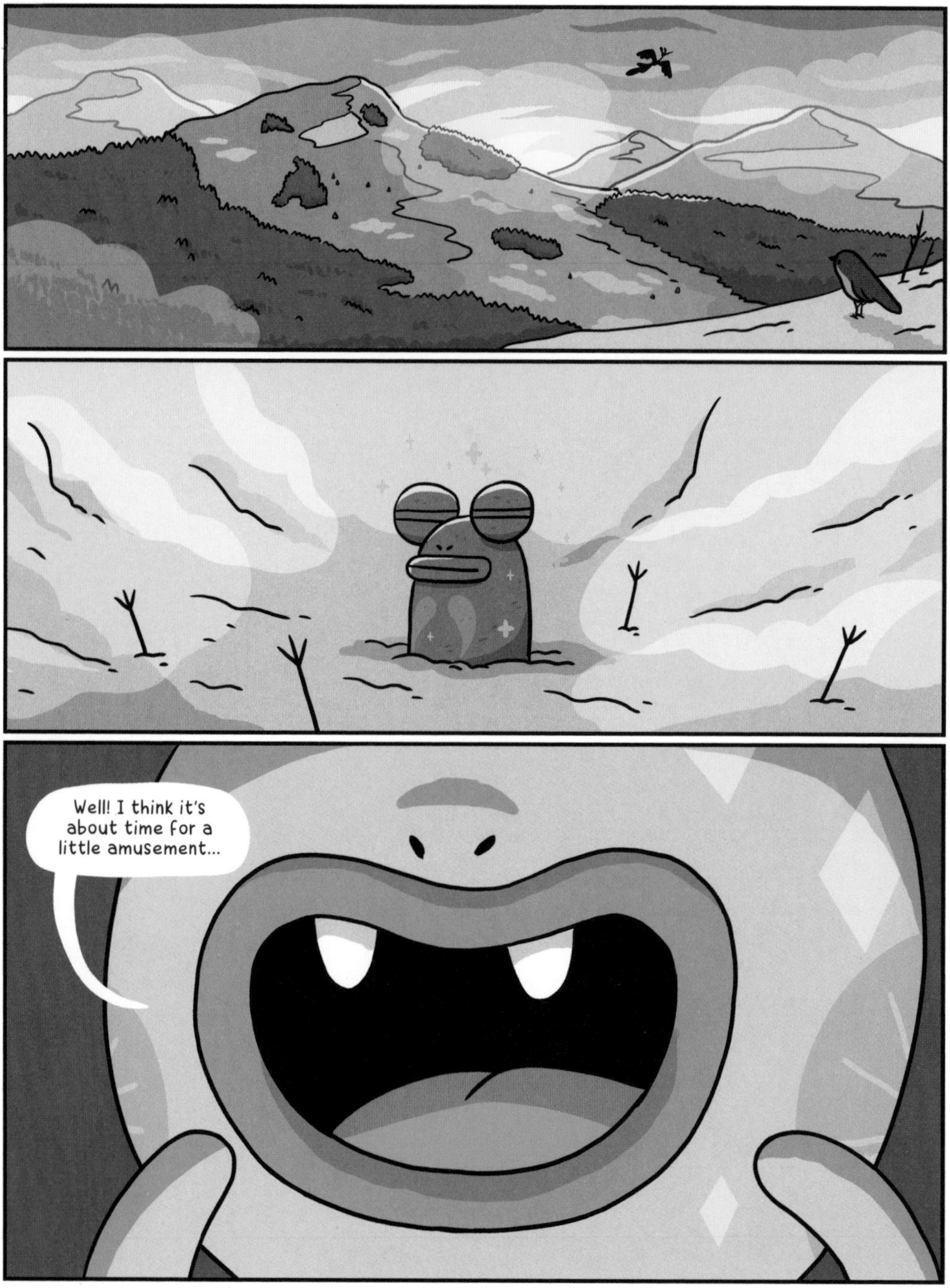
Well! I think it's about time for a little amusement...

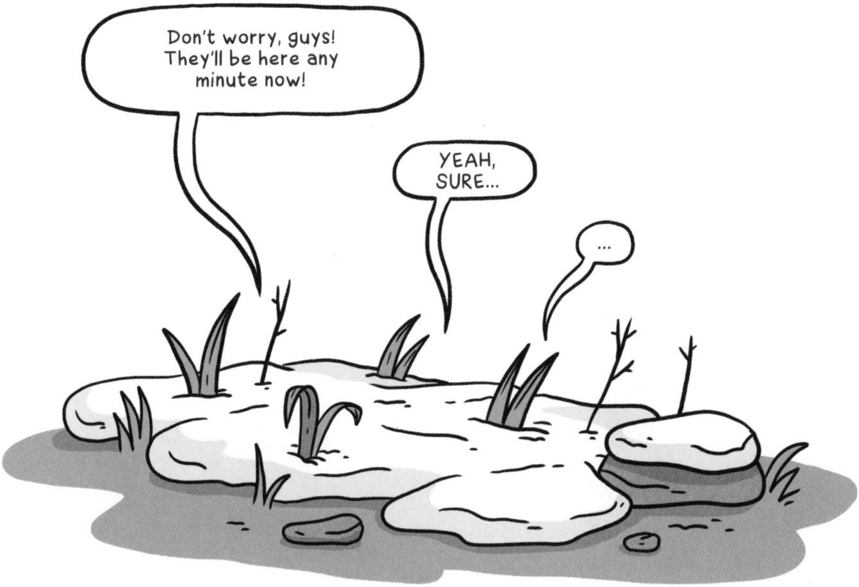
Don't worry, guys! They'll be here any minute now!
YEAH, SURE...
...

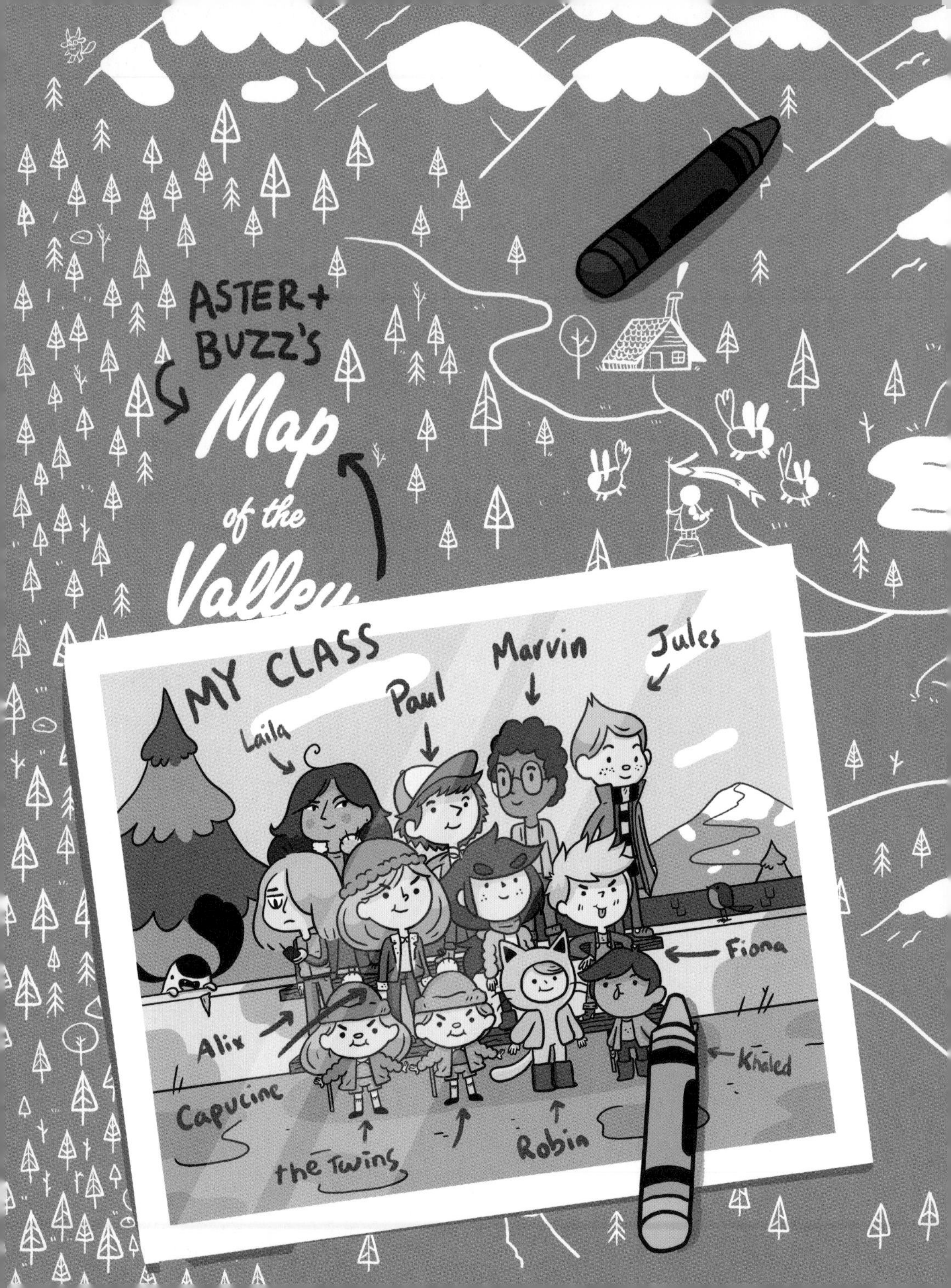
ASTER + BUZZ's
Map
of the
Valley
MY CLASS
Paul
Marvin
Jules
Laila
Fiona
Alix
Khaled
Capucine
Robin
the Twins

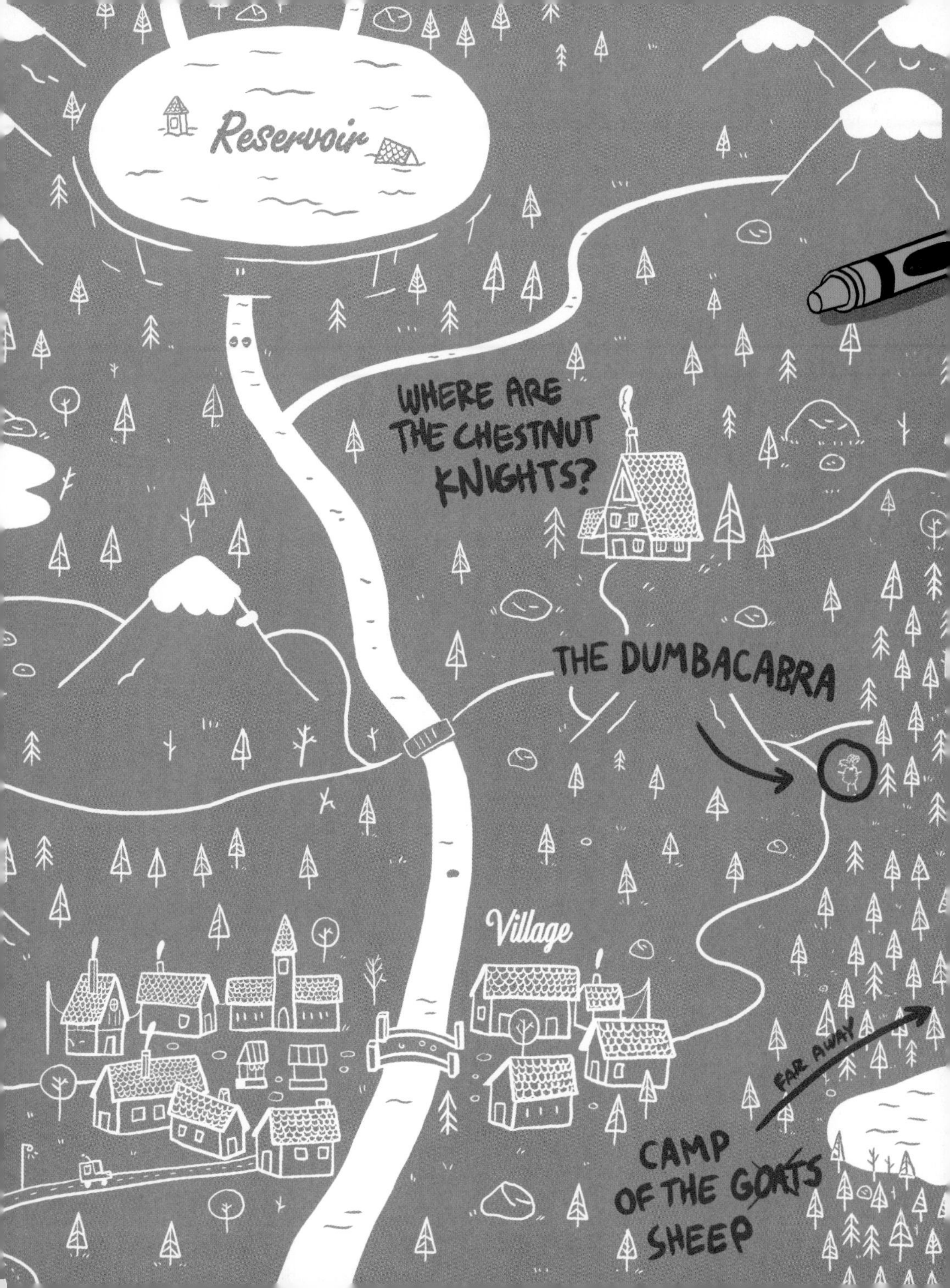
Reservoir
WHERE ARE THE CHESTNUT KNIGHTS?
THE DUMBACABRA
Village
FAR AWAY
CAMP OF THE GOATS SHEEP

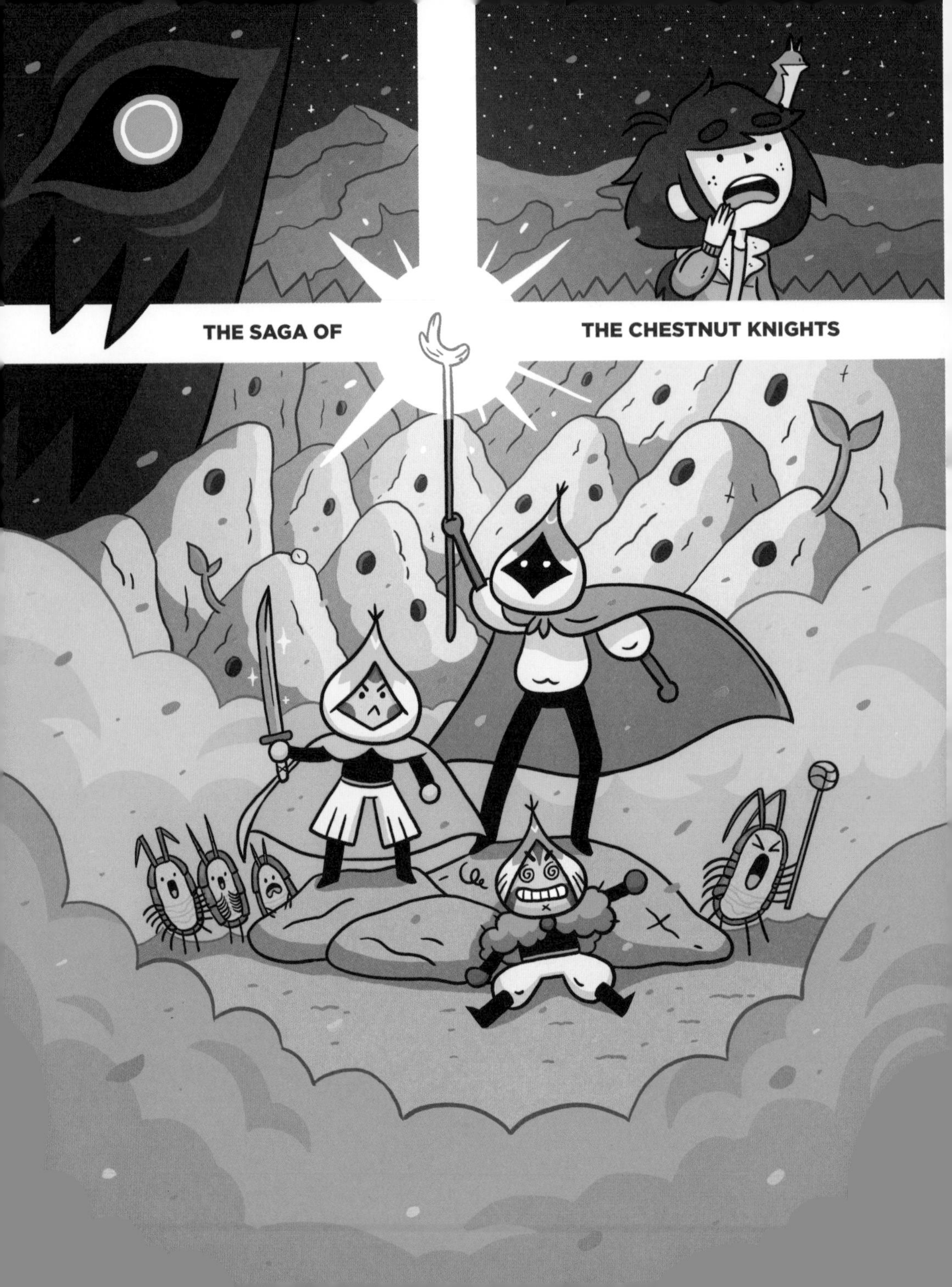
THE SAGA OF
THE CHESTNUT KNIGHTS

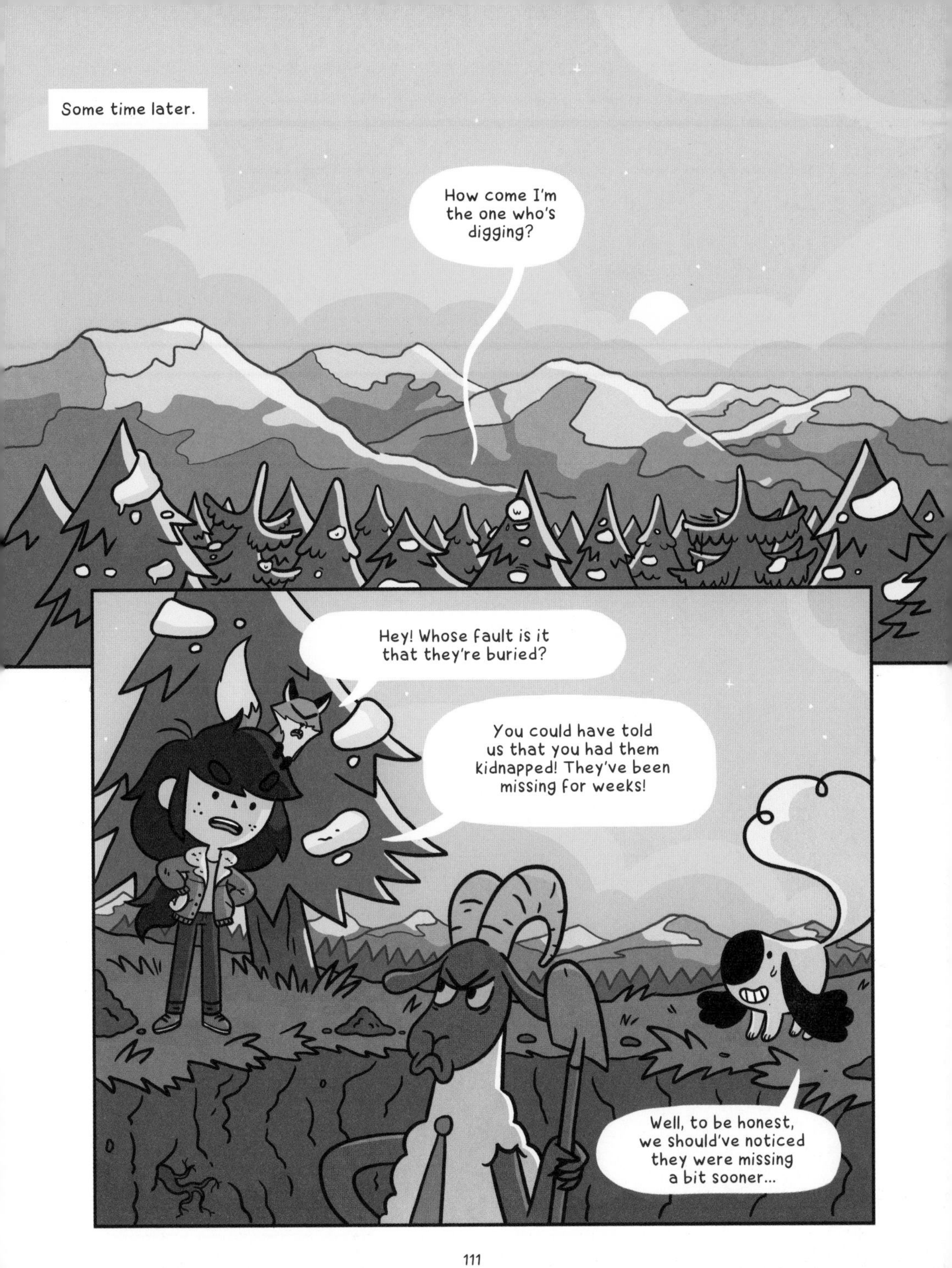

Some time later.
How come I'm the one who's digging?
Hey! Whose fault is it that they're buried?
You could have told us that you had them kidnapped! They've been missing for weeks!
Well, to be honest, we should've noticed they were missing a bit sooner...

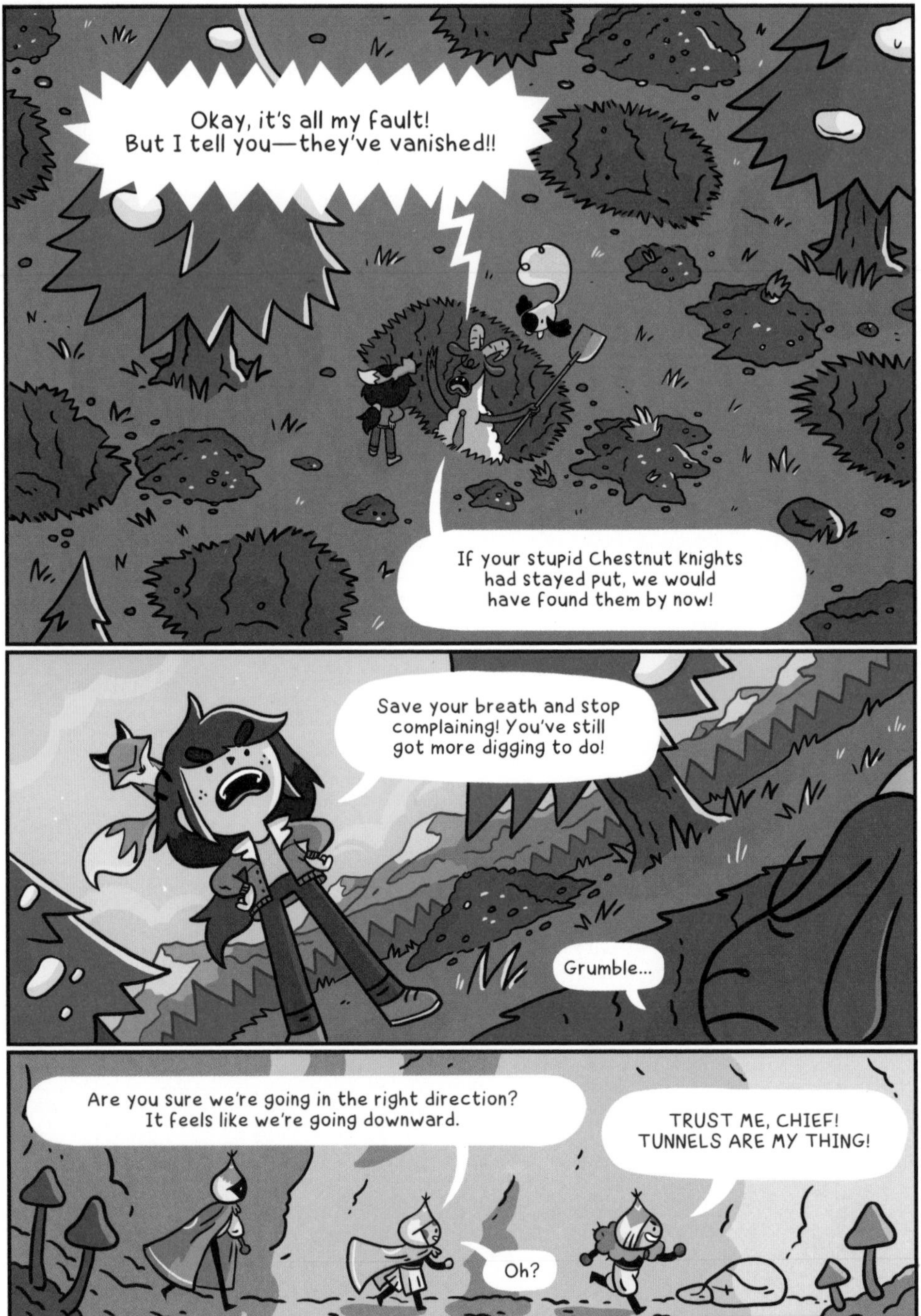
Okay, it's all my fault! But I tell you—they've vanished!!
If your stupid Chestnut Knights had stayed put, we would have found them by now!
Save your breath and stop complaining! You've still got more digging to do!
Grumble...
Are you sure we're going in the right direction? It feels like we're going downward.
Oh?
TRUST ME, CHIEF! TUNNELS ARE MY THING!

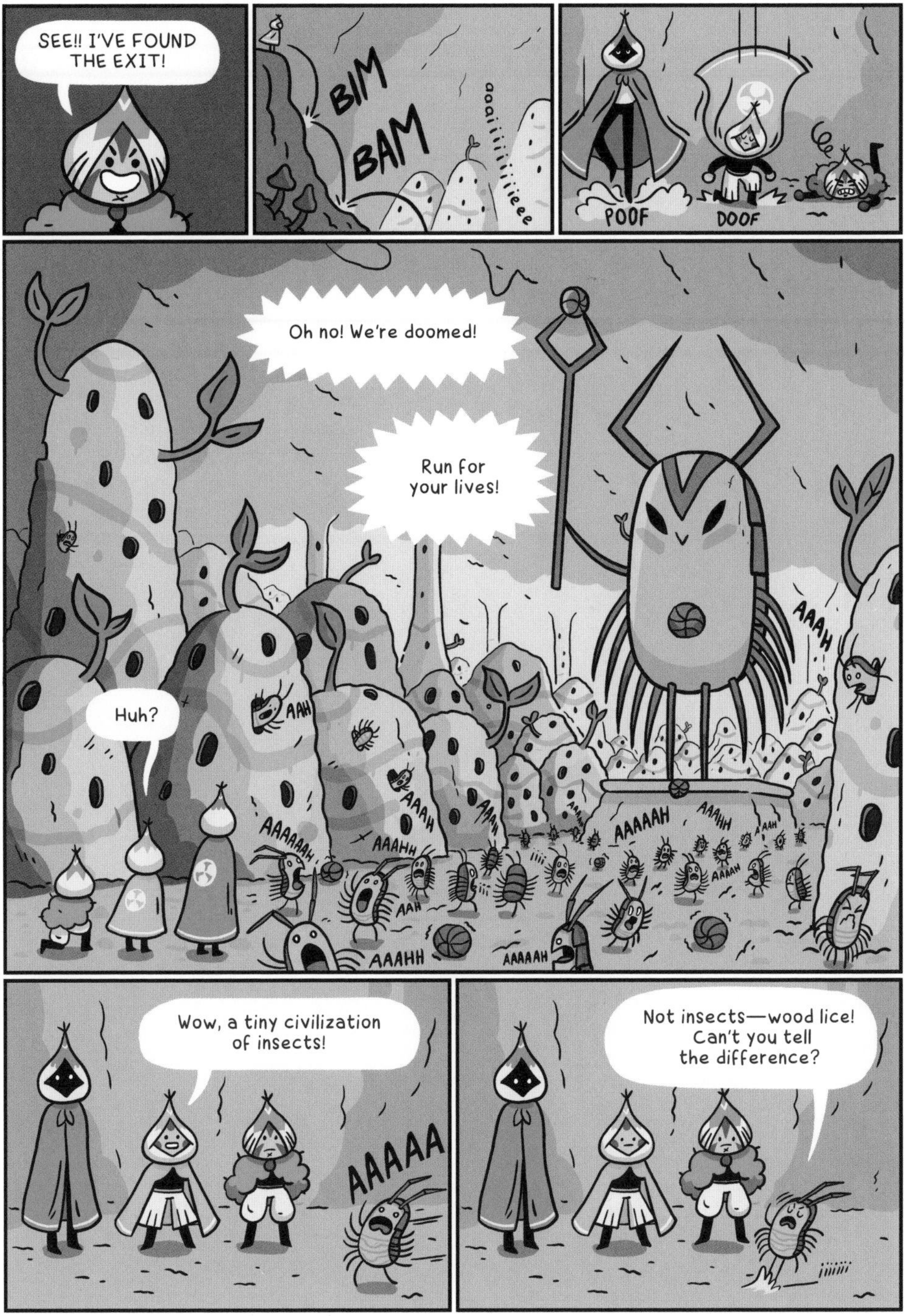
SEE!! I'VE FOUND THE EXIT!
BIM
BAM
aaaiiiiiiiiiieee
POOF
DOOF
Oh no! We're doomed!
Run for your lives!
Huh?
AAH
AAAH
AAAAAAH
AAAHH
AAAH
AAAAAH
AAAHH
AAAH
AAH
AAAHH
AAAAAH
AAAH
Wow, a tiny civilization of insects!
AAAAA
Not insects—wood lice! Can't you tell the difference?
iiiiiii

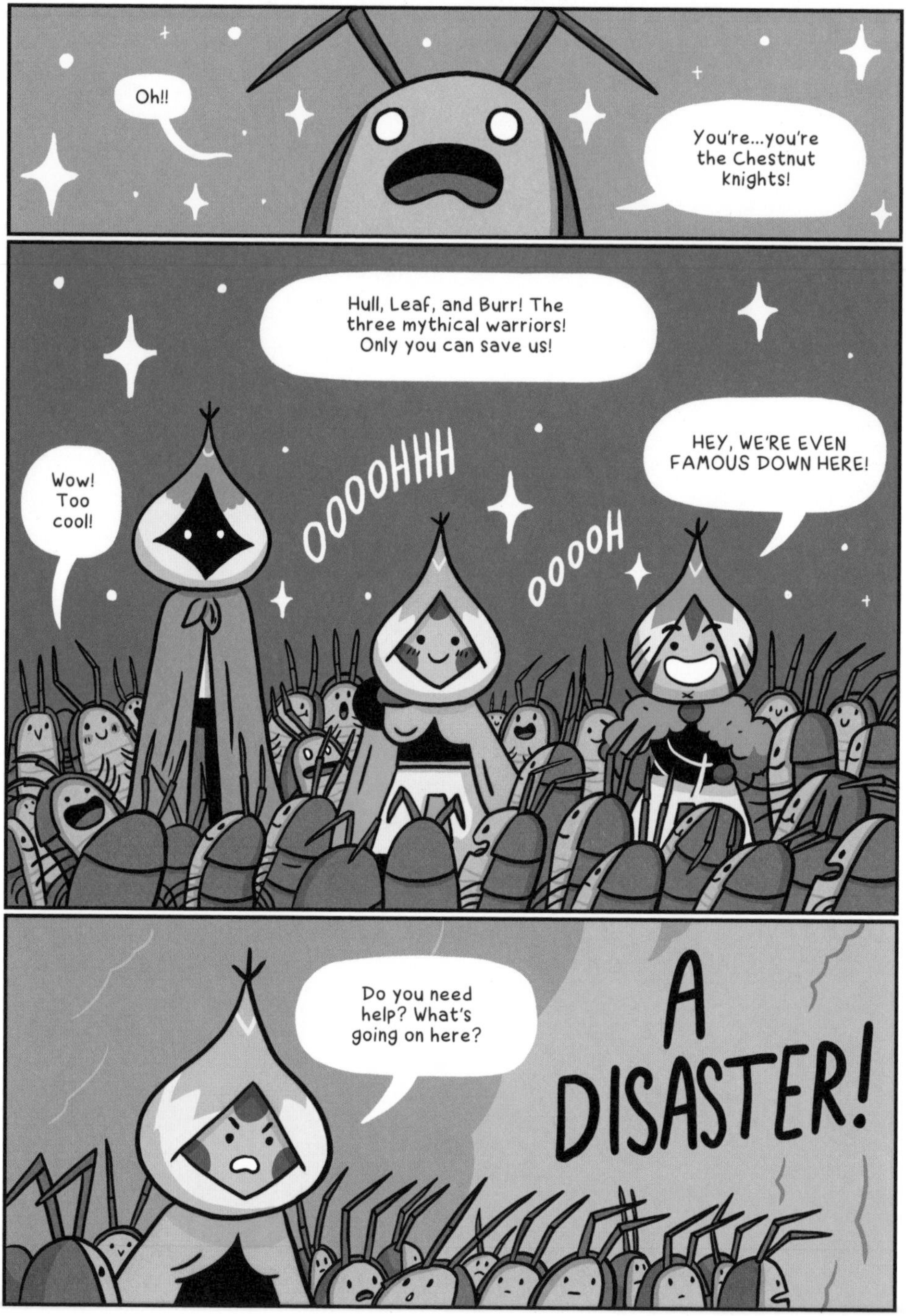
Oh!!
You're...you're the Chestnut knights!
Hull, Leaf, and Burr! The three mythical warriors! Only you can save us!
Wow! Too cool!
OOOOHHH
OOOOH
HEY, WE'RE EVEN FAMOUS DOWN HERE!
Do you need help? What's going on here?
A DISASTER!

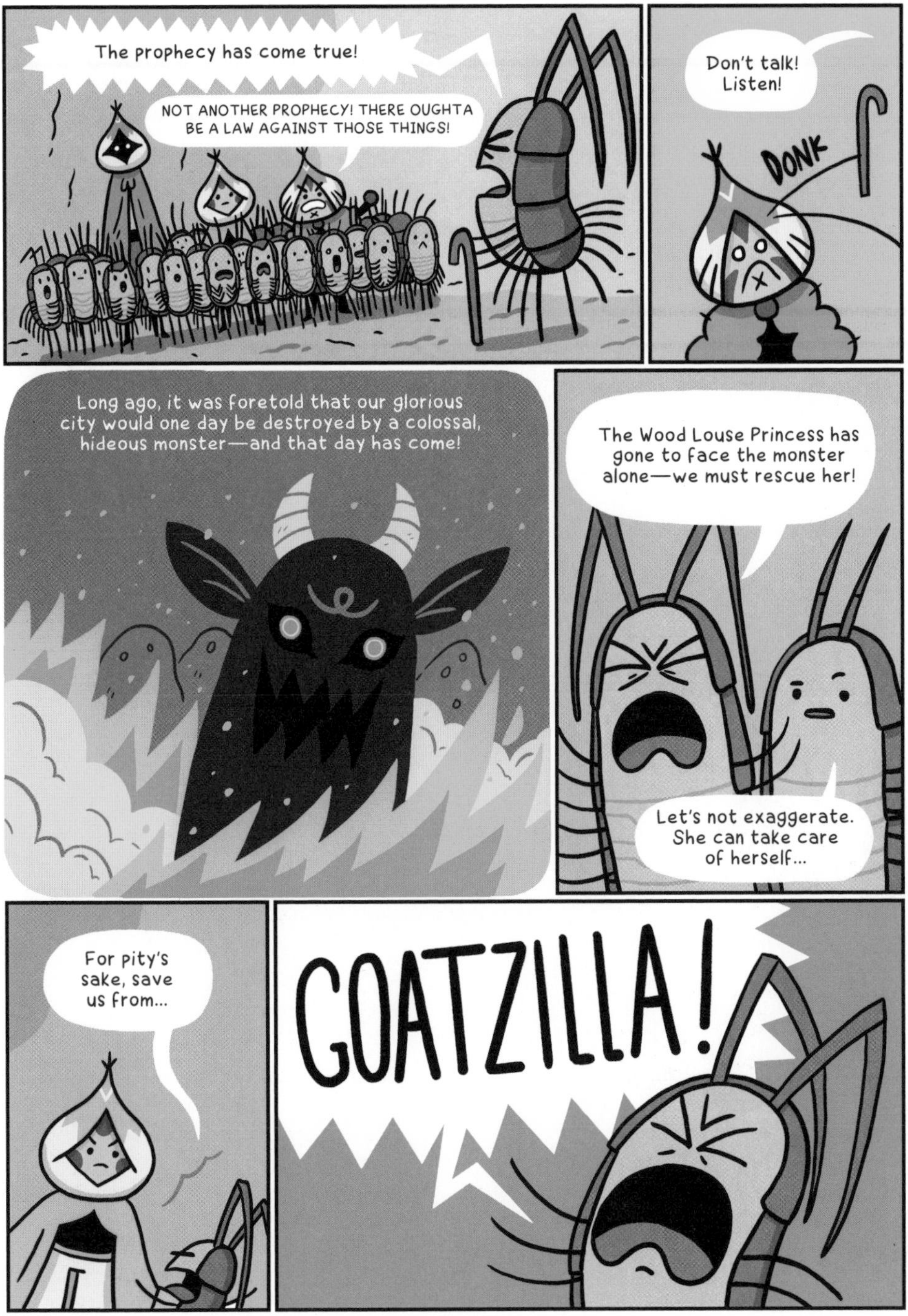
The prophecy has come true!
NOT ANOTHER PROPHECY! THERE OUGHTA BE A LAW AGAINST THOSE THINGS!
Don't talk! Listen!
DONK
Long ago, it was foretold that our glorious city would one day be destroyed by a colossal, hideous monster—and that day has come!
The Wood Louse Princess has gone to face the monster alone—we must rescue her!
Let's not exaggerate. She can take care of herself...
For pity's sake, save us from...
GOATZILLA!

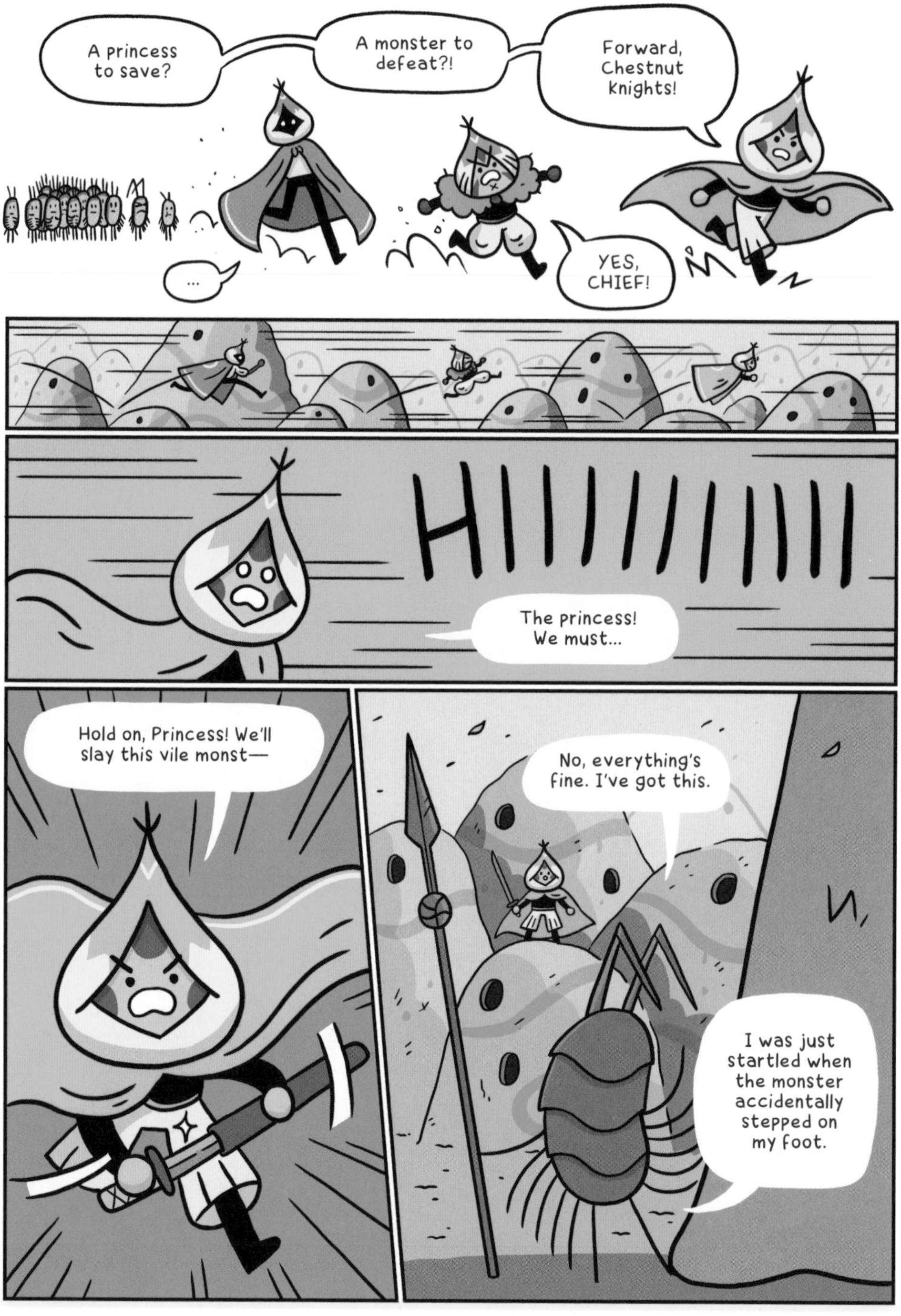
A princess to save?
A monster to defeat?!
Forward, Chestnut Knights!
...
YES, CHIEF!
HIIIIIIIII
The princess! We must...
Hold on, Princess! We'll slay this vile monst—
No, everything's fine. I've got this.
I was just startled when the monster accidentally stepped on my foot.

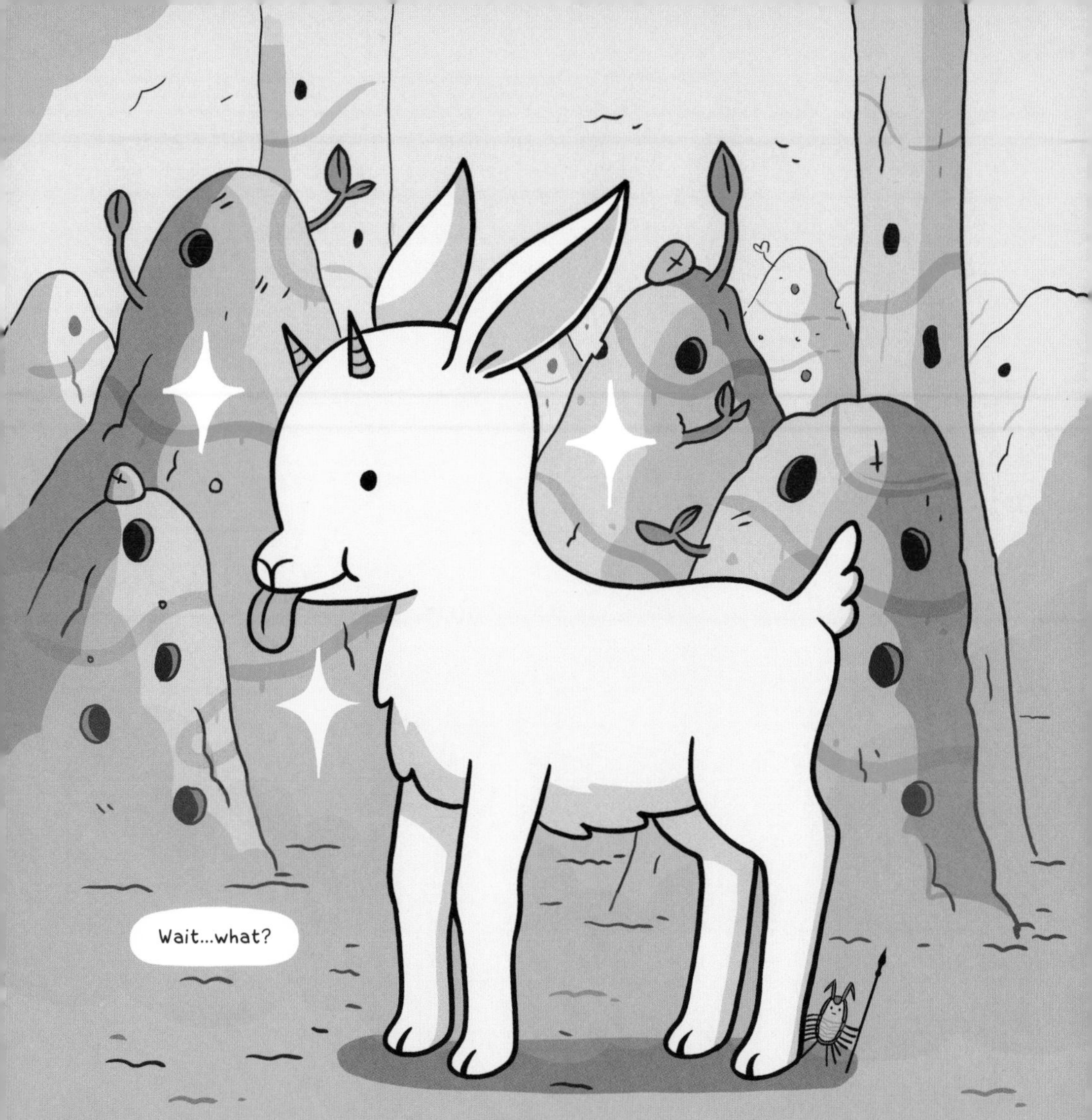
Wait...what?

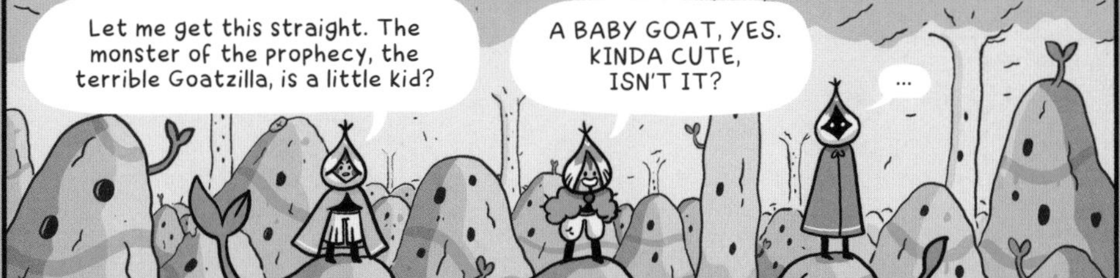
Let me get this straight. The monster of the prophecy, the terrible Goatzilla, is a little kid?
A BABY GOAT, YES. KINDA CUTE, ISN'T IT?
...

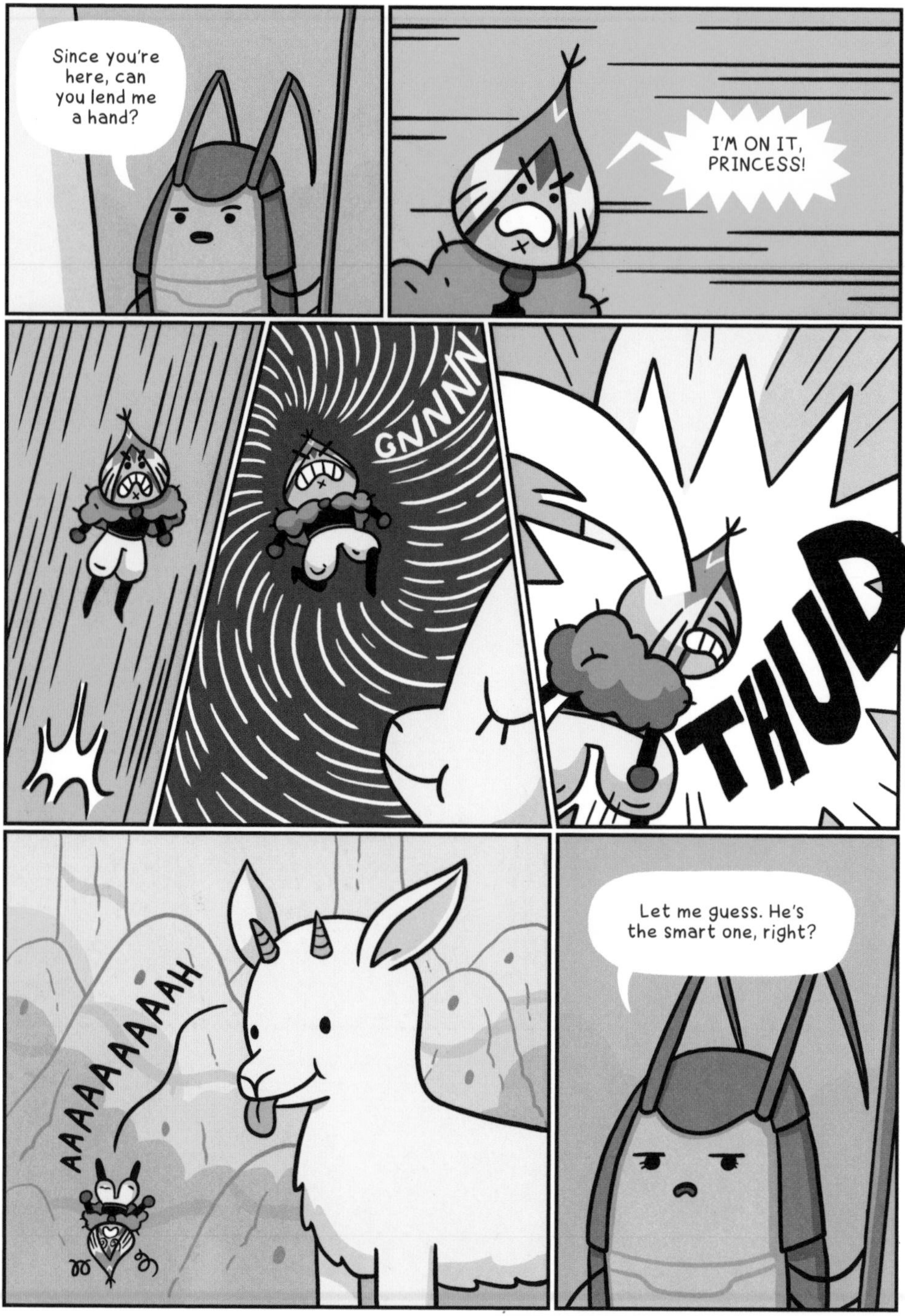

Since you're here, can you lend me a hand?
I'M ON IT, PRINCESS!
GNNNN
THUD
AAAAAAAAAAAAH
Let me guess. He's the smart one, right?

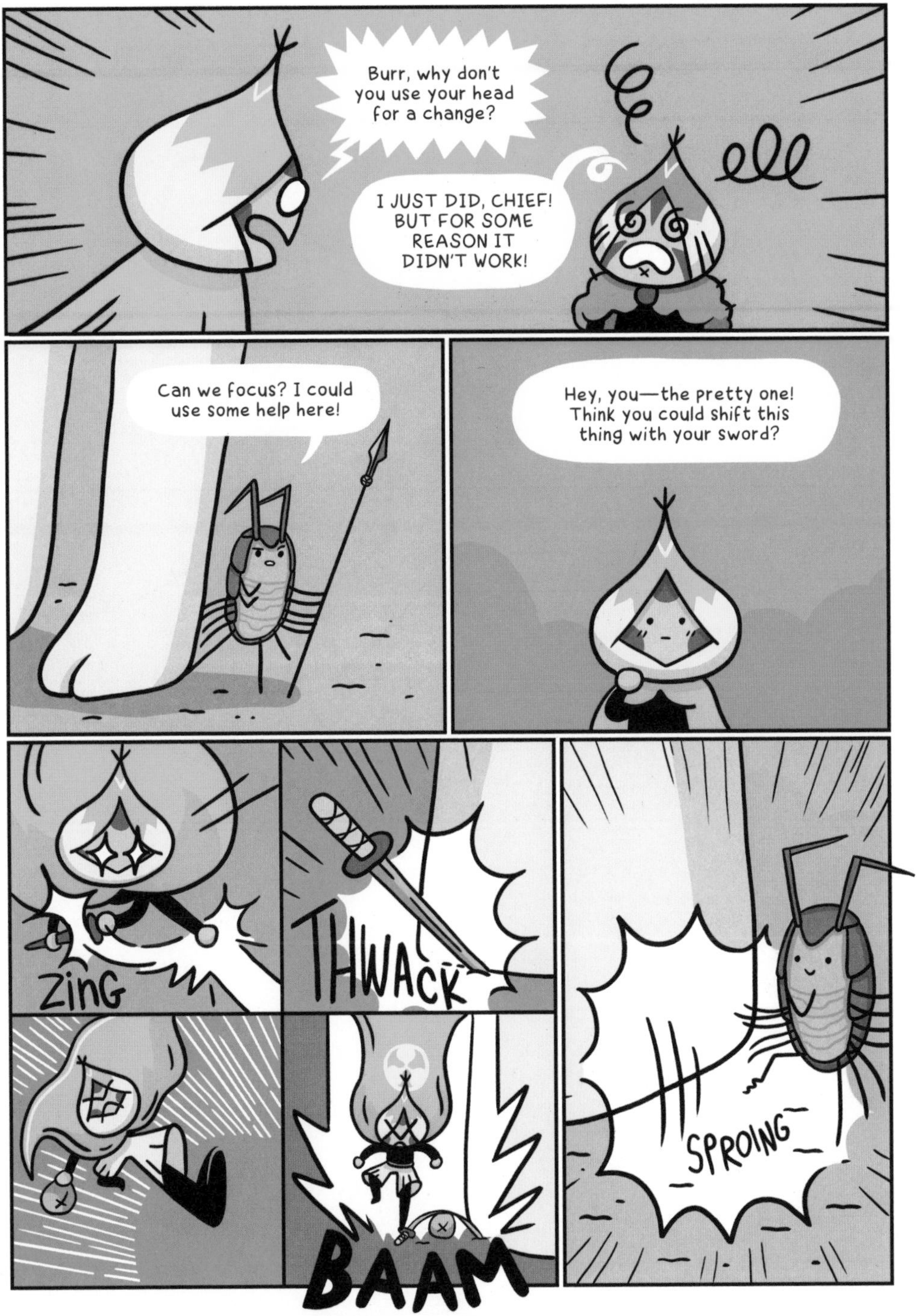
Burr, why don't you use your head for a change?
I JUST DID, CHIEF! BUT FOR SOME REASON IT DIDN'T WORK!
Can we focus? I could use some help here!
Hey, you—the pretty one! Think you could shift this thing with your sword?
ZING
THWACK
BAAM
SPROING

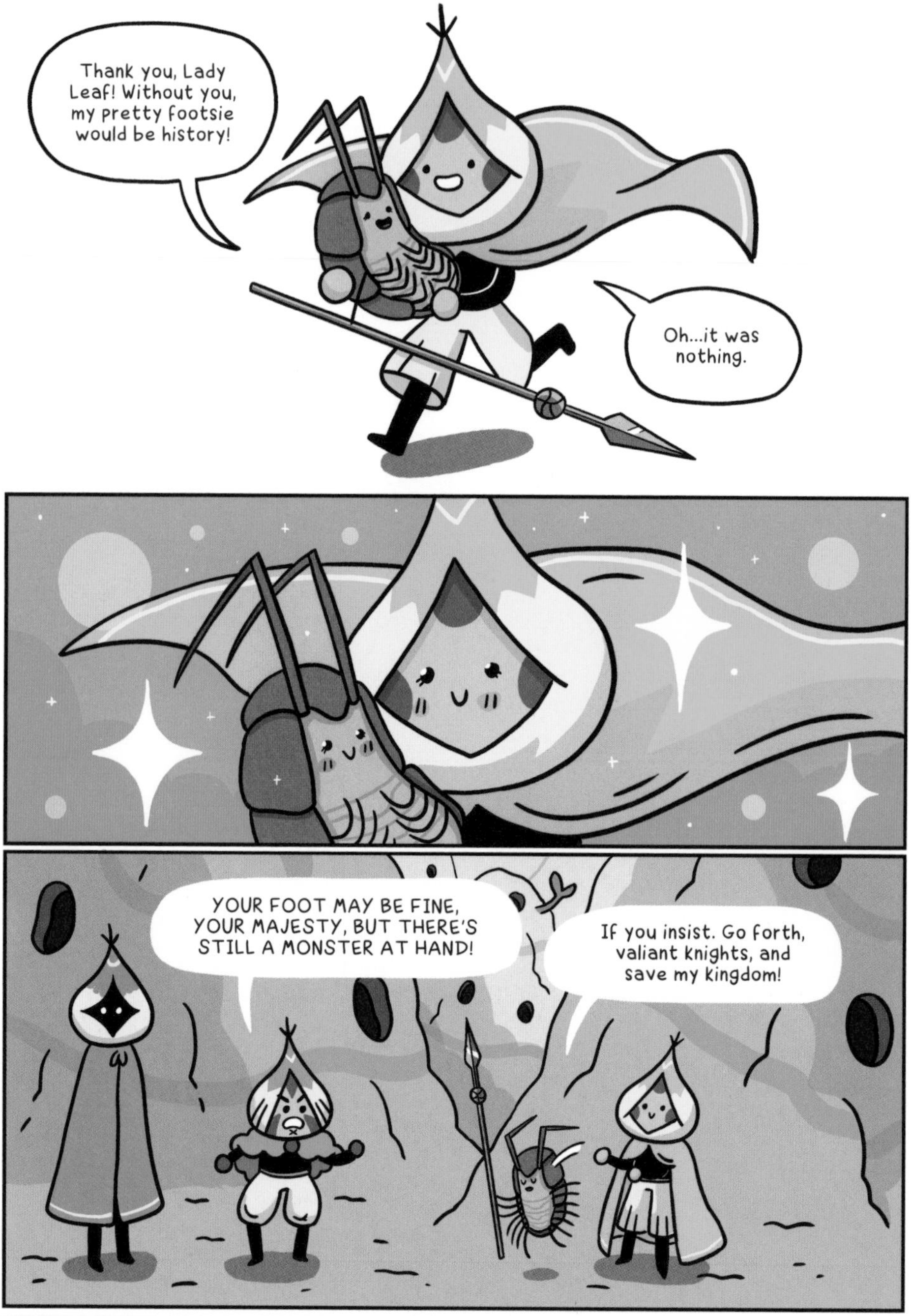
Thank you, Lady Leaf! Without you, my pretty footsie would be history!
Oh...it was nothing.
YOUR FOOT MAY BE FINE, YOUR MAJESTY, BUT THERE'S STILL A MONSTER AT HAND!
If you insist. Go forth, valiant knights, and save my kingdom!

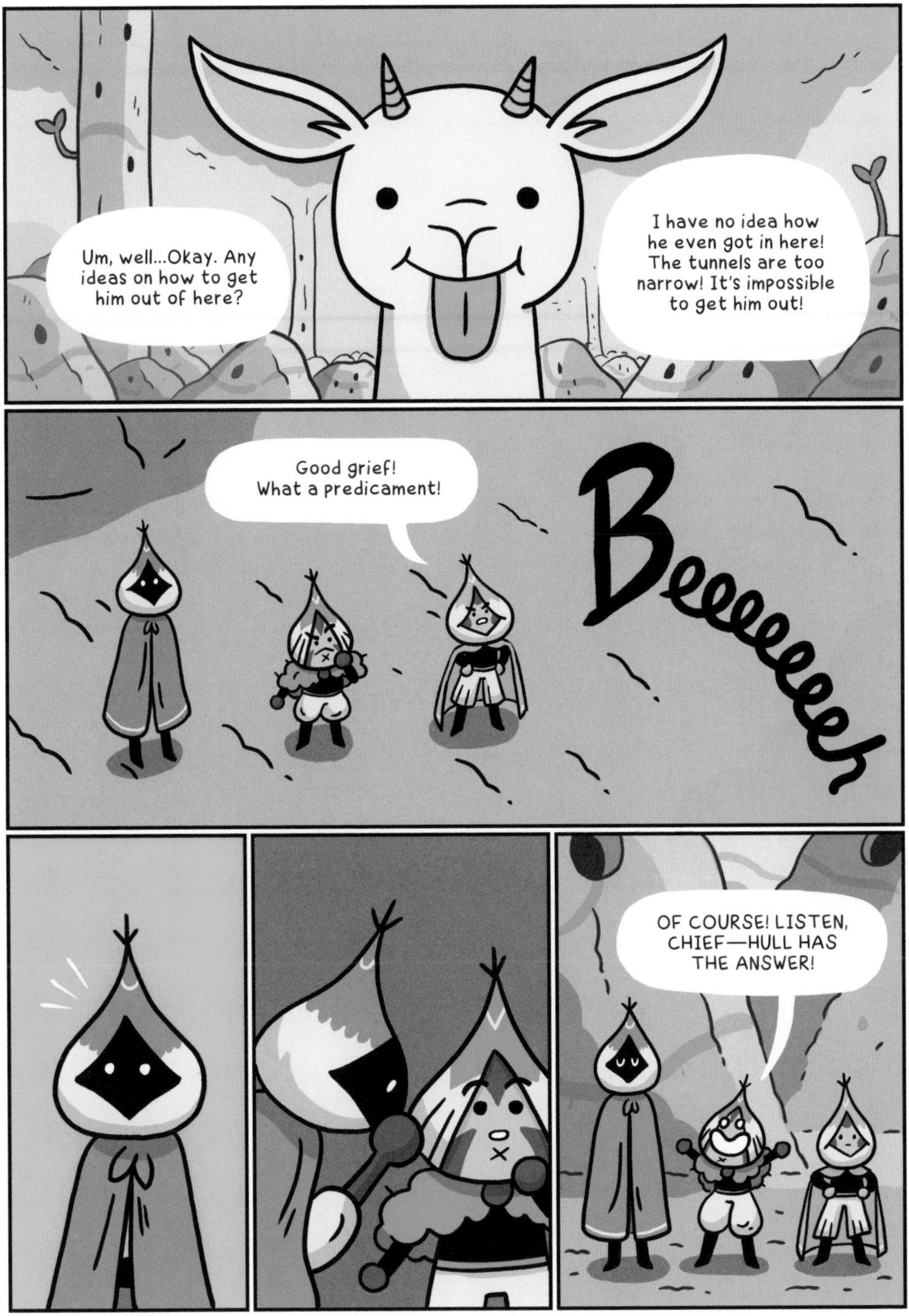
Um, well...Okay. Any ideas on how to get him out of here?
I have no idea how he even got in here! The tunnels are too narrow! It's impossible to get him out!
Good grief! What a predicament!
Beeeeeeeh
OF COURSE! LISTEN, CHIEF—HULL HAS THE ANSWER!

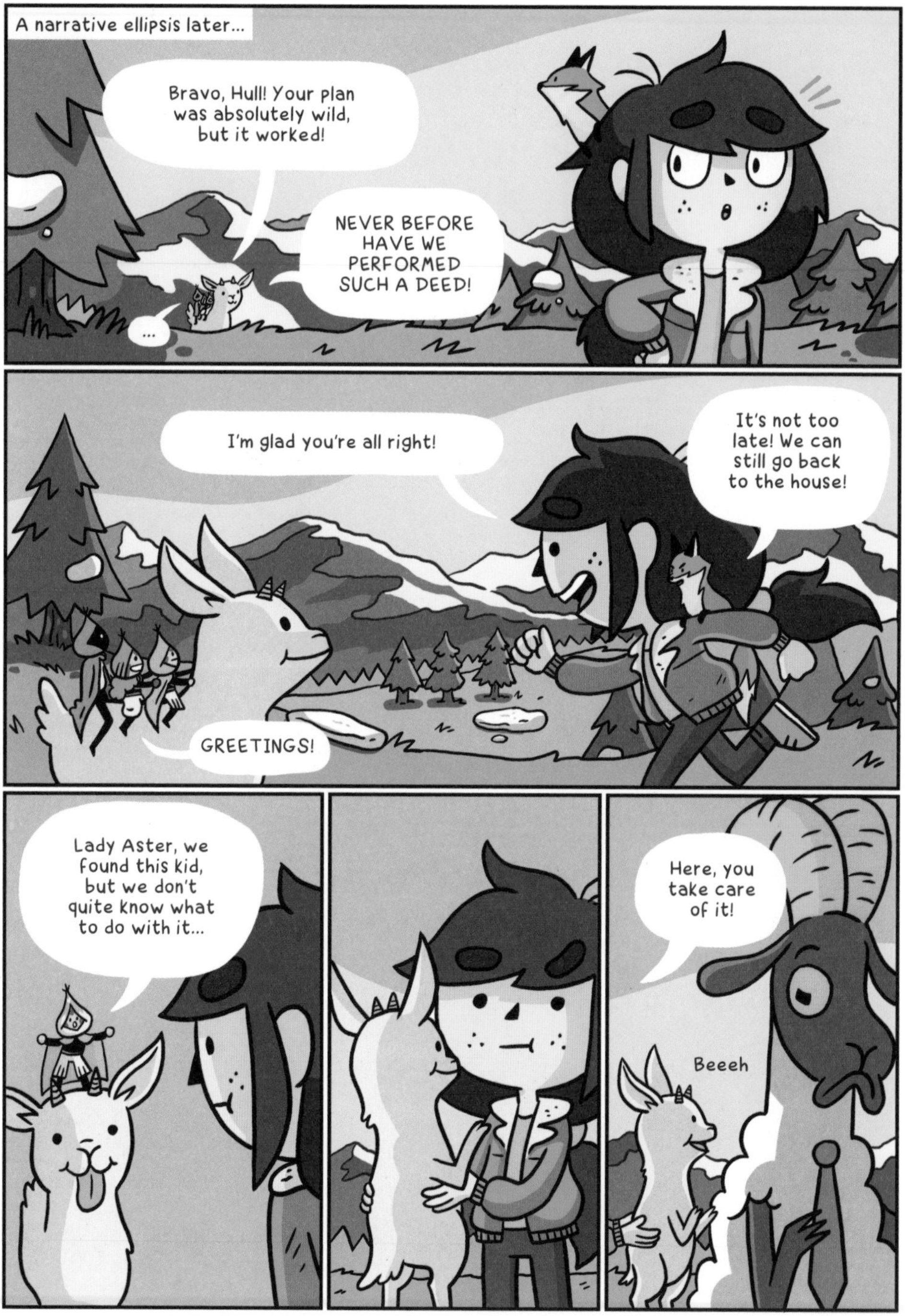
A narrative ellipsis later...
Bravo, Hull! Your plan was absolutely wild, but it worked!
NEVER BEFORE HAVE WE PERFORMED SUCH A DEED!
...
I'm glad you're all right!
It's not too late! We can still go back to the house!
GREETINGS!
Lady Aster, we found this kid, but we don't quite know what to do with it...
Here, you take care of it!
Beeeh

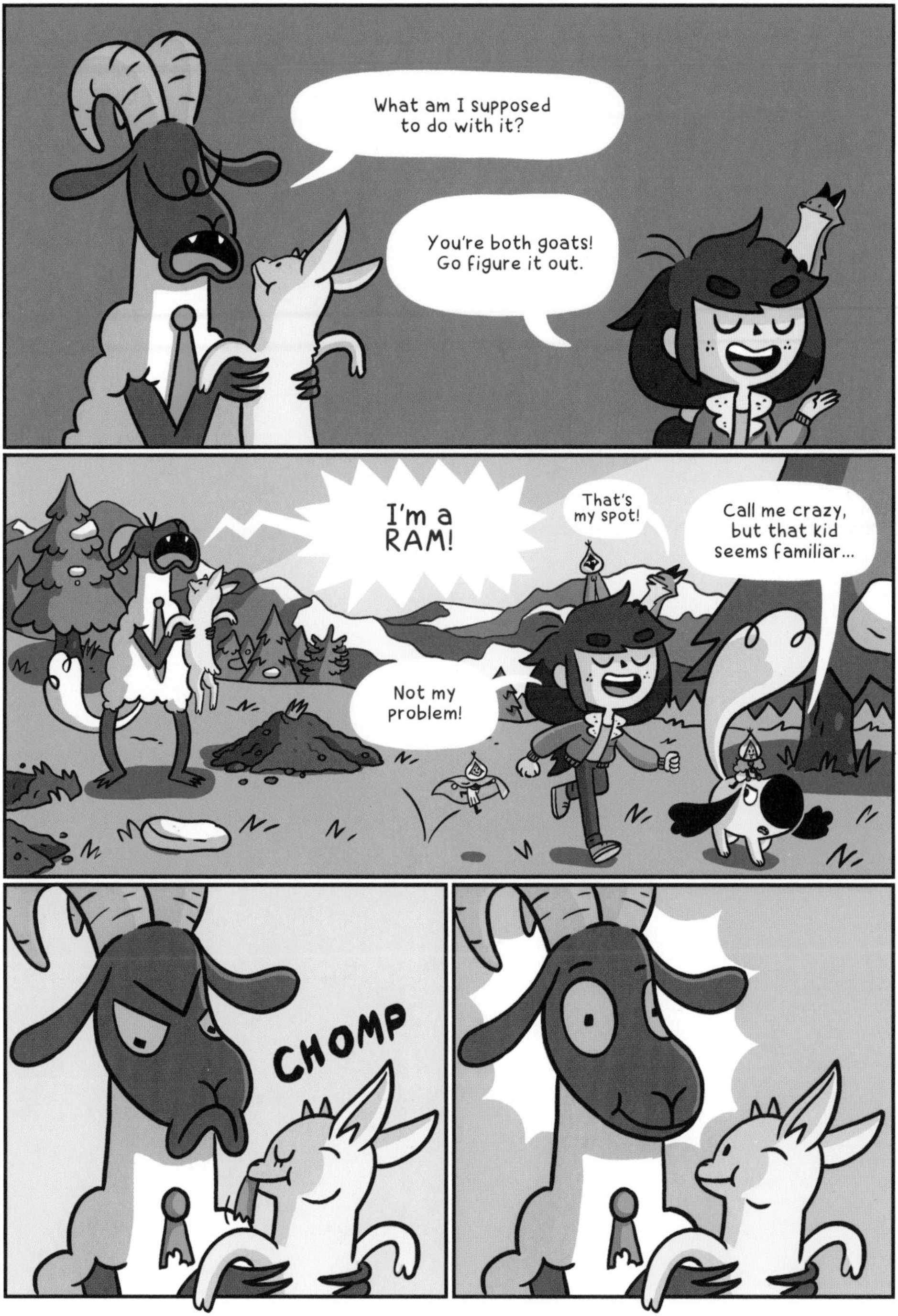
What am I supposed to do with it?
You're both goats! Go figure it out.
I'm a RAM!
That's my spot!
Call me crazy, but that kid seems familiar...
Not my problem!
CHOMP

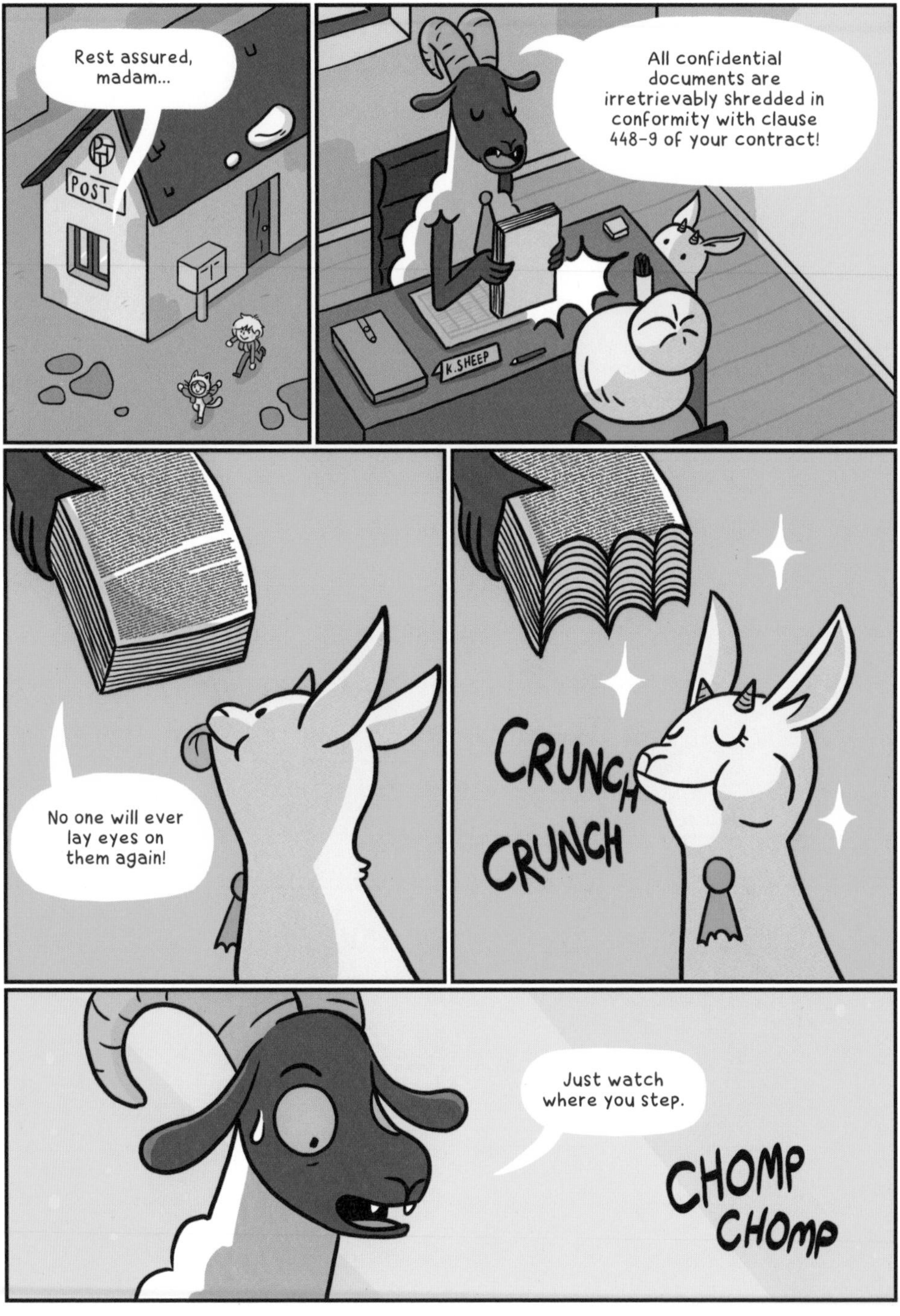

POST
Rest assured, madam...
All confidential documents are irretrievably shredded in conformity with clause 448-9 of your contract!
K.SHEEP
No one will ever lay eyes on them again!
CRUNCH
CRUNCH
Just watch where you step.
CHOMP
CHOMP

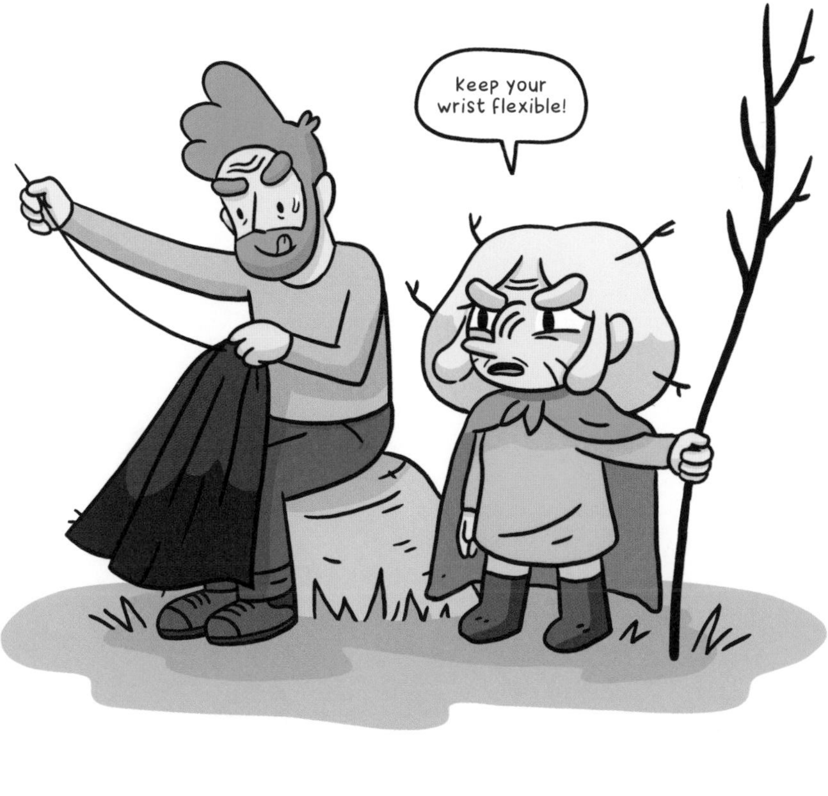
Keep your wrist flexible!

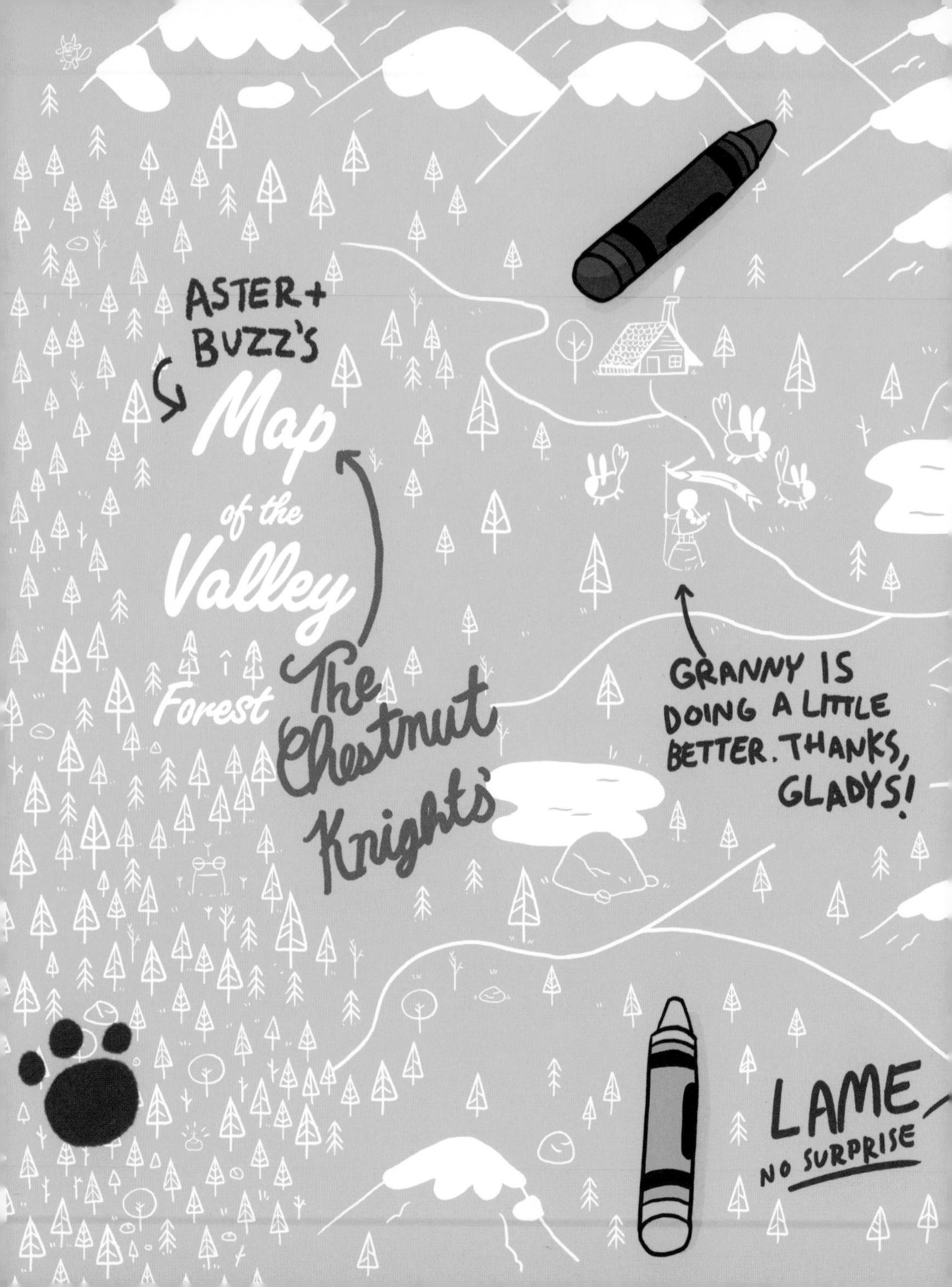

ASTER + BUZZ'S
Map of the Valley
The Chestnut Knights'
Forest
GRANNY IS DOING A LITTLE BETTER. THANKS, GLADYS!
LAME
NO SURPRISE

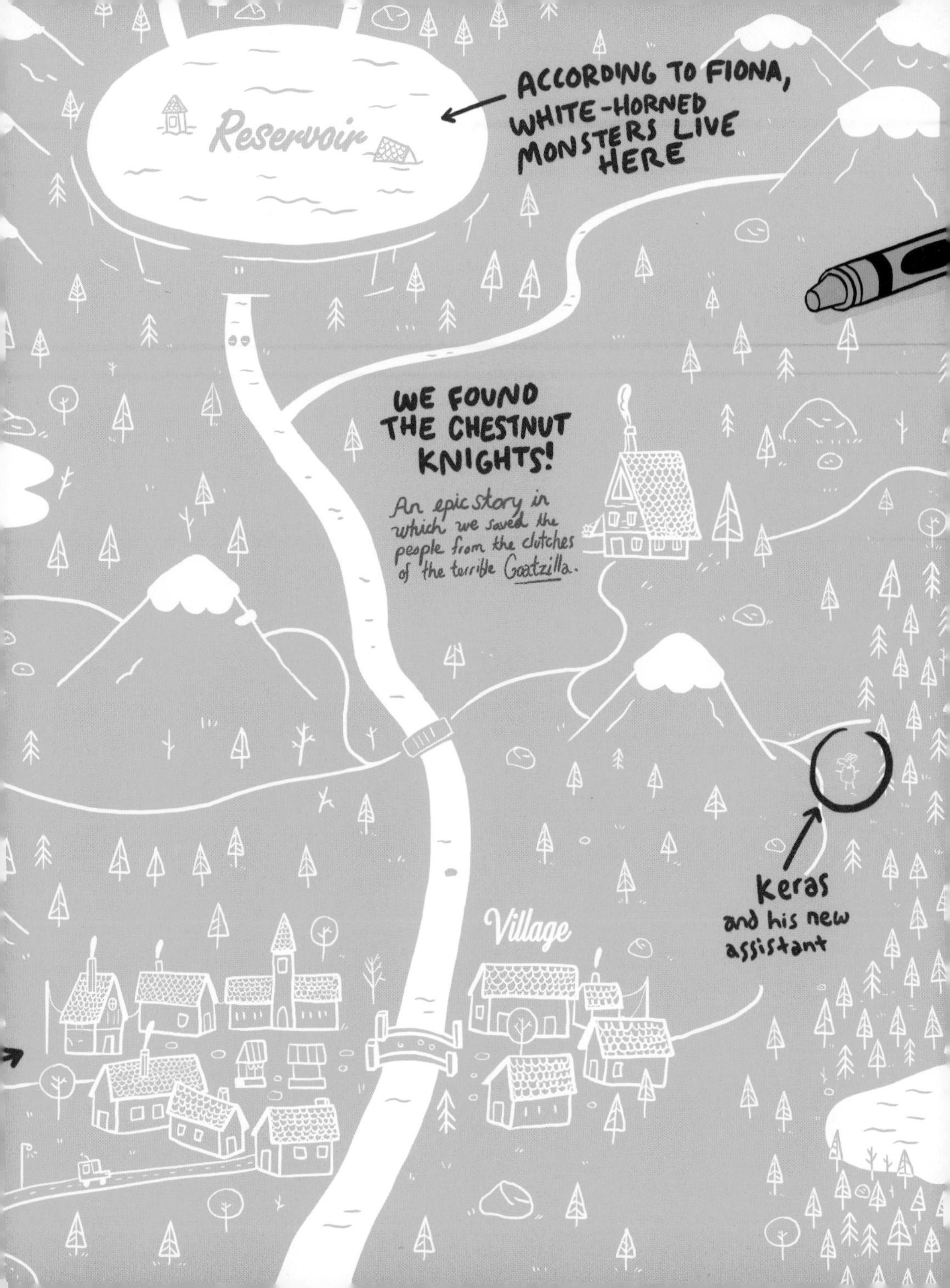
ACCORDING TO FIONA, WHITE-HORNED MONSTERS LIVE HERE
Reservoir
WE FOUND THE CHESTNUT KNIGHTS!
An epic story in which we saved the people from the clutches of the terrible Goatzilla.
Keras
and his new assistant
Village

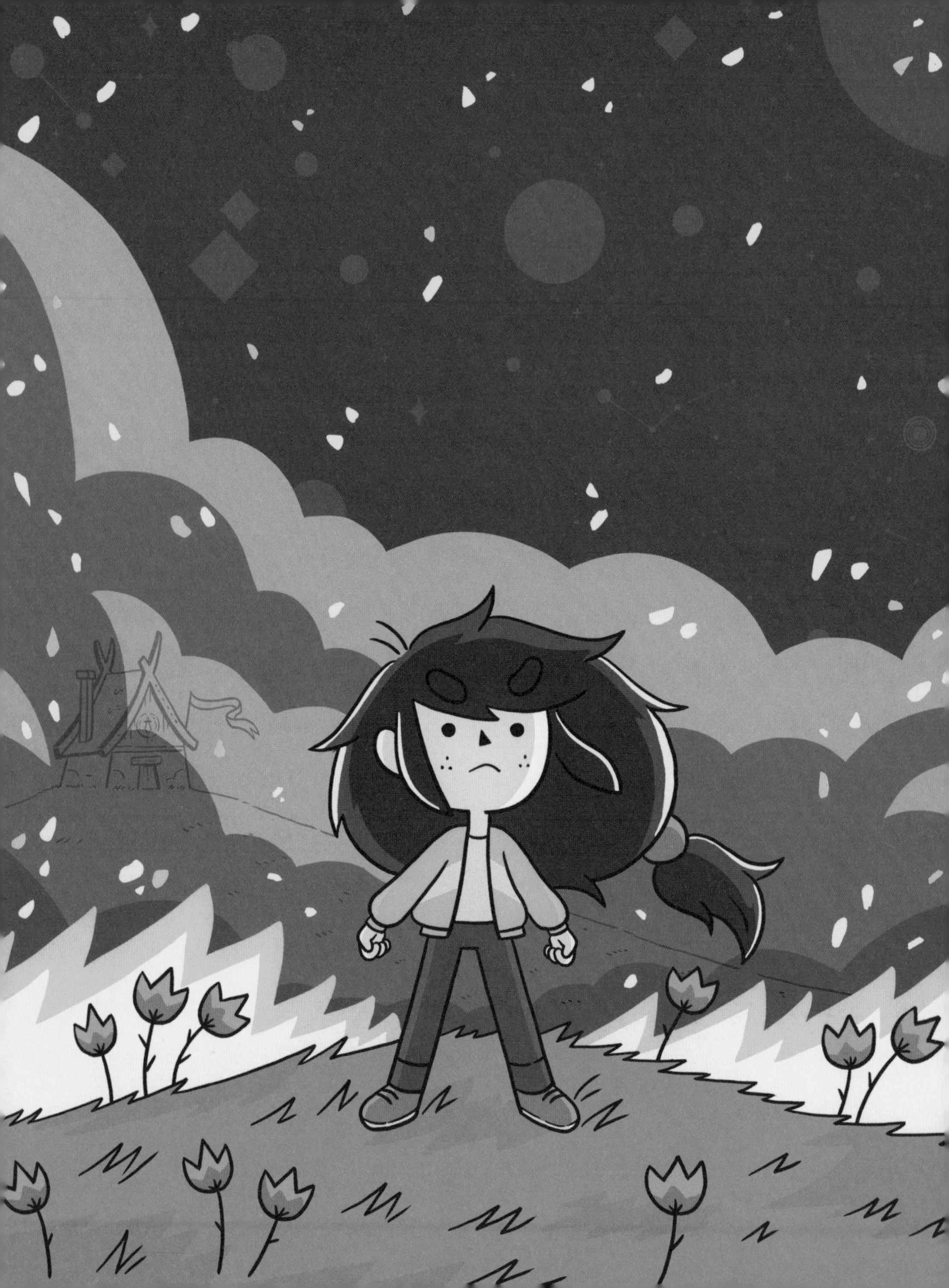

THE END OF EVERYTHING
(AND WHAT HAPPENED NEXT)

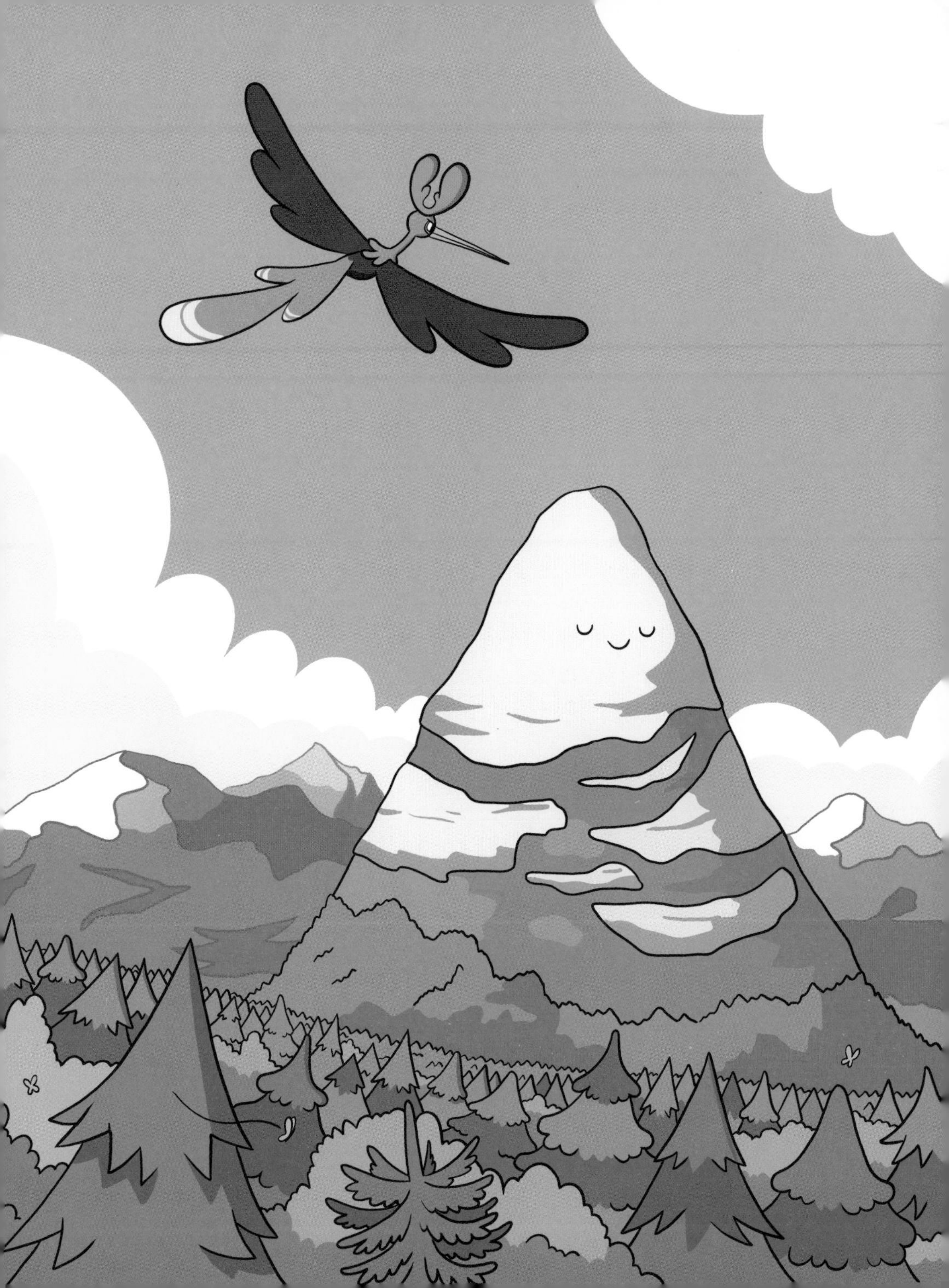

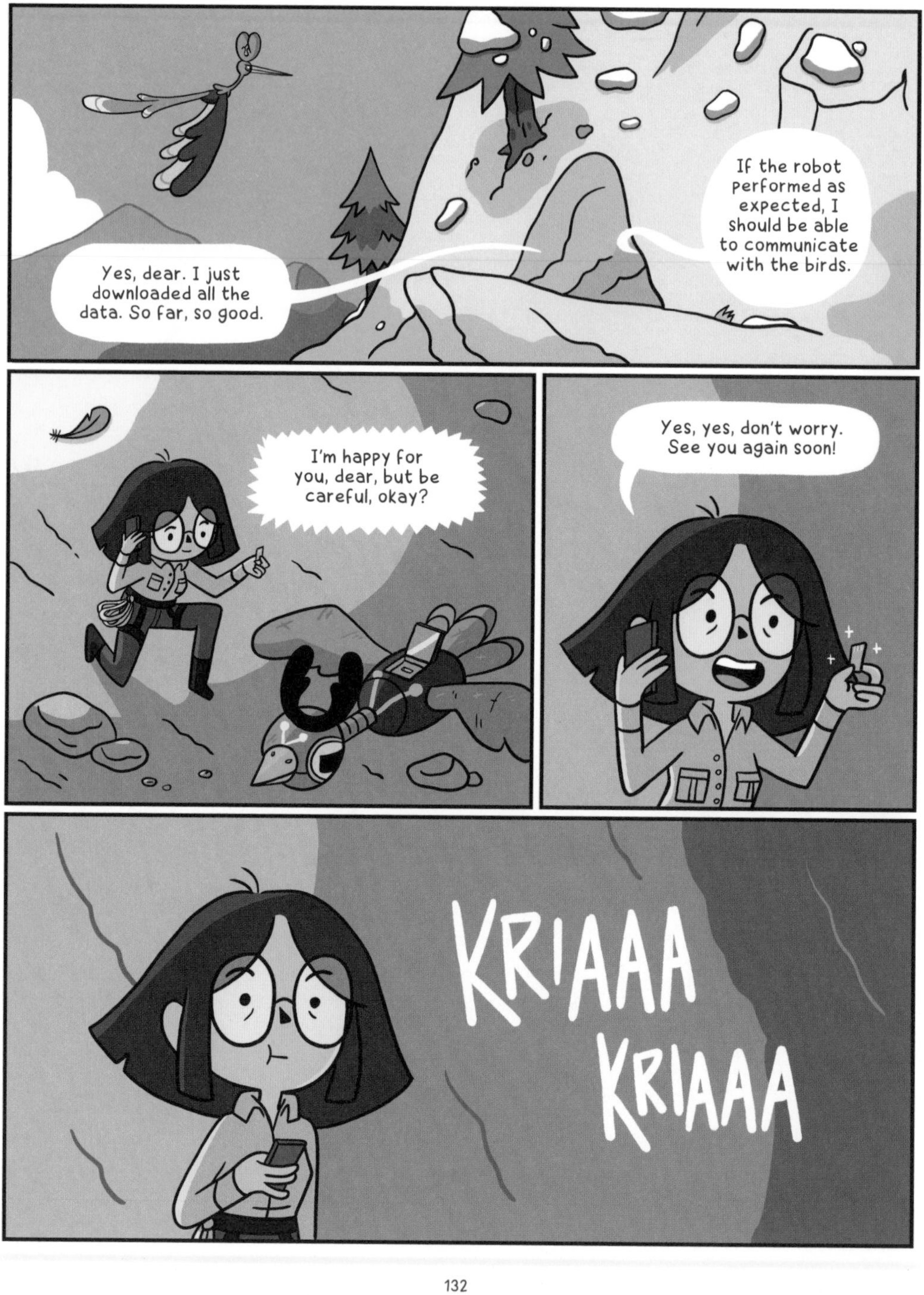
If the robot performed as expected, I should be able to communicate with the birds.
Yes, dear. I just downloaded all the data. So far, so good.
I'm happy for you, dear, but be careful, okay?
Yes, yes, don't worry. See you again soon!
KRIAAA
KRIAAA

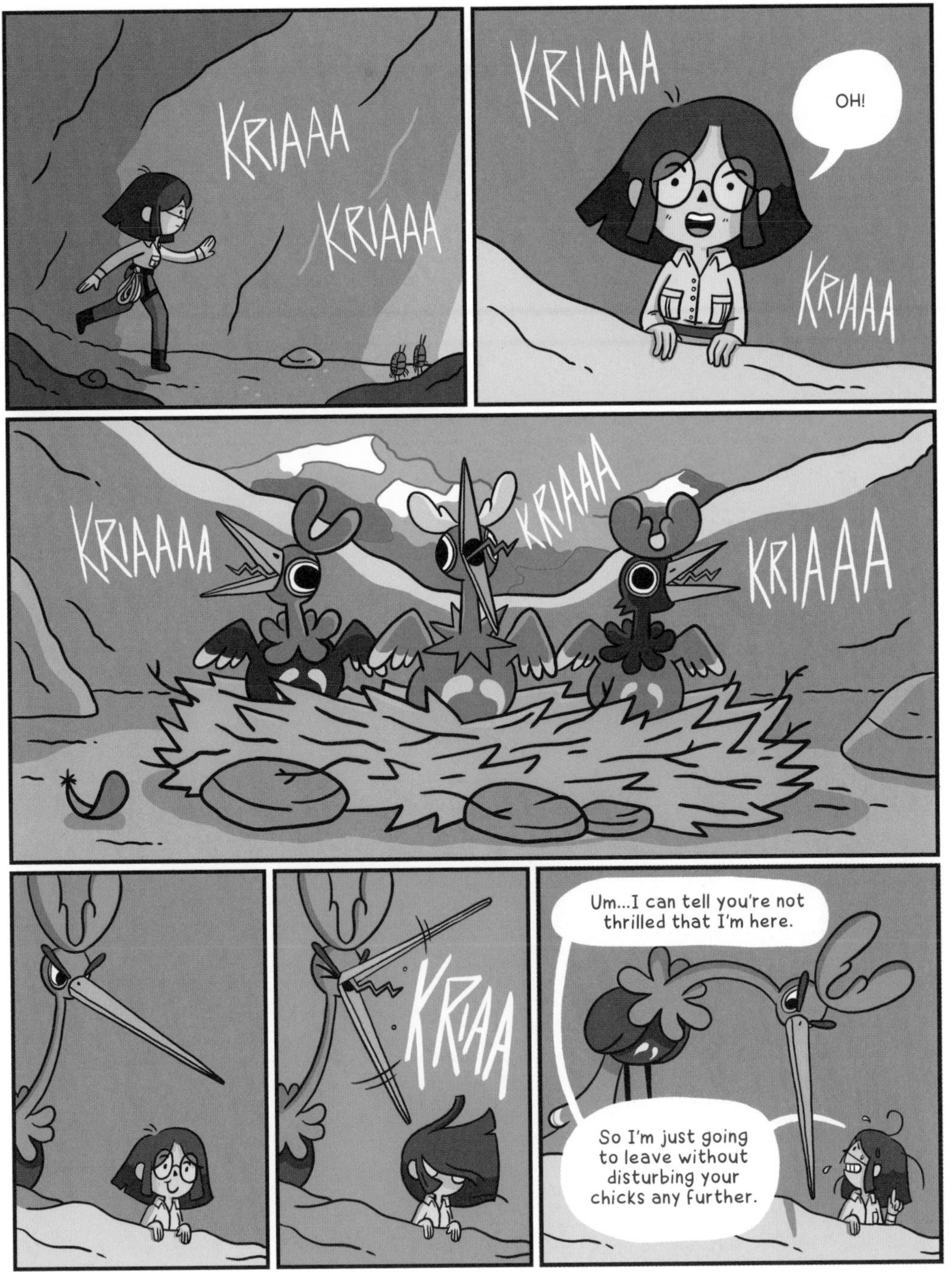
KRIAAA
KRIAAA
KRIAAA
OH!
KRIAAA
KRIAAAA
KRIAAA
KRIAAA
KRIAA
Um...I can tell you're not thrilled that I'm here.
So I'm just going to leave without disturbing your chicks any further.

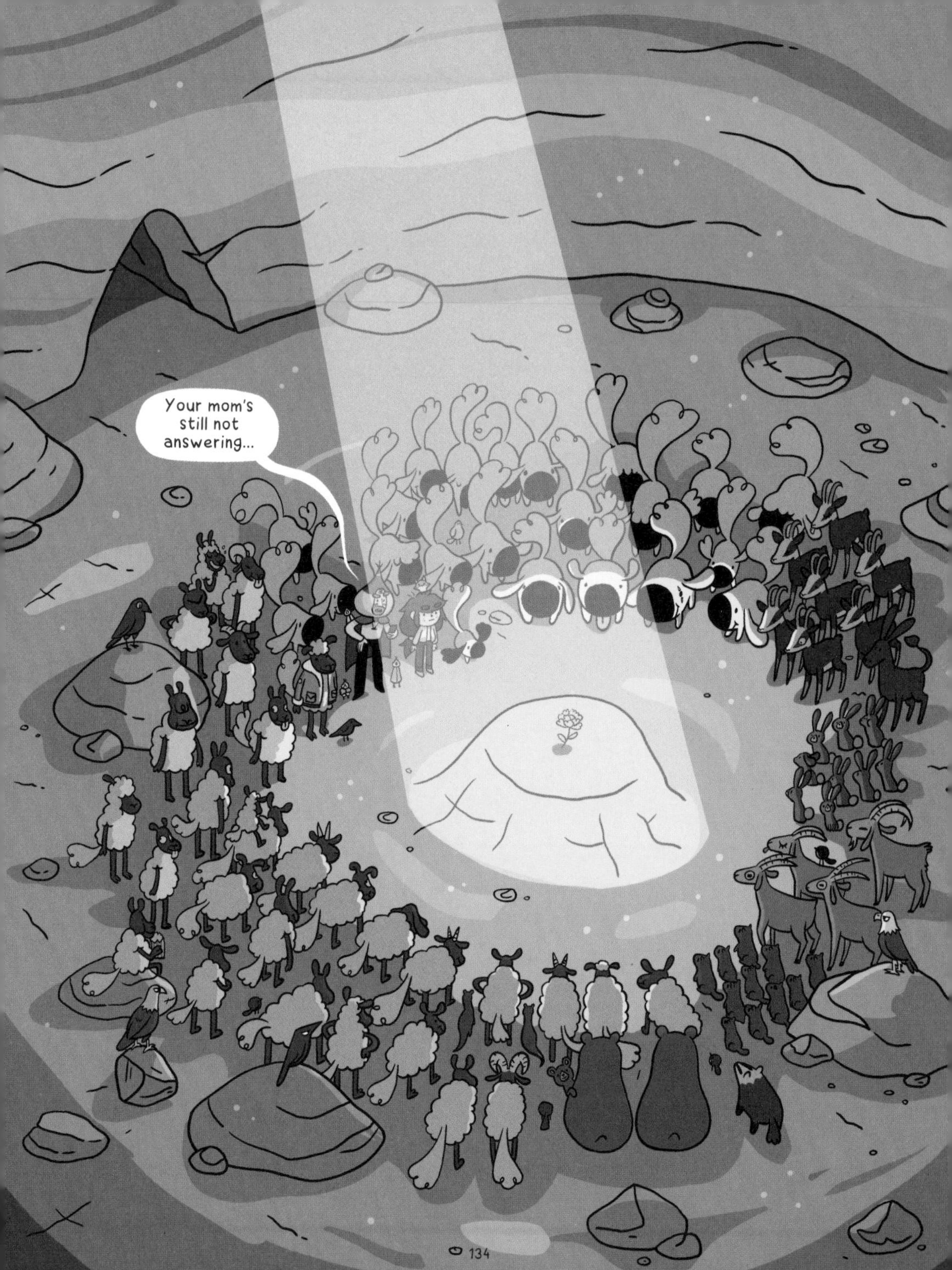
Your mom's still not answering...

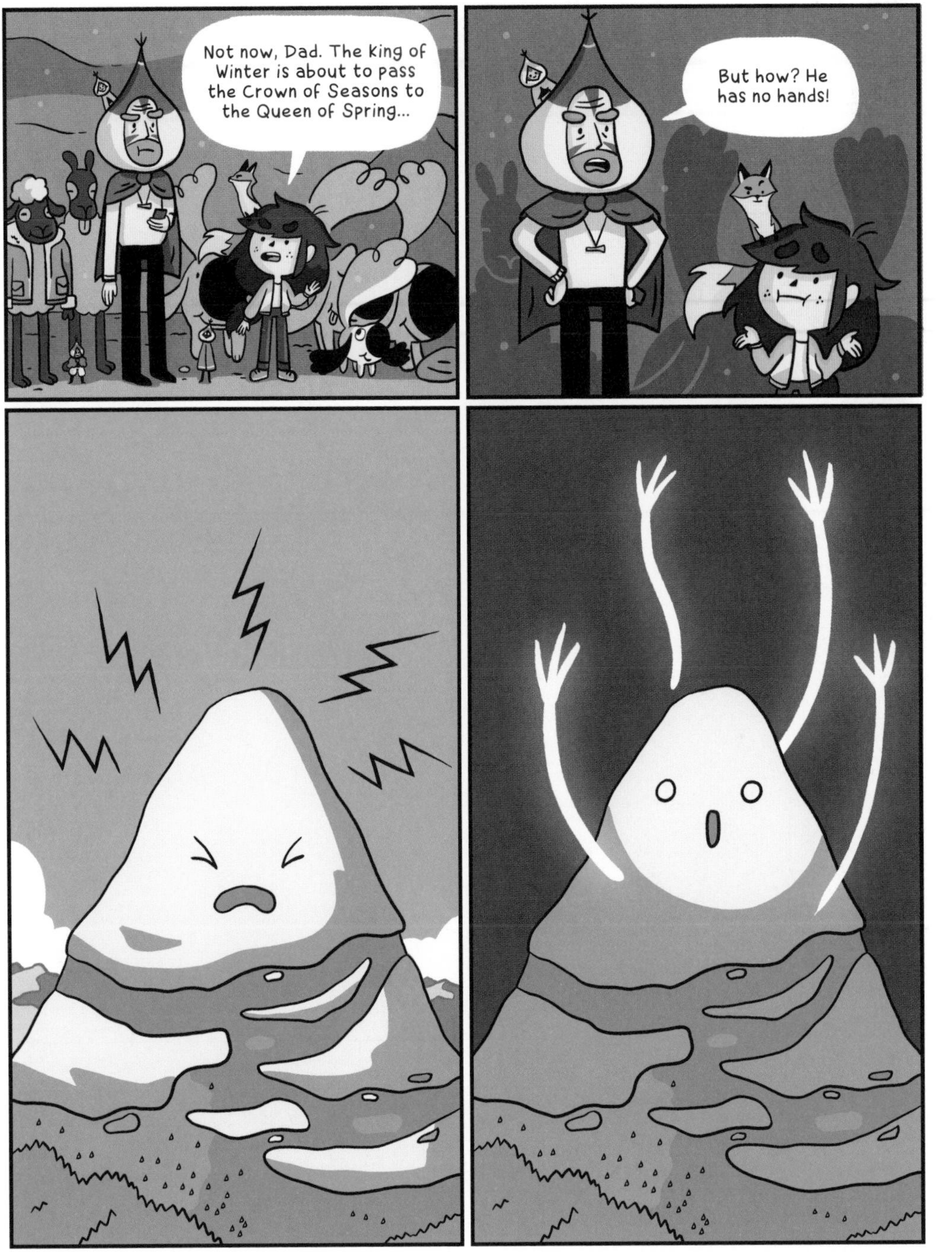
Not now, Dad. The King of Winter is about to pass the Crown of Seasons to the Queen of Spring...
But how? He has no hands!

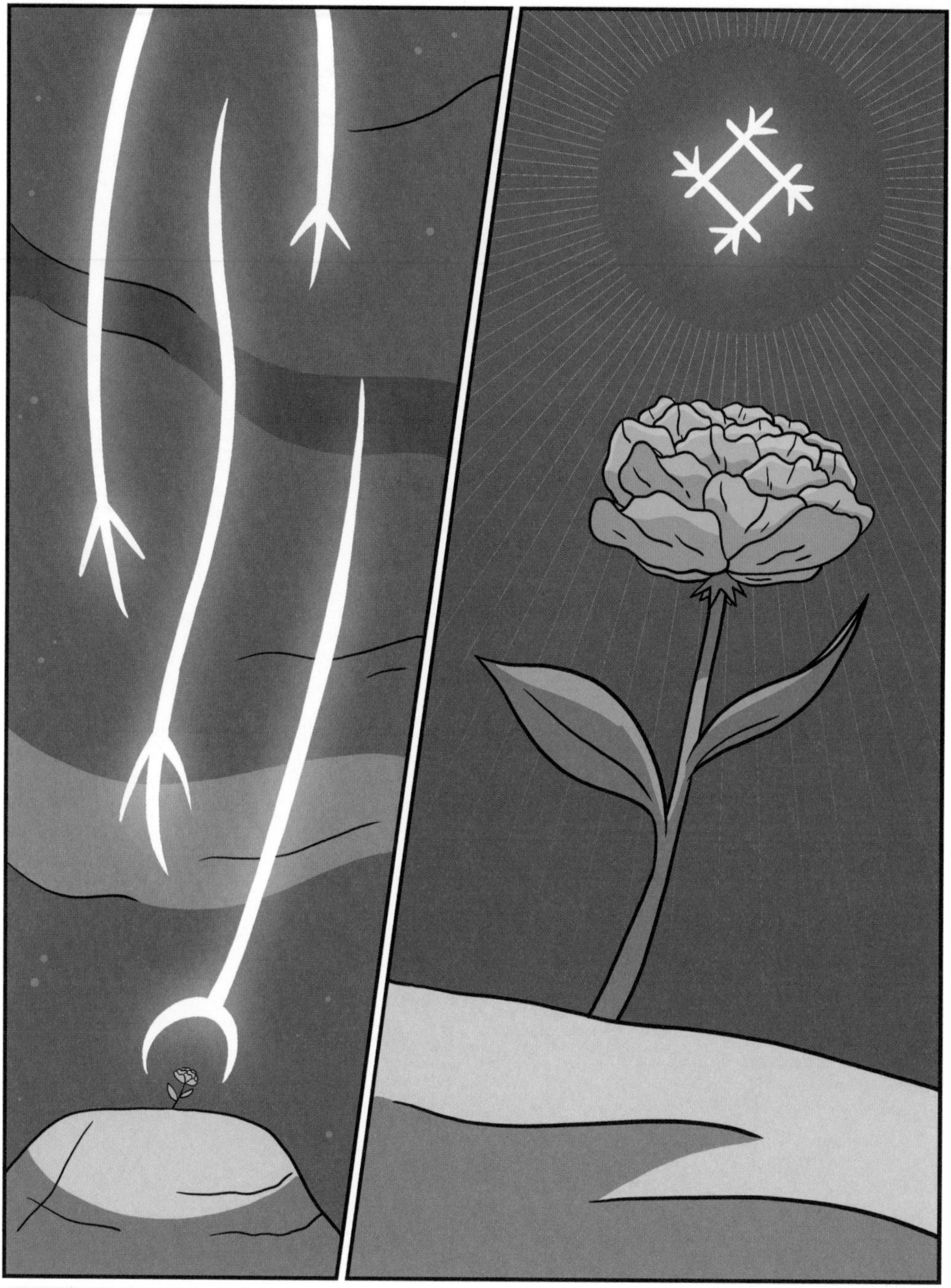

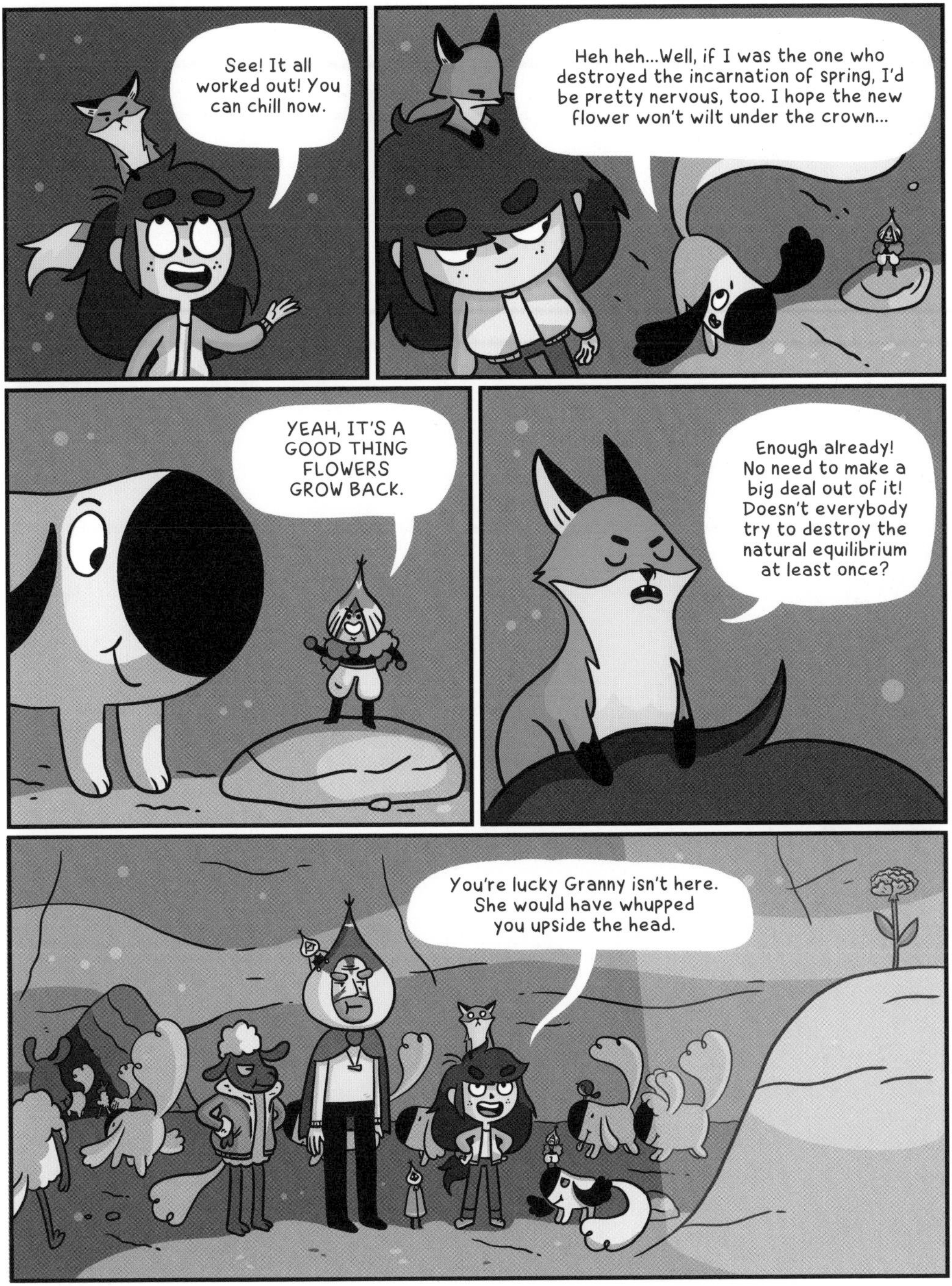
See! It all worked out! You can chill now.
Heh heh...Well, if I was the one who destroyed the incarnation of spring, I'd be pretty nervous, too. I hope the new flower won't wilt under the crown...
YEAH, IT'S A GOOD THING FLOWERS GROW BACK.
Enough already! No need to make a big deal out of it! Doesn't everybody try to destroy the natural equilibrium at least once?
You're lucky Granny isn't here. She would have whupped you upside the head.

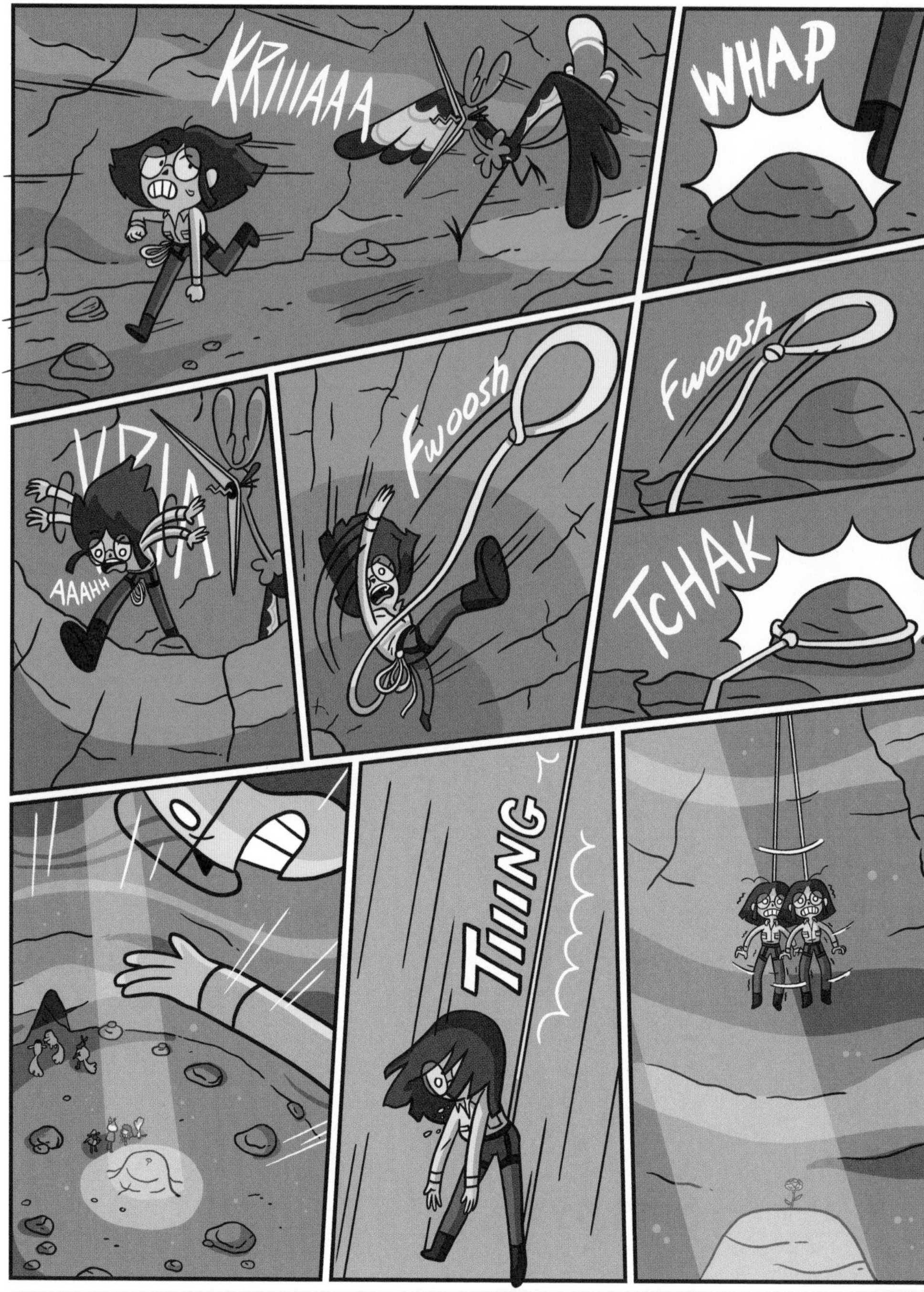
KRIIIAAA
WHAP
AAAHH
Fwoosh
Fwoosh
TCHAK
TIIIING

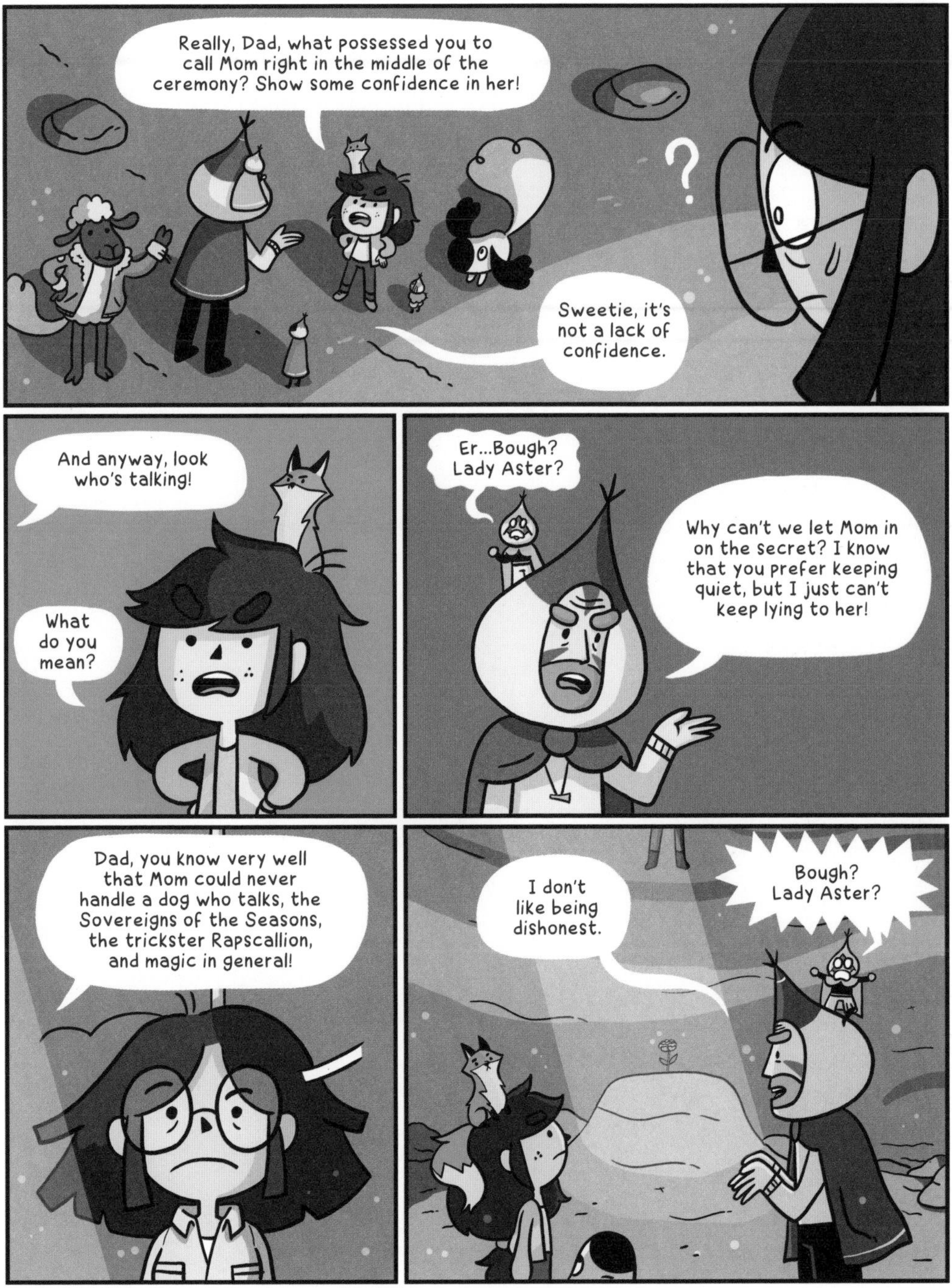
Really, Dad, what possessed you to call Mom right in the middle of the ceremony? Show some confidence in her!
?
Sweetie, it's not a lack of confidence.
And anyway, look who's talking!
What do you mean?
Er...Bough? Lady Aster?
Why can't we let Mom in on the secret? I know that you prefer keeping quiet, but I just can't keep lying to her!
Dad, you know very well that Mom could never handle a dog who talks, the Sovereigns of the Seasons, the trickster Rapscallion, and magic in general!
I don't like being dishonest.
Bough? Lady Aster?

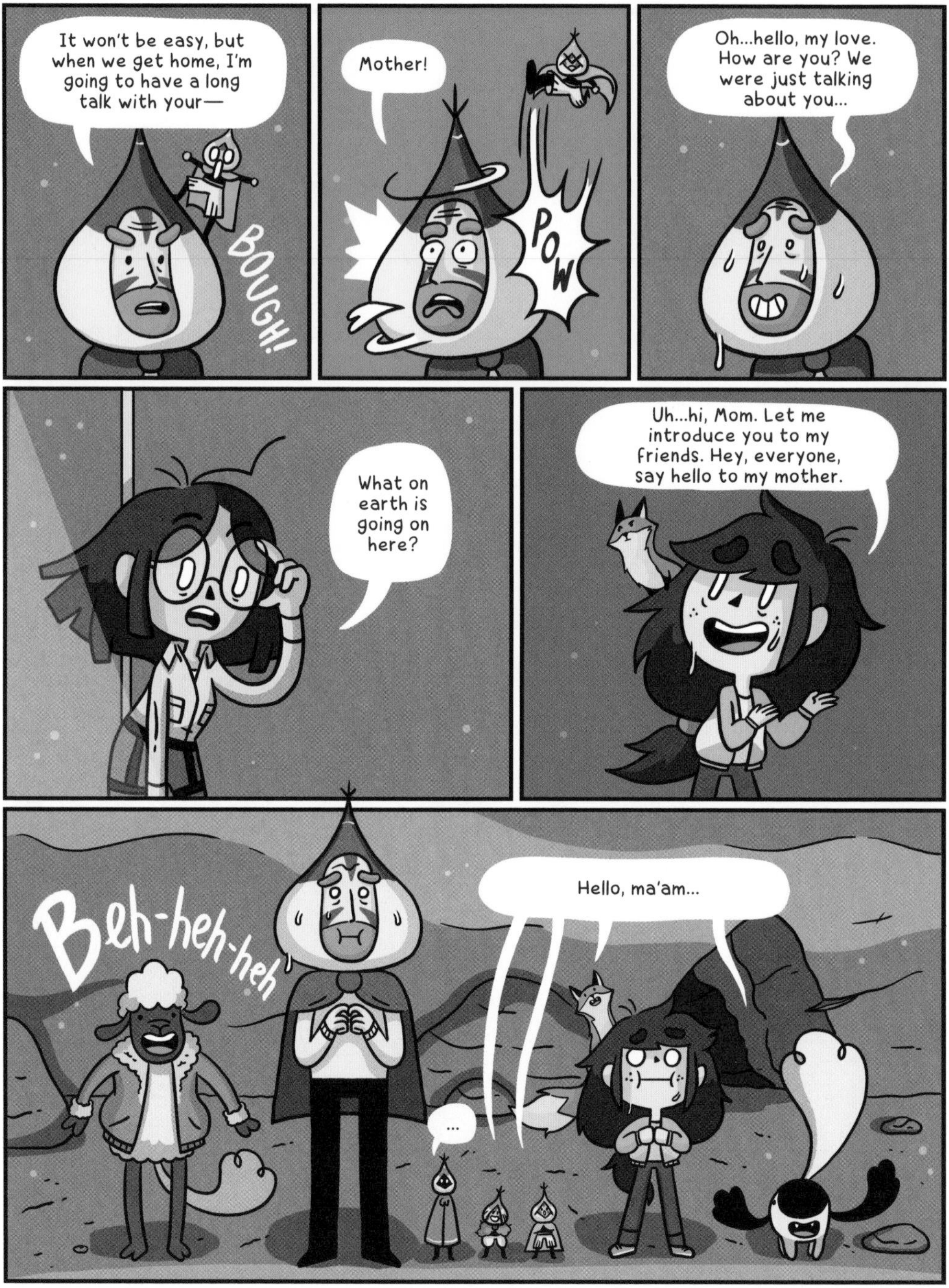

It won't be easy, but when we get home, I'm going to have a long talk with your—
BOUGH!
Mother!
POW
Oh...hello, my love. How are you? We were just talking about you...
What on earth is going on here?
Uh...hi, Mom. Let me introduce you to my friends. Hey, everyone, say hello to my mother.
Beh-heh-heh
Hello, ma'am...
...

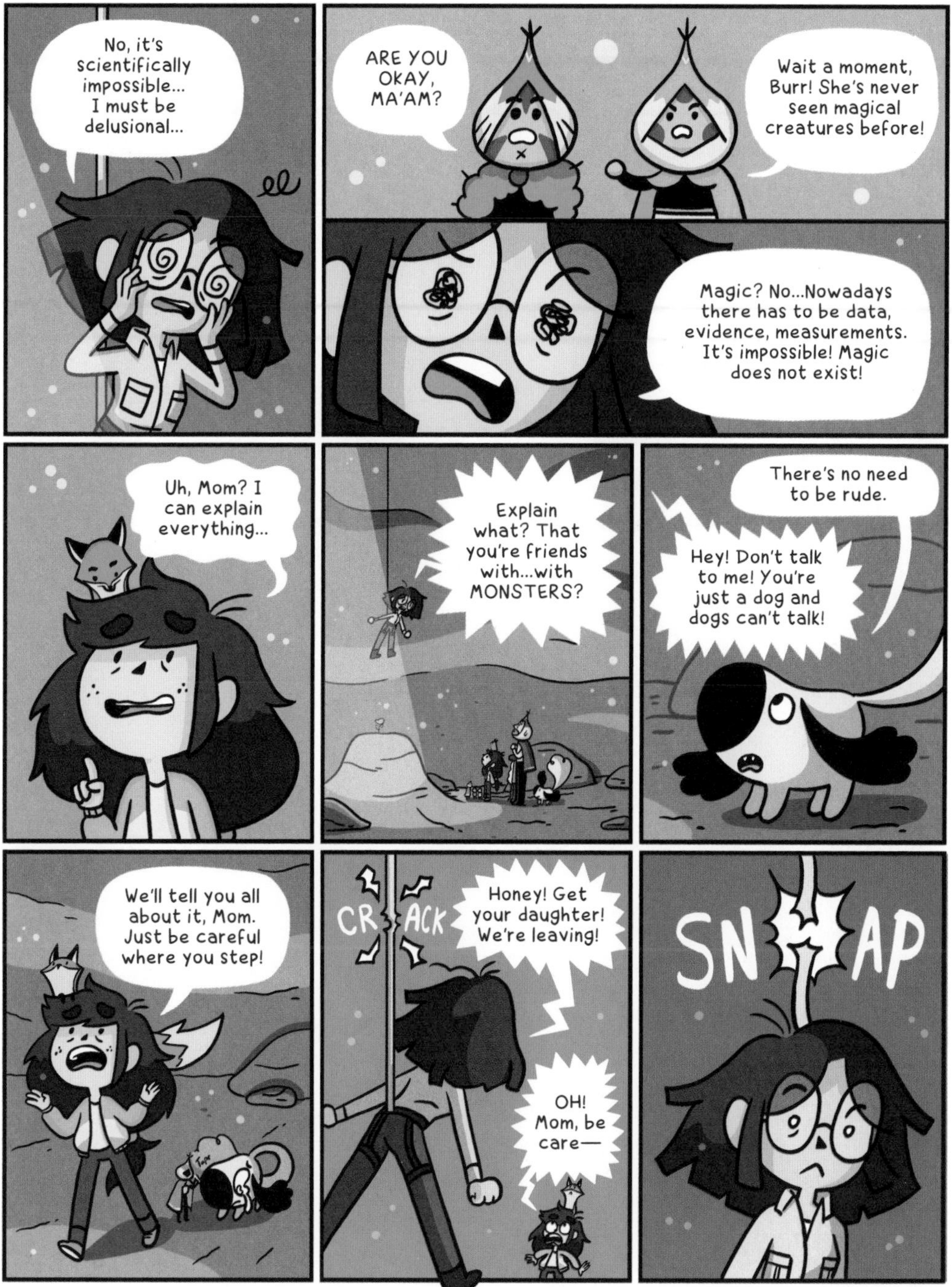
No, it's scientifically impossible... I must be delusional...
ARE YOU OKAY, MA'AM?
Wait a moment, Burr! She's never seen magical creatures before!
Magic? No...Nowadays there has to be data, evidence, measurements. It's impossible! Magic does not exist!
Uh, Mom? I can explain everything...
Explain what? That you're friends with...with MONSTERS?
Hey! Don't talk to me! You're just a dog and dogs can't talk!
There's no need to be rude.
We'll tell you all about it, Mom. Just be careful where you step!
CR ACK
Honey! Get your daughter! We're leaving!
OH! Mom, be care—
SN AP

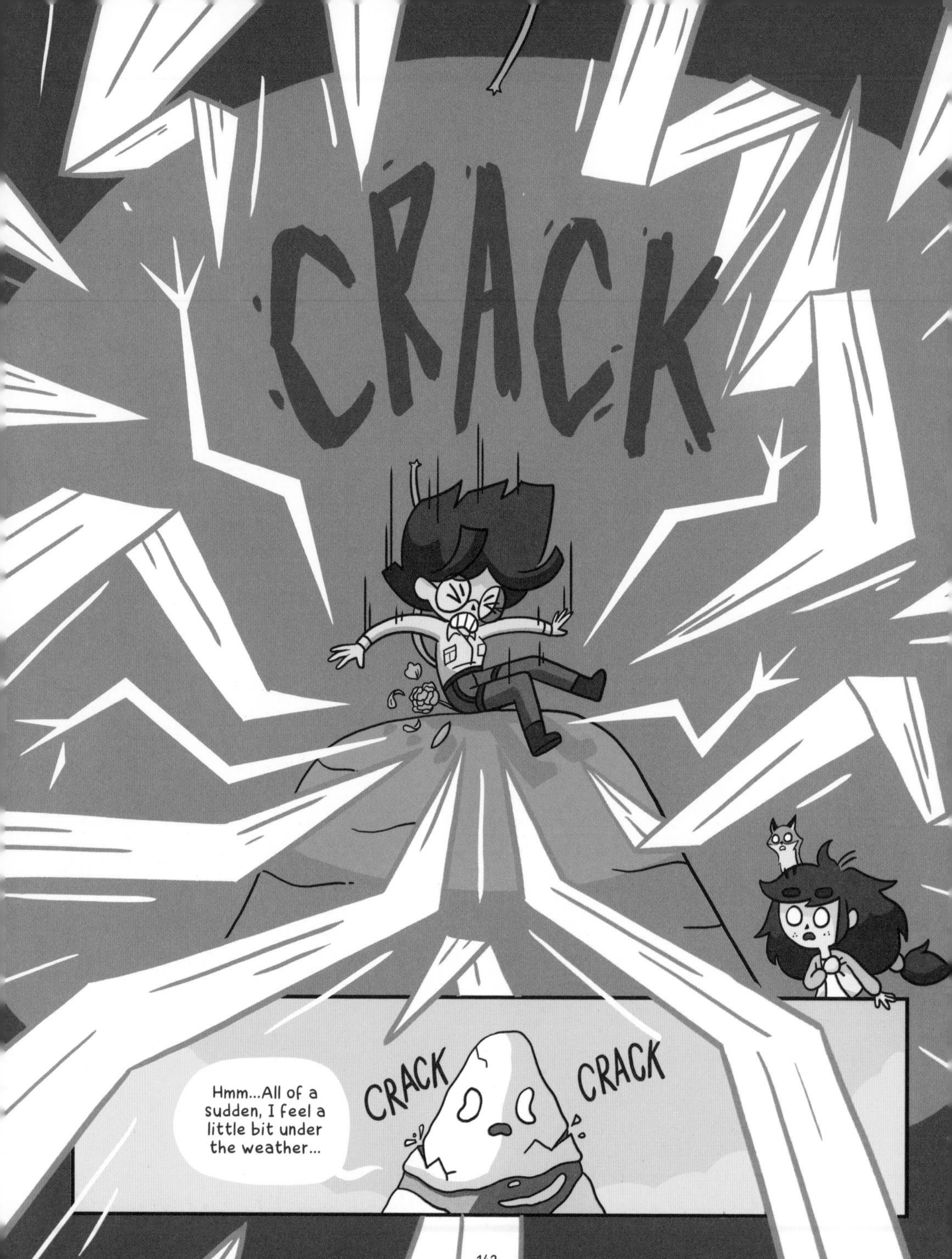
CRACK
CRACK
Hmm...All of a sudden, I feel a little bit under the weather...
CRACK

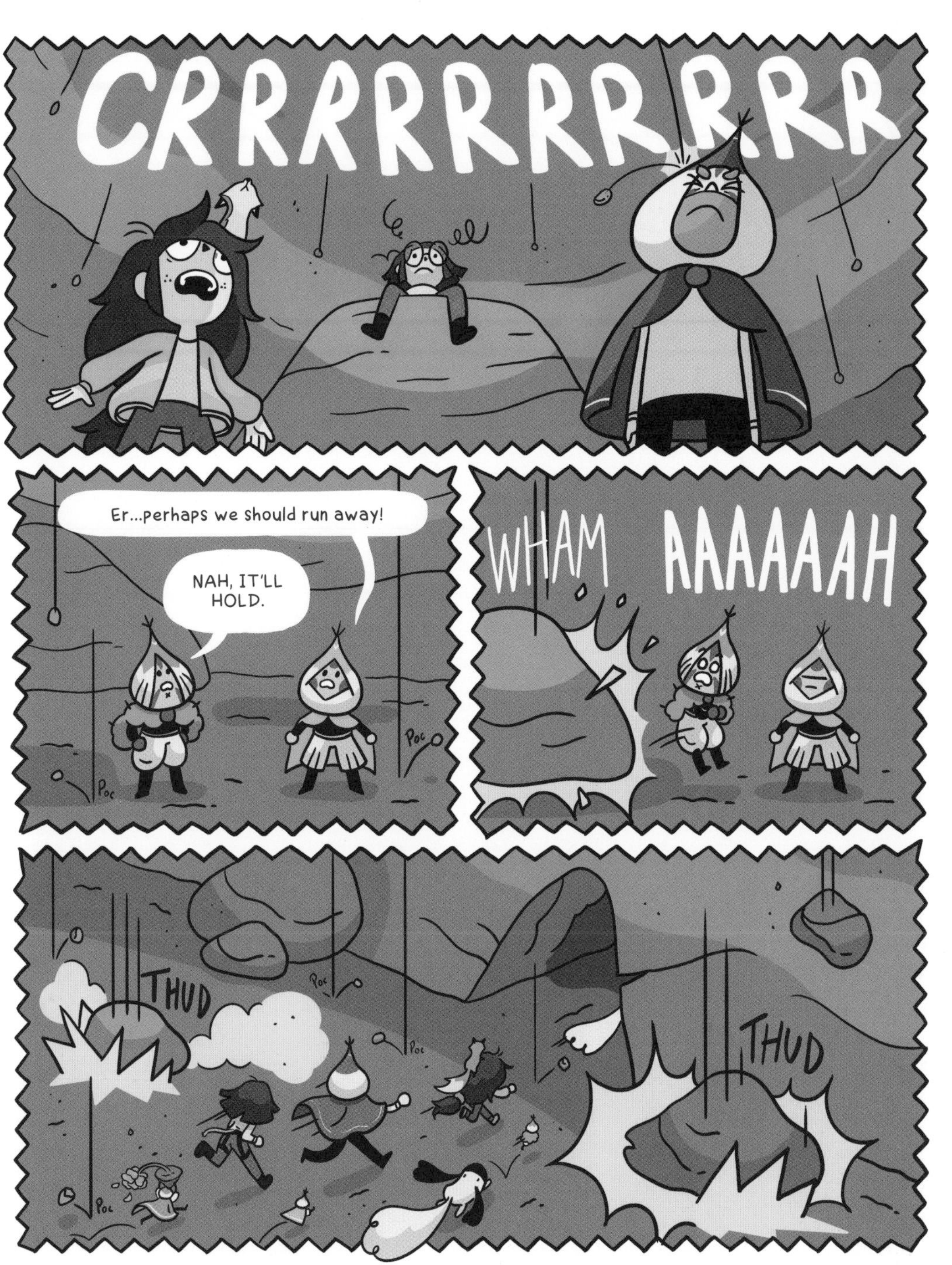
CRRRRRRRRRR
Er...perhaps we should run away!
NAH, IT'LL HOLD.
Poc
Poc
WHAM
AAAAAAH
THUD
Poc
Poc
Poc
THUD

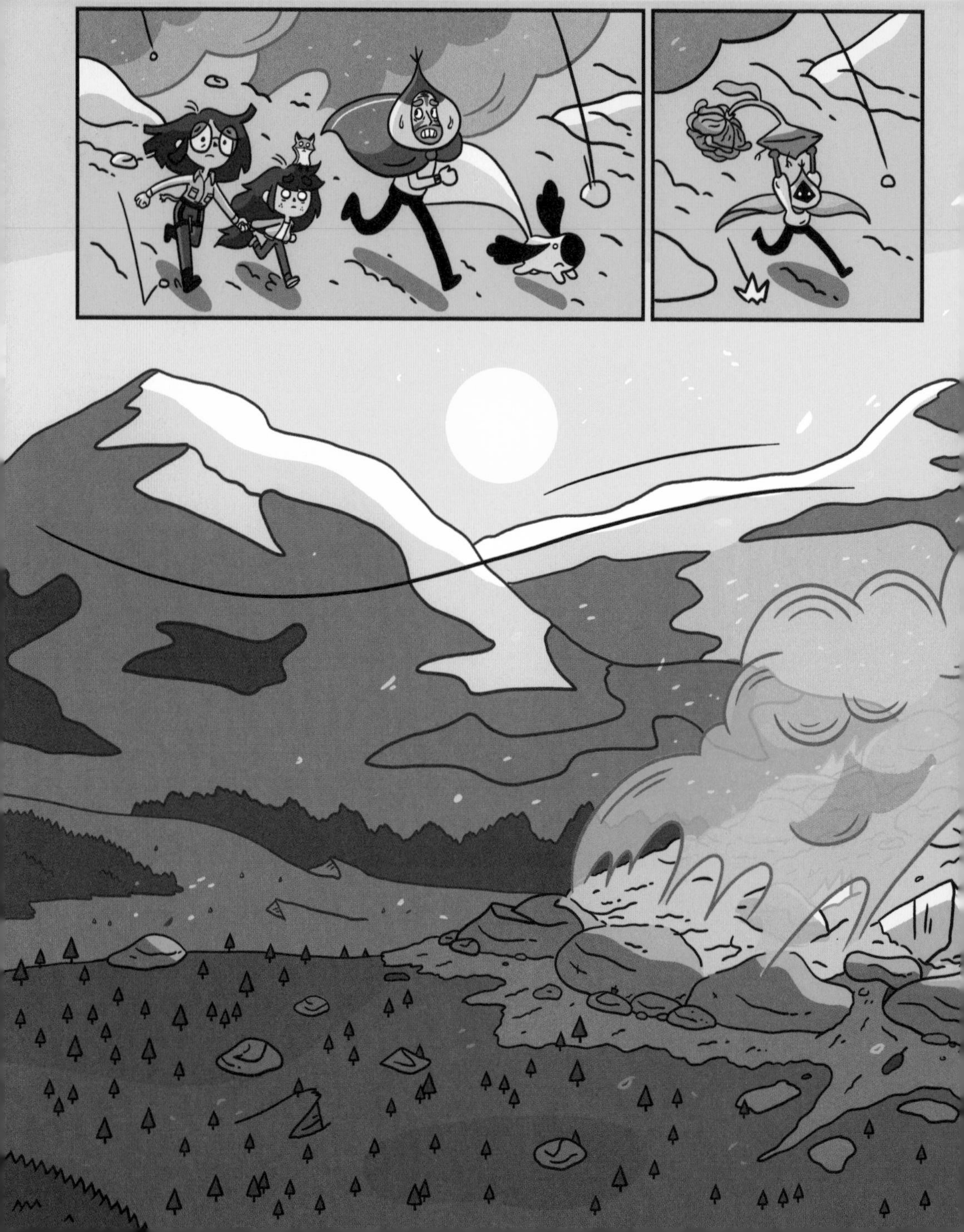

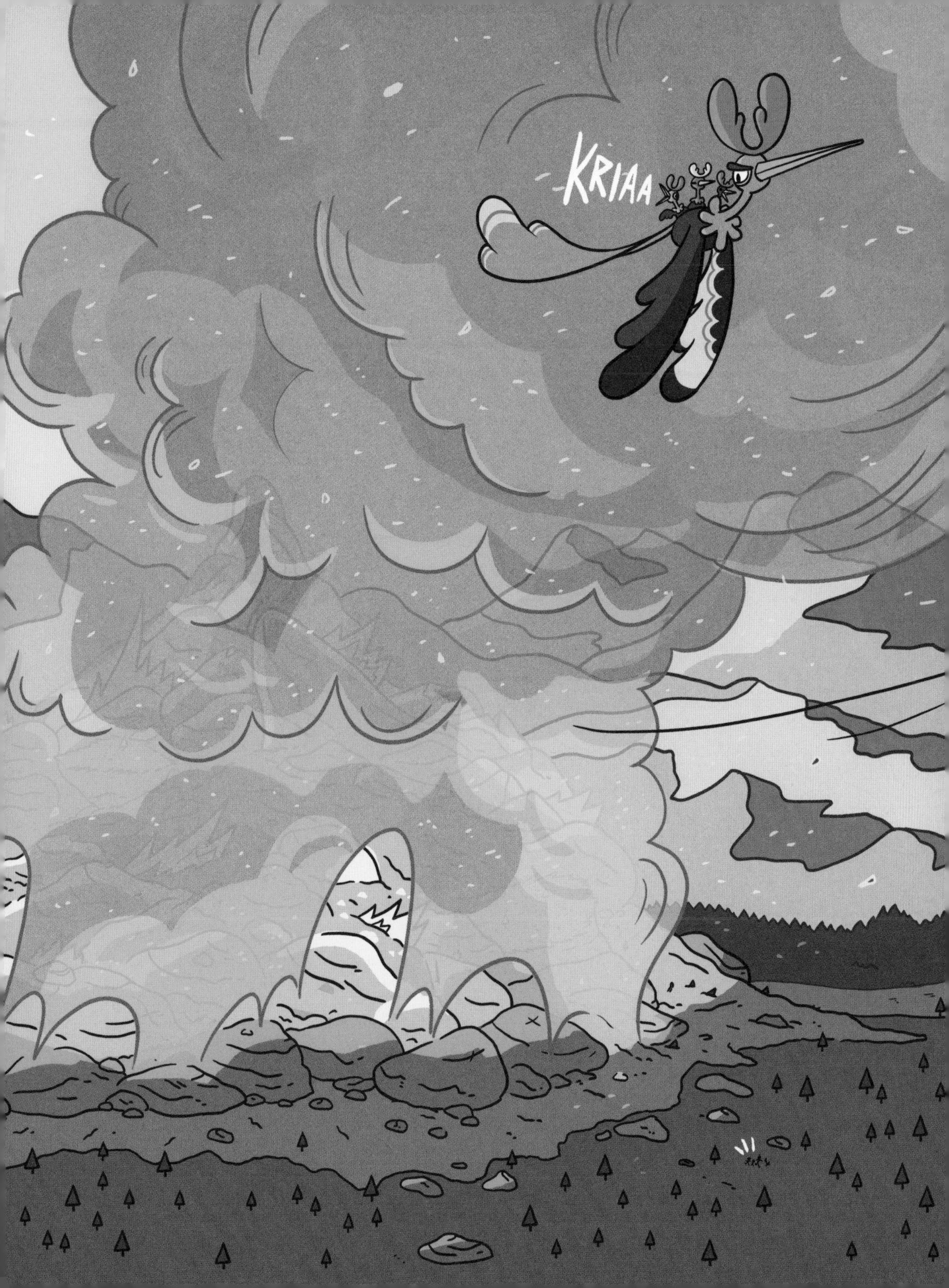
KRIAA

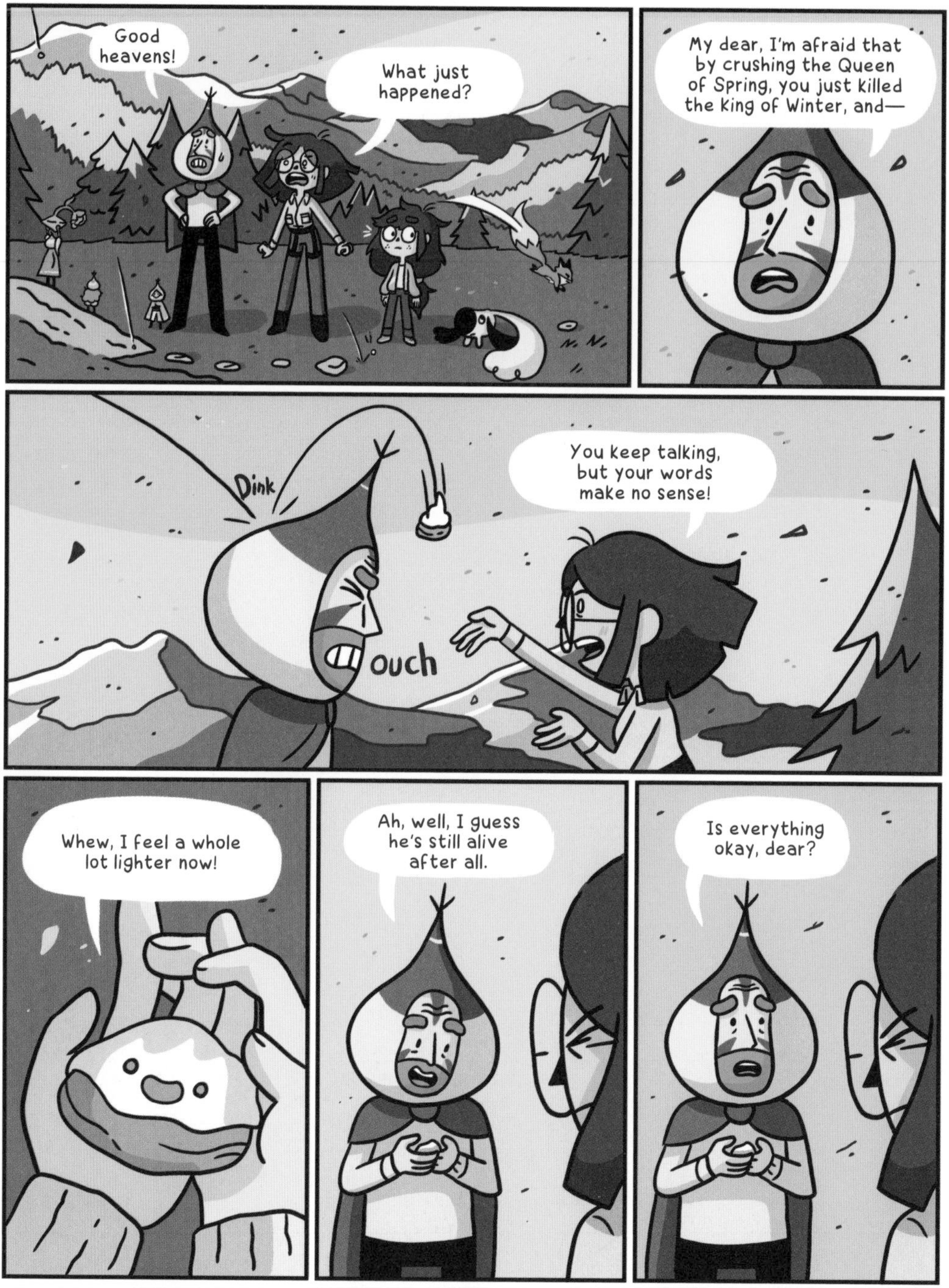
Good heavens!
What just happened?
My dear, I'm afraid that by crushing the Queen of Spring, you just killed the King of Winter, and—
Dink
ouch
You keep talking, but your words make no sense!
Whew, I feel a whole lot lighter now!
Ah, well, I guess he's still alive after all.
Is everything okay, dear?

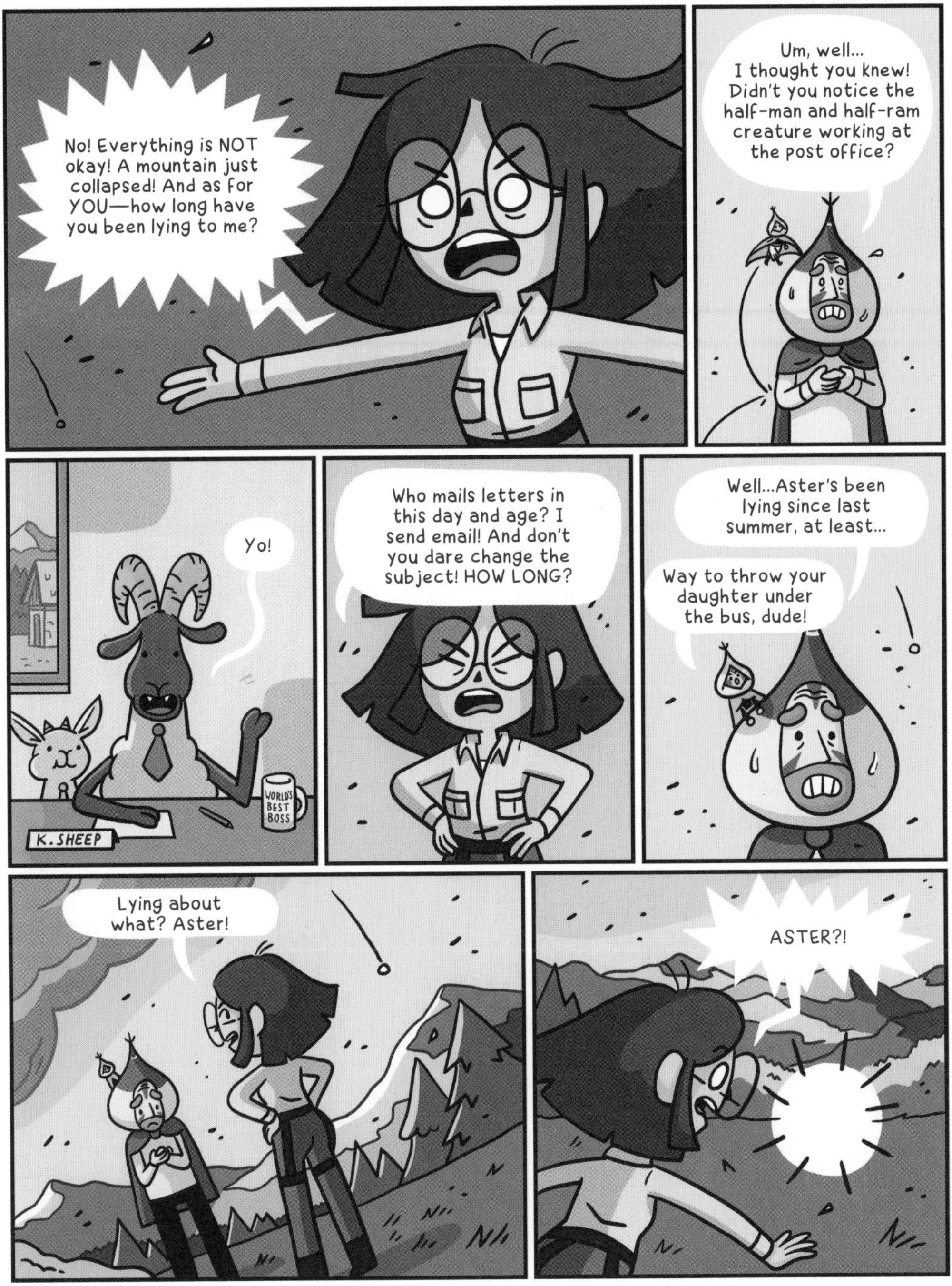
No! Everything is NOT okay! A mountain just collapsed! And as for YOU—how long have you been lying to me?
Um, well... I thought you knew! Didn't you notice the half-man and half-ram creature working at the post office?
Yo!
WORLD'S BEST BOSS
K. SHEEP
Who mails letters in this day and age? I send email! And don't you dare change the subject! HOW LONG?
Well...Aster's been lying since last summer, at least...
Way to throw your daughter under the bus, dude!
Lying about what? Aster!
ASTER?!

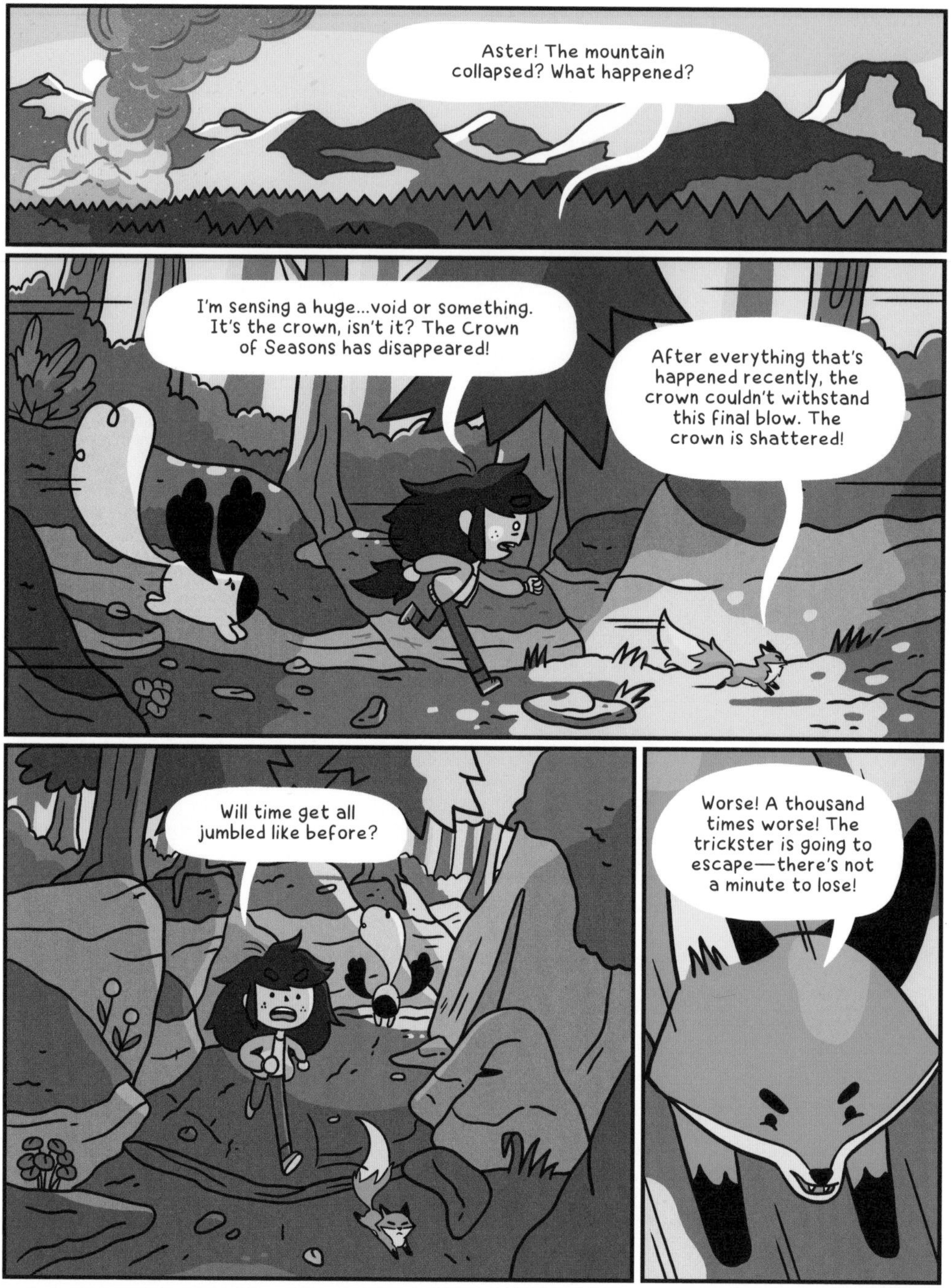

Aster! The mountain collapsed? What happened?
I'm sensing a huge...void or something. It's the crown, isn't it? The Crown of Seasons has disappeared!
After everything that's happened recently, the crown couldn't withstand this final blow. The crown is shattered!
Will time get all jumbled like before?
Worse! A thousand times worse! The trickster is going to escape—there's not a minute to lose!

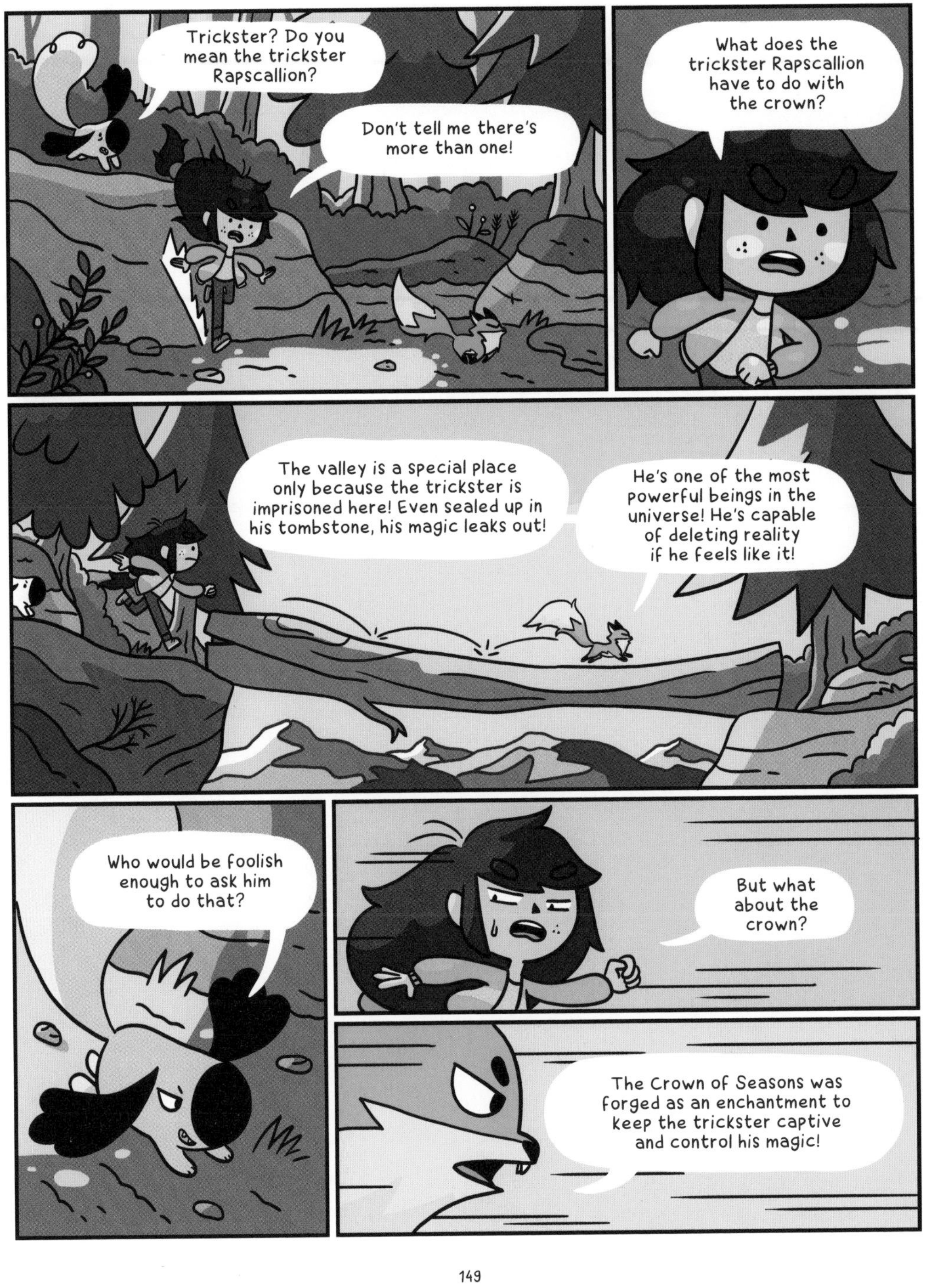
Trickster? Do you mean the trickster Rapscallion?
Don't tell me there's more than one!
What does the trickster Rapscallion have to do with the crown?
The valley is a special place only because the trickster is imprisoned here! Even sealed up in his tombstone, his magic leaks out!
He's one of the most powerful beings in the universe! He's capable of deleting reality if he feels like it!
Who would be foolish enough to ask him to do that?
But what about the crown?
The Crown of Seasons was forged as an enchantment to keep the trickster captive and control his magic!

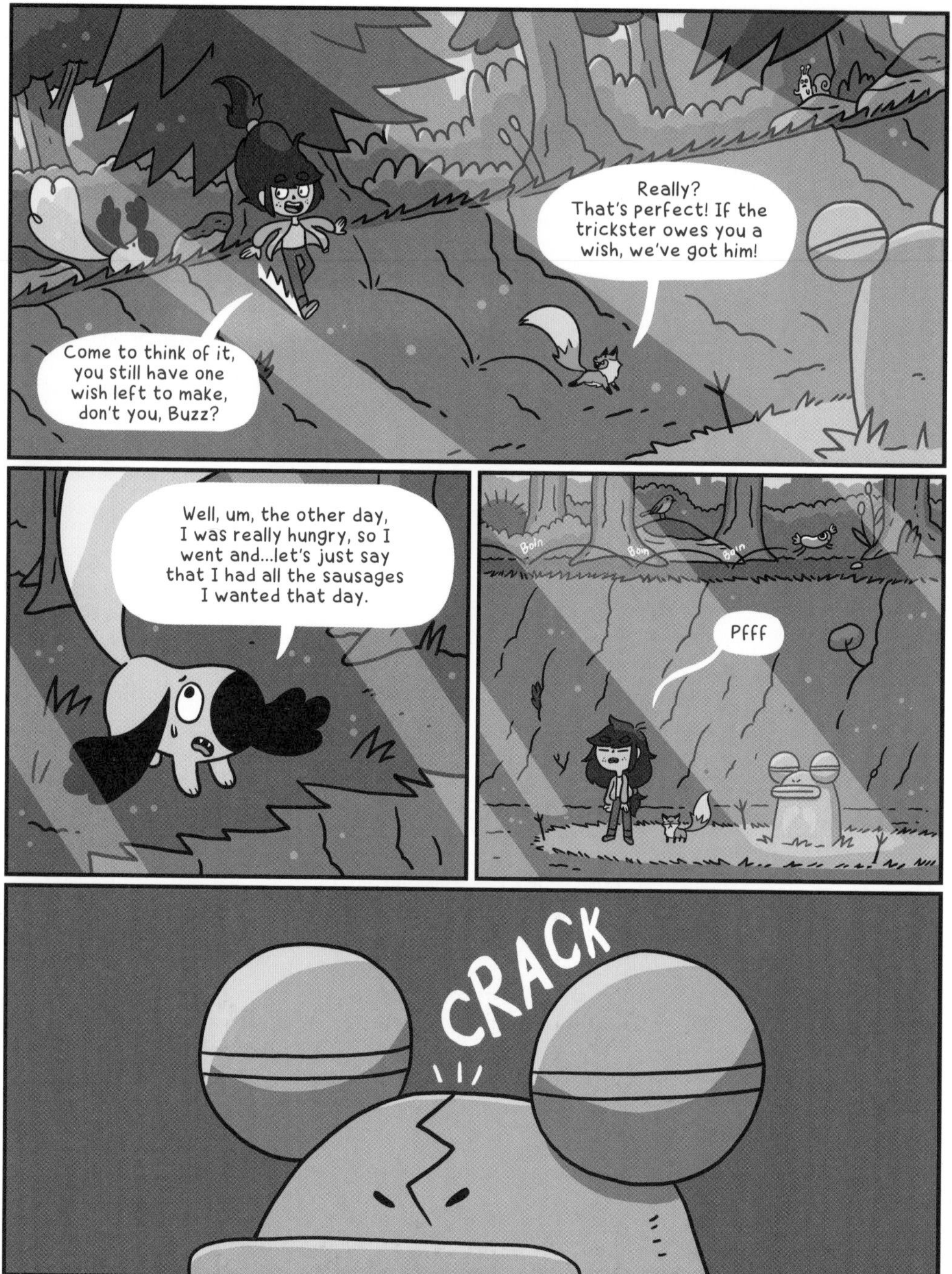
Come to think of it, you still have one wish left to make, don't you, Buzz?
Really? That's perfect! If the trickster owes you a wish, we've got him!
Well, um, the other day, I was really hungry, so I went and...let's just say that I had all the sausages I wanted that day.
Boin
Boin
Boin
Pfff
CRACK

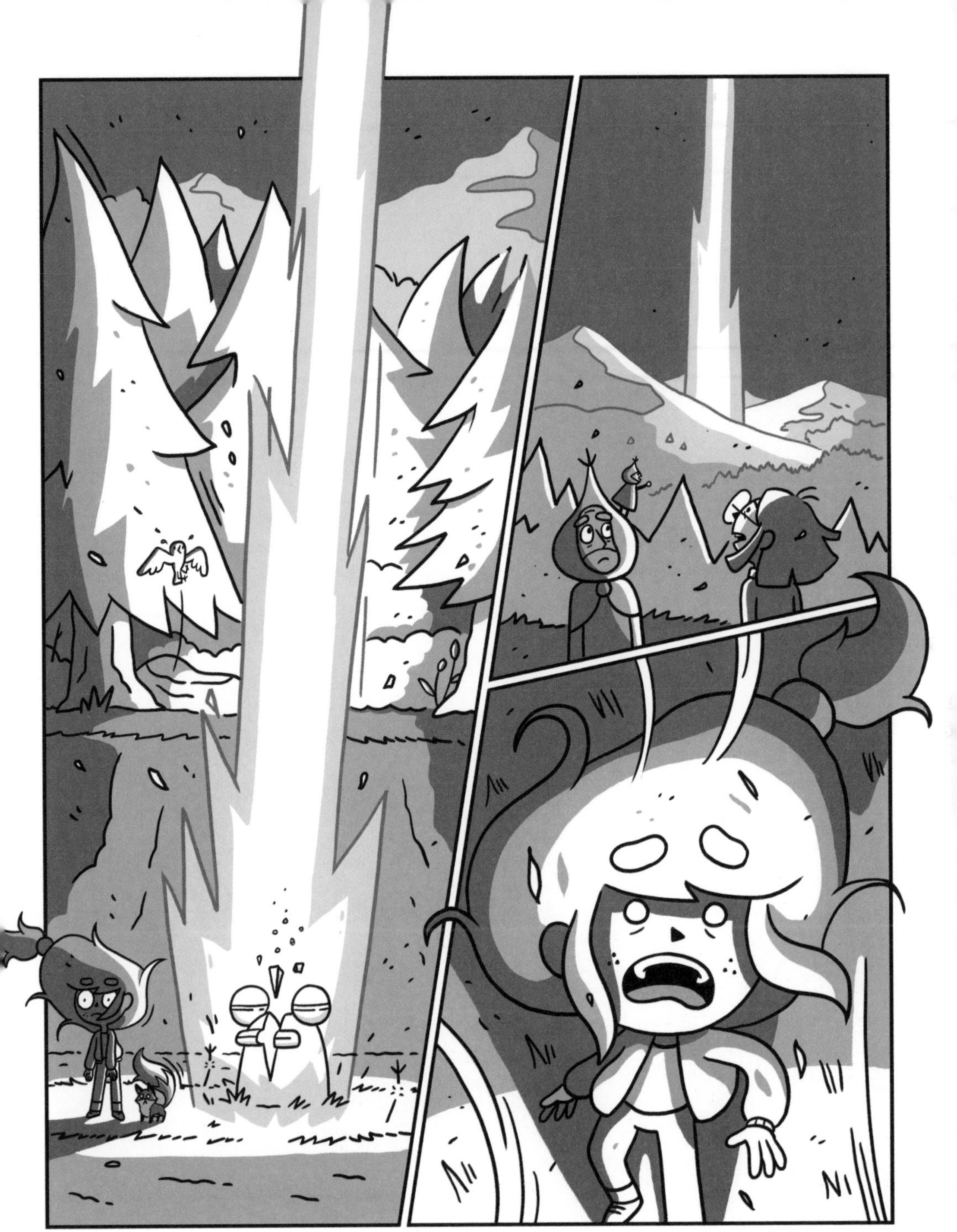

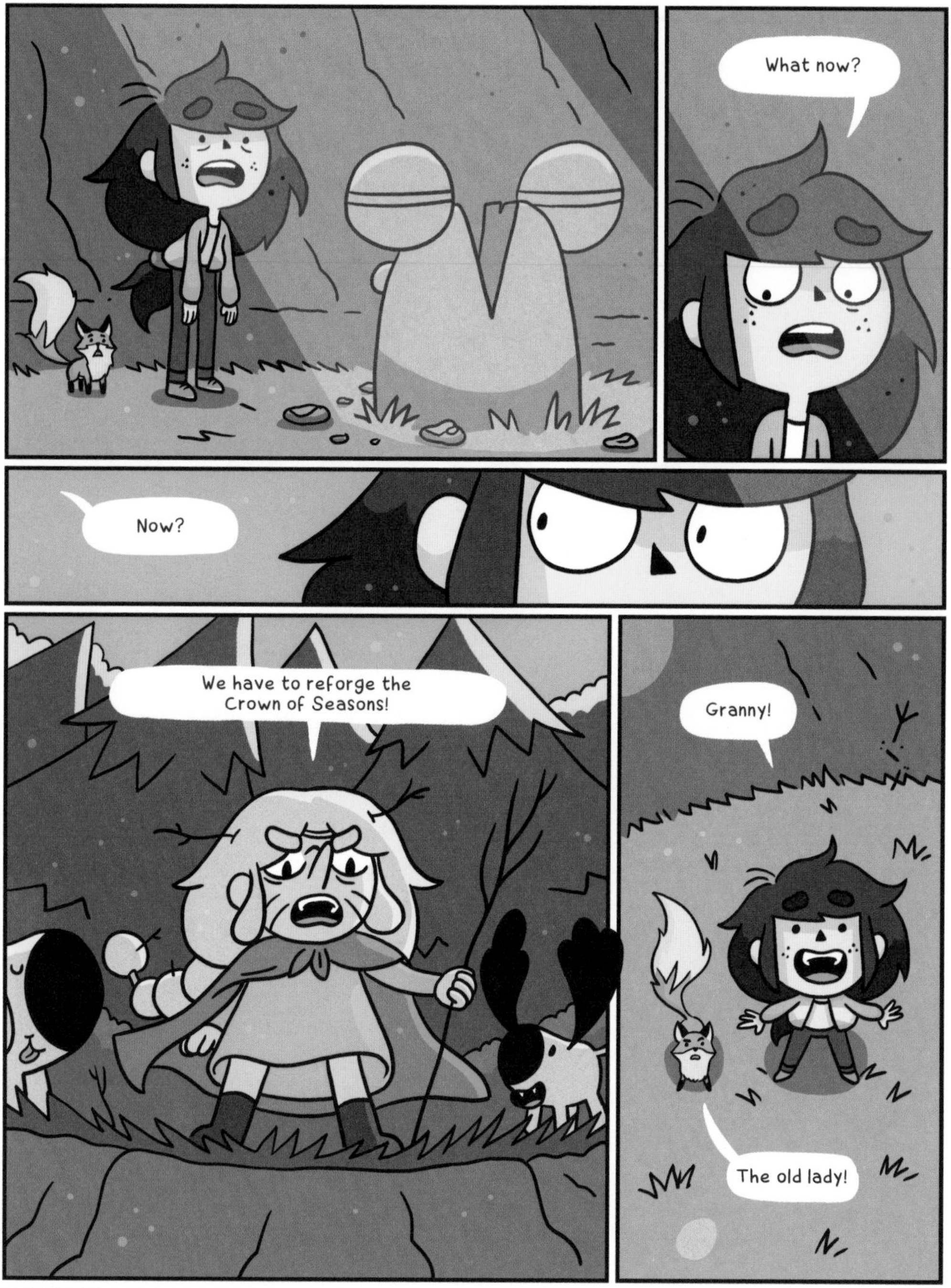
What now?
Now?
We have to reforge the Crown of Seasons!
Granny!
The old lady!

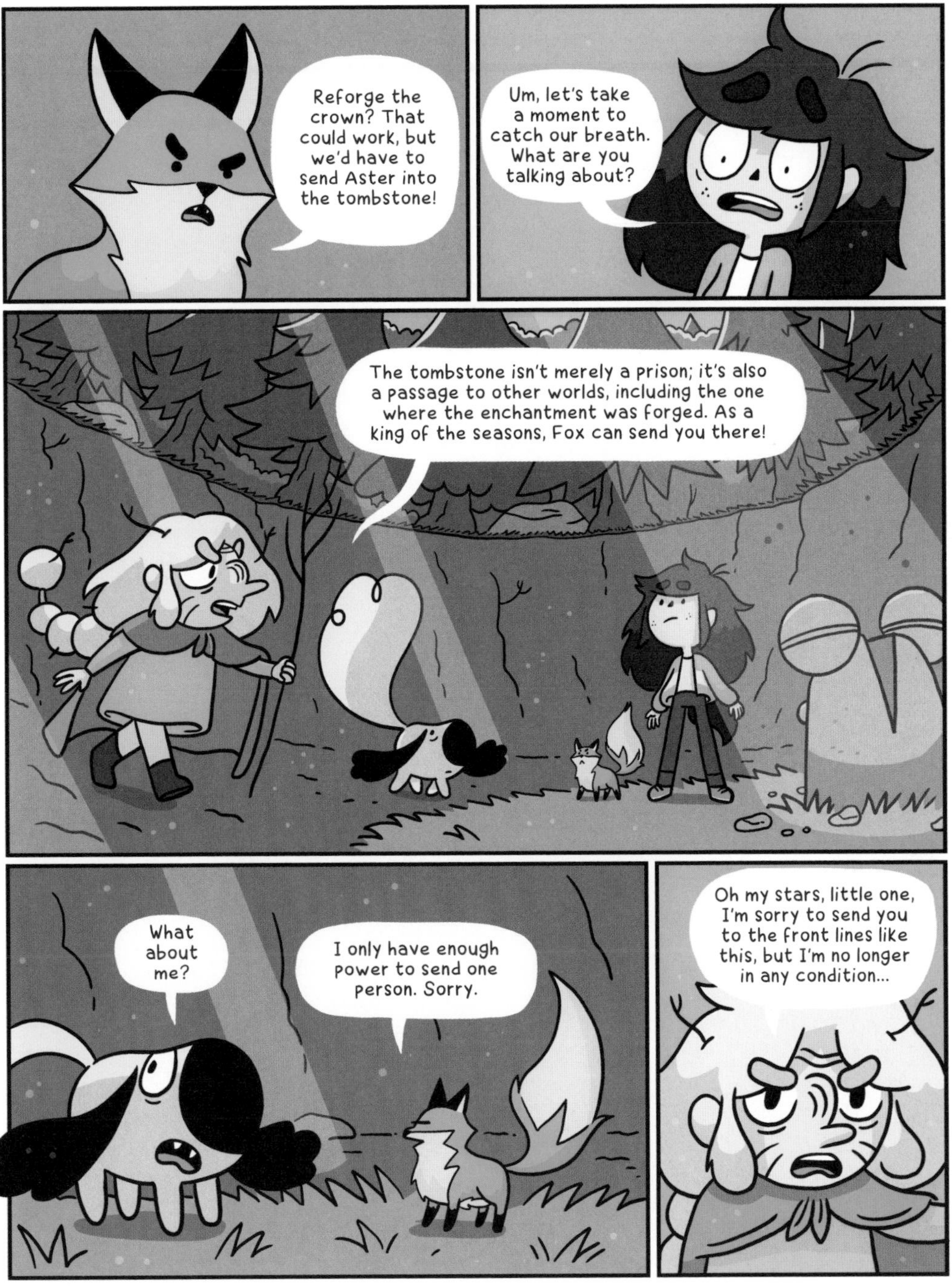
Reforge the crown? That could work, but we'd have to send Aster into the tombstone!
Um, let's take a moment to catch our breath. What are you talking about?
The tombstone isn't merely a prison; it's also a passage to other worlds, including the one where the enchantment was forged. As a king of the seasons, Fox can send you there!
What about me?
I only have enough power to send one person. Sorry.
Oh my stars, little one, I'm sorry to send you to the front lines like this, but I'm no longer in any condition...

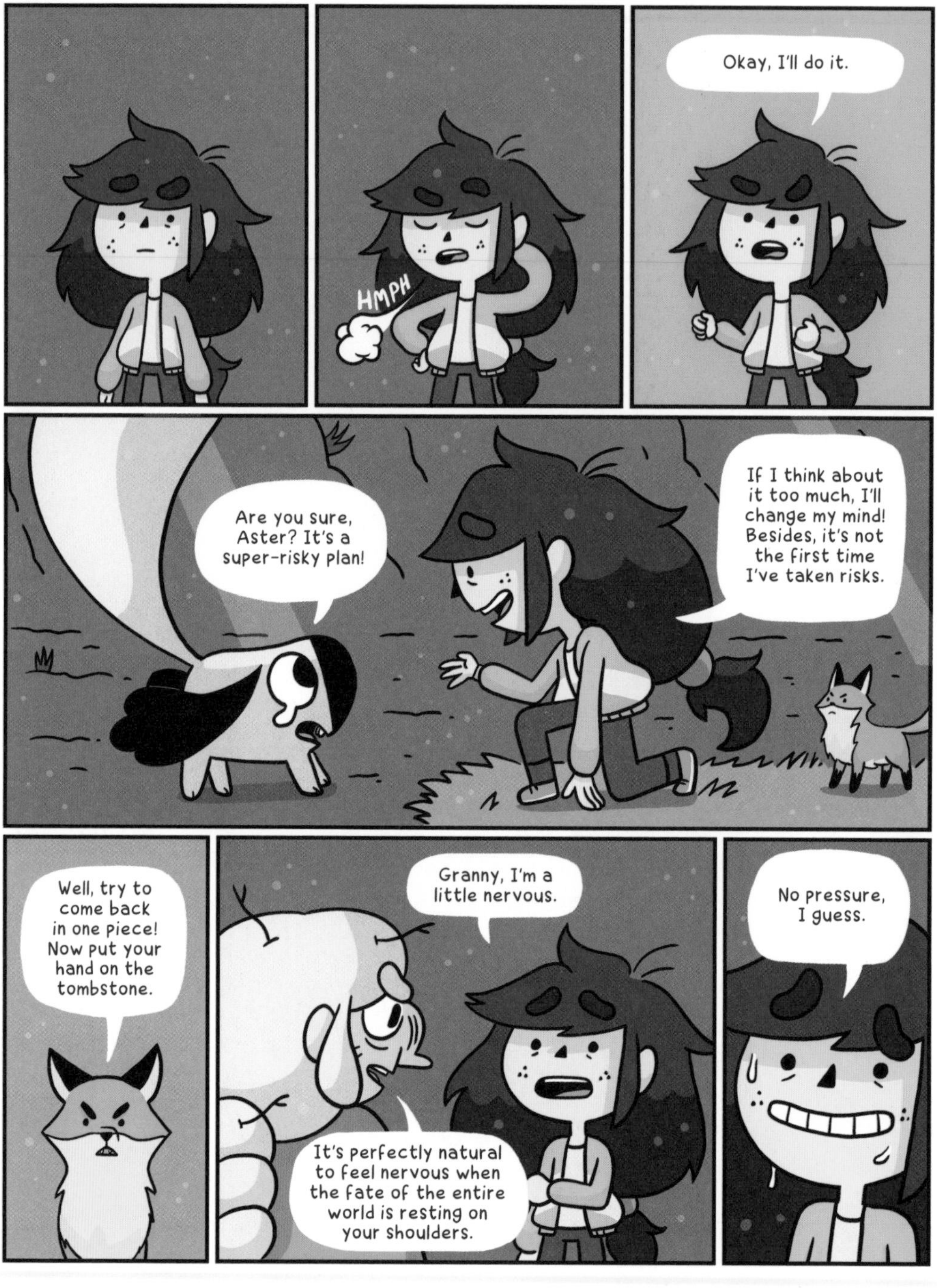

Okay, I'll do it.
HMPH
Are you sure, Aster? It's a super-risky plan!
If I think about it too much, I'll change my mind! Besides, it's not the first time I've taken risks.
Well, try to come back in one piece! Now put your hand on the tombstone.
Granny, I'm a little nervous.
It's perfectly natural to feel nervous when the fate of the entire world is resting on your shoulders.
No pressure, I guess.

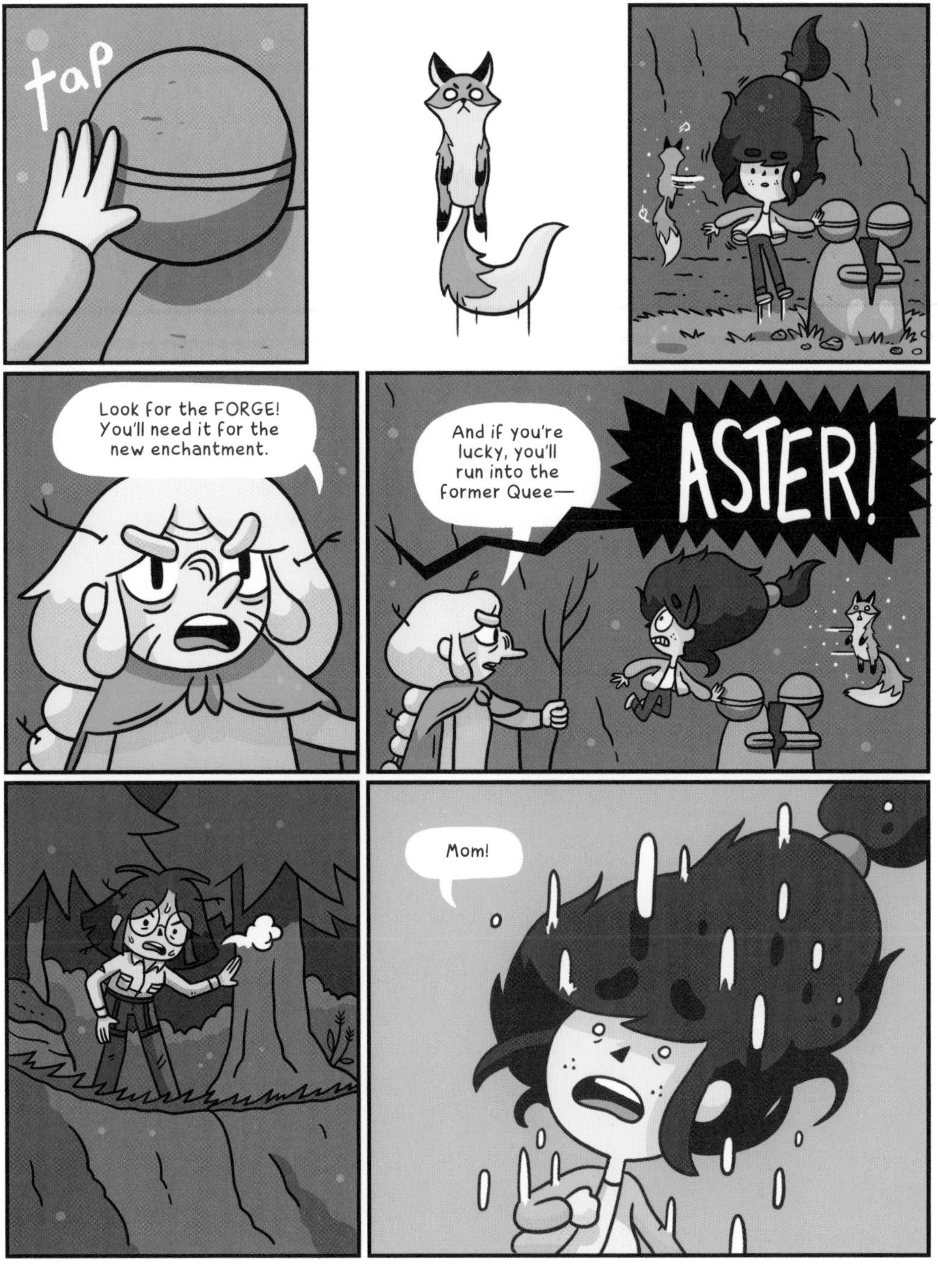
tap
Look for the FORGE! You'll need it for the new enchantment.
And if you're lucky, you'll run into the former Quee—
ASTER!
Mom!

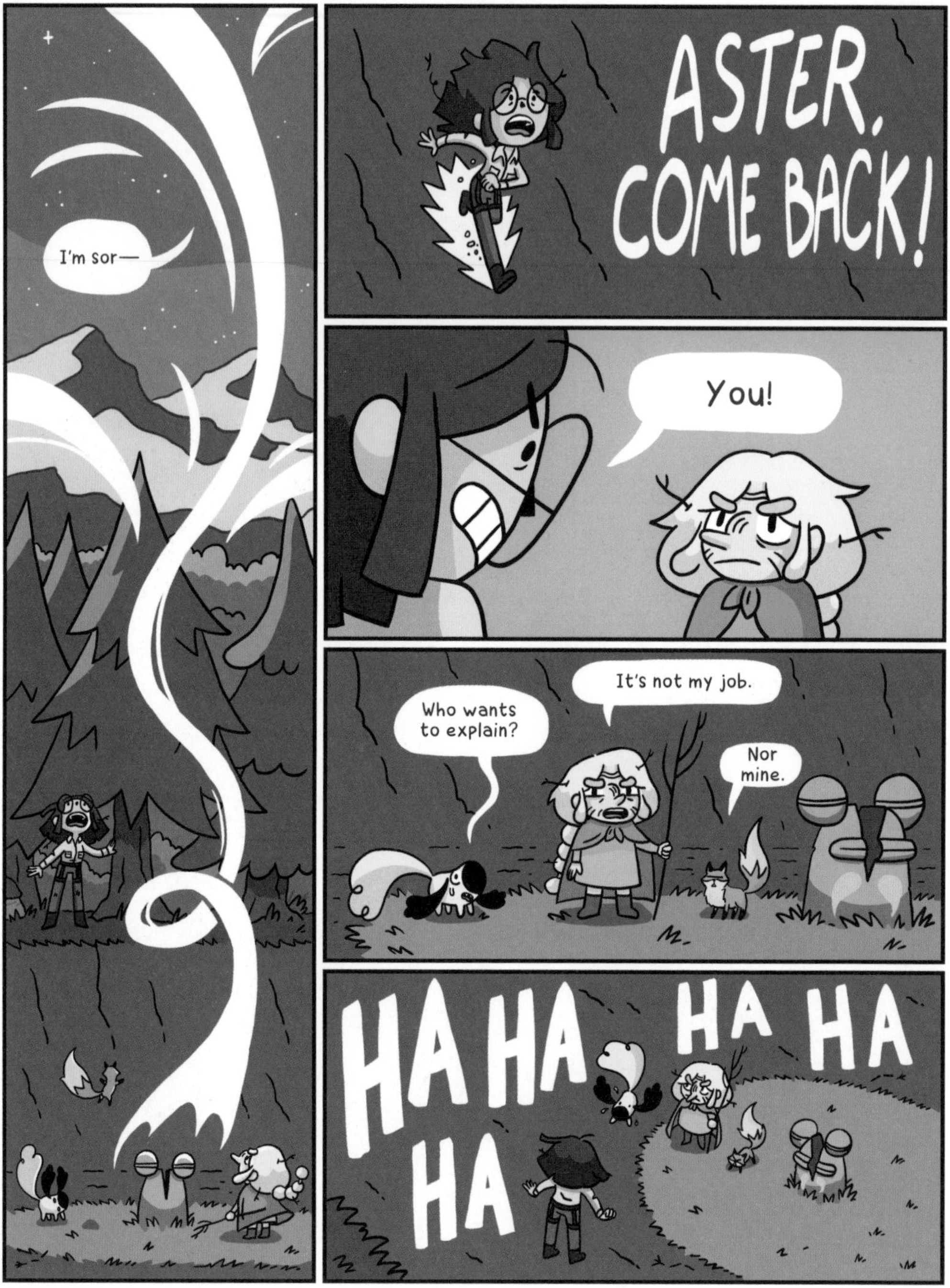
I'm sor—
ASTER, COME BACK!
You!
Who wants to explain?
It's not my job.
Nor mine.
HA HA HA HA HA HA

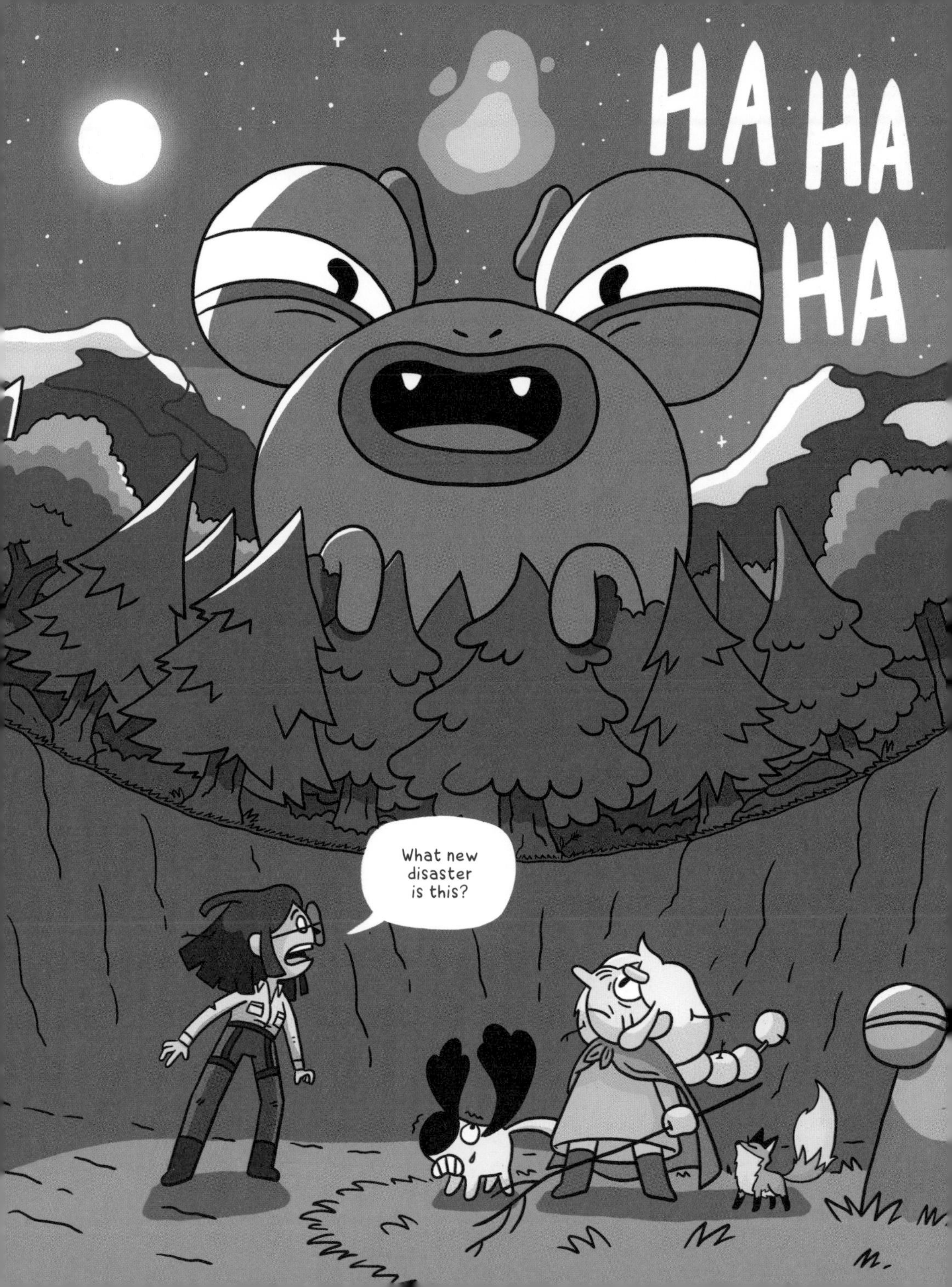

HA HA HA HA
What new disaster is this?

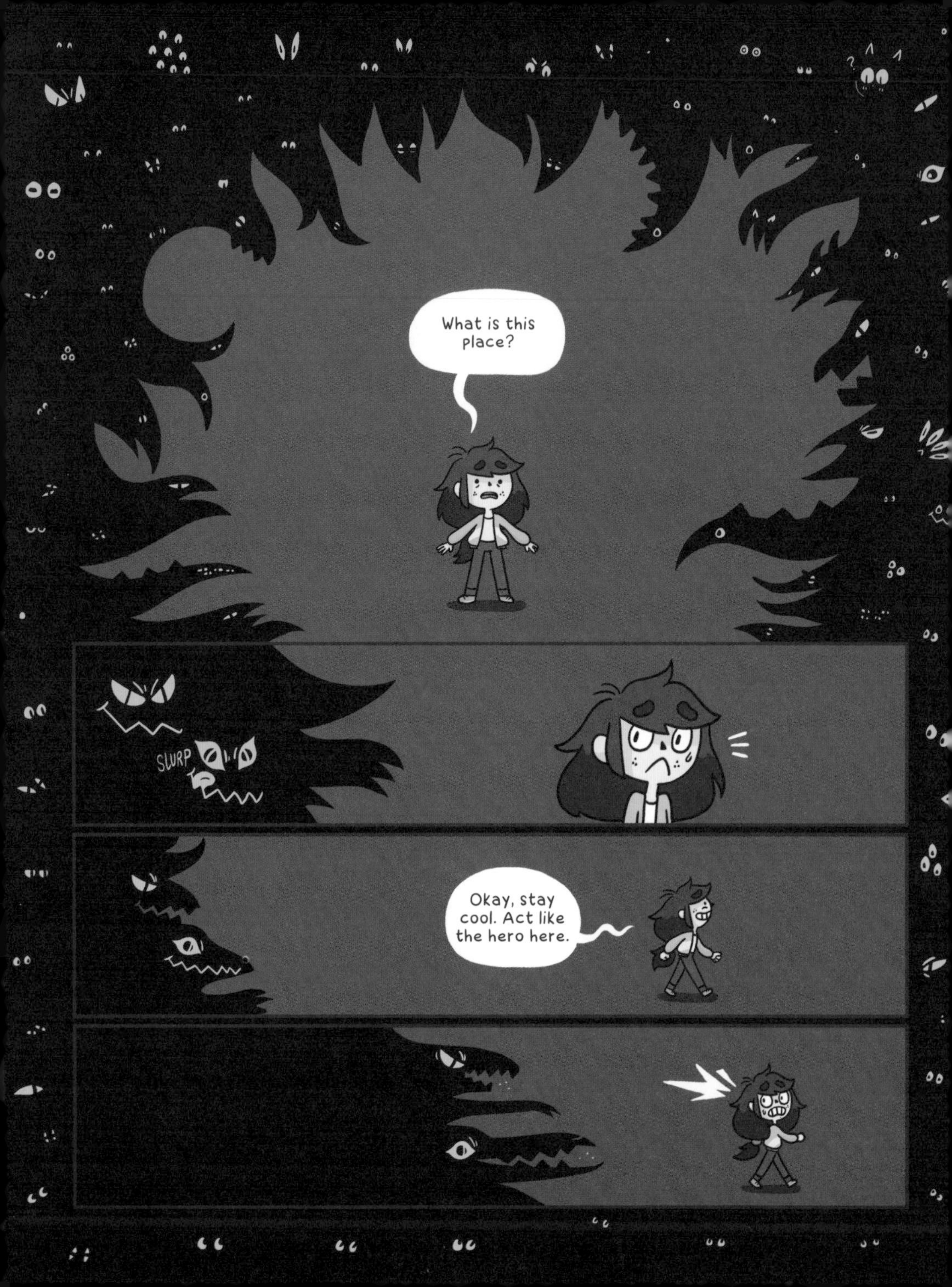
What is this place?
SLURP
Okay, stay cool. Act like the hero here.

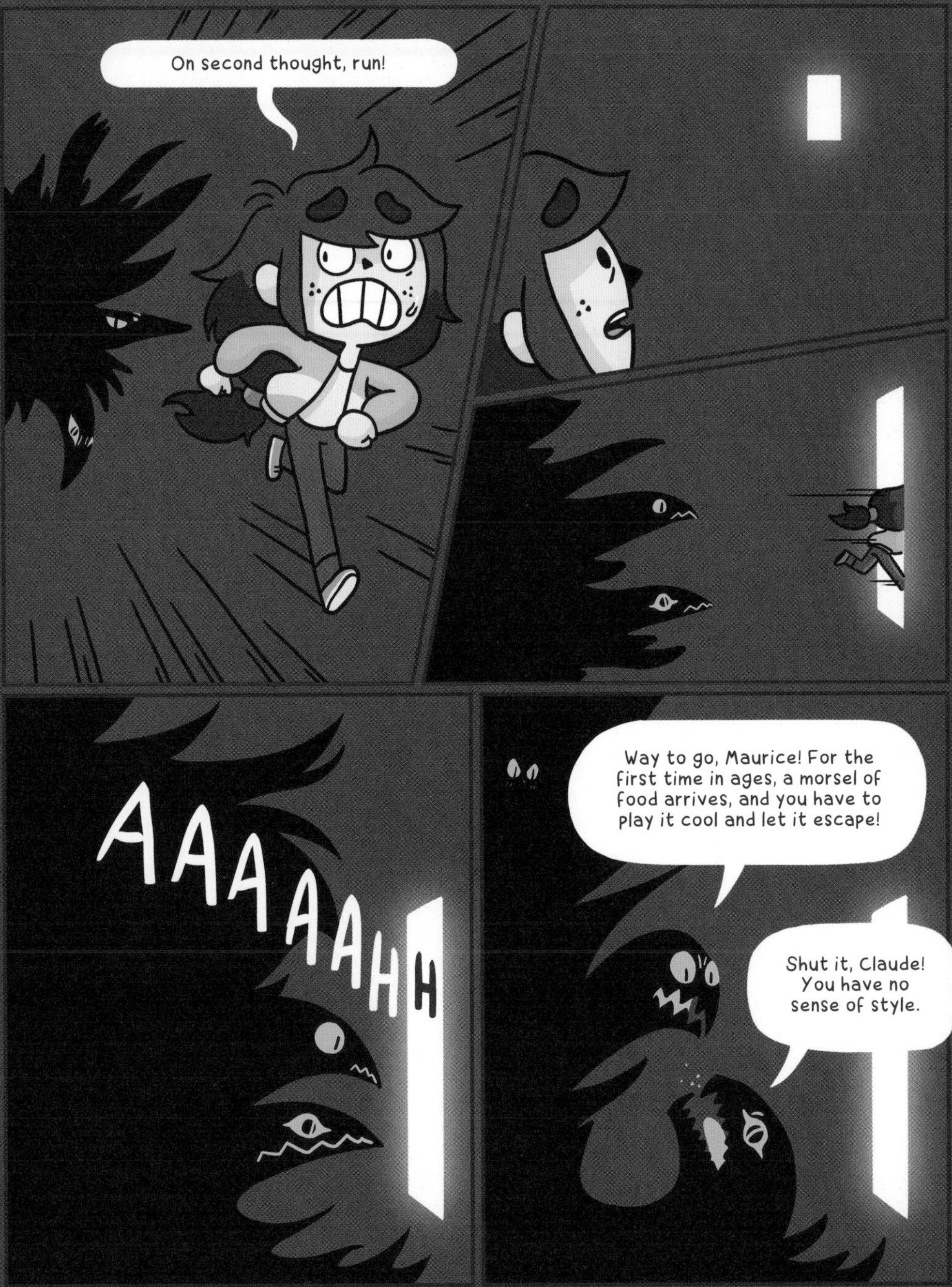

On second thought, run!
AAAAAAHH
Way to go, Maurice! For the first time in ages, a morsel of food arrives, and you have to play it cool and let it escape!
Shut it, Claude! You have no sense of style.

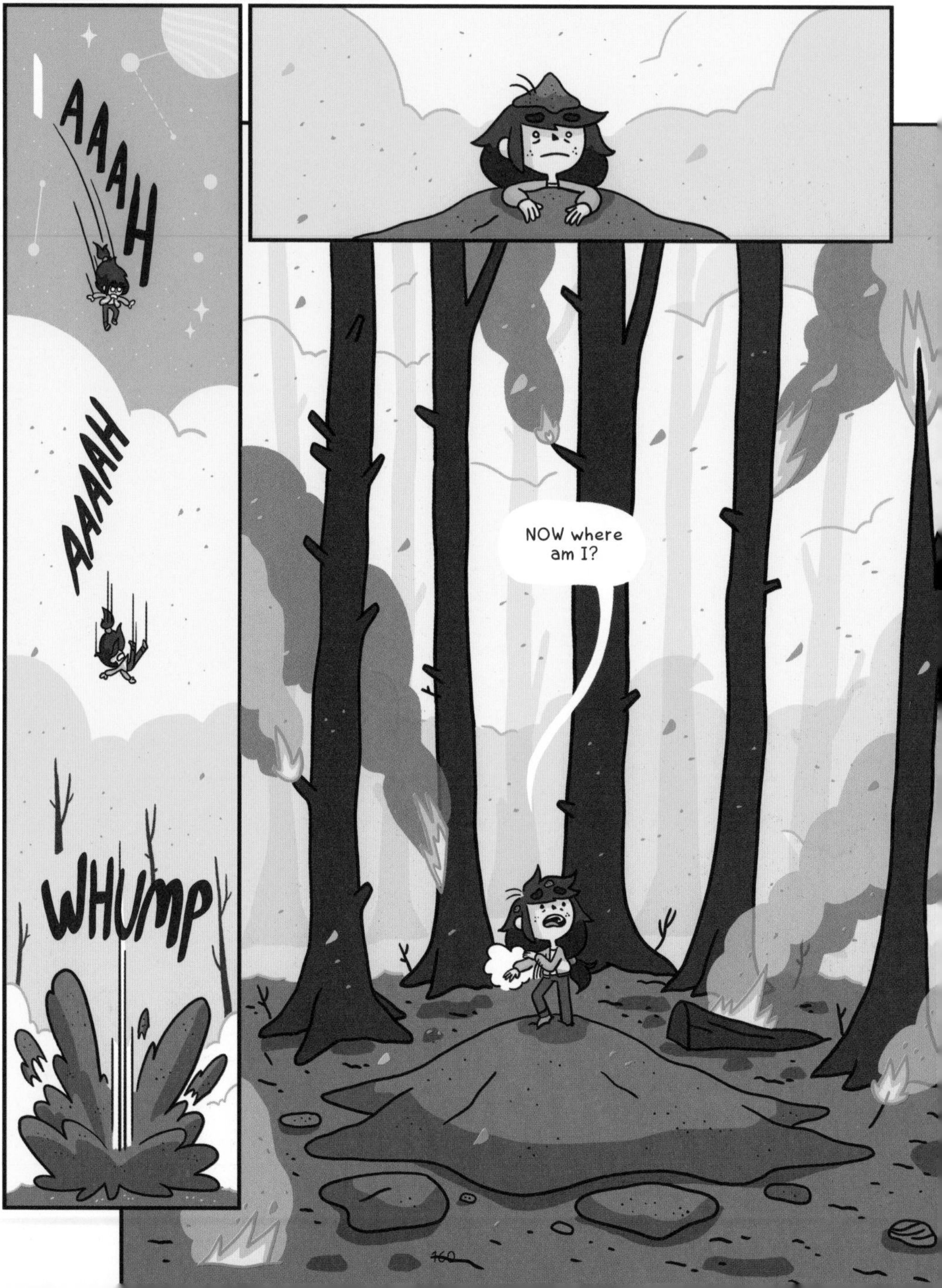
AAAAH
AAAAH
WHUMP
NOW where am I?

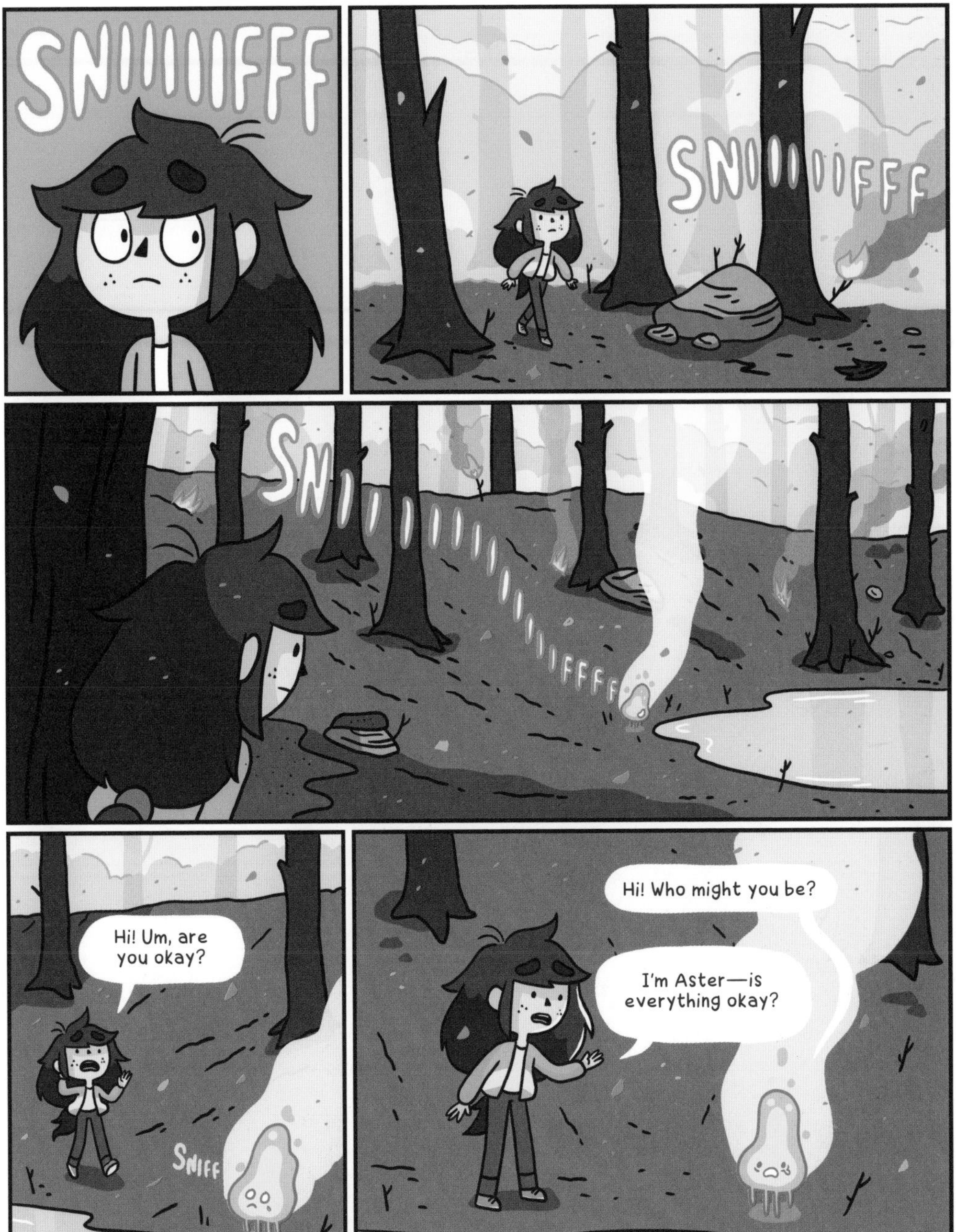
SNIIIIIFFF
SNIIIIIFFF
SNIIIIIIIIIIIIIFFFF
Hi! Um, are you okay?
SNIFF
Hi! Who might you be?
I'm Aster—is everything okay?

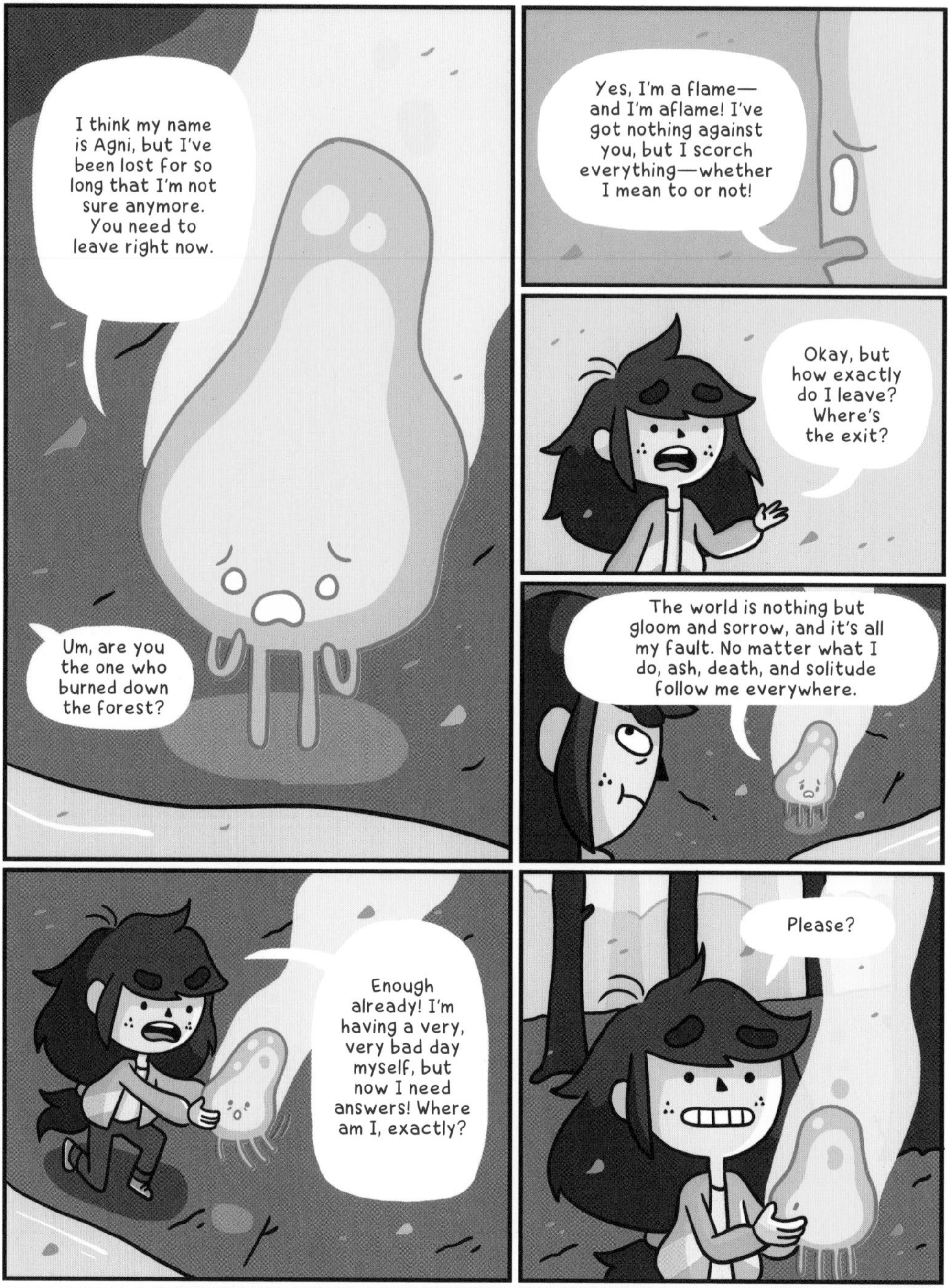
I think my name is Agni, but I've been lost for so long that I'm not sure anymore. You need to leave right now.
Um, are you the one who burned down the forest?
Yes, I'm a flame— and I'm aflame! I've got nothing against you, but I scorch everything—whether I mean to or not!
Okay, but how exactly do I leave? Where's the exit?
The world is nothing but gloom and sorrow, and it's all my fault. No matter what I do, ash, death, and solitude follow me everywhere.
Enough already! I'm having a very, very bad day myself, but now I need answers! Where am I, exactly?
Please?

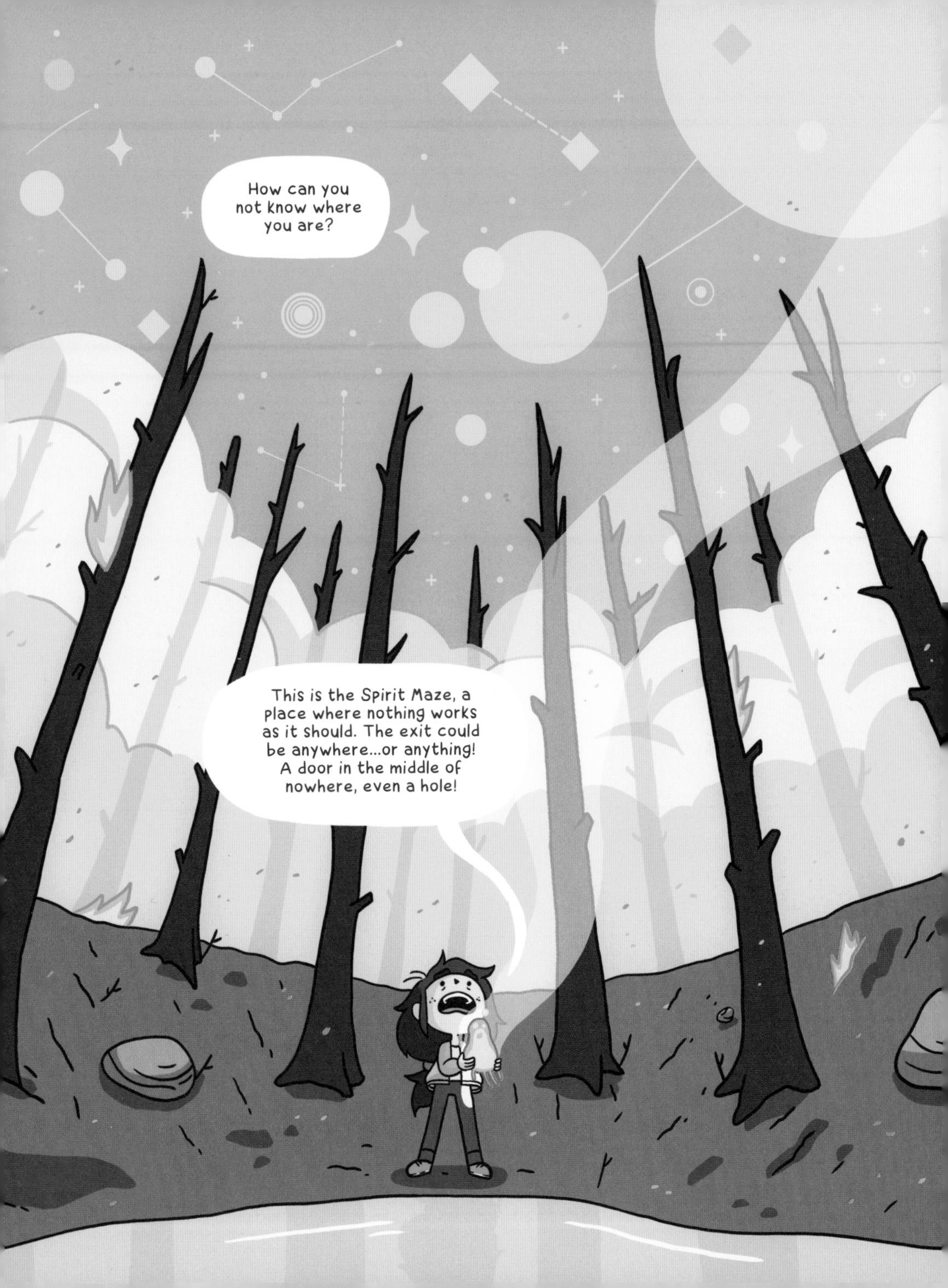
How can you not know where you are?
This is the Spirit Maze, a place where nothing works as it should. The exit could be anywhere...or anything! A door in the middle of nowhere, even a hole!

Hold on a moment!

...but at least it's a start! Now tell me, do you know of a forge around here somewhere?

We may be in the Spirit Mazethingy...

A forge? Wait, now that you mention it... But first, I need to know something...

Argh—what?

How is it that I haven't burned you?

AAAAAH

Tchııııııııı

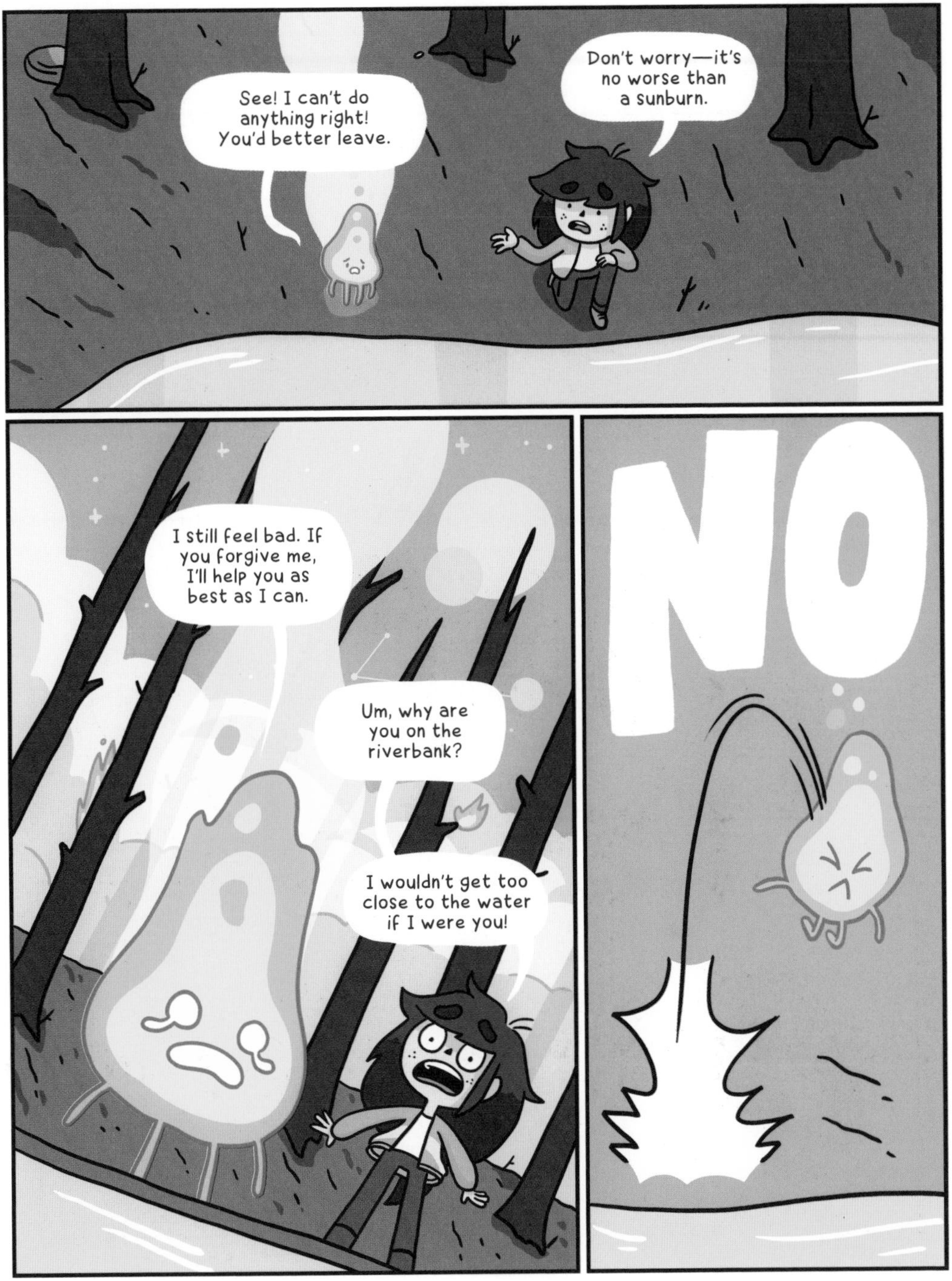
See! I can't do anything right! You'd better leave.
Don't worry—it's no worse than a sunburn.
I still feel bad. If you forgive me, I'll help you as best as I can.
Um, why are you on the riverbank?
I wouldn't get too close to the water if I were you!
NO

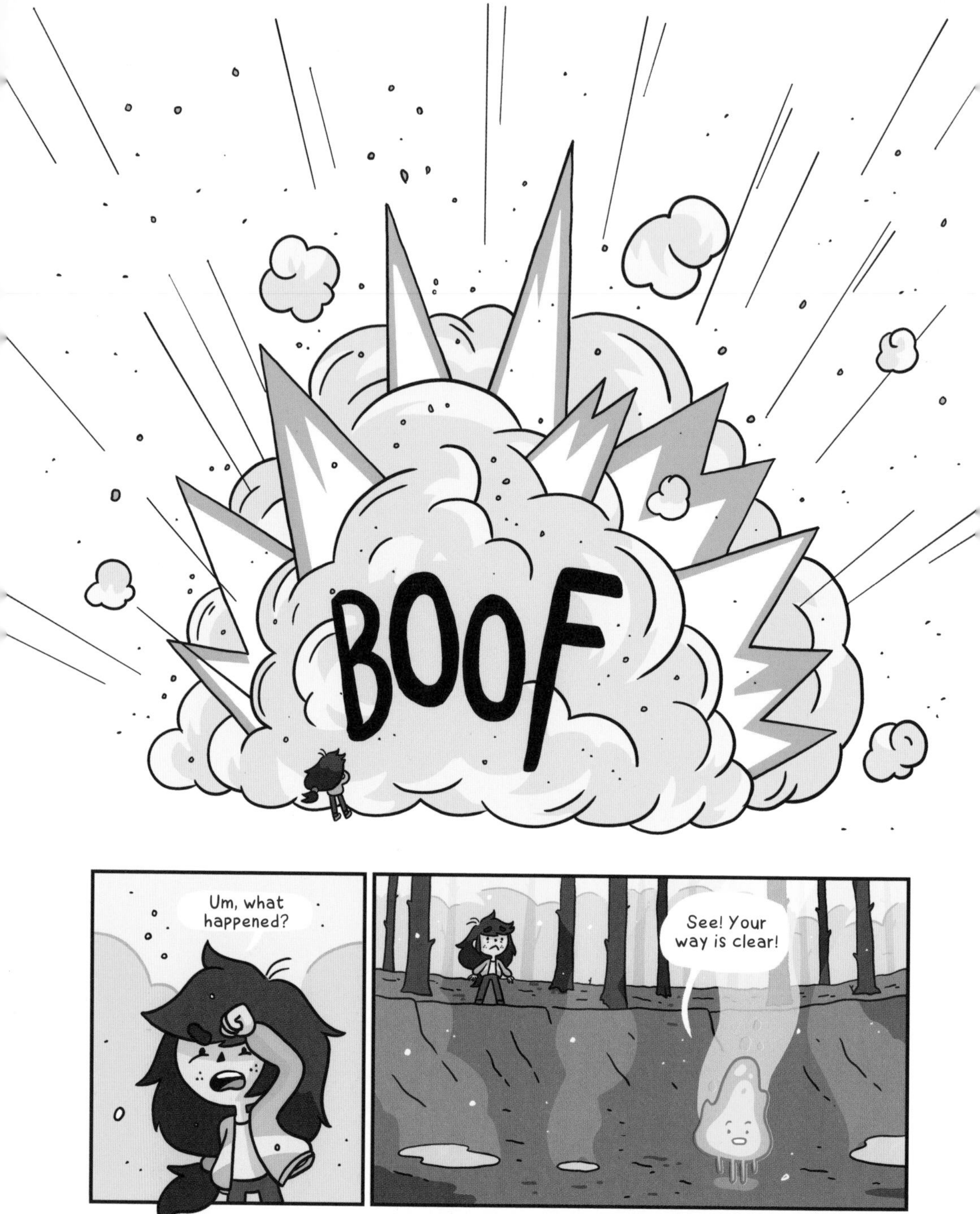
BOOF
Um, what happened?
See! Your way is clear!

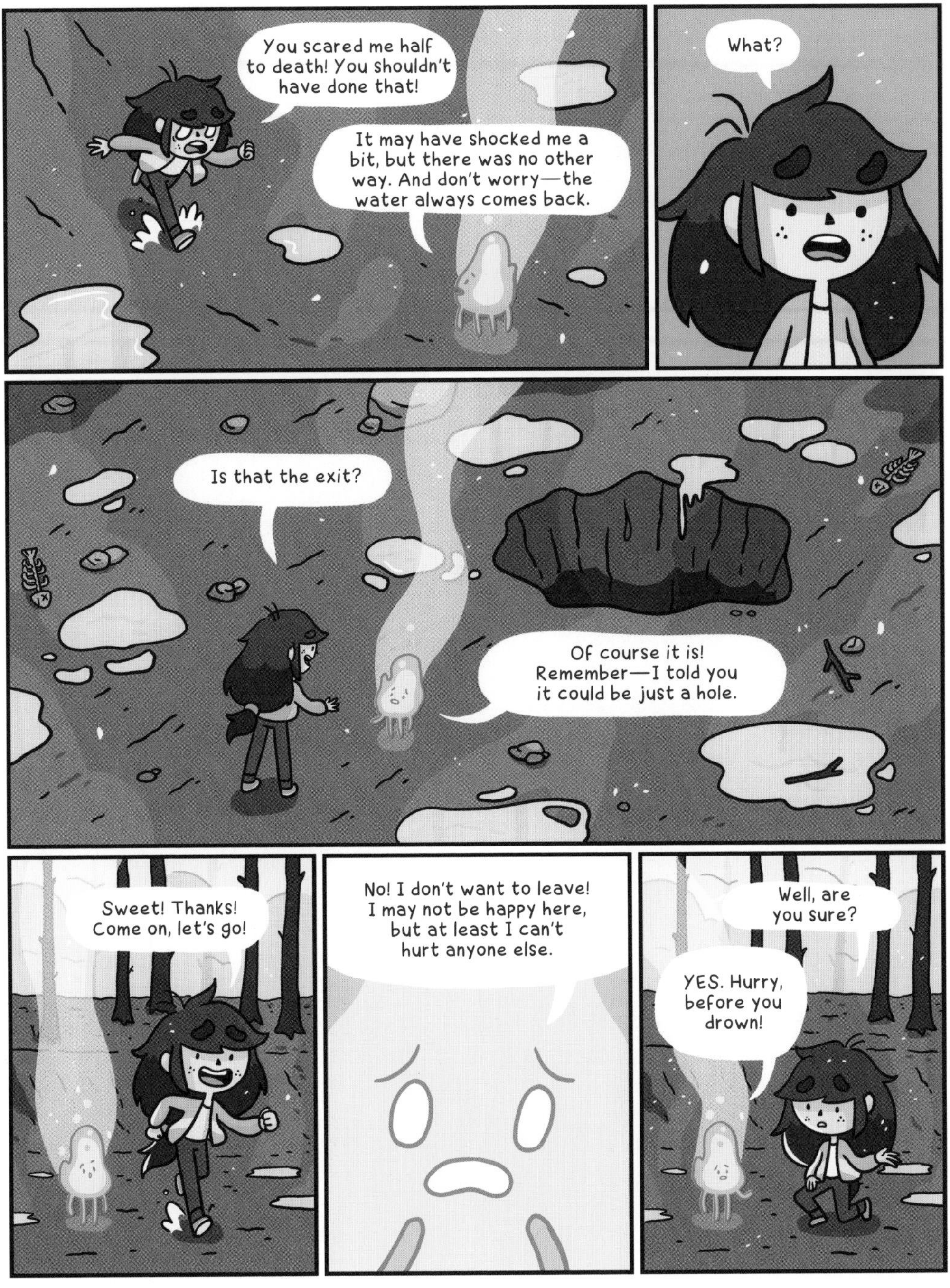
You scared me half to death! You shouldn't have done that!
It may have shocked me a bit, but there was no other way. And don't worry—the water always comes back.
What?
Is that the exit?
Of course it is! Remember—I told you it could be just a hole.
Sweet! Thanks! Come on, let's go!
No! I don't want to leave! I may not be happy here, but at least I can't hurt anyone else.
Well, are you sure?
YES. Hurry, before you drown!

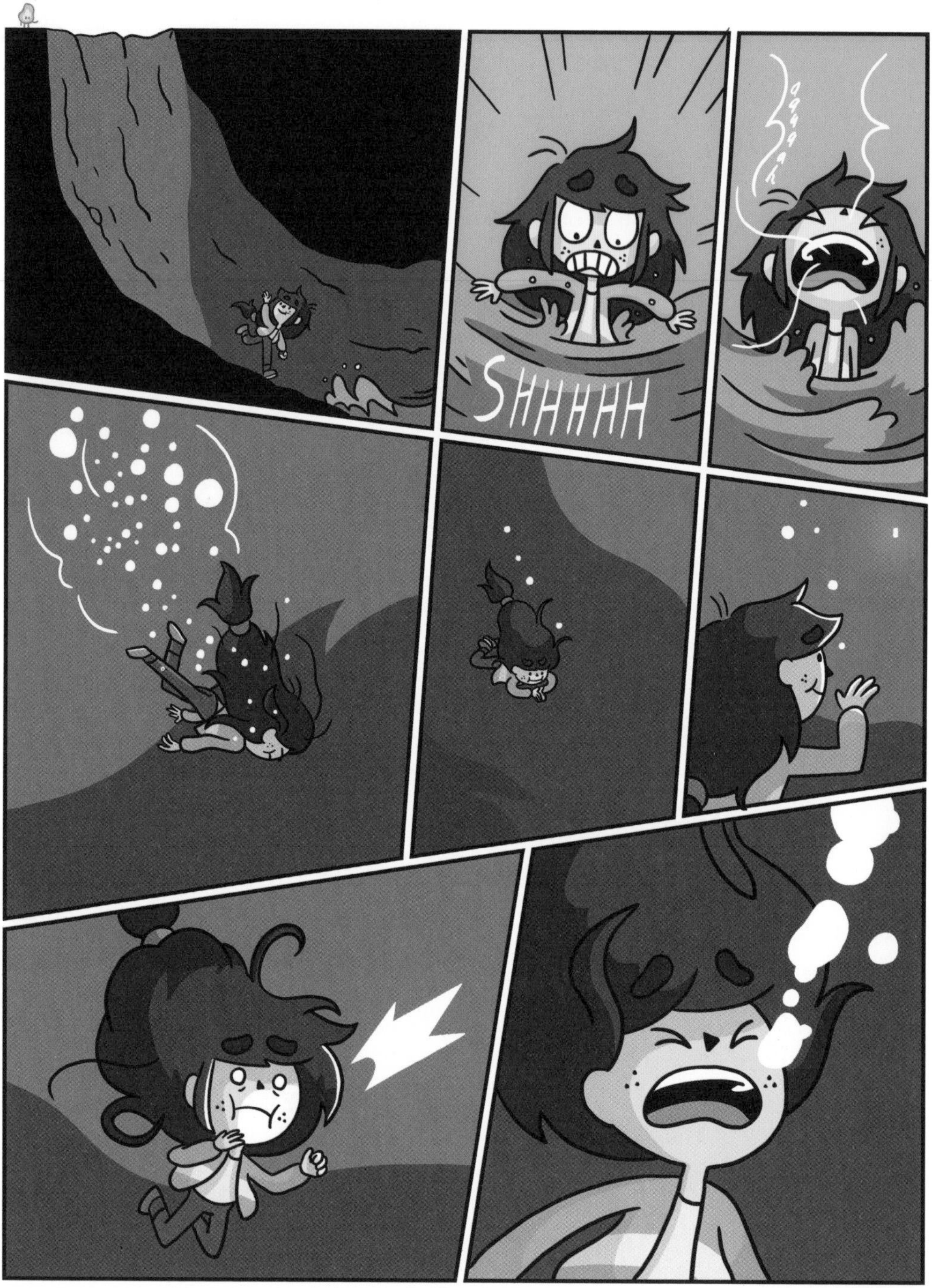
SHHHHH
aaaaaah

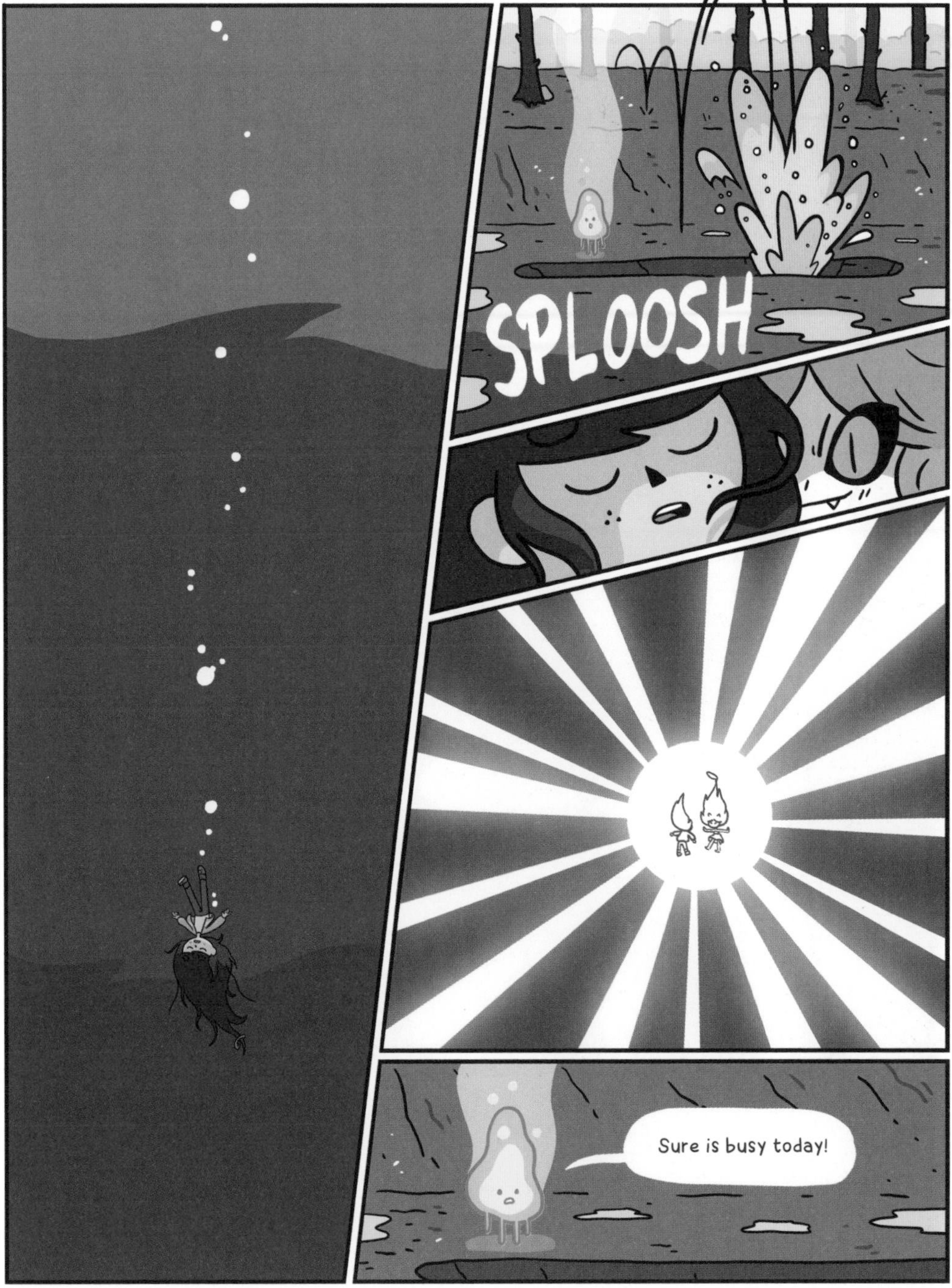
SPLOOSH
Sure is busy today!

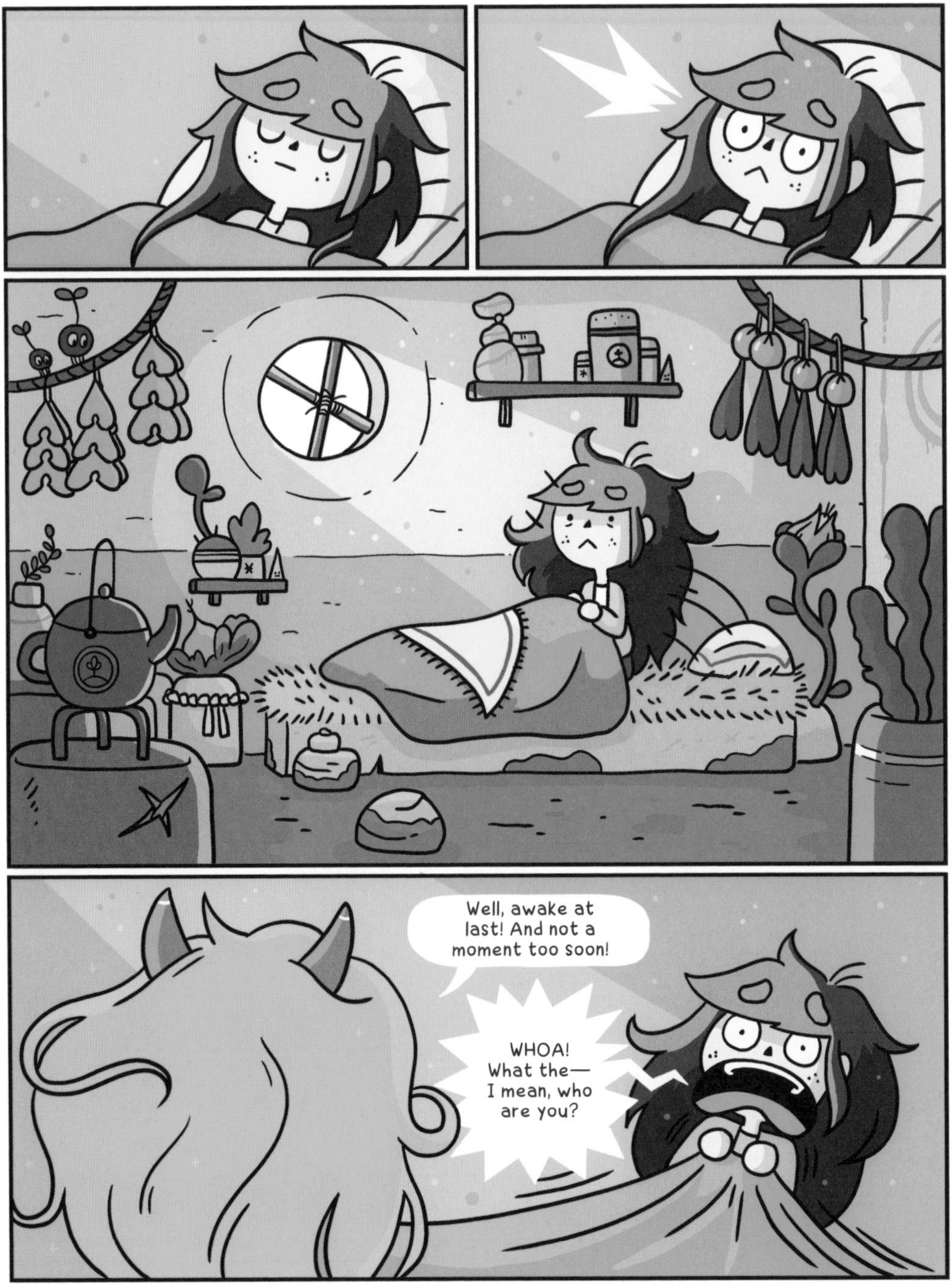
Well, awake at last! And not a moment too soon!
WHOA! What the— I mean, who are you?

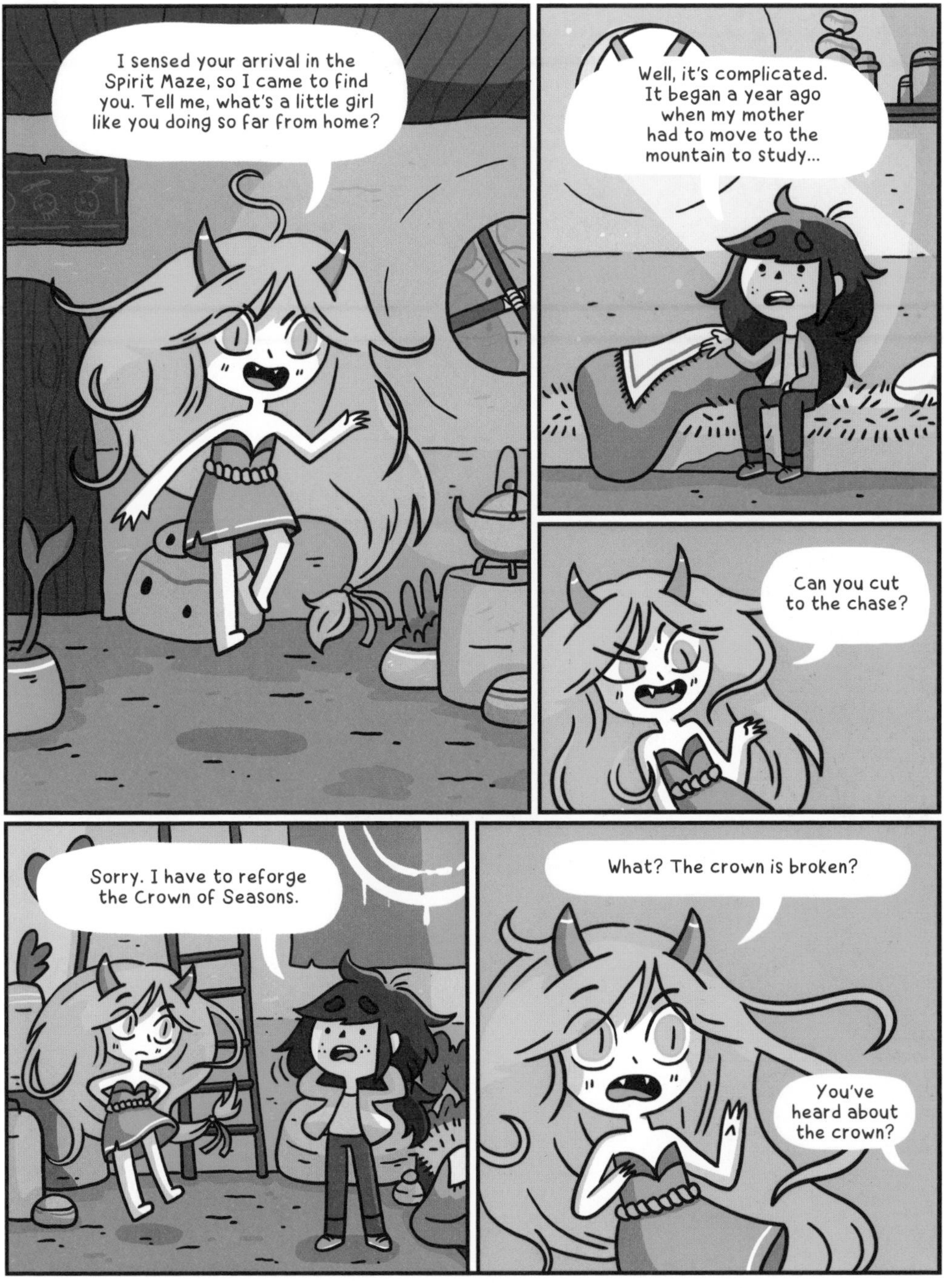
I sensed your arrival in the Spirit Maze, so I came to find you. Tell me, what's a little girl like you doing so far from home?
Well, it's complicated. It began a year ago when my mother had to move to the mountain to study...
Can you cut to the chase?
Sorry. I have to reforge the Crown of Seasons.
What? The crown is broken?
You've heard about the crown?

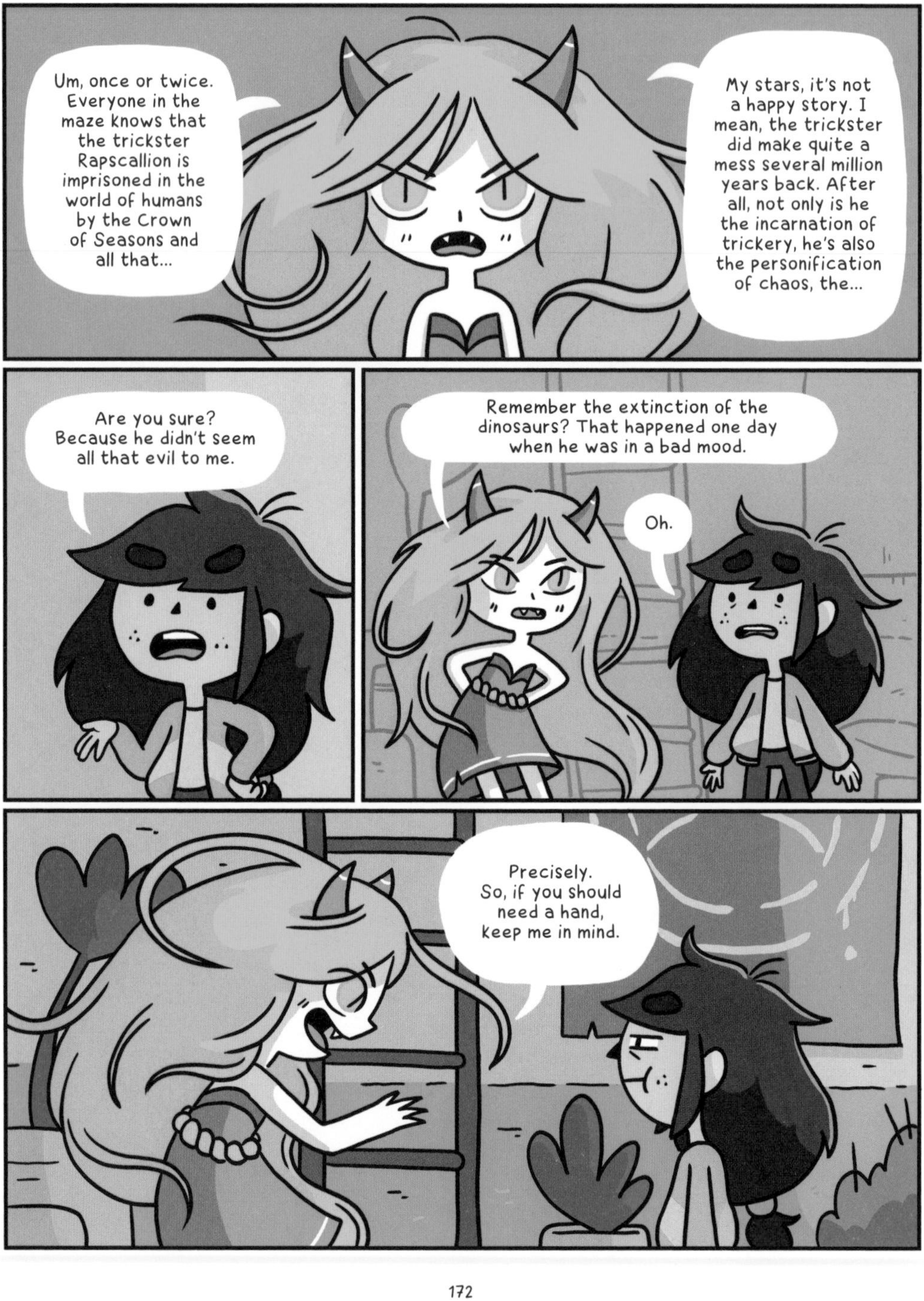
Um, once or twice. Everyone in the maze knows that the trickster Rapscallion is imprisoned in the world of humans by the Crown of Seasons and all that...
My stars, it's not a happy story. I mean, the trickster did make quite a mess several million years back. After all, not only is he the incarnation of trickery, he's also the personification of chaos, the...
Are you sure? Because he didn't seem all that evil to me.
Remember the extinction of the dinosaurs? That happened one day when he was in a bad mood.
Oh.
Precisely. So, if you should need a hand, keep me in mind.

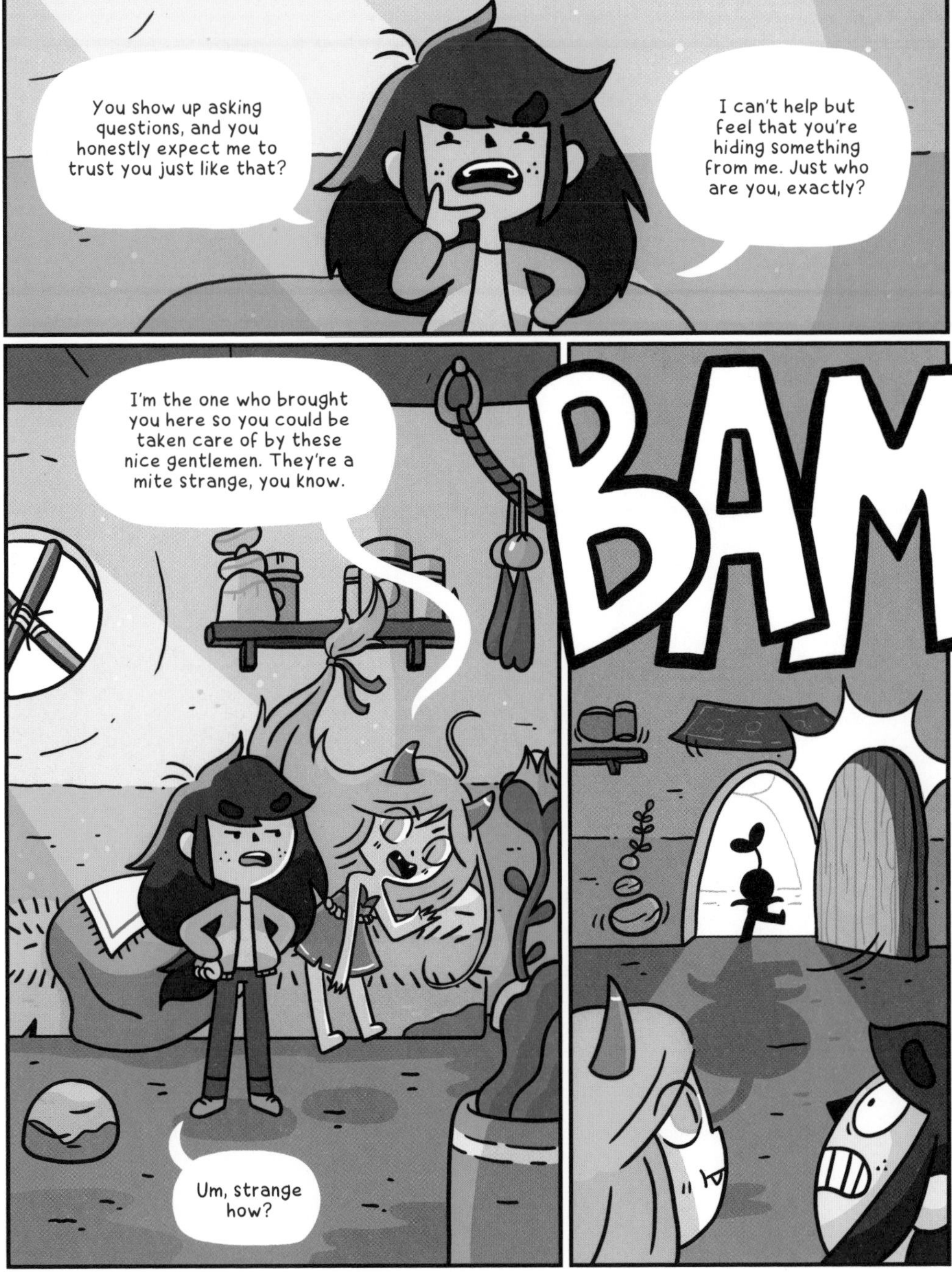
You show up asking questions, and you honestly expect me to trust you just like that?
I can't help but feel that you're hiding something from me. Just who are you, exactly?
I'm the one who brought you here so you could be taken care of by these nice gentlemen. They're a mite strange, you know.
Um, strange how?
BAM

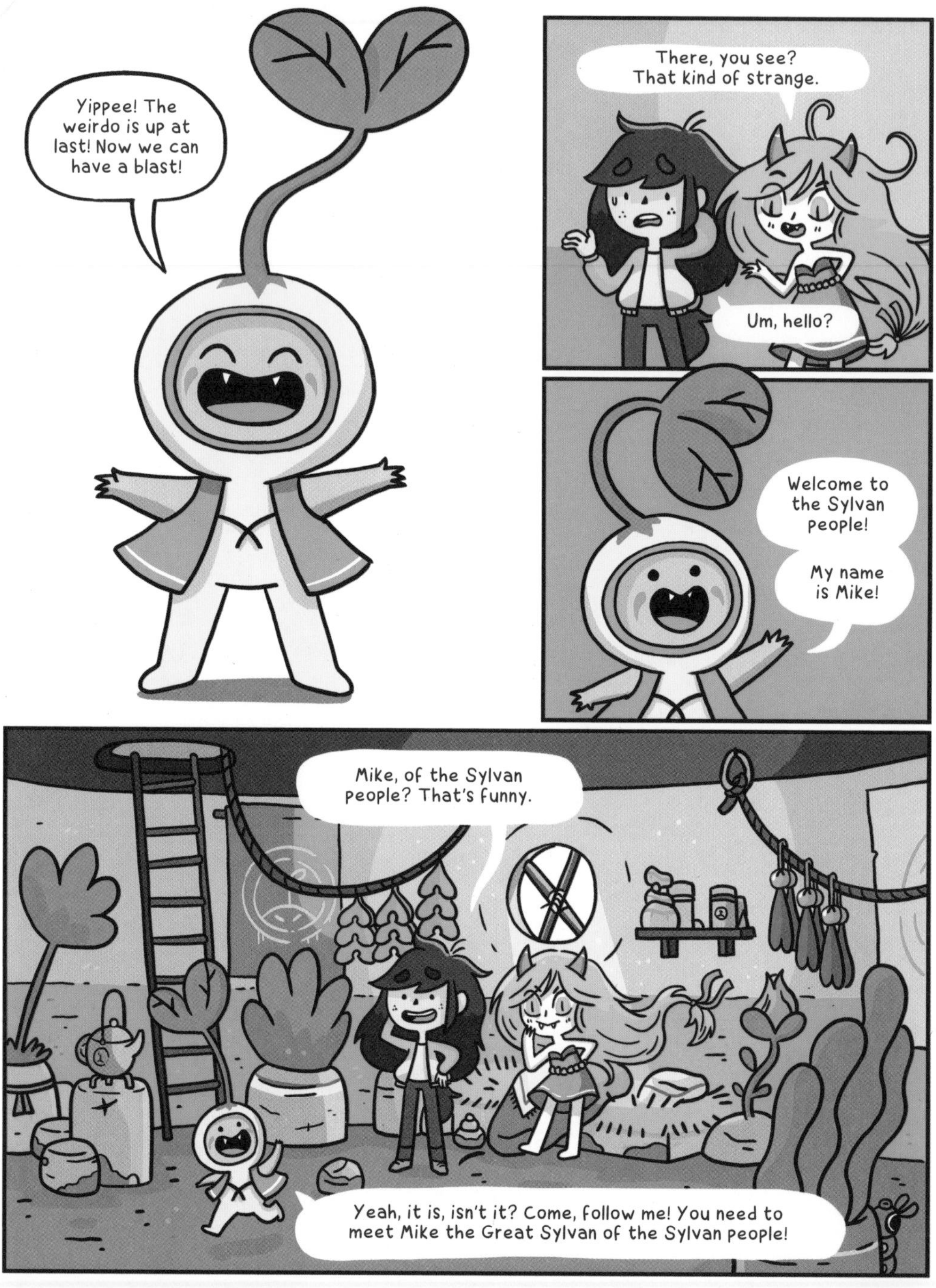
Yippee! The weirdo is up at last! Now we can have a blast!
There, you see? That kind of strange.
Um, hello?
Welcome to the Sylvan people!
My name is Mike!
Mike, of the Sylvan people? That's funny.
Yeah, it is, isn't it? Come, follow me! You need to meet Mike the Great Sylvan of the Sylvan people!

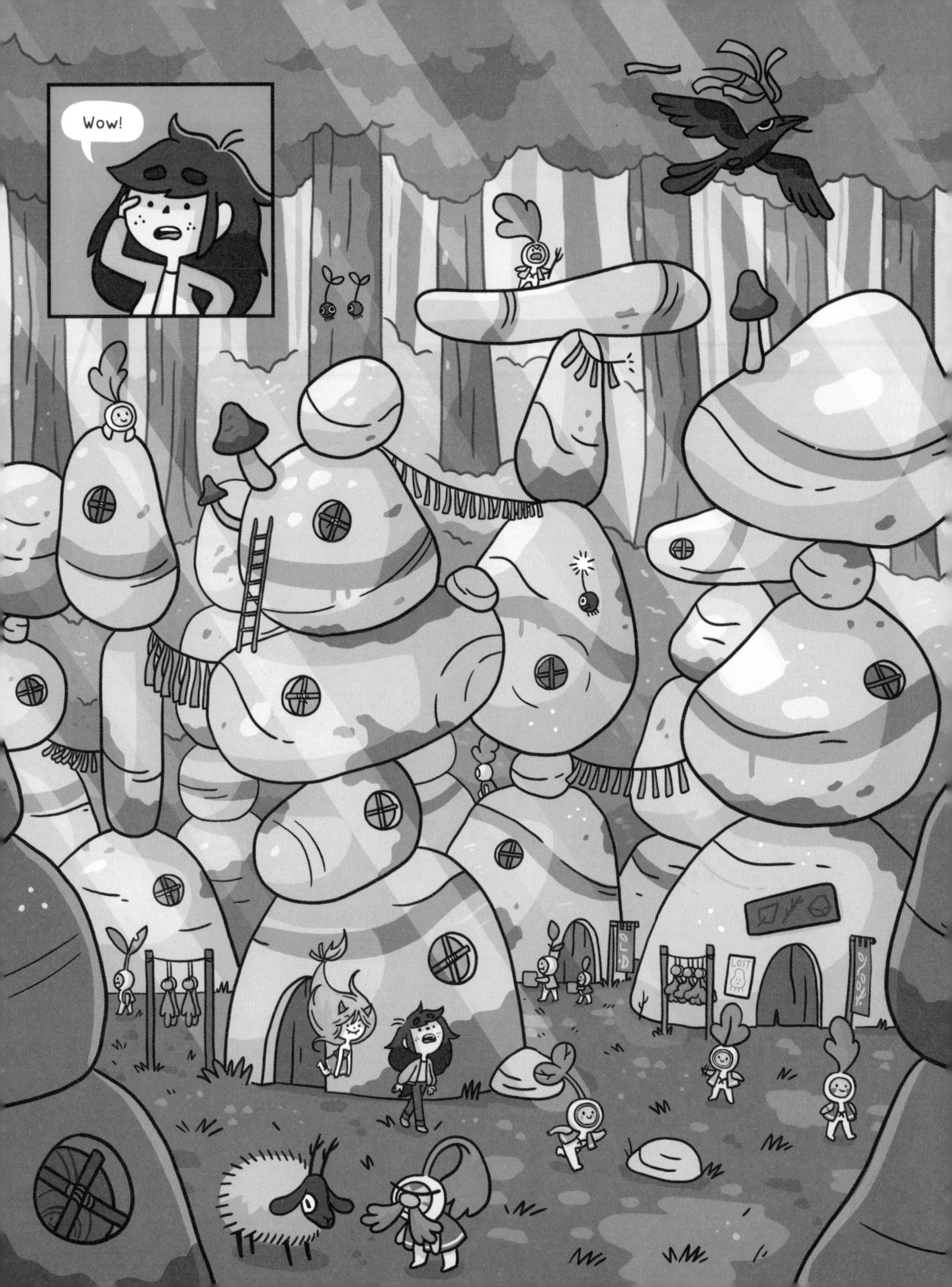
Wow!
LOST

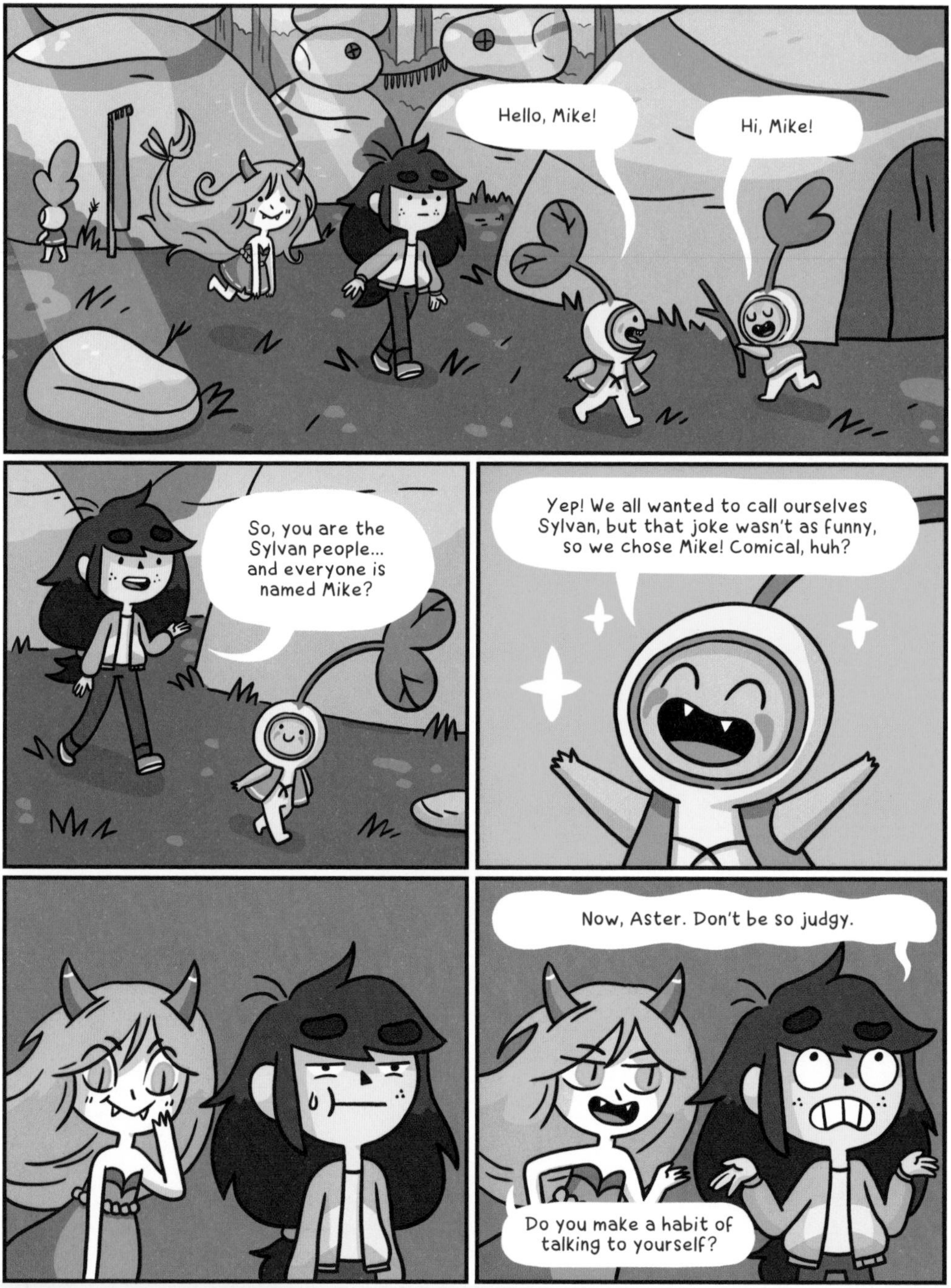
Hello, Mike!
Hi, Mike!
So, you are the Sylvan people... and everyone is named Mike?
Yep! We all wanted to call ourselves Sylvan, but that joke wasn't as funny, so we chose Mike! Comical, huh?
Now, Aster. Don't be so judgy.
Do you make a habit of talking to yourself?

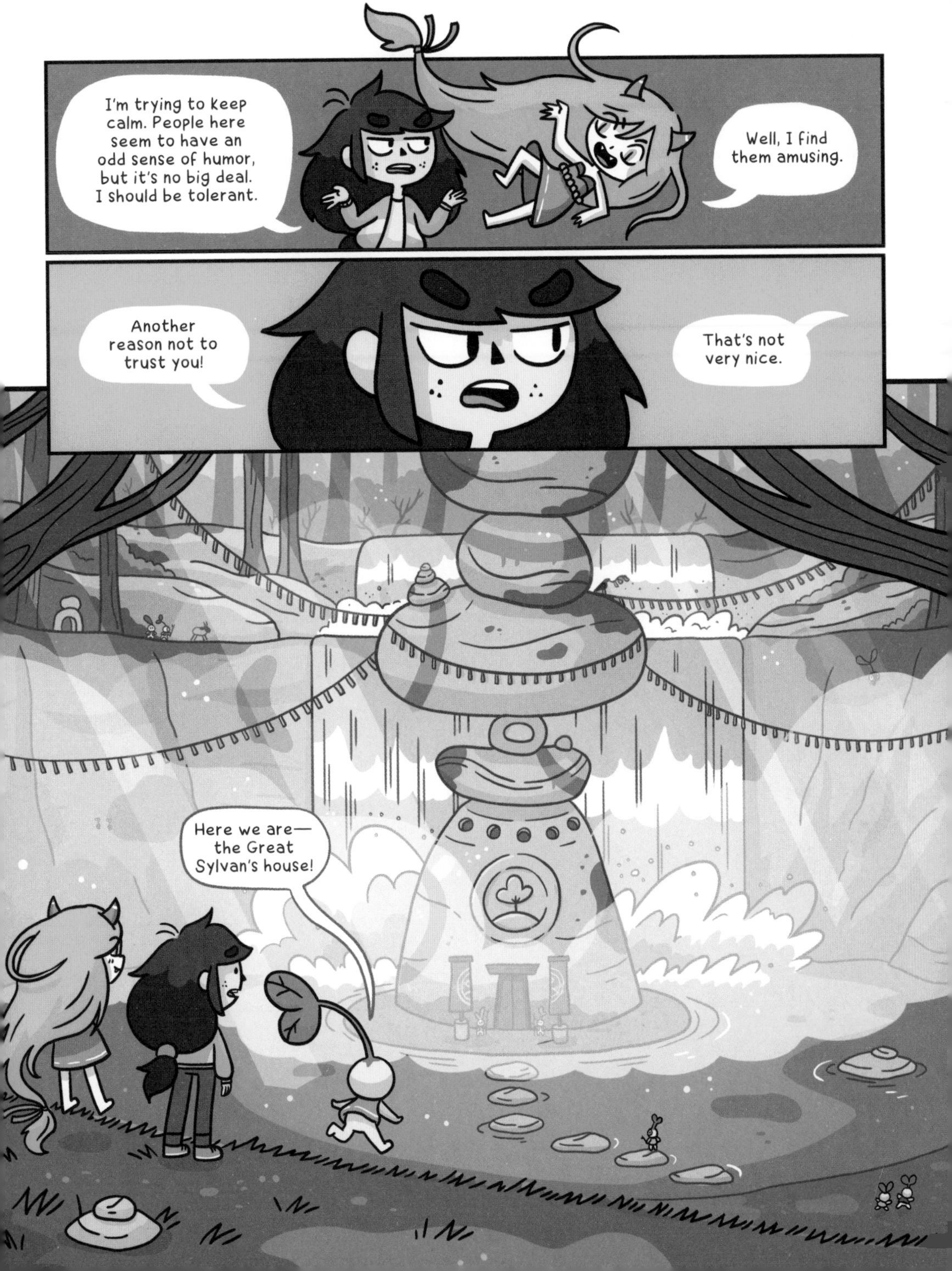
I'm trying to keep calm. People here seem to have an odd sense of humor, but it's no big deal. I should be tolerant.
Well, I find them amusing.
Another reason not to trust you!
That's not very nice.
Here we are—the Great Sylvan's house!

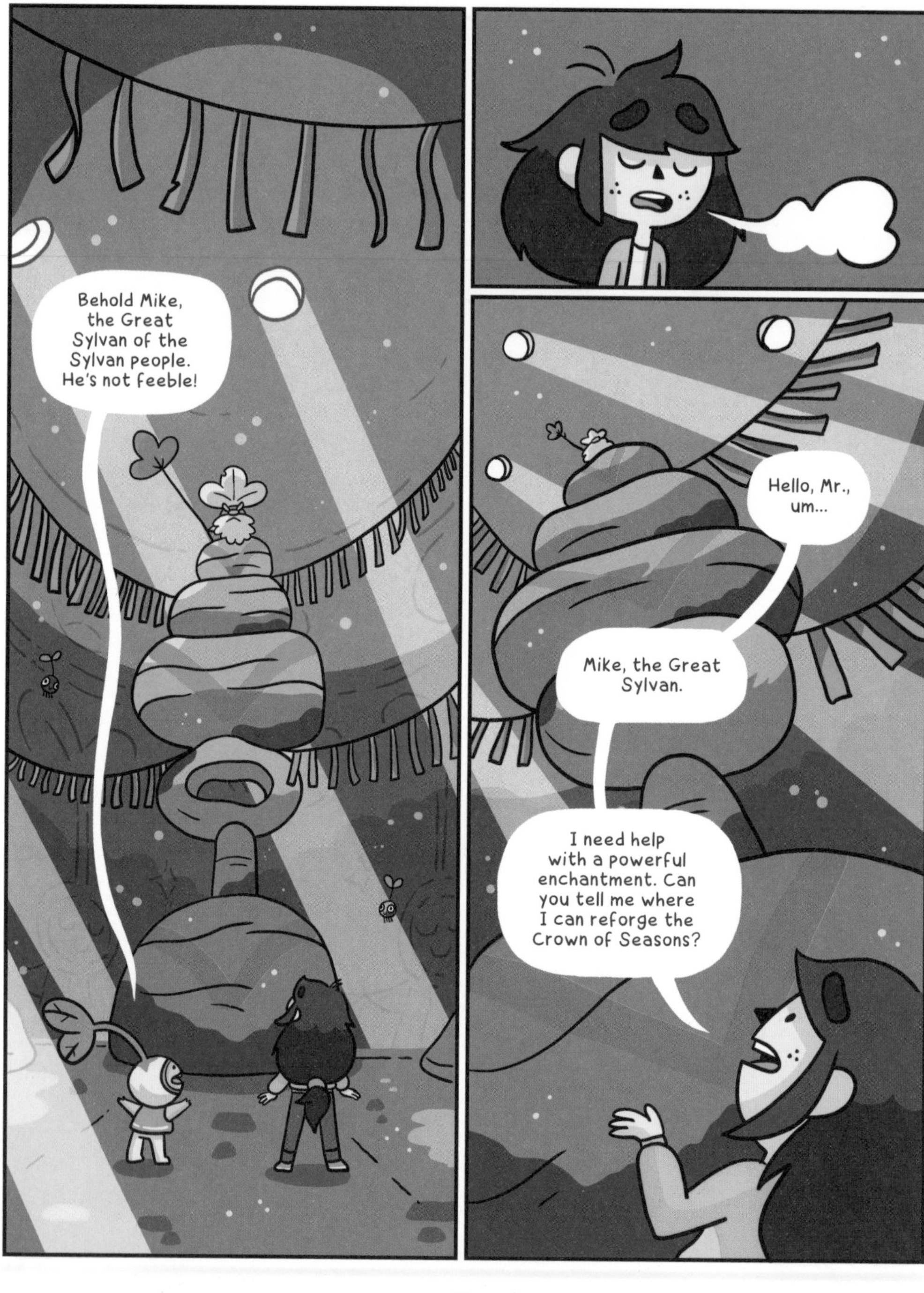
Behold Mike, the Great Sylvan of the Sylvan people. He's not feeble!
Hello, Mr., um...
Mike, the Great Sylvan.
I need help with a powerful enchantment. Can you tell me where I can reforge the Crown of Seasons?

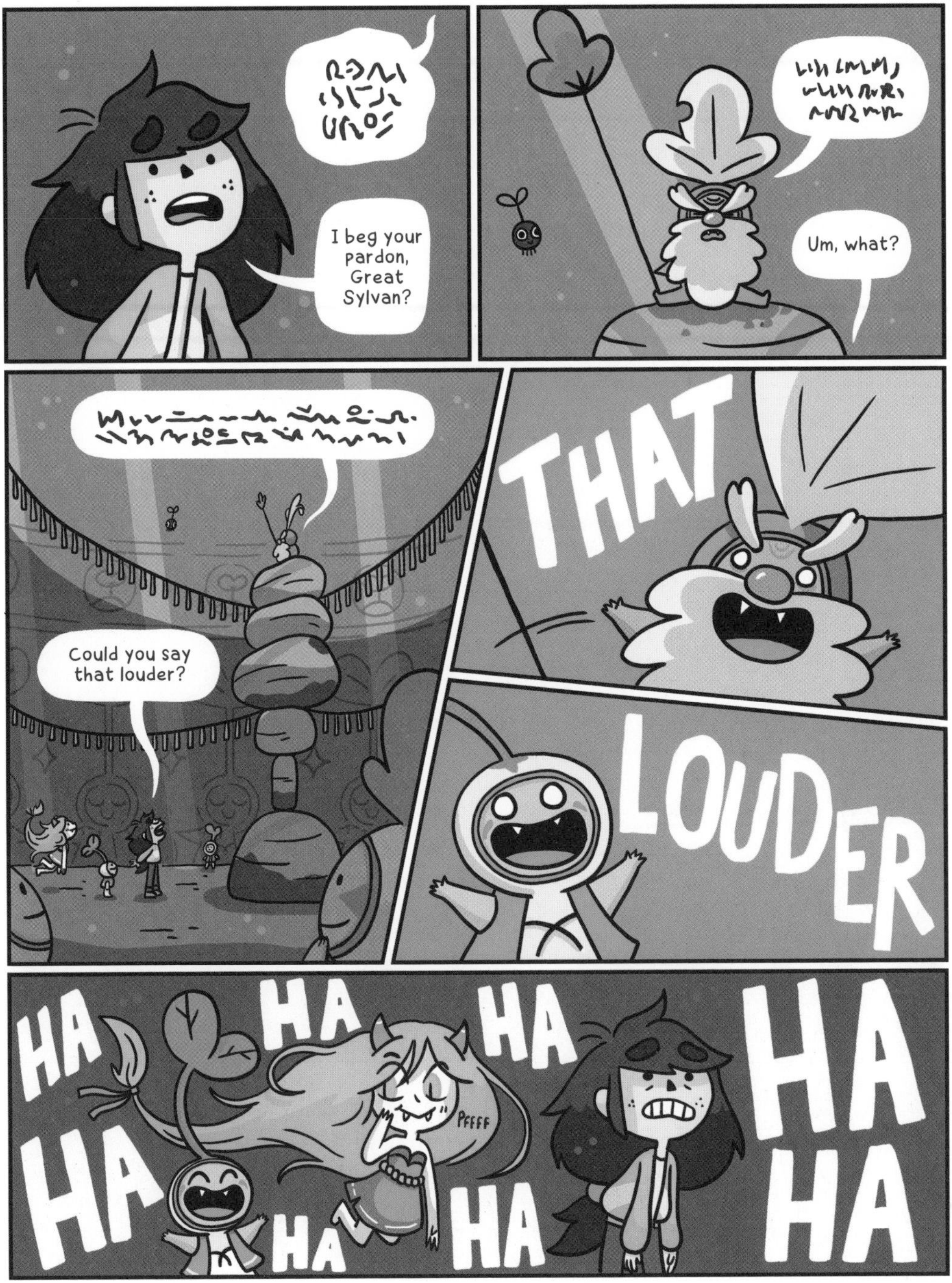
I beg your pardon, Great Sylvan?
Um, what?
Could you say that louder?
THAT LOUDER
HA HA HA HA HA HA HA HA HA HA
PFFFF

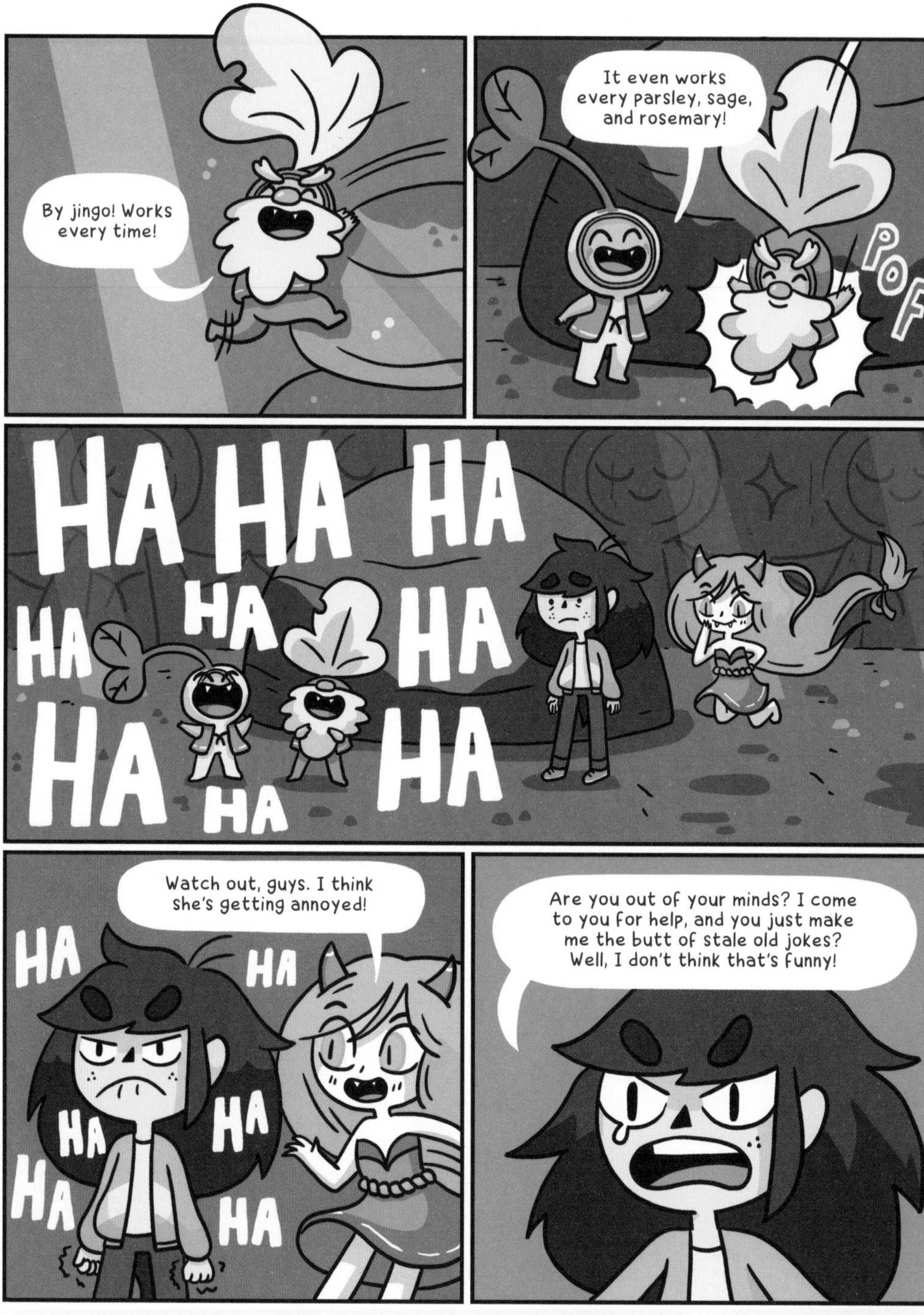
By jingo! Works every time!
It even works every parsley, sage, and rosemary!
POF
HA HA HA
HA HA HA
HA HA HA HA
Watch out, guys. I think she's getting annoyed!
HA HA HA HA HA HA
Are you out of your minds? I come to you for help, and you just make me the butt of stale old jokes? Well, I don't think that's funny!

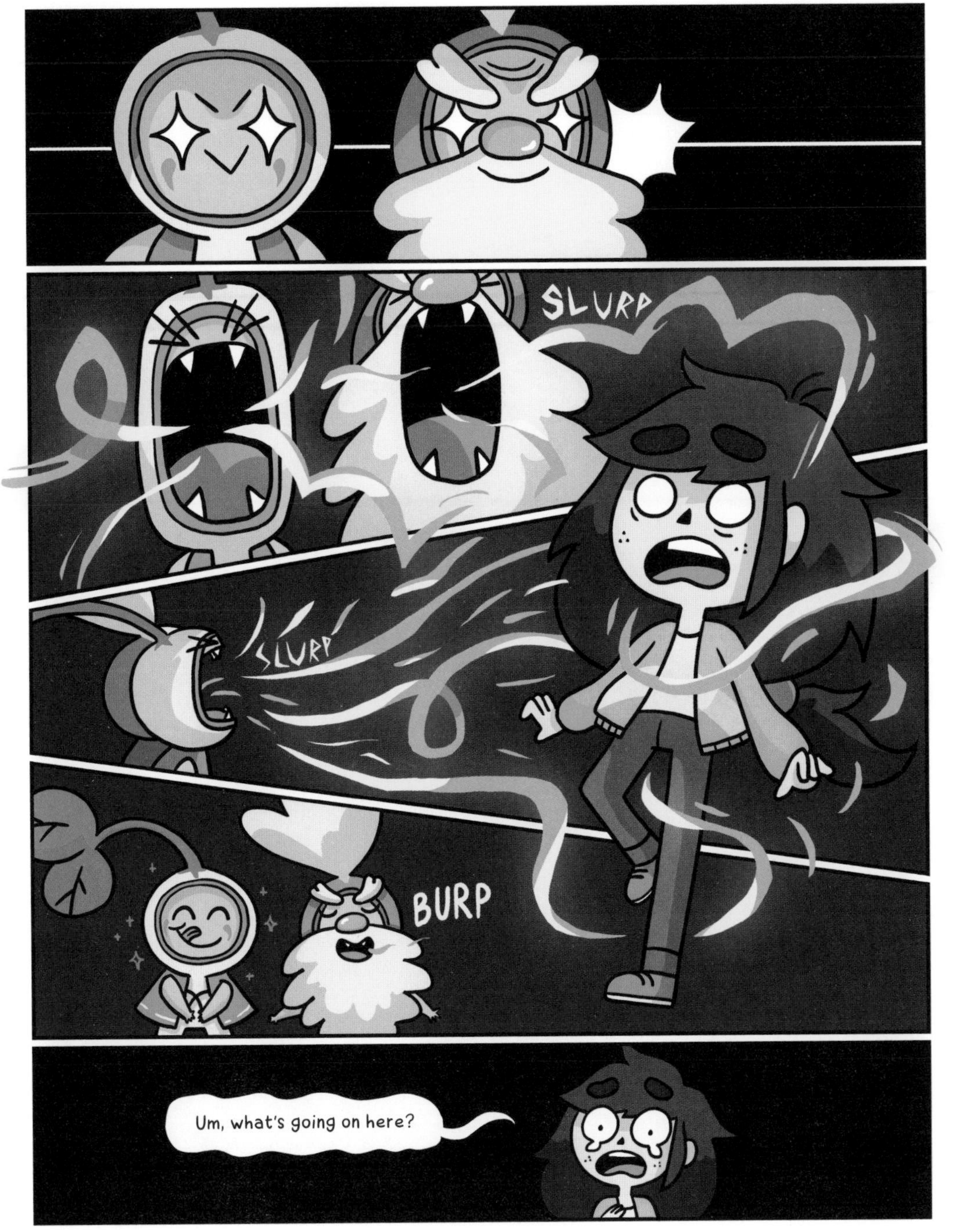
SLURP
SLURP
BURP
Um, what's going on here?

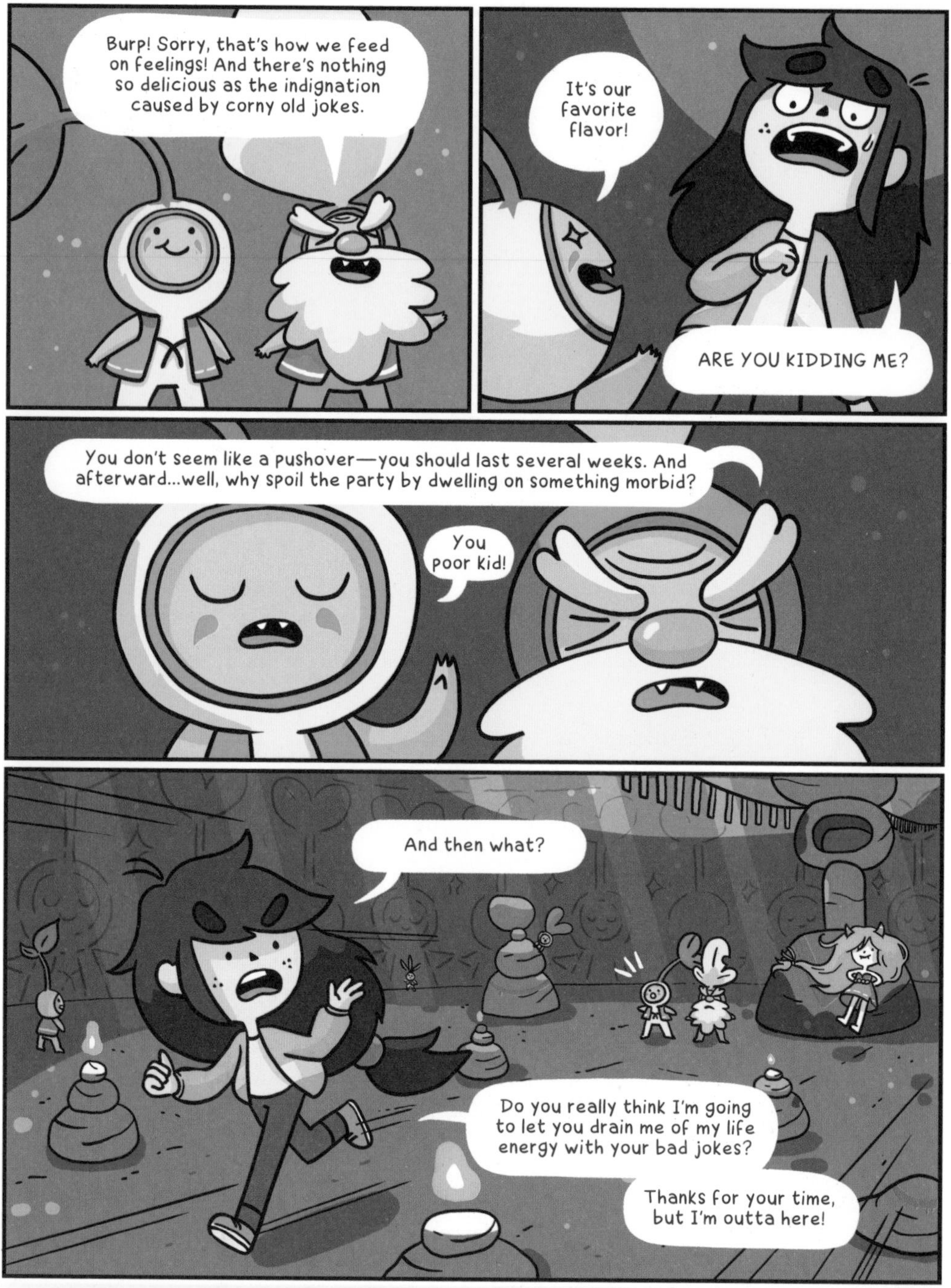
Burp! Sorry, that's how we feed on feelings! And there's nothing so delicious as the indignation caused by corny old jokes.
It's our favorite flavor!
ARE YOU KIDDING ME?
You don't seem like a pushover—you should last several weeks. And afterward...well, why spoil the party by dwelling on something morbid?
You poor kid!
And then what?
Do you really think I'm going to let you drain me of my life energy with your bad jokes?
Thanks for your time, but I'm outta here!

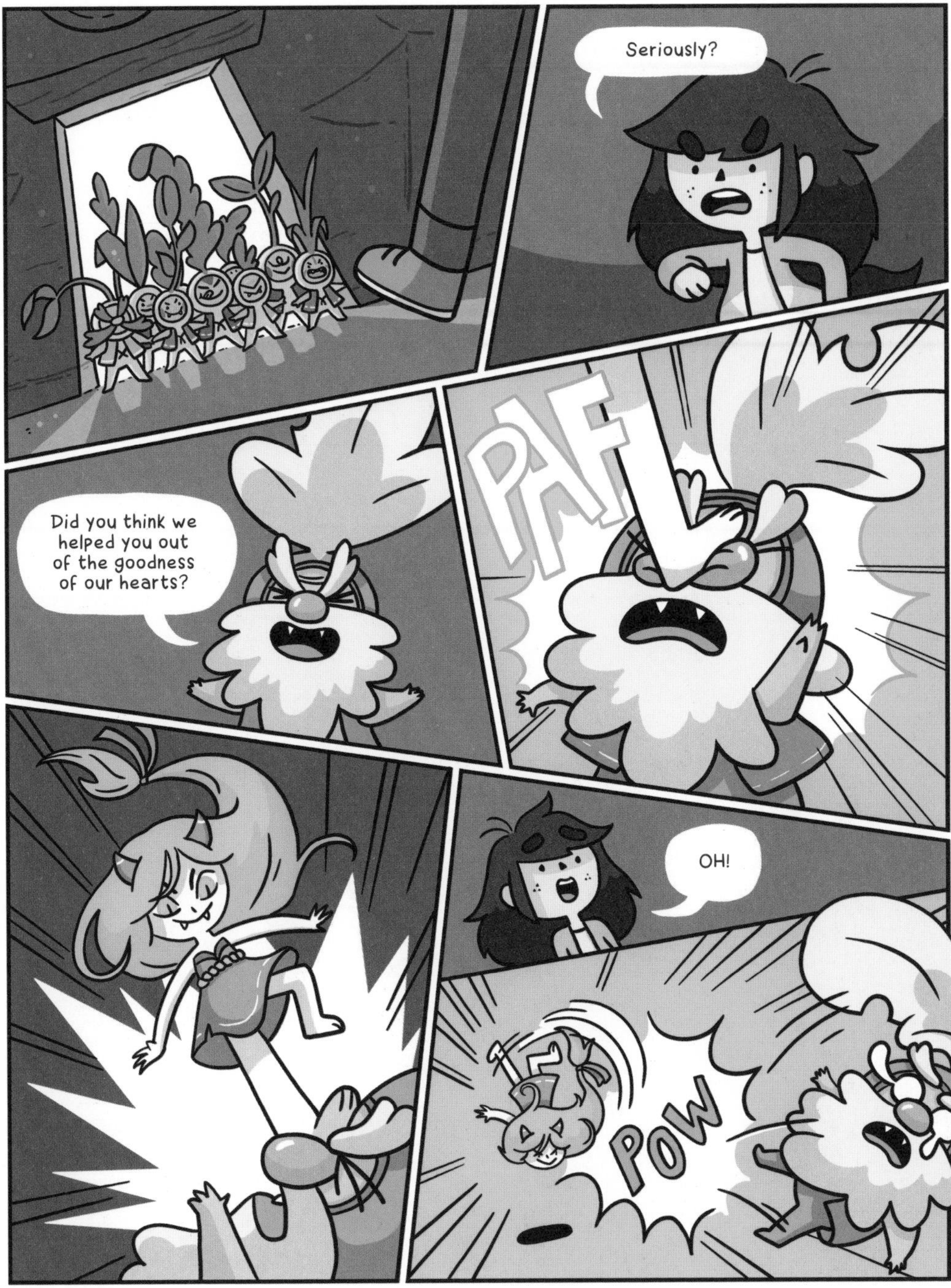
Seriously?
Did you think we helped you out of the goodness of our hearts?
PAF
OH!
POW

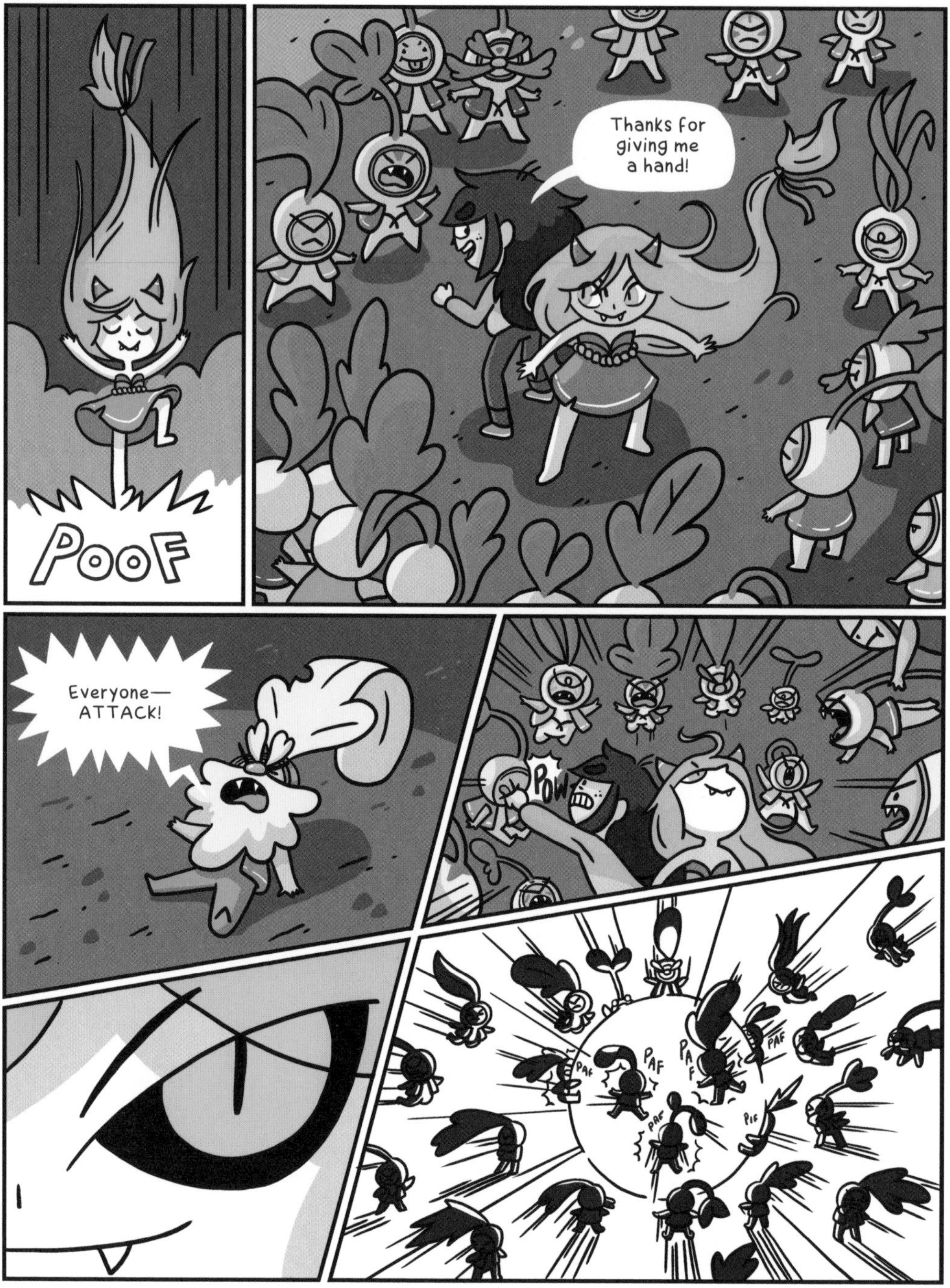
POOF
Thanks for giving me a hand!
Everyone—ATTACK!
POW
PAF
PAF
PAF
PAF
PAF
PIF

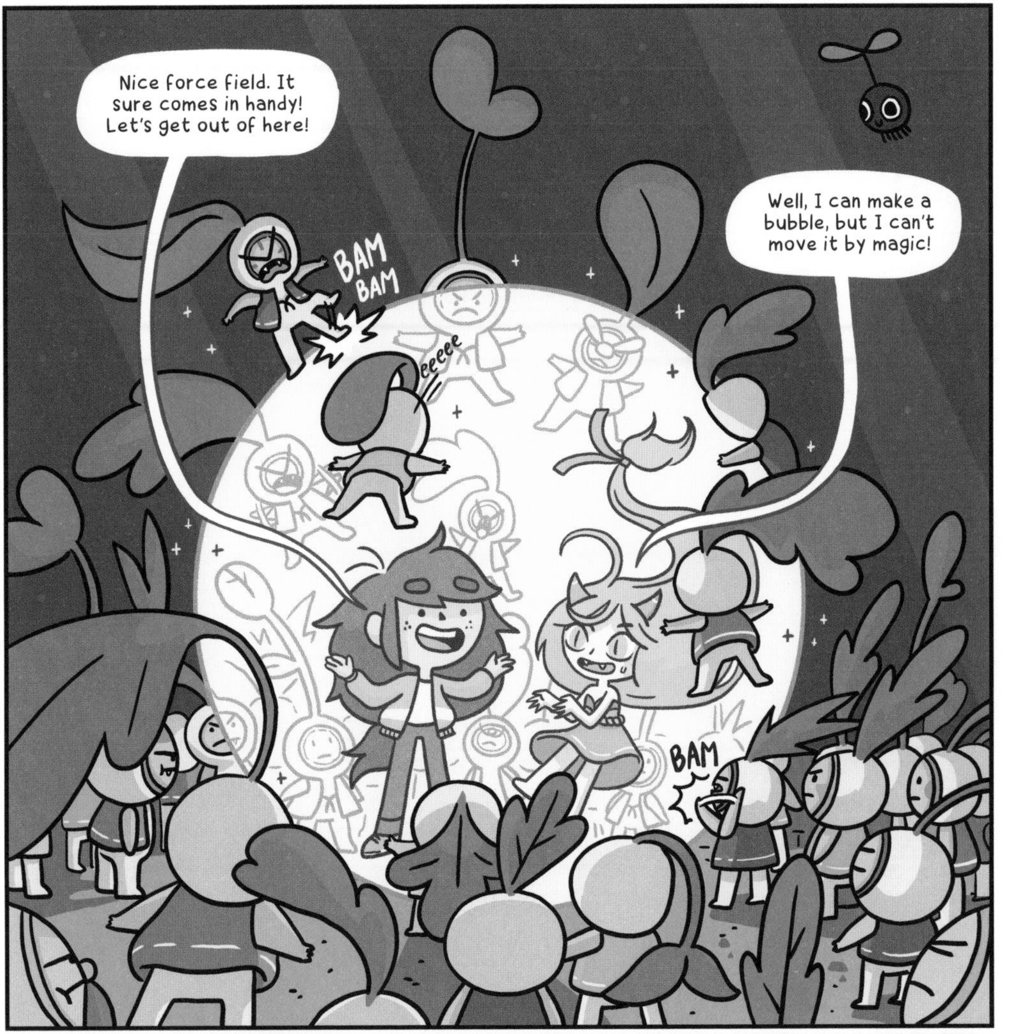
Nice force field. It sure comes in handy! Let's get out of here!
Well, I can make a bubble, but I can't move it by magic!
BAM
BAM
eeeee
BAM

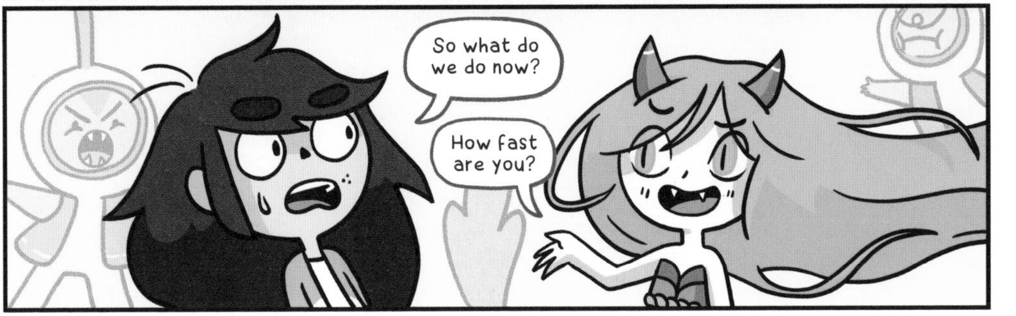
So what do we do now?
How fast are you?

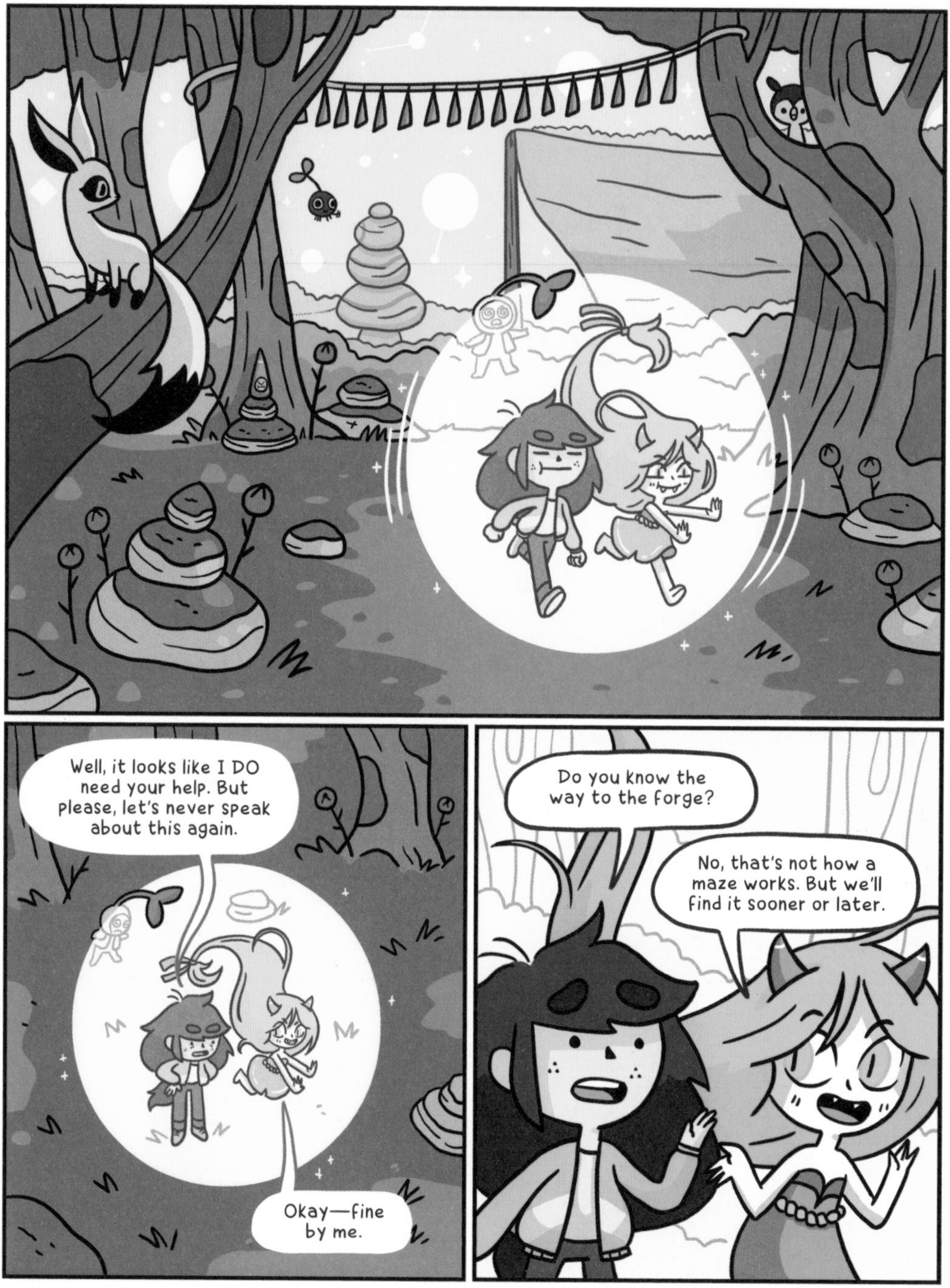
Well, it looks like I DO need your help. But please, let's never speak about this again.
Okay—fine by me.
Do you know the way to the forge?
No, that's not how a maze works. But we'll find it sooner or later.

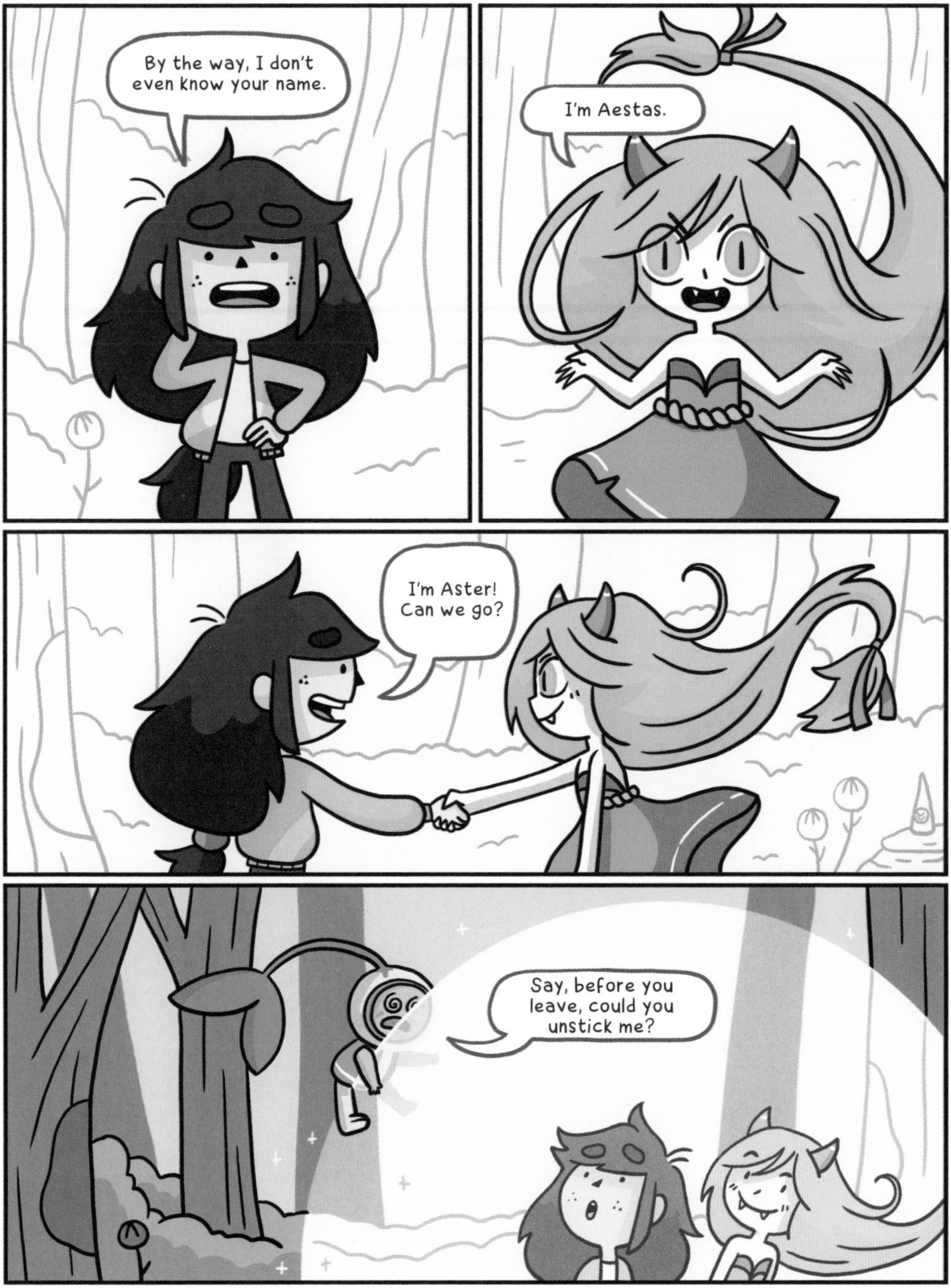

By the way, I don't even know your name.
I'm Aestas.
I'm Aster! Can we go?
Say, before you leave, could you unstick me?

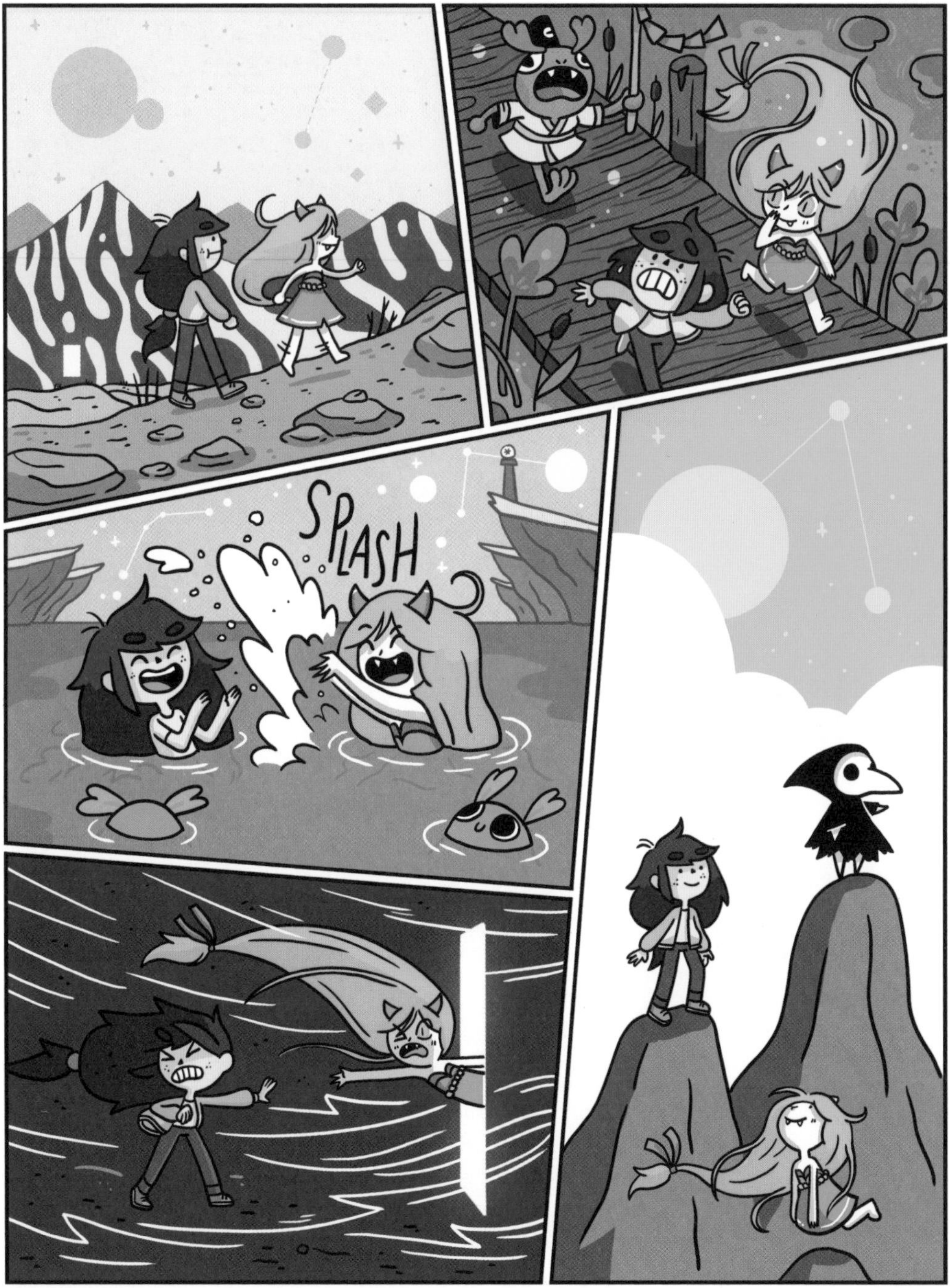
SPLASH

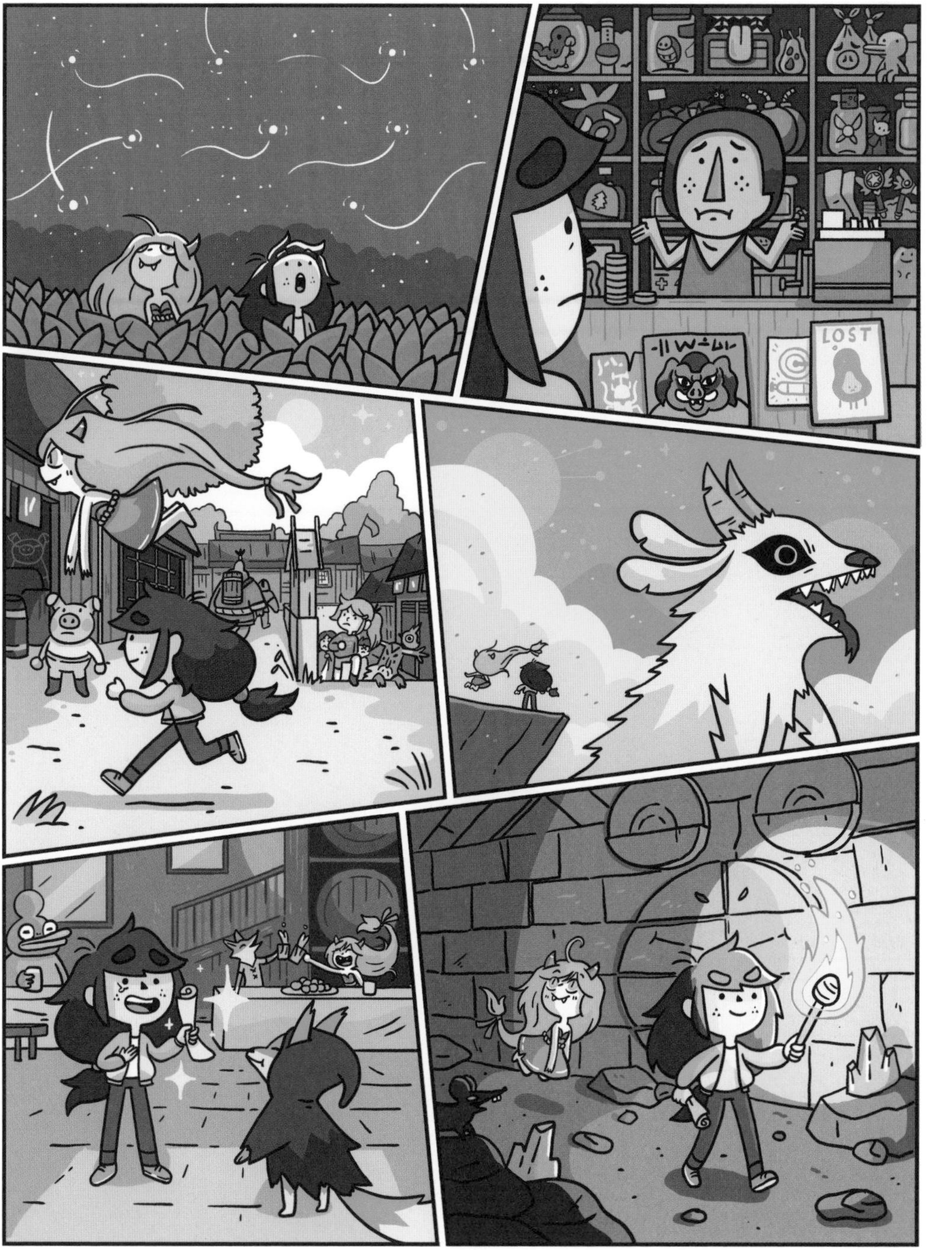
LOST

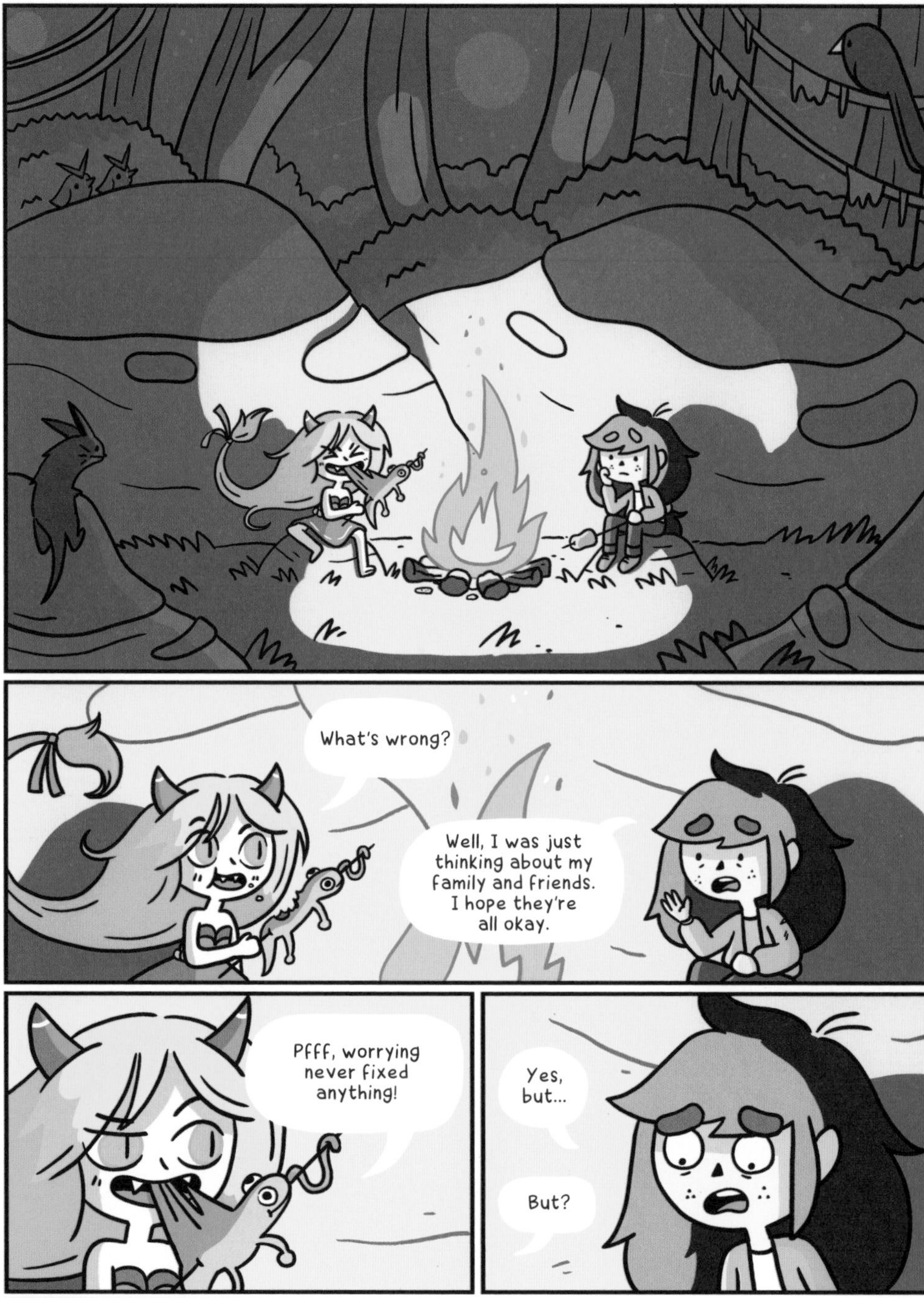
What's wrong?
Well, I was just thinking about my family and friends. I hope they're all okay.
Pfff, worrying never fixed anything!
Yes, but...
But?

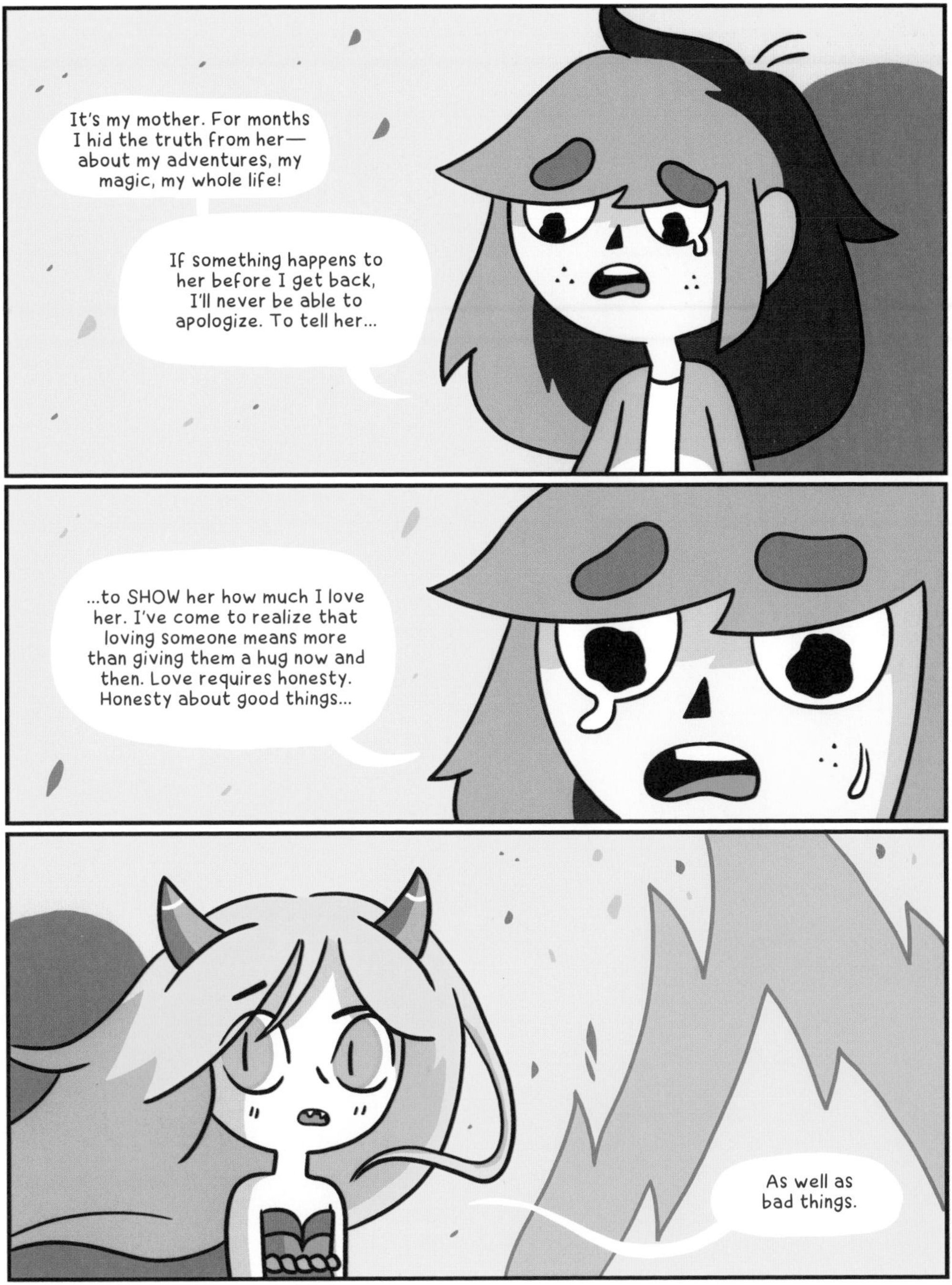
It's my mother. For months I hid the truth from her—about my adventures, my magic, my whole life!
If something happens to her before I get back, I'll never be able to apologize. To tell her...
...to SHOW her how much I love her. I've come to realize that loving someone means more than giving them a hug now and then. Love requires honesty. Honesty about good things...
As well as bad things.

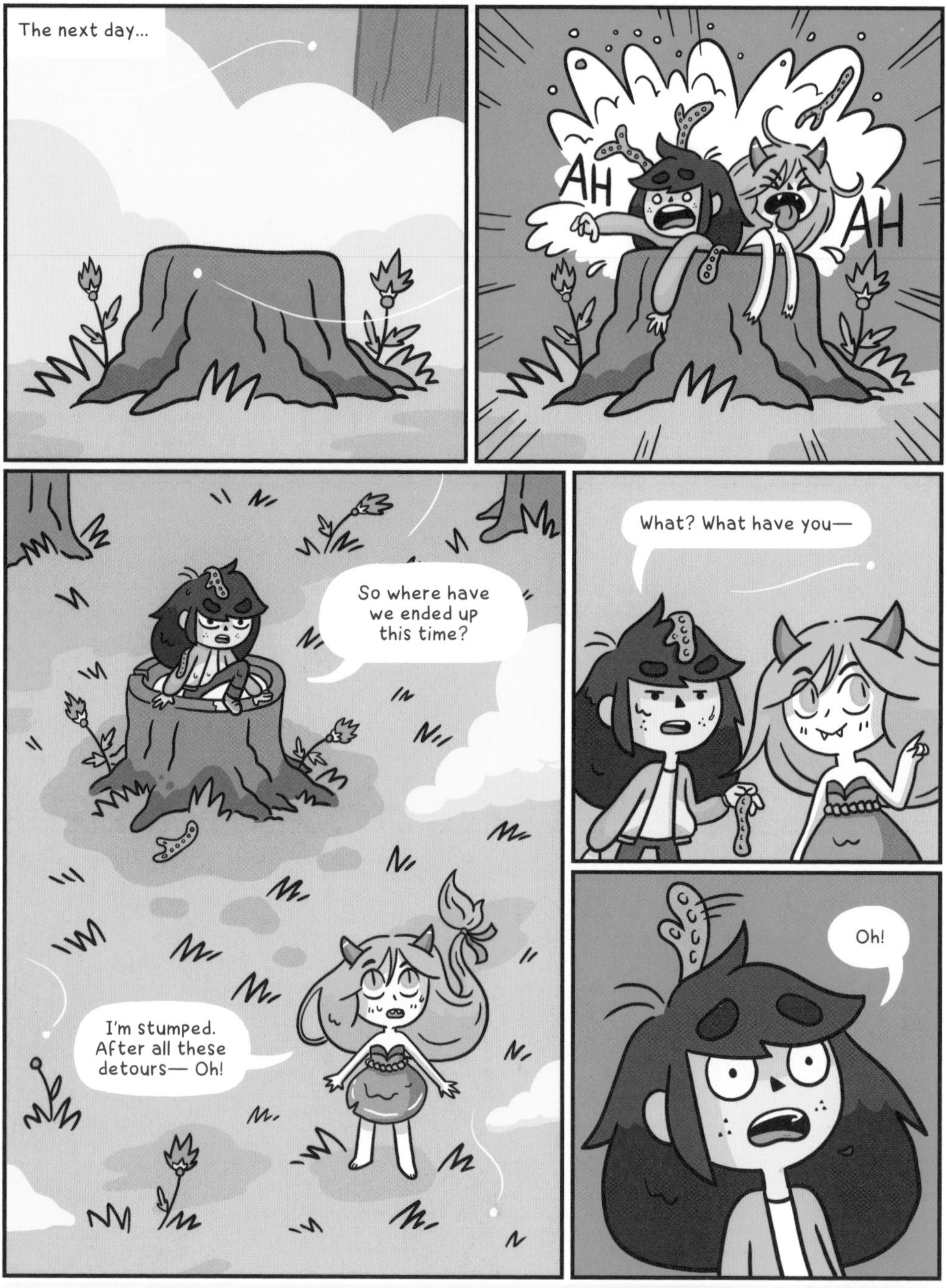
The next day...
AH
AH
So where have we ended up this time?
I'm stumped. After all these detours— Oh!
What? What have you—
Oh!

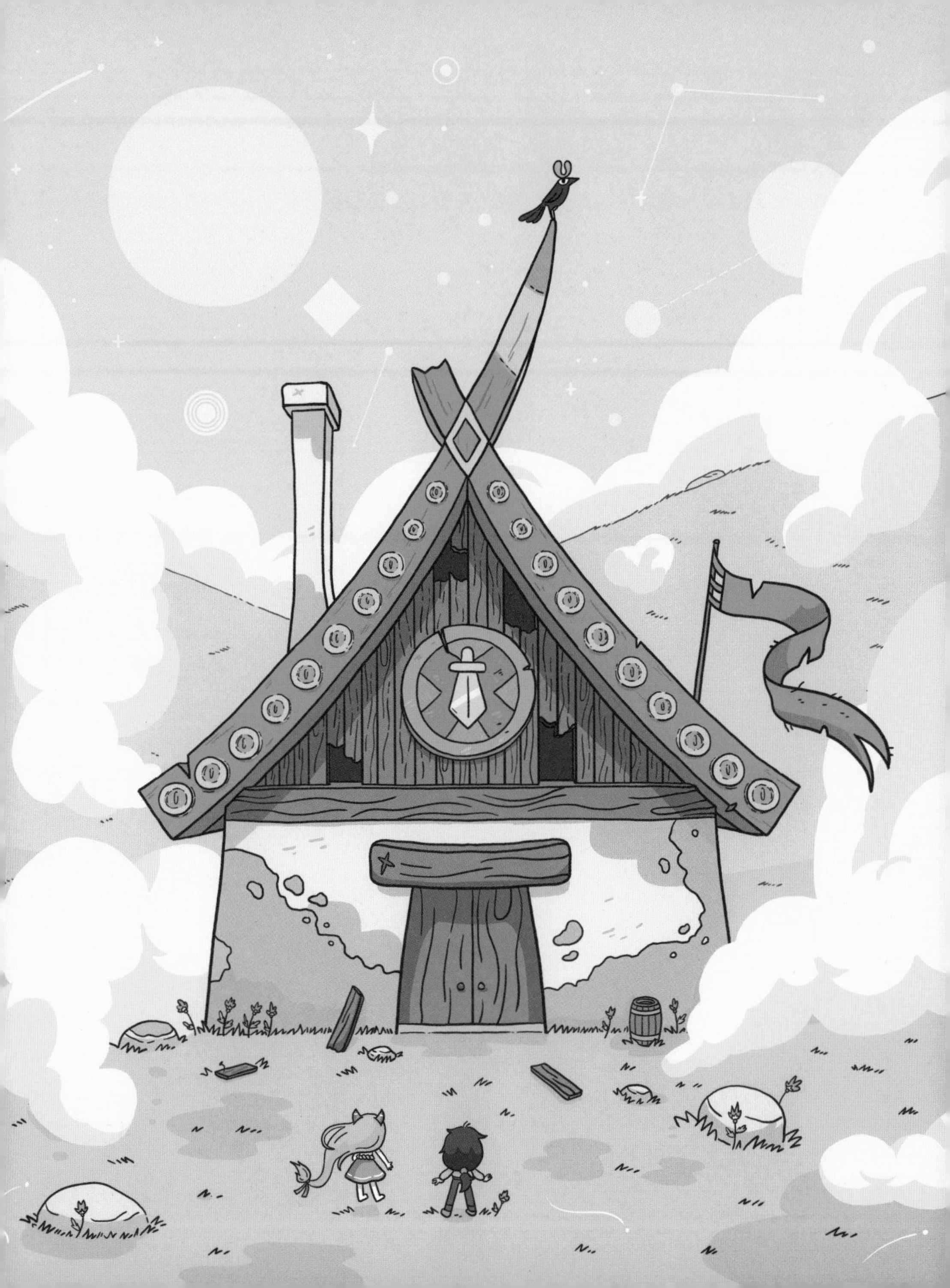

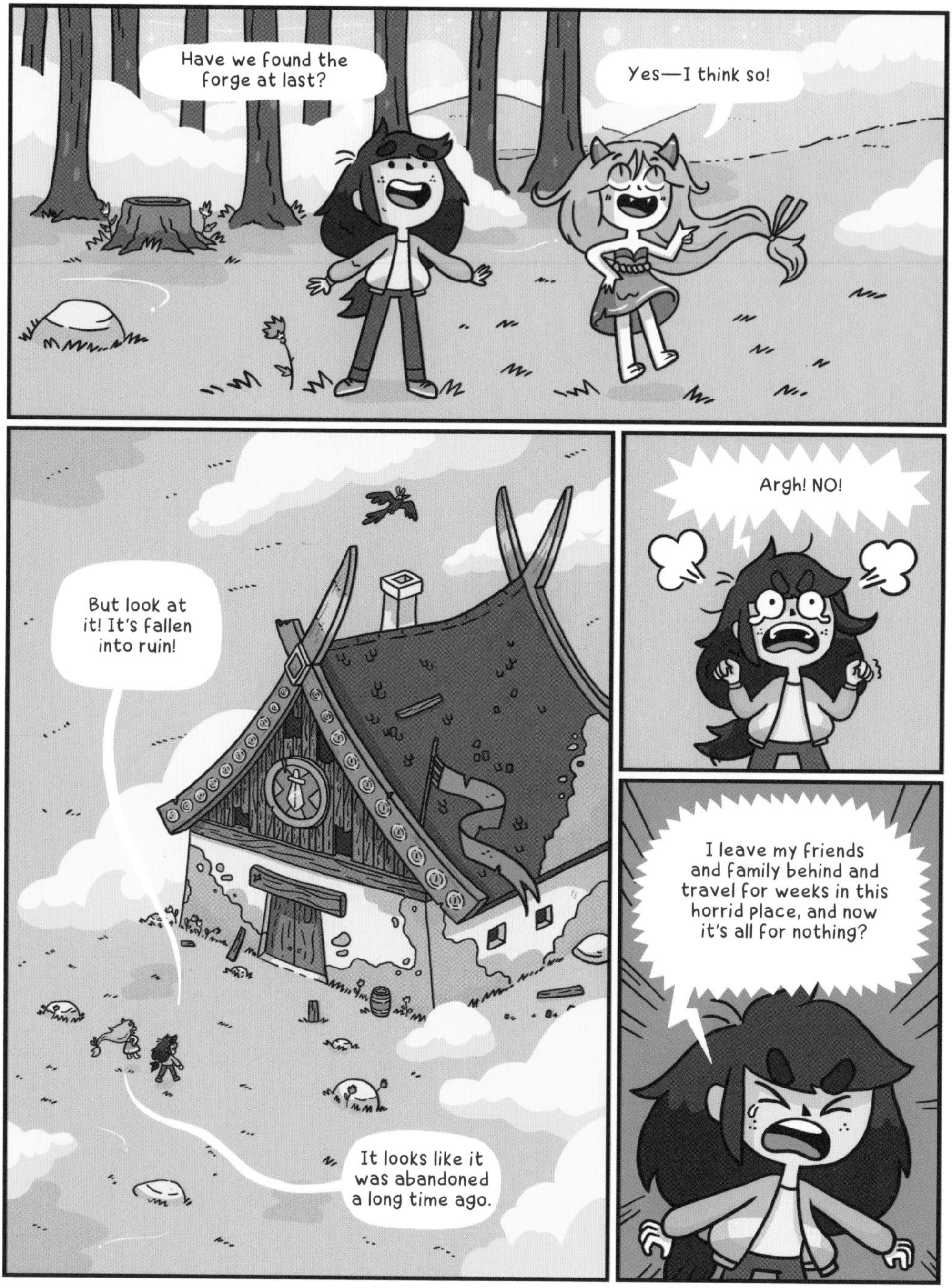
Have we found the forge at last?
Yes—I think so!
But look at it! It's fallen into ruin!
It looks like it was abandoned a long time ago.
Argh! NO!
I leave my friends and family behind and travel for weeks in this horrid place, and now it's all for nothing?

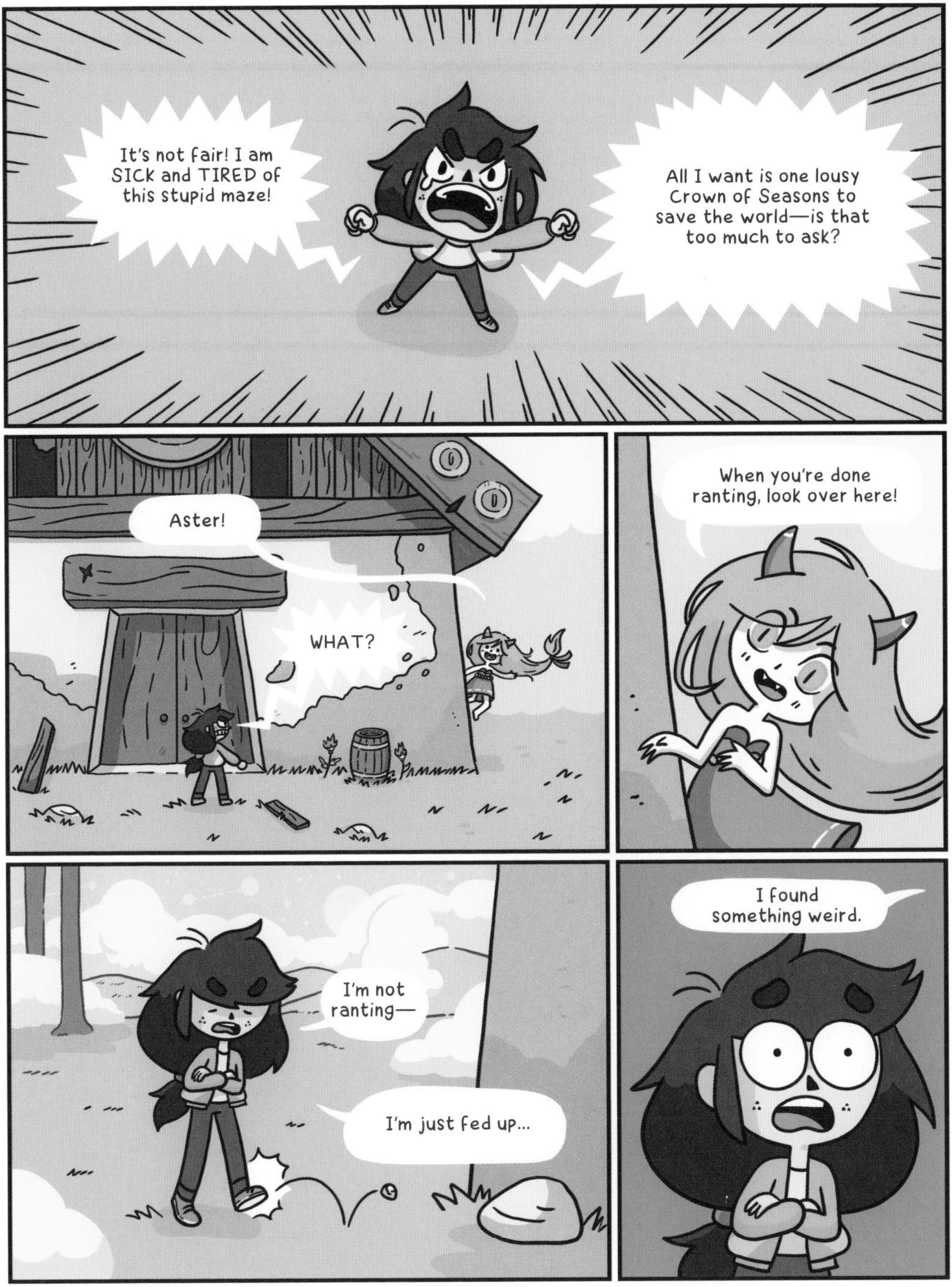

It's not fair! I am SICK and TIRED of this stupid maze!
All I want is one lousy Crown of Seasons to save the world—is that too much to ask?
Aster!
WHAT?
When you're done ranting, look over here!
I'm not ranting—
I'm just fed up...
I found something weird.

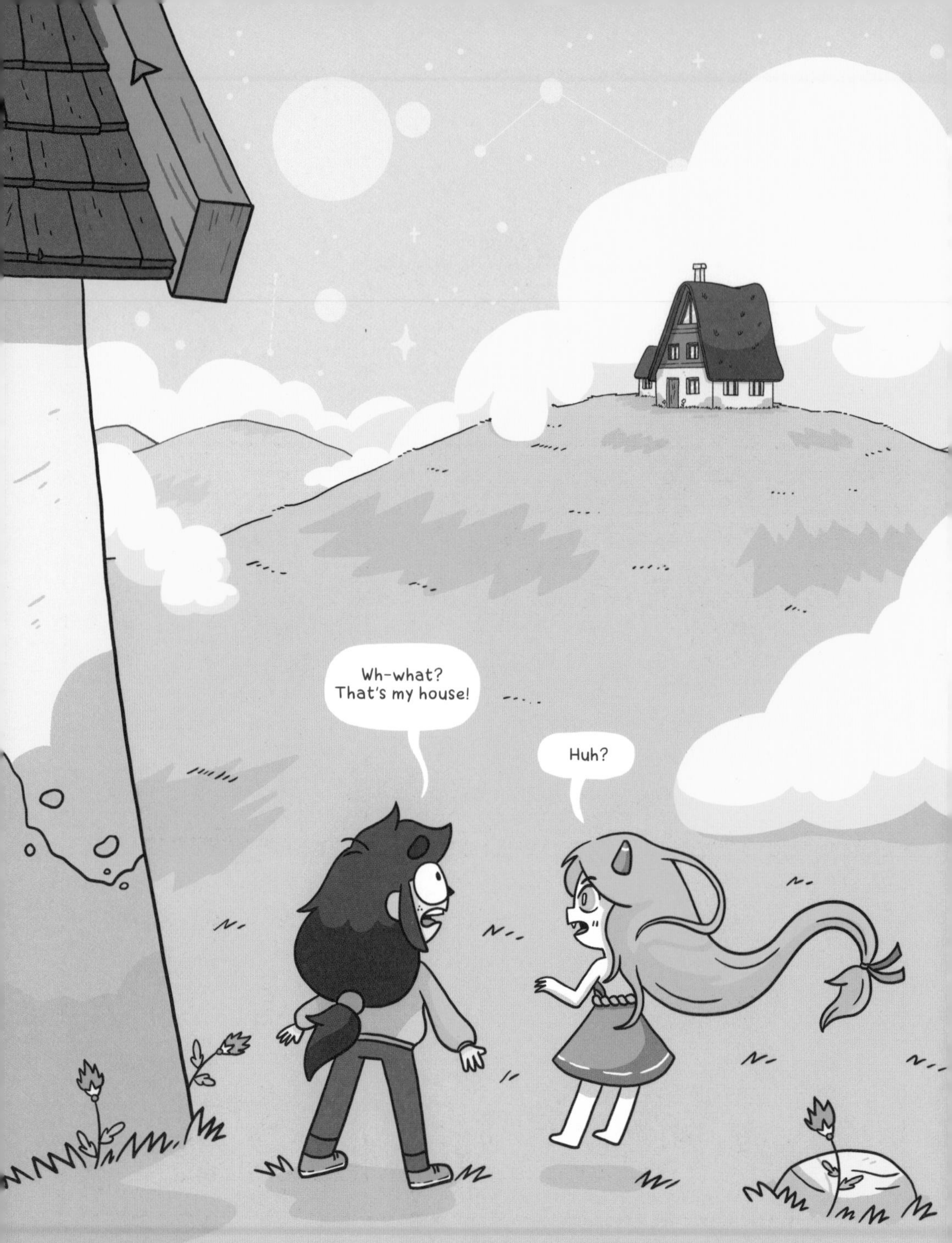
Wh-what? That's my house!
Huh?

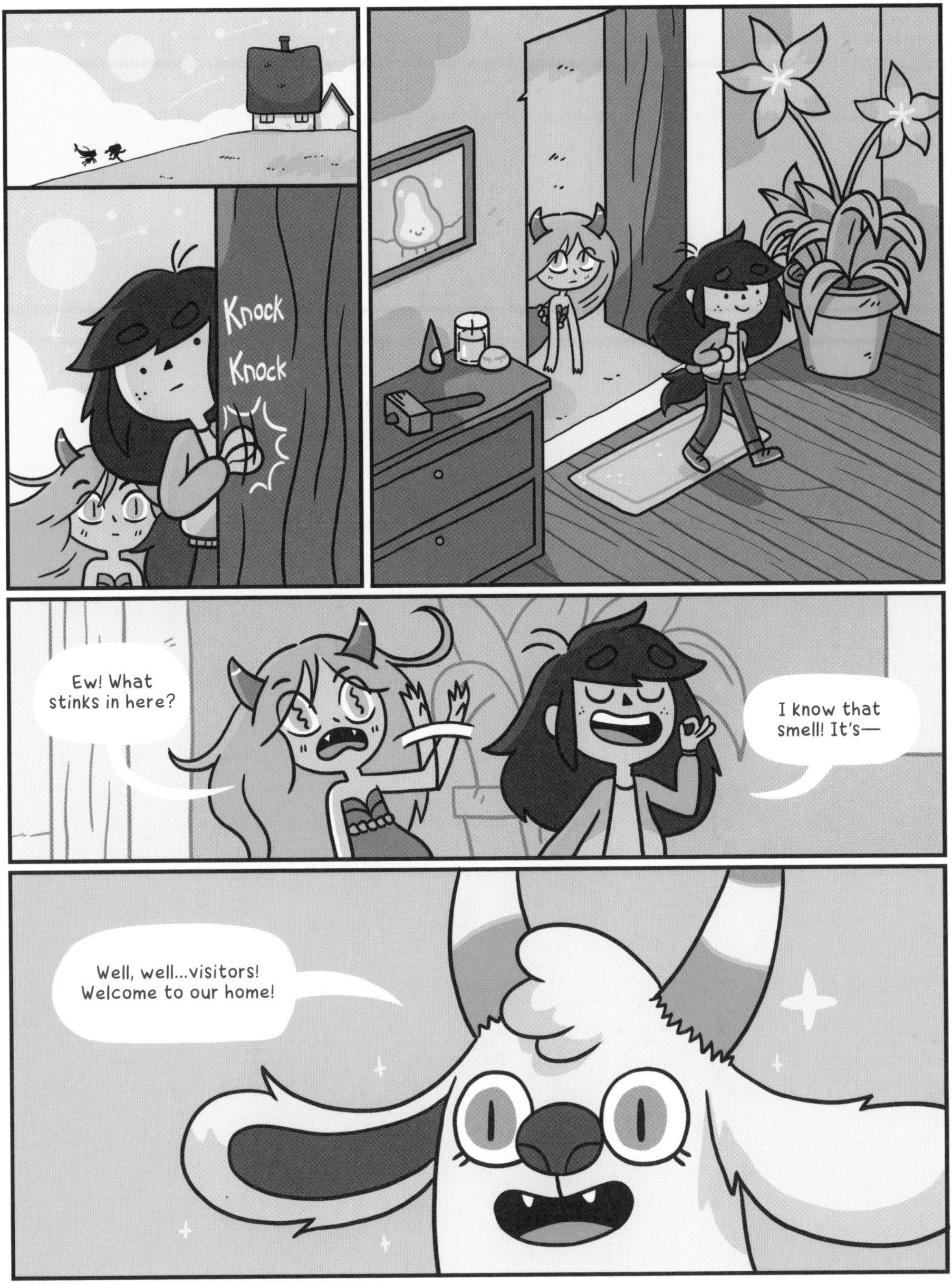
Knock
Knock
Ew! What stinks in here?
I know that smell! It's—
Well, well...visitors! Welcome to our home!

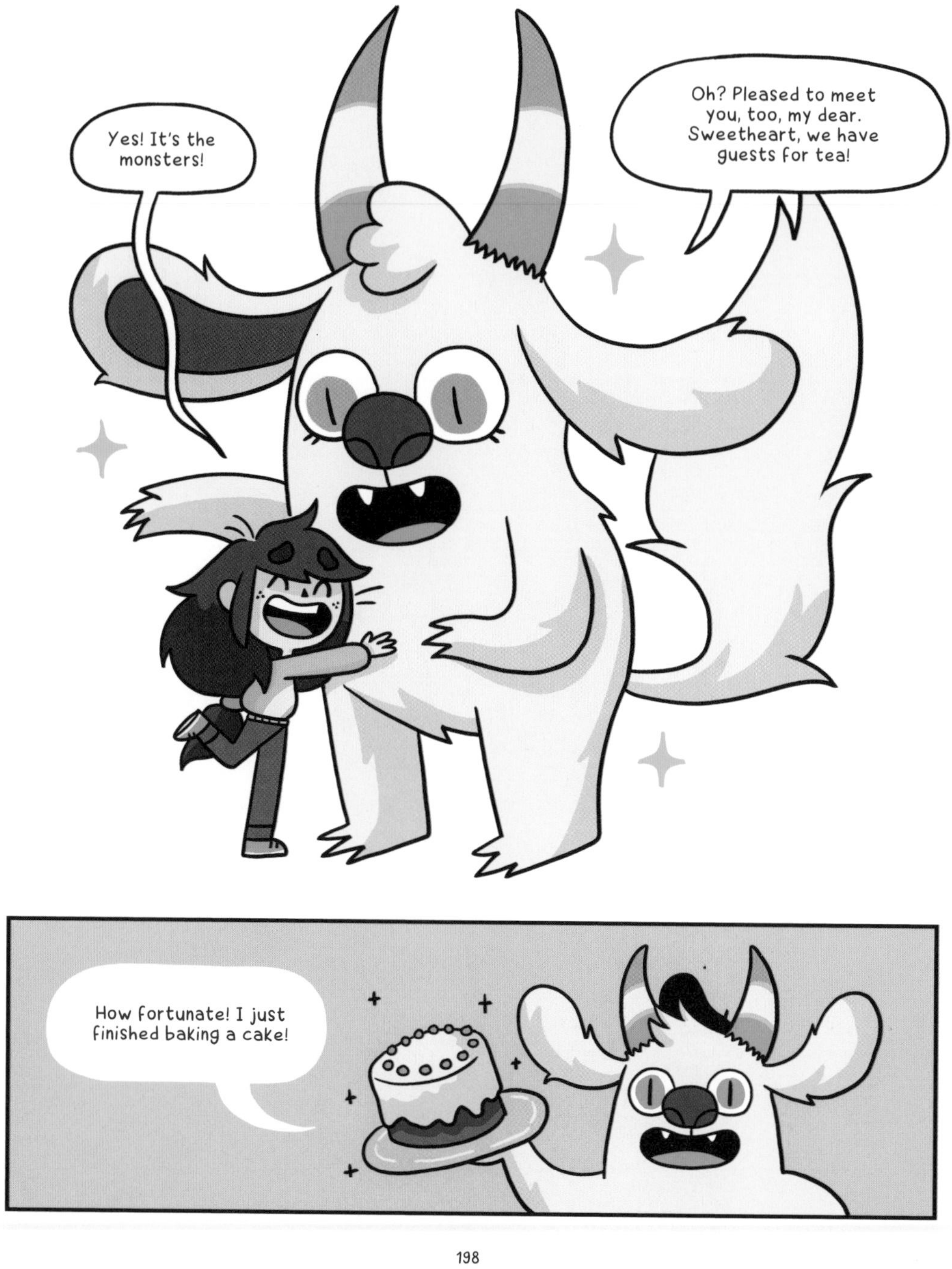
Yes! It's the monsters!
Oh? Pleased to meet you, too, my dear. Sweetheart, we have guests for tea!
How fortunate! I just finished baking a cake!

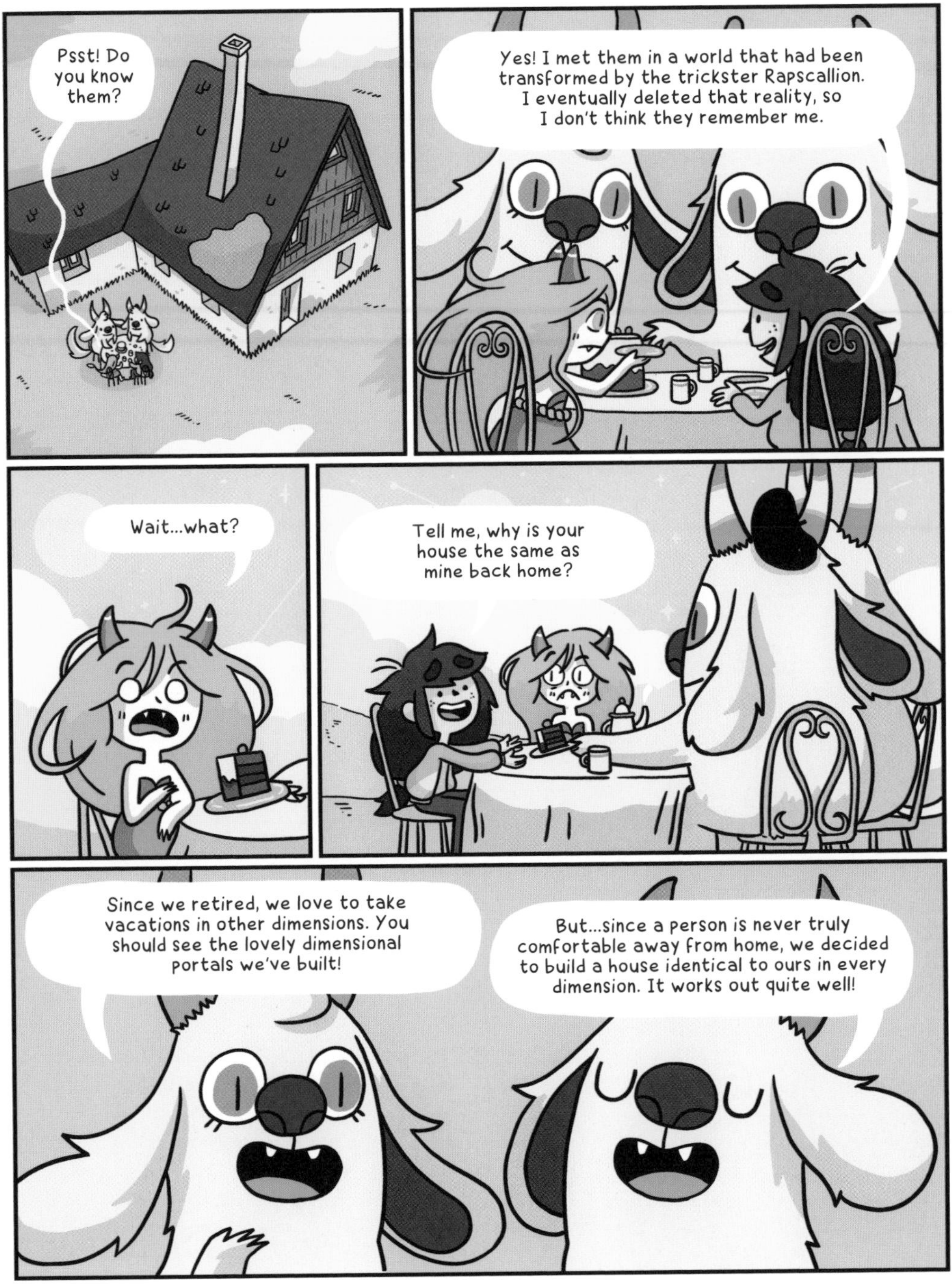
Psst! Do you know them?
Yes! I met them in a world that had been transformed by the trickster Rapscallion. I eventually deleted that reality, so I don't think they remember me.
Wait...what?
Tell me, why is your house the same as mine back home?
Since we retired, we love to take vacations in other dimensions. You should see the lovely dimensional portals we've built!
But...since a person is never truly comfortable away from home, we decided to build a house identical to ours in every dimension. It works out quite well!

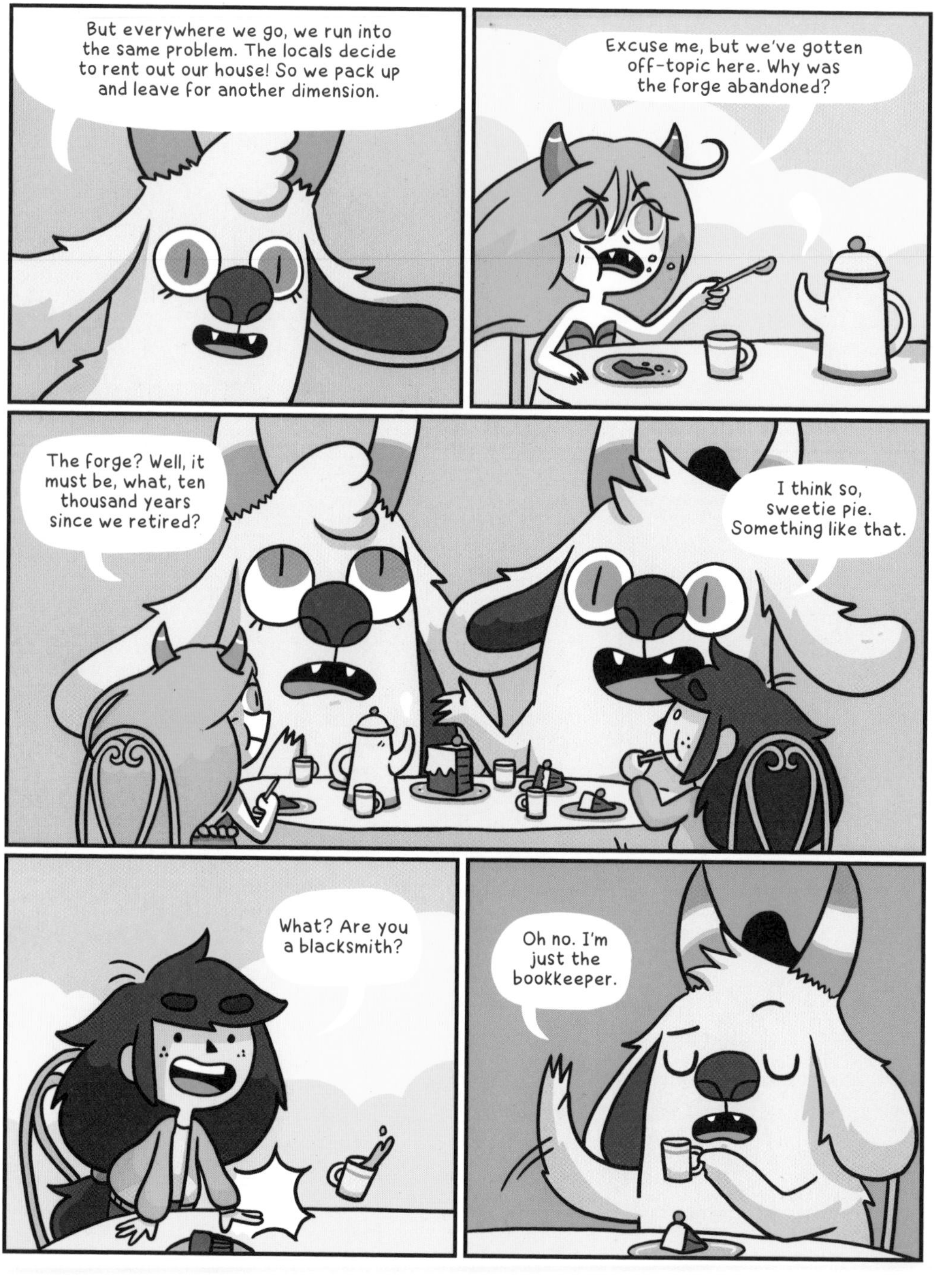
But everywhere we go, we run into the same problem. The locals decide to rent out our house! So we pack up and leave for another dimension.
Excuse me, but we've gotten off-topic here. Why was the forge abandoned?
The forge? Well, it must be, what, ten thousand years since we retired?
I think so, sweetie pie. Something like that.
What? Are you a blacksmith?
Oh no. I'm just the bookkeeper.

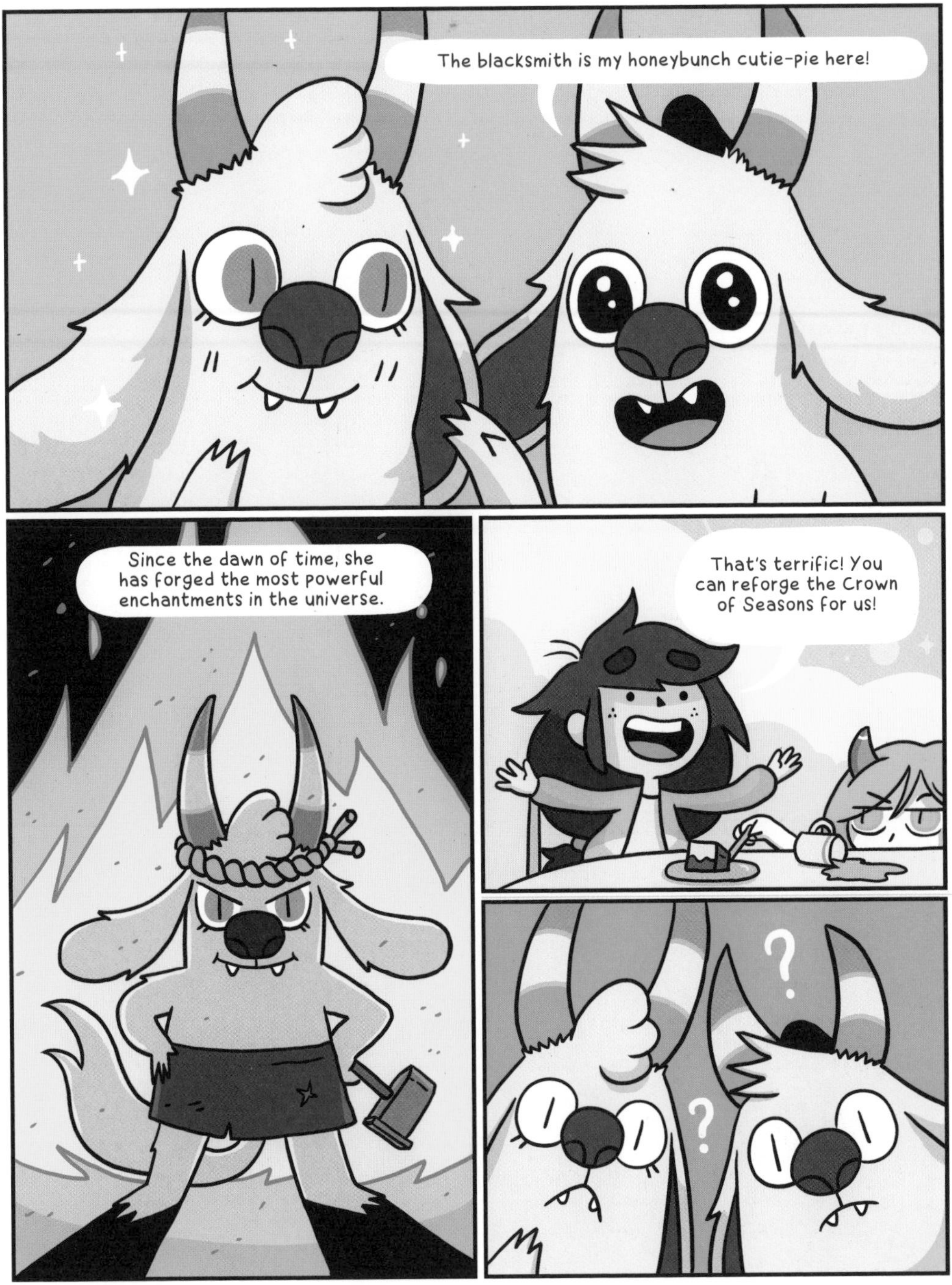
The blacksmith is my honeybunch cutie-pie here!
Since the dawn of time, she has forged the most powerful enchantments in the universe.
That's terrific! You can reforge the Crown of Seasons for us!
?
?

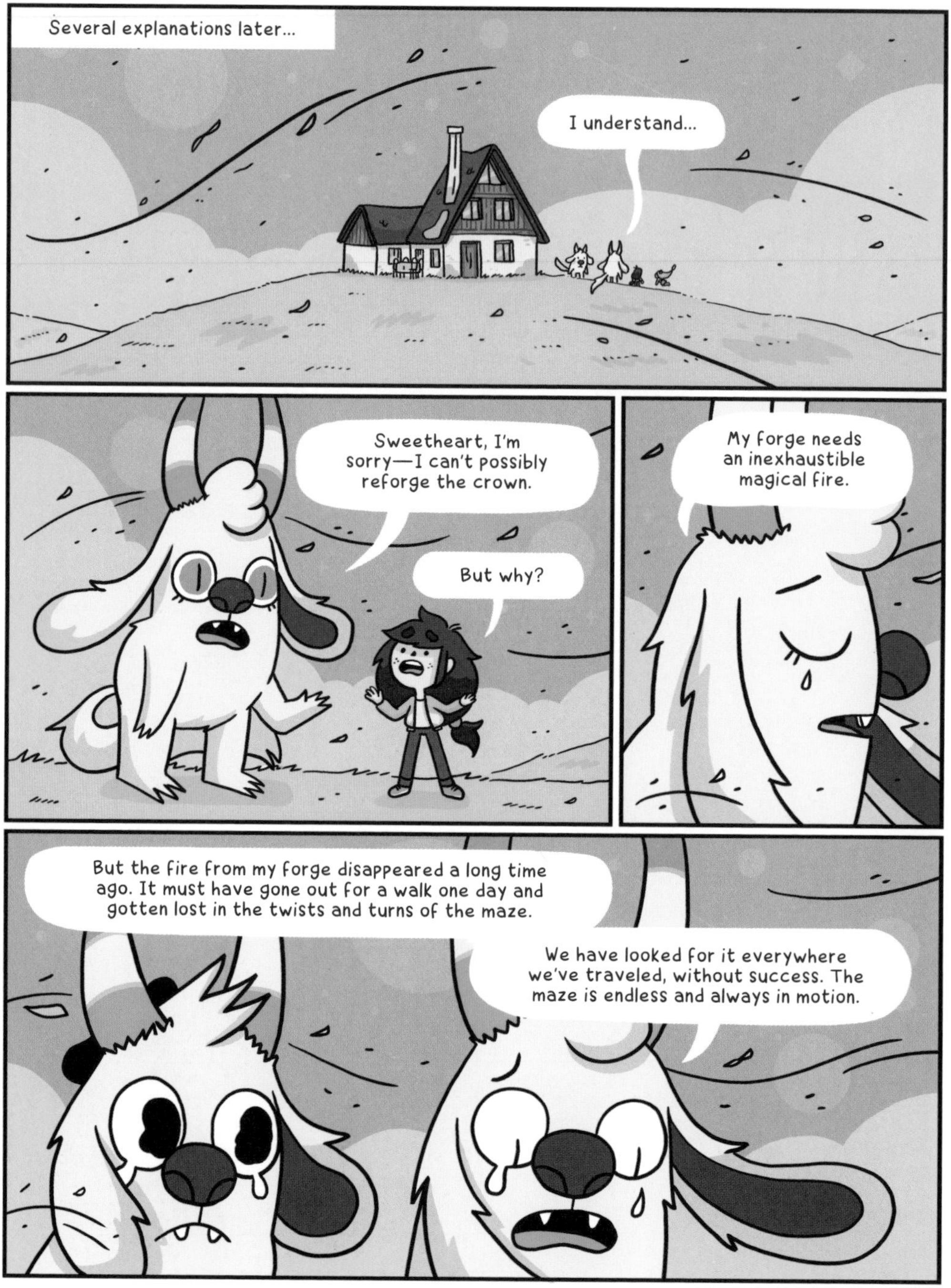
Several explanations later...
I understand...
Sweetheart, I'm sorry—I can't possibly reforge the crown.
But why?
My forge needs an inexhaustible magical fire.
But the fire from my forge disappeared a long time ago. It must have gone out for a walk one day and gotten lost in the twists and turns of the maze.
We have looked for it everywhere we've traveled, without success. The maze is endless and always in motion.

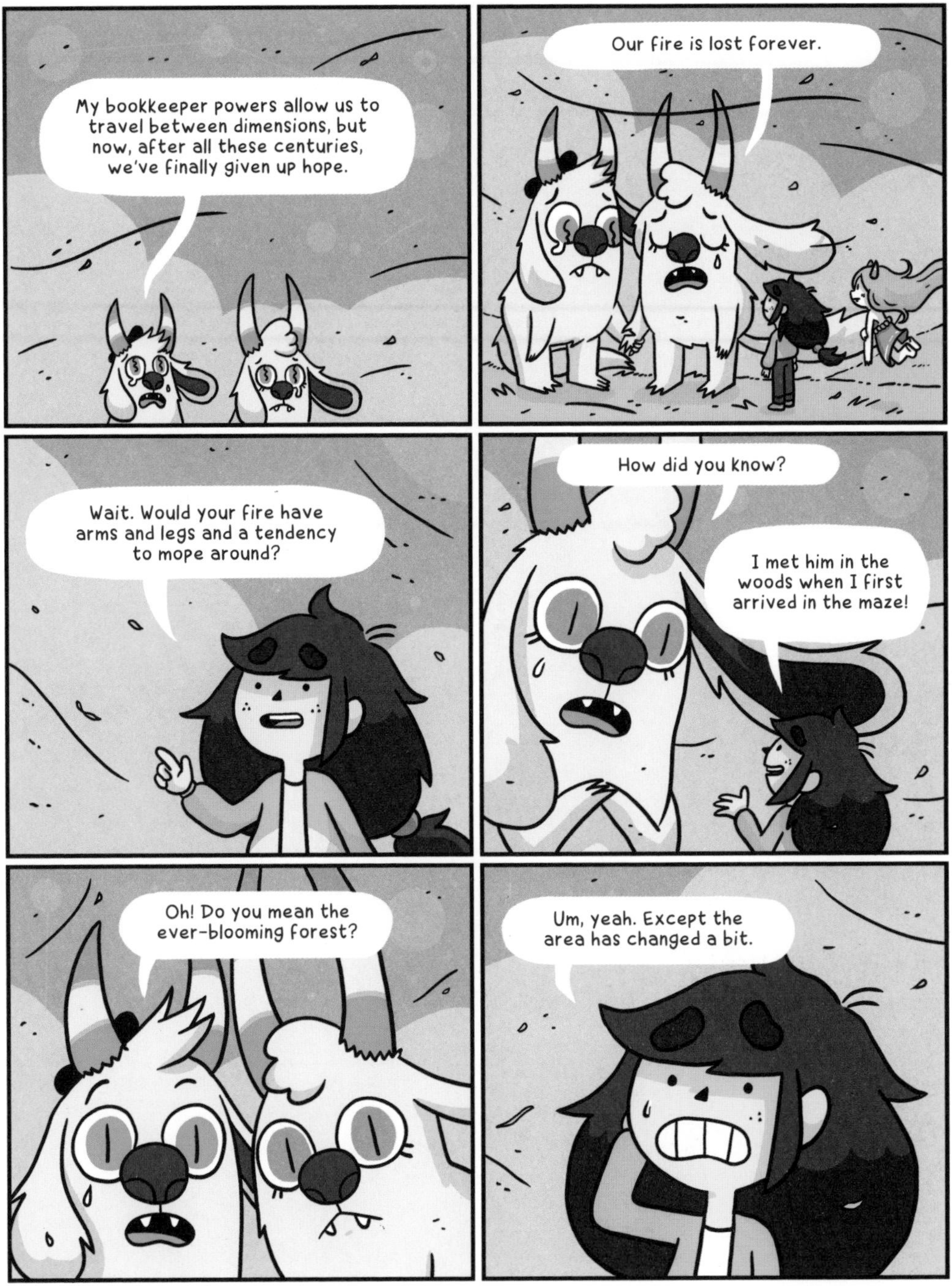
My bookkeeper powers allow us to travel between dimensions, but now, after all these centuries, we've finally given up hope.
Our fire is lost forever.
Wait. Would your fire have arms and legs and a tendency to mope around?
How did you know?
I met him in the woods when I first arrived in the maze!
Oh! Do you mean the ever-blooming forest?
Um, yeah. Except the area has changed a bit.

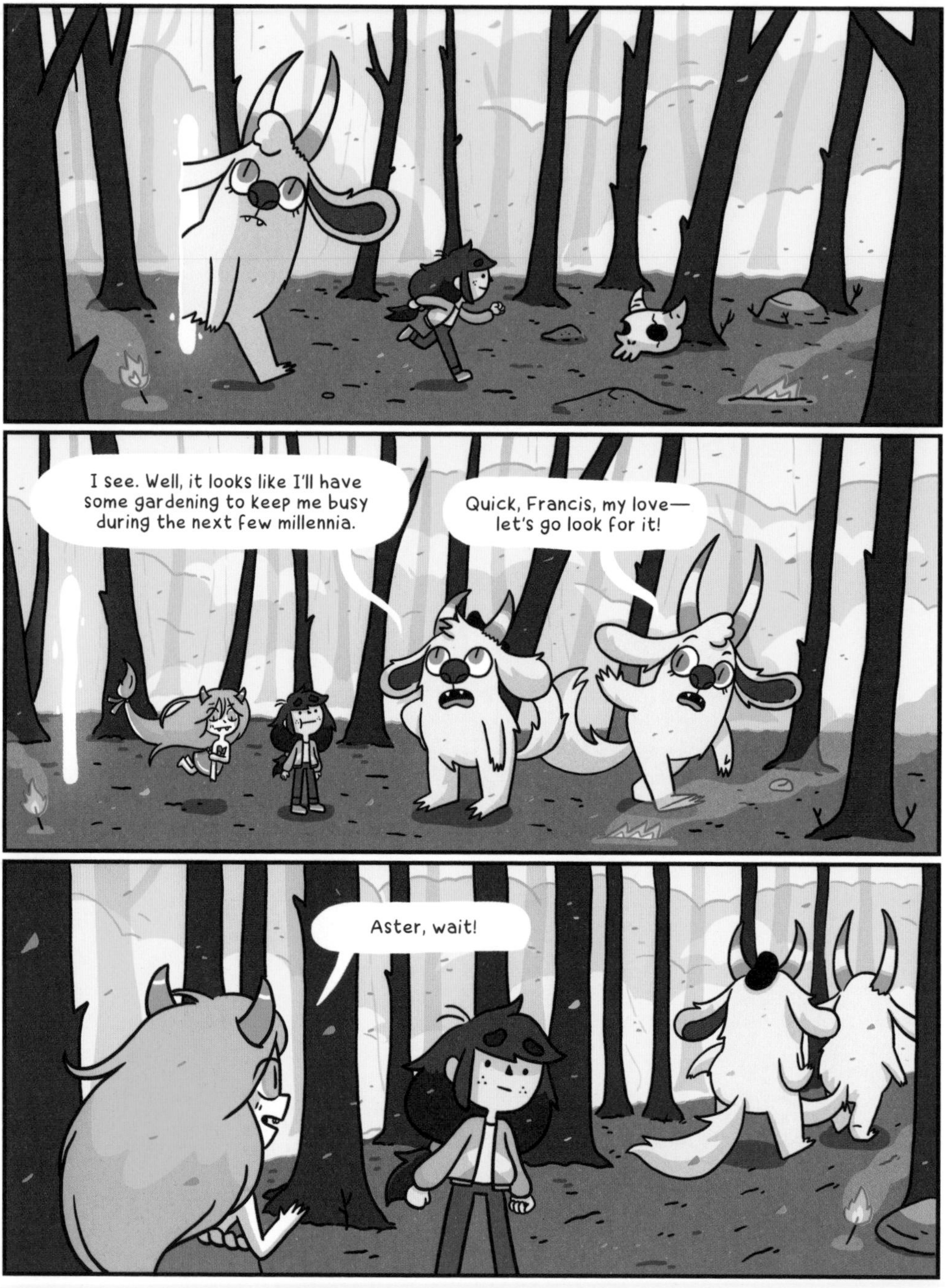
I see. Well, it looks like I'll have some gardening to keep me busy during the next few millennia.
Quick, Francis, my love— let's go look for it!
Aster, wait!

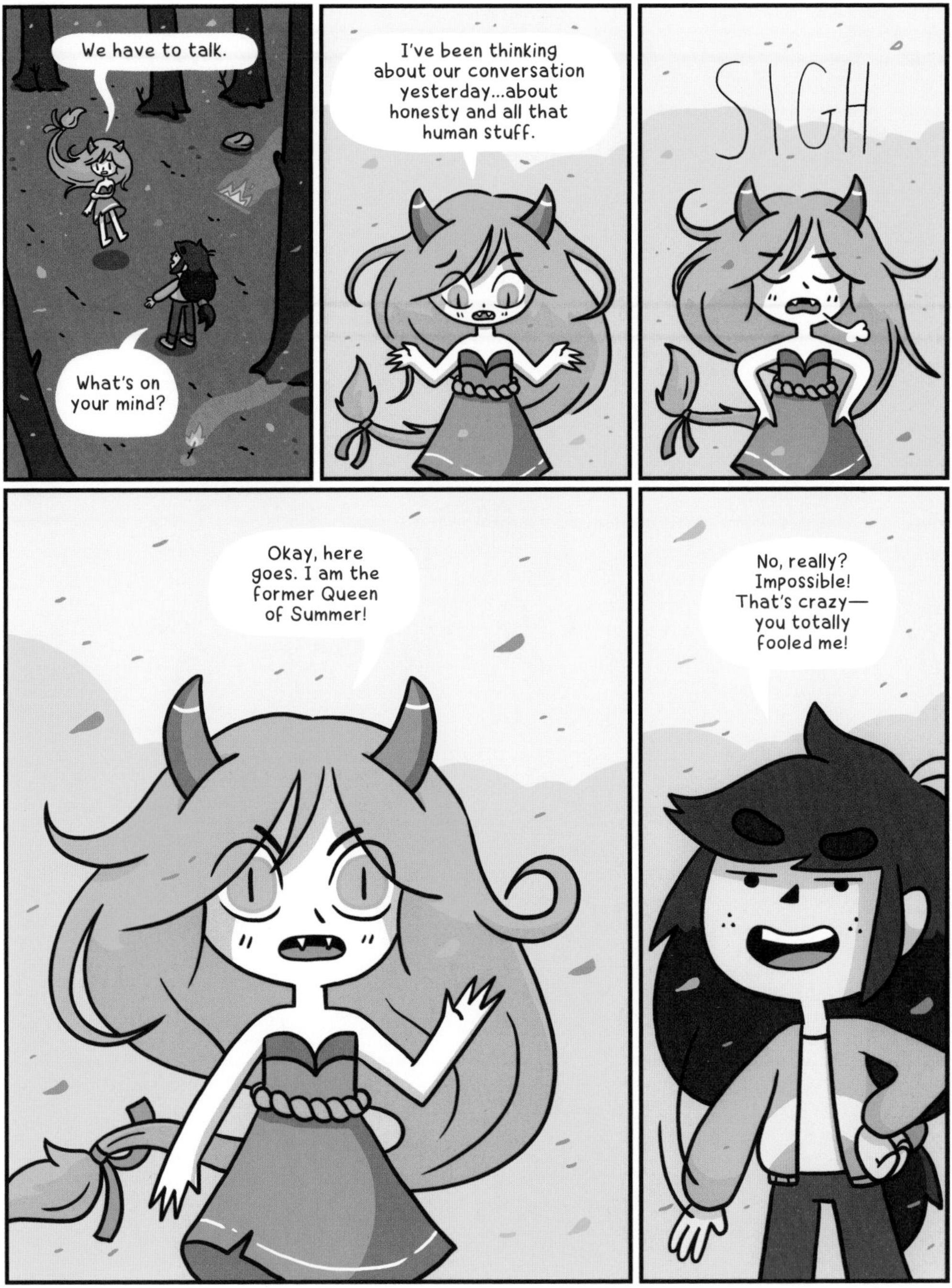
We have to talk.
What's on your mind?
I've been thinking about our conversation yesterday...about honesty and all that human stuff.
SIGH
Okay, here goes. I am the former Queen of Summer!
No, really? Impossible! That's crazy—you totally fooled me!

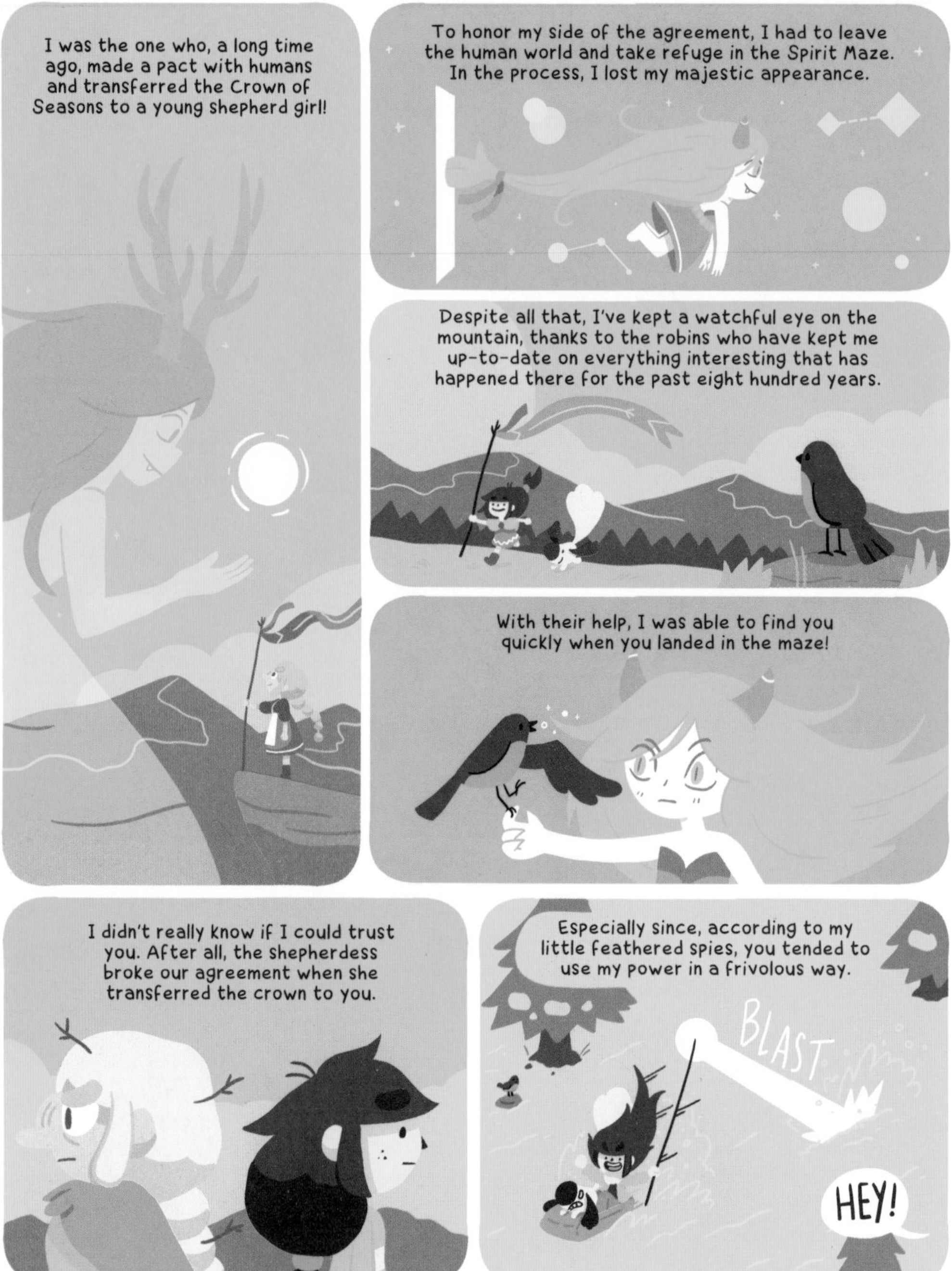
I was the one who, a long time ago, made a pact with humans and transferred the Crown of Seasons to a young shepherd girl!
To honor my side of the agreement, I had to leave the human world and take refuge in the Spirit Maze. In the process, I lost my majestic appearance.
Despite all that, I've kept a watchful eye on the mountain, thanks to the robins who have kept me up-to-date on everything interesting that has happened there for the past eight hundred years.
With their help, I was able to find you quickly when you landed in the maze!
I didn't really know if I could trust you. After all, the shepherdess broke our agreement when she transferred the crown to you.
Especially since, according to my little feathered spies, you tended to use my power in a frivolous way.
BLAST
HEY!

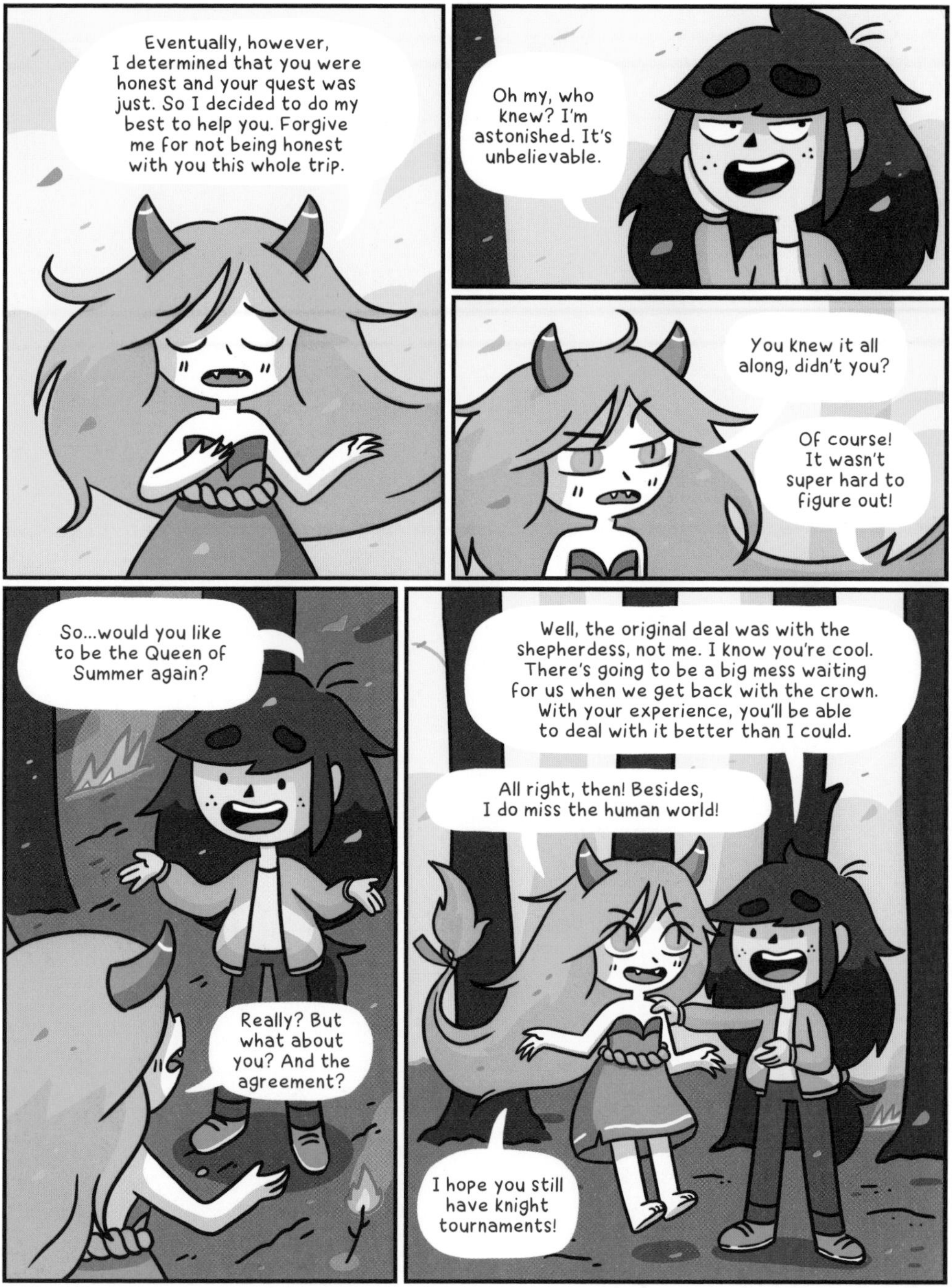
Eventually, however, I determined that you were honest and your quest was just. So I decided to do my best to help you. Forgive me for not being honest with you this whole trip.
Oh my, who knew? I'm astonished. It's unbelievable.
You knew it all along, didn't you?
Of course! It wasn't super hard to figure out!
So...would you like to be the Queen of Summer again?
Really? But what about you? And the agreement?
Well, the original deal was with the shepherdess, not me. I know you're cool. There's going to be a big mess waiting for us when we get back with the crown. With your experience, you'll be able to deal with it better than I could.
All right, then! Besides, I do miss the human world!
I hope you still have knight tournaments!

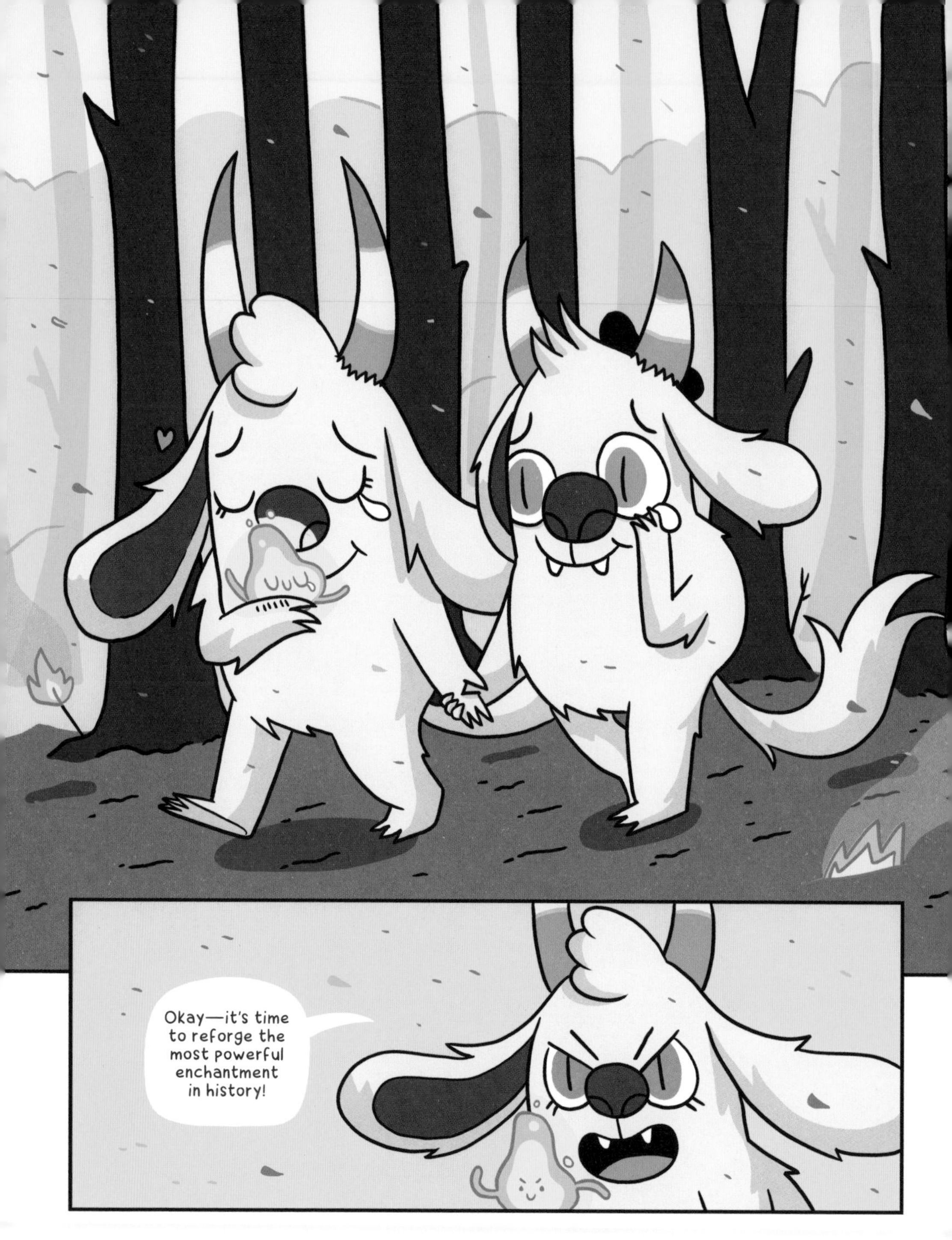
Okay—it's time to reforge the most powerful enchantment in history!

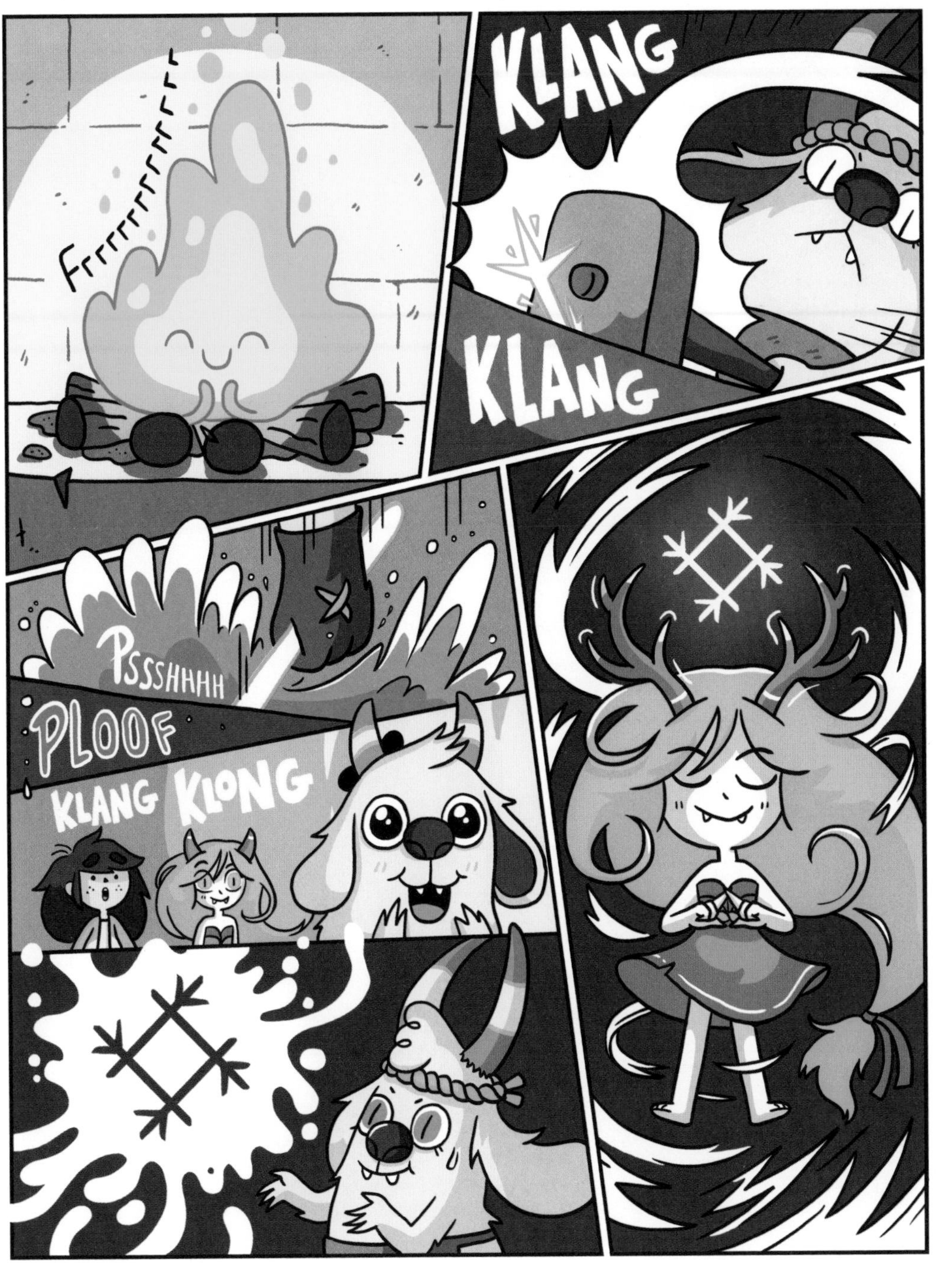
Frrrrrrrrrrr
KLANG
KLANG
PSSSHHHH
PLOOF
KLANG KLONG

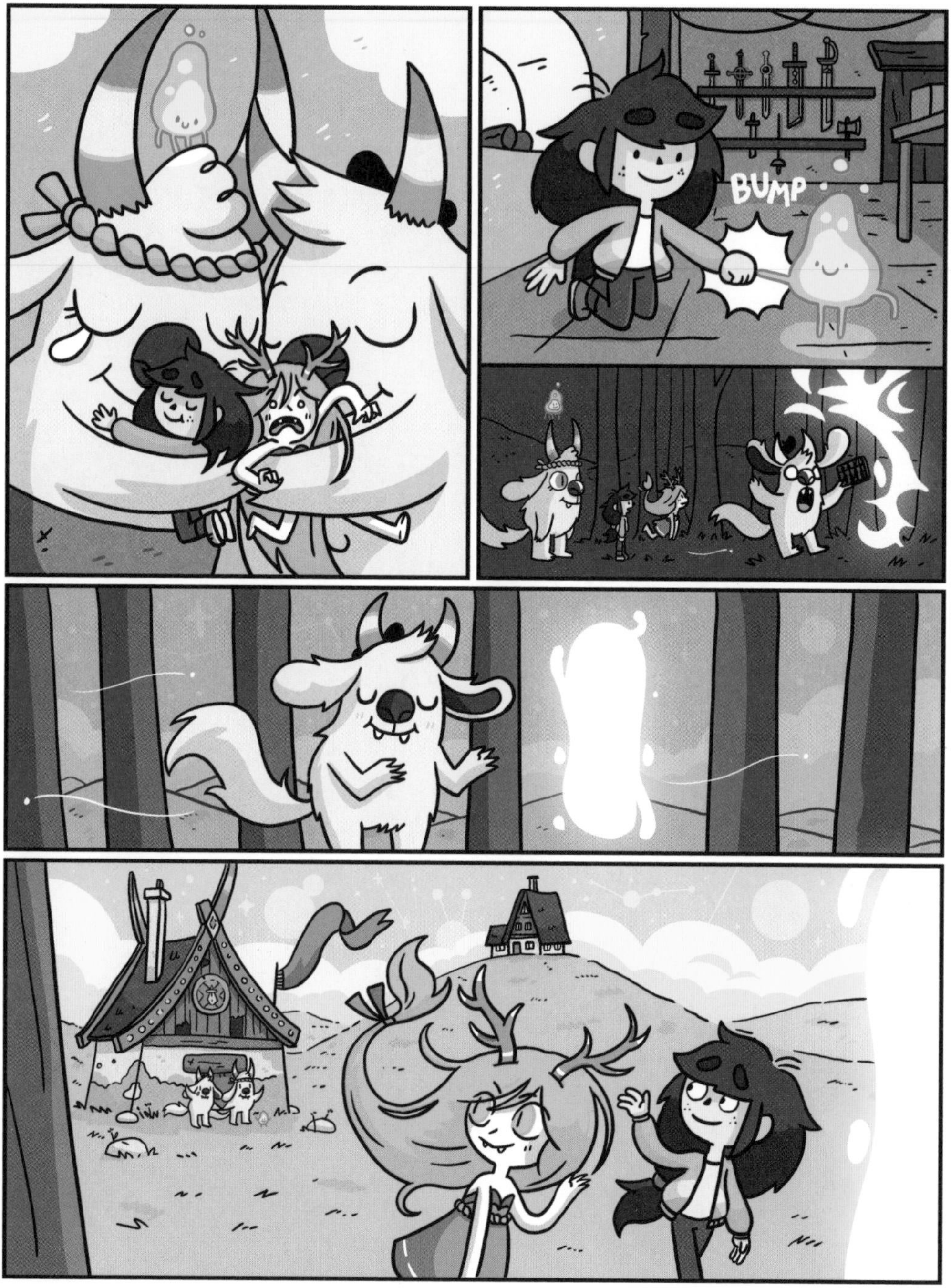
BUMP

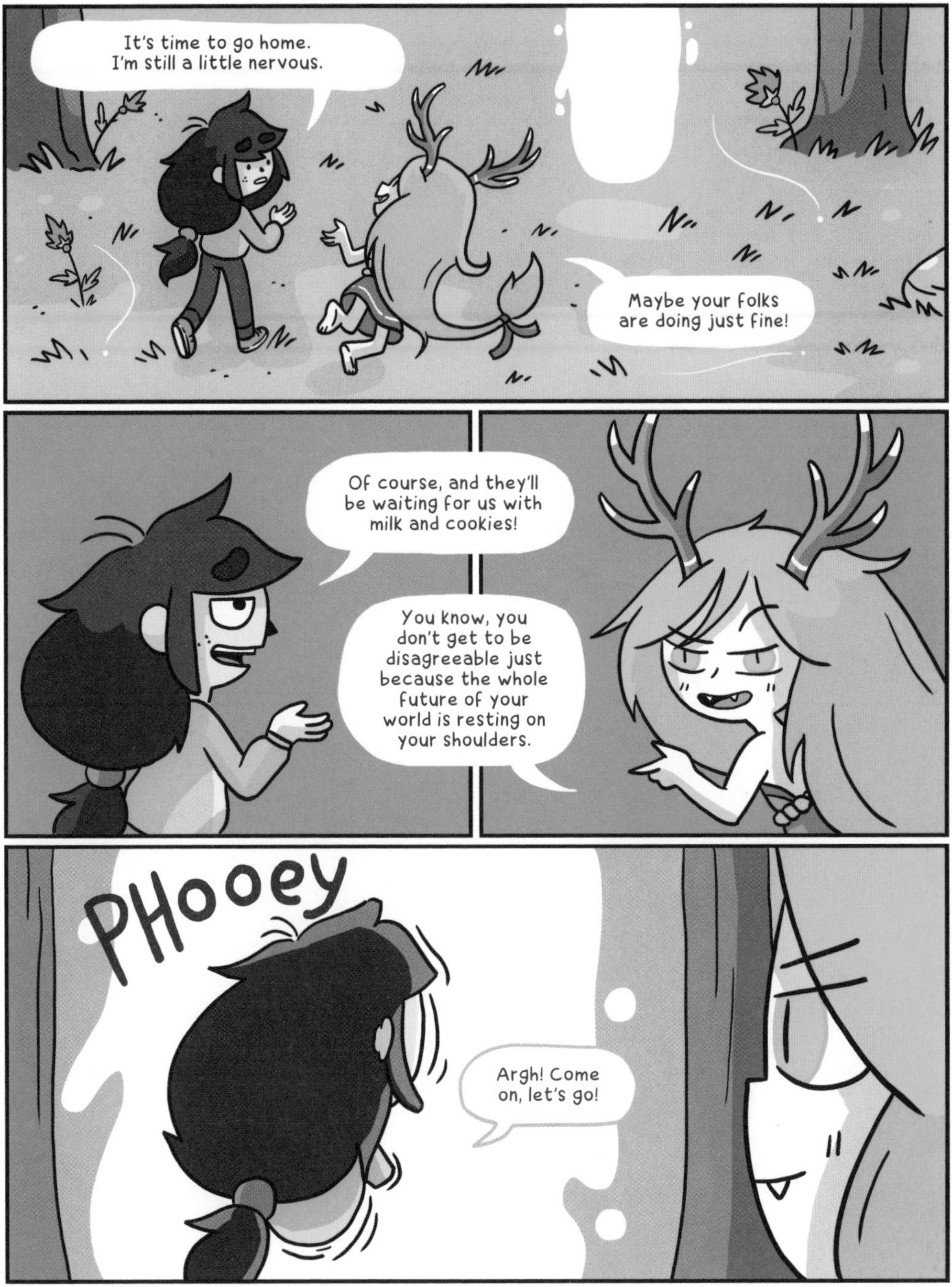
It's time to go home. I'm still a little nervous.
Maybe your folks are doing just fine!
Of course, and they'll be waiting for us with milk and cookies!
You know, you don't get to be disagreeable just because the whole future of your world is resting on your shoulders.
PHooey
Argh! Come on, let's go!

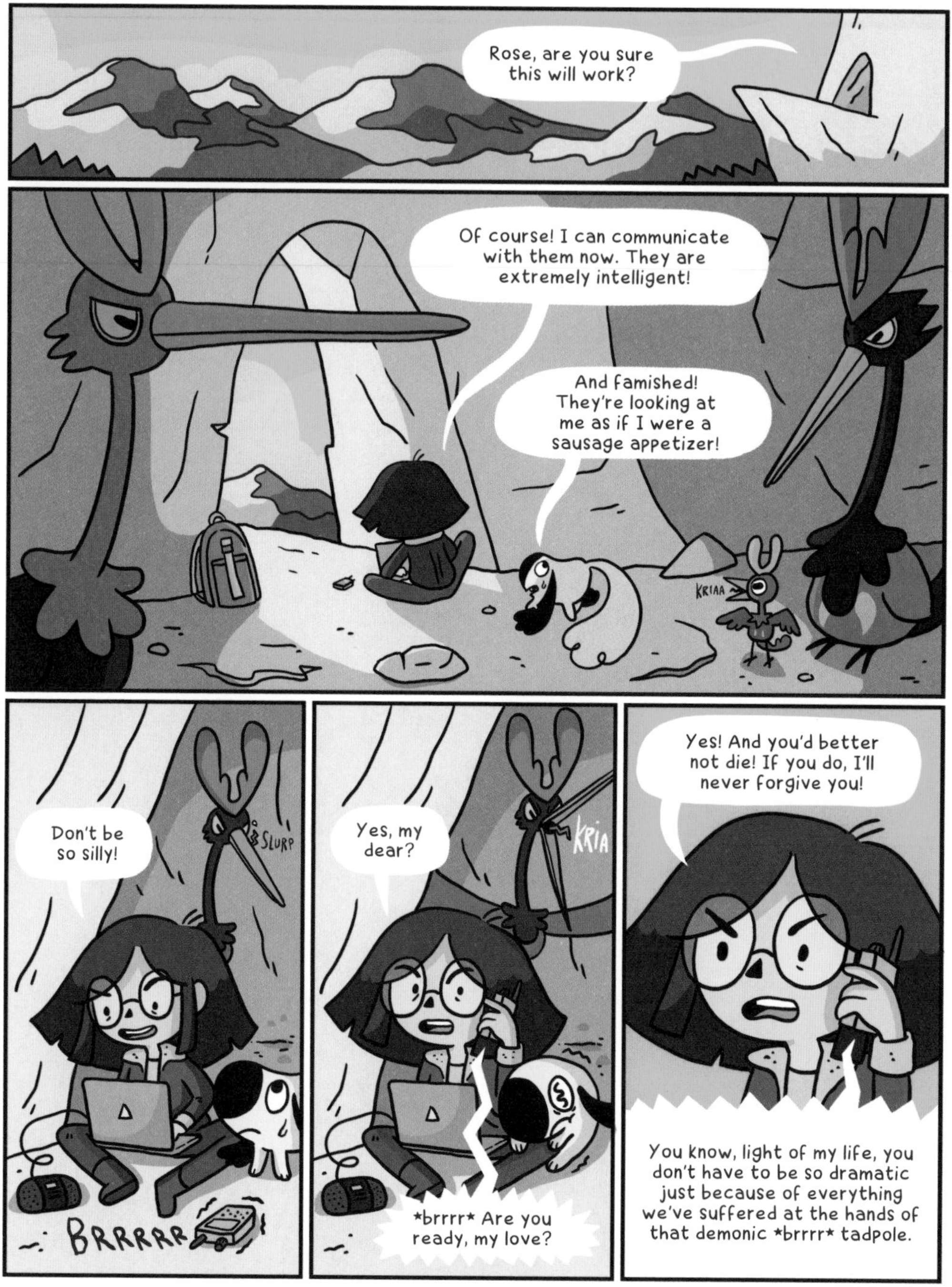

Rose, are you sure this will work?
Of course! I can communicate with them now. They are extremely intelligent!
And famished! They're looking at me as if I were a sausage appetizer!
KRIAA
Don't be so silly!
SLURP
BRRRRR
Yes, my dear?
KRIA
brrrr Are you ready, my love?
Yes! And you'd better not die! If you do, I'll never forgive you!
You know, light of my life, you don't have to be so dramatic just because of everything we've suffered at the hands of that demonic *brrrr* tadpole.

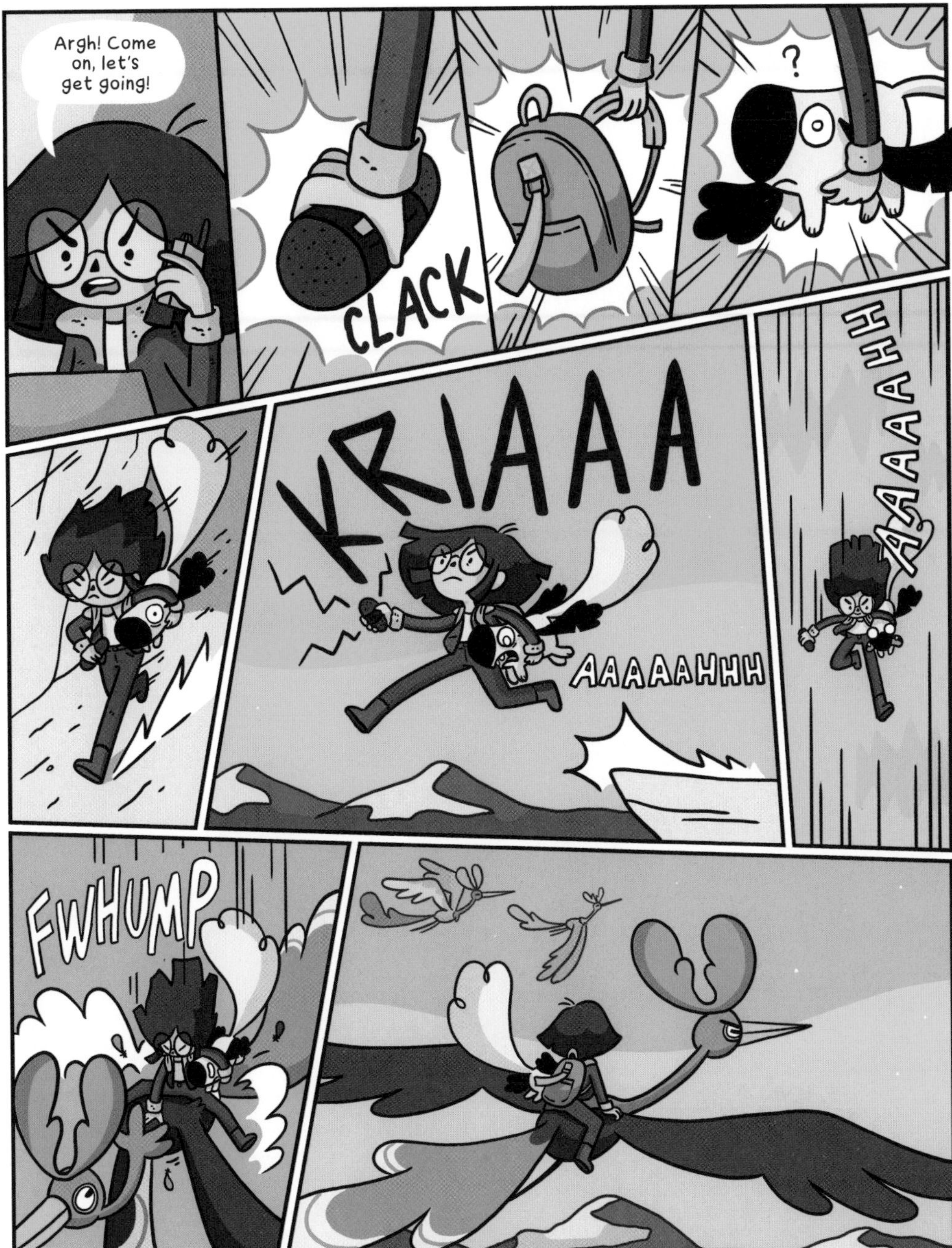
Argh! Come on, let's get going!
CLACK
?
KRIAAA
AAAAAHHH
AAAAAAAHH
FWHUMP

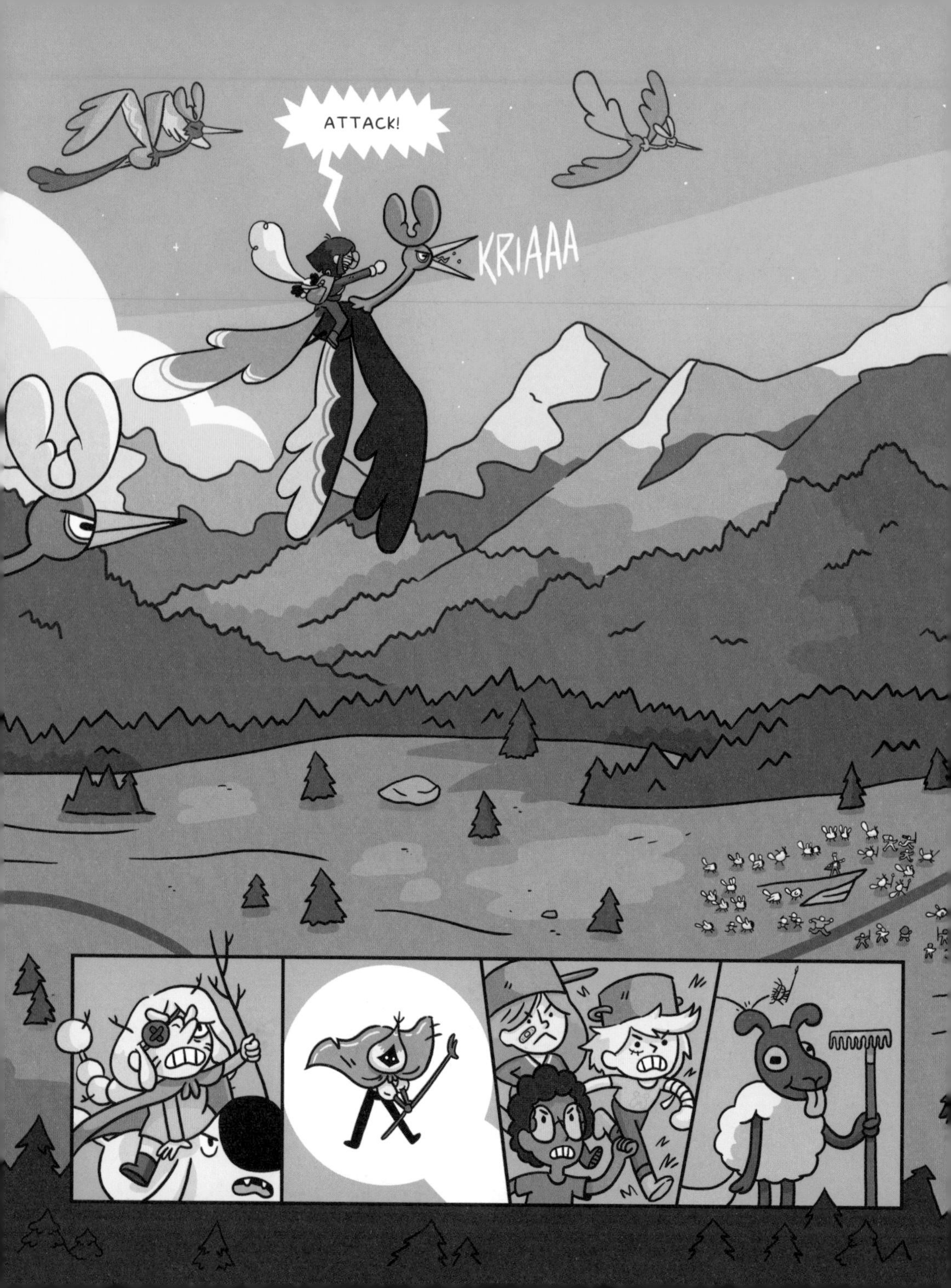
ATTACK!
KRIAAA

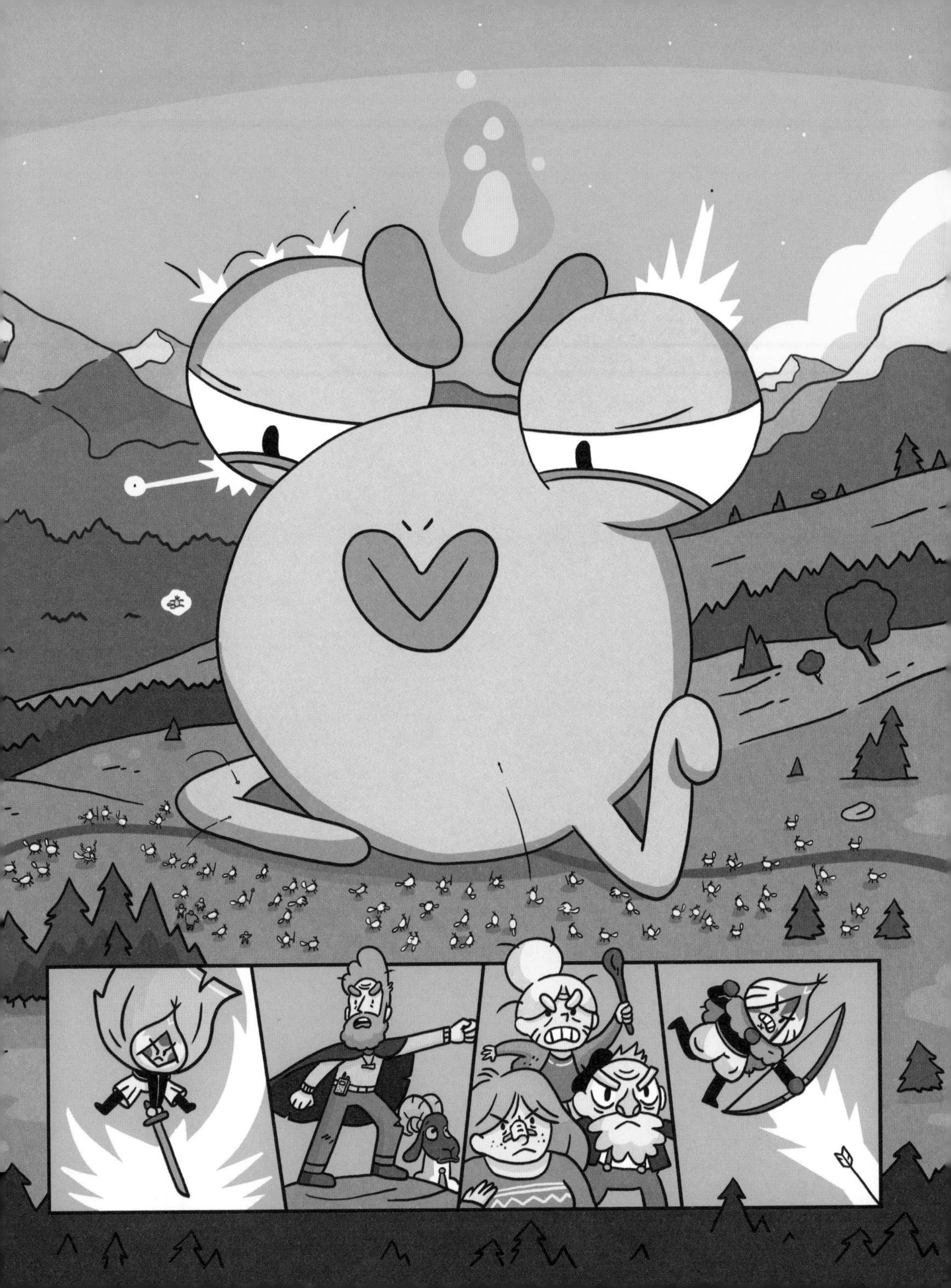

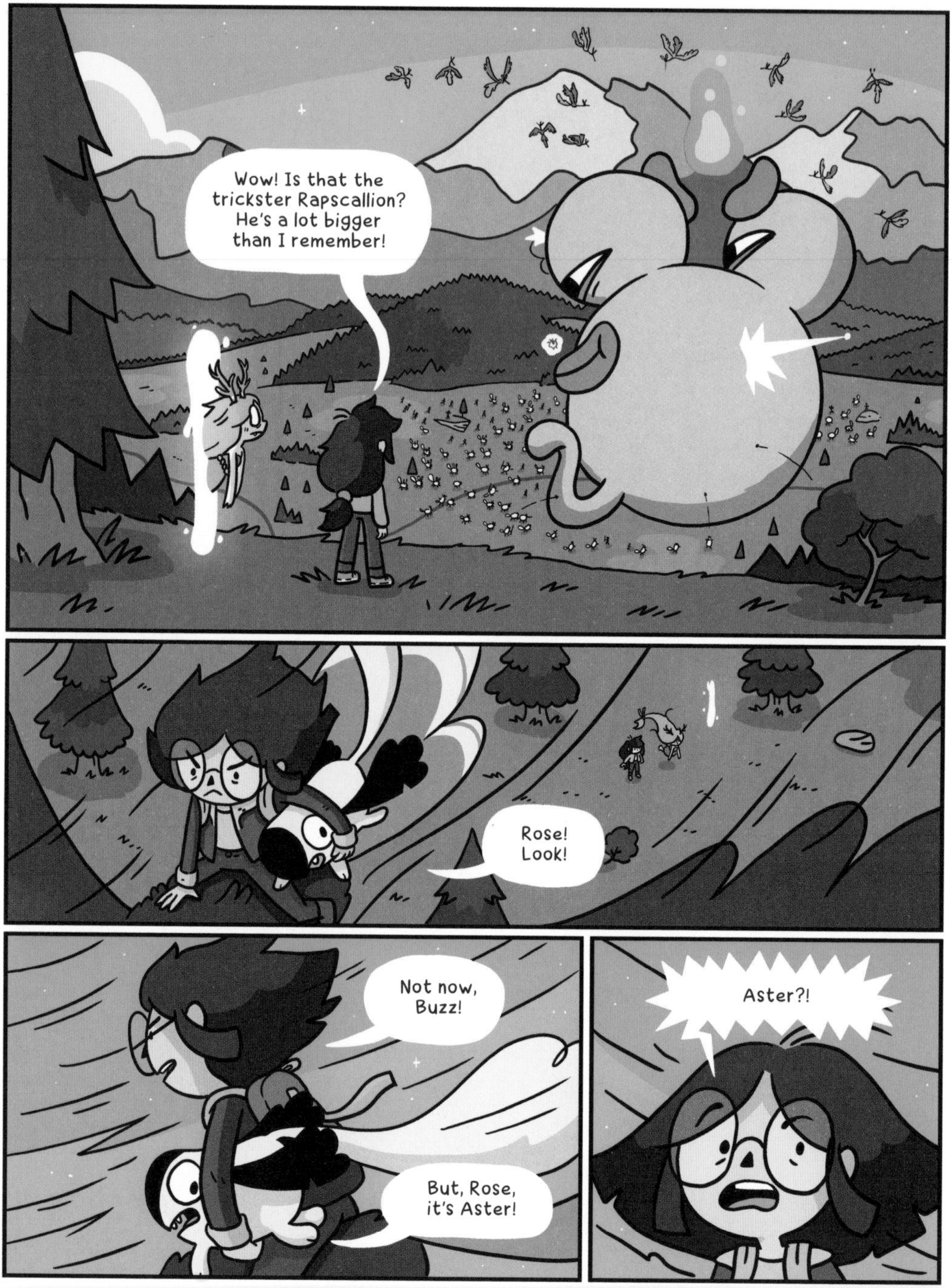
Wow! Is that the trickster Rapscallion? He's a lot bigger than I remember!
Rose! Look!
Not now, Buzz!
But, Rose, it's Aster!
Aster?!

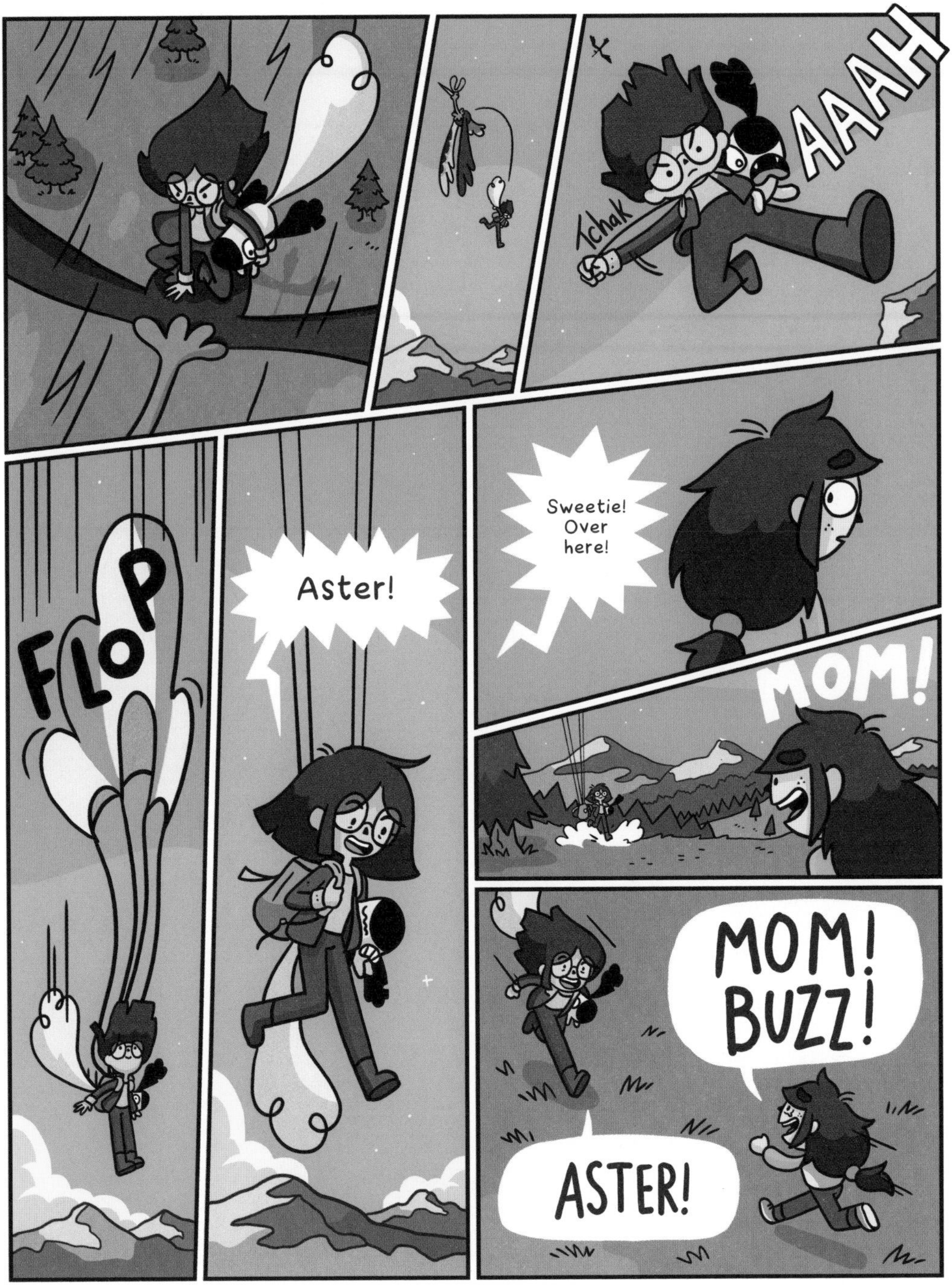

Tchak
AAAH
FLOP
Aster!
Sweetie! Over here!
MOM!
MOM! BUZZ!
ASTER!

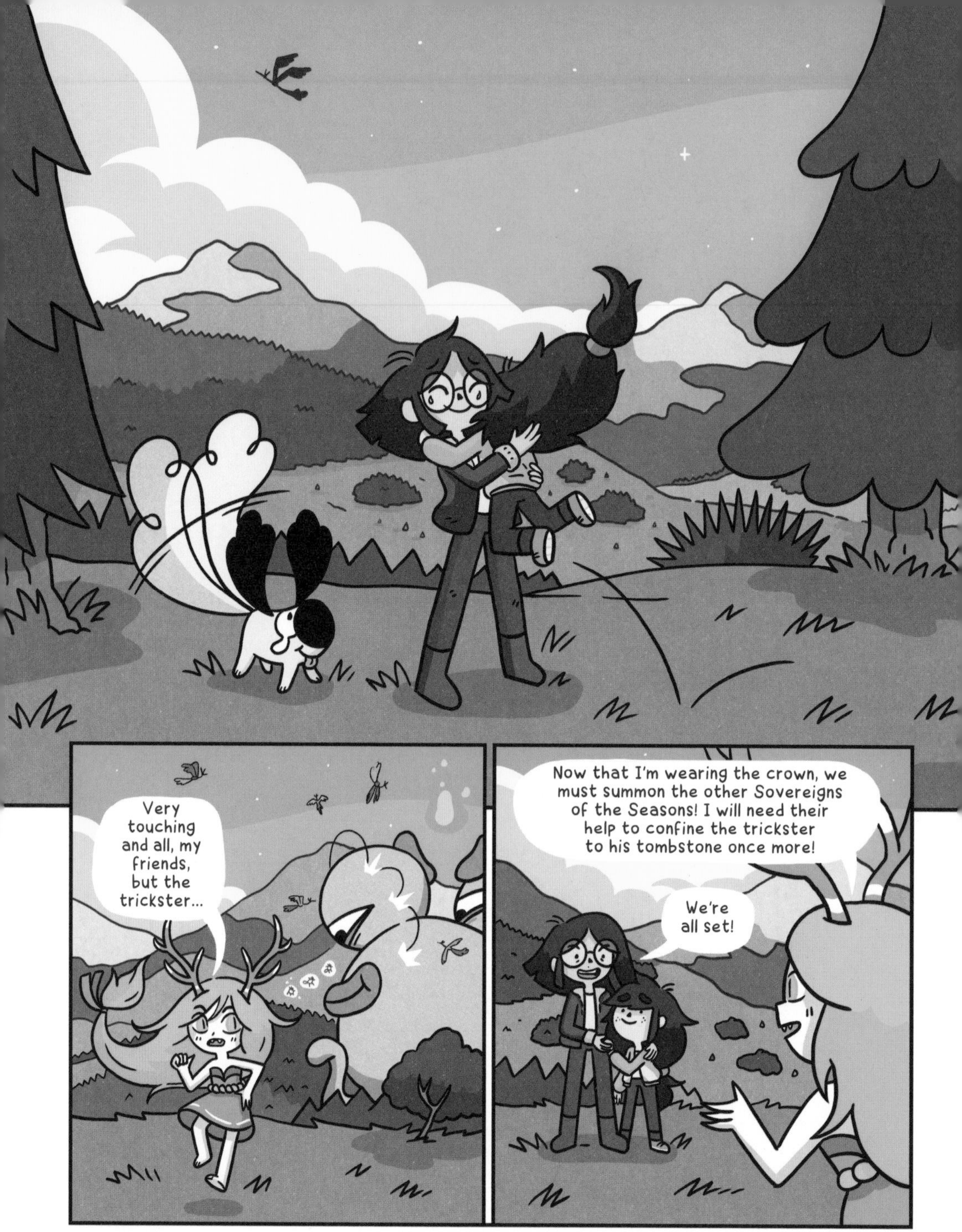
Very touching and all, my friends, but the trickster...
Now that I'm wearing the crown, we must summon the other Sovereigns of the Seasons! I will need their help to confine the trickster to his tombstone once more!
We're all set!

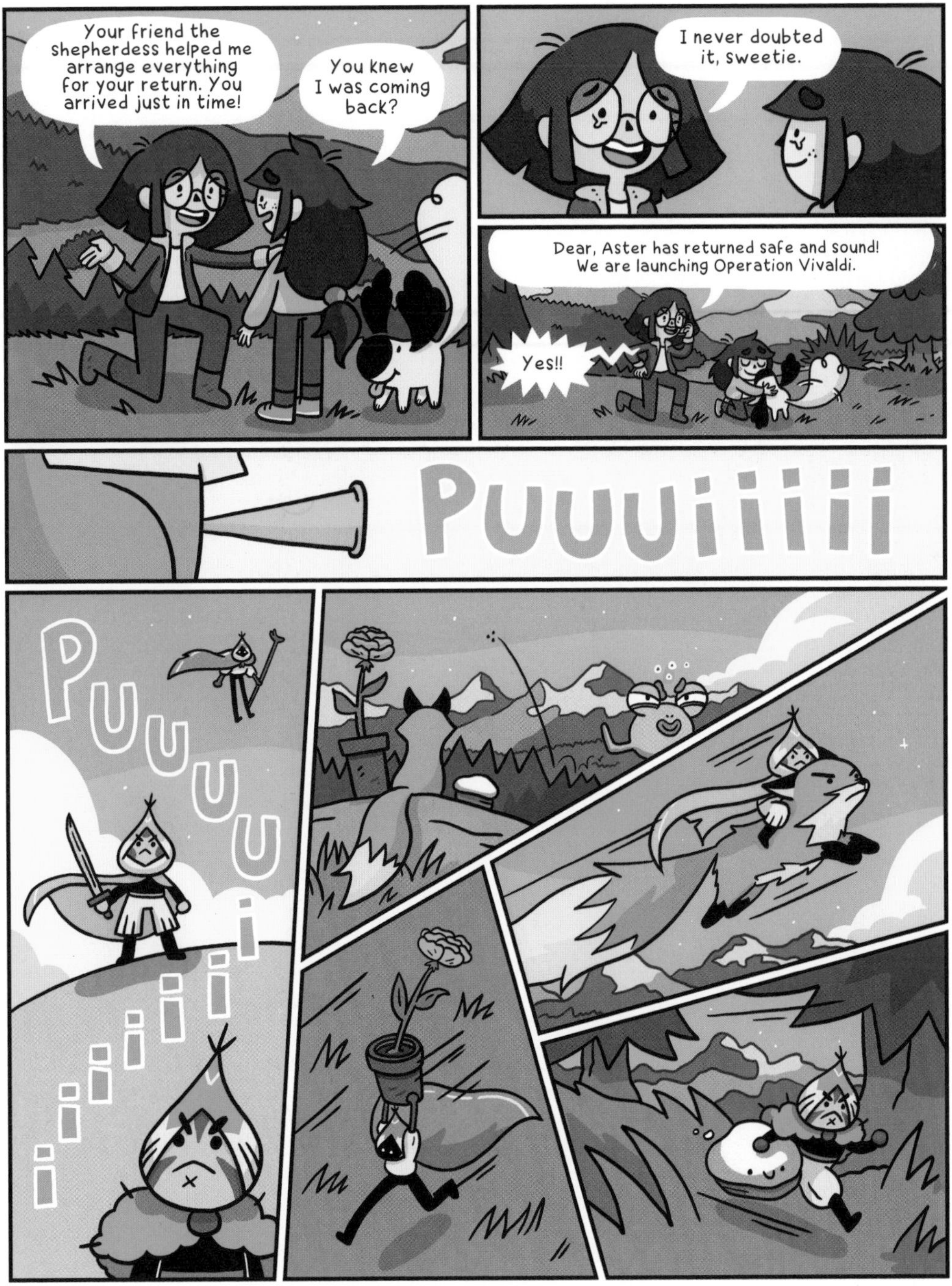

Your friend the shepherdess helped me arrange everything for your return. You arrived just in time!
You knew I was coming back?
I never doubted it, sweetie.
Dear, Aster has returned safe and sound! We are launching Operation Vivaldi.
Yes!!
Puuuiiiii
Puuuuuiiiiiiii

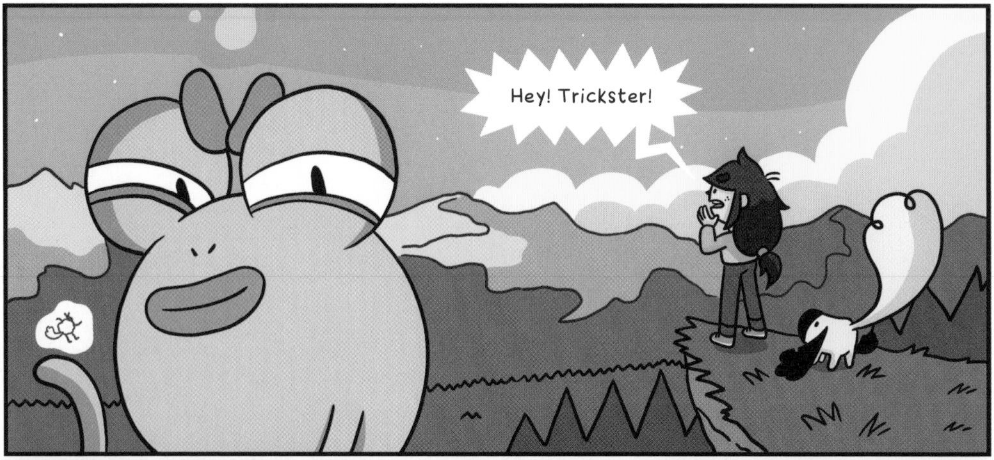
Hey! Trickster!

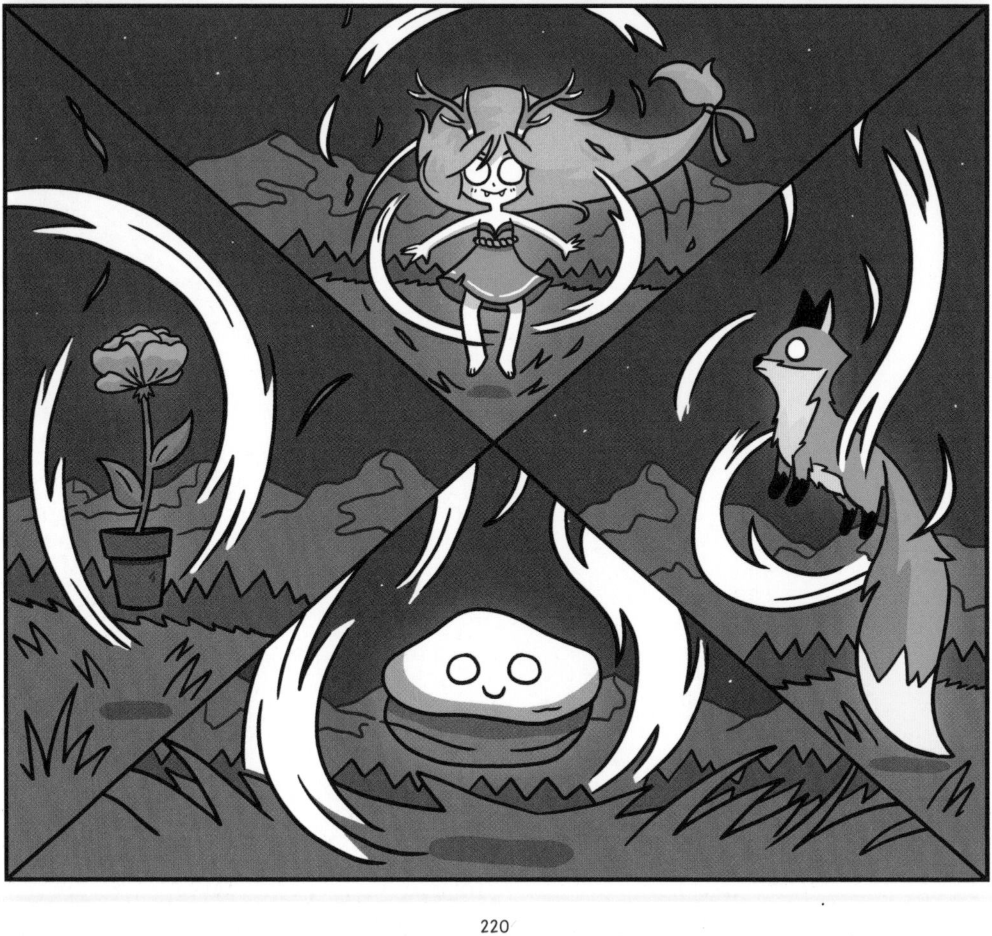

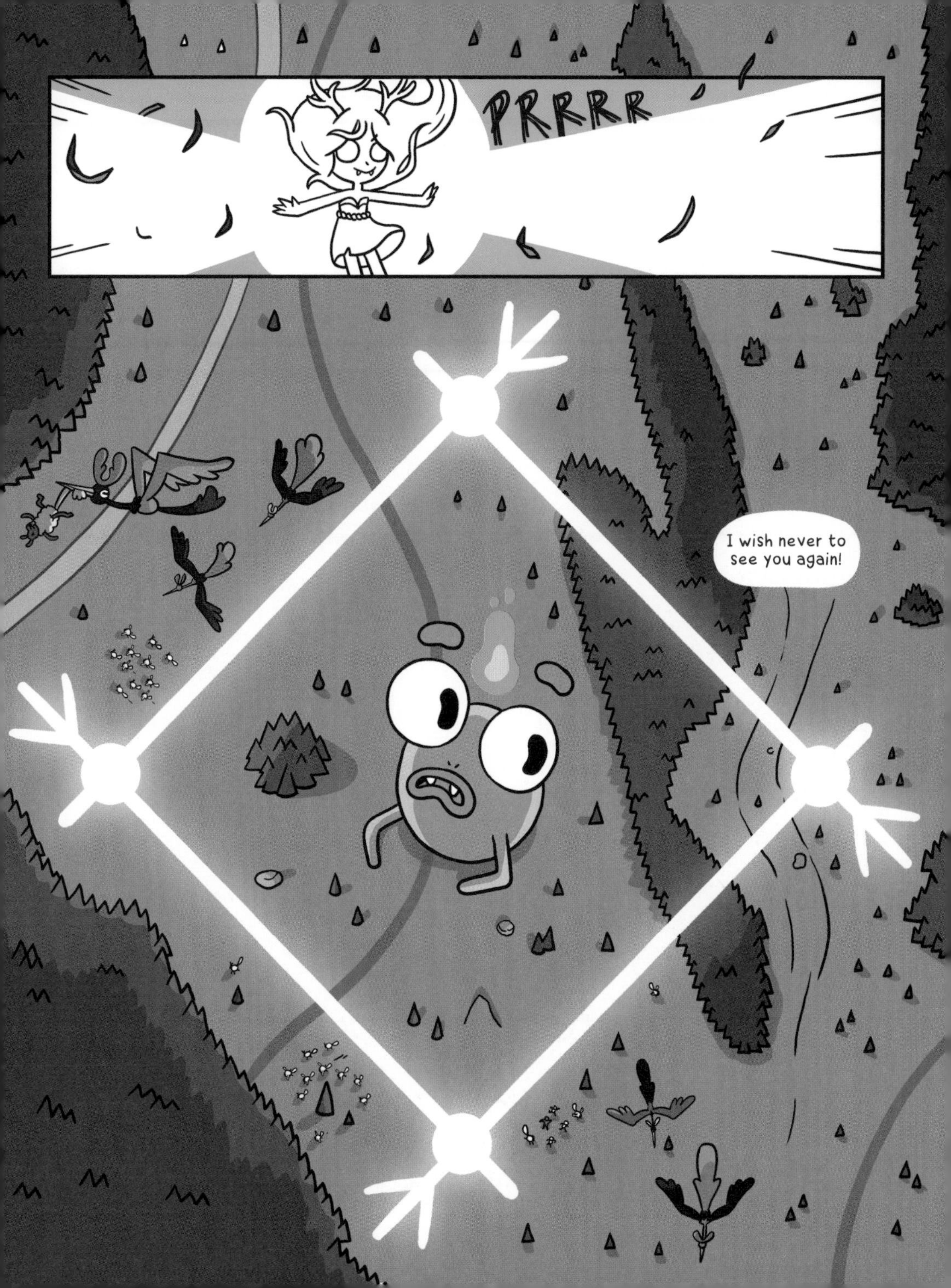
PRRRR
I wish never to see you again!

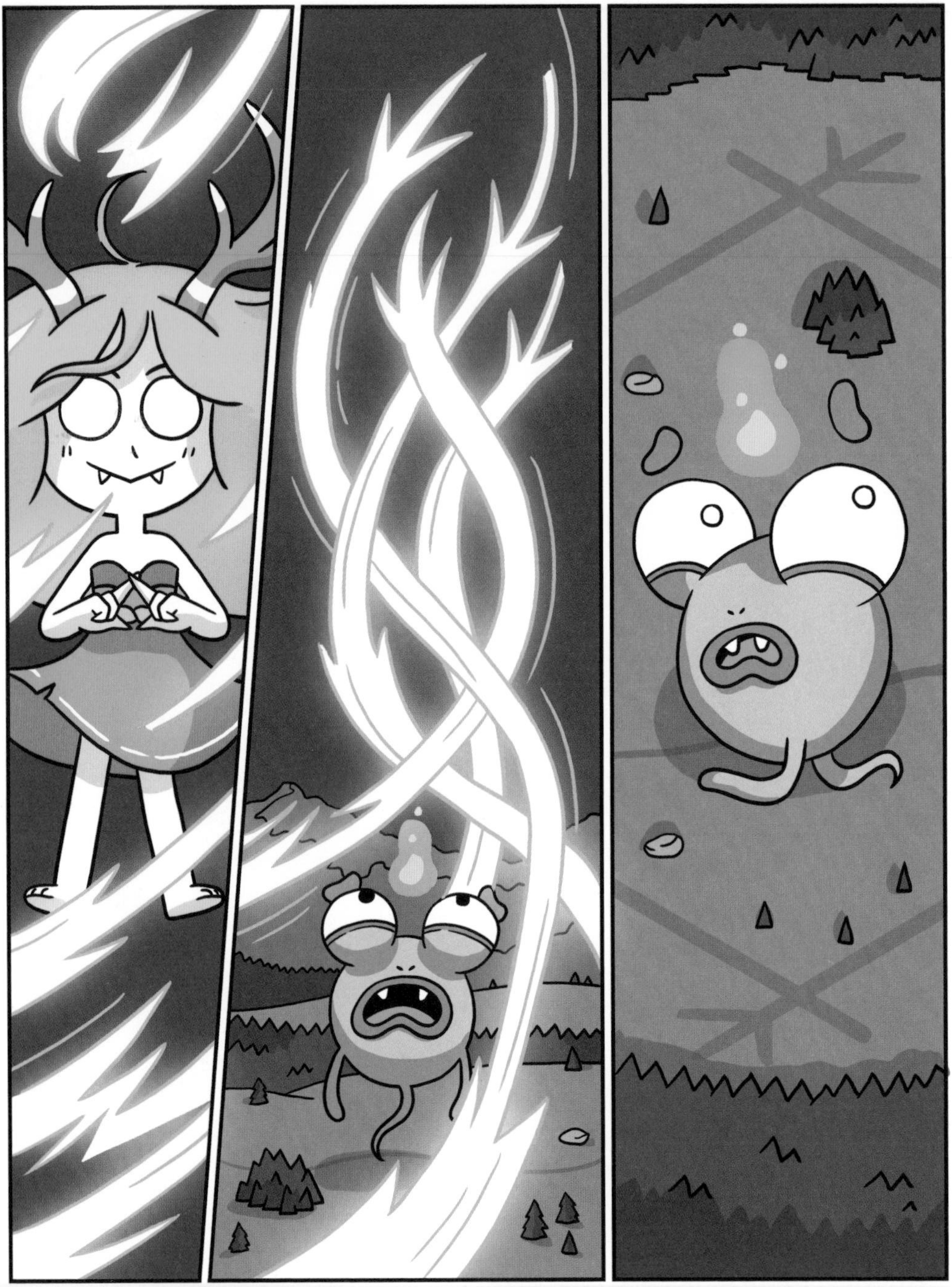

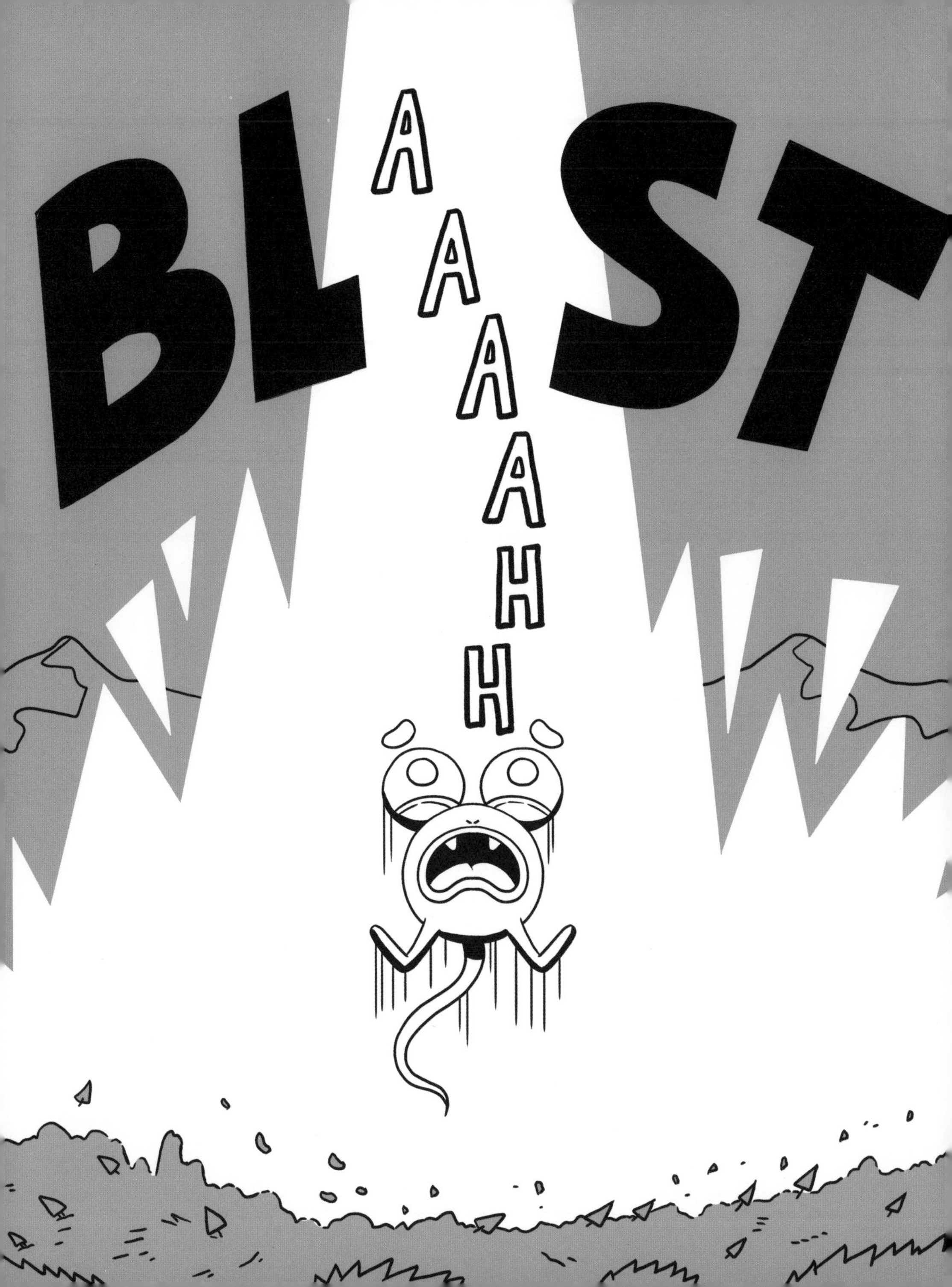
BL
AAAAAHH
ST

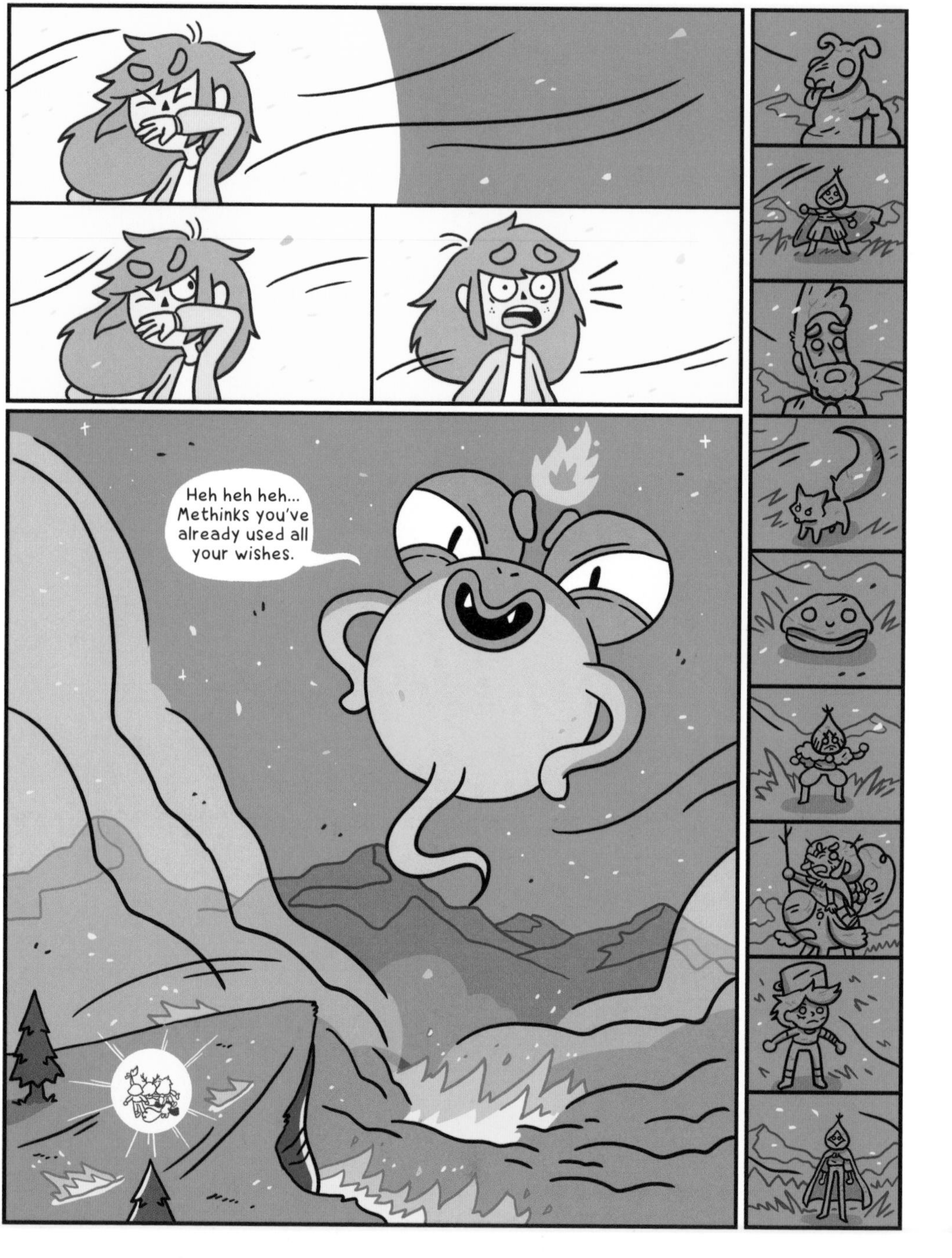
Heh heh heh...
Methinks you've already used all your wishes.

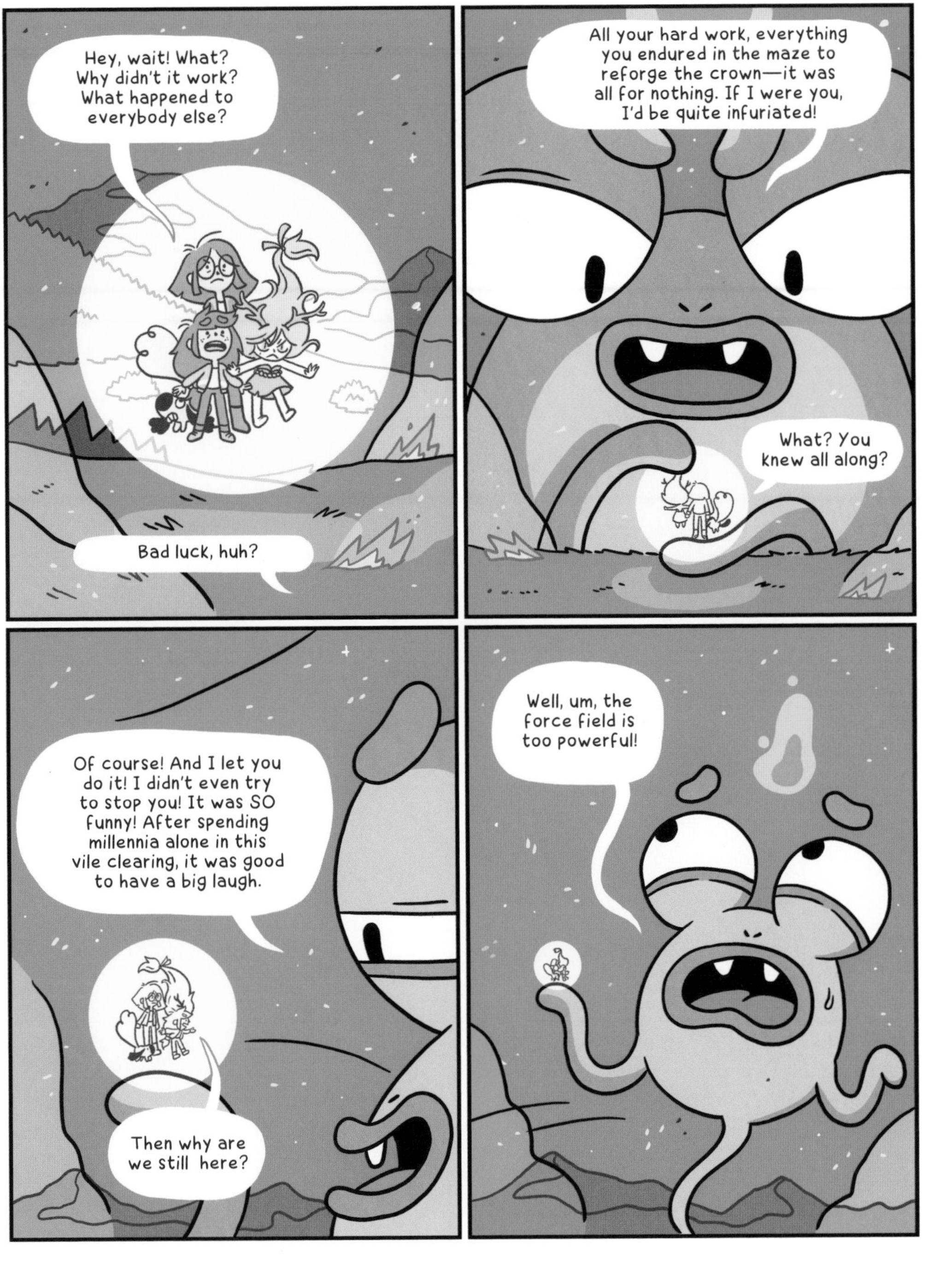
Hey, wait! What? Why didn't it work? What happened to everybody else?
Bad luck, huh?
All your hard work, everything you endured in the maze to reforge the crown—it was all for nothing. If I were you, I'd be quite infuriated!
What? You knew all along?
Of course! And I let you do it! I didn't even try to stop you! It was SO funny! After spending millennia alone in this vile clearing, it was good to have a big laugh.
Then why are we still here?
Well, um, the force field is too powerful!

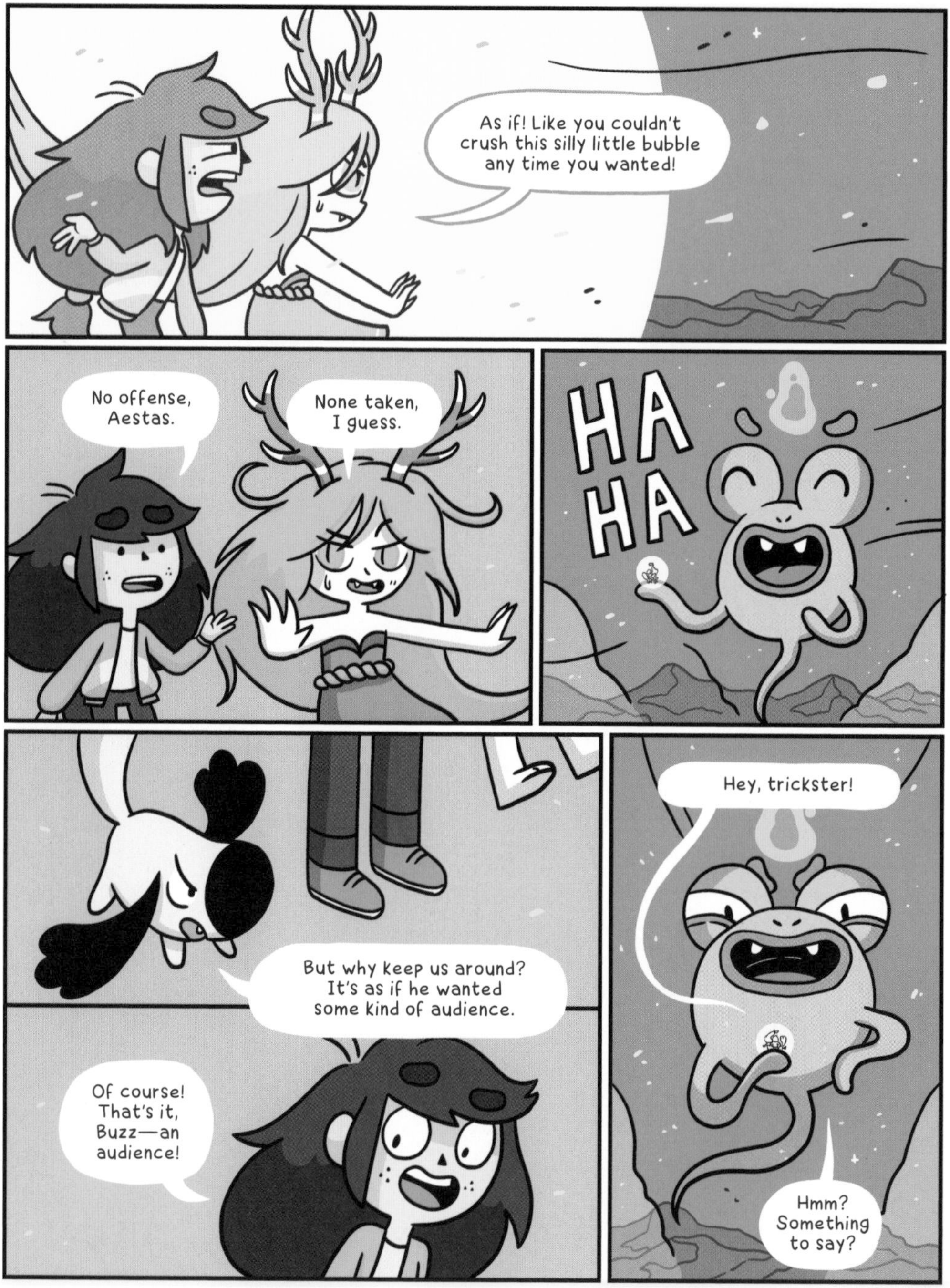

As if! Like you couldn't crush this silly little bubble any time you wanted!
No offense, Aestas.
None taken, I guess.
HA HA
But why keep us around? It's as if he wanted some kind of audience.
Of course! That's it, Buzz—an audience!
Hey, trickster!
Hmm? Something to say?

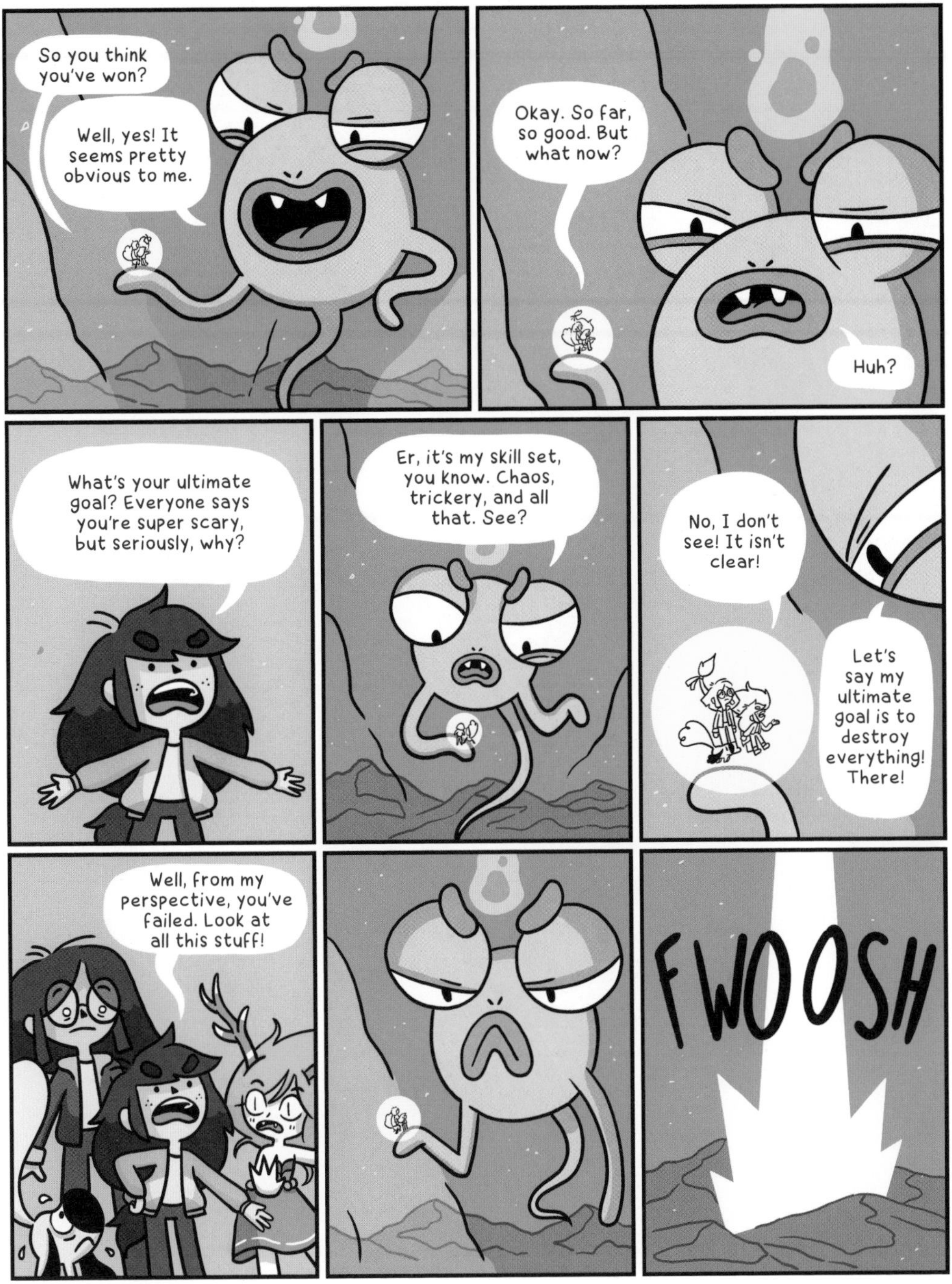
So you think you've won?
Well, yes! It seems pretty obvious to me.
Okay. So far, so good. But what now?
Huh?
What's your ultimate goal? Everyone says you're super scary, but seriously, why?
Er, it's my skill set, you know. Chaos, trickery, and all that. See?
No, I don't see! It isn't clear!
Let's say my ultimate goal is to destroy everything! There!
Well, from my perspective, you've failed. Look at all this stuff!
FWOOSH

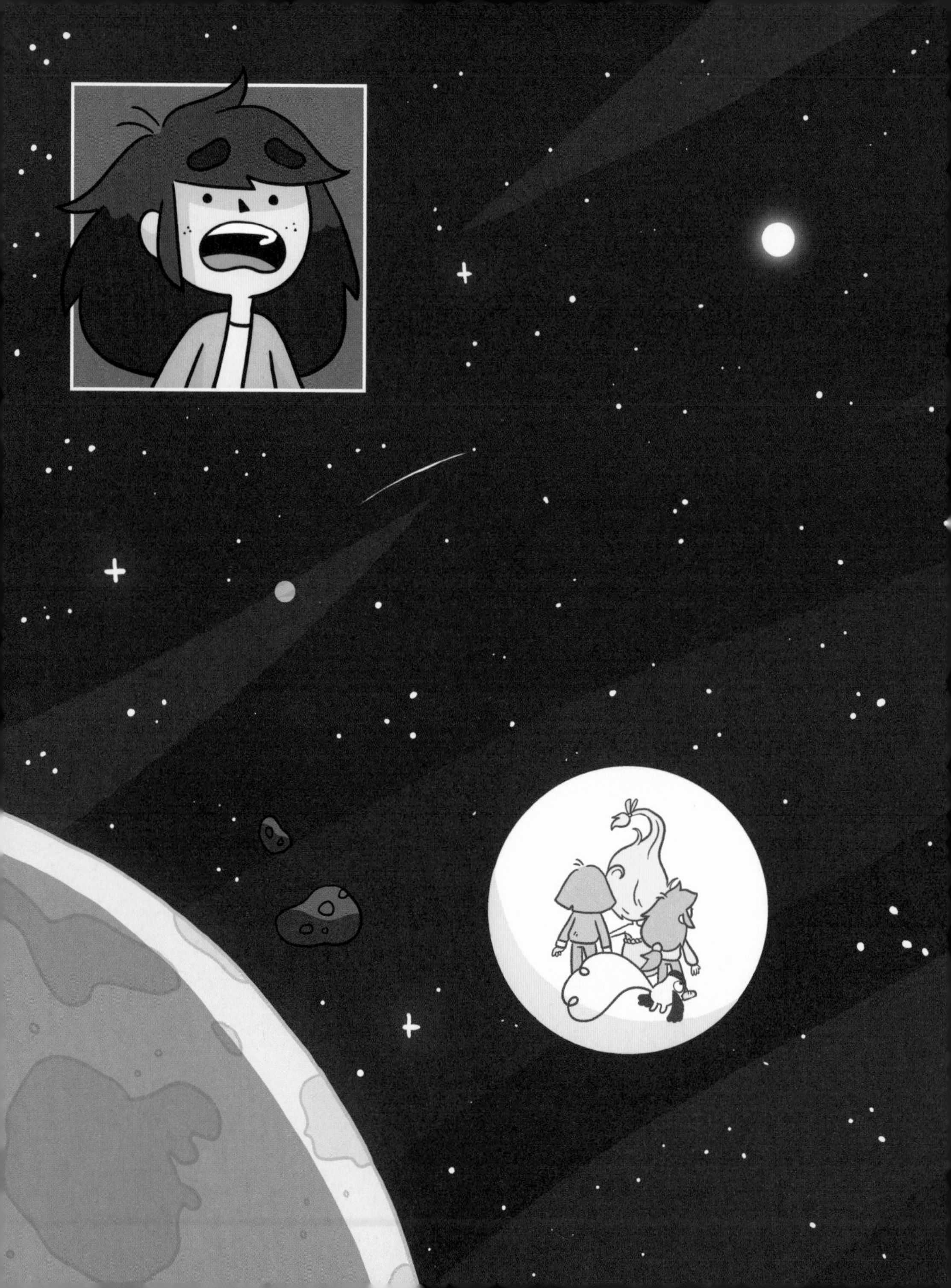

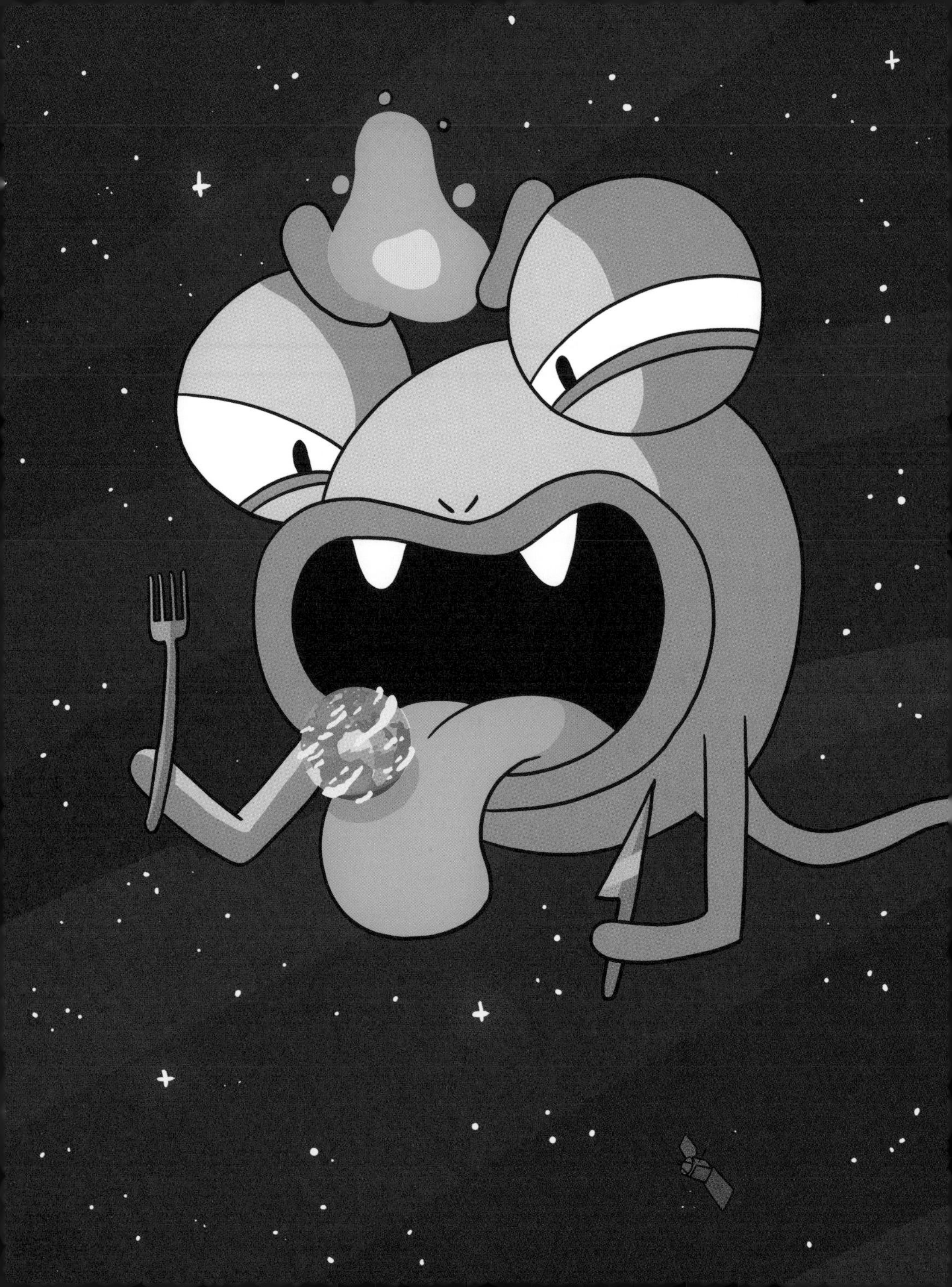

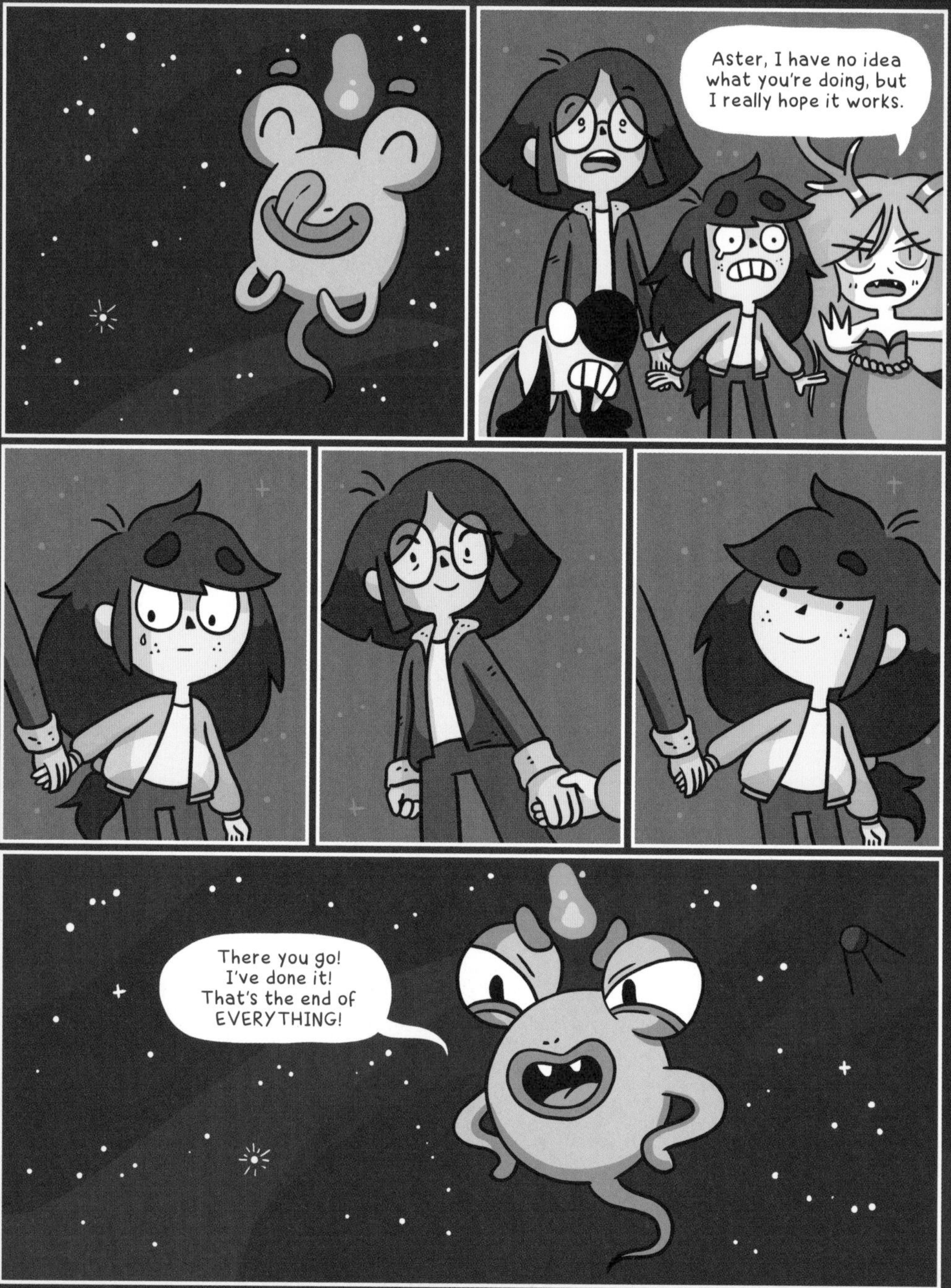
Aster, I have no idea what you're doing, but I really hope it works.
There you go! I've done it! That's the end of EVERYTHING!

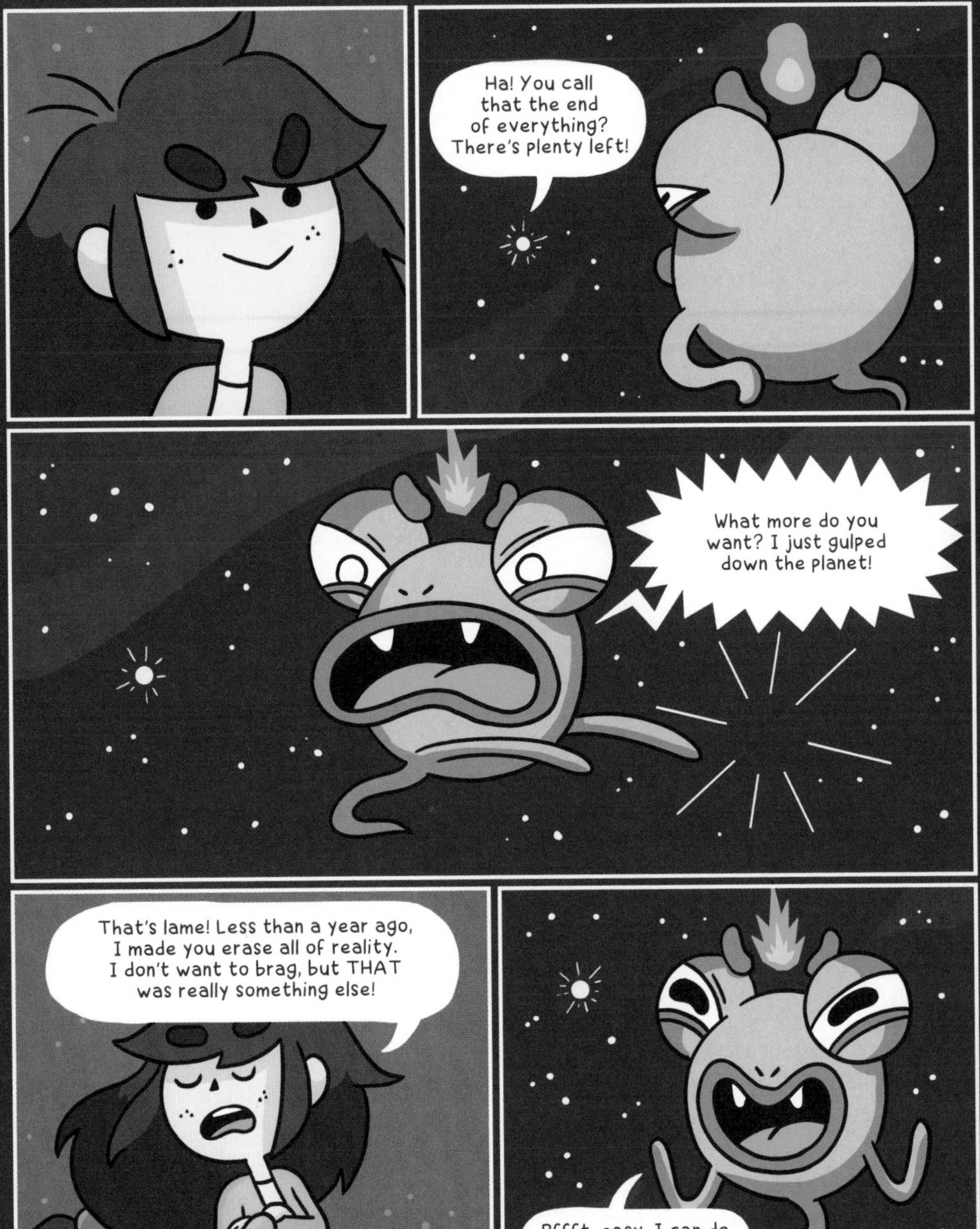
Ha! You call that the end of everything? There's plenty left!
What more do you want? I just gulped down the planet!
That's lame! Less than a year ago, I made you erase all of reality. I don't want to brag, but THAT was really something else!
Pffft, easy. I can do that anytime I want!

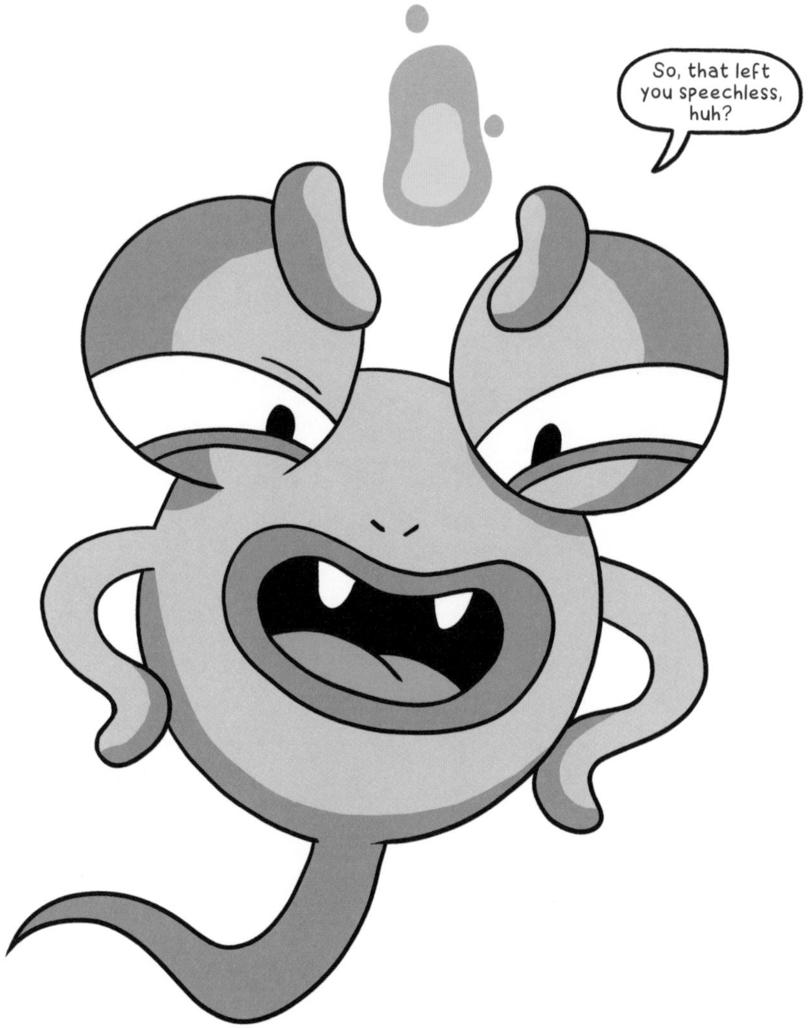
So, that left you speechless, huh?

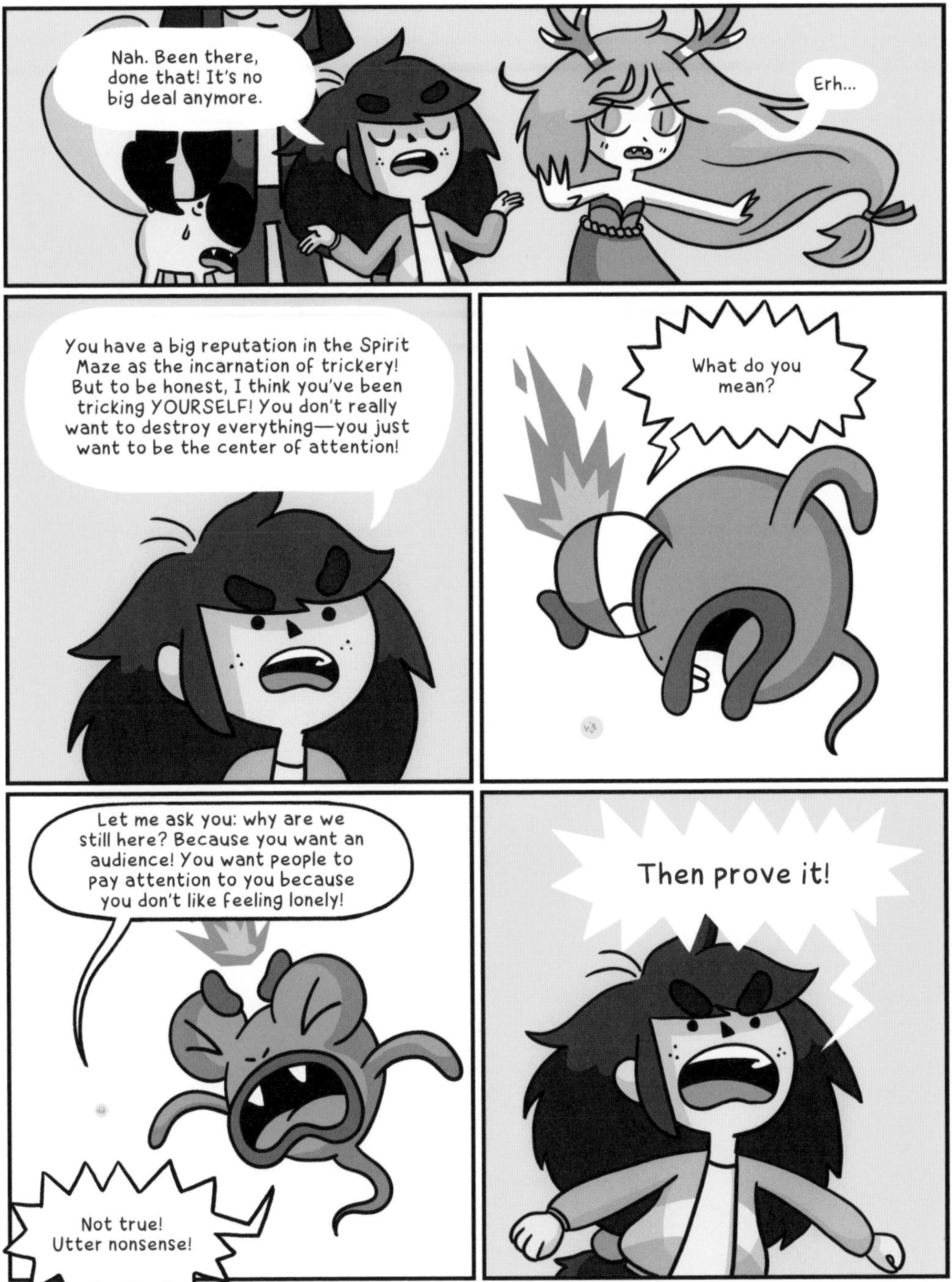
Nah. Been there, done that! It's no big deal anymore.
Erh...
You have a big reputation in the Spirit Maze as the incarnation of trickery! But to be honest, I think you've been tricking YOURSELF! You don't really want to destroy everything—you just want to be the center of attention!
What do you mean?
Let me ask you: why are we still here? Because you want an audience! You want people to pay attention to you because you don't like feeling lonely!
Not true! Utter nonsense!
Then prove it!

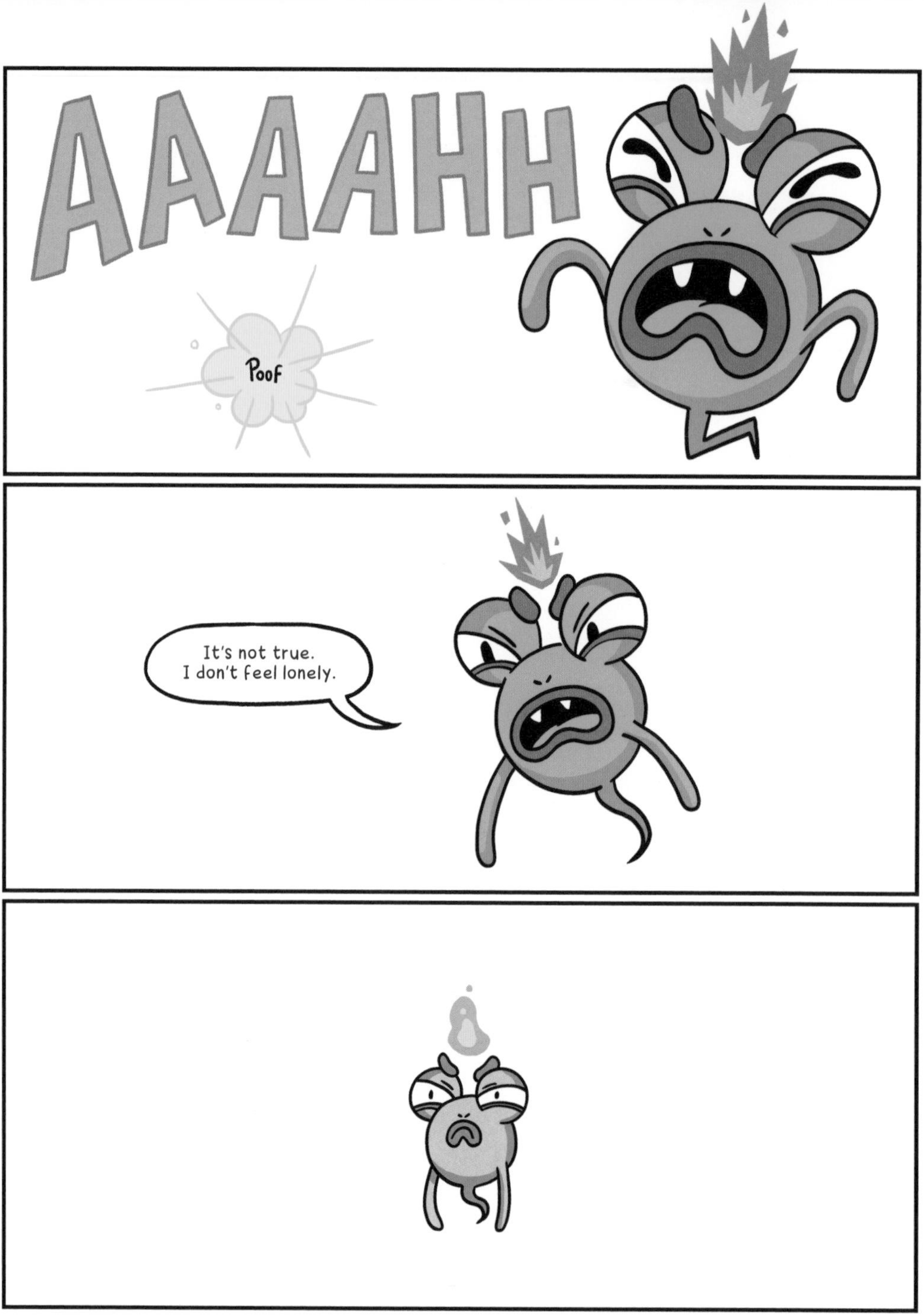
AAAAHH
Poof
It's not true.
I don't feel lonely.

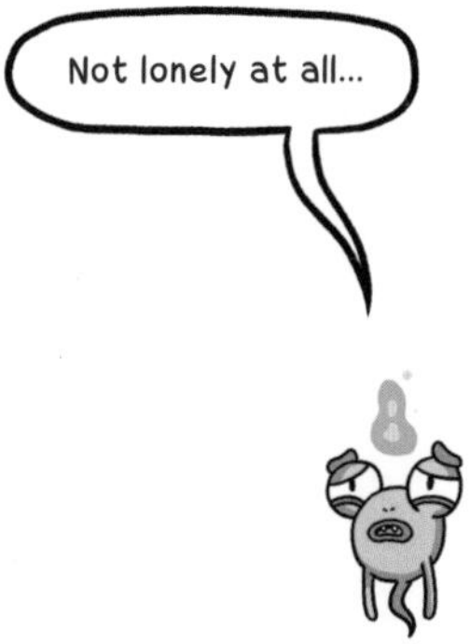
Not lonely at all...

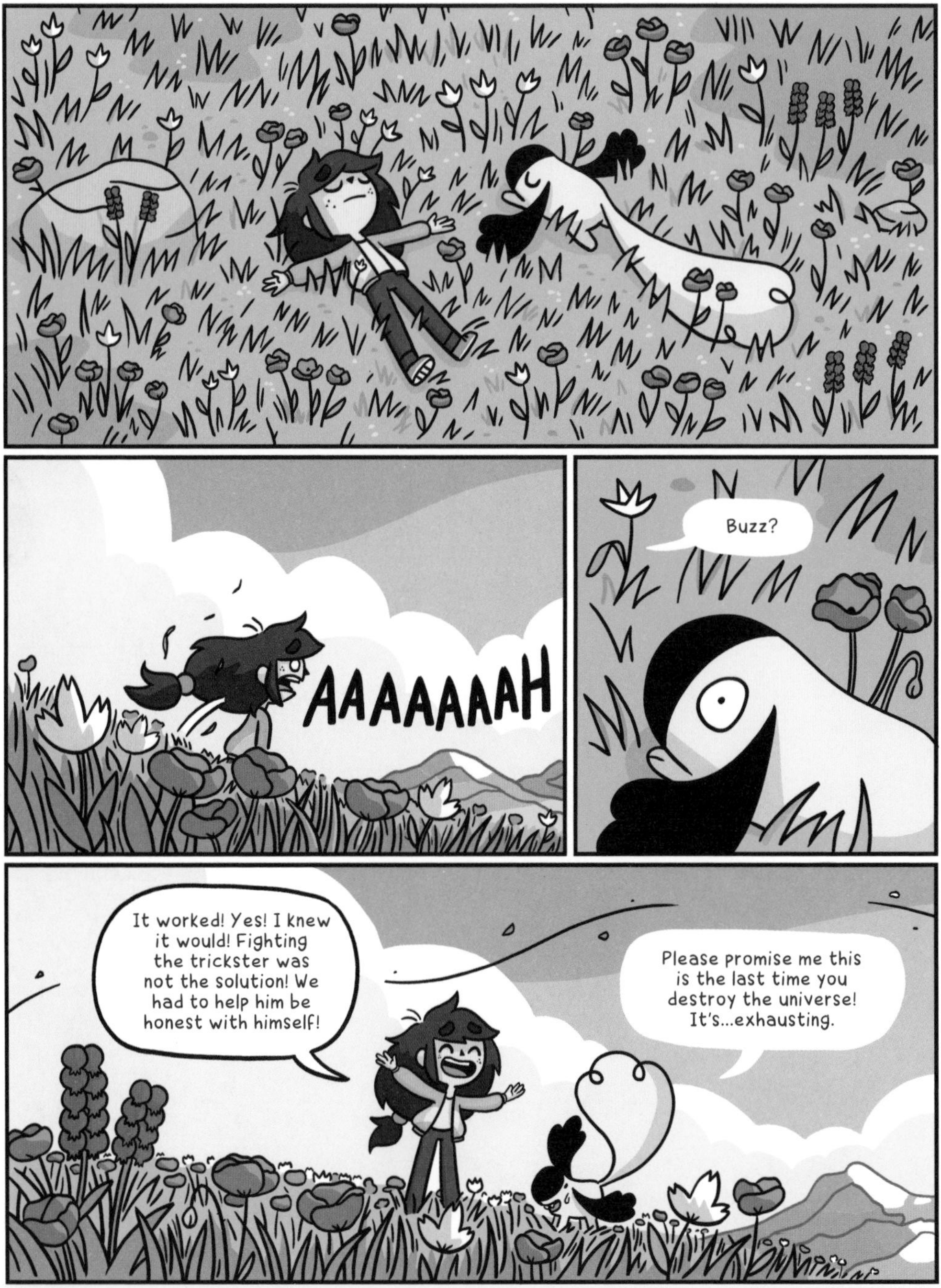
AAAAAAAH
Buzz?
It worked! Yes! I knew it would! Fighting the trickster was not the solution! We had to help him be honest with himself!
Please promise me this is the last time you destroy the universe! It's...exhausting.

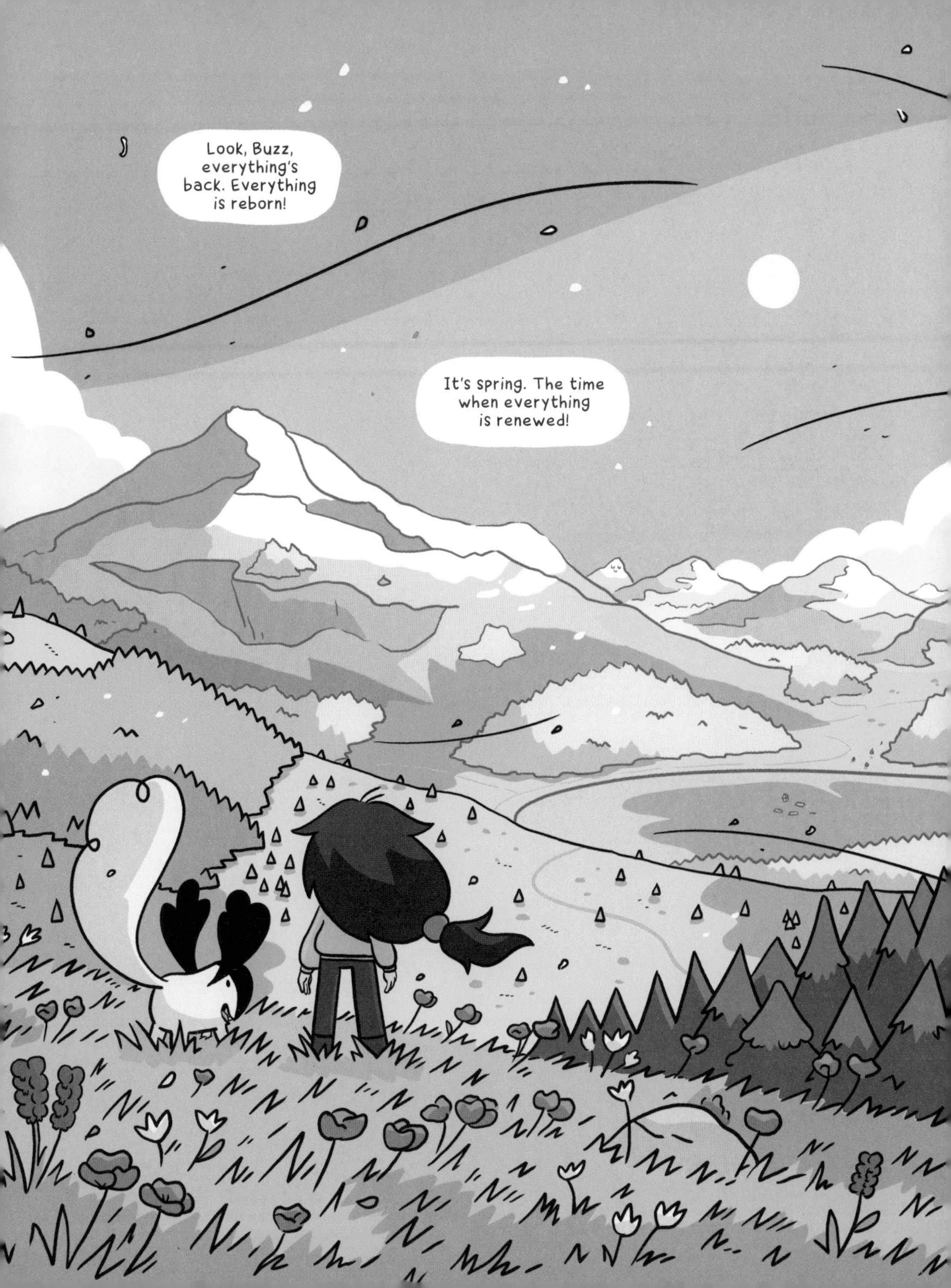
Look, Buzz, everything's back. Everything is reborn!
It's spring. The time when everything is renewed!

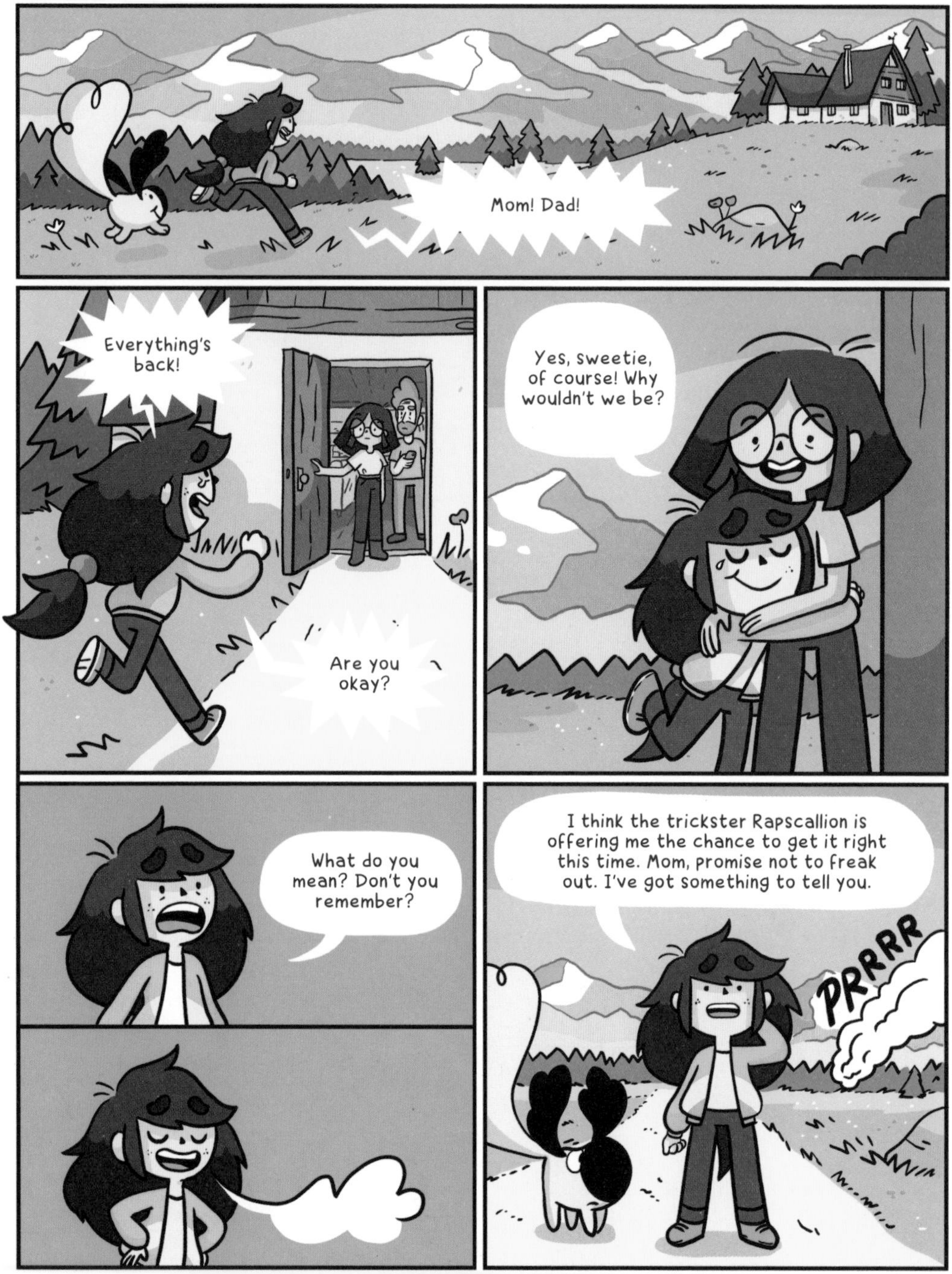
Mom! Dad!
Everything's back!
Are you okay?
Yes, sweetie, of course! Why wouldn't we be?
What do you mean? Don't you remember?
I think the trickster Rapscallion is offering me the chance to get it right this time. Mom, promise not to freak out. I've got something to tell you.
PRRRR

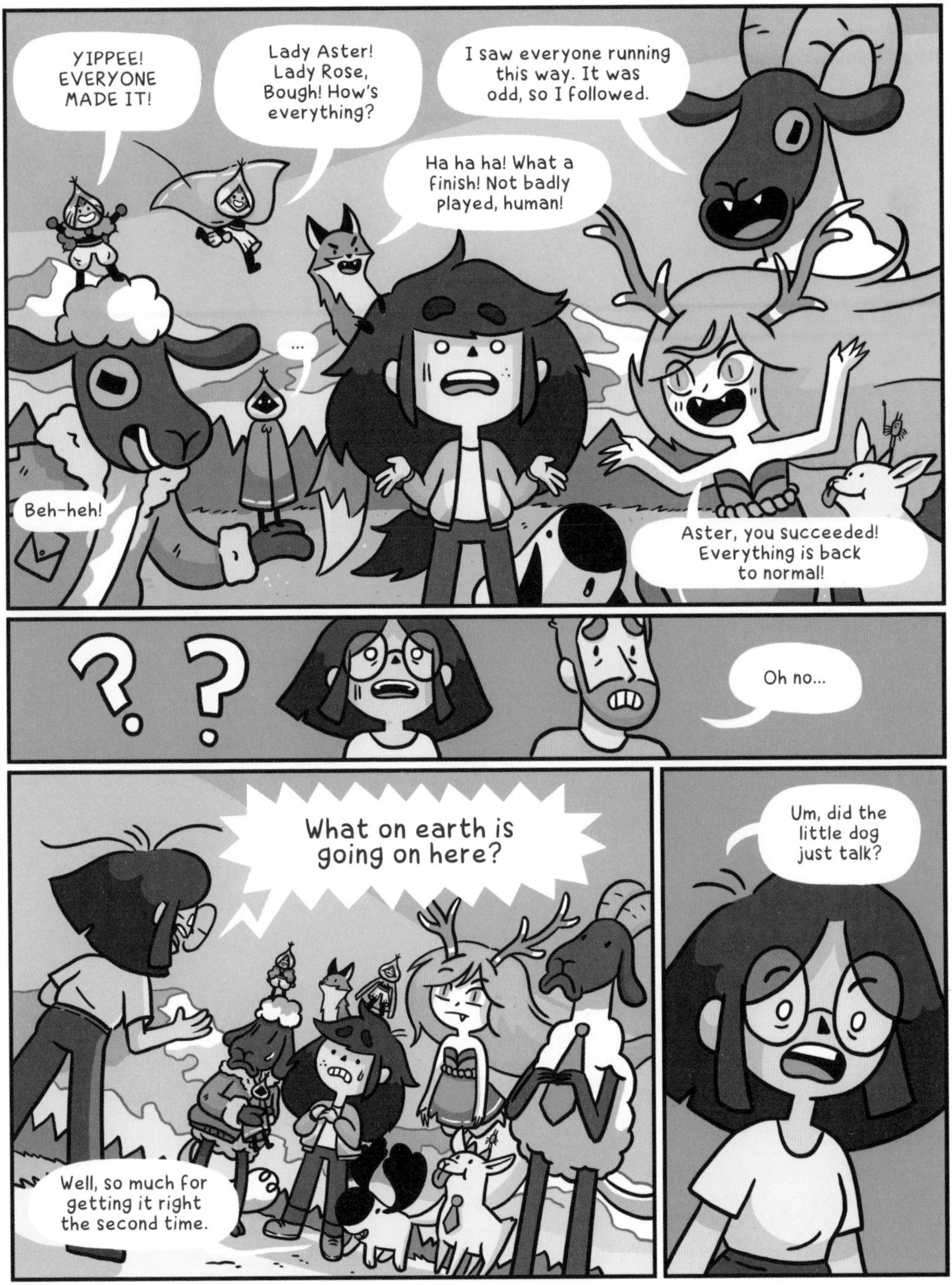
YIPPEE! EVERYONE MADE IT!
Lady Aster! Lady Rose, Bough! How's everything?
I saw everyone running this way. It was odd, so I followed.
Ha ha ha! What a finish! Not badly played, human!
...
Beh-heh!
Aster, you succeeded! Everything is back to normal!
? ?
Oh no...
What on earth is going on here?
Well, so much for getting it right the second time.
Um, did the little dog just talk?

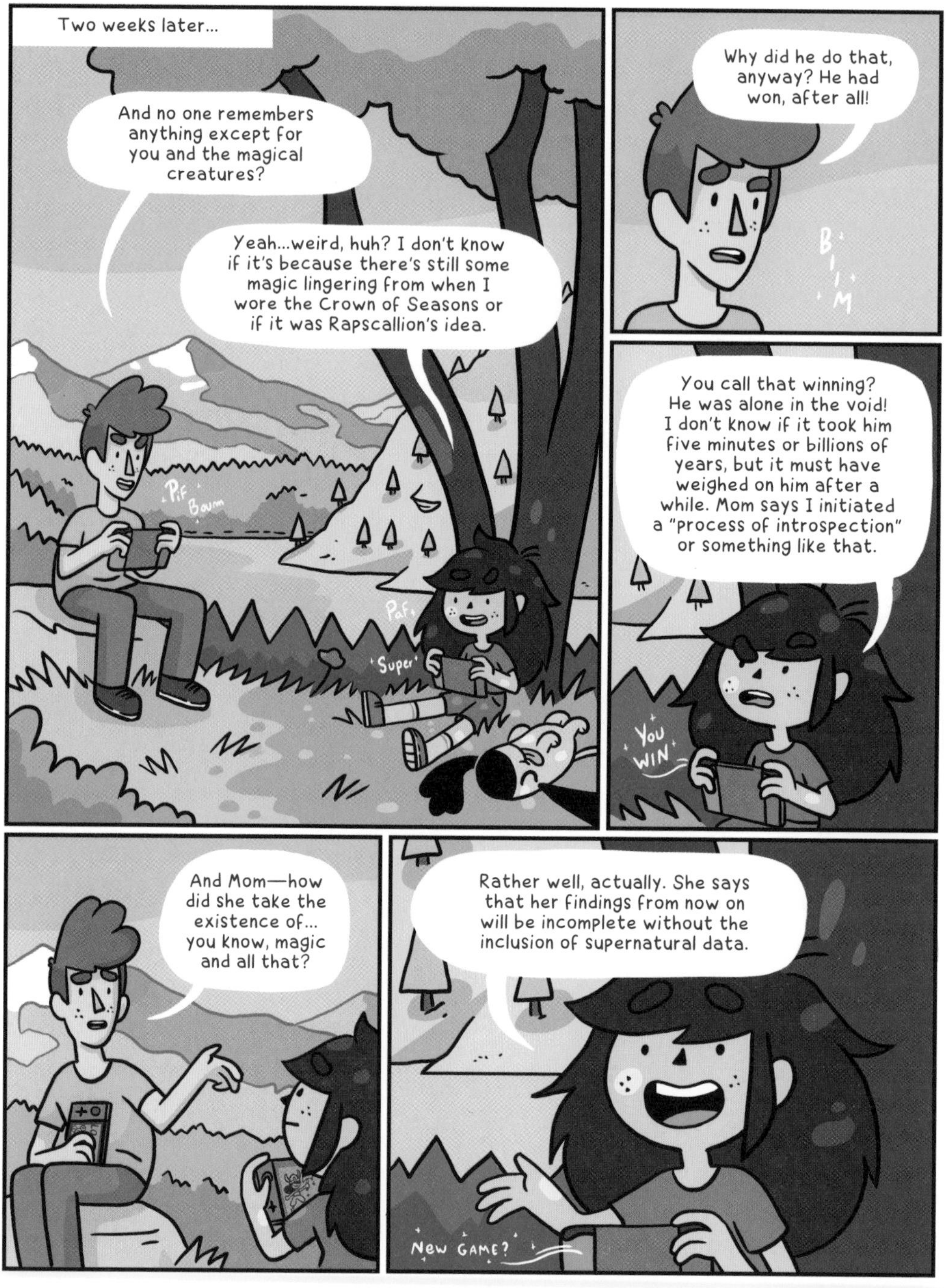
Two weeks later...
And no one remembers anything except for you and the magical creatures?
Yeah...weird, huh? I don't know if it's because there's still some magic lingering from when I wore the Crown of Seasons or if it was Rapscallion's idea.
Pif
Boum
Paf
Super
Why did he do that, anyway? He had won, after all!
BIIM
You call that winning? He was alone in the void! I don't know if it took him five minutes or billions of years, but it must have weighed on him after a while. Mom says I initiated a "process of introspection" or something like that.
You WIN
And Mom—how did she take the existence of... you know, magic and all that?
Rather well, actually. She says that her findings from now on will be incomplete without the inclusion of supernatural data.
New GAME?

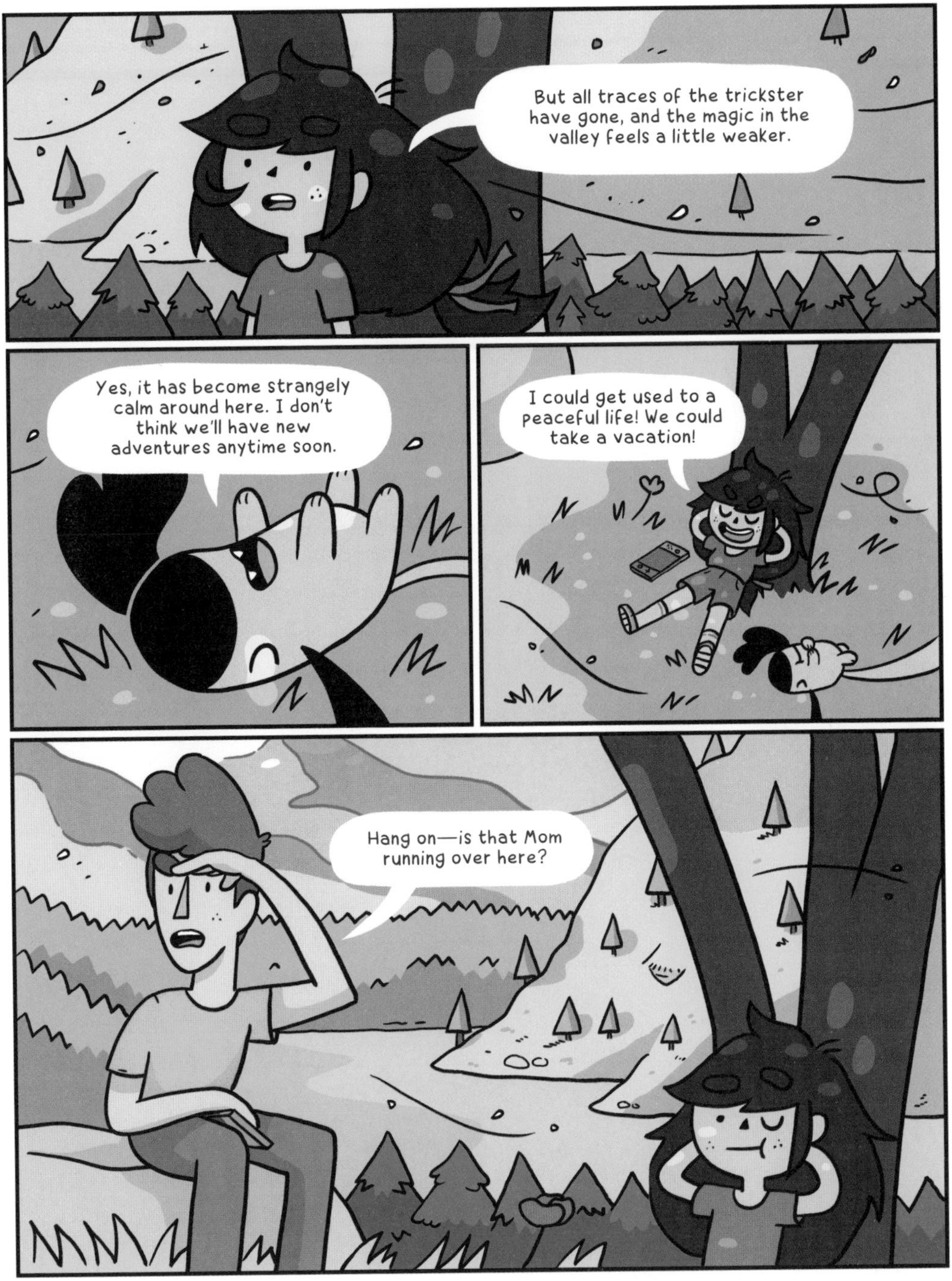
But all traces of the trickster have gone, and the magic in the valley feels a little weaker.
Yes, it has become strangely calm around here. I don't think we'll have new adventures anytime soon.
I could get used to a peaceful life! We could take a vacation!
Hang on—is that Mom running over here?

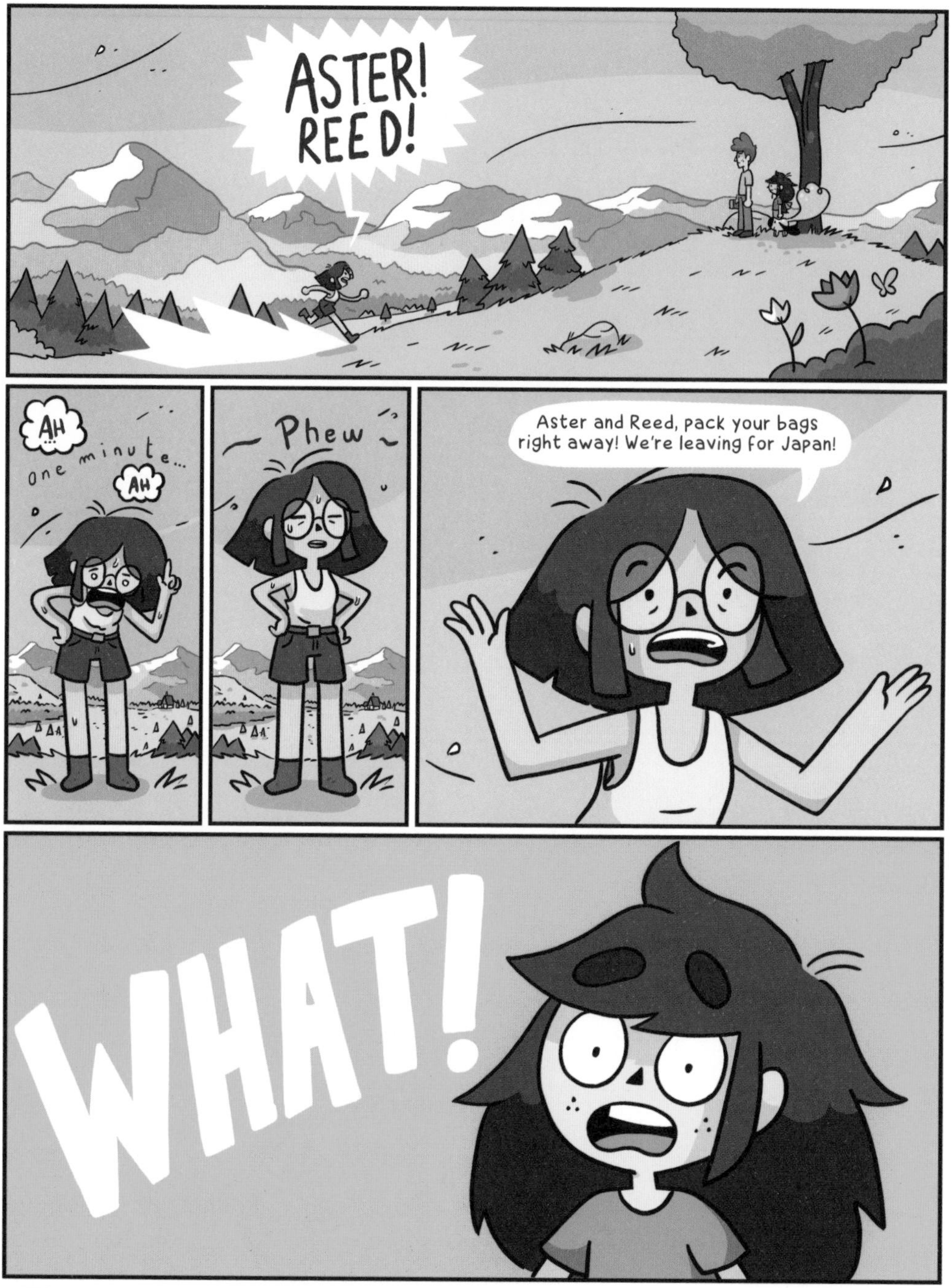
ASTER! REED!
AH
one minute...
AH
Phew
Aster and Reed, pack your bags right away! We're leaving for Japan!
WHAT!

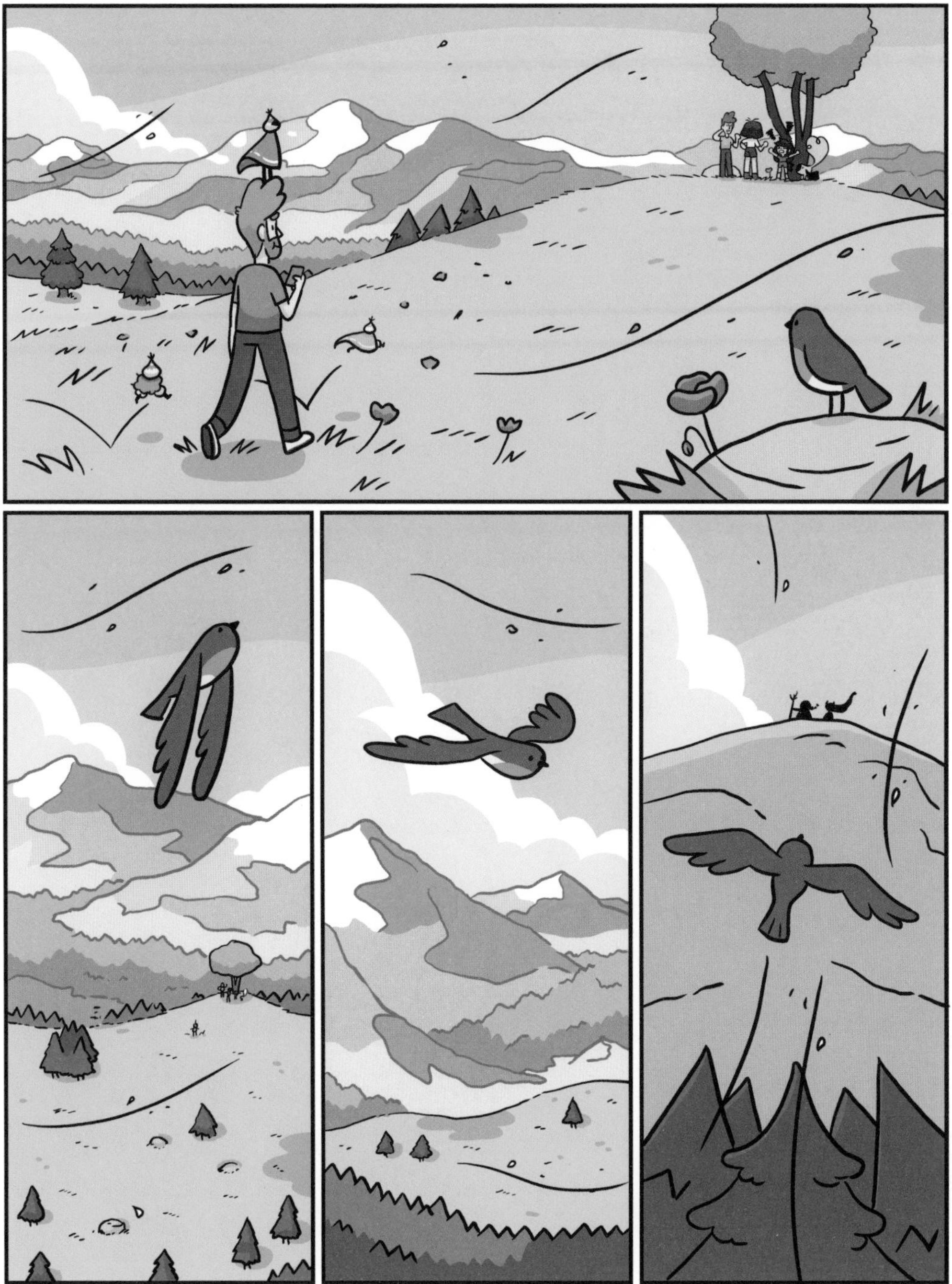

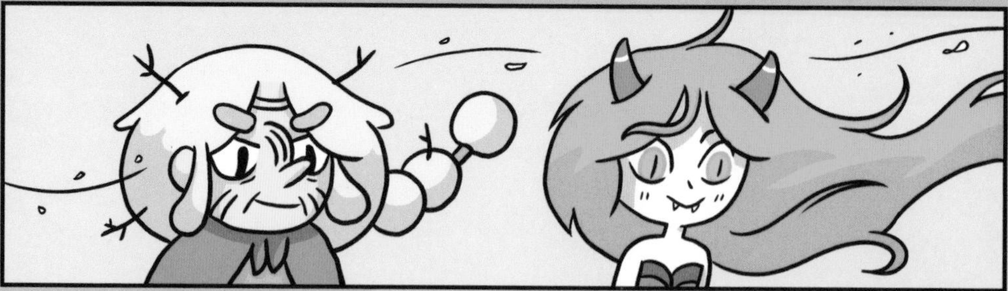

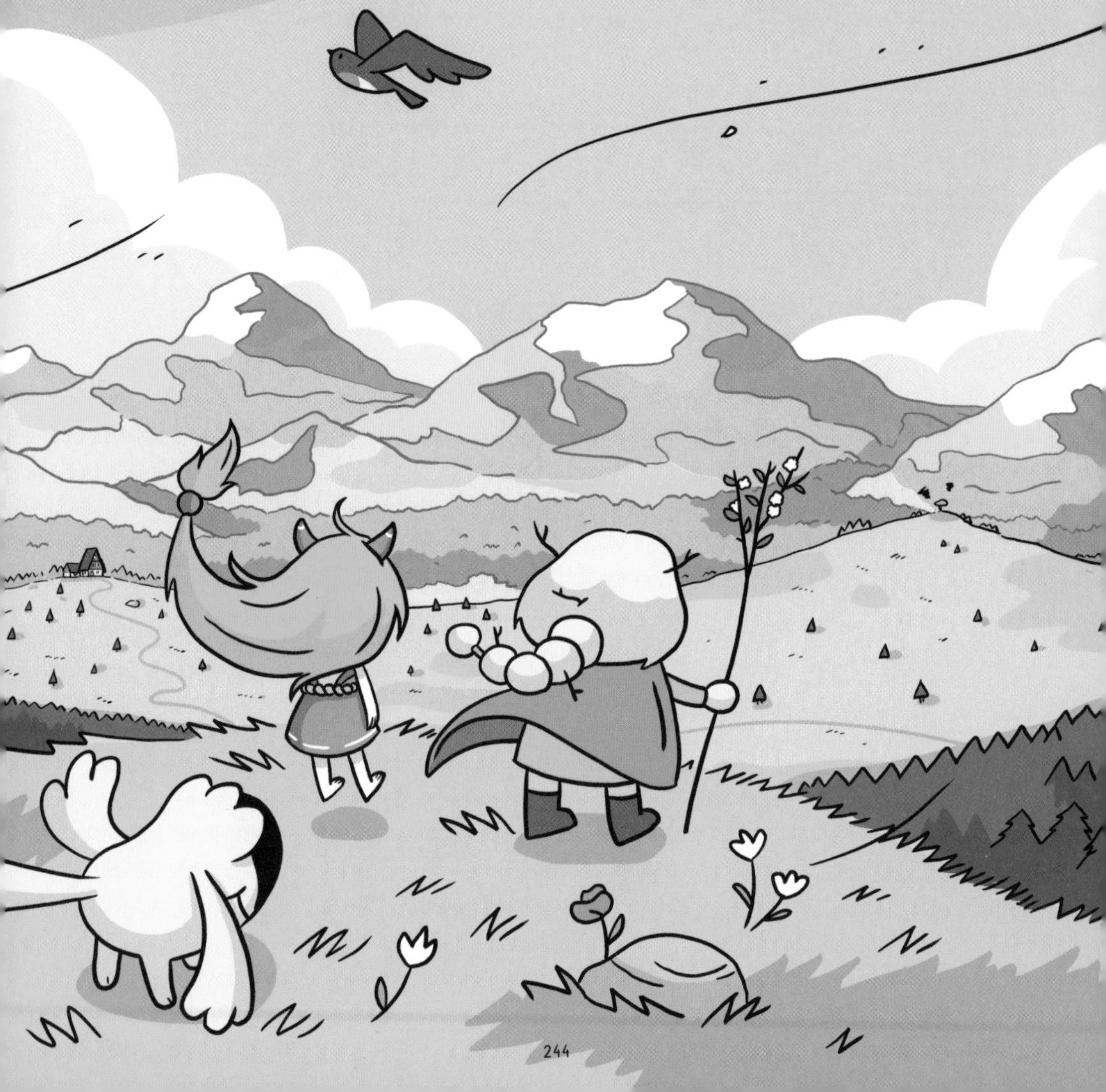

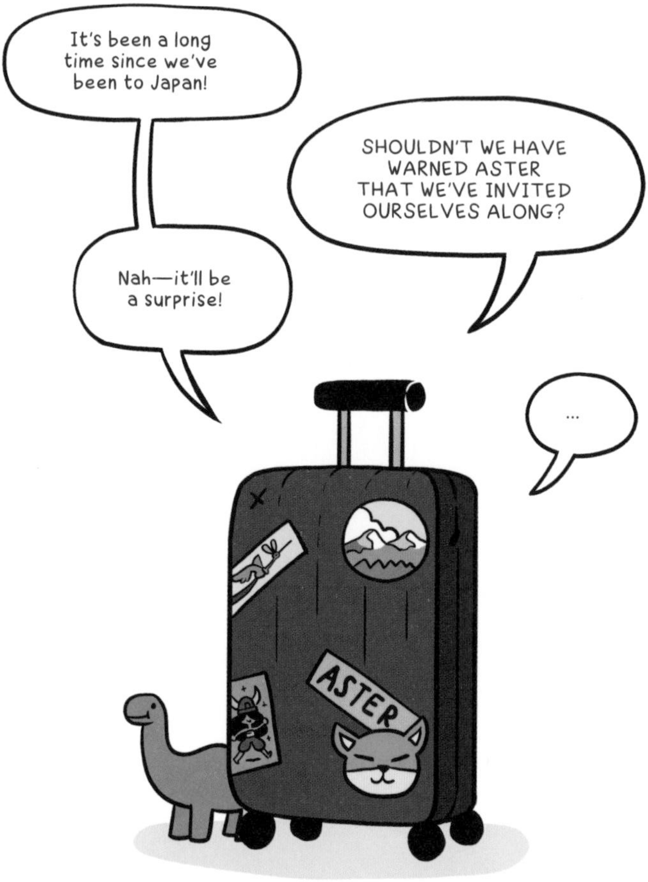
It's been a long time since we've been to Japan!
SHOULDN'T WE HAVE WARNED ASTER THAT WE'VE INVITED OURSELVES ALONG?
Nah—it'll be a surprise!
...
ASTER

Aster and the Mixed-Up Magic was thumbnailed with pen and paper, then inked and colored in Photoshop. The book is lettered in Hawthorne.

Thom Pico was born in Périgueux, France. His enthusiasm for writing has led him to a number of different projects, including theater and youth workshops—before karensac offered to collaborate with him on their comic book project.

karensac was born in Grenoble, France. Always passionate about comics, she won the Angoulême Prix Révélation Blog for her online work in 2015. Aster and the Accidental Magic was her first graphic novel.

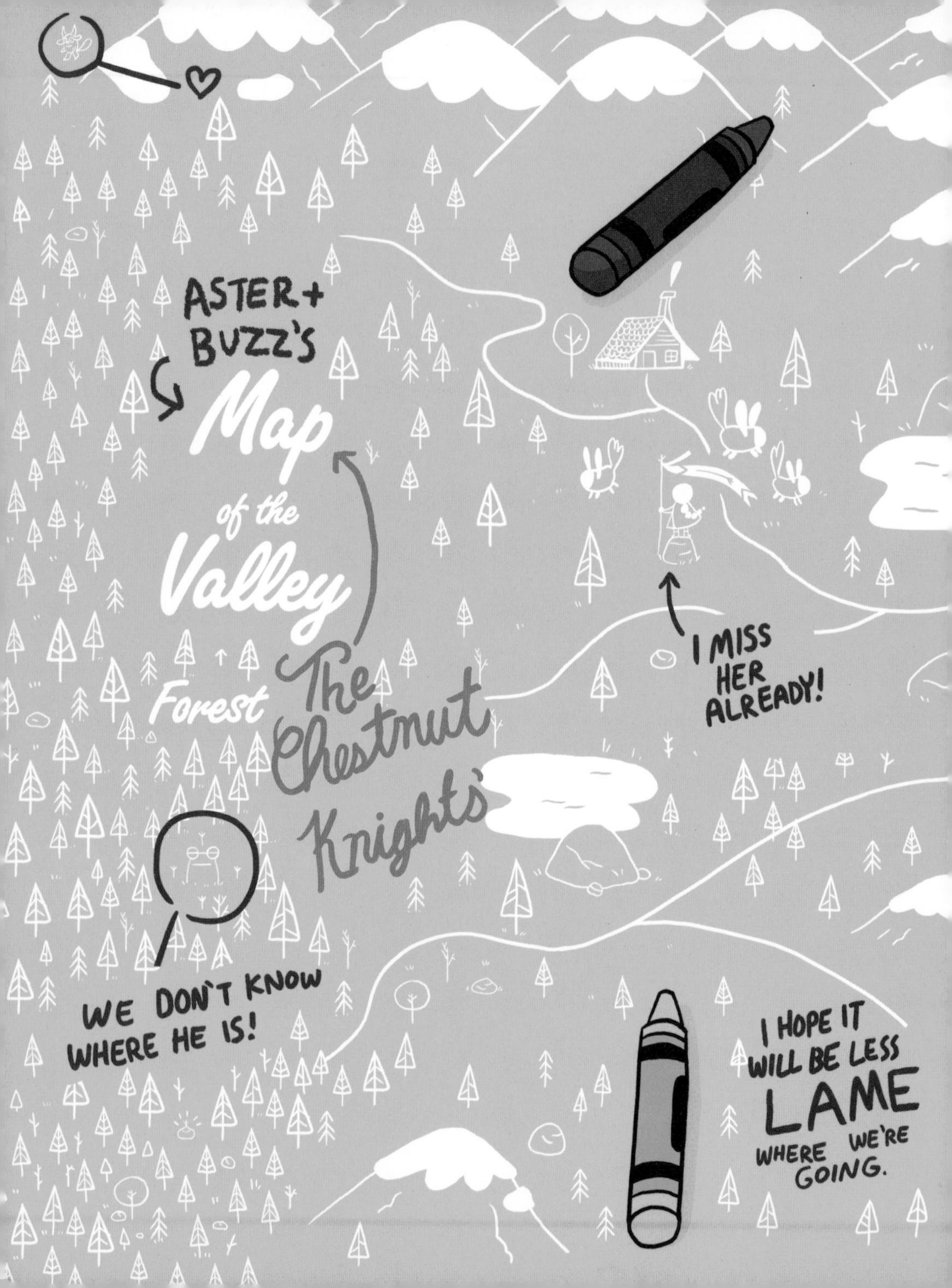
ASTER + BUZZ'S
Map
of the
Valley
Forest
The Chestnut Knights'
I MISS HER ALREADY!
WE DON'T KNOW WHERE HE IS!
I HOPE IT WILL BE LESS LAME WHERE WE'RE GOING.